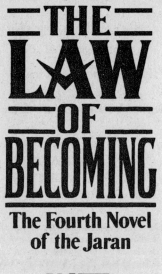

THE LAW OF BECOMING

The Fourth Novel of the Jaran

KATE ELLIOTT

DAW BOOKS, INC.
DONALD A. WOLLHEIM, FOUNDER
375 Hudson Street, New York, NY 10014

ELIZABETH R. WOLLHEIM
SHEILA E. GILBERT
PUBLISHERS

For Jeanne, Kit, and Sheila,
the three spinners who helped me
give birth to this book.

And with thanks to Morten Stokholm,
who gave me much needed advice
about certain laws of the universe
that I know too little about, to
Michael Zimmerman for the bread
pudding, to Ann Marie Rasmussen, my
medieval connection, to my early
readers for giving me confidence,
and, as always, to Jay.

"In this world below the dome of heaven, nothing that is or does can be eternal, for the law of the harvest is the law of becoming. All that is sown must be reaped, and all that is reaped must be sown again back into the world from which it sprang. Thus every change becomes another turn in the great wheel of years."

—from *The Revelation of Elia*

PROLOGUE

1

The Plains

He woke before dawn and snuck away from the tents to watch the sun rise, both of them solitary—he and the sun. He had done so every morning since his mother died. On cloudy days only the light changed, paling into day. When it rained, the night leached away reluctantly, spilling into the soil. In the deep winter blizzards snow settled like a blanket over everything. But on other mornings, clean, sharp mornings like this one, the sun rose like a splintering blow, sundering day from night all at once and with the promise of brilliance to come. The promise was for him. At least, that was how he thought of it; he lived here in night, but someday that would change. It had to.

"Vasha! Come here at once!"

Vassily turned away from the east and the light and trudged back into camp. Mother Kireyevsky cuffed him on the ear. "Have you milked Tatyana's goats yet?" she demanded. "Uncle Yakalev needs your help this instant! Lazy boy! You're a disgrace!"

A chill edged the morning, but it was no worse than the looks he got from old Tatyana and her son when he caught up with the flock. They spoke not one word to him, not even to greet him. He settled down to milk the goats. When he had finished, he slung four heavy flasks of warm milk over his shoulders and carried them back in toward camp. Passing the herd of *glariss* yearlings, he made the mistake of looking straight at the Vysotsky cousins where they stood watching over the herd.

"Watch your eyes, pest!" shouted the elder, who was only three years older than Vasha himself.

"Bastard!" The younger casually picked up a rock and threw it at Vasha, and he ducked away, but not in time. The rock stung his cheek. The Vysotsky cousins jeered and laughed. "Thought you were better than us, didn't you?"

they called, the familiar refrain. "Now you're the lowest one of all."

The fire flared within his heart, but Vasha hunkered down and walked on, fighting it back. It did no good to scrap with them. He had learned that quickly enough: His punishment from Mother Kireyevsky would be severe and swift. Tears of shame burned in his eyes, shame that they all despised him, shame that he had to act like any common servant, shame that he had never made any friends before, when his mother still lived. She had closed him off from everyone else. She had wrapped herself around him, and she had told him over and over again that he was special, that it was the others who were less than he was. It wasn't fair that she had lied to him.

He swallowed the tears, forcing them down as he came back into camp. His throat choked on them. *Never cry,* his mother had said, *you are a prince's son. Don't play with those Vysotsky boys; they aren't good enough for you. When your father comes, then they'll understand exactly who you are and how much power you have.* Well, they did understand who he was: He was a bastard, the only child in the tribe who had no father and who never had had a father, despite what his mother claimed. They understood exactly how much power he had, which was none.

Mother Kireyevsky used him as a servant, and the elders themselves had refused to make his mother headwoman of the tribe, as she should have been after her own mother, his grandmother, had died. Because they had all despised his mother as well. They had rejoiced when she had died two winters ago. And he had learned how to survive their contempt and to endure alone.

As he crossed behind Mother Kireyevsky's tent, he heard messenger bells and saw, out beyond the other tents, a figure swinging down from a spent horse. He would have liked to stop and look, but he knew someone would tell on him if he faltered at all, so he walked on.

"Vassily!" His cousin Tamara called to him. "Give me those flasks. Go to Mother Kireyevsky at once!" Her face was flushed.

He was too shocked to do anything but obey, but as he circled the tent and ducked under the awning a sudden foreboding washed over him. *Now what had he done wrong? What was she going to punish him for?*

"Aha!" said Mother Kireyevsky, catching sight of him. "You will attend me here, Vasha. You will do exactly as I say, you will not speak one single word, and you will serve *komis* to our guest. Do you understand?"

He nodded, mystified. She hurried away, and he knelt down and waited. What could this be about? When guests came to visit at Mother Kireyevsky's tent, he was banished from the family circle because he represented a shameful stain on the Kireyevsky line.

Mother Kireyevsky soon returned, bringing with her the messenger—who was a *woman!* Dressed in soldier's clothing, too! Vasha dutifully offered the woman a cup of komis, which she accepted without looking at him. Tamara brought her food, and she ate with relish and politely complimented his cousin on the meat and the fine texture of the sweet cakes.

Then, just as Vasha moved to offer her a second cup, Mother Kireyevsky said the fateful words. "Ah, you are Bakhtiian's niece."

Vasha almost dropped the cup, but the woman took it from him as if she did not notice his shaking hands. As the rest of the cousins and aunts and old uncles filtered in to listen, they lapsed into a long discussion of the disposition of the Kireyevsky riders in the great jaran army, the army led by the great general and prince, Ilyakoria Bakhtiian. This dragged on endlessly while Vasha stared surreptitiously at Bakhtiian's niece—Nadine Orzhekov—from under the screen of his dark hair. As if by examining her he could divine something—anything—about the man who was the greatest leader the jaran had ever had, the man who commanded the combined jaran tribes in their war against their ancient enemies, the khaja, the settled peoples.

"Vasha!" said Mother Kireyevsky tartly, no doubt divining his purpose in her turn and deciding now, at last, to dismiss him. "Bring more sweetcakes."

For an instant, Vasha's gaze met that of Nadine Orzhekov. She had a sharp, penetrating eye, but she did not appear to scorn him. Of course, she did not yet know the truth. He hurried away.

When he returned, Mother Kireyevsky did an unheard of thing. "Vasha, set those down. Then you will sit beside me."

Sit beside her! Stunned by this sign of favor, he obeyed, sinking down beside her and folding his hands in his lap. He risked another look at their visitor. *Bakhtiian's* niece! She looked no different, really, than other women, except that she dressed and walked like a soldier. Her black hair was caught back in single braid and her cheek bore a recent scar. Again her gaze met his, measuring, keen, but this time he forgot himself enough that he did not drop his away immediately.

"Vasha!" scolded Mother Kireyevsky. He stared at his hands. Then the horrible truth came out. "Inessa Kireyevsky was not married when her mother died, although by this time she had an eight-year-old child. She had no husband. She never married."

"But then how—" Nadine Orzhekov broke off, looking at him. *How could she then have a child?*

Shame writhed through Vasha. He felt it stain his cheeks, a visible mark of the disgrace that his mother had brought on her tribe.

"Luckily," Mother Kireyevsky was saying, "she died a year after her mother died."

"Leaving her son," said Orzhekov. Vasha could not bear to look up now, knowing he would see contempt, not curiosity, in her gaze.

"Leaving a boy with no father, dead or otherwise, and no closer relatives than distant cousins. That line was not strong." Mother Kireyevsky's voice rang like hammer blows, unrelenting. Gods, why was she humiliating him like this? What was the point? Hadn't he been brought low enough already, that she had to make sure that Bakhtiian's niece knew of the scandal as well? Would she never be satisfied?

Like a spark, like his thoughts had triggered the words in her, Nadine Orzhekov spoke. "Why are you telling me this?" Then, secure as he could never be, she carelessly took another sweetcake.

Vasha felt more than heard Mother Kireyevsky take in a breath for the momentous pronouncement. "Inessa claimed to know who the child's father was. It was her last wish, as she lay dying of a fever, that the boy be sent to his father. If it is at all possible. . . ." His hearing hazed over as a roar of fear and hope descended on him, claiming him. Mother Kireyevsky continued to speak, but he did not hear her words, not until she pounded the final strokes: "She claimed that his father was Ilyakoria Orzhekov."

Into the silence, Nadine Orzhekov's reply was so light-hearted, caught on a laugh, that it seemed false. "My uncle, Bakhtiian."

Vasha hunkered down. He knew what must come next. Now Nadine Orzhekov would repudiate the connection. She would laugh.

"Of course he must return with me," said Orzhekov cheerfully, as if she had just been offered a prime stud. "I'm riding back to the army now. I will take responsibility for his well-being myself."

Shocked, he looked up right at her. Did she mean it? Nadine Orzhekov eyed him coolly, disapprovingly.

"You are recently married yourself," said Mother Kireyevsky, eyeing the scar on Orzhekov's cheek.

"Yes," replied Orzhekov in a cold voice. "I also command a jahar. You may be assured that the child is safe with me. What is his name? Vasha is short for—?"

"Vassily."

"*Vassily!* *Now* she looked astounded, where none of the rest of his sordid history had shocked her. "How did he come by *that* name?"

Stung, he forgot himself. "My mama told me that that is the name *he* said to give me."

Mother Kireyevsky slapped him, and he hunched down, berating himself. Idiot twice over, for speaking at all and for giving Nadine Orzhekov any reason to think ill of him, to think he might actually *believe* the fiction that his mother had claimed was the truth: not just that Ilyakoria Bakhtiian was his father, but that Bakhtiian had known of her pregnancy and even told her what name to give the child. Only he *did* believe it. It was all he had to believe in.

". . . and he's always been full of himself," Mother Kireyevsky was saying, "thinking that he's the son of a great man. You needn't mind it. Of course Bakhtiian can't recognize him as his son—it's all quite ridiculous, of course, that an unmarried woman . . ." Mother Kireyevsky was practically babbling, fawning over Bakhtiian's niece in her desperation to be rid of him. "Of course he has no father, but we're grateful to you for taking him—"

"He looks like him," said Orzhekov curtly, cutting her off. "As I'm sure you *must* know." She sounded disgusted, and in a blinding moment of insight, Vasha realized that she was disgusted with Mother Kireyevsky, not with him. "But in any case, I must go. I'll need a horse—"

A horse! He was leaving!

"He's got nothing," said Mother Kireyevsky. "Her tent and a few trinkets."

"He gave my mother a necklace," said Vasha abruptly, emboldened by Orzhekov's sympathy. Because he so desperately wanted her to believe him, to prove to her that it was all true, that it must be, because he knew things that a common boy would never know. "It's gold with round white stones. *He* brought it from over the seas. From a khaja city called Jeds."

"Go get your things, Vasha," snapped Mother Kireyevsky, and he flinched, but she did not hit him again.

And when a horse was saddled and his pathetic handful of belongings and his tattered blanket tied on behind the saddle, and he mounted up and waited for Nadine Orzhekov, he realized all at once that Mother Kireyevsky would never hit him again. The thought terrified him. He had never in his life strayed farther than herd's distance from his tribe. He was scared to leave, and yet he wanted nothing more than to go. No one came to see him off. That quickly, they rid themselves of him and went back to their lives, free of the burden of his presence.

They rode out in silence, he and Bakhtiian's niece. He concentrated on his riding, and on keeping his hands steady and his mind clear, because fear threatened to engulf him, fear and excitement together.

Finally, she spoke. "How old are you, Vasha?"

He took heart at her straightforward question. "I was born in the Year of the Hawk."

"Oh, gods," she murmured, as if she was talking to someone else. "Eleven years old. Eleven years old."

"Is it true?" he asked. "Is he really my father? My mama always said so, but . . . but she lied, sometimes, when it suited her. She said he would have married her, but she never said why he didn't, so I don't think he ever would have. Only that she wanted him to." He knew that, like Mother Kireyevsky, he was babbling out of desperation, but he couldn't stop himself. He recalled his mother so clearly, her pretty face, her warmth, her scent, her cutting words to her cousins and the others in the tribe, to men who courted her, to women who tried to befriend her; her constant harping on the man she had loved and borne a child to—a man who had never in all the years afterward returned or even sent a message. "Every tribe we came to, she asked if they'd news, if he'd married. He never had, so she said he still meant to come back for her. Then after my grandmother died, the next summer we heard that he'd married a khaja princess. Mama fell sick and died. Both the healer and a Singer said she'd poisoned herself in her heart and the gods had been angry and made her die of it." He gulped in air, it hurt so badly to think of her, of her dead, of being alone. "No one wanted me after that."

And why should the Orzhekov tribe want him? Why should Nadine Orzhekov take responsibility for him? Perhaps she needed another servant in her camp. Better to know the worst now.

"I think you're his son," she said so calmly he thought at first he had heard her wrong.

"But how can I be?" he demanded. "He wasn't married to my mother."

She sighed. "I'll let *him* explain that."

Him. It hung before him like a talisman, and though their journey was a strange one for a boy who had never before traveled outside of his tribe, that *him* hung before Vasha as a fog disguises the land, all through the days that they rode, with strange companions and into khaja lands, toward *him.*

Their party came at last to a vast army camped before a huge, gleaming khaja city, and Nadine took Vasha beside her, riding forward alone to come into camp at sunset. He had never seen so many tents, so many horses, so many people—women and children and countless men armed for war—all in one place. They dismounted at the very center of camp, and two men led their horses away. Nadine herded him forward toward the great tent that loomed before them. Terror clutched hold of him, and he slunk back behind Nadine when she stopped under the awning of the tent. She greeted the two guards and rang a little bell three times. The guards eyed him curiously but said nothing.

A cool, commanding voice answered from inside the tent. "Send them in."

A shudder shook through Vasha, so hard that at first he thought he could not walk. But Nadine Orzhekov was all he had. When she swept the entrance flap aside and ducked in, he followed tight against her, practically hugging her side. Vasha had never felt more afraid in his life.

Two men stood on either side of a table in the outer chamber. In that first instant, glimpsing them—one dark and stern, one fair and breathtakingly handsome—either one could have been the man he had dreamed of all these years. Dressed simply, and yet gifted with the commanding presence a general and great leader must have. Both tall. Both of them radiant. He could have fallen at the feet of either of them, and been happy to gain their notice. He clenched his hands and fought back tears. And remembered that his mother had always spoken of Bakhtiian as a dark-featured man.

Like an answer to his thought, the dark man started forward and embraced Nadine. "Dina! Have you just ridden in? Where is the prince?"

"About two days behind us, with the pack train. I rode ahead, Uncle."

Oh, gods. Bakhtiian looked past her. It took every ounce of courage that Vasha possessed to hold his ground against that severe gaze. Bakhtiian had dark hair, a beard, and eyes that pierced right through him. "Who is this?" he demanded of his niece, without taking his eyes off of Vasha.

"I see I've come at just the right time," replied Nadine sarcastically. "Where is Tess?"

"Come here. What's your name?"

Vasha gulped down a breath and stepped out from behind Nadine, into the full force of Ilyakoria Bakhtiian's stare.

"Vasha, this is Bakhtiian," said Nadine brusquely. "Pay your respects."

All the years of waiting and dreaming weighed on him. He had never believed it would come to this. How badly he wanted to make a good impression. "I am Vassily Kireyevsky," he said softly, because it was all the volume he could manage. "My mother was Inessa Kireyevsky."

"Inessa Kireyevsky! Gods." Bakhtiian stared at him, and Vasha wanted only to drown, to spin away into the air, into nothing. The haze descended once again, and although he knew the others went on talking, he paid no attention to them, he only stared at Bakhtiian, memorizing him, the man he had never seen and yet knew as well as . . . his own father. But a spark rose burning within, fighting his paralysis: Bakhtiian *remembered* Inessa Kireyevsky. That was hopeful.

The curtain into the inner chamber stirred and opened, and a woman stepped out. "Isn't Inessa Kireyevsky the one you lay with out on the grass, under the stars?" Her voice was low, touched with a kind laughter, generous and full.

Bakhtiian did not shift his gaze from Vasha, and the boy felt smothered under the weight of his stare. "You've a good memory, my wife," he said in that same even voice that smothered the turmoil in its depths.

"For some things," she replied.

An odd accent graced her voice, light, even pleasing, but obvious. Vasha tore his gaze away from Bakhtiian and stared at her: at her brown hair and her fine, exotic features. Her calves and feet were bare, but a silken robe of gold covered the rest of her. The fine sheen of the fabric caught the light, shimmering as she moved forward through the chamber. She was pregnant. She was *not* a jaran woman.

"You're the khaja princess!" he blurted out.

"Yes." She examined him. "What's your name again? Vasha?"

Her interest seemed benevolent enough, although he was not sure he could trust her. "Vassily Kireyevsky."

"How old are you, Vasha?"

"I was born in the Year of the Hawk."

"And you've no father? Did your mother never marry?"

He hung his head in shame. Again, the truth had to be told. He wanted so desperately for them to like him. "My mother never married. That's why my cousins wished to be rid of me."

"Inessa never married?" said Bakhtiian, sounding skeptical. "I find that hard to believe."

To Vasha's surprise, it was Nadine Orzhekov who came to his defense. She rested a hand on his shoulder. He hadn't even known if she liked him. "They treated him poorly enough. They didn't want him. That's why I thought he'd be better off here. Especially since Inessa claimed up until the day she died that you were the boy's father."

Bakhtiian flung his head back. He looked astonished. He fairly crackled with life. "How can I be his father? I never married her!"

"Vasha," commanded the khaja princess. "Come here." He obeyed, walking over to her. She placed a finger under his chin and gently tilted his head back, the better to examine his face. She was—not beautiful like his mother, but strong, with her odd khaja features, and she measured him kindly, with compassion in her eyes such as he had not seen since his grandmother died.

At that moment, he fell in love with her.

"It could be," she said generously. "There's a strong enough resemblance, once you look for it."

"But, Tess—"

She cut off her husband ruthlessly. "Don't be stupid, Ilya." Then she lifted a hand and brushed Vasha's dark hair lightly. "Vasha, do you know why your mother never married?"

He risked a look at Bakhtiian, who stood glowering at them. He swallowed, but knowing the princess expected him to speak, he managed to. "Because she thought that Bakhtiian was coming back to marry her. But he never did. And she never wanted anyone else." All at once he realized that these words might offend the princess. He flushed, sick with worry. Bakhtiian's fixed expression cowed him, and he was too afraid to look at the princess.

But the princess, when she spoke, merely sounded puzzled. "Surely this was inevitable?" she asked the others. Her hand traced a path down Vasha's neck and came to rest on his shoulder. He melted against her, seeking shelter, and she gave it to him, tightening her arm around him.

Bakhtiian just stared. "Gods, I didn't think she meant it when she told me she was pregnant."

"Is it just a coincidence that he's named Vassily?" asked the princess calmly.

In reply, the other man came to life, the fair one who stood over to one side of the princess, saying nothing, only watching. Given an instant's choice between them, Vasha would have guessed that the fair man—on beauty alone—must be Bakhtiian, but he was someone else and thus did not count. Until now. "Do you mean to say," he asked hoarsely, "that you told her to name the child after me?"

Frightened by this outburst, Vasha huddled closer in against the princess. As if in answer, she looked down at him. "Vasha. Is that what you wish? To be our son?"

The ground dropped out from under his feet. He could not speak, not even to beg for what he wanted more than anything in the world.

Like a slap, bringing him back to earth, Bakhtiian snapped

at his wife. "Tess! We can't take him in. That's absurd. I'll raise no objection if Nadine wishes to foster him, but—"

"You already made the choice, Ilya. You lay with her. She bore a child."

"But, Tess—"

"Gods, Ilya, just look at him. By the laws of Jeds, this boy would be recognized as your son."

Bakhtiian stiffened, and Vasha recognized, even through his stupor and the pain of his hope, the bearing of the general who had united the jaran tribes. "This isn't Jeds," he said in a taut, threatening voice, "and neither are the laws of Jeds my laws."

Gulping in air, Vasha recovered himself. That was that, of course. As he had known it must be. But still. . . .

"That may be," said the princess with terrible gravity, "but by the laws of Jeds, and by the laws of Erthe, I acknowledge him as your son, and by that connection, as my son as well." Her hand tightened on his shoulder, claiming him, and the world seemed to go white in deference to the fierce passion of her words, each one a force in and of itself. "And by the law of the jaran, by my stating it in front of witnesses, it becomes true."

She had just claimed him as her son.

She had just claimed *him* as her *son!* Which made him, by the laws of the jaran, Bakhtiian's son as well.

He burst into racking sobs and collapsed to his knees in front of her.

A little while later, she knelt down beside him, stroking his hair, murmuring soothing words. "Vasha. Shhh. Don't cry. Come now, stand up. Here's something to drink."

His nose was running, and he wiped at it, at his cheeks, with his sleeve and hid his face with his arm until the worst of it was gone. Then, on unsteady legs, he rose.

Only to face a worse apparition: that of Bakhtiian standing, looking angry and perplexed, holding out to him a cup filled with steaming tea. Vasha hesitated.

"Take it," snapped Bakhtiian.

Long used to obedience, Vasha obeyed. His hands trembled as he took the proffered cup from the hands of his— from *him*. He shook so badly that a little bit of liquid slopped over the side, stinging his hand. "Thank you," he murmured.

For some reason the comment made Bakhtiian give an exasperated sigh. "I need to go—" he began.

"No, you don't," said the princess mildly. "You need to stay here."

He grunted, annoyed, and turned his back on them to go stand at the table. He lit another lantern and rolled out a thick slab of parchment that bore many little marks on it, and stared grimly at it, ignoring them.

Vasha drank down the tea. Gods, he was thirsty! The lantern light shadowed the man, but the thing studied lay illuminated. He gathered up his courage. "Is that a map?" he asked softly of the princess.

Bakhtiian glanced back at him. Vasha flinched, afraid he had said something he oughtn't. Despair swamped him. Now that he was here, he could see how foolish dreams were: He had what he wanted, what his mother had told him was his rightful place, only Bakhtiian didn't want the unwanted child any more than the Kireyevskys had.

"Yes," said Bakhtiian curtly. "It is a map."

There was a long pause.

Grudgingly, Bakhtiian spoke again. "Come look at it."

Vasha took one step and halted. The princess took his arm, and thus encouraged by her closeness, he went to stand next to his ... to his *father*. Together they examined the map.

2

Earth: One Year Later

Anatoly Sakhalin sat on a pillow and stared out the window. His hands lay open on his knees, but it was only by main force of will that he kept his body relaxed. On the street below, bordered by flowers and divided into two paths by a line of scrubby trees running down the middle of the paved surface, women and men passed at odd intervals, intent on their own business but greeting each other as they passed. Close to the trees other people flew by, legs pumping the strange two-wheeled creatures called *bicycles*. Here in the vast city called London, they all wore such strange clothing that Anatoly could not always be sure which were women and which were men. The sun shone down, and squares of light patched the rug on which he sat.

The *flat* lay quiet behind him. That had been their first fight. Twenty days ago he had walked off the *ship* into Diana's arms, and since that time she had kept him next to her every instant. For the first eight days, they had stayed at her family's house, and although he liked her rather loud and enthusiastic relatives, they had all, it seemed to him, conspired with her to keep him always under her eye. Then Diana had returned to the city and he, of course, went with her. When she rehearsed, he sat in the *theater* and watched. When she performed, he did the same thing, or waited in her dressing room. She ate with him, slept with him, stuck next to him as a father dogs his daughter's first steps or as anyone leans over a new-built fire, coaxing it to burn on a windy day.

Gods, it infuriated him. She was sheltering him, damn her. Today he had refused to go with her to the theater. And when she had protested, when she had scolded him, he had finally said what he had known in his heart at that first embrace on the *transfer station,* twenty days past.

"You don't want me here!"

Any fool could read the look that crossed her face. "But

you are here, Anatoly," she had said, not denying it, damn her twice, "and I'm responsible for you."

In reply, he had seated himself on the pillow, turning his back to her, and refused to be budged. Eventually she had left.

He felt no triumph in the act, but, by the gods, a prince of the Sakhalin was not a child to be watched over! And yet, the bitter fact remained: Not one soul out there in London, except the members of the repertory company who had spent a year with the jaran, cared or even knew about the Sakhalin tribe, Eldest Tribe of the jaran. None of these khaja had heard of Ilyakoria Bakhtiian, who even now led the jaran army on a gods-inspired mission to unite jaran and khaja lands. Anatoly had left that army to follow his wife to her country, and a damned strange country it was, too.

He had taken a long and confusing and often inexplicable journey to get here to this city called London, to this province (or was it a kingdom?) called England, to this *planet* (that had been explained to him, but he remained skeptical about the truth of the explanation since he was well aware that the khaja honored different gods and thus must believe a different story of the world and of creation than the jaran did) called Earth. And the worst of it was, for all his skill at tracking, for all that he had chased the Habakar king a hundred days' ride into unknown territory and found his way back with no trouble to Bakhtiian's army and known lands, he did not know where he was. As terrible as it was to admit it, he did not think that, if he wanted to return, he could find his way back to the plains by himself.

But he refused to return, because it would give his grandmother and Tess Soerensen the satisfaction of knowing they had been right to counsel him not to follow his wife.

These khaja were like grazel, he reflected as he examined the scene outside with distaste. They preferred to clump together in huge herds rather than roaming in smaller, freer groups as did wild horses and the jaran tribes. He felt closed in. And it smelled funny, too.

Like an echo of his thoughts, a familiar scent caught at him, and he turned his head to look back into the flat. While not a particularly large room, it had been furnished with little enough furniture that it almost gave the illusion of a tent as spacious as his grandmother's. In the doorway leading into the hall, a vision appeared, a woman dressed as any proper, well-born jaran woman would dress. Standing there, she seemed a sudden and stark reminder of what he had left behind.

"I beg your pardon," said Karolla Arkhanov. "May I come in?"

He rose at once. "Cousin," he said, acknowledging her in the formal style.

She walked into the room, skirted the couch, and sat down on a pillow opposite him on the rug. Her children trailed after her, the fair-haired, sullen, small boy and the gorgeous daughter who carried the infant Anton in her arms.

"Mama," said Ilyana in an undertone, shifting her baby brother in her arms as he squirmed to get free and down on the carpet, "we're supposed to be in school."

"Hush," said Karolla, slanting a quick glance at her daughter. The girl did not look like her mother at all. Karolla was a pale, undistinguished, weary-looking woman, and Anatoly found it odd and rather disturbing that she acted more like her husband's servant than his wife. "It's a khaja thing, this *school*. There's no reason you need to go."

The girl set her lips tight, but to Anatoly's surprise, she did not protest. The boy flung himself down on the carpet and stared at the flowered wall, or at nothing.

Anatoly got up and went over to Ilyana. "Here, I'll take the little one," he offered. Anton was a robust boy, not quite walking yet; solemn, a little grumpy, but coaxable. Anatoly liked holding him. He set the baby on his knee and turned back to Karolla, careful not to look at her directly. "Cousin, I apologize for ... my impertinence, but as my wife says, the children must learn khaja ways as well as jaran ways if they are to get along here." He pretended not to see the grateful glance Ilyana threw his way. Valentin stared dreamy-eyed into the air and did not appear to hear him. Anton wiggled off his lap and crawled over toward his mother, thought better of it, sat up, and began chewing on his fat fist.

Watching him, Anatoly conceived the first element of his campaign to win his wife back. They must have a child, preferably three or four.

"Go on, then, if you want to," said Karolla suddenly into the silence.

Ilyana leapt to her feet, grabbed Valentin's wrist and yanked him up, and tugged him out of the room before he seemed aware that his feet were moving. Anatoly heard their feet pound down the stairs. At their defection, Anton broke into hiccuping little sobs, and at once Karolla pulled him to her lap and let him nurse.

"We shouldn't be here," she said in a confiding voice. "The gods cannot approve."

Irritated, Anatoly nevertheless was far too well-bred to show it. The two situations were scarcely comparable. He had, as was fitting, followed his wife to her people's tribe. That his wife was also a Singer and thereby touched by the gods (although here on Earth they called her an *actor*) had made his duty all the more clear, and indeed, while the pressure for him to stay with the jaran had become intense, once decided he had not faltered from his choice to follow her.

"We are here," he said mildly, finally, "and surely that is the duty the gods have given us."

"To live exiled from our people?" asked Karolla bitterly. Then she answered herself. "But I have always lived in exile from my tribe, since I chose to follow my father and my husband."

Unnatural acts both, thought Anatoly, but he did not voice the thought aloud, not wishing to hurt her feelings. "These khaja are strange," he said instead. "Stranger even than the Habakar and the Xiriki-khai."

"What will you do here?" she asked.

"I will study the lay of the land," he replied. And thus was born the second element of his campaign, the second prong of attack.

Karolla glanced toward the window and away. "I don't like it out there," she said softly.

Anatoly didn't think he would like it much out there either, but the longer he sat here, the clearer it became that he must go.

"But as long as Bakhtiian can never come here," added Karolla in a whisper, "then I am content."

Anatoly risked a glance at her, puzzled by her odd comment, but he could not read her expression.

Karolla excused herself finally and left. Anatoly rose at once and strapped on his saber.

Then he thought better of it, and took it off. He would rather go outside without his shirt than without his saber, but Diana had told him time and again that on no account was he to wear it outside of the flat. He had yet to see anything that looked like a weapon on any of these khaja, indoors or out.

He went down the stairs, touched his hand to the *door panel,* and flinched back slightly when the door opened. Then he descended the five stone steps to the path. He was outside, alone in the great khaja city.

It was noisy. It smelled. But he had thought the same thing about every other khaja city he had been in. It was time to look for the differences, the things that made Diana's people, Diana's land, different from the cities of Karkand and Salkh and Jeds.

No horses. No wagons pulled by draft animals. The broad paved paths nearer to the houses were meant for foot traffic. In the center of the street (Diana had made him memorize the name: *Kensington Court Place*) the bicyclists pedaled past. He walked, although he still found it strange to walk and not ride.

On the greater road, next to the huge expanse of trees and short green grass called Kensington Gardens, huge red wheelless wagons called *buses* hummed along above the paved road at a sprinting clip, disgorging and engulfing riders, while the boxier *lorries* seemed, like merchant's wagons, mostly to be transporting goods. These great wagons puzzled Anatoly because they had no wheels and no scent. Diana called them *solar powered,* and had explained that Mother Sun (only she also claimed that this was a different Mother Sun from the one the jaran knew, so how was he to know whether this was more khaja superstition or the truth?) gifted them with the power to move, and that Father Wind granted them an *air cushion* on which they floated above the ground. He kept walking.

Fruits and vegetables lay in bins, smelling sweet and earthy. At another shop, slabs of meat hung open to the air, but as he approached, confused by their lack of smell, he felt the warning tingle of a *field generator;* Diana had explained to him that, like glass, it protected objects from the open air. He stepped back quickly, not trusting khaja sorcery. Well, he knew it wasn't sorcery, but he still didn't trust it. Above awnings, huge images of people and things lay flat against the buildings, holding on by some agency he did not understand (Diana called them *projections* or *billboards*) and here and there, in shop windows and in little tableaus and often moving around, he saw people—whole and living and breathing like himself—

that he could see right through. It seemed to him that there were far too many things in Diana's country that weren't solid, that didn't have weight. Once he caught the smell of horses, from somewhere out in the park, but they had the close, pungent scent of khaja horses, boxed into stables. He did not choose to investigate that way . . . yet.

It was just past midday, hot, a little sticky. A few clouds obscured the sky, and now and again they drew a welcome blanket over Mother Sun's bright face. Farther along, where the park gave out onto more (more!) buildings, an arch and a statue of a soldier mounted on a horse graced the corner of the park. Pausing here, he felt the ground tremble deep beneath his feet, the dull rumble of the subterranean creatures called the Underground that swallowed and disgorged travelers. But he wanted to go on, not down. He could not *read* any of the signs, but he could manage to cross the great roads alongside other people. That was the other thing: London was an inconceivably great city, filled with people, many of whom walked briskly along beside him or passed beside the walkers on their bicycles or clambered on and off buses or climbed up stairs into the light from the passages below. Yet it did not have the intense, galloping pace of Jeds, whose streets had been crowded with wagons and horses and animals and people in a hideous roar of activity that had reminded Anatoly of the chaos of the attack on Karkand.

He followed a straight broad avenue down past what could only be a palace—although compared to the graceful, light palaces of the Habakar kingdom, this one seemed heavy, dense, and drab—circling past a monument boasting a golden winged woman at the top, and farther yet, to a square guarded by stone *lions* where some poor soldier stood frozen in stone so high up on a column that Anatoly supposed him sick from the height. At last he came to the river.

Boats passed quietly on the waters which lapped at stone banks. A path led along the bank. He followed it. It smelled of water here. The sun played light over the slow course of the waves. Passengers on a barge waved at him, and he lifted a hand in greeting, felt at once awkward, and then cheered when a child called out an incomprehensible but perfectly friendly greeting. A breeze lifted off the waves and laughed in his hair, which he had cut short again. He had sheared off his braids on the day he had boarded the thick iron arrow that had lifted far above the land and brought him (in time and taking him to other metal ships along the voyage) here. One of the braids he had sent back to the jaran, hoping it would reach his sister. One he had given to Diana. The third he kept with him, to give in time to his firstborn daughter.

He was alone in the middle of a great khaja city. Yet he was not lost. He knew exactly how to make his way back to Diana's tent—to her flat. So it was possible physically to explore. Now he must learn the khaja language. Although from all he had seen, he wondered if he would ever understand them. They seemed completely indifferent to his foreignness. They carried hand-sized thin slates called modelers, or computers, with them everywhere as if they were holy charms. But it was the total absence of weapons that puzzled him most, as if they either knew nothing of weapons or were prohibited from carrying them, and Anatoly knew very well that only khaja *slaves* or the lowliest jaran servants were forbidden to carry weapons.

Coming out from underneath a bridge that spanned the river with massive grace, he saw a great bridge that looked like a fortress. And there, closer, almost beneath its feet, stood a real fortress.

The river shouldered up against a wharf and bled into the moat that surrounded the castle's outer walls. He stopped dead and examined it. Here stood something he understood.

He ventured out along the wharf. Water lapped at an arched gate set into the wall below, but a bridge led him across the greenish moat waters which smelled of dense rotting vegetation. Walls enclosed him. Passing through an inner archway, he found himself on a broad green lawn shaded by trees. In the middle of this ward stood a white-bricked tower capped with a rounded turret at each corner. Like any citadel, it looked imposing. Wooden stairs led up, and openly, into the tower. Why would they build such a thing and yet let people pass in and out so freely? Here and there on the grounds he marked uniformed men, dressed in brilliant red and gold or somber black and red, who stood with the posture of soldiers, but they carried no weapons, although one of them held a burnished black staff.

Anatoly wove in and out among other people who seemed, like him, merely to be looking. He followed a clump of them up the stairs, and suddenly he came into a cluster of rooms where he felt, at last, at home. Armor and weapons stood displayed along the walls. He knew better than to touch anything. Yet just the sight of it eased his worries. These khaja knew and understood war, that much was obvious. He understood vaguely from things Diana and the Prince of Jeds (no longer the prince, but still alive) had said to him that there were people, not human people but *zayinu,* the ancient ones, who ruled Diana's people. Diana called them *aliens;* the Prince called them Chapalii. Perhaps these Chapalii had forced the humans to lay aside their weapons—it would make sense, if they had conquered them—but let them keep a few here for some strange zayinu reason.

It was dusk by the time he went back outside, pondering all that he had seen. Glowing lanterns without flame lit the streets, so it was no trouble to find his way back, although by the time he turned the corner onto Kensington Court Place his legs ached from so much walking. A man ought not to walk so far. He ought to ride.

He placed his palm on the panel, and as the door opened he heard her voice and then her feet pounding down the steps.

"Anatoly!" Diana jerked to a halt at the base of the steps. He stilled, watching her. Her expression passed from fear to relief and straight into anger. "Where were you?" she demanded.

At the door above, Ilyana peeked out.

Anatoly brushed carefully by Diana and took the steps at a dignified pace up past Ilyana and on to their own flat. Another actor, Hal, lived here also, but he had gone to stay with a friend for the month, to give them privacy. Diana practically trod on his heels following him up.

"I was terrified!" she yelled at him even before the door shut behind her. "How dare you go out like that on your own! You could have gotten lost! Anything could have happened!"

He went all the way forward to the sitting room, to the window, and laid a hand on the cool glass, staring down at the lamplit street below. He felt . . . satisfied. Fuming, she stood behind him.

Finally, he turned. "But I did not get lost. And why should I not go out? Is there some law that prevents me?"

"No, but—"

"Then I don't understand why you are angry," he added,

understanding full well. "Unless you want me never to do anything on my own."

Her blue eyes shone even brighter, sparkling with unshed tears. She made a face, grimacing, and looked wretched, and for an instant he felt guilty, making her feel this bad, but restrained himself, knowing that to hesitate in attack is always fatal.

"Oh, Anatoly," she said, throwing her arms around him. "I was so worried."

Anatoly decided it wouldn't hurt his cause to embrace her back.

"What are we going to do with you?" she murmured into his ear. Unlike so much of her world, Diana was solid; she had weight. She had warmth. But he said nothing, just held her. After a bit she pushed away from him, sniffed once, and regarded him pensively. She had tied her hair back with a ribbon, and he reached up and unbound it, liking it better when it flowed around her face and along her shoulders. She hesitated, then went on. "Yevgeni Usova thinks he can get you work at the cobbler shop."

"I think not!" he retorted. "A prince of the Sakhalin does not make boots for other people. And certainly not side by side with an arenabekh, and a lover of men, at that."

"Anatoly! That is one thing you will not say in my tent. Do you understand?"

"Yes, my wife," he said meekly.

She sighed and folded her arms on her chest. "I don't know what to do with you."

But he already had some ideas. "Do you khaja mean to go to war with the zayinu, the Chapalii?" he asked. She started, looking guilty, but did not answer. "Did the Prince of Jeds—not Tess Soerensen, but her brother—not give up Jeds in order to come here to fight the Chapalii?"

She shrugged. "We want our freedom, it's true."

"Well, then, I'm trained to fight. Why shouldn't I offer my services to Charles Soerensen?"

Diana sighed and rested a hand on his sleeve and stared out at London, at the gently glowing streetlamps, at the steady light glimmering through windows, at the distant lambent glow above the rooftops of a million more lights of the vast khaja city. "The way we will train to fight and the way the jaran fight, well, Anatoly, they aren't very alike any more."

But her words heartened him. She was a Singer, an artist, touched by the gods to perform her art. But as much more as she knew of this art called acting, he knew of war. He had seen the khaja weapons. They looked the same. Even supposing they had other weapons, ones that weren't solid, that didn't have weight, still, he could learn to use them. And if, as slaves, these khaja had not used weapons in a long time, then they would need a person trained as a soldier.

Every campaign must have an objective. Bakhtiian and Charles Soerensen had an alliance of some sort. Soerensen had told him as much. Just as Anatoly had gone ahead into Habakar territory, hunting down the Habakar king and gathering intelligence for the army, now here, too, he would act as Bakhtiian's scout, as the vanguard of Bakhtiian's army in alliance with Charles Soerensen in his revolt against humanity's alien masters.

PART ONE

The Web Of Fate

▼

Seven Years Later

CHAPTER ONE

With the Jaran

Sonia had a new loom. She had strung the warp, taut vertical lines of coarse thread that striped the distant horizon and the lightening expanse of the sky. Seen through the warp, the rolling hills and endless grass of the southern plains did not look fractured but rather like a promise of the weaving to come. As she did with every new weaving, Sonia had sited the loom so that the weaver and the unadorned warp faced east, to catch the rising of Mother Sun.

Tess Soerensen watched as the sun rose, splintering its glory into the yarn. The grass turned gold. A wandering river, twisting and turning through the land like a child's careless loops, flooded with gold briefly before shading to a humbler tone of murky blue. In the distance, a solitary rider approached camp at a gallop, eerie for the sight as yet untouched with sound. The quiet that permeated these vast plains was in itself a kind of sound, a note of expectation combined with a deep abiding peace. Although, Tess reflected, perhaps what people heard as peace was only nature's monumental indifference to the tides of history that rose and fell on its shores.

Sonia poured a cupful of milk onto the ground and threw a handful of earth into the air, where the wind caught it for an instant before it sprayed in a hundred hissing droplets into the grass. Then she took her shuttle out of its case and knelt to begin the weaving. Tess sat beside her, helping when necessary.

"In the long ago time," Sonia began, telling a story to help pass the time as she threaded the weft through the warp, beating it down, "a pregnant woman began to weave a blanket for her unborn child. And as she wove, she pulled down threads of moonlight and sunlight, threads of the wind and threads of river water and of earth, and patterned the blanket as her child's life, as she wanted her child's life to become. But soon

enough she was no longer content just to weave the new
child's life but began to weave the lives of all of her children
and of her husband and her sisters and mother and father and
aunts and uncles and at last of her entire tribe. And because
such a blanket can never be finished, the child could not be
born."

Tess listened distractedly. In the end, after many trials, the
weaver's ancient grandmother had to unravel the weaving for
her, and thus was the child delivered, to live its own life.

Tess felt like that weaver. With a net of invisible threads, she
wove the destiny of the jaran. Her loom had no substance, except perhaps for the implant embedded in her cranium that allowed her access to a vast network of information and structural
ramparts on which and out of which she could build the matrix—weave the pattern—that had become her task. Her warp,
strong and straight, was the tribes of the jaran. Across it she
wove the strands of human space, of the Chapalii Empire, of
the rebellion against the Empire that Tess's brother even now
laid the groundwork for, of the infinite twists and turns any
event might take as it became part of the texture.

But she could never be sure that what she was doing was
right.

"You're quiet," said Sonia.

"Unquiet," retorted Tess, "in my heart."

Sonia smiled without faltering as she wove. "My sister,
you think too much. You must accept the task the gods have
given you to do, and then do it."

They had had this conversation a hundred times before
over the twelve years they had known one another. No doubt
they would repeat it a thousand times more in the years to
come. But Sonia knew only part of the truth.

The threads of starlight Tess used in the weave were invisible to the jaran. She kept them that way. She had devised a
complicated web that concealed and revealed the true nature
of her life, her origins, her purpose here, in alternating
strands, so that no one strand was so weak, foundering on
half-truths, that it might break and thus collapse the entire
fragile edifice.

Strand One (revealed): Tess Soerensen was the sister of
Charles Soerensen, formerly Prince of Jeds, a flourishing
city-state far to the southwest of the plains, and now a fugitive in his mother's country of "Erthe," far across the seas.
Having given up his princely seat, Charles had gone to fight

against the Empire that had conquered and subjugated Erthe, hoping in time to free his mother's land from the Chapalii yoke.

Strand Two (concealed): Earth was not a country far across the seas, but a planet orbiting a distant star, up in the heavens. Far from giving up any pretense to power, Charles had indeed passed the princedom of Jeds into Tess's hands, but only to resume with full force the dukedom granted him by the same conquering Chapalii.

Strand Three (revealed): The Chapalii were not human. They were *zayinu,* the ancient ones.

Strand Four (concealed): The Chapalii were aliens. Their interstellar Empire had swallowed Earth and her sister planets a hundred years before, bringing a period of peace and stability and a number of technological advances to the mostly human population of the amalgam of planets known as the League. But Earth and the League were subject states. They were not free.

Strand Five (revealed): Charles Soerensen meant to lead a rebellion against the Chapalii Empire, and so Tess (as Prince of Jeds) had allied herself with Ilyakoria Bakhtiian, the leader of the united jaran tribes.

Strand Six (concealed): The jaran, Jeds, the lands the jaran had already conquered, all lay on an interdicted planet called Rhui, in the Delta Pavonis system. Charles needed the mostly untapped resources of Rhui for his rebellion. To this end, he and Tess had agreed to do what they could to aid the jaran in uniting as much of the western continent of Rhui under one authority—jaran authority—as possible, so that when they needed the resources of Rhui a decade or a century from now, these resources could be swiftly commandeered.

Strand Seven (revealed): Tess was married to Ilya Bakhtiian.

Strand Eight (concealed): Well, she really was married to him. That had happened before the rest of the plan sprang to life. But she had concealed her true origins from him. He didn't know she came from another planet. He didn't even know that *he* lived on a planet, much less that there *were* other planets with other life or that the universe existed on any but an abstract, philosophical scale even as it rested within the hands of the gods themselves.

By what right did she keep from him, from Sonia, from all

of them, knowledge of the stars? She could list the rationales easily enough, one, two, three:

If she hadn't come here, accidentally, in the first place, they would never have known or suspected anyway; their technology was medieval and their mind-set, however flexible, however laudable in many ways, was primitive.

If Ilya, the greatest leader his people had ever known, knew the truth and how inconsequential it made the vision that had driven him, even before Tess had arrived, to unite the jaran and begin his conquest of khaja—of settled—lands, it would destroy him; it would cut out his heart.

And anyway, now that she and Charles and the rest of the cabal were set on this plan, they had to proceed in complete secrecy; they could not afford to arouse Chapalii interest in any fashion; and so, since Rhui was interdicted, it must stay that way, and there must be no awkward questions asked or betraying traffic to and from the planet other than that initiated years before when Charles had first established a foothold here as a kind of sanctuary from his duties as the first human duke, the first and only human to be granted a rank within the labyrinthine imperial Chapalii hierarchy.

But she still wondered. Should she tell them the truth? And if so, when? And if not, how long could she stay with them, truly? Because in the end she *would* have to return to Earth.

"Mama! Mama!"

Tess smiled, turning to greet her son. Yuri's enthusiastic hug almost bowled her over. She laughed and steadied herself with one hand on the grass. With an impish grin, Yuri untangled himself from her and regarded Sonia gravely.

"I beg your pardon, Aunt Sonia," he said, but Sonia merely smiled in answer and kept weaving. Yuri squatted down to watch her shuttle, and Tess just studied him, this wonderful boy whom she loved with an unsettlingly fierce passion, he and his older sister. Yuri was a sturdy five-year-old, still growing out of his baby fat. He had the world's most equable temperament, quite unlike either of his parents, and a penchant for silliness. Sitting so still, though, his gentle child's profile showed him serious and intent.

"Where is Natalia?" asked Tess.

"I don't know," he replied with a younger child's blithe irresponsibility. "What pattern are you weaving, Aunt Sonia?"

"The Moon's Horns," she answered.

He grunted, content, and slipped onto his knees in order to watch her more closely. The rising sun shone gold lights through his brown hair. He fit there, beside Sonia, with uncanny ease. At five, he had greater patience for weaving than Tess had, but she was used to patterns taking shape more swiftly, nets and structures that she could build and dismantle at whim. She was trying to learn patience, but she hadn't mastered it yet.

Instead, Tess rose, touched Sonia on the shoulder and gave Yuri a kiss, and walked down the hill toward camp. The wind fled in waves along the grass, great ripples darkening the ground for a moment as they spread and, at last, faded into the distance. Far off, she saw the amorphous mass of the horse herd and farther still, a glint of white marked the edge of the grazing line of sheep.

A hundred sounds drifted on the breeze, plaiting her footsteps into a greater whole. Tess hummed to herself. She smelled meat cooking. A hawk screamed above, and she tilted her head back to watch it soar on the cold blue bell of the sky. Already it was warm. By afternoon the camp would be well sunk into summer stupor; that was why everyone was so active now, in the cool of the morning. The bright spiral of the tents wound out before her, losing shape as she neared the bottom of the rise and the camp rose up and took shape as an inviting maze before her.

A whoop startled her out of her thoughts. She held her ground against the charge of three horsemen. Girls, to be more exact, on what were supposed to be quiet old sleeper horses. Her daughter grinned at her as she galloped by, chasing her reckless cousin. Tess winced. She could not get used to that child riding that way at such an age. She wasn't even eight yet.

At a more sedate pace, riding a kind of distant herd on the trio, came another rider. He pulled up beside Tess and swung down in order to give her a kiss.

"Your daughter is wild," she said accusingly.

"She is not!" Ilya laughed. "She is merely determined. Lara is the wild one, as you well know. Natalia and Sofia are just trying to keep up with her."

"Lara is wild because her father spoils her," said Tess, determined to have a pleasant argument with her husband.

"Just as I spoil Natalia?" asked Ilya. Then he grinned, knowing full well what she was about. He caught her face between his hands and stared soulfully down at her. "No more than I spoil you, my heart."

Tess rolled her eyes. "You're impossible to argue with when you're in this kind of a mood." But she kissed him anyway and then greeted his stallion, Kriye, who nosed at her sleeve, affronted by her lack of attention to him. He was an incredibly vain horse, as he, of course, had every right to be, and smart enough to know what he deserved.

They walked along, following in the general direction the girls had taken.

"I saw a rider coming in," Tess said. "What news?"

"He rode from Yaroslav Sakhalin's army," said Ilya. "Sakhalin has received submission from the prince of Hereti-Manas, but he has reports that the prince of the neighboring land of Gelasti is raising an army, perhaps with Mircassian soldiers among them."

"Does the Mircassian king intend to support Gelasti?" Then she shrugged. "Well, why not? He hopes they will act as a buffer. If you are forced to waste your strength on Gelasti and the neighboring principalities, then it will go harder once the main force of Mircassia's army takes the field against you."

"It isn't that simple," began Ilya. She gave him a look. "But I feel sure," he added hastily, "that you have more to say."

"No. Not right now. I want to speak again with the merchant from Greater Manas who arrived here last month. The better we understand the relationships between the princely houses of the Yos princedoms, the better we will be able to exploit what seems to me are any number of internecine quarrels within their ranks."

"Spoken like your brother," said Ilya softly.

"No doubt," replied Tess dryly. She felt a stab of guilt. She much preferred war in the abstract, discussing it, directing it, from out here on the plains, never having to see her words put into action. "Did Vasha send a letter?"

Ilya's shoulders tensed. "Just a few lines, that said nothing."

"And?" she asked, hearing the silence he did not want to fill.

"No mention of him by Sakhalin at all, but appended to Vasha's letter was a lengthy diatribe from Katerina on how badly he's getting along." He paused. Tess waited him out.

Finally, on a let out breath, he finished. "I shouldn't have let him go."

"You should have. Ilya, he had to leave, to go out on his own. You can't keep him in camp. He has to grow up, to become his own man. Otherwise—"

"Otherwise?" Ilya demanded. This was not the argument Tess had wanted, but she braced herself to carry on with it anyway. "He will never be accepted as my heir in any case, Tess, so what does it matter?"

"He must be accepted as himself. Whatever else comes, will come. We can't know what that will be."

"He doesn't get along well with other people."

"You have been protecting him, Ilya. He *has to* learn to fend for himself."

"He can't fend for himself. He's too young. He's hotheaded and he plays the prince's son too often."

"He's a good boy, Ilya. You know that, damn it. I admit he has too high a sense of his own consequence at times, but he's willing to learn. But for God's sake, he's nineteen now. He'll never become a man unless you are willing to let go of him."

"But what if he—?"

"You have to let him make his own mistakes!"

Ilya relapsed into a stubborn silence. Irritated, Tess eyed him, feeling equally stubborn. After a bit, she began to enjoy the sight of him fulminating. He did it so splendidly.

His lips quirked. "I don't want to argue with you," he said in a stifling tone.

"You don't *want* to, but you like to," she retorted instantly. "Well, my love, Vasha is riding with Sakhalin's army now. He's out of your hands for the time being." She forcefully restrained herself from adding: *And it's just as well.*

"I'd better go see what's happened to those girls," said Ilya, choosing evasive action.

But an instant later, two riders came pounding back to meet them. A flushed Natalia, flanked by an even redder Sofia, pulled up before them.

"Lara's broken her arm!" Natalia announced in a satisfied voice. "She tried to jump old Flatrump over the hide that Grandfather Niko has staked out, and he balked and threw her. Serves her right."

"How charitable of you, Talia," said Tess. "I did not, of

course, see you following after her at the same ungodly pace."

"I didn't try to jump!" protested Natalia. "Mother! I'm not *stupid.*" She patted her bay on the neck. "She's too stiff to jump."

"Who balked?" asked Ilya. "Niko?"

Natalia giggled. "No. But he's scolding her right now."

"And setting her arm at the same time, I hope." Tess sighed. "Talia, let me tell her mother. Please."

Natalia bit down so hard on a grin that her cheeks puckered in. Even Sofia, a preternaturally solemn child, smiled. "It's too late. Her father saw it all."

"What did he say?" asked Tess, dreading the worst. Sofia giggled and clapped a hand over her mouth. Natalia preened for a moment, well aware that she held important information like a great treasure. She had her father's black hair and dark coloring, and spirited eyes. She wasn't really wild, but it terrified Tess that she didn't seem scared of anything. "He said that he'll have to get her a real horse, one that won't balk."

"Gods," muttered Tess.

"Father . . ." began Natalia coaxingly.

"No," said Ilya.

"But—"

"No. When you are ready, not before."

Natalia, thank goodness, did not pout. "Oh, all right," she said, all reasonableness now. "Lara made a fool of herself, anyway."

"A practical attitude," mumbled Tess. The two girls rode off to spread the news, looking gleeful. "It's true that you spoil your children," Tess commented, "but unlike Feodor Grekov, at least you know where to draw the line."

"Your flattery is boundless, my wife."

"You and Kriye are very alike, you know. You both demand a certain amount of praise. Otherwise you grow peevish." But she had made the mistake of amusing him. He looked at her out of the corners of his eyes, playing at modesty while she flattered him in tone although certainly not in words. He knew how to look at her just so. Her heart took that familiar awkward lurch and she smiled, agreeably overwhelmed by the sudden warmth of her feelings, and shook her head. "Oh, stop it," she said.

"Stop what?" he asked innocently.

She ran a hand up his sleeve, brushed under his beard with her knuckles, and traced his lips with the tips of her fingers. His eyes sparked. "Never mind," she said softly, knowing he knew she was laughing at him. After twelve years, she felt so comfortable with him on this level that it was as if she had always known him. It was the same way with the children: They were now so completely a part of her consciousness of the world that she could scarcely recall the day when they did not exist.

She just held his hand for a moment. Even out here, such simple shows of affection might be considered unseemly. Then she dropped his hand and turned to face the camp. "We'd better go stem the tide which is no doubt swelling even now."

Ilya raised dark eyebrows and examined the vast sprawl of the camp. "I'm sure if it was quiet enough we could hear Nadine roundly cursing Feodor for all the ills of the world, not to mention Lara's wildness."

"She's such a sweet girl, though. Most of the time."

"But aren't all of us like a fine weaving? The pattern the world sees often hides the threads." Tess stared, his words were so close to what she had been thinking earlier. He had one hand on Kriye's withers, and he stared over the horse's shoulders toward camp, that huge, living entity that was itself an unfinished, ever-changing pattern. "We don't see the warp and the weft that created us, but only the bright design. And some, like Lara, are woven in two faces, a different one on each side of the weaving."

Was he thinking of her as he spoke? Did he suspect how much she was keeping from him? Tess wasn't sure that she wanted to know the answer to those questions.

CHAPTER TWO

With Yaroslav Sakhalin's Army

The rim of the sun crested the eastern hills and flooded the clouds striping the horizon with a pale light. Vassily Kireyevsky shaded his eyes and looked down at the villa. It was a typical Yossian nobleman's house: a great house with a central courtyard ringed by a wooden palisade. Outbuildings and livestock pens lay within the palisade, but the fields that fed the inhabitants were outside the protecting wall. A barred gate marked one wall. Four towers studded the corners. In the central courtyard two women emerged through a door and carried buckets out to the well to draw water.

"It's well fortified," said Stefan casually, leaning his chin on his arms where they rested on dirt. His tone irritated Vasha. Next thing, he would say that the whole expedition was foolhardy.

The three boys lay close together on a spine of rock on a ridge overlooking the villa. Behind them, at the steep base of the hill, Ivan held onto the horses, his duty as the youngest of the four.

"We don't have to get into the house," Vasha pointed out. "We only have to get past the palisade in order to get to the horse pens.

"Well worth the risk," said Stefan sarcastically, since even from this height they could see that the ponies and horses confined within the pen were the usual sorry excuse for mounts that the khaja bred.

"We can manage without you," retorted Vasha, stung. But Stefan didn't stir, and would not. He and Vasha had been the best of friends for too long now for him to abandon Vasha, especially since he had volunteered to come along just as enthusiastically as Ivan and Arkady had.

"Look!" said Arkady in a sharp whisper.

Out of the east came a rider, galloping. But Arkady was looking southwest. In the distance, four wagons jerked and pitched along a rutted road, whipped along at a brisk pace, aiming for the villa. Four armed men marched alongside the wagons. A flag went up on one of the villa's towers, and the palisade gate swung open just as the rider pounded up and entered.

At once, activity erupted throughout the compound. Men yoked cattle to wagons. Two girls at the bird coops fought feathers and flapping wings to cage the birds inside tiny pens. A trio of boys linked the horses up on strings and led them out to the big gate. Women streamed in and out of the great door leading into the villa, bearing chests and bundles of clothing. It all looked quite disorganized and frantic. A child sat in the dirt beside the door and wailed.

"If that rider's brought news that the jaran army is advancing," said Stefan, "then we'd better go back."

"Not before we get a prize to take with us," said Vasha stubbornly.

Stefan shot him a look but mercifully said nothing more. It was all very well to advise caution, but Vasha knew that Stefan was as frustrated as he was, too young to ride with the army, too old to be satisfied to stay in camp. Vassily had seen khaja boys—men—led in as prisoners or fallen on the field of battle who were no older than he was. And Stefan's twin sister Elena, and Vasha's own cousin Katerina, had already ridden with the archers; of course, they were already women even if they were all nineteen; it was different for them.

"But if they've news of the army," said Arkady suddenly, "then they won't expect us to be here. Look at them run around. They must think they have time to escape." Sharp-eyed, he squinted toward the villa. "Besides the four on foot, I only see two archers in the northeast tower and one other khaja with a spear. Only that messenger is armed and mounted, and he just has a short sword. It should be easy to steal some of those horses."

"What do you think those other wagons are?" asked Stefan, jerking his head toward the four wagons that approached from the southwest. "Why are they guarded?"

"What does it matter?" asked Arkady. "Only women ride in wagons anyway. And khaja women don't know archery."

Vasha studied the situation a moment longer. From this height, he surveyed the fields that stretched out around the palisade. At the base of the ridge, a line of trees rimmed a stream that flowed down from the heights.

"Come on." He scooted backward from the rim. Jumping to his feet, he leapt down the slope, his boots sliding on shale as he picked up speed. Arkady followed, falling flat out once in his haste and rising with a grin. Stefan picked his way down more carefully.

"Well?" demanded Ivan.

"They'll all have to emerge through a single gate," said Vasha, "and advance along the road, with those wagons, so that will string them out. If we time it right, there'll be some confusion when they meet the four wagons coming in. They'll have to turn around, trade places, discuss what to do next. We'll approach along the stream and break in when they're distracted. Whichever horses are farthest north and east we'll strike for and cut away. Ivan, you'll hold back and be in charge of—"

"I'm always left behind!"

"You're the best one of us with horses," said Vasha, "so you'll be responsible for herding them in the right direction once Arkady and I have cut them loose. Stefan will cover our action and strike in if necessary."

They all nodded. It had been Vasha's idea, and anyway, they all knew who his father was. They had agreed to come as friends, they were friends, but while they might question his authority they could never supersede it. Satisfied, Vasha swung onto his mare and urged her forward. She hesitated one instant as if to say: *What fool notion have you got into your head now, young man?* But Misri loved him too well to refuse, even if she was, perhaps, wiser than he was. She pricked her ears forward and led the other horses along the hillside.

Farther down, a scrubby vale of woods cut through the ridge and led out onto the flat where the villa lay. They cut through the woods, keeping the trees between them and the villa, and found the stream that wound out into the valley. In short order they had advanced far enough out onto the flat to observe the palisade gate at fairly close quarters while remaining hidden in the trees. The palisade loomed large from this angle, but they had all seen higher walls fall to the jaran army, and in any case, this was a mere villa, scarcely worth stopping for. More likely if a jahar of the army did pass through here, the house would simply be burned. They might not even bother to knock down the palisade. Of course, the khaja themselves all seemed to be leaving, so perhaps the work would be done for them.

Stefan leaned toward Vasha. "They'll turn that into a messenger station," he said in a low voice.

A flash of irritation sparked through Vasha, smothered quickly by envy and the usual admiration. Stefan always thought of things like that. Of course he was right.

"The wagons are coming in!" said Arkady. His mare, as high-strung as he was, minced under his restless hands. Ivan looked pale, but he was steady.

Vasha took in a big breath. Out on the road, the four wagons from the southwest jerked to a halt as the first line of wagons retreating from the villa slowed down and halted in their path. An armed guard and one of the men from the villa shouted at each other, gesticulating. The first clump of horses emerged through the palisade gates.

"Come on!" ordered Vasha, starting Misri forward. She caught his excitement and went eagerly. Arkady had to rein his mare back to restrain her from bolting forward.

"There could be arrows from the palisade walk," said Stefan quickly, hanging back.

"Yes!" snapped Vasha, "but look how those riders are swinging out. They're leading the horses around the wagons. By the time we reach them, they'll be out of range of the walls. Come on!"

They forded the stream and broke out of the trees. At once, the horses broke into a run and Arkady let out a whoop. They pounded over the grass. Vasha's heart beat fiercely, and he grinned. The khaja boy herding the horses hesitated, seeing them. Vasha drew his saber, and on either side of him, he felt more than saw Arkady and Stefan draw theirs as well.

More men burst out of the gate. At the wagons, the guards turned and a man shouted.

Arkady edged out in front. He made a tight turn between the khaja boy and the lead mare, shoving against the boy so hard that the khaja fell off his horse. Vasha and Stefan fanned out on either side. For a moment, nothing happened. Some of the khaja men went down on one knee submissively, watching them. Others simply stared. One fell down flat, as if he'd been struck down.

"Look!" shouted Arkady abruptly. The lead mare sidled

away from him. "To the northeast. Dust. More riders approaching."

"Into the trees!" ordered Vasha, and they pushed the horses back toward the line of trees. After a moment, the lead mare decided to go with them, and the rest followed her.

"Faster!" shouted Stefan, craning his neck around to look toward the approaching riders. "Those are soldiers!"

Catching their mood, the horses began to run. Arkady was laughing desperately, the way he did when he got excited. Ivan rode out to meet them, and they drove the horses on, passing through the trees and splashing noisily through the stream.

Vasha hesitated, struck by an instinct and also because he was a little angry that everything had gone so easily, that it had been khaja soldiers, not jaran, who these khaja were afraid of. And he was curious: Who so frightened them that they would let four unknown riders steal seven horses without a fight?

"Go on!" he shouted to Stefan. "I'm going to scout."

Stefan could not protest. Once over the stream, the horses broke into a run, clearly enjoying their stampede. Stefan *had* to follow, and Ivan chivied the herd along from the rear. But Arkady turned back.

"I said—!"

"Oh, they can manage. We'll catch up. Anyway, I want to see." Arkady laughed again. Like the horses, he relished the excitement.

At the villa, the khaja now streamed back *into* the palisade. Two riders came racing out through the gate and headed southwest, passing the wagons, which still blocked each other. With a great deal of tugging and swearing, the wagons from the villa lurched out onto a field where their wheels promptly mired in mud while at the same time the four wagons from the south inched forward along the road toward the safety of the palisade, trying to skirt the two wagons that still blocked the path. Even at this distance they could hear shouting and cursing. The dust thrown up by the approaching riders drew closer. The fleeing messengers shrank and dwindled into the west.

"Look there," said Arkady. "Some idiot is trying to escape on foot."

Overlooked in the chaos, a single, small figure swathed in

robes and veils clambered down from the second of the four arriving wagons and scuttled out across the field toward the safety of a clump of high grass edging a ditch. The boys watched with interest as the black-clad figure made the ditch safely and threw itself down where they could no longer see it. Wagons jerked forward and all at once a shout rose up and the men fighting the wagons mired in the field let go of them and in a great streaming cacophonous wave the four southern wagons, the guards, and the remaining people outside ran and rumbled for the gates. The gates swung to and closed just as a party of eighteen armed and mounted men outfitted in khaja fashion rode up and stopped outside of arrow range.

From the ditch, nothing.

At once, four men detached themselves from the group and galloped southwest along the road, following the messengers. The others rode over to the abandoned wagons and leisurely cut through the traces, two men dismounting to rummage through the goods while the others kept watch on the gate and the towers.

Arkady gulped down a cough. "Maybe we should go," he said tentatively, sounding torn.

But Vasha was transfixed by the scene before him. A few arrows peppered the ground before the raiders, but they were out of range. Why were the khaja fighting amongst themselves when they must know that the jaran army advanced steadily on their lands? Why weren't they uniting, as the jaran tribes had, to fight their common enemy? Did they not know? Not care? Were their own hatreds stronger than their fear of the jaran? Or were these raiders simply out for a quick profit before running before the jaran army? If they would not help each other, then it was no wonder they gave way before a united and single-minded force. Piecemeal and divided, they could never hope to defeat the jaran.

Black stirred in the rushes at the edge of the ditch closest to the boys, like an animal creeping out from its den. The fugitive at least had the sense to move slowly, a bit at a time, and to keep low, and he wasn't afraid to hold still for long periods of time, trusting to stealth over speed. Knowing full well he could not outrun mounted men.

"That's not a man," said Arkady in a low voice. "It's a woman."

"She has a veil," agreed Vasha, squinting as the figure

wiggled along a bare patch of ground and then lost itself in a waist-high field of grain.

"And she has breasts under that cloth." Arkady managed to smirk and blush at the same time. Then his eyes widened. "Look, they're setting their arrows on fire."

The bandits began to fire flaming arrows into the compound. The skirmish had begun. Smoke trailed up from a thatched roof. Animals bellowed. The human noise drifted out to them like the distant roar of a waterfall.

Whether the fugitive chose that moment to panic, or simply judged herself far enough away for a dash to freedom, Vasha could not know. Or even—at that moment—where she thought she was escaping to. But she reached the edge of the grain field, jumped up, and ran, flat out. Shocked, Vasha stared. Unlike any other khaja woman he had seen, she wore not just skirts but belled black trousers under her skirts and robe, and because of them she *could* run. But horses ran faster, and the bandits had seen her. Two of them broke away in pursuit.

Arkady moved before Vassily did. His mare danced forward and as Arkady urged her on, clearing the stream with a single clean jump, Vasha and Misri skirted a dense clump of underbrush and made it out to open ground while Arkady was still thrashing through.

The two bandits closed in on her. They shouted, seeing the two boys emerge from the trees, drawing the attention of their comrades. At that instant, Vasha realized that the fugitive must have seen him and the others as they stole the horses, that she was following them, because she veered toward them even though it meant crossing the path of the nearest bandit. She clutched at her waist and drew a long knife, dodged the mounted man and kept running while he jerked his horse around. Four more men broke away from the main group of bandits.

Driving his mare at a dead run, Arkady reached her first. As if they had rehearsed it, she stuck the knife in her teeth, reached up just as Arkady drew his mare in, and he swung her on behind him and turned all at once. Vasha cut across the path of the second bandit. He saw the man's face, the glint of gold in his teeth, his blue eyes and the bronze embossing on his leather breastplate. Vasha wore no armor at all, except for the thick padding afforded by the embroidery on his sleeves and along the collar of his gold shirt. He felt paralyzed.

The man swung at him, and Vasha parried instinctively. He had never fought anyone before who meant to *kill* him. Parried, and struck back, heard Arkady yell something. Misri side-stepped and Vasha cut again, a head cut that unbalanced the bandit and sent him reeling back . . . open. An arrow, and then another, skidded past his vision.

As if someone else saw it, Vasha realized in the next instant that four riders were bearing down on him. The gate to the villa swung open and a ragtag, screaming clot of fighters burst out, charging the remaining bandits. But the arrow fire came from *his* side. An arrow lodged in the bandit's shoulder and dangled there while Vasha stared dumbly and the bandit, righting himself, cursing, fought to stay on his horse.

"Let's go," Vasha shouted. Misri moved with him as if with one thought. Arkady was already two lengths in front, headed for the trees. Behind, the bandits hesitated, torn between the sortie from the villa and the lost fugitive.

Out in front of the trees, Ivan sat on his stockstill mare and shot, calmly, accurately, swiftly, just as his sister and cousins had trained him to do.

Arkady was laughing again.

An arrow sprouted in Ivan's shoulder. Ivan went white and swayed, but he did not drop his bow, although the arrow nocked there slipped over his bay's withers and fell to the ground. Vasha came up alongside him and grabbed the bow out of Ivan's hands. Gritting his teeth, Ivan reined his mare around and followed the others into the trees.

Behind, a melee cluttered the muddy ground before the villa. With halberds and scythes, the defenders gave as good as they got, but it was easy to see that before long numbers would win out.

They followed the trail left by the horses. Stefan had encouraged them back up the vale into the hills and along the base of the ridge. Their fugitive said not one word, only watched them with dark eyes, her face hidden by a scarf. After what seemed like forever, they found Stefan, who had run the horses into a shallow defile and boxed them in.

"Ivan," said Vasha curtly, dismounting. "Let Stefan get the arrow out and bind that wound."

Ivan obeyed meekly. He bit on a strip of leather, sweating and pale, while Stefan eased the arrow out and staunched the ɔleeding. Surprisingly, the woman ripped strips of cloth off of her robe and gave them to Stefan to use as a bandage. Otherwise she stayed away from them. Her hands looked soft and smooth, and her nails were tipped with gold paint. She did not speak, and Vasha was not inclined to ask her questions, knowing that pursuit might be close behind.

When they mounted again, she stuck next to Vasha and without words made it obvious she intended to ride with him. She had a decent seat on a horse, but he felt incredibly aware of her close up behind him. Her presence embarrassed him. Why did she choose him now? Why had she run to them at all? Did she know they were jaran? But how could she know, since none of them had yet been granted the privilege of wearing the red shirt of the jahar. They wore boys' shirts still, green or gray or the gold he wore, with embroidery on the sleeves.

Then he looked closely at Ivan and saw how pale the younger boy was. "Ivan, you can truly ride?" he demanded, his fear making him angry. "You'd better get up behind Stefan."

Ivan bit down on his lips. "Just because I'm sixteen doesn't mean I'm a baby. I'm fine. I can ride. It doesn't hurt too much."

"It's a clean wound," added Stefan, and because he had been trained in healing by his grandfather Niko, Vasha accepted his judgment.

Chastened, they rode on. Before too long, they came across the forward units, battle-hardened veterans who looked more amused than angry to see them out in front of the lines, where they assuredly should not be.

"Look what we've caught us, Riasonovsky," said the man who commandeered them, leading them back to his captain. "It's Bakhtiian's son, doing a little horse stealing out in front of the lines."

Riasonovsky was a light-haired man with steady eyes. Vasha knew his type: Risen from the ranks to command his own hundred, he undoubtedly did not suffer fools gladly, nor did he have to. Bakhtiian gave his generals complete authority over their own armies, and the general of this army, Yaroslav Sakhalin, was notorious for strict discipline and an unswerving instinct for the right men to promote. Everyone knew that he had thrown a Suvorin prince out of a command and into the ranks for not following orders to his satisfaction during a battle. So Riasonovsky, wherever he might have come from before, was not afraid of Vassily.

"Bakhtiian's son must be all of six years old now," said Riasonovsky calmly. "What's that to do with these four boys?"

Vasha flushed.

"How dare you—!" began Arkady.

"I am Bakhtiian's son," cut in Vasha, "as you well know."

"You are Vassily Kireyevsky, and if Bakhtiian was ever married to your mother, I wasn't aware of it."

"I do not expect to be insulted like this!"

"I do not expect to have boys out in front of my lines causing trouble for me! And I expect you to hold a civil tongue in your head, young man."

Vasha was furious, but he knew better than to say anything that would put him in a worse light, and, mercifully, Arkady said nothing stupid. Stefan kept quiet, and Ivan just looked white and weary. The old veteran snorted, vastly amused, and Vasha felt humiliated as well.

"Well, Zaytsev," finished Riasonovsky, who clearly had better things to worry about, "escort him back to Sakhalin, where he's supposed to be. And don't trouble us again, Kireyevsky. Gods!" He turned away to talk to his scouts.

Stefan shot Vasha a look, but that was all that was needed to plunge Vasha into a morbid gloom. Stefan would never say so now, not in front of the others, but his eyes spoke as loudly as words: *I told you so.*

The veteran, still chuckling, led them to the back of the unit and rode out toward the northeast hills, beyond which the bulk of the army lay. "My cousins and I stole horses from the Vernadsky tribe back when we were lads. Got one of us killed, too. That was before Bakhtiian united the jaran." But then his gaze slipped to the black-clad figure sitting, silent, behind Vasha. The woman had scarcely stirred and not made a single sound since they had reached the jaran line. "We never stole women, though," he added, and those words hurt, they were spoken so hard.

"We didn't steal her!" Vasha was appalled. "We would never do anything like that. She ran after us. If we'd left her, khaja bandits would have taken her, and you know what they would do—!" He broke off, furious and ashamed that any man would think such a thing of him. Especially an old soldier like this: Vasha desperately wanted the old rider to think well of him. He wanted all the riders to think well of him, to think that he was one of them, that he deserved to be.

"Well," said Zaytsev thoughtfully, "no doubt trouble rides in on its own horse. Sakhalin will have to judge the case."

They rode the rest of the way in silence. Vasha smothered his dread by riding close by Ivan and asking him if he felt well enough so often that the boy finally set his lips and refused to reply.

The army was on the move, so no one remarked the five riders and seven extra horses passing back through the line. But there was no such luck when the old rider handed them over to one of Sakhalin's personal guard and went on his way with a casual farewell. Yaroslav Sakhalin was waiting for them. He wasn't alone.

Sakhalin rode beside the wagon that his much younger cousin drove. Konstantina Sakhalin was Mother Sakhalin of her tribe in all but name: Her grandmother was still etsana, but she had been failing for years now, ever since her favorite grandson had left the tribes, and Konstantina had taken over most of her duties. Worse, far worse, on the other side of the wagon with her bow and quiver rode Katerina Orzhekov. Vasha's cousin, more or less. Ivan's sister.

"Ivan!" Katerina exclaimed, seeing them approach.

Sakhalin sighed, looking exasperated. "Where have you been? I do not recall giving you permission to scout. But perhaps you decided to override my authority?"

Vasha rode out in front of the others, to spare them the worst cutting edge of Sakhalin's anger. Yaroslav Sakhalin was not a man worth angering. "I just—" he began, and faltered. The whole expedition seemed incredibly stupid, now.

"What is that behind you on the horse?" demanded Konstantina Sakhalin.

"Oh, Vasha!" cried Katerina. "What are you doing with a khaja woman? It's bad enough you'd ride off like an idiot, but this! Ever since Tess took you to Jeds with her, it's as if you want to be khaja yourself."

Vasha flinched. "We didn't *steal* her! Gods, Katya, you can't possibly think that—"

He broke off when the khaja woman moved. She slipped off the horse and flung herself down before the wagon. Not before the men, of course, but before Konstantina Sakhalin. She spoke, a flood of words. Vasha was mortified to hear how light and youthful her voice sounded and yet how collected.

"Can you understand her?" Konstantina asked Katya.

"I don't know this language," said Katya, but she dismounted and went over to the khaja woman and put out her hand. "But of course we must offer her sanctuary. I feel *sure*," she added scathingly, "that Vasha will explain himself."

As if Katya's hand bore a promise, the khaja woman sat back on her heels. She pulled aside her scarf, and all four boys gasped. She was young, no older than they or Katya, and, in an exotic khaja fashion, pretty. She was also laden with gold jewelry, as if she bore her own ransom with her. They stared, until Konstantina sharply reminded them to mind their manners.

"Well," said Yaroslav Sakhalin curtly. "That's settled then. My men will take the horses. Kireyevsky, I've had enough of you and your insubordination. I'll give you one hundred riders as escort. I'm sending you back."

Vasha felt the world go white. He thought his heart would stop. "But you can't!"

"I can and I will!" snapped Sakhalin. "I don't have time for any boy's nonsense, especially not yours." The words cut like a red-hot blade. "Your companions will stay with me. Perhaps they'll do better without your bad example, since you always seem to be the ringleader." His gaze rested briefly on the seven stolen horses. "The prize looks pretty damned worthless in any case." Not even Arkady, rash though he was, was unthinking enough to protest Sakhalin's judgments.

But Stefan said quietly, "If Vasha goes back, then so do I."

"Stefan!" protested Vasha. "Don't ruin it for yourself. Or you other two, either." Looking guilty, Arkady said nothing.

"I will go back with you," said Stefan stubbornly.

Sakhalin shrugged. "So be it." He turned back to Vasha. "I told Bakhtiian you weren't ready to ride with the army. I'm not sure you ever will be. Despite what you may have hoped to gain, I don't find that this little raid of yours has convinced me otherwise."

"You may go," echoed Konstantina, whose word was equally law. "Who can you spare to ride with him, Cousin?"

Sakhalin was a brilliant general. Everyone knew that. But

he also had an uncanny instinct for how to handle men, either by rewarding them or by making sure their shame was complete. "Riasonovsky's jahar deserves a rest from the front. I'll send a rider to call him back in. He can escort the boy back to his—" There, always, the hesitation. He could not bring himself to say the word, *father.* "To Bakhtiian."

At that moment, Vasha thought, there was nothing, nothing, that could make the situation worse.

Ivan made a choking noise in his throat. He turned paler than pale, swayed and, fainting, fell from his horse.

CHAPTER THREE

Earth: *There*

Ilyana tilted her head back and blinked twice, and at once she was out of the funerary chamber and back walking—floating more, since neither she nor the vision of Egypt she walked within were real—along the terrace colonnade of the temple of Hatshepsut, where huge painted statues of the Queen stood in front of square pillars. Myrrh trees graced the terrace, and the pink-stained limestone cliffs of Deir el-Bahri rose into the stark sky above. The Valley of the Nile lay beyond and below, and farther, the river itself stretched north and south like the trail of some great beast.

Ilyana descended both of the stairways and at a dizzying speed raced out along the causeway across the flood plain toward Karnak. Her bare feet slapped down on the coarse dusty stone of the avenue that led to the great temple of Amon. Ram-headed sphinxes gazed into and beyond her, quiescent but aware. She passed the first great pylon, through a courtyard, and into the great hypostyle hall. Row upon row of huge columns supported the stone and wood roof, all of them covered with the carved and painted reliefs of gods and pharaohs, beasts and birds and cartouches swollen with hieroglyphs. Dust glimmered and swam where light filtered through the stone window gratings.

Around her, the temple unbuilt itself. Columns vanished, and the complex lost parts of itself to the slippage of time running backward until she stood before the vague outlines of the Middle Kingdom temple, square and simple.

And rebuilt. First the architect Ineny under Tuthmosis I, who enclosed the old temple with a wall, added two of the great pylons to serve as monumental gateways, added an entrance court and statues of Osiris. Then, to the east, Tuthmosis III constructed the Festival Hall and a small temple to Amon-Re, and finally a great hypostyle hall where the New Kingdom pharaohs were crowned was added, as well

as two other temple groups, one to the local deity and one
to the goddess Mut.

Ilyana turned and walked back out into the blast of the
noonday sun to follow the procession of Amon's boat along
the avenue of the sphinxes that led to the temple of
Amon-Re at Luxor. Ahead of her, the boat sailed on the
shoulders of the priests. Their hawk and jackal masks muted
their voices, but she could see the pale linen of their robes
slide around their bodies and the sere brown skin of their
hands, holding up the god's boat. She let herself feel the sun
searing her back and the dry heat of the air, the parching
dust, and the distant breath of the river.

Ten years ago she had not even known that this fantastic
complex of temples existed. She had never heard of an ancient land called Egypt, nor had she known such marvels—
such tools, such technology—existed that she, not the real
Ilyana but an ephemeral construct of herself, might walk
through these buildings without actually being there.

A sphinx yawned and reared itself up, stone limbs crackling, and regarded her quizzically. "Yana," it said, "it's past
time to go home. The system is going down in five minutes."

"Thanks, Kori," she said. She reached out, farther, farther,
toward the great gateway, through the fading priests and
Amon's boat, and dove through. Egypt whirled away in a
great blaze of light and she veered, flying, for the metal
gleam of the docking bay, the artificial construct embedded
in the teaching programs so that children would learn to
make the transition from *there* to here as safely as possible.

On the farthest rose-tinged rim of the horizon, a red light
winked on and off. She leapt, closing in on it. It was, of
course, the portal she had long ago built so that she could
spy on Valentin. Right now it stood on a spinelike ridge of
rock, a corbeled arch lined with flashing neon whose other
side hovered over the brink of an abyss. Frowning, she
slowed and stepped cautiously through. She never knew
where she would find her little brother. Usually it was no
place good. Cold pierced her to the bone, and she clamped
her eyes shut against a stab of wild color. Abruptly, there
was no ground beneath her feet. She opened her eyes, caught
in an instant of stillness.

From a great height, she plunged. Wind screamed past her
and the fall thrust pressure against her flesh. It was painfully

hot. Each breath stung. Hills undulated out on all sides, a rich golden haze. Nothing but gold, as if the ground were plated with gold leaf. A dark filigree wound over a distant curve, the only break in the monotony.

As the ground neared, she recognized her surroundings: an endless desert of sand dunes. She caught a glimpse of the tail end of a caravan swaying away over a dune. The ground rose to meet her. Of course, in Valentin's construct, she had no ability to manipulate. She was herself a kind of artificial intruder. When she slammed into the sand, would she be wrenched back into her body? Would her construct-self, her *nesh*, be obliterated? If she was lucky, the worst thing that would happen would be that she would return from *there* to here and throw up all over the couch. But she had heard of more horrible fates.

A sharp gust of wind pulled her free of gravity and with a disorienting twist she landed lightly on her feet.

"Ah! Gods!" she yelped and began jumping back and forth from foot to foot. The sand burned. The heat baked her.

At once a whole crowd of camels, spitting and slobbering, materialized around her. They reeked. They were disgusting. Valentin always was obsessed by sensory detail.

"Valentin!" she shrieked, more horrified by them than by the prospect of smashing into the dunes. The camels honked and chewed and farted. A thick yellow gobbet of spit landed on the skirt of her tunic, staining it dark, and remains of it slid down and fell toward her feet. She yelped and jumped to one side to avoid it. "Valentin! You worm! Stop this right now! They're closing the system in five minutes!"

A low haze swelled on the horizon. The sky darkened. The sun turned in an instant from brilliant white to a bloody ball of fire smothered in a rising wall of dust. A howl rose like the scream of a thousand agonized animals from the sands, pierced by a whistle.

The storm hit. Ilyana collapsed to her knees and covered her head. Sand battered her. Sharp waves of pebbles flung hard by the wind pelted her on her bare arms and through the thin weave of her tunic. The wind roared and the stones rattled and clashed in a perfectly hellish din.

And was silent.

Ilyana spit sand out of her mouth and cracked her eyes open. Sand leaked from her hair and weighted down her braids. Grit coated her tongue. It tasted stale and metallic. The camels, thank the gods, were gone, but now instead of the curve of dunes she saw only a rock-strewn flat plain, empty of life. The raw blue of the sky hurt her eyes. There was no sun, but it was as light as day.

On a six-legged beast, a rider approached across the flat. Ilyana clambered to her feet and brushed off her tunic, the sleeveless shoulders, the fitted waist, the culotte skirt. But even though the cloth was navy blue, encrusted by sand she just looked clothed in brown.

A demon rode the six-legged creature. It had bulging eyes and red-rimmed tusks and an inventive assortment of claws on its four arms. It pulled up its beast in front of her. Its curled hair gleamed like iron. Fire licked out from its tongue.

"Valentin," said Ilyana in disgust, "as you know, this doesn't impress me. Now come on. The system is closing down for the day. You *know* that. If you break the rules again, they're gonna suspend you from *guising* completely. You're already on limited runs."

Flames licked threateningly from the demon's mouth.

Ilyana sighed, exasperated. Valentin was never a *person* in his constructs. His *nesh* was always an animal or some strange animalistic demon, like this one, culled from mythology or from his own nightmares, which were plentiful. Ilyana had experimented as most children did with other guises, guising as different animals and real or imagined aliens, even just in other human bodies, but for the last year, as she had grown more and more interested in exploring the great monuments of Earth and Ophiuchi-Sei and the other human planets, she had mostly stayed herself.

"And anyway," she added, "we have to go to that reception for Father tonight."

"I *won't*" said the demon petulantly, and it vanished in a swirl of smoke. She caught a glimpse of Valentin's unguised *nesh,* a slight, sallow-eyed boy of thirteen, but his image faded and with a jolting wrench and a tear in her chest she found herself back on the other side of the archway. Bells rang, echoing up from the abyss. She dove for the docking bay, sealed herself through the lock, and felt the shift of pressure, the reorientation to the gravity of the real world. The inner lock unsealed and M. Lissagaray popped the seals off her eyes and she shook the gel tips off of her hands and swallowed bile.

"That was a bit close," said M. Lissagaray tartly. "Chasing your brother again?"

On the other side of the aisle, Kori had already grabbed her duffel from underneath her couch and stuffed all her tack into it. "Heyo, Yana. You wanna go blading this afternoon? You look green."

Reflexively, Ilyana checked the skirt of her tunic, but, naturally, no gobbet of camel spit stained it. It looked crisp and clean, unrumpled by her sojourn on the couch. "I can't," she said reluctantly.

Kori made a face but said nothing. M. Lissagaray moved away to untangle Zaid from his wires and tips; Zaid was one of those unfortunates who twitched constantly while in nesh. Ilyana sighed and regarded Kori enviously. Kori was also sixteen, but she was perfect. She was smart and tall and strong, she wore her coarse black hair in gorgeous locks, and she had a flawless mahogany complexion every bit the equal of Jane Zhe, the actress who played Infinity Jilt, girl pirate of the never-never, on the interactives. Ilyana hated her own paleness. She stuck out here.

Kori sat down next to her and put an arm around her shoulders. "Valentin, again?" she asked. "Maybe your mother is gonna take him to see a physician."

"Yeah," said Ilyana sarcastically. "A brain doctor. Gods, Kori, I think he's gone loony."

Kori shrugged. "You wanna come over after supper? We can do our trig homework together."

Yana bent out from under Kori's arm and stuffed her tack into her duffel: It was not a true duffel, of course, with shiny gray or black sides, but an old carpet her mother had sewn into a bag. It embarrassed her. Especially because all the other kids thought it was *new* just because they'd never seen anything like it before.

"No, I really can't." Ilyana laced the bag shut. "My . . . my dad, I gotta go to a reception tonight. . . ."

"Neh. Sounds terrible. My cousin Euterpe said yesterday she'd seen something on the net about it. All kinds of important people—maybe even Charles Soerensen. Heyo. How about tomorrow?"

"Yeah," agreed Ilyana. "Now I gotta go see what trouble Valentin's gotten himself into."

"I'll come with."

Ilyana glanced at her friend, but she knew better than to think Kori's offer came from anything but compassion and a simple desire to help. Kori had been the first friend she'd made, eight years ago, moving into this neighborhood. "Thanks," she said.

They waved good-bye to M. Lissagaray, who was decelerating the nesh-drives, and went down to the school courtyard, where the other kids hurried out the gates, heading home. They cut through the maze to the junior wing. The door wafted open into the junior nesh-pods, and the smell of vomit hit the two girls. Kori gagged audibly and choked it down, looking apologetic.

"Oh, gods," muttered Ilyana, washed by humiliation. "This is so embarrassing." But she was also terrified. Kori followed her as she wound to the back, where M. Tioko, with infinite patience, swabbed down a deathly pale Valentin. He had thrown up all over *everything*. Luckily there was no one else in the room.

M. Tioko did not look up as he wiped Valentin's mouth clean. "There's a spare set of clothes in the closet." Kori dropped her duffel and headed for the closet.

"Valentin," said Ilyana. His eyes were shut. "This is the fourth time this month!" He did not respond.

Now M. Tioko did glance up. He was a good, decent person and Ilyana trusted him. And anyway, he was about the only person besides her who really cared about Valentin anymore. "He's overdosing," he said in a tired voice. "He's got to be guising at home, or some time away from school, because I've got him on a strict schedule here."

"But I *made* Mama get rid of the nesh-drives," Ilyana protested.

"What about the two other families in your house?"

"They're actors. They don't nesh at all. And anyway, I . . . I talked to them about it. You can't cut off his time here?"

M. Tioko tossed the wet cloth into a hamper, which immediately sucked it into the cleaning tubes. "He'll go into withdrawal, which will be worse, and we can't deal with that unless your parents agree to put him under medical supervision."

Which they never would. Ilyana flushed, feeling cold with worry. Valentin just lay there, breathing shallowly. He looked so sick. He looked so young. Most of the neshaddicts that the nets did those awful docuwraps about were mid-aged, in their seventies or eighties. Valentin was barely thirteen. It just wasn't fair.

Kori returned with the clothes. "All right, girls," said M. Tioko with a resigned half-smile. "Thanks. I'll send him out when he's changed and cleaned up his couch."

Valentin cracked an eye, tilting his head back like a one-eyed bird to squint at his sister. "I *won't* go," he muttered. "I'm gonna stay late at school and do my leftover geo homework. So there."

"Can you send him out to me as soon as he's done?" Ilyana begged, hating the sound of her voice.

M. Tioko nodded and waved them away. As they left the room, they heard him start in. "Now, Valentin, stop that shamming and get into these clean clothes—"

Ilyana blinked away tears brought on by the sudden light of the courtyard.

"Heyo, look, it's Uncle Gus!" Kori whooped, grabbed Ilyana's hand, and tugged her along after.

Heat flooded Ilyana's cheeks. Gods, how she hated her complexion, which betrayed everything. She wanted to die right now. She fixed her eyes on the pavement.

"Little squirt. How you doing?" Gus gave Kori a hug.

"I didn't know you was back," said Kori.

"*Were* back. Yeah, the tour ended early, so I came back home. Hello, Ilyana. Pleased to see you again."

Ilyana lifted her eyes just enough to see where he had stuck his hand out, so she lifted hers, and they shook hands.

"I hope you're well," added Uncle Gus solemnly.

She mumbled something in the affirmative, as reply. She wanted to shrivel up into a worm and just die. Kori's Uncle Gus was a dancer and a choreographer, very well known and quite well connected, and the last time she had seen him he had been politely but firmly extricating himself from her dear father's attempt to seduce him.

Uncle Gus took pity on her, released her hand, and turned back to his niece. "And I'm getting married."

Kori shrieked, and then laughed. "To who? To who? Oh, not another dancer—!"

He chuckled. "To whom. To whom. You kids and your grammar. Not to a dancer, to a nice woman I went to university with years ago and just met up with again during the tour. She's doing soil research right now on Tau Ceti Tierce."

"A scientist!" Kori snorted. "What? You had to bring someone in to keep Mama company?"

"She's at the flat now," he said. "I was hoping you could come right home and meet her." But then, because like Kori and everyone else in her family he was a sympathetic and perceptive soul, he hesitated. "But perhaps you are off to do something with Ilyana."

"No, no," said Ilyana quickly, cutting off Kori's reply. "I'll see you later." She backed onto the grass until she shouldered up against the hedge. Kori lifted a hand in farewell and then dropped it, seeing very well that Ilyana meant them to just go on. She took her uncle's arm and, chatting away, they walked off under the archway to the bike rack.

This time, it wasn't the sun that brought tears to Ilyana's eyes. Why couldn't she have had a family like that? Or like Diana Brooke-Holt's family, who always made her welcome even if Ilyana knew she would never really be one of them? Or like a real family: mother and father, aunts and uncles, siblings and cousins and grandparents, all living in one set of tents. . . .

She winced at her lapse. Not *tents,* but flats or houses or a complex, all the things they had here on Earth. But even back where she had been born, even back on the planet Rhui, with the jaran, she had never had a *real* family. She had always been different. Just a mother and a father—when her father was around—and one sibling. That was all. It wasn't healthy to live like that, without cousins and aunts to surround you, without a grandmother and ancient wizened great-aunts to give a child sweets and whisper to her the secrets of weaving and tell her at bedtime the old stories of the moon and the sun. Well, now she had another brother and a sister, and yet another on the way, but still, they were alone.

Disgusted at herself, she sniffed, hard, and wiped away her tears. It didn't do any good to cry. They all depended on her.

"Heyo," said Valentin from the maze, startling her. He emerged, blinking hard against the sunlight. But he didn't look as pale and sickly as he had in the nesh-pod. "I'm sorry," he said, and touched her arm fleetingly. "But I won't go anyway," he added quickly. "I hate those receptions. You know I do. They're disgusting. Dad is disgusting."

"Stop it! It doesn't matter what he is—"

"—he's still our father," he finished in a mincing voice, which changed abruptly. "And I wish he'd go away again."

"Well he *won't* go away!" she shouted. "Don't be stupid, Valentin. I know you hate him, but he's still our father. He *tries* to be nice."

"Oh, he is nice, when he wants to be." Valentin sat down on a bench and slid his blades onto the soles of his shoes. "He's just so wonderful. Everyone says so."

It bothered Ilyana that Valentin had so little balance that he had to sit to pull on his blades. She tugged hers out of her duffel and stood first on one foot, then the other, and sealed the blades onto the latches on her boots. With a like gesture, they slung identical duffels each over a shoulder to hang along their backs. Then they skated on the path out under the archway, toward home.

"I just want to live in nesh forever," Valentin said, and Ilyana felt cold fear stab straight through her heart.

CHAPTER FOUR

A Transaction

Hills and forest broken by fields and villages and an occasional town—such were the khaja lands that Vassily and his escort rode through, day after day after day, heading north. Some of these Yossian princes and dukes had mustered armies and fought Sakhalin; most of them had died or fled, and two, with their captured children and wives, had been sent north to pledge loyalty to Bakhtiian. Rather like he was being sent north, except that Bakhtiian was probably more merciful to the khaja princes than he would be to Vasha.

But that was too distressing to think about for long. Vasha knew how to hunker down and go on without staring his worst troubles in the face.

The land lay quiet. More, Vasha thought, because the khaja were still shocked by the sudden and devastating appearance of the jaran army than because they were now at peace. Sakhalin sacked cities that resisted and spared those that surrendered immediately. More and more, the khaja surrendered. He ought to have taken that tack with Sakhalin, he ought to have just obeyed, but to be sent out to groom horses with fifteen-year-olds! It was too much to endure.

"Shall we go over to the merchants' camp?" Stefan asked, his question a welcome relief. They'd done with watering the horses and had hobbled them for the night, and it wasn't their duty this evening to stand guard.

Vasha sighed, glancing back toward the jahar's camp, where the captured khaja woman's tent had been set up by older riders. Her name was Rusudani, and she was evidently a daughter or niece or cousin of Prince Zakaria of the Yos princedom of Tarsina-Kara. That was all he knew about her or was, at this rate, ever likely to know.

"You can't talk to her anyway," added Stefan, reading his mind.

"And you can't talk to Merchant Bathori's wife, either,"

retorted Vasha, stung, "even if you do make eyes at her shamelessly."

"Can too talk to her. She speaks Taor. So there."

"But you never have, so what difference does it make?"

Stefan punched at him, and Vasha punched back, and they sparred a bit until they both broke off, laughing and out of breath.

"Come on, let's go," said Vasha. "The merchants' camp is the only interesting place here, since we can't go into that town."

"We could sneak out ..." suggested Stefan, but Vasha only shook his head. Riasonovsky had laid down strict rules for his charges, and Vasha did not intend to get into any more trouble.

They skirted the horses and started off along the river. At dusk, the river bank melded with the water and the moon's reflection swam on the rippling current. On this side of the river lay the princedom of Hereti-Manas, across it that of Gelasti, but the land looked exactly the same to Vassily. A ford lay down at the bend in the river, and on the other bank stood the town of Manas the Smaller, itself a kind of younger cousin to the city of Greater Manas, the prince's seat.

Here where they camped, the merchants' wagons covered a whole grassy area, bounded by trees on one side and on the other by the high grass and reeds of the damp ground nearest the river. Insects riddled the air, except where fire and smoke drove them away. Riasonovsky had a third of his men on watch, but many of the rest had wandered over to the little bazaar the merchants had set up. A fair number of people, mostly women and old men, had forded the river from Manas the Smaller to come to bargain and barter and buy.

Even the newest boy sent to the army from the plains could have as many copper coins as he could carry, so Vasha and Stefan had money. They paid two copper coins each to the merchant from Parkilnous who doled out *kava* in tin cups. They lingered at the edge of his stall, sipping at the hot, bitter drink while they surveyed the makeshift bazaar, which they had come to know well in the twenty days since Riasonovsky had agreed to let the little caravan of five merchants and their entourages and goods travel with the jahar.

Master Larenin, the Parkilnese merchant, sold spices and seeds and nuts and beans, as well as salt, and the exotic smells alone were reason enough to linger by his stall. A Jedan man, Benefract, displayed his usual array of utensils and pots. Skins and worked leather and furs, some of which were traded for local varieties, came from the stall of the Yossian merchant Hunyati, who hailed from the Yos kingdom of Dushan.

But Vasha found Sister Yvanne's tables most interesting. Sister Yvanne sat, as she usually did, in a heavy brocaded chair and supervised while two young men (Vasha wasn't sure if they were her sons, her nephews, her apprentices, or her slaves) did a brisk business in what Katerina had condescendingly informed him were religious goods. Tiny silver knives, pendants to hang from gold and silver chains, rested on cloth. There were boxes, too, some of them small enough to hang on necklaces, other, larger ones made and decorated in different styles: cloisonné enameling, painted wood, even one that appeared to be carved from black bone. Once Vasha had seen Sister Yvanne open one (they each had some secret way of opening) for a customer; he could have sworn there was a bit of frail yellowed bone tucked inside, a fingerbone, perhaps. There were also leatherbound books in any one of several languages, stamped with gold leaf titles. The ones in Rhuian and Taor read *The Recitation*. Strangely, Sister Yvanne only sold this one particular book, and commentaries on it. She did not have a whole sampling of books such as a book merchant in Jeds might have.

"Look," said Stefan, elbowing Vasha. "There she is." He hastily handed his empty cup back to Master Larenin's apprentice and sidled over toward Sister Yvanne's tables.

She was the very young and very pretty wife of Merchant Bathori, a fat, middle-aged man who always seemed to Vasha to have been recently dipped in lard. *She* stood staring at the tiny silver knives, wringing her hands together and biting prettily at her lower lip, while Sister Yvanne eyed her with evident disapproval. Each woman wore a scarf to hide her hair, but while Sister Yvanne's drab gray scarf matched her shapeless robes and covered her hair entirely, the young woman's scarf was gaily bright. Wisps of pale hair escaped from under it to curl around her face.

"How can she stand to be married to that horrible old man?" Stefan whispered. "I didn't think the khaja men marked women."

"No, but a girl's parents might sell her to a rich man, or

a rich girl might be sent with some of her riches to a noble one. That's how the khaja do it."

"Oh." Stefan looked mollified. "Poor woman. At least it wasn't any of her choice. Still, it must be awful. Can you imagine—?" But he broke off, unable to voice what he didn't want to imagine, or at least, what he *did* want to imagine, only for himself. He blushed and finally looked away from her, recalling proper manners. At least enough people moved about the bazaar that no one bothered to notice two young men loitering. Or if they did, they noticed Stefan, who was not just good-looking but had enough healer's training to warrant respect. No one bothered to notice Vasha; he was just another dark-haired, slender boy a bit too old to still be helping with the horses. Surely that was what the khaja travelers thought of him. It galled.

At last Merchant Bathori ambled over, leaving his own stalls where he sold cloth. The way he casually rested a hand where the back of her skirt curved out over her buttocks, the way he publicly patted and squeezed her, made Vasha's skin crawl. Stefan, glancing over, jerked his gaze away. *She* did not seem to mind, however. Perhaps she had grown used to it.

Vasha watched the transaction. The young woman wanted one of the tiny silver knives. But the odd thing was not that Bathori did not want to buy it for her—he seemed amenable—but that Sister Yvanne did not seem to want to sell it to her. They were the only two women in the merchants' train. Surely as women they would have befriended one another. And what merchant refused a sale?

The khaja were very confusing.

"Vasha! What are you doing out here?"

Vasha started and turned around, tensing. Even since he had arrived at Sakhalin's army six months ago and seen Katerina again, he had felt awkward and stupid around her. She had been his dearest cousin, and his first lover, before she had left two years ago to ride with a jahar of archers in Sakhalin's army. At first she had been happy to see him, but that had all changed. Now he wished she had stayed with Sakhalin instead of choosing to act as Rusudani's escort back to the main camp.

"What are you doing here?" he retorted.

"I may go where I please, which is more than I can say for you!"

"No doubt you're still feeling clever because Sakhalin gave you the imperial staff."

"Oooh. That still rankles, does it? But why should Sakhalin vest authority for the journey in your hands when he won't even trust you in his army? Because he's sending you home in disgrace?"

"Thank you for reminding me, since I'd obviously forgotten it."

"Oh, Vasha," she said plaintively, her mood changing abruptly, as it often did. "Why did you have to act so stupidly?"

But Vasha was too angry with her to listen to her sympathy now. He pointedly turned his back on her and looked back at the dispute going on between Sister Yvanne and Merchant Bathori. To his astonishment, a new party had entered the fray: Rusudani. She no longer concealed her face, but like all the women in Yos lands, she covered her hair with a scarf. She had a softer, rounder face than Bathori's wife, and she was small, with plump hands, a delicate olive complexion, and dark eyes. The sight of her always made Vasha horribly embarrassed; not just that he thought her so pretty, but that he remembered what it was like to have her holding on to him so very very closely when they had ridden together away from the bandit raid, escaping back to the army. She had not so much as looked at him once since coming under Katerina's wing.

"She wanted to visit the bazaar," said Katerina, sounding disgruntled, "so of course I came with her, since we're the only women here. One never knows how the khaja will treat a woman alone." But with her long knife at her belt and her quiver with arrows and unstrung bow, Katerina looked like a woman any person, even a khaja, would treat with respect. "Even if she *is* a princess."

"A noblewoman," he replied, "but you can't know she's a princess. She could just be a lesser relation to Prince Zakaria." He trailed off because Katerina gave him such a superior look.

"She has a prince's manners, Vasha, as you ought to know."

"Because I have them myself?"

"At the most inappropriate times."

"Thank the gods I'm not as meek and humble as you are!"

"You two!" said Stefan. "My ears hurt."

"Anyway," Vasha added quickly, wanting to change the subject, "why shouldn't she be safe? There are other women riding with us, Sister Yvanne and Merchant Bathori's wife."

Katerina snorted. "Bathori's *wife?*" She blinked several times in quick succession. "Don't you know anything?"

"But she rides in the finest painted wagon, over there," protested Stefan, abruptly defensive, "which must be hers, and Bathori goes in to her every night."

"I have no doubt he does," said Katerina rudely. Both Vasha and Stefan blushed furiously, and Stefan, abashed, looked down at his boots.

"Katya!" exclaimed Vasha. "What's happened to you?" Her coarseness shocked him more than her disdain for everything he did and said.

"You couldn't understand," she said bitterly. Then, like lightning, her mood shifted, and he saw tears in her eyes. Her lower lip trembled, and for an instant he thought she was going to start crying. Once, he would have been her first and most precious confidant.

"No doubt I'm too stupid to know," he snapped, annoyed that she had abandoned him.

Her face stiffened at once. She brushed the ends of her braids back over her shoulder and strode away, over to the table.

"Oh, Vasha!" said Stefan, exasperated.

"Be quiet." Vasha crossed his arms and stared after her, unwilling to admit to any wrongdoing. She had started it, after all.

And there was enough to distract him. At Sister Yvanne's table, a strange spectacle unfolded. Rusudani pulled back the sleeve of her long tunic and displayed her wrist to the Sister. The change this small gesture wrought was miraculous. At once, Sister Yvanne agreed to give up one of the tiny silver knives, and Merchant Bathori exchanged coins with her.

But then the transaction changed yet again: Rusudani turned and addressed Bathori's wife, and soon Bathori joined in until all three of them were, evidently, haggling over something. By degrees, Stefan inched closer to the conversation, and Vasha followed him, grateful to have any chance to see Rusudani.

Bathori was a great haggler. In the twenty days the merchants had traveled with them, Vasha had watched him wear down his customers with sheer volume of words. This time,

he spoke infrequently and deferred more and more to
Rusudani. After a bit, nodding her head, she reached into the
complicated layers of robe, skirt, and trousers that she wore
and brought out a purse. From that purse she removed five
coins. Four she gave to Bathori and the fifth to Bathori's
wife.

Bathori's wife curtsied and said, in clear Taor, "Lady, I
am called Jaelle." Then the two khaja women walked away
together, Jaelle trailing three steps behind Rusudani.

Katerina still stood by the table. She glanced at Vasha and
Stefan, turned her back toward them, and spoke briefly with
Bathori and Sister Yvanne in Taor, the trade language many
of the children of the Orzhekov tribe had learned during
their time in Tess's *school*. Toward Katerina, the khaja merchants' demeanor was not just deferential but fawning.

"No wonder she has such a fat head," said Vasha.

"What? Are you still angry with her?"

"What do you think! I have every right to be!"

"No need to be angry with me, too," retorted Stefan. "I
know how much she loved you before, Vasha, but she *has*
been two years with the army. Surely she must prefer to
spend her time with the women." He paused, and then said
it anyway. "And with older men, now."

"Not with a rash, stupid boy like me? Well, I don't care
what she thinks about me."

"Of course you don't."

But Vassily waited, anyway, while Katerina finished her
conversation with the two merchants and walked back to
them. She had developed a kind of saunter that he detested.

"So," she said, coming up beside them, "Bathori's *wife*
has gone to be handmaiden to the princess. But maybe
Bathori can find a new *wife* there." With her chin, she indicated a section of the bazaar where a cluster of khaja women
with uncovered hair loitered around a circle of small wagons, each wagon crowned with a tent over the bed of the
wagon.

The wagons had come over from Manas the Smaller,
Vasha supposed to cart goods back into town. He hadn't
seen the little tents go up, and now he realized that a fair
number of jaran riders stood around there as well, drinking
hot kava and oilberry wine from Merchant Larenin's wagons
and flirting, most of them with discreet good manners, with
the khaja women. Vassily knew about khaja women: It was

commonly believed among the tribes that khaja women covered their faces, kept their eyes cast down, and in general were afraid of men, quite the opposite of how real women were supposed to behave. It was just another example of what barbarians the khaja were. But these khaja women were much more like jaran women. A horrible suspicion took hold of Vasha.

"Do khaja really marry again so quickly?" Stefan asked. "Does he even *know* those women, or anything of their families? How can he? I suppose without the mark on a woman's face the khaja have no real respect for marriage, then, if it can be given up so easily...."

Katerina's look silenced him. Vasha could tell, anyway, that Stefan was babbling, something he never did except when a powerful emotion took hold of him. "I'm going to bed," said Katerina, and left them.

Meanwhile, Merchant Bathori excused himself from Sister Yvanne and strode purposefully over to the clot of khaja women. They clustered around him while he talked. As he finished, all but three of the women laughed and filtered back to flirt with the soldiers once again. Bathori himself dismissed a pale-haired older woman in favor of the two younger ones, one raven-haired, the other with features similar to those of his former wife, although her complexion was not as fine. The three of them began to haggle.

Suddenly, the raven-haired girl unlaced her blouse and bared her breasts, right there in front of everyone. Stefan choked. Vasha could not help but stare. The other khaja women went on with their talking and flirting without blinking an eye, but every man within sight of her—every jaran man, that is—stopped stock-still in shock. Well, she had fine, full breasts and ample, pleasing flesh. Bathori examined her the way a man would examine a horse he was planning to acquire. He squeezed her breasts, then her buttocks through her skirt, and patted her briskly as if to pronounce himself satisfied.

The blonde woman looked disappointed but shrugged and walked away. Without any sign that she cared one whit that every man there was trying not to stare at her—or perhaps even pleased that it was so—the raven-haired girl laced up her blouse and began haggling with Bathori again.

"I will never understand the khaja," said Stefan. The words caught in his throat. He looked mortified.

"She's a whore," said Vasha.

"What's a whore?"

"A woman who sells having sex with men for coins or goods. I saw them in Jeds."

"No. You're lying. I don't believe it. I know khaja are barbarians, but—" He broke off. Like the other children in Tess Soerensen's school, Stefan had received a rigorous education. It wasn't khaja he couldn't believe it about. It was the conclusion he must then draw about Jaelle, the pretty young woman he admired. "But she couldn't be," he finished plaintively. "What would drive a woman to behave like that? How could her mother and aunts ever let her come to such a pass?"

"Tess says that many khaja lands don't even have etsanas."

"I hate the khaja," said Stefan suddenly. He turned and stalked away.

But Vasha did not move. It was true that the khaja were barbarians. It was no wonder that the gods had given Bakhtiian a vision, that their favorite children, the jaran, must rule over these less-favored lands. But still, now that the jaran ruled khaja lands, it did no good simply to condemn, simply to sneer, at khaja ways. A ruler must set down true and good laws, of course, and hold to them, but simply crushing the khaja would not make them good subjects.

But he shied away from thoughts that might lead him to think too keenly about his father.

Most of the riders had abandoned the whores, shocked by the raven-haired girl's display. The few left looked quite drunk. Vasha wandered back by Sister Yvanne's wagons and paused there to peer at the silver knives. He had seen these in Jeds, too, had even been in the great holy church there, but he had never gotten a satisfactory explanation for them. Tess had an annoying habit of only answering those questions she wanted to. Why would anyone want a tiny image of a knife rather than a real knife, which was useful?

By the light of two lanterns, Sister Yvanne and her two assistants were carefully bundling up their wares and putting them away.

"The jaran may be barbarians," Sister Yvanne was saying tartly to one of her boys, a black-haired young man dressed in gray robes similar to those the Sister wore, "but at least *Hristain* has granted them a proper sense of modesty, though

I fear they are sadly lacking in humility. But we may yet be successful, Brother Saghir, in our mission, if God favors us."

"What is *Hristain?*" Vasha asked. "Isn't that the name of your god?" He started because they both started, surprised that he could understand them.

"You speak Taor, most honorable young man?"

"Yes, my lady," replied Vasha, uncomfortable now. He didn't like the way she fixed her eye on him. It reminded him too much of the way she had looked at the poor woman Jaelle, disapproving but also, in a perverse way, hopeful.

"We speak of our Lord, the Anointed One," she went on, making a funny little gesture with one hand in front of herself. "*Hristain* is one of His titles. Indeed, in the language of the true church, it is His name. In this book is written the recitation of His word. May I tell you of His sundering?"

"Uh, no, I thank you." Vasha backed away. She had a light in her eyes that reminded him of his father, and he didn't want to think about his father.

He fled back to the jahar's camp, and found Stefan easily enough, standing morosely in the darkness beyond the firelight outside Rusudani's tent. Both of the khaja women knelt outside the tent. Rusudani was speaking, but in such a low voice that Vasha could only just see her lips move, not hear her words—which he couldn't have understood in any case, since she did not speak Taor. She held her little knife in her right hand and with her left clutched a book. Vasha thought that she was, perhaps, praying.

And while Rusudani spoke, her new servant, Jaelle, lifted the tiny knife she had just acquired and brought it to her lips and kissed it ardently. She had tears on her cheeks.

CHAPTER FIVE

Home

Ilyana skated home from Kori's house with her duffel banging against her back. Her homework was done, it was fine summer weather, and she held a bouquet of fresh flowers from Kori's mother's garden in one hand. She paused at the Cornwall Gardens playing field to watch a group of rebellious university students, probably from Imperial College, playing soccer. As university students liked to do during the summer, they were flouting the dress protocols, marking their teams with shirts-and-skins rather than arm flags.

And sure enough, a bystander called out, "quisling peep!" There was a pause in the action, but none of the skins players made any move back to their shirts until the protocol 'car drifted into view, humming down to hover about twelve feet above the center of the field. Even from the edge of the street, Ilyana could feel the uncomfortable pressure of the air field. No one moved for a moment. Finally the young women and men sauntered back to the sidelines to pull on their shirts. Ilyana admired their insouciance. It lent the trivial nature of their defiance some excitement.

She tugged self-consciously at the hem of her shorts. Her knees and calves were showing, but she was still classified as a child, so it ought not to matter. And the protocol 'car didn't have Chapalii stripes, which meant it was human officers, and especially in the summer they tended to go easy on people. The 'car banked, skipped on an air current, and moved away, and the game resumed, with arm flags now. Ilyana peeled a wet leaf off her left blade and skated on.

Coming down Kensington Court Place, she called a greeting to a neighbor and stopped in front of her door. She unsealed her blades, caught them under an elbow, and placed her left hand on the doorplate. The front door opened. At once she knew that her good mood was not to last. As if she had really believed it could.

Valentin sat on the bottom step, feet planted on the entry-way tile. He looked cross. Way, way up at the top of the flight of steps that angled around and around, she saw a face peering down from the third level, withdrawn quickly when it saw her movement below.

"Who's that?" she asked, jerking upward with her chin. "It wasn't Hyacinth or Yevgeni."

Valentin shrugged. "Hopeful actor, probably. How should I know? Why should I care?"

"Just that they're spying!" said Ilyana in a loud voice, hoping the person upstairs could hear her. "What are you doing down here?"

He shrugged again, but said nothing.

"Answer me!"

He had dark shadows under his eyes, set off by the pallor of his face, and he was thinner than ever. Ilyana bit down on adding: *You've got to eat more!* because she had learned that to draw attention to that problem only made it worse. Valentin made a face and stared down at his bare feet. He had grown prettier with puberty, maybe because he was just undernourished enough that he hadn't quite yet grown into that awkward half-man stage, but it was an unhealthy, waiflike prettiness. It attracted the wrong kind of attention.

"Oh, gods," said Ilyana, feeling a sick thread of doubt claw through her. "Dad didn't invite over that awful groping old woman again, did he?"

Valentin shut his left eye and squinted at her through his right one. "Neh. I didn't mind her. I made her pay for it with nesh time."

"Valentin!" Ilyana shrieked. She wanted to punch him and protect him, at the same time. Somehow, her father managed to attract the most horrible old perverts, maybe just because he was willing to do anything he had to in order to get better acting parts and more access to the people who held the reins of power in the entertainment tribe. "Or are you just joking me?"

For a second she thought he was going to say: "Oh, what do you care?" But the last time he'd tried that she'd slapped him once hard. Finally he traced the red curlicues fired into the tile with a toe. But he didn't answer.

Like a winter storm blasts in, bleakness hit. "Oh, Valentin," she whispered. "Did you really?"

His toe moved, but none of the rest of him did. "I just

gotta have the nesh time, Yana," he said finally without looking at her. "I don't care anymore what I have to do to get it."

She sat down next to him, and he made room so she could. She set her blades to one side and slipped the duffel off to sit on the step above. The marble felt cold through her shorts. She put an arm around his thin shoulders. "Valentin, you don't got to. I don't know—I could ask Diana. She'll take you to see a doctor. If I go, too, and explain, they'll have to waive the consent. Everyone knows both our parents are crazy—"

"Then they'll take Anton and Evdokia and the new baby away from Mother."

"It would serve her right," muttered Ilyana fiercely.

"How can you say so?" demanded Valentin, flaring. "It would kill her."

"It will kill you—!"

"I don't care! It's better than here. I hate it here!"

They both heard the exhale of the door opening on the landing above. Ilyana started and twisted to look up, but Valentin did not move. He had the ability to remain utterly still, like a statue, like a body unanimated by soul.

There, on the landing, looking down on them as an angel regards mortals from on high, stood their beautiful father. The most beautiful man on Earth. Everyone said so. Well, he never said so, but he didn't have to. And his reputation was all the more astonishing because golden-blond hair and a pale complexion and that peculiarly piercing blue of the eyes hadn't really been fashionable for a hundred years or more. He had made it so, or at least, for himself.

"Hello, heartling, you're back early." His expression, severe, softened as he regarded her.

Always, she betrayed herself. Always, she smiled, and her heart melted. "Heyo, Daddy," she said, just like a little girl again, wanting to make him proud of her. "We finished all week's homework, too. Kori and I are gonna apply to go Frejday to see the rehearsals of her Uncle Gus's new piece, the one about Shiva and Parvati."

He didn't have to say anything. He could simply radiate approval. She basked in it. Then his gaze shifted to Valentin's back. The world darkened. Her fingers, still cupping Valentin's shoulder, tightened, as if with this shield she could protect him.

"You must apologize to your mother, Valentin," said Vasil emotionlessly.

"Come on," said Ilyana to her brother in a low voice, nudging him with a knee. She didn't have the strength right now to play spectator to this endless battle of wills. "You can take the baby out to the garden while I make dinner."

There was a long hesitation, but finally Valentin stood up. As if that was his cue, Vasil disappeared back inside the flat and the door inhaled shut behind him.

"What did you say?" Ilyana whispered as they climbed the seven steps together, pausing on the landing. Valentin shrugged. She growled at him, then snaked her foot forward toward the toe panel. Hesitated. Always, that split second hesitation before going inside. Always, she had to consciously press the panel with her foot, rather than reflexively tapping it, because she dreaded what was inside. The door whisked open.

Scent and smell and sight, all conspired in this wave that swelled over her every time she came home. Humiliation and loathing together.

All the internal walls in the flat had been torn down, leaving it a single space. In this space her mother had put up her great circular felt tent, surrounding that tent with two smaller tents as well as a cunningly devised fire pit that really wasn't one but looked like one. Not one transparent window looked onto the street or onto the garden and the alley. Not one stretch of plain white wall betrayed that they lived in a khaja building, in a great khaja city, on a planet far distant from the planet and the lands which had given them—well, all of them but the two littlest ones—birth. Because her father was a famous actor, they had resources to draw on. Her mother liked to think it was because he was a Veselov and she an Arkhanov, princely scions of the most important tribes in the jaran, that they had access to such tribute, but Ilyana knew better. Because her father was rich and courted by the rich, he had done what his wife wished: He had paid or bartered to have projection walls installed in place of the windows and the regular walls. So that when you stepped into the flat, you stepped into another world: You walked into a jaran camp.

Other tents sprawled out on two sides, and occasionally a person moved between the tents. Beyond the tents, herds of animals grazed. On the other two sides, instead of looking at the street below or at the blank wash of wall, you looked out at an endless horizon of grass and hill, and the wind brushed the grass in wave upon wave upon wave, sweeping layers of bright and dark across the plains in a pattern that never repeated itself. The distance was so real, so four dimensional, that even knowing better Ilyana still caught herself at times on the verge of walking out into it.

The carpet she stood on had been handwoven of grass. It gave beneath her feet just as a mat of trampled grass would, and its dry scent stirred in her nostrils. The ceiling lofted above, disguised by an infinite projection of sky, sometimes cloudy, sometimes bright, and always with a sun different than Earth's sun, and with a moon larger than Earth's moon.

Vasil's patrons and flunkies loved this flat. It was part of his reputation. Even Valentin, entering, relaxed, but Ilyana tensed. She hated it. She despised her mother for hiding here. Because of the fire codes, one old-fashioned latched window had been left in the streetside wall. A seamless holo projection covered it, but now and again, when everyone else was asleep or out, Ilyana would sneak it open, as if to let in a whiff of London—the curved, supple roofs, the unearthly lights, the breath of here and now.

"Your mother is resting," said Vasil as the door shut behind them. He ducked inside one of the small tents; Ilyana shared the other small tent with Valentin. By the fire pit, little Evdokia crouched next to a pot of water in which she washed vegetables with four-year-old solemnity. Anton stood by the corral, the stretch of wall that disguised the door into the bathroom, beating on a pillow with a piece of wood shaved to look like a saber. One of the flunkies was here, in the corner where the big carpet loom was tacked down on the ground; she was an aspiring actress who had decided instead that she had been given a mystical calling to apprentice at traditional weaving with the great actor's wife. Ilyana thought the sloe-eyed young woman looked ridiculous dressed in cast-off jaran clothing, but her presence meant that Ilyana didn't have to spend hours every night weaving and spinning.

"Here," said Ilyana, giving her duffel to Valentin. Then she went into the great tent. The projection walls were fantastic, of course; it was practically impossible *not* to believe in the illusion. But inside the tent even Ilyana could forget for an instant that she had ever left the tribes.

Weavings curtained the interior. Embroidered pillows were piled neatly in one corner. The bronze warming stove sat on its stag-headed legs next to a carved wooden chest inlaid with bone and gold. Leather flasks hung from the ceiling poles, and the great leather vessel used for fermented milk sat on a metal trivet, surrounded by its attendant dishes and a wooden scoop. Ilyana opened the chest and got out wooden bowls and spoons. She set them on the rugs, which were layered three deep in the outer chamber of the tent, and then pushed past the curtain, stepping up onto the six deep carpets of the inner chamber of the tent.

Karolla Arkhanov reclined on a raised wooden bed. Sitting on a stool by her feet was another flunky, this one a producer's daughter who had recently managed the transition into being allowed into the intimacy of the family quarters of the tent by virtue of having accidentally been in the flat when the new baby had come five days ago. She had made herself useful by boiling water and pounding the birth rhythms on the drum, and had thus been granted a status which she evidently deemed glorious but which Ilyana knew was the equivalent of a favored servant. Right now she was spinning, and rocking the baby's cradle with rhythmic pushes of one foot while Karolla gave her a desultory lesson in khush.

"Here is Yana," said Karolla. Yana went obediently over to her mother, gave her the flowers, and kissed her on either cheek, in the formal style. She nodded at the flunky, who bobbed her head enthusiastically in return. Thank the gods that Rory wasn't there; he was the first, and the worst, of the flunkies, and had, in fact, made himself useful to her parents, but recently he had been eyeing Ilyana with unbearably sexual interest. At least the women, whatever their inclinations, were polite and discreet.

The baby was sleeping. Ilyana knelt and brushed her fine pale skin with a finger. The newborn had no hair, but she had a thumbnail-sized red blemish below her left ear. Because of this blemish, Karolla refused to name the baby until she was blooded again—until her menstrual cycle started. It was an old superstition, and it embarrassed Ilyana even while the flunkies and patrons thought it charming.

"Do you want Valentin to take the baby outside, for some fresh air?" Ilyana asked her mother, switching to khush.

There was a silence. "Valentin has been rude," said Karolla gravely. "Our visitor was forced to leave."

"Uh, who was it?" Ilyana flicked a glanced toward the producer's daughter. Karolla had no sense of privacy. All the serious flunkies used language matrices to learn khush and put up with Karolla's verbal lessons as part of the game of playing court.

"M. Pandit," said the producer's daughter, who went by the unfortunate nickname of "Nipper." Valentin always said, coarsely, that it was because she liked to be bitten, but Ilyana had overheard someone at a party say it was because her grandmother had raised her in Old Japan. Ilyana didn't know what her real name was.

Ilyana shrugged, kissed the baby, and retreated outside, gathering up the bowls and spoons as she went. M. Pandit was a new visitor, and while Ilyana didn't much like her, she hadn't pegged her yet. Definitely not a flunky: M. Pandit had a greasy aura of power around her, as a potential patron would have, though she was not, as far as Ilyana knew, connected with the vast entertainment tribe in any way. Neither did she seem to be interested in Vasil Veselov in *that* way. With a few notable exceptions, those were the only three reasons anyone ever came to visit the Arkhanov camp.

Valentin sat chatting with Evdokia by the fire, encouraging her to count the vegetables as she washed them. He didn't help, of course. Their mother would have an absolute fit if either of the boys helped to cook: Jaran boys didn't cook; they learned to help with the herds, to work with hides and leather and harness, to embroider, to fight, to do men's work. There was very little men's work to do here, but Karolla managed not to see that, and since she rarely went to other people's homes, she never saw that both women and men cooked here on Earth. She was content that Anatoly Sakhalin instructed the boys in fighting and in embroidery. She was resigned to the fact that the children had to attend khaja school. She ruled over her flunkies, received homage from her husband's admirers, and had babies.

Ilyana fetched a shank of lamb from the pantry hidden behind the bank of potted shrubs that flanked the "spring" from which they got water and hunkered down beside Evdokia to slice it up for stew.

"I went upstairs," said Evdokia in a soft voice, "an' Portia and I played with—" She broke off and glanced over toward the weaver, lowering her voice further. "—real toys. Yana, when can we live in a real flat? When do I get to go to school like Portia?"

"I don't know, little one," replied Ilyana, feeling suddenly sick with guilt for her afternoon of freedom at Kori's house. She should have been home, spending time with the little ones. The gods knew, they needed it. "Maybe not till you're six. Go pour that water out down the drain, heartling." Obediently, Evdokia trotted off. "Valentin," hissed Ilyana, lowering her voice so that it barely sounded. "What did you say to M. Pandit?"

"Didn't say anything to her," retorted Valentin. "I just told Mother that she's an oily old quisling and anyway she's just sniffing round here 'cause she thinks her smart young trophy husband is interested in Dad, and she dun't want him to be."

"Valentin!" Ilyana squealed, and clapped a hand over her mouth. In some ways Valentin was grossly ignorant, but in others he was far, far too knowing. "How could you? Why do you think that anyway?"

Valentin rolled his eyes. "You were at that awful reception, Yana. Didn't you see her? Didn't you see Dad making eyes at her husband?"

"No. They had those great reproductions of Greek and Roman amphitheaters in the salon. I just stayed there the whole time." No one had bothered her there, a quiet girl lingering by three-dimensional models that most of the adults ignored. "Anyway, if M. Pandit is a quisling, then what can her trophy husband do for Dad? He never makes eyes at anybody unless he thinks they can do something for him."

"I don't know *everything,* Yana! You outta pay more attention."

"Why?" she asked, and then they both clamped their mouths shut when their father emerged from the spare tent. He looked at them but, mercifully, decided to go in to his wife instead. Evdokia returned, Anton tagging along behind.

"Can we go out, Valentin?" Anton asked querulously. "I'm bored."

Valentin glanced at Ilyana. "Oh, all right," he said.

"Voice tag yourself for forty minutes," said Ilyana. "Then it'll be dinnertime."

"Can I go, too?" begged Evdokia.

"You're too little," said Anton with all the scornful superiority of an eight-year-old.

"Yes, you can come," said Valentin swiftly. "Let's get out of here before Dad comes back out and says we can't." They vanished out the door—a stretch of gold and blue horizon that opened into the startling blank flatness of hallway and then merged back in with the endless land again—and it was suddenly quiet. The flunky at the loom shifted position now and again. Ilyana chopped up the vegetables, humming to herself.

The sudden appearance of her father startled her, he arrived so silently. He crouched down beside her. "I have to attend an opening tonight, and your mother is too ill to go with me." It was a convenient fiction: Her mother was almost always "too ill" to attend functions, even if in this case it was true, the baby just having come. He settled a hand tenderly on her knee and smiled at her. "Will you come with me?"

"What kind of opening?" she asked reluctantly, even while she knew it was already decided.

"Oh, nothing too overwhelming, I think. Not as bad as the last one, anyway." His smile became conspiratorial, including her in the memory of how stultifyingly official the last reception had been. "It's an exhibition of photography."

"Photography? Like the two-dimensional stuff?"

He chuckled warmly. "Some of it, I suppose. I don't know all the technical terms."

"Father," she asked suspiciously, "why are you going to an art exhibit? Are you angling for someone to do a portrait of you?"

Now he really laughed. It was such a rare sound that Ilyana cherished it. "I don't think so. There've been so many, after all. But you will come with me, won't you? It's at the Little Tate, and there's that nesh-enhanced exhibit of the Floating Gardens of Babel in one of the adjoining galleries."

It was actually the Hanging Gardens of Babylon, but she didn't correct him. "Oh, all right," she said, not immune to bribery. Then she felt a pang. "But I really should stay home with Valentin and the little ones."

"I'll send them upstairs."

"Valentin doesn't get along with Anatoly Sakhalin, Father. You know that."

It was the wrong thing to say. Her father clenched one hand, and his gaze fixed on the haze of the false fire. "Certainly Anatoly Sakhalin has his own views of the world, and a certain position to maintain as a prince of the Sakhalin—" Which was to say that Vasil did not like him much, either. "—but if Valentin behaved like a boy and not like indolent khaja chattel, Sakhalin would not despise him. Valentin has to become a man someday."

Ilyana winced, her father's tone was so biting. "But, Daddy . . ." she began.

He cut her off. "It is kind of you to plead for him, Yana, but if you continue to protect him, he will never grow up."

Tears stung at her eyes. She bent down and chopped furiously at the vegetables. It wasn't fair. Why could no one see that Valentin had taken it hardest of all, torn out of the tribes and transported to this strange new world? It had happened to Valentin twice now, first losing his father before he could understand what had happened and then losing the aunt and uncle who had sustained him through those difficult years when Karolla had lived in the Veselov tribe alone, her husband an outlaw. Their father had returned to them, but Vasil had never forgiven Valentin for not accepting him instantly, even though it was too much to expect from the wary five-year-old child Valentin had been back then. And Vasil had compounded the offense by taking them away from the jaran forever.

Her father's hand touched her hair and stroked down to cradle her neck and jaw, the way he had comforted her when she was a child. "I . . . I . . ." she said through her tears, but she could not go on.

"Tell me, heartling," he said quietly.

"I'm worried about Valentin. I'm worried about him guising too much."

He withdrew his hand. "There is nothing wrong with Valentin that he can't cure by acting as he ought! We will not discuss this any further, Yana. You're making excuses for him. And he still hasn't apologized to your mother." But, relenting, he kissed her on the forehead and then stood up. "We'll leave after supper."

She sighed, brushed away her tears, and dumped the vegetables into the stew.

One of the reasons Ilyana hated going to receptions with her father was that he never, ever, traveled like most people did, on public lines. He always had to hire a private carriage, no matter how expensive, no matter how exclusive it made him look. Vasil Veselov liked being exclusive. He liked pressing the sumptuary laws to their edge, never quite crossing into the pale. Not even Kori's Uncle Gus or her Aunt Parvati, who was a member of Concord Parliament, took private carriages. Gods, even Charles Soerensen, the only human who had gained a rank within the Chapalii Empire, traveled like everyone else did. Everyone knew that.

Ilyana wore a plain blue silk tunic and a calf-length silk skirt, ornamented with a belt of wooden beads and a single gold necklace, but her father, to her horror, got himself up in jaran clothes: the scarlet shirt gaudily embroidered down its arms and along the collar, the black trousers and black leather boots decorated with gold tassels, and gold bracelets and enough necklaces to make him gleam. He looked positively barbaric.

Their arrival at the Little Tate Gallery caused a sensation. The carriage sank down beside the broad steps and spit out a tongue of stairsteps down which Vasil made his entrance onto the street amidst the crowd of arriving pedestrians. Ilyana slunk along next to her father, trying to disappear, while he was pointed at and swarmed and in general made much of. He had a word or a touch or a glance for every soul who came within ten feet of him. They bogged down in the gallery foyer until a tall, red-haired woman plowed through the crowd and made an opening for herself before them.

"Veselov! I'm honored to see you here! I'm Margaret O'Neill." She stuck her hand out, the khaja way of greeting.

"I remember you," he said, taking hold of her hand and lifting it to his lips, an affectation he had picked up from old-time "moving" flat films.

She snorted, giving him time to finish the gesture before she extricated her hand and turned to look at Ilyana. "Charmed, I'm sure. This is—" She hesitated, and a peculiar expression swept her face and vanished. "Ilyana, isn't it?"

"Ilyana Arkhanov," said Ilyana crisply. "I'm sorry, M. O'Neill, but have we met before? If we have, I beg your pardon for not remembering."

"Call me Maggie." She smiled, and Ilyana liked her immediately. "You were younger though. I last saw you— what?—eight years ago when we were all leaving Rhui. I don't expect you would remember me. Here, come inside. There might even be a photo of you, Ilyana."

"Of me?" Ilyana's heart sank, weighted down by an awful sense of foreboding. Maggie O'Neill. Leaving Rhui eight years ago. They passed through the double doors and into a well-lit gallery cut by zigzagging white panels and spittled with big white cubes. Maggie O'Neill's records adorned these surfaces. Her records of the jaran.

With leaden feet Ilyana stalked over to the nearest cube and gaped at the three-dee film grown up from its surface. A young jaran woman played and sang, accompanied by an intent young man on a drum. Ilyana could understand her, of course; she didn't need to read the words scrolling by along the rim of the cube or listen in to the translation plug. The Singer sang the story of Mekhala and how she had brought horses to the jaran tribes, freeing her people but in turn binding herself in marriage to the wind spirit who had aided her.

"Isn't this *marvelous?*" said a man in passing to his companion. "And they made it a flesh-only viewing, too. It's all of a piece with the subject and materials."

Ilyana hunched down just a little lower and sidled over to the nearest panel. Old-fashioned flat photos were displayed here, but somehow the primitive subject matter looked right on the two-dimensional surface. She reached out to touch a photograph of a woman, heavy in a felt coat, seated before a loom, then withdrew her hand abruptly. There, two boys stood by a cluster of sheep, faces dirty, smiling at some joke. And there, a light-haired girl sat on horseback, a bow slung over her back. And there, a troop of riders marched off to war, gloriously armed with spears tipped with flags and rank upon rank of sabers.

All her unwanted old childhood memories came rushing back, overwhelming her. She could hear the harness jingling and the noise of the horses, and then she realized that there was another white cube behind this panel boasting a living, moving three-dee, this one of a jahar riding endlessly off, ready for battle.

"And look, Amber," said a woman's voice breathlessly behind her. "I *told* you braving the crowd would be worth it. Isn't that Vasil Veselov in the flesh? Goddess, look how he's dressed. I could just die."

Ilyana cringed. She edged away toward another panel and pretended to examine a panoramic photo of a jaran camp spread out along a flat horizon of gold. She could hear conversations from the other side of the panel, but she felt protected here, invisible. She had lost track of her father.

"I don't know, Youssef, I think all the fuss a little ridiculous myself. Consider the genre as well. I just don't think the primitive recording techniques add anything to the subject, even though I'm sure they're meant to be a commentary on the planet's interdicted status."

The comment elicited only an uninterpretable grunt.

"M. O'Neill, how nice to see you again," said a familiar, sharp voice that Ilyana couldn't quite place.

"Ah, M. Pandit. How wonderful to see you. I'm so *pleased* you could come." Maggie O'Neill's voice sounded so deadpan that Ilyana couldn't tell whether she was being sarcastic or polite. "But a little surprised to see you at this kind of event."

"My husband is interested in the arts," replied M. Pandit. "I can't help but be interested as well in an exhibition of this kind. The planet of Rhui is interdicted by Chapalii protocol dictates, after all, and under Duke Charles's order, as well. I'm just surprised that this kind of material would exist at all. Of course, we all know about the unfortunate death of his sister on Rhui. Such a shame. But one can't help but be interested in seeing pictures of a planet few of us will ever visit, especially knowing that Terese Soerensen spent her last days there. That she might even have been—why, here, look at these native women. How easily any of *us* might blend in among them."

Ilyana had a sudden vivid memory of Tess Soerensen kissing her good-bye, in the formal style, on either cheek. She had really liked Tess Soerensen. But she also had a premonition that Tess's image would appear nowhere in this room.

"So true," said Maggie in fulsome tones. "As you know, Marco Burckhardt has been doing anthropological surveys of the native populations on Rhui for many years now. I happened to spend some time with him, and I did a little recording of my own. I did so feel that it might be important to make a permanent record of some of the Rhuian natives. I think it illuminates something of our own past to us, don't you? I couldn't resist showing it here."

"Especially not with a native brought back from Rhui, in defiance of the interdiction." M. Pandit's tone was menacing.

Maggie laughed easily. If she was cowed by M. Pandit's veiled threats, Ilyana could not hear it in her voice. "Yes, there were compelling medical reasons, as well as aesthetic ones ... but I won't go into that here. Also, as you know, Veselov originally was contracted to the Bharentous Repertory Company, a bit of an—experiment—by Owen Zerentous, but he went on to—ah—bigger and better things. I'm lucky to have him here today. His presence can only add luster to my exhibit. He's so very famous now, you know, as well as quite handsome. But they were all in general a good-looking people."

Ilyana bit down on a smile, liking Maggie O'Neill even more; she was being so obviously sardonic with the stiff, nosy old M. Pandit, not caring about Pandit's ominously authoritarian curiosity. Ilyana wished she had such confidence.

"Ah, there you are, Jazir," said M. Pandit abruptly in an altered tone. She almost purred. "M. O'Neill, have you met my husband?"

There was a strange, brief silence, like a skip of breath. "No, I haven't," said Maggie finally. "How do you do?"

Ilyana suddenly caught sight of her father, standing at the end of the row of panels, staring, staring, at a still three-dee portrait of a black-haired, bearded man dressed in the simple red and black of a jaran soldier, one hand resting casually on his saber hilt, his glance thrown to one side. The jaran man looked intensely severe. But Ilyana knew, seeing him, recognizing him with a stab that ran right down through her and flooded her with prickles, that he was caught forever in the moment just before he smiled at someone unseen, beyond the range of the camera.

How could she not know? She bore his name. The extraordinary fervor of her father's concentration as he stared at the image of Ilya Bakhtiian troubled her. Vasil never showed this kind of emotion outside of his acting; it might give other people power over him. She knew, as she knew when the air changes, heralding storm, that something was about to happen. With a jolt, she uprooted herself and hurried over to him.

In time to see him lift his eyes and focus on a group of three people on the other side of the panel. One was Maggie O'Neill. At first Ilyana didn't recognize M. Pandit because the emerald uniform disguised her, overwhelmed her. A quisling uniform. M. Pandit was one of the human officers

in the Protocol Office—oh, they didn't call themselves quislings, of course. Everyone else called them that behind their
backs. M. Pandit wore three platinum bars on the lapel of
her uniform, and Ilyana gulped down a sudden lump in her
throat. Three bars. It was the highest rank a human officer
could attain in the service of the Chapalii—the highest rank,
that is, except for the ennobling that Charles Soerensen had
inadvertently achieved.

Between the two women stood a young man, one arm
folded passively around M. Pandit's elbow. He was a good-
looking young man, as befitted a trophy husband, with short
dark hair and a neatly trimmed beard, deep brown eyes and
a narrow, defined face. His expression was serious. But then
he glanced up at Vasil Veselov, smiled brilliantly and briefly,
and looked down again.

In that brief gesture Ilyana clearly saw the resemblance.
He looked enough like Ilyakoria Bakhtiian that anyone
might laugh good-naturedly over the odd coincidence. Anybody but her father, who gazed with unnerving steadiness at
the other man. Anyone but M. Pandit, who skewered the famous actor with an aggressive stare.

Anyone but Ilyana, who had long ago learned to recognize
trouble coming. And she had a very, very bad feeling about
this.

CHAPTER SIX

Spider's Web

The jaran camp drowsed under the afternoon sun. The dusty air hung in a heat haze over the tents, and the cloudless sky seemed to breathe in and out with the pulse of the sun.

Tess liked these lazy afternoon days. Time suspended; there was no past or future, nothing but an endless present with her children playing nearby, her husband sitting beside her under the awning, usually in quiet council with one or another of his commanders, her sister twenty steps away weaving, her tribe—for that was what the jaran were to her, now—surrounding her. On these long afternoons she could easily sit motionless for an hour at a time without anyone thinking it strange.

So she sat now, scrolling through information about Chapalii shipping schedules recently sent to her by her brother. The screen, which didn't exist physically, seemed to float in the air about an arm's length in front of her, and periodically she blinked twice to move the information on. The implant in her cranium produced these images and processed the information, and she used her eyes as the interface, processing visually.

"All encryption is cyclic," she said aloud.

"Hmm?" murmured Ilya. He was reading, or dozing, beside her, sprawled comfortably on pillows. They weren't quite touching—it was too warm for that—but she felt the length of his body all along hers, his back to her side.

"Encryption. Ciphers, also called codes. They're cyclic, so they can eventually be decoded, be broken and deciphered, but a cycle could be so long that by our standards it's essentially unbreakable. . . ."

He shifted around to look at her. "You think about the oddest things."

She made the mistake of glancing at him. The two sights, her screen of numbers and linked spatial codes and his face, blurred together and made her head hurt. She blinked four times hard and the implant switched off. "Ouch," she said reflexively. Even after years of living with the implant, it still caught her out at times.

"Staring at the sun again?" he asked lightly.

"No."

He watched her for a little while in silence. For a moment, he seemed on the brink of asking her a question. But he didn't.

"I'm just thinking about why merchants use encryption," she continued, and he let her go on, knowing she liked to talk things out. "To conceal their manifest of cargo, or to avoid a prince's tax they don't want to pay. Plotting treason. Or if their cargo is particularly valuable, they might want to discuss and plan out the route of travel in secret, so that no bandit or competing house would know where to lie in wait for an ambush."

"You've been talking to too many merchants."

"Actually, I was thinking about something my brother said to me in his last letter." She hesitated. Charles sent information embedded in the tiny cylinders used to seal the handwritten parchment and paper letters that were his overt communications. Even these handwritten letters, although not the main part of the information he continually fed to Tess, were themselves partially encrypted so that Ilya could read them without suspecting that he was seeing only part of the message. But seeing Ilya's expression now, Tess wondered if he knew that he was being served only part of the truth. "About Chapalii merchants. He *thinks* they may be using ciphers, but he wonders why they would use them. Especially since the emperor controls all the shipping routes with an iron hand."

"You know that the emperor controls these routes? Or only believe that he does? We watch the merchants travel from one city to the next, from Hamrat to Parkilnous to Jeds, and we may think they travel on a set pattern fixed by years of tradition or by a king's will, but then if you speak with these merchants you see that the truth is not so simple. Sands shift and cover old roads and watering holes. Alliances shift and turn two princes into enemies where they had once been friends. A grandson may choose to rebel against his grandfather's set ways, and he may try a new road and find that it leads to disaster, or to riches. And yet again one family may have trodden the same paths for generations, never changing. By walking the same road, each girl after her mother, each boy after his father, so does that road become their family and each of them lives on forever in the ones who come after."

Insects droned in the quiet. Harness jingled and stilled. "Are you going to give up conquest for philosophy, my love?"

A smile tipped his lips. "Your own brother once told me that knowledge is power. Is philosophy not a form of conquest?"

"I thought it was more like a search."

"Isn't that the same thing?"

Tess touched his cheek, but it was so damned hot that even that contact was too sweaty to prolong. "Only for you, my heart. Ilya—?"

"Yes?" He smiled now, a real smile. He looked so youthful that it was uncanny, even though she knew why he wasn't aging at a normal rate. Still, at forty-five, he wasn't quite yet old enough that the few strands of gray sprinkling his hair weren't enough; that the gray hadn't increased in eight years had not yet excited suspicion. But it would. Soon enough, seeing time somehow suspended in him, people would begin to wonder how he stayed so young.

"Nothing," she replied.

"A wise ruler," added Ilya after a few moments, "maintains stability so that merchants may trade and increase his wealth through taxes as well as their own through profit. If these same merchants follow the rule of law, then it is in any emperor's interest to let them carry on their trade, which they understand best just as he understands how best to rule, without his interference."

"True," mused Tess. She examined him, where he lay so close: the coarse black hairs of his mustache which curved down around his lips to meld into his beard; the lines on his forehead, wrinkles brought on by frowning. Ilya had never developed laugh lines. An odd light dwelt in his eyes, as it had always done. He had never bothered to conceal it; thus had the gods marked him as one of their own. He could not have concealed it in any case. He lived in the world differently. For Ilya the world was one great long vision illuminated by the gods' touch and through it he walked according to some hierophantic time.

"Is there something wrong with me?" he asked suddenly, touching his face with his right hand.

"Nothing cooler weather and a little privacy couldn't cure," she said with a grin.

"Mmmm," he replied. He sat up. "Here comes Niko."

Tess jumped to her feet and hurried out into the sun to give her arm to Niko. Even that short movement made her break into a sweat. "It's too hot to walk around, Niko," she scolded.

"I'm bored," said Niko, "and there are twelve children singing loudly in my wife's tent. Including yours. So I have come here to play a game of *khot* with your husband."

He moved slowly, and although for years she had stood eye to eye with him, now he stooped enough that she could look down on his head. Ilya set out pillows. Tess helped Niko ease down to sit and then filled a cup with lukewarm tea for him and arranged a plate with sweetcakes and fruit. Carefully, stiffly, glancing once at Tess to make sure she did not interfere with the labored movements of his hands, Niko untied a leather pouch from his belt and set it on the carpet. Although *khot* could be played on a grid drawn in the dirt with sticks, Ilya had a gracefully carved wooden board which he brought out from the tent along with his own stones. Then the two men settled down to play. Tess reclined back on her pillows, blinked, and set up her program again. The quiet snap of stones being placed on the board serenaded her.

Twelve years ago, Charles had obtained the allegiance of a Chapalii merchant house. Eight years ago, Tess's old friend Sojourner King Bakundi and her husband Rene Oljaitu had managed to talk Charles and the Keinaba house elders into letting the two humans apprentice to the Keinaba family. Bit by bit, information trickled in. Charles—or, that is, a consortium of people who worked with him—had collected it and other stray strands of information, packed it on a cylinder, and sent it to Tess. She had loaded the packet into her implant and now she picked her way through. It was rather like cutting a path through a dense jungle. The vegetation obscured the landmarks.

First and foremost, any great empire thrives on movement: stable lines of supply, of trade, of information. This movement must be unobstructed for officials on imperial business, and monitored and restricted for others on a scale that varied depending on the necessity of these functions to imperial strength and the likelihood of such restrictions causing dangerous levels of dissent.

In order to effectively sabotage the movement of ships and information in the Chapalii Empire, Charles had to figure out the logic of their transportation and communications web.

"Damn," muttered Ilya suddenly, jolting Tess back to the real world. "Why do you always beat me, Niko?"

"Because you still try to use force and the weight of numbers to take territory, rather than building a spider's web which looks fragile but in the end spreads its tendrils everywhere and takes over the board." Niko chuckled. "Shall we try again?"

Ilya grunted. Tess heard the sweep of stones being collected, a cascade as stones were poured back into their pouches, and then, starting again, the taps at uneven intervals as the two men took turns setting their stones on the board.

In the twenty-first century, humanity had braved the stars with a sublight drive. Soon after this momentous occurrence, the Chapalii had appeared and given the humans and their fledgling League the key to the vector drive, which allowed them to travel through space rather as ships had once sailed the seas between the continents of Earth. It reminded Tess all at once of the game of khot, if one warped the board so that the grid had a three-dimensional curve rather than a two-dimensional flat expanse. Relay stations (the stones) created the windows (the lines of the grid), the singularity in the time-space continuum through which ships traveled. The velocity and angle of entry—the vector—determined where and how far the ship would then travel in that "window" between two points in normal space. Thus, with this network of relay stations, the Chapalii Empire controlled a system of movement that encompassed navigable space.

That much humans knew for sure about the vector drive, that, and that their routes of passage were strictly controlled by the Protocol Office. Tess could not help but wonder, though, if the relay stations created the windows or merely allowed them to be accessed. As far as human scientists had discovered, the windows existed naturally somehow, since it was remotely possible—if terribly dangerous—to navigate with the vector drive without the aid of relay stations, devising calculations by instinct, skill and sheer good luck. Perhaps in a long, slow outward expansion the Chapalii had mapped the network of windows and marked them for their own, creating a web on which they could traverse the stars. Like a spider's web. The thought triggered a series of connections deep in her implant, and abruptly an old Machine Age flat poem wavered onto the screen:

A noiseless, patient spider,
I marked where on a little promontory it stood isolated,
Marked how to explore the vacant vast surrounding,
It launched forth filament, filament, filament, out of itself,
Ever unreeling them, ever tirelessly speeding them.

"Better," said Niko, breaking the silence. His voice was still lucid, but heavy with age. "But you've still let me encircle you. Shall we try again?"

Ilya grunted, too irritated, too intent, to reply in words. Stones poured.

Tess flickered her attention back to the screen and the spider.

. . . . Ceaselessly musing, venturing, throwing, seeking the
*   spheres to connect them,*
Till the bridge you will need be formed, till the ductile an-
*   chor hold,*
Till the gossamer thread you fling catch somewhere—

Only Walt Whitman was talking about the soul, which wound her around to that days-ago conversation with Ilya, in which a woven pattern had seemed to her to express as much about her own and little Lara Orzhekov's personalities as any straightforward listing of attributes might.

Unless one thought of the web of windows linking planets and stations each to the other across the "measureless oceans of space" as the soul, the breath, of the Empire. Like a great net, pulsing with the inspiration and expiration of its own being.

Ilya chuckled suddenly, distracting her. Like an echo ringing faintly after his laugh, she heard bells. She blinked hard four times and the screen snapped into oblivion, leaving her with a lingering aftervision that dissipated as a belled messenger rode through it, pulled up, and dismounted, handing his reins over to one of the day guard.

Without looking up from the game, Ilya lifted a hand, and the soldier approached. He was a young man, his black hair twisted into three braids, his cheeks ruddy from the heat. He knelt just under the shade of the awning, bells chiming softly, and sat back on his heels, resting his palms on his thighs. He looked content enough to wait, out of the sun. Tess poured him some tea, and he thanked her prettily and sipped at it with commendable restraint.

Ilya and Niko finished the game, which, naturally, Niko won. As far as Tess knew, Ilya had only ever bested Niko at khot two times in his life.

Niko shook his head. "Ilyakoria, I despair of ever teaching you the serenity that will allow you to master the game. Yet somehow the lesson you cannot learn on the board you have learned to apply in war, so I have not utterly failed."

Ilya glanced up sharply at the old man. "You have not failed at all, Niko," he said harshly, and then subsided when he saw the smile on Niko's face. "You will stay here, of course, and listen to the report."

"Of course," murmured Niko, still looking amused, although Tess also saw that he was beginning to look tired.

Ilya turned to the messenger. "Your name?"

"Daniil Obolensky, of Zvertkov's army," said the young man promptly. "I bring two pieces of news. The first is of a revolt in Salkh, led by a bricklayer dressed in rags who claims to have heard the word of their God through a fog that set upon him in the night—"

"And no doubt gained the backing of their discontented noblemen as well," muttered Ilya.

"That is so," agreed the soldier, "according to the messenger who got through to us. The jaran garrison was set upon, although some tens are still barricaded in the citadel and others escaped to the ruins in the sands which the khaja will not visit for fear of demons."

Tess sighed, though she said nothing. Ilya listened intently. For eight years Salkh had remained a sore point in the southern Habakar district of the growing jaran empire, under jaran suzerainty but never quite yielding.

"What action has Zvertkov taken?" asked Niko.

"He has called back the advance troops from the Heaven Mountains to throw a perimeter around the city. But he has only just established himself in the city of Kalita, which lies thirty days' ride across the wastelands from Khoyan, which itself lies twenty days' ride across desert from Salkh, so he does not wish to withdraw any significant portion of his army back across these wastelands. By his order, I delivered these tidings as well to Prince Mitya as I passed through Hamrat in Habakar. The prince has sent two thousands south to help establish the perimeter. Otherwise he awaits your word."

"Did Prince Mitya send word to me on how he intends to deal with Salkh?" Ilya asked, looking annoyed that such a matter had been brought to his attention rather than summarily dealt with.

The rider dipped his head, acknowledging the unspoken censure in Bakhtiian's question. "Prince Mitya adds these words: 'While I would otherwise simply destroy Salkh and its people for their rebellion, my wife begs that I spare the city, since in it rests a great and ancient temple to her God founded by a holy man whose daughter many daughters removed is her mother.' "

Ilya grunted. "Tell Prince Mitya this. 'You will level Salkh until it is no higher than the sands which surround it. If you first set the town on fire, then the holy sanctuary may be spared if it is built of brick; if it is spared, then it alone may be allowed to stand while what remains is leveled, to show our mercy toward those who submit to the will of the gods.' "

"What about the inhabitants of Salkh?" Tess asked. Ilya glanced at her. Tess knew it puzzled him, her concern for a thousand, ten thousand, insignificant lives, but he was used to her quirks by now.

"Those who led and countenanced the rebellion will be executed." He hesitated and considered Tess for a moment, frowning. "Artisans and craftsmen may be dispersed to where they will do the most good. Those with special skills will be sent to Sarai. Of the rest, they may be made servants of the empire or sold into slavery, as Prince Mitya and his wife and ministers see fit." He nodded once, decisively, to show that the matter was ended. Tess said nothing. It was a more merciful fate than some cities had met. "The other message?"

The rider reached under his coat of bells and carefully

drew out oiled cloth, which he unwound. Two thick slabs of paper lay protected within. He offered the first to Tess.

" 'From Kirill Zvertkov to the Prince of Jeds,' " he recited from memory. " 'Greetings, and a treaty from the merchants of Byblos, who lay at rest in the caravansaries of Kalita and were brought before me. After two days of feasting we agreed to the following terms.' "

Supple with oil, the parchment unwrapped smoothly. Jaran commanders usually used foreign scribes, writing in Rhuian, to record their treaties. Tess could tell by the formality and flowing curves of the calligraphy that this was done by a Habakar scribe now in the service of the jaran conquerors. Underneath the Rhuian, a second hand had roughly traced in a translation, in the script (derived from the Jedan script) which Tess had devised for khush, the language of the jaran.

" 'By the authority invested in me by Ilyakoria Bakhtian, dyan of the jaran, and by Tess Soerensen, Prince of Jeds, I, Kirill Zvertkov, commander of the Army of the Right Hand, hereby authorize this treaty. As Kalita is the northernmost city to which the merchants of Byblos travel, so shall they henceforth send detailed reports to the jaran army as they travel of the worth of the local merchants and the routes of the caravans and the strength of the princes both in soldiers and in wealth, and reports as well of the movements of any soldiers in the lands through which they travel. As well, the merchants of Byblos shall tell at every city through which they travel of the great strength of the jaran army and of the favor shown us by Mother Sun and Father Wind, such that no prince and no people can stand against us. In return, wherever the jaran ride that is south and southeast of Jeds, we will destroy any trading station that does not hold allegiance to Byblos.' "

When she had finished, the messenger handed her the second note. This one, a little drier, crackled as she opened it. Inside was a brief letter written in a hand Tess recognized, one she had trained herself, that of Shura Sakhalin.

" 'Here follows a description of the merchants of Byblos,' " she read aloud, " 'given by Kirill Zvertkov, commander of the Army of the Right Hand and husband of Mother Veselov, and written down by Shura Sakhalin, eldest granddaughter of Mother Sakhalin. The men of Byblos are small of stature, with red-brown skin. They come from lands far to the south of Kalita. They wear loosely draped finespun cloth of white with blue or purple borders and they comment constantly on how cold it is, although it seems hot enough to me. They have no women with them. Neither do they travel with soldiers, trusting to their god, Son-of-Falcon, to protect them as he does all travelers. They wear delicate necklaces of gold and of jewels unknown to me. They all know how to read and write and tally accounts, a gift granted to their people by a goddess named Bird-Woman, whose claws left tracks in the mud, the first writing. By this veneration of birds I judge them to be civilized people."

Finishing, she made no comment. They all sat a while in silence. No wind stirred the tents at all. The heat of the sun seeped down through the grass and into the earth as if it had weight. A child's pure voice lifted in a song, and soon a ragged chorus joined it, nearing them.

"Go to the tent of Eva Kolenin," said Tess finally to the rider, remembering her manners. "She will feed you and give you a place to rest. Her husband is Konstans Barshai, who is the captain of Bakhtiian's jahar. In the morning you will return to us, and we will give you messages to take back to Zvertkov."

The rider inclined his head and took himself off, bells whispering as he walked away from them. He passed an unruly pack of children, two of whom broke away from their companions and ran over to the tent.

"Mama! Papa!" cried Natalia, dancing around under the awning in excitement. "Mother Orzhekov says there is to be a *birbas* in ten days, with ten tribes, or more!"

Yuri sat down in his mother's lap, and then reached over and stole a sweetcake out of his father's hand. He smiled sweetly, and Ilya let him keep it.

"Sit down, Talia," said Niko. "You're making my head hurt. Here, you can play a game of khot with me. At least you're more of a challenge than your father."

Natalia flung herself down opposite Niko, her back against her father, and transformed herself into a paragon of stillness. "I am not! He beats me all the time."

"But you will be," replied Niko mildly.

"Niko," broke in Tess, "are you sure? You look tired—" Niko shot her a look that said, perhaps, more than he meant it to, or perhaps not: *Let me play khot with the child while I still can.*

"What do you know of Byblos?" asked Ilya suddenly.

Tess considered. "I don't even know if it's a trading house, a city, or a kingdom. I confess I know very little about the lands south and southeast of Jeds, except that they must be very hot. It was clever of Kirill to word the treaty like that."

"Indeed," said Ilya coolly. Tess glanced over at him. Was it possible that he was *still* jealous of Kirill? Surely not. Ilya admitted few women and fewer men into his circle of absolute trust. His aunt, his female cousins and especially Sonia, his niece Nadine, a courtesan of Jeds named Mayana, Niko's wife Juli Danov, Dr. Cara Hierakis, and Tess, of course: Nine women that made, but Tess could only think of five men. Three men had been with him since the beginning, Niko, Josef Raevsky, and Tadheus Lensky; the fourth was his first and most valuable ally, the great general and prince Yaroslav Sakhalin. But eight years ago by some invisible process impossible to understand or describe, Kirill had become the fifth.

"Yuri, you're too hot," said Tess, abruptly irritated that Ilya might find any praise she gave Kirill to be suspicious. Yuri opened his mouth to complain, thought better of it, and popped in the rest of the sweetcake instead. Then he pressed his sticky fingers onto her cheek and giggled. "Off!" He grinned and jumped up, unaffected by the heat, and ran out into the sun to greet Mother Orzhekov.

Ilya's aunt Irena, etsana of the Orzhekov tribe and the most powerful woman in the jaran tribes now that Mother Sakhalin was failing, took Yuri's hand, dropped it, and said a few words to him which immediately caused him to look abashed. He ran off in the direction of the river. Mother Orzhekov advanced without any loss of dignity, even when she licked her fingers clean.

Tess rose at once and gave her a kiss on either cheek.

"I won't sit down," said Irena, twitching her skirts away from the half-empty tray of sweetcakes. At sixty-two, she still had strength and vigor. "I have only come to tell you that a birbas has been arranged for ten days from now, at the great wilderness to the west of Sarai. We have not had a princely birbas for two years now."

Ilya inclined his head, looking, before her, incongruously very like the messenger had looked before him. "That is well, my Aunt," he agreed. "How many tribes will come?"

"Those who can," she said. "It will be good training for the men who will return to the armies this fall, and for those young women and men who will ride out for the first time."

"In Sarai," added Ilya, "we can ask the merchants what they know of Byblos."

A horrifying thought struck Tess. What if it wasn't her praise for Kirill—the old rivalry between the two men for her love—that had annoyed Ilya? What if it was a lingering suspicion that she knew more than she would ever tell him? What if Ilya didn't truly trust her?

And why should he, in any case?

CHAPTER SEVEN

In the Princedom of Hereti-Manas

In six days they came to Greater Manas, but Riasonovsky made sure to camp well upstream from the town. Even so, a delegation ventured out to pay their respects and to bring food and drink for the riders and grain for the horses, as was prudent. A jahar had been through these parts just the day before, they reported, so no doubt the khaja were unpleasantly surprised to see another one so soon.

But when the prince's chamberlain saw Rusudani, than he sent a man back to town immediately. It was barely full dark when a new delegation emerged from the gloom, this one headed by the prince of Hereti-Manas himself.

Vasha dragged Stefan away from his self-imposed watch over the two khaja women and stood in the shadows beside Riasonovsky's tent, where Riasonovsky and Katerina received Prince Sigismar.

"I ought to be with them," Vasha muttered, but he stayed in the shadows, not wanting to make a scene, knowing what reception he would receive.

Sister Yvanne acted as interpreter, and when the khaja prince had acknowledged Katerina as befitted a princess of the jaran and Riasonovsky as befitted a soldier who could, at the merest breath of treason, order his head cut off, Katya allowed Rusudani to be brought forward. Her servant, Jaelle, trailed after her, looking nervous.

At once, Prince Sigismar came forward and gave Rusudani the embrace of a kinsman. They began talking in the Yossian language common to these lands.

"Sister Yvanne," said Katerina, "you will translate all the words of the prince into Taor, and Jaelle, you will translate the words of Rusudani into Taor, so that we may understand what they say to each other. Tell them that this is what I intend."

Sigismar knelt in front of Katerina. "I beg you, my lady,"

he said through Sister Yvanne's translation, "allow me to receive Princess Rusudani into my family, since the news I
bring her is sad, that she is so recently bereft of two brothers
who, alas, chose to follow a rash cousin into the war against
your own people. They perished with the other Yos princes
at the battle at Salho River. But Princess Rusudani has been
in the convent since she was a child, so she is an unwitting
accomplice to their crime. As well, her father, Prince
Zakaria, gave no aid to the rebels, so she is free of taint from
his side, and her mother, Helena Mirametis, has been dead
these past seven years. Her father's sister is my own wife. It
is right that she be embraced in the bosom of her own kins-
woman in this unhappy time. She is young, and untutored in
the ways of the world. You know that I have been the faithful servant of the jaran since your people first appeared in
Yos lands."

Vasha crept forward to better examine the participants.
Rusudani knelt next to her kinsman, her gaze cast toward the
ground. Her face was quiet and composed. If she grieved for
her brothers, Vasha could not read it in her expression.
Katya stared hard at the other woman and then, looking up,
caught sight of Vasha and beckoned him forward. She was
seated on a pillow next to Riasonovsky, outside his tent, and
Vasha knelt on one knee in order to hear her. She covered
her mouth with a hand and whispered into his ear.

"Did you hear what he called her mother?" she said in
khush, so that only they could understand. "Helena *Mirametis!*"

It took him a moment to register the name, but when he
did, he sat back on his heels in shock. Rusudani's face was
as still, as sweetly rounded, as that of an angel carved above
the doors of a khaja church. With her hands clasped in front
of her and her eyes half closed, she appeared to be praying.
Prince Sigismar eyed his jaran hosts uneasily.

"What have you discovered?" asked Riasonovsky of
Katerina, leaning forward. He, too, was seated on a pillow.

Katerina was gracious enough to allow Vasha to answer.

"Only the kings of Mircassia and their children are
granted the family name Mirametis. Which means—"

"That Princess Rusudani's mother was the daughter of
King Barsauma of Mircassia," finished Riasonovsky
brusquely. "Then she is a more important hostage than we
could have imagined. What is a *convent?*"

"A holy community, where women live together to serve their god," said Vasha, eager to show off his knowledge and perhaps to impress Riasonovsky. "There is one in Jeds, called Jedina Cloister, but I could not visit inside of it, since men are forbidden."

Riasonovsky folded his arms across his chest and returned his gaze to Prince Sigismar. The old prince fidgeted under that grim stare, his face gray in the firelight.

"Princess Rusudani," said Katerina finally, "I am grieved to hear of your brothers' death, although I must condemn their allegiance to the princes who fought against us. But I hope your father has other sons and daughters by your gracious mother, may her memory be praised, who may console him in his grief."

Rusudani glanced up. Her expression was so guileless that Vasha had a wild urge to warn her not to speak, but she did so anyway. "I thank you, my lady," she said in her soft voice, and the servant, Jaelle, translated the words into Taor. "I did not know my brothers well. They lived away from the women's quarters and had their own pursuits, as men do, and I was given to the convent early. And it is true that my father has children by his second wife, but they are very young. Please do not blame them for my brothers' actions."

Prince Sigismar looked grayer than ever. Katerina smiled triumphantly.

"I beg you, Princess Katherine," said the khaja prince, naming Katerina in the Yos style, "to consider my petition."

"Princess Rusudani travels with us to Sarai," said Katerina. She inclined her head. "But you may send a chest of clothes to her, if you will, so that she may dress in the way of your people while she lives among mine."

It was a polite way of dismissing him, and he recognized it. A cautious man, Vasha judged him, who had seen fit to bow before the storm rather than battle against it. "May I pray with her?" he asked, "as is the custom among my people?"

Katya nodded.

He turned and grasped her hands, and spoke in a low voice, quickly. Rusudani shook her head, troubled by his words, and pulled her hands out of his as he went on more passionately. Sister Yvanne cut him off.

"I have reminded Prince Sigismar that I have pledged to

tell you each word he speaks," Sister Yvanne said, "though you must know, Princess Katherine, that I am of his kind and not of yours."

"All of you live on the sufferance of the jaran, Sister Yvanne."

"I live on the sufferance of God, my lady. I wish only for permission to accompany you past Parkilnous, to Sarai itself, where God calls me to take my mission and those of my holy brothers."

"I will consider it," said Katerina. "What did he say to her?"

"He reminded her that she is now the sole heir to her mother's holdings."

"Which are?"

"He did not say."

"Ask him," ordered Katerina.

When Sister Yvanne repeated the question, Prince Sigismar looked remarkably mulish. Rusudani answered, hands clasped still, lifting her gaze to look on Katerina.

"My uncle meant only to remind me of my duty to my family, Lady Katherine, but I am pledged to God, and would have spoken my final vows next spring. Worldly ties mean nothing to me." Her servant translated the words. Vasha thought for a moment that Rusudani was about to look at him, to include him in her answer, but she did not. Plunged into gloom, he scarcely noticed as Prince Sigismar took his leave and Rusudani was escorted back to her tent. Why should Rusudani notice him in any case? He was nothing, no one, not even acknowledged as Bakhtiian's son by men like Yaroslav Sakhalin.

He realized his hands were shaking and that, despite the cool night air, he had broken out in a sweat. Oh, gods, what was Bakhtiian going to do when he returned in disgrace to Sarai? What would happen to him?

But no answer revealed itself. Katerina went away to her own tent, and Zaytsev, the old veteran, chased Vasha and Stefan away, reminding them that it was their turn to be on guard duty by the horses. They wandered back and forth along the lines, the horses a calming presence. Stefan whistled softly. He seemed infuriatingly cheerful.

"How did Jaelle learn to speak Taor?" he asked after a long while. "She speaks it so well."

"How should I know? The same place she learned to speak Yos, I suppose."

"Oh, Vasha, I'm sorry."

"What for?" Vasha snapped.

Stefan shrugged, and Vasha looked away from his sympathy, afraid that he was about to blurt out something stupid.

"Kireyevsky! Danov!"

Vasha turned to see Riasonovsky striding toward them out of the darkness. Now what had he done? Had Riasonovsky come to berate him for speaking out of turn?

"Saddle horses," said Riasonovsky. "We need every man to search."

"Search for what?"

"The khaja woman, the Mirametis. She's run away, leaving the other one in her bed as a decoy."

Vasha flushed, and his heart raced. "But she said—"

Riasonovsky gave him a look, and Vasha swallowed the rest of his words. What she said and what she meant in her heart were clearly two different things. Stefan was already saddling horses, and soon other riders arrived and they rode out with them, branching off as a pair to search down by the river.

The moon hung high, lighting their way. Thin threads of pale cloud lay tangled across the sky in an unpatterned web, and the moon hid behind them at intervals, but never for long. The breeze here tasted more of the ambling river water than anything else, lazy, drowned in earth. But Vasha could also smell the late summer reeds and the last faint odor of the soil steaming under the summer sun. Misri moved cautiously, and Stefan's halfblood mare walked beside her with stolid equanimity.

"Where will she go?" asked Stefan in a half whisper.

"She must be running to Prince Sigismar. Isn't there a ford by the khaja town?"

"Surely she'll know we'll look there."

Vasha shrugged. "How else can she cross? We crossed by that ford two days ago. She might backtrack. She could walk back to Manas the Smaller."

"Why would she run to us at first, when we found her, and then run away now?" Stefan asked, reining his mare to a halt at a thin stretch of rocky beach. The river sang to them in three voices: a little boy's voice among the pebbles, high and sweet, the constant steady murmur of a young lover, with grandfather's bass roar underlying it all.

"Maybe she just wanted to escape those bandits. Gods, perhaps they weren't bandits at all. They might have been anyone, another khaja faction. How are we to know? And she didn't know then that her brothers were dead."

"I still don't understand why that is important."

"I suppose you were lost in staring at the servant woman instead of listening! She is King Barsauma's granddaughter. And Mircassia is the greatest kingdom between Parkilnous and Jeds."

"But I thought in khaja lands the inheritance always passed through the male line. Does King Barsauma have no sons of his own?"

"He had at least two, but I remember that when I was in Jeds we got news that one had died unexpectedly."

"Hush, look there!"

There was one place they had not expected to look: out in the river itself. But the moon slid out from behind the concealing clouds and betrayed her, a shadowy figure with bulky shoulders, up to her chest in the water.

Vasha swore and urged Misri forward. She flattened her ears, but she rarely disagreed with him, and anyway, she had no fear of water. She plunged into the water with great splashes, the bank gave out from under them, and they went in hard. Water streamed around him, hitting in gusts. At once, snorting, Misri came up and began to swim, and Vasha flung himself off the saddle and clung to her neck, trying not to hinder her. The figure moved swiftly, seeing them, and struck out into the current.

Behind, Vasha heard Stefan call out. He was soaked through and his boots dragged him down. His saber caught against one of Misri's legs and he shifted, trying to thrust his body away from her to free her to swim, but there was nothing to push against but water until the current caught them and swept them steadily downstream toward the ford. The girl thrashed with her arms, but she somehow moved as much across the river as down with it.

Warned of the treacherous bank, Stefan and his mare had made a better start. They forged out across the river and Vasha barely saw them gain the other side about the same time as the slight figure of Rusudani struggled out of the water just as his feet scraped bottom, lost ground, and found

purchase again. By the time he and Misri had scrambled up
the bank, dripping, Stefan had the girl cornered on a stretch
of beach upstream. Vassily saw them clearly with the moon
so bright between a rent in the clouds that he could almost
make out their features. She had a knife in her hand, but she
did not move. She had tied her extra clothes onto a roll on
her back.

Vasha led Misri down the bank, picking carefully along
the brushy slope, slipping once to send a spray of dirt and
pebbles into the water. She just stood there. She wore only
a shift. The cloth clung to her form, outlining every curve,
the more so because her thin shift was white.

From far away, Vasha heard a man call out a challenge. The
river rippled by. Stefan held his position in front of her.

"Thank the gods," he said as Vasha came up beside him.
"Now what do we do with her?"

"Take her back to camp." But she still held the knife up.
They stood there, not knowing what else to do. She faced
them. Stars shone through the rents in the cloudy web above.
Air lifted off the river and brushed Vasha's face, chilling his
ears and neck. He shivered. His shirt stuck and slid against
his skin as he shifted. Water squished in his boots. His toes
were cold.

Like an echo, Rusudani shivered as well. With sudden decision, she sheathed her knife, unslung her roll of clothing,
and covered herself in a kirtle that draped from her shoulders to her knees.

They all looked at each other for an unguarded moment.
Vasha risked looking her straight in the face. She appeared
resigned, but not beaten, and she met his gaze firmly, so that
he looked away first, heart in his throat at the clear beauty
of her face. Slowly, they walked down to the ford where
they met some of the soldiers. Zaytsev arrived and took
over.

"Get dry clothes on," he said to Vasha and Stefan, and
they went obediently.

Katerina met them by the tents. "Where did you find her?
Gods, you're both soaking wet."

"We went in the river," he said. He shifted from one foot
to the other to keep warm, not wanting to shiver in front of
her. "Do you think she was trying to escape to Prince
Sigismar?"

But now Katerina looked smug. "I just spoke to her,

through her interpreter. She says that she wanted only to return to the convent. She wants only to serve her god."

"Do you believe her?"

Katerina shrugged. "What difference does it make? If she is truly the daughter of a daughter of King Barsauma, then she is a cousin twice over to the prince of Filis, Basil Atvandis. And Mircassia and Filis are the last great obstacles lying in the army's path before we reach Jeds. She is a valuable hostage."

"But you granted her sanctuary, Katya!"

"She is a hostage, nonetheless. It's a good thing you ran off to steal horses."

But that stung. And she knew it did; he could see it in her face. "You didn't need to say that," he said quietly. More clouds had drifted in by now. The sky grew as dark as Vasha's thoughts.

"You didn't need to antagonize Yaroslav Sakhalin the instant you rode in six months ago."

"It wasn't my fault! He hates me because I'm a bastard. As soon as I arrived, he sent me to groom and care for the horse herd like any common boy."

"Every boy who comes to the army starts with the horse herds. You wanted to be treated differently. That's what's wrong with you, Vasha."

"And you don't take advantage of the deference shown you because you're an Orzhekov?"

"I've proven my worth," she said, her voice shaking. She turned and stalked off.

"Maybe if you two would just lie together you wouldn't fight so much," said Stefan, pulling a hand through his wet hair.

Vasha was too angry to reply. His head ached. "It isn't fair," he said finally, "to say that I wanted to be treated differently."

Stefan coughed.

"Well! Is it?"

"I'm going to change into my dry clothes," said Stefan.

"I just hate being treated like a servant!" Vasha shouted after him. The air had warmed a little with the promise of rain. Insects chittered. An animal slithered through the brush. Vasha slapped at a fly on his cheek and, cursing, slogged after Stefan, water still squelching in his boots.

Stefan was waiting with his saddlebags, and they changed

quickly under the trees, slapping away bugs until they were both laughing.

"I suppose," said Vasha, chastened, "that we ought to go back to the horse lines. It's still our watch."

"Yes," said Stefan, and nothing more. Vasha went glumly. It hurt, that Stefan agreed with Katerina. But they hadn't lived in the Kireyevsky tribe. The memory hit him so hard he almost staggered. His mother ... dead, and the whole Kireyevsky tribe had turned against him, and cast him out of the etsana's tent and sent him to sleep with the herds together with the other servants.

"Never again," he mumbled.

"What?"

"Nothing. Who's there?"

It was Zaytsev. "There you are, boys. Have you given your report to Riasonovsky? He's waiting for it."

Vasha gulped down a retort and simply nodded. They strung up rope next to the horses and hung their clothes out, hoping it wouldn't rain. Crossing through camp, Stefan led them by angles past Rusudani's tent.

"Don't make a fool of yourself," said Vasha, catching Stefan's elbow and dragging him past the tent once he had seen that Rusudani was not outside. A ring of guards stood around the tent, and he didn't want them to think he was ... well, he didn't want them to think anything about him.

"I'm not making a fool of myself!"

"You are, too. You stare at her like a stupid grazel."

"And you don't stare at the princess? Now I suppose you think that Bakhtiian will want you to marry her, so that he has a claim to the Mircassian throne."

"Why shouldn't he?" For the first time, Vasha felt abruptly hopeful. "It would be easier to conquer Mircassia with an alliance than with soldiers."

"I have to piss," said Stefan, and detoured into the underbrush. Vasha waited, brooding, knowing Stefan well enough to hear in his silence the words Stefan would not say but that other people would say: Why should a bastard receive any blessing, any favor, from the man who could not truly be his father, not by jaran laws. Only by khaja ones.

"Anyway," said Vasha toward the bushes, "why shouldn't he marry me to a khaja princess? Do you think the jaran would ever follow me, truly? They'll follow Aunt Nadine's children, or Aunt Sonia's. But not me. So why shouldn't he provide for me by granting me a kingdom, as he did for Mitya."

Stefan swatted branches aside and came out, buckling his belt. "Mitya has a better claim to be Bakhtiian's heir than you do."

"I *know* that! But why shouldn't he, anyway?"

"Is that what you want? Truly?"

Standing knee-deep in thick grass, Vasha heard Father Wind's thick voice talking in the deep-leafed trees. Through a gap in the trees, Vasha saw a few torches and lanterns still burning, marking the merchants' camp. Behind them, three fires burned down toward coals, orange flames shooting up from banks of glowing red. Occasional noises sounded on the night air, a voice, a twig snapping, farther off the startled lowing of a cow in a nearby village or the uff-uff of one of the bad-tempered little guard beasts that the khaja loved.

"Yes," said Vasha finally. "Not that one thing, only of itself, but to be at the center of something, like Father and Tess are, and to build a web of alliances as strong as a weaving, that can never be ripped apart."

"But then why did you steal the horses?"

"I don't know. Why did you come with me?"

"I don't know." Stefan grinned. "We did manage it, though, even if it did make Yaroslav Sakhalin furious. I'll bet he never stole horses when he was a boy."

"I'll bet he did."

"Bet he didn't."

"Who's going to ask him?"

Stefan laughed. "Come on. We're supposed to report to Riasonovsky."

They walked on, sidestepping riders sleeping curled in blankets on the ground.

"Do you really think Yaroslav Sakhalin never tried to steal horses or even grazel when he was a boy?" Vasha asked finally as they came up to Riasonovsky's tent. They heard voices inside, two men talking together. By the light of the lantern hung within the tent, they saw two shadowy outlines, men standing by the tent flap.

"None of those Sakhalins stole horses. They didn't have to."

"What about my cousin Galina's husband? They say he was pretty wild when he was young."

A hand snaked out abruptly from the tent and yanked

aside the tent flap, revealing Riasonovsky and a fair jaran man dressed in Sakhalin colors. "Who says that?" asked the second man. He grinned. "Well met, Vassily Kireyevsky. I heard you were riding this way. As it happens, I'm returning to Sarai as well. I've just told Riasonovsky that I and fifty of my men will be riding north with you. Galina is expecting our second child, as you know."

Vasha's first thought was that Riasonovsky could not have looked more expressionless had he been a Habakar holy man in the grip of a God-induced trance: He had seen one himself, and would have sworn that the holy man was dead, except he was sitting upright and unsupported, and had miraculously come back to life two days later.

His second thought was that no one could possibly have as bad luck as he had.

"Well met," he stammered. "I didn't know you were riding through these lands."

Andrei Sakhalin smiled. As the feckless youngest son in a string of good-looking and hard-fighting boys (the eldest being his famous brother Yaroslav), he had profited by the others' loyalty and service to Bakhtiian: When Galina Orzhekov, eldest granddaughter to Mother Orzhekov, came of age to be married, it had been agreed by the etsanas and the dyans of the Orzhekov and Sakhalin tribes that a Sakhalin prince ought to be granted the alliance. That prince had originally been meant to be Mother Sakhalin's grandson, Anatoly, but he had been poisoned with love for a khaja Singer and had disappeared into khaja lands. That left Andrei, who was suspected of being light-minded; he was also thirteen years older than the girl, but he was unmarried. Galina had done her duty, not that she had any choice in marriage in any case.

"I hear you stole horses from the khaja," added Andrei.

Vasha flinched and barely nodded.

Andrei chuckled. "Good for you. I stole horses from the khaja once, when I was a boy. They were filthy creatures—the horses, that is. Thank the gods I never got close enough to the khaja to tell what they were, although why do we even need to? Their stone tents reek from a morning's ride away. I would have tried stealing grazel from the other tribes, which would have been more interesting, but even by then Yaroslav had pledged to aid Bakhtiian in uniting the tribes, so we were forbidden from trying anything that might have started a feud." He sighed, looking wistful. "Ah, well." He turned back to Riasonovsky. "I'll bring my men over in the morning. I need fodder for the horses."

Without further ado, he swept out of the tent, winked at Vasha, and walked out into the darkness.

There was silence.

"What is he doing here?" Vasha asked finally.

Riasonovsky grunted. "Going back to Sarai," he said in a voice that made it obvious that he had nothing more to say on the matter. "Your report?"

They gave it, succinctly, and he dismissed them, leaving them to stand awkwardly out in the darkness. They looked at each other.

"What will happen to us when we get back to the tribes?" Stefan asked softly, the question Vasha most dreaded to hear. Suddenly his throat was choked with fear.

"Grandfather Niko will make sure that you get sent out to a good jahar, maybe Kirill Zvertkov's or Tasha Lensky's. Somewhere you could make a name for yourself."

"I wouldn't go. You'd never manage without me."

"You might not have any choice," Vasha said hoarsely. "I don't know what's going to happen to me. Oh, gods, Stefan . . ." Then, because it was cowardly not to say it, he forced himself to, though his voice was the merest whisper, almost lost on the breeze. "What if my father casts me out? What if the tribe disowns me?"

"Tess wouldn't disown you."

Vasha just shook his head. Tess was khaja, after all, not jaran. In the end, it was the jaran council that would speak.

"Well," repeated Stefan stubbornly, "I won't go anyway, no matter what happens."

CHAPTER EIGHT

Ardhanarishvara

Ilyana woke early on Frejday, feeling a pleasant sense of anticipation. The dust-eater purred at her feet. When she shifted to
get up, it slid away under the bed (a real bed, which Diana's
Aunt Millie had built for her). She swung her feet down and
kneaded the soft pile of rug with her toes.

"Up! Valentin, it's morning time—" She broke off. Valentin's sleeping pillows lay empty, his blankets still folded
neatly in their center. Ilyana dressed quickly and ducked outside. Anton sat by the fire, drinking milk. "Where is
Valentin?"

"I dunno." Anton slanted a glance up at her, gauging her
mood. "Doing something you don't want him to, probably."

"Anton!" Infuriating beast. Ilyana could see trouble building with Anton; he was getting more and more bored with
his life and the restrictions set on him, and he had long since
learned to be underhanded in his dealings. "Have you seen
him?"

"No."

Gritting her teeth, she went to her mother's tent. Karolla
was still asleep, and Vasil, with the baby snuggled in a sling
against his chest, was playing a counting game with
Evdokia. Ilyana slunk out quietly. Evdokia got so little attention from their father that she didn't want to disturb her now.
She went back to the pantry, drank some milk, and went out
to the hallway.

No Valentin at the bottom of the steps, where he liked to
sit and brood. She sighed and stared up the twisting flights,
wooden banisters polished to a dark sheen. From the next
level she heard, faintly, Hal and Diana and Anatoly singing
a song together, and Portia giggling. Their door was cracked
open, and Ilyana smelled frying bacon, so strong and tantalizing that she had to swallow. But Valentin wouldn't be
there, not if Anatoly Sakhalin was there, too. Higher, at the

top, she knew that Hyacinth would not yet be awake and Yevgeni would already have left for the shop where he worked. She cursed under her breath and went out back to the garden.

The garden consisted of a bed of flowers and a vegetable patch, with a five-meter-square lawn in the back. Hal took the younger kids out there on afternoons he was free (and the weather was good) and taught them baseball. One dwarf Myriad grew by the back gate, an arthritic old tree developed in the heady days of hybridization; the pear and apple limbs still bore fruit, but the peach and apricot only leafed out and then faded. Valentin liked to sit in its shade, but he wasn't sitting there now.

Back by the house the cellar doors lay shut, but the bolt was retracted. Mired to the earth by a sudden sense of dread, Ilyana forced herself forward, heaved up one door, and took the steps down into the darkness. It remained cool and dank down here, even with the filter running. Various kits, chests, cupboards, and power nodes cluttered the cellar. None of the residents of the house really bothered to straighten it up except at the winter reset. Beyond this storage the bulk of the cellar simply drifted into a melange of beams and plascrete reinforcements and darkness.

In the farthest back corner, she found Valentin shivering. He was all over gooseflesh. His fingers twitched spasmodically under gel tips and his left foot, curled awkwardly under his rear, was tangled in a wire. He had old-fashioned goggles on, although he could not have seen her in any case. The tray of nesh-drives sat on the ground just out of his reach. Either he had slid away from it, or he had stationed himself out of reach on purpose.

Ilyana bit down so hard on her lower lip that she swallowed blood before she realized that she had broken her skin. She wanted to scream. She really wanted to panic. Had he been here *all* night? But she blanked out her emotions and knelt down to begin the sequence of drive deceleration. It wouldn't do any good to run the *return* sequence that would alert the person in nesh that it was time to get out. She had to compel him into a narrowing sequence of paths, like jaran hunters on a birbas driving game into a shrinking center, and thus push him into the "air-lock" that would return him to *here*.

She picked up the monocle that allowed an outside observer a fail-safe to peer into the nesh environment and squinted into it. A bewildering array of images rushed by her. The sun rose over a golden, infinite plain and shivered, transforming as a wave like heat passed over the scene so that a paler sun gleamed coldly down at midday on an army retreating in disarray through a frozen wasteland of snow and trees. Tower Bridge slid by in twilight. A vast spaceship loomed and faded. Infinity Jilt blasted through a space lock and crossed the threshold into a council chamber whose walls were a hundred swaying slender tree trunks that shot up into a sky filled with the lights of the aurora borealis, shifting, weaving, a spider dropped silken strands down and the delicate threads caught and bound a crippled bird that dragged its shattered wing along the ground and it fought against the binding and Valentin began to retch, dry heaves.

Ilyana dropped the monocle and pulled the goggles off his eyes. He was doubled over, wires knotting, and she ripped them off his fingers. He was shaking hard and gagging and vomiting, but nothing came out, only a little spittle. His shakes turned into shivers. The cellar light snapped on and Ilyana started back, gripping Valentin's hands protectively. His fingers were blue with cold. He was back, in this world, but he wasn't yet aware.

"What is this?" asked Anatoly Sakhalin.

Trust him never to let any covert action go undetected, not in this house.

"Oh, gods," said Ilyana under her breath. Still holding Valentin's hands, rubbing them, she looked back over her shoulder.

Sakhalin regarded her and Valentin in silence. Like all the Sakhalin princes, he was a good-looking man, and Ilyana found him imposing, even though he always treated her politely. She adored Diana. Anatoly made her feel—well, anyway, a man like him never noticed girls like her. She flushed.

"I'm sorry," she said.

"I am also sorry," he replied in khush, walking forward now, "that there are not Singers here trained to guide a boy's journeys. He is sorely in need of help."

Hope flared. "He needs to see a *dokhtor*," she said hurriedly, before Valentin regained his wits. His retching had subsided into hoarse coughs. He sounded like he was cough-

ing his lungs out. Ilyana flinched at each convulsion. He began to blink frantically as he reoriented.

"Then the etsana must order it done," he said, and hope
died. Karolla Arkhanov was "etsana" of the jaran exiles, and
she would never admit anything was wrong with her eldest
son. Anatoly crouched on the other side of Valentin, examining the boy with a frown on his face. "But if the dokhtors
here are also Singers, I have not heard of it, and it is the
Singers who must sing to the spirit of the wounded, to grant
it healing."

"Wounded?" Ilyana stuttered.

Valentin's hands tightened on hers and his gaze focused
on her face. "Yana?" he whispered. He swallowed, hard.
"Damn it. Why did you do that? I was just going good." The
harsh cellar light made his skin look stretched and white.

"Do not speak to your sister with such disrespect," said
Anatoly mildly, still in khush. Valentin began coughing
again. "These khaja machines are poison to you," added
Anatoly, in the same deceptively bland voice.

"What do you know?" Valentin retorted, made belligerent
by the aftereffects of the guising. "You've never lived anywhere but on the surface world."

"What is the *surface world?*" Anatoly asked, looking at
Ilyana.

"Never mind," said Ilyana hastily. "Won't you and Diana
try to help me get him to a dokhtor?"

"He doesn't need a khaja dokhtor. He needs a Singer. He
should have been apprenticed to a Singer years ago. That is
why the khaja machines have poisoned him, because they
make ghosts of the gods' lands and lure spirits like his
there."

"But we don't *have* a Singer—" began Ilyana just as
Valentin said, "See, he knows I don't need a doctor."

"Can you walk?" Anatoly stood. He picked up the nesh
tray, weighing it in both hands, and sniffed at it. "It smells
of nothing," he commented. "It is only ghosts."

"You don't know anything!" gasped Valentin, struggling
to his feet, but his legs gave out on the first try and then
Ilyana yanked him back down.

"Just sit down!" she snapped. "That's a bootleg model,
Valentin. You're not supposed to be neshing outside of
school."

"That is true," added Anatoly. "and you must do as your

sister says. As far as what I know, Valentin, I know enough
to have tried these khaja machines before passing judgment
on them. If you will, Yana, I will get rid of this."

Valentin fought against her, but he was too weak, too thin,
and still too freshly emerged from guising to have any hope
of getting free of her grip.

"Thank you," she said and glanced up in time to see
Sakhalin smile at her and then, abruptly, modestly, look
away from her as any proper jaran man would from a
woman. Ilyana felt her face burn, but, thank the gods, he
left, carrying the nesh-drive. Men didn't treat girls like that;
that was how they responded to women. Confusion boiled
through her heart and then dissipated as Valentin stopped
struggling and just lay there, looking bleakly up at her.

"Oh, gods, Valentin," she said, letting him go. "Where did
you get that? Don't you know bootleg machines can be dangerous?"

But he had gone silent now. She recognized the look.

"Let's go upstairs and get you ready for school. I'm going
to have to nesh a message to M. Tioko, though. Valentin, if
you were guising all night—!" She stopped, too full to go
on. What was she going to do with him? Oh, gods, and she
and Kori were supposed to leave soon for the rehearsal.
What if Valentin was too sick to go to school and she had to
stay home with him? At once, she felt ashamed of her own
selfishness, and then angry at Valentin for acting this way.
"Come on!" She grabbed his wrist and hauled him to his
feet. He coughed a final time and followed her meekly.

"He hates me," said Valentin suddenly.

"Who—? What? Anatoly Sakhalin? You're feeling sorry
for yourself, Valentin. He doesn't hate you at all." She
voiced off the cellar light and they climbed the stairs and
blinked hard in the morning sunlight.

"He can't like me," mumbled Valentin, and clammed up
again.

"Where've you been?" demanded Anton when they
slipped into the flat. In the camp, phantom jaran busied
themselves about their morning tasks. Nipper had arrived
and she waved at them and went back to carding wool, sitting cross-legged on the ground next to the fire. She had the
baby now. Its pale head peeped out above the brightly
woven sling.

"Go eat something," said Ilyana.

"I'm not hungry," said Valentin.

"You've been guising again," said Anton.

"Shh!" hissed Ilyana, but Nipper was too far away to eavesdrop.

"I want to go play soccer tonight," said Anton.

Valentin sighed. "Oh, all right, I'll take you," he said, paying out on the blackmail. "Let's just go to school now, Anton. You're not going to school today anyway, are you, Yana?"

"Valentin—"

"I'll tell M. Tioko. I promise."

She bit at her lip. "All right. But go. Before—"

"Ah, there you are, Yana," said her father, emerging from the big tent. Valentin grabbed Anton by the wrist and led him away.

"Good morning," said Ilyana cautiously. Vasil looked sunny this morning. That was always suspicious.

"It isn't often you get a day off school and I get a day off rehearsal at the same time," he said cheerfully. "How about I come with you today?"

The ceiling could have fallen in on her and she wouldn't have felt any more crushed. "That would be wonderful, Father," she said brightly. "But I don't know if they're running open rehearsals . . ."

"Oh, I've already cleared it with the stage manager. Don't worry about that. Take Evdokia upstairs. She's to sit with Portia until your mother wakes up. She's very tired today."

Sometimes, in her more uncharitable moments, Ilyana wondered if her father was really as solicitous and considerate as he seemed, or if it was all acting. A snap sounded from the door panel, and the double chime of a nesh message sounded.

"Receive sight only," said Ilyana, and watched as Kori appeared, standing in the front of the door, her image so real, so three-dimensional, that she could just as well have been standing there. "Transmit sight," added Ilyana, and Kori's eyes tracked round the room and caught on Ilyana. She grinned.

"Uncle Gus and I are leaving now. You wanna skate over and come with us?"

Ilyana winced, wondering if Kori or her uncle knew about Vasil's plans. "I gotta take Evdi upstairs, so I guess I'll meet you there."

"See you, then. And out." Kori vanished.

Vasil agreed to take regular transport, thank the gods, but Ilyana knew people were staring at them. They got off the Underground at Covent Garden and walked to Covent Annex, which snuggled up behind the Royal Opera House. The porter at the stage door recognized Vasil at once—he had performed here when he was still with the Bharentous Repertory Company—and they let themselves into the back of the auditorium. Kori sat in the back row, watching as Uncle Gus and the other dancer chatted with the musicians, and two members of the tech crew paced and repaced the stage, marking out the light and nesh coordinates.

"First tech rehearsal?" Vasil asked Kori in a low voice.

If Kori was surprised to see him, she didn't show it. "Neh. Second. Yesterday was first, but the new lighting system kept shattering the nesh so they're trying different settings today. Uncle Gus says the designers and the nesh tech had a terrible argument yesterday but it was really only because the light designer's grandmom just hit the Decline, so he needed to be angry with someone."

"Is that Ajoa Sen?"

"Neh. He got the commission to do the first run at Concord, so he's gone for at least two years. It's Kwame Jones Bihua."

"He did the lights for the *Mahabharata*," said Vasil instantly. Ilyana had long since noted that her father had an astonishingly poor memory for people who couldn't do him any good, especially if they had no essential power which they might turn to his benefit, but, conversely, he had total recall for anyone whom he deemed useful. He showed particular notice to lighting and costume designers. In return, they treated him well.

Uncle Gus glanced up, saw them, and lifted a hand in acknowledgment, then went back to his discussion. After a bit, they took their places, Gus stage right and his partner stage left. The woman dancing the part of Parvati was long-limbed and tall and voluptuous, a typical dancer, graceful and confident in a way that gave Ilyana the usual pangs of envy. She was barefoot, the soles of her feet in pale contrast to the lush mocha color of her skin, and she was dressed in a sari spangled with tiny shimmering mirrors, an anklet of bells around each ankle. She triggered her nesh, and *she* appeared center stage. Behind her, upstage center, stood a small shrine draped with a garland.

When Ilyana had first come to Earth, she had not been able to distinguish a person from her nesh, if both were indoors. It was easier outside. The right kind of light betrayed many things, including the lack of weight. Inside, Ilyana had learned subtle cues: For instance, the mirrors sparkled and flashed to angles of light that didn't match the way the lights illuminated center stage. The dancer stamped her feet and spun, both of her spun, and the mirrors shot splinters of light all through the auditorium while the bells shook and rang. She stopped and bells whispered to silence.

Gus triggered his nesh. He wore plain rehearsal clothes, and he stood a foot downstage so that his nesh stood alone in front of his partner's nesh while he turned once and twice. They both squinted expectantly toward the back of the auditorium. An unspoken command reached them. Gus took one step back, and the two neshes intermingled. It looked strange at first, Gus superimposed on the woman, she on him, and yet each separate on either side. Their stillness radiated out like a force in the hall. Ilyana held her breath. Then a drum opened a beat, a sitar and flute entered, and Shiva and Parvati began to dance.

Ilyana rested her arms along the silken back of the seat in front of her and stared. The Hindu god Shiva was many things; among others, he was Lord of Dance, who, dancing, set the universe in motion. He was also a renowned lover. His second wife, Parvati (who was the reincarnation of his first wife), was so beautiful that he loved her divine body without respite for a thousand years. Ancient artisans in India carved statues of Shiva and Parvati integrated into a single body. Thus had Uncle Gus named this piece "Ardhanarishvara," the Lord whose Half is Woman.

As he and his partner danced in perfect separation so their nesh dance commingled, blending together until their arms became the four arms of a single being, their bodies sculpted and flowing so that at times they were hermaphroditic and at times sexless and at times a seamless unity, as any divine beings might love, coalescing into a new form that partook half of the female and half of the male. Parvati's braid, as thick as a child's arm, floated up as she—as they—spun, wrapping around her—around their—waist like a belt, like a symbol of their joining, and fell back again. Their hands made the most expressive gestures, nuanced and emotional, speaking of longing and love and bliss. Ilyana was amazed by how strong and supple the dancers' feet were.

Ilyana forgot time, caught in the endless cycle of birth and death, destruction and rebirth, union and sundering, the melody itself repeating with different rhythmic intonations and the dance repeating and changing and then her breath caught and suddenly it was over.

Two new people walked onto the stage and an intense discussion ensued. Ilyana sat back and grinned at Kori.

"That," proclaimed Kori, "is why I'm gonna be a scientist, not a dancer. I could never be anything but Augustus Gopal's niece. Isn't he grand?"

Ilyana realized that her cheeks were hot. "Do you think that'll get past the Protocol Office?" she asked, not that the dance was explicit, just that it suggested so much.

Kori grunted. "Already cleared. It's not as if they really touch, after all." They remained silent for a moment. Then Kori added, in a very low voice, "Do you think that's what it's like?"

Ilyana's cheeks burned. "I dunno!" she retorted. A second later she realized that her father was missing.

She looked around, but he wasn't in any part of the auditorium that she could see. "Where'd he go?"

"Shh," said Kori. "They're starting again."

The music began again. The dancers started, but now they worked in fits and starts, fine-tuning the nesh and the lighting and whatever else they had to niggle with. Vasil did not return. After a while, Ilyana leaned up against Kori and whispered, "I gotta go use the loo," and crept out like a spy or a refugee.

She didn't have to use anything, but it bothered her that her father had vanished like that. Why would he make such a business of coming with her and then disappear? If he had wanted to act the whore with Gus Gopal he certainly couldn't do that with the dancer on the stage the whole time; not that Uncle Gus had ever shown any sign of being interested in Vasil. Ilyana often suspected that her father simply did not *believe* that any person could be uninterested in him. Maybe that was why he was so attractive: sort of like a self-fulfilled prophecy.

She slunk back into the dressing rooms, but there was no one there. She tried below, remembering the layout of this theater from the times the Bharentous Repertory Company had performed here, with Vasil as part of the company, and she and Valentin had explored the place. Those had been good days, before Valentin had discovered neshing. Or at least, most of those days had been good. The Company had given Vasil stability and Karolla some measure of support, and Owen had always been able to squash Vasil's worst pretensions without alienating him.

She climbed the metal stairs to the attic storage rooms, not expecting to find him—why would he come up here?—but recalling with sudden clarity the musty smell of the costume attic where she and Valentin would hide, burrowing beneath mounds of old moldering costumes and choking down giggles when their father or Yomi, the stage manager, came looking for them. Old habit made her cautious and quiet.

The hallway was unlit. She found the door more by touch than by sight. It was an old swing style door. With a slight pressure from her fingers, it opened silently into the vast murky loft of the costume attic. A thin slit of windows cut through at the eaves. Dust spun like snow there, blending into twilight and thence into the swollen shadows that filled the rest of the space. Racks of clothes like lines of summer trees ranged along one side of the space. Barrows rose behind them, burial mounds for forgotten costumes. Some creature was rustling around up here, a mouse maybe or a cat or . . .

Her eyes adjusted at last.

Like Shiva and Parvati, commingling in nesh, two people stood back among the costumes, intertwined, kissing. Dust settled in silence, leavened by the soft rustling of their feet, shifting, and their breath forming into sounds that were not quite words and yet not only sighs. One was her father. She knew his shape instantly. The other she did not recognize, except that the cut of the clothing he wore seemed oddly familiar but unidentifiable in the dimness. Did they not realize she was here? Or did they simply not care?

Ilyana had seen her father flirt. She had even seen him insinuate a hand on a lover's arm or thigh, a half-hidden, intimate gesture, always brief. But she had never seen him actually in the act before. She was mortified. She couldn't stop watching. She just stood there, rooted into the ground, staring through the darkness at them, at the way a hand snaked up a thigh and buttocks to come to rest on the small of the back, at the way a finger interposed between lips and was itself kissed and made part of their joining, at the way their bodies flowed against each other, pressing, moving, seeking a new fit.

Vasil's lover arched back just enough so he could play with the buttons on Vasil's tunic, and somehow, with the angle altering subtly, Ilyana felt as if she had just succumbed to a sudden hallucination. A dark-haired, bearded jaran man, undressing her father with slow sensuality. It couldn't be . . . except she knew those clothes. But no other jaran had left Rhui. The other man had Vasil's tunic half off. Ilyana didn't know what to do. If she moved now, they would surely notice her. If she didn't move, then she would see everything, things no child ever ought to know about their parents, her father and Ilya Bakhtiian—

Ilyana's heart pounded in her ears like the stamp of feet. For an instant, she could believe it, even though she knew it wasn't true. For an instant, she thought it was still her heart beating so loudly.

The door swung open behind her, just missing her back, and a wash of noise and the press of bodies bore in behind it and thrust her forward as on a rising tide into the room.

A light snapped on, flooding the attic with unforgiving brightness.

M. Pandit came to rest not three steps from Ilyana. She had a half-dozen thugs dressed as quisling officers with her.

"Separate them," she said in a frigid voice.

The thugs swarmed past Ilyana, but by the time they reached the two men, Jazir had already jumped away from Vasil. Pandit's husband was indeed dressed as a jaran rider: scarlet shirt, black trousers, black boots. Under the hard light, he looked absurd.

The thugs surrounded Vasil, who looked more dazed than anything, and began to beat him up. Outnumbered and outweighed, Vasil covered his face with his arms and dropped to the floor. They kicked him, eerily silent about their task.

"Hey!" yelped Ilyana, and bolted for him.

Pandit grabbed her by the shoulders and yanked her to a stop. "Get out of here," she said.

Ilyana kicked her. Pandit grabbed Ilyana's right arm and wrenched it up behind her back until the pain made her cry, and she watched her father get kicked and beaten through a haze of tears.

Jazir circled around the thugs and slunk over to M. Pandit.

"I didn't—" he began.

With a sour frown, M. Pandit fingered the fine red silk of his shirt. "This is obscene." She let go of the shirt and brushed her fingers together as if she was trying to wipe off slime. With her other hand she tightened her grip on Ilyana's arm.

Ilyana yelped. "It hurts! You old pig."

Pandit slapped her. She had strong hands. Then she turned back to her husband. "Get out of those things and go home."

So briefly that Ilyana almost didn't see it, he winced. Then he smoothed over his expression, turning the full force of his gorgeous brown eyes on his wife. "Don't be angry with me."

"Go." She turned her attention back to the thugs. "Not his face, you idiots. That's enough in any case. You three, escort my husband home." They left. The remaining three stationed themselves equidistant around their quarry.

"You may stand up," said M. Pandit in a calm voice. "I trust you have learned your lesson."

Vasil unbent stiffly. "Gods," he said, blinking at the floor. Gingerly, he touched his fingers to a bruise already forming on his naked left shoulder. He swore, and then explored his face. Finally he looked up. His eyes widened, seeing Ilyana, and he swore again. "Let go of her!" he demanded, and Ilyana saw him reach instinctively for his saber. Which was, of course, not there.

Pandit let go of Ilyana's arm, and Ilyana gasped in relief and ran over to her father.

"Not so hard," he said, flinching when she hugged him. She choked down a sob and turned to look at M. Pandit.

"Now." Pandit lifted a hand, and the thugs retreated, coming back to stand behind her. "I don't like other people seducing my husband, especially not you, M. Veselov, with your obvious attractions. I don't intend to risk that you or he will be rash enough to try this again. Therefore, you will leave Earth. Your family does not have to leave, just you. But I can make life very difficult for you if you don't go of your own free will. Do you understand me?"

Vasil had found a bruise on his left cheek and seemed to be more interested in exploring the extent of the damage than in listening to Pandit's threats.

"You can't just make us leave!" cried Ilyana.

Pandit blinked, looking bland. "Of course I can. I can do

many things. I can destroy your father's face and career. You're a particularly lovely child. I can see that you disappear into a servitude that you would not enjoy."

At this, Vasil did look up.

"But that's illegal," said Ilyana.

"You may be assured that I know what is illegal and what is not. There is always a black market for handsome boys and girls. Both you and you brother would serve my purpose, your brother especially, since he would be easily controlled. The younger children don't seem blessed with looks, unfortunately, although at their age that might not matter to some people."

"You wouldn't dare," said Vasil suddenly. "It goes against every law of the gods to treat children in such a fashion."

"I am not concerned with the law of the gods, M. Veselov. I am concerned about my husband. Because I'm generous, I'll grant you one month to make your plans."

"But, Father—!" began Ilyana.

"Hush," said Vasil. He looked remarkably intent now, as if the threats to his children had focused his thoughts.

"Do you understand me?" M. Pandit asked.

"Perfectly," replied Vasil coolly.

She left. Ilyana heard footsteps ringing down the steps, and then they faded and she and her father were alone.

"How *could* you?" she demanded, letting go. A horrible wrenching misery took hold of her. Everything they had built here, her friends, her school, a place for the little ones, all gone because her father wanted to pretend that he was— well, anyway, she didn't understand what her father wanted or what drove him. He was hugely successful, everyone said so, and yet she could never shake the feeling that he had left something behind on Rhui without which he was doomed to remain incomplete.

"She reminds me of Ilya," said Vasil suddenly, softly. "He made me leave because he was afraid that Tess was falling in love with me." He winced. "Gods. I'm going to look like hell for the next ten days. I'll have to cancel my appearance at Cannes."

"But what are we going to do?" She sniffed hard, strangling tears.

"Oh, gods," he said under his breath, and assayed a step, and another, flinching each time. "We'll go, Yana."

"But I don't want to leave! Daddy, I don't want to leave! Please, don't make us go."

"Oh, I'm sure we can come back in a year or two or three. She'll forget. And I won't bother *him* anymore. These khaja are very strange. They let two men or two women marry, so why should she object to me taking him as a lover? I don't understand them."

Ilyana knew that if she tried to say anything more, she would begin to cry in earnest, so she said nothing. What could she say, anyway? Nothing that her father would hear. Her feet felt heavy with the weight of her desolation. She didn't want to leave, but he would never leave his family behind, especially not knowing that M. Pandit had her eye on them. She dragged along after her father. Even beaten badly enough that it hurt him to move, he seemed unaffected by the whole episode. It didn't matter to him if they left Earth.

Ilyana had to stop, the illumination hit her like a blast of light. Nothing mattered to him, not really. Nothing had, since they had left Rhui.

"What are we going to tell Kori and her Uncle Gus?" she asked finally as they paused at the door.

Vasil smiled. "That I fell down the stairs." He winked at her. Ilyana giggled. He held her to him, and she laid her head against his shoulder. "Gods, you're getting tall." He examined her quizzically. His left eye was purpling. "M. Pandit is right. You're a beautiful girl, just as you should be."

Uncomfortable, Ilyana extricated herself from him and snapped off the light. They negotiated the steps, made their excuses to Kori and her uncle, and went home in a private car.

A package waited at the door for M. Veselov: a set of jaran clothes, scarlet shirt and black trousers, pressed and impeccably folded, and black boots polished to a supple sheen.

Ilyana helped her father upstairs. "Put in a call to Owen Zerentous," he said as soon as they crossed the threshold. "Voice only."

CHAPTER NINE

Recompense

"Are you sure," Diana asked for the fifth time, "that you want to come with the Company? I don't know how long we'll be on this tour, or even exactly where we're going, if it's true that we actually get to go to Duke Naroshi's palace. You know you and Portia are welcome to stay here with my family. You know they'll be glad to have you."

"Gods!" Anatoly Sakhalin jumped to his feet and stalked to the edge of the brick patio. Beyond lay the bright patchwork of the flower garden, exhaling in the sun, and beyond that the fields of rye and barley and the stark frame of the great greenhouse. The wooded hill that had given the farm its name loomed above the greenhouse. Behind him, through the open patio doors, he could hear the cheerful rumble of Diana's family as they chatted and worked and prepared family dinner inside the house. He smelled bread baking, and a soufflé. Portia shrieked with laughter. A bee droned lazily through the flowers, and from the lawn to the west of the house he heard the crack of a cricket bat and one of the cousins yelling.

"You don't want me to go with you," he said.

"Well, what will you *do?* We'll probably be confined in a small area, we'll be rehearsing and performing all the time, everyone else there will be part of the Company."

He turned to look at her. She wore the face he liked least: She was going to be reasonable, to appeal to practicality, to rationality, whatever that meant. Anatoly was damned tired of being reasonable. He had been reasonable for five years now, after the fiasco with the Couture Festival, and the only thing it had gotten him was a daughter, although Portia was certainly worth every otherwise monotonous year that had passed.

"How can I be any more confined than I am now?" he demanded. "At least I will get to see something of the lands away from Earth."

"If you would bestir yourself to get some kind of occupation, then you wouldn't be so confined!"

"I have an occupation! One I trained for for many years. I am a soldier, and I offered my services to Charles Soerensen when I left Rhui."

"Not this again! You are so inflexible and stubborn, Anatoly! This isn't Rhui. This isn't the jaran. You're as bad as Karolla, living in the past."

"I beg your pardon!"

"Oh, I know, I know. You get along very well here. You take your classes and ride at the stables and fence and teach at the Academy. You've learned how to get around and I swear you know how to use all the obscure bits of technology better than I do—!" That made her chuckle, and he saw her soften; she always did, eventually, when they fought. This time he was not inclined to forgive her. "No one can ever accuse you of not being single-minded. Or of not being smart enough to do what you want."

"Thank you," he replied sarcastically.

She stood up, defensively crossing her arms on her chest. "Then why can't you admit that you aren't a jaran soldier anymore? You've got to make a new life for yourself. It's been seven years since you left Rhui!"

"I *am* a jaran soldier."

"Ah, Goddess, you're impossible!"

They lapsed into an angry silence, glaring at each other. Diana's Aunt Millie, laughing at something someone had said behind her, stepped out through the patio doors, halted, frowned, and went back inside, leaving them alone on the patio again.

Diana sighed, finally, running a hand over her eyes. He could see that she was close to tears. "Oh, Anatoly, why do we have to argue all the time?"

She was in a mood to soothe him, but he wasn't in a mood to be soothed. "You have done nothing to help me. Why did you ask me to leave Rhui when you never intended that I become a part of your tribe?"

She bit down hard on her lower lip and did not reply, but he saw tears brimming in her eyes and he pressed his advantage.

"You only had the baby to placate me."

"That's unfair! I love Portia!"

"But you wouldn't have agreed to have her, would you, if it hadn't served to distract me from the discovery that all those enterprises I had gotten involved in, that all of them were just using me as a pet, as a . . . what do you call it? . . . a sideshow freak? If you truly cared for me, you wouldn't ask me to stay behind, as if I were a servant. A man does not stay behind when a jahar goes riding; he rides. It's insulting, Diana. As if you think I can't take care of myself. You could think about me for once, instead of only thinking of yourself."

"Only thinking of myself!" she gasped. "How dare you? If you think I haven't struggled all these years . . . how dare you say that! I've had to make sacrifices, too."

"That is all I am to you now, an obstacle. You would rather leave me behind with your family who will smother me with their kindness and conceal your shameful infatuation within the walls of the tent. So I won't embarrass you again, because I know you were mortified after I showed those whimpering festival producers what a battle is really like. No one patronizes a Sakhalin!"

"I stood up for you!"

"Only because you had no choice! Not because you truly meant it!"

She burst into tears. "You can't even see that it's been hard for me, too," she choked out, and she broke past him and ran out along the graveled path that led toward the greenhouse.

Anatoly contemplated the ruins of their argument with grim satisfaction. After a moment he realized that his hands were shaking, and he clenched them.

Aunt Millie stepped out onto the patio and surveyed him. He lifted his chin and faced her stubbornly. "Routed the enemy, I see," she said conversationally.

"I didn't—!"

"Now, Anatoly, come inside and help me wash the vegetables for the salad." Once he would have protested that men did not cook, but that excuse was not tolerated at Holt Farm. He followed Aunt Millie inside meekly and took up a station beside her at the double sink. Most of the rest of the family—and there were a lot of them—had adjourned to the west lawn to watch the cricket game. Through the west window he saw Portia sitting on her grandfather's lap, golden head resting on Granfa's arm and two fingers stuck in her mouth. She was tired.

"You're discontented," observed Aunt Millie.

"It isn't right that Diana should want me to stay behind," he said promptly, taking the dispute as to where it should have been essayed in the first place. "This could be a chance for me to use my skills, the only chance I've truly had so far."

"It could be," she agreed mildly. She was a big-boned woman, quite unlike her niece, appealingly strong, with powerful hands and arms from decades of carpentry work. "But I can't say that you further your cause by driving Diana to tears."

"She fights just as well as I do."

"Certainly she can be just as cruel and cutting when she wishes to be, but she doesn't have your years of tactical and strategic training, so, I would give the advantage in that department to you, I'm afraid."

He had the grace to look ashamed.

"I know from my own experience that it's sometimes impossible to forgo a chance to make a person whom you're angry with cry just because it feels like recompense for your anger. But that isn't the way to build a marriage. If I say that Diana has had to struggle these last years, I don't say it to belittle what you've gone through, Anatoly. But you have to accept that she has had to make as many adjustments as you have." She paused and looked at him with what he knew was a keen eye. "Do you disagree?"

Anatoly was not in the habit of disagreeing with aunts and etsanas, and in any case, he had discovered over the years that Aunt Millie did not give advice often, or lightly. Nor was it wise to ignore her. He tried to sort out his feelings, but they were far too chaotic. He settled for the direct approach. "I'm very angry. I want to go."

She nodded, and he was relieved to see that this confession contented her. "Then that is what you must tell Diana."

They washed and cut broccoli in silence for a while and finally, driven by the quiet, he blurted out, "No one seems to understand. If I were still with the jaran, I would be a dyan, a commander, of my own army. These are the years that a soldier does his best fighting, and I'm wasting them away."

"So you're frustrated. I understand that. But, Anatoly, you

know that you've received treatments that will allow you to live far longer than you could have expected to on Rhui."

"My body has received these treatments, and my mind benefits from them, but my mind still lives on Rhui. That is, I mean—" He flushed, angry at himself for repeating the worst of Diana's accusations against him, when that wasn't what he had meant.

"I know what you mean: Intellectually you understand that you'll live longer, but in your own mind, emotionally, you still age each year the way you always expected you would. Or at least, is that what you mean?" She smiled.

Relaxing, Anatoly smiled back. "Close enough. I can't help but think that I ought to be doing something, but I'm not."

"That is up to you."

Diana sat at the other end of the long, long table at dinner, with Portia next to her, and Anatoly had no chance to get her alone until evening. He ran her to ground when she came downstairs and went out onto the front lawn after putting Portia to bed.

"Diana," he said softly, coming up behind her. He did not touch her.

She shrugged without answering, without turning to face him.

"I beg your pardon for the things I said. I was angry because I want to go with the Company."

Now she turned, looking startled. In any light, she was beautiful. Dusk softened her expression, and for an instant he could believe that she had forgiven him everything.

"Thank you," she said. "I appreciate you offering an apology and explaining yourself."

He flinched as if slapped, but he kept Aunt Millie uppermost in his mind and he forced himself to stay calm. "Diana. I had hoped we could—"

"Kiss and make love and wake up in the morning as if nothing, no argument, had happened, like we always do? I'm tired of running that same cycle over and over and over, because we aren't getting anywhere new."

She paused. It was so quiet that he felt as if he could hear the exhalation of the sky, the music of the stars, and the slow drag of the moon on the distant tides.

A gleam of bitter humor surfaced in her face. "But I am

willing to enter negotiations," she added, "if it's worth it to you, to build something we can live with."

"Of course it is worth it to me! How could you think otherwise? I left everything for you, Diana!"

"How could I ever forget it?" she whispered, ducking her head down, as if to avoid a blow.

"My heart," he murmured, and caught her shoulders and pulled her into him. It was the only sure way he knew to show her that he loved her. For a moment she resisted. Then she muttered something uninterpretable under her breath and abruptly wrapped her arms around him and kissed him. They stood that way, under the stars, for a long time. No one disturbed them.

CHAPTER TEN

Sarai

The Orzhekov tribe crossed the great sea of grass in an untidy line, a thread pulled across a golden tapestry. Out on the plains, it was easy to love the passage from one pasture to the next for its own sake, to feel at one with the migration of the wind, to believe that the journey itself was endless, that no destination, once reached, was ever final.

Tess urged Zhashi along the line. In the back of one wagon, Yuri slept soundly despite the constant movement, his head cushioned on an arm, his body swaying to the rhythm of the wagon's ride. She lifted a hand to greet Niko as she passed him as well. He could no longer ride long distances and had to drive wagons now. But he smiled at her. The duty seemed not to bother him.

"Dammit," she said, coming up beside her husband in the vanguard, "it hurts me more to watch him get old than it does him to get old."

Ilya glanced at her, then went back to surveying the ebb and flow of grass along the low hills, rippled by the wind while the clouds sailed with majestic disinterest above. "So do we all grow old and die," he said finally. "He has lived a long life, and has seen a child born to his granddaughter. No doubt, having lived lawfully and well, the gods will allow him to be born into his next life as a woman."

Tess laughed. "No doubt that will be his reward."

"You don't think so?" Ilya asked, looking truly puzzled. It was at moments like this that Tess remembered how different they were. Abruptly distracted, he reined Kriye aside and headed out away from the tribe, motioning her to follow.

Mystified, she did. They came to the crest of a rise and there, below, lay Sarai, distant enough that the line of trees along the river looked narrow and low. Ilya dismounted.

"Here is the spot where you marked me, and I you," he said. He looked not as much joyful as smugly satisfied.

"How can you possibly tell?"

Looking down on him, she saw how the sun lit his hair and shone, for an instant, on his face before the clouds muffled its light. "How can you *not* tell? You khaja have been crippled by your maps and your timepieces and your walls."

"Our maps have been very useful to you!"

"That is true. But nevertheless, you are like the prisoners in the cave, your legs and necks shackled by your maps and your walls so that all you can see is the shadows thrown by the fire on the wall of the cave. You think they are the truth, but they are only a shadow of the truth, which lies—" He gestured to the sky and the plain and the distant spiral curl that was the growing city of Sarai. "—out here, under the gaze of the sun and the moon and the stars."

"Well!" Tess laughed again. "That is why you have so often been accused of loving khaja learning too much! I thought you didn't like Plato."

"I don't." Ilya grinned and swung back up on Kriye, who sidestepped away and was in general feeling lively. "But I must use the weapons I am given or else lose all." As soon as Ilya was on Kriye's back, the stallion broke away and ran along the crest until Ilya finally reined him in and turned back. Zhashi snorted and lowered her head to graze, disgusted by this masculine idiocy.

But Tess enjoyed watching it. Ilya and Kriye together made a beautiful picture. And they liked being admired. "Vain creatures," she said to Zhashi, who found the subject too uninteresting to reply to.

She inspected Sarai, which from this height and distance bore more resemblance to the ruins of a whorled seashell than to a city. She blinked her implant on. If she had been alone, she would have used voice triggers to bring up the program she wanted; instead, she had to sort backward through the entrance architecture by focusing her eyes on and blinking at each subfile she wanted, as if she was descending a long staircase. It took longer, but it was silent.

They had laid out the pattern first, a great spiral at whose center rested an oval plaza, the heart of the city. Through her implant, the image overlaid on Sarai-as-she-was-now, Tess saw that pattern marked on the ground as she and David ben Unbutu had envisioned it, a city blending both worlds, jaran and khaja. At last, she focused past the pattern and examined the actual city.

On one side of this plaza spread the khaja city, on the other, the haphazard strings of jaran camps. Swathes of parkland cut through the khaja city. Following David's plans, the surveyors had marked out areas where khaja settlers—mostly artisans and laborers and merchants brought in from conquered territories—could build their own houses. Within those districts an untidy array of houses and hovels and villas rose in clumps, warrening together by clans or religions or some other designation Tess hadn't yet figured out. These districts grew in fractured rings out from the innermost city, where the first of the public buildings now rose beside the plaza.

"It looks like the marketplace is finished," said Ilya.

The image of the marketplace took form and commingled with the actual marketplace, a vast space of arches roofed with stone and wood open on the sides. Tess smiled to herself and a new image asserted itself, that of David's third tier design, a fanciful combination of arches and fluttering cloth and elegant thin spires all bringing more loft and air to the market. But they could not build such a thing now. Not yet.

She let her eyes roam, spiraling out and seeing the image of the city that was meant to be: a glorious shell open to the sky, with the broad oval paved in white stone and a great fountain at its center, with a forum and a second marketplace and a palace for the bureaucracy (since it was certainly not anything Ilya would agree to live in) and an audience hall and a granary and guild halls and a library (her addition) and a stadium and a theater modeled after the one at Ephesus, and at this point she and David had spent more time laughing over what utopian absurdities they could think up than actually planning anything useful.

"What do you see?" asked Ilya casually.

Tess started, blinking down hard on the third tier construct and reining Zhashi—who had caught her sudden shift of mood—in with a touch of her knees. Her eyes caught an unfamiliar gleam of pale tile, and she gasped.

"The bathhouse roof is on! It must be finished!"

Her enthusiasm surprised a laugh out of Ilya. "Very well. Perhaps we'd better go down and investigate."

Tess slanted a sidewise glance at him, but mottling his face and form she saw instead David's five-hundred-year projections for the growth and spread of the city, an ugly sprawl that reminded her bitterly of what the jaran had already lost, and what they had yet to lose. She blinked the implant off and, frowning now, followed Ilya down the slope.

They rode into Sarai along a paved thoroughfare that began abruptly in the middle of grass and ran straight into the city. Fifty riders from Ilya's jahar fell in around them and escorted them to the park on the jaran side of the oval in which the great tent of the Orzhekov tribe stood, the permanent symbol of Orzhekov authority. To the right, half-hidden by stands of young trees, sat the Sakhalin tent topped by a red pennant edged with gold, and to the left, farther back behind a young planted wilderness that would in time hide them from view, rose the tents of whichever of the other Elder Tribes were in residence at any given time. Right now, Tess counted three flags: the golden sword of Veselov, the blue horse of Raevsky, and, of course, the green tent striped with gold that marked the Grekov tribe.

Tess dismounted and unsaddled Zhashi and rubbed her down while Ilya went to greet his cousin Kira and her daughter Galina, who had stayed in Sarai. Then, handing the mare over to a boy who would lead her out to pasture, Tess followed Ilya inside the great tent.

It was vast, more like a great round hall than a nomad's tent. It also boasted a slatted wooden floor and huge beams rising above, on which the felt roof rested and from which tapestries hung, decorating the long inner hall and closing off a series of smaller private rooms along the sides, although any one of those private chambers was the size of many an etsana's tent.

Ilya laughed, and she saw him at the opposite side, kneeling beside Galina's firstborn, a chubby three-year-old.

"Gods," said Tess as she greeted her eldest adopted sister, Kira, "it's hard to believe that little Galina is old enough to be having her second child."

"Even if she did have to marry that worthless Sakhalin prince?" asked Kira tartly.

"Well, it isn't my fault that Anatoly Sakhalin disappointed both his grandmother's and my plans and Galina ended up with his uncle instead."

"Anatoly Sakhalin would have been a better match," agreed Kira, perfectly willing to malign her son-in-law. "At least Andrei spends more time with the army than here. Hush, now. She cares for him, so that's all that matters."

Galina waddled over and Tess embraced her. "You're looking well, little one," she said, and everyone laughed, since Galina was hugely pregnant. "What news?" she asked Kira, but they were interrupted by the arrival of the rest of the family from the wagons: Sonia and Stassia and the children, and Irena Orzhekov.

For a while, bedlam raged. The gods had smiled kindly on the Orzhekov tribe. Not only had they granted one of their sons a vision that had led him to unite the tribes and lead the jaran to conquer their rightful subjects, the khaja, but they had also gifted Mother Orzhekov with five daughters (one adopted) and many healthy grandchildren, and particularly many fine girls to carry on the line. In fact, Tess reflected, sitting on a pillow with a still sleepy Yuri heaped in her lap, most of the Orzhekov line was here right now, which was why even with the muffling properties of the tapestries and the felt walls, their mingled voices rang with such an overpowering swell of noise.

Irena's eldest daughter Kira and her husband Sevyan had six children, of whom only one had died in infancy; Kira's eldest son Mitya was now governing prince of Habakar, but her daughter Galina was here as were the other two girls and one boy. Stassia, the second daughter, and her husband Pavel had eight formidably robust children; two boys and one girl were out with the army, but of the other five girls, one was married and four still young. Anna, who had died over fourteen years ago, had left a boy and a girl; her husband, Gennady Berezin, was a long-standing member of Ilya's jahar.

Sonia's elder children Katerina and Ivan were with Yaroslav Sakhalin. Little Kolia—well, no longer little now, since he was thirteen this year—was outside with Dania Tagansky helping with the horses while his baby sister Alyona, the daughter of Sonia and her second husband, Josef Raevsky, sat on her mother's knee and wailed at some imagined slight. Tess's adopted brother Aleksi was gone; he had ridden out two months ago to lead the expedition along the Golden Road. But his wife Svetlana Tagansky and their three children were here. Feodor Grekov had his younger daughter riding on his hip. Tess guessed that Nadine would be outside, already gleaning reports from whatever couriers had ridden in recently; as for Feodor and Nadine's elder daughter, Lara, neither she nor Natalia nor Aleksi's younger daughter Sofia were in evidence. No doubt trouble was brewing.

"That is disturbing news indeed," said Irena Orzhekov calmly to Kira. "Alyona, my heart, you must cease crying this instant."

Yuri reflexively stuck two fingers in his mouth and sucked on them intently, watching his three-year-old cousin decide whether it was worth continuing to cry. Aleksi's wife Svetlana, with her youngest child in tow, swooped down and spirited Alyona off Sonia's lap. Yuri settled a hand possessively around Tess's elbow as Alyona's indignant wails faded away when she was taken outside.

"What is disturbing news?" asked Sonia, resettling herself more comfortably next to Tess. Stassia squatted next to them, and Kira threw a pillow down so that both she and her mother could sit.

"Mother Sakhalin is failing. The healers agree that she is in her last days," said Kira. She and Stassia resembled their mother, with lean faces and bright blue eyes and pale blonde hair washed even lighter with silver.

Tess nodded gravely with the other women, but her eyes caught on Ilya where he stood by the entrance, conferring with Konstans Barshai. Konstans was ten years younger than Ilya, and yet they looked, where the sun filtered through and cast stripes of light along their figures, illuminating their dark hair, their beards, to be about the same age. Except it was Ilya and his cousin Kira who were born in the same year.

"At least the succession is not only assured, but in safe hands," said Irena. "Konstantina Sakhalin will be a worthy Mother Sakhalin. What concerns me, Kira, is this news of Arina Veselov."

"Arina?" Tess's attention snapped back to the council. "Is something wrong with Arina?"

"She is pregnant," said Kira. "As we suspected."

Tess gasped.

"As she would not admit," added Sonia. "But how could she have risked it? Not only her tribe's elders and Varia Telyegin but Tess's *Dokhtor* Hierakis all warned her that this time it would probably kill her."

"Well," said Kira solemnly. "We shall soon find out. Varia Telyegin says she has had strong rushes all morning."

"Then she hid it for a long time," said Tess, since they

had only been out on the plains for four months, "or else she's early again."

"Early or late," said Irena, "if she dies, there is no woman in the direct Veselov line to become etsana. The tribe will never have Vera Veselov—"

"I doubt she would give up being dyan in any case," put in Tess, "a position for which she is far better suited."

Irena Orzhekov's lips quirked slightly, while Sonia rolled her eyes and Stassia made a face. "Although it pains me to agree with you on this matter, I fear it is true," said Irena. "So be it. Who then will become etsana of the Veselov tribe? Mira Veselov is only eleven years old."

"Could someone hold it in trust for her, until she is old enough, and proves herself worthy?" Tess asked.

"This is also what I am thinking," said Irena. "I am thinking that Galina should. In time she will become Mother Orzhekov, if the gods will, and in this way she would gain experience and yet there could be no suspicion involved that she hoped to supplant Mira herself."

"And it would give her good-for-nothing husband a bit more responsibility, which he sorely needs," said Kira sourly.

"Kira!"

Kira glanced around to make sure that Galina was out of earshot. "I am sorry to say that my son married a timid khaja girl and my daughter a son of the Sakhalin tribe, and of the two I far prefer the little khaja princess, barbarian though she may be. Begging your pardon, Tess."

"Granted willingly." As an afterthought, all five of the women looked at Yuri. He stopped sucking on his fingers and slowly drew them out of his mouth. He squirmed closer against his mother, folded both his hands around her elbow, and hung on. "You'd better go, Yurinya. This is women's business."

He opened his mouth to screech, caught Irena Orzhekov's eye, and decided against it. With a pronounced sigh, he heaved himself to his feet and wandered away, dragging his feet until he caught sight of his father. Tess watched him trot over—he had an endearingly uncoordinated lope that could not quite be dignified with the word "run"—and attach himself to Ilya's leg. Startled, Ilya looked down at him, up toward Tess, and then scooped the boy up and set him on his shoulders. Together, they walked outside with Konstans,

Yuri ducking as they went under the threshold. Yuri was already chattering away, and Tess cringed, hoping that he was not repeating in some fragmented fashion the conversation he had just heard: He had an astonishingly good memory for a five-year-old.

"We have decided to postpone the birbas for at least ten more days. There has been the usual nonsense with the Grekov tribe, who are determined to quarrel with the Raevskys, this time over right of place in the birbas," added Kira.

All the women except Sonia shook their heads. Tess dipped her head down to hide a smile.

"Why are you smiling?" asked Sonia suddenly.

Tess chuckled. "I don't know. Maybe only to wonder how I could have been so naive as to imagine that the four of you hadn't planned it all from the beginning, for Feodor Grekov to mark Nadine. I just find it so amusing to see you all so irritated that it hasn't worked out as you'd planned."

"She has given birth to two fine girls," retorted Sonia, nettled.

Kira snorted. "If you call Lara fine. I would call her wild, myself."

"I grieve for the little boy they lost," said Irena, "but nevertheless, Tess is right. The gods always find ways to remind us that we aren't nearly as clever as we believe we are. I will have to consult with—" She hesitated, reading her eldest daughter's expression. "Is Mother Sakhalin so ill that she can't be consulted?" she asked, startled enough that Tess caught a hint of alarm in her voice.

Kira bowed her head. "Three days ago she fell into sleep and has only woken twice briefly since."

Irena rose, shaking out her skirts. "Then we must go at once to her tent. After that, we will visit Arina Veselov. Tess, you will come with me. Sonia and Stassi, you will remain here now and then attend Mother Sakhalin this evening. From now until she dies, one of us should remain at her tent at all hours."

"I'll see that our tents are put up," said Stassia, rising.

"Oh, Stassi," said Sonia, "let me supervise the tents today. The sight of food makes me ill. You promised yesterday you would see to dinner until I'm feeling better." The other women paused and examined her with critical eyes.

"Aha!" said Tess. "You *are* pregnant, aren't you?"

Sonia laughed. "You know the answer to that as well as I do. But I must say, Tess, that—'"

"No! I've had two. That's enough!"

It was an old argument that had been raging for over two years now, ever since Yuri had turned three. Tess had avoided it for a time by going to Jeds, but on her return it had simply resumed with more force.

"Don't tease her, Sonia," said Irena mildly. "Although I admit I now understand why the khaja princes are so weak, and why their houses die out so quickly, if they think two children are enough to secure their line."

Tess sighed. It was all very well to have a mother and older sisters, but it also meant that she had to bear up under the brunt of their advice and scolding.

"Come, Tess," said Irena. Tess followed her away, making a face at Sonia over her shoulder. Sonia only laughed.

They walked toward the Sakhalin tent across an expanse of flourishing green grass. It was lawn grass, truth to tell, not the coarser plains grass that grew everywhere outside the central grounds of the park. In the year he had spent here on the site of Darai, David had devised many ingenious marvels, working with Habakar and Vidiyan engineers brought to Sarai by the army. One of them was the unobtrusive irrigation system, which was almost as marvelous as the citywide plumbing system, both of them built with the technology and manpower at hand. It was amazing what one could accomplish with enough hands and enough time and enough patience. Tess had schemed for this lawn. She would have taken off her boots just to feel the soft grass between her toes, but Irena would probably think her odd for doing so. In any case, they crossed over a small canal, skirted a line of saplings, and came to the Sakhalin tent. The sight of it sobered Tess.

Elizaveta Sakhalin was dying.

Inside, incense could not cover the sour-sweet smell of illness. Mother Sakhalin lay on pillows, breathing shallowly. She looked impossibly tiny, as if the illness itself was shrinking her. Her skin was so pale and dry that Tess was afraid the slightest touch would mark her permanently. Irena knelt down beside the old etsana and took her ancient, veined hand in her own. She regarded the old woman calmly. A Sakhalin girl hovered in the background, and the Sakhalin healer sat quietly opposite Mother Orzhekov.

Tess remained standing. She sniffed back a tear and caught a second on a finger. But she wasn't really crying for Mother Sakhalin, although she grieved to see her so close to death. Even as Mother Sakhalin had grown old, had grown weaker, and finally failed, Tess knew she was seeing the beginning of Niko's decline, and that was far harder to contemplate.

Niko would not thank her for interfering with the natural course of life, and yet she could not help but wonder if she ought to try to give longevity to all the jaran. Yet even with the treatments that extended youth, a swift decline set in at around one hundred and ten years. Inevitably, this scene was played out in every family, with every individual. Even if Cara Hierakis found a formula that would double the human life span, still, in the end, mortality faced them all.

The sweetish smell caught in Tess's throat, and she gagged.

Mother Sakhalin stirred. Her hand fluttered in Irena's gentle grip. Her eyes opened and closed and opened. Her gaze had lost its sharp intelligence; it pained Tess to see how lost and confused the old woman seemed. Mother Sakhalin glanced around the dim chamber as if looking for something that wasn't there, and her fingers moved, clutching Irena's hand.

"Anatoly," she said in a hoarse whisper, "*kriye*, dear one."

She fell back asleep.

Irena let go of her hand and sat back on her heels. "Kira said she was woken twice before from this sleep."

The healer nodded. "With the same result. It is always the boy she asks for."

Irena rose. She carried with her such vast reserves of serenity that Tess could not imagine seeing her flustered. "My other daughters will come as well," she said to the healer. They took their leave.

Outside the tent, blinking as they adjusted to the sunlight, Irena spoke without looking at Tess. "It is hard for you, I can tell, my daughter. But I hope you remember that a woman who survives her childbearing can expect to see her husband die before her." Tess shuddered. Irena rested a cool hand on Tess's arm, a fleeting, comforting gesture. "But it is true that he is holding up well under the weight of his years and his vision. Perhaps the gods have chosen to grant him youth past the normal measure, so that he may better lead his armies as far as the gods want him to." She dropped her hand and walked on, as if she knew that Tess did not want to speak of these matters.

At the Veselov tent, Arina looked peaceful enough. Her eyes lit, when she saw Tess, and she extended a hand. Tess grasped it and sat down beside her.

"You are well?" asked Tess, feeling stupid as she said it.

"I am fine," said Arina, but she looked worn and pale, her small body dwarfed by her pregnancy. Even her gorgeous black hair hung lankly down over her shoulders as if it had lost an essential spark of life.

"I wish you hadn't done this," Tess blurted out. "I'm very worried for you, Arina."

Arina's expression softened. "I am not as worried as you are. But it was nice of you to come so swiftly. You must just have ridden in."

"Oh, gods, I ought to be reassuring you, not you, me. Everything will be all right."

Arina smiled. "You can only say that because you have not been in camp with the Grekovs and the Raevskys arguing around you. Why, at least once a day some one or other of them comes to me to complain."

Tess laughed, and they chatted for a while on these other, safer topics, until the healer Varia Telyegin chased her out.

"She didn't seem to be having any pains," said Tess when they were outside, and out of Arina's earshot.

"They stopped just before you came," said Varia, "but that, too, discourages me."

"Do you truly not believe she can survive the labor?"

"She has scarcely been able to walk for eight years now. How can she be strong enough to give birth to this child? None of her other births went easily—not of the two children who yet live and certainly not the one six years ago when we lost the baby and almost lost her."

"But that happened to me," said Tess obstinately, "and I went on to give birth to two healthy children afterward."

Varia only shook her head.

"There is nothing we can do," said Irena as they walked back to the Orzhekov encampment, growing now as tents were set up beside and behind the great central tent. "Arina has been a wise etsana, for all that she came so young into the position, but she has a weakness for men. First, to let her cousin Vasil return when he had been exiled."

"Yes, but he's gone now," said Tess impatiently, not liking the way Irena was looking at her. Tess suspected that Irena suspected many things about her and Ilya and Vasil, all of which were probably true.

A smile cracked Irena's stern expression, then vanished. "And second, she badly wanted to tie Kirill closer to her by giving birth to many strong children."

"But Kirill loves her!"

"That is true enough. I confess I misjudged him early on. I believe now that even were she never to give birth to any more children, she could not shake his affection and loyalty to her. But Arina has always lived in the shadow of your tent, Tess."

Tess winced. "But—"

"I am not blaming you, my daughter. I doubt if Arina Veselov does either. She is far too wise and generous for that."

"Certainly she has always been generous," muttered Tess, feeling guilty.

"That does not change the fact that her life would have been very different if you had not come to the jaran."

"I wish—" began Tess, and broke off. Irena regarded her evenly. Tess finally produced a lopsided smile. "I wish you wouldn't tell me things I don't want to hear."

Irena stopped, placed a hand on each of Tess's shoulders, and kissed her on either cheek. Then, without another word, she walked into the great tent, leaving Tess standing outside.

Ilya strolled up, as if he had been waiting for her. "And?"

"I'm sure you've heard the worst from Kira, and there isn't any better news to replace that with. Let's go see if the baths truly are finished."

"You and your baths. I think the only reason you wanted Sarai founded was so that you could have those baths built."

Tess smiled, because David had accused her of the same thing, six years ago.

They went in relative solitude: an escort of only twenty riders. She walked, the better to inspect the foundations of the fountain being built in the center of the great plaza. About a dozen men were digging here, installing pipes, and they ceased work immediately and knelt, bowing their heads, when she approached. Their subservience made her uncomfortable, but Ilya climbed right down into the pit and inspected the workings with interest. Tess watched the laborers eyeing him from under the brim of their caps, but none spoke a word except in answer to his direct questions.

"Very clever," he said finally, climbing out. They strolled on across the oval, which was already paved in smooth stone. Tess had insisted that David site the archives, which she called the library, directly opposite the Orzhekov tent, so that the two faced each other across the white expanse of the plaza, although the Orzhekov tent was set back so far in the park that only the gold banner and the slope of the roof were visible above the screen of new trees that would eventually grow to hide it entirely from view.

Jaran guards stood impassively at the great double doors that led into the main reading room. Tess set a foot on the stairs and gazed up. The library had been the first building they had built, and they had built it in unseemly haste, taking only five years to do it. And she had business within, important business. Of all the buildings here, of all the buildings dreamt of, it was her favorite.

She withdrew her foot from the stairs. "No, I want to see the baths first."

"You want to see the *khepelli* priestess," said Ilya.

Tess shot him a glance but did not reply. Instead she kept walking, circling the elegant marble dome, a smaller version of the Pantheon, and its ringed portico and meeker octagonal annex, the scriptorium.

Behind the library stood the huge baths complex. They were a vile luxury, and Tess found them utterly enchanting. They were divided into four sections: the cold pool (which stretched outdoors), the Greater Baths, the Lesser Baths, and the Imperial Baths, together with the annexes, the lavatories and (the most obscene addition) a bank of showers.

The Imperial Baths were reserved for jaran, but at midday, except for the guards, they were empty. They paused in the foyer.

"I will wait out here, then," said Ilya, "or perhaps go back to the archives."

"You will not!"

Ilya glanced at their escort. "Tess," he said in an undertone, "it is unseemly for a man and a woman to bathe together."

"It is not. Your aunt need never know in any case." He looked unconvinced but he hesitated, so she turned to

Konstans. "Konstans. Take the men outside and place a ring around the building."

Konstans looked amused. "Does this mean I may bring my wife here some evening?"

Ilya flushed.

"If you move swiftly, now, and don't say anything about this to anyone else. Out."

They went.

"I don't—" began Ilya.

"Yes, you do. We've been traveling for ten days to get here. There you stand in all your dust, and the truth is, the only thing that stops you from going in with me and enjoying these miraculous baths is your own embarrassment. Ilya, your armies have swept through more princedoms than I can count, and you're afraid that back at camp they're going to gossip about you because you bathed with your wife!"

"You have never been scolded by my aunt for improper behavior."

"I have, too! She doesn't scare me. Much." She threw up her hands. "I'm going in. You may follow or not, as you wish."

She passed through the vestibule and walked across the silent exercise court that fronted the baths themselves. Inside, in the dressing room, she stripped. She had just taken off the last of her clothes when Ilya appeared.

"I was thinking—" he began, and broke off, seeing her naked.

Tess rolled her eyes. "You aren't this shy in my blankets."

Crossing into the warm baths chamber, she eased herself into the circular pool and just floated there a while, enjoying the lap of gentle waves against her arms and chest. Then she swam a slow lap, luxuriating in the warmth and the sensuous slipperiness of the water against her skin. She dove under and surfaced next to the stairs, to find Ilya sitting on the steps, half in the water, looking . . . uncomfortable.

"I forgot," said Tess, suddenly illuminated. "You don't know how to swim." She caught back a laugh, because she could tell he was in an uncertain mood.

"Damn you." He took her by the arm and hauled her in against him, and Tess instantly revised her evaluation of his mood.

"Mmmm." said Ilya after a while. "It is no wonder the khaja are so weak. We bathe in cold streams and rivers, where we certainly aren't tempted to linger on doing this sort of thing."

"Are you complaining?"

"Not at all."

Even the floor was warm, because of the hollow pipes running underneath that conducted hot air from the furnace. The finest grade of stone had been chosen for these rooms, so that although the floor was hard, it had an almost silken smoothness rather akin to the flow of Ilya's skin under her hands.

"You were thinking," she said later, lying half on top of him, idly tracing the curves of his face with a finger, studying its lines, as she liked to. He shifted his hips, easing away from where her knee pushed hard against his thigh.

"I was thinking," he said slowly, "that it is time for me to return to the army. The horses are fat from the spring grass, and if Kirill can push west quickly enough, we can catch the king and army of Micassia between two pincers and so make an end to him. Then only Filis and its prince will remain between us and Jeds. We could reach Jeds by midwinter, if all went well."

Tess froze. All of her pleasure evaporated. She rolled off him and plunged into the pool, swam across it, and clambered out the opposite side, dripping water, and hurried away under an archway and into the chamber with the cold pool, which was likewise deserted. She dove in. The numbing cold of the water stung her, and she surfaced, gasping. Waves surged out from her and swelled out under the arches that opened onto the outdoor portion of the pool, where they dissipated under the sun. She heaved herself up and sat on the lip of the pool. After a little bit, Ilya came in.

"I'm sorry," she said before he could say anything. "You're right, of course."

He sat down beside her, dipped a foot in the water, and hid a wince. Then he threw himself in, shattering the surface into a thousand drops of spray. He came up, sputtering, and wiped his eyes. "Naturally you and the children will come to Jeds as soon as the way is clear."

"Naturally," she echoed, missing him already. But this, too, was part of the life she had chosen.

"I beg your pardon." Konstans's voice broke into their conversation. "Mother Orzhekov has sent a message." Tess spun to look behind her, but Konstans stayed discreetly out of view. "Mother Veselov's baby is coming, and it isn't going well."

"Oh, hell," said Tess, leaping up. "I'll come at once."

CHAPTER ELEVEN

A Prince of the Blood

Andrei Sakhalin liked to talk.

"We have passed into the kingdom of Dushan, another of the Yos lands, although King Zgoros of Dushan has less power and less land than Prince Sigismar of Hereti-Manas, and was himself a vassal of Prince Dragos of Zara before he became our vassal."

"How can a king be a vassal to a prince?" asked Stefan.

Vasha and Stefan flanked Andrei Sakhalin, one on each side, while they watched the merchants' train of wagons ford a river, carts bucking and heaving over the shallow rocky bed.

"The khaja are not like us," said Andrei. "They give themselves names, king or prince or priest, but the names mean nothing unless they hold land to themselves and have soldiers enough to keep others from stealing it."

Stefan snorted. "You can't steal land."

"But they're bound to the land," interposed Vasha, feeling a flicker of interest in the conversation, "because they are farmers."

"They're not all farmers," objected Stefan. "Some of them are merchants."

"What Vassily means to say is that their wealth is bound into the land they hold," said Andrei, "and so without land, even a mighty king will rule nothing, and his mother's name will be forgotten. That is why they cannot stand against us. We do not forsake the names the gods gave us. The Sakhalin will always be First of the Elder Tribes, even if Mother Sakhalin has only one tent and ten grazel."

On the far bank, the princess and her escort appeared, and Vasha watched as Princess Rusudani and her servant and her ten guards picked their way across the ford. Vasha could not help but notice what a good seat on her horse Rusudani had, especially compared to Jaelle, who still after all these weeks rode with the uneasiness of a person who distrusts horses. He envied the khaja, suddenly; by khaja law, his position was assured.

Sakhalin began talking again, and Vasha let the words wash over him, drowning his fear in noise. "But King Zgoros of Dushan was grateful to ally himself with us, since his own father had been forced to kneel before the prince of Zara. When the younger Prince Dragos of Zara was killed fighting at the River Djana last year, King Zgoros sent an envoy to Bakhtiian to ask that his youngest son Prince Janos be granted the Zaran throne, since in his great-grandfather's time the prince of Zara was the nephew of the Dushan king and subordinate to him. In those days, the Dushan king was preeminent over all the princes in Yos lands, Zara, Hereti and Manas, Gelasti, and Tarsina-Kars, and allied as an equal with Mircassia. But an ambitious nephew of a younger line stole the land and put in a claim for himself, and the other princes supported him, so Zara was again torn from Dushan's grasp. That is why—" Sakhalin broke off.

Vasha jerked his gaze away from Princess Rusudani and looked over at the Sakhalin prince.

Andrei, too, was studying Rusudani, his eyes narrowed. His face bore a calculating look, which surprised Vasha, since Andrei seemed to chatter more than to think.

"Is it true that the khaja princess has no brothers or uncles?" Andrei asked suddenly.

"As far as we can tell. The two brothers died at the Salho River, and there must be the one uncle left, who would be King Barsauma of Mircassia's heir."

"I heard a different rumor, in Dushan, that all of King Barsauma's sons had died, the last only recently, and that he has but a nephew left, a boy who is feebleminded and crippled."

"How do you know so much about the khaja?" asked Stefan, who returned his attention to the Sakhalin prince as soon as the women passed down the road and out of view.

"It is my duty to know a great deal about the khaja, and it should be yours, as well. You come from a good family, Stefan Danov, and your grandfather Nikolai Sibirin is a respected healer, a man of influence. If you fight bravely and listen well, there is no reason you could not command a jahar in time."

"I'm gong to be a healer," said Stefan quietly, but Andrei had already turned to Vasha.

"What do you think, Vassily Kireyevsky? Should such a valuable khaja princess be allowed to marry back into the khaja lines, or should some clever young jaran prince marry her to keep her power within the tribes?"

Vasha flushed. It was as if Andrei, like a Singer who can divine the words of the gods, had known his ambition. "I think any jaran man who wishes to marry her had better speak with Mother Orzhekov and Mother Sakhalin before he marks her," he stammered. "What if she refuses to marry any man who does not dwell in the same church as she does?"

Andrei rolled his eyes. "Women do not have a choice in marriage. Why should it matter to them in any case? They may pray to their gods as they wish. When Prince Mitya's khaja wife brought in builders and priests to lift up a temple to her god in their new city, no one spoke against her."

Vasha smiled, thinking of Mitya, the one bright spot in this whole gloomy journey. "I think the Habakar do not mind so much, because so many people of different lands travel through their kingdom, and their kings and rulers marry women from so many different places. But I think the khaja who follow Hristain's church think differently."

Andrei smiled indulgently. "Well, my boy, it does not matter what these khaja think, since they are subject to us. They will follow the laws we set down." He urged his horse forward and fell in with the rearguard as it cleared the river and headed down the road. A few ramshackle old wagons and clots of travelers on foot trailed behind them, khaja stragglers who were not part of the official party but who crept along in their wake, hoping to find safety by sticking as close as possible to Riasonovsky's soldiers.

Andrei went on talking, as always, telling them old stories about the mischief he and his brothers and cousins used to get into and newer stories about the skirmish he had recently fought in and the story of the Djana River battle (for the third time) and how Yaroslav Sakhalin's army had routed the combined forces of the Zaran and Gelasti princes and their allies.

In this way, Vasha reflected, Andrei was refreshingly different from Ilya and Tess. Tess rarely told stories. Mostly she taught, but even then the words she used and the knowledge she related seemed more characterized by the silences between the words than by the words themselves. When Ilya spoke, even the most casual remarks bore so much weight that one could not afford to miss any least syllable he uttered. But Vasha did not want to think about his father.

Katya had used to be like Andrei Sakhalin, just going on and on and not seeming to care if you were listening with your full attention all the time, but since their last fight, she did not speak to Vasha except when civility demanded.

He sighed. But even as the last bit of air escaped his lips, a thought struck him with such force that he gulped in air again. Had Andrei Sakhalin been suggesting to him that he take matters into his own hands and mark Princess Rusudani? Just like that? A woman could not erase the mark from her face, nor could a man withdraw a stroke of the saber once it was cut. And once he had married her, he would hold position and power through her that could not be taken away from him.

Then he imagined what his father would say.

Even so, the idea nagged at him for the rest of the day. When they stopped for the night, Vasha went along with Stefan who every evening without fail helped Jaelle with her most onerous chores. Tonight the young woman handed Stefan four buckets without a word, as if she now expected his help. Rusudani sat on a stool outside her tent, sewing. Vasha wanted to linger, to see if she would possibly, just possibly, ask Jaelle to talk to him, but it wasn't fair to make Stefan go down to the river by himself. Once they were out of sight of the tent, Vasha took two of the buckets from Stefan.

They walked down to the river, batting away flies and underbrush on the overgrown path that led down to the bank, shrouded in bushes and overhanging trees. It was sticky hot this evening, and there was no breeze to move the air.

Vasha slapped his neck and cursed. "I don't understand why you do this every night."

"I don't know," mumbled Stefan in a voice that made it obvious that he did know.

"Has she asked you to lie with her yet?"

Stefan flashed him an angry glance. "Be quiet! Didn't you ever listen to Tess? I've been thinking a lot about what she told us about khaja women. I didn't believe it then. Who could believe that people could be such barbarians?"

He trailed off where the path gave out. They slid down a ragged slope and knelt to fill the buckets with water. The river burbled along. On the dim bank opposite, trees bent down over the waters and the sky rose, night-gray with clouds, above the vegetation.

Stefan's voice dropped to a whisper. "If it's true that khaja women are taught not to take lovers, then why should Jaelle ask me to lie with her? And if she is a *whore,* then if I show my interest in her by giving her a gift, as I would with no shame if she was a jaran woman like Katya, then she will think I am buying her. So I wish you would stop asking me about it."

"I'm sorry." Vasha felt like an idiot. He should have seen how upset Stefan was. "If you feel that strongly for her, you could . . . marry her."

Stefan snorted. He hung the buckets from notches on a heavy pole and stood up underneath them, balancing the weight on his shoulders. "Everyone knows that Anatoly Sakhalin made a fool of himself by marking that khaja Singer impulsively. Gods, I've even heard Grandfather Niko say that same thing about Bakhtiian."

"You did not!"

"Did, too!" Stefan scrambled back up the slope. Water sloshed in the buckets but only a tiny wave splashed over and spilled. "Even if it was possible, I would talk to my sister and mother and grandmother first. She would have to come live with us, wouldn't she? It wouldn't be fair to a khaja woman if she had to come to live with the tribes for the rest of her life, if her new sisters and aunts didn't want her."

"Well, it isn't true about my father, anyway."

Stefan paused two steps up the path and looked back. "Is, too," he said in an undertone. "Grandfather Niko says that everyone knows that he was desperately in love with Tess, but she wouldn't have him. Or at least, not until later."

"Is not."

Wind stirred in the trees, bringing with it the sound of harness, a ring so faint it almost drowned under the noise of the river.

"But, Vasha, they all saw—" Stefan broke off. The ring of bridle sounded again, closer now. Vasha leapt up the path and stopped in the shadows beside Stefan. There was only silence and darkness, but then they heard the noise again. A shadow moved. A man appeared, dismounted, out of the trees. He looked up and down the bank. He had the bulky shape of a man dressed in chainmail. He was not jaran.

A hissed whisper drifted out, and he quickly retreated back into the bushes. A horse snorted and stilled. Then nothing, only the rush of river water flowing by.

Stefan bent his knees to set the buckets on the ground silently. Twigs snapped. They froze.

A figure formed in the shadows along the path leading back to the jaran camp. Andrei Sakhalin halted beside the two young men. He lifted his chin and indicated the opposite shore.

"Those are khaja soldiers. You two, go back to the princess's camp and stay there all night. I will let Riasonovsky know." His voice was the merest shadow, scarcely audible. "Take the buckets, so they won't know anything is amiss. We don't want her to try to escape again." He stepped aside to let them pass, and they went quickly, heeding his urgency.

As they came out of the woody bank and into sight of the camp fires, Stefan gulped in air, as if he had forgotten to breathe. "Do you think they've come to steal Princess Rusudani?"

"I don't know. We couldn't even tell how many men there are."

They crossed through the unobtrusive ring of guards that surrounded Rusudani's tent.

Vasha paused by the old veteran Zaytsev. "Be on alert," he said. "We saw some khaja soldiers across the river."

Zaytsev took in this information without batting an eye. "Does Riasonovsky know?"

"Yes. Sakhalin went to warn him."

Zaytsev grunted, and Vasha hurried to follow Stefan, who had set the buckets down beside the smaller tent. From here, the two young men could see the princess sitting within the halo of lantern light, reading aloud from a book while Jaelle sat at her feet, mending a torn blouse. It was so quiet that Vasha heard Rusudani's words clearly, each syllable, although he understood none of them. She recited more than read, and her voice was clear and plain. He admired her for sitting with such composure, a hostage in an enemy camp. She could not know what fate awaited her, but she did not seem to fear it.

Not like he did.

Abruptly she looked up, straight at them, although surely it was too dark to make them out clearly. The lantern's gleam gave her eyes a lustrous cast, and her face was fair, her expression tranquil, perhaps a little stern. Vasha's heart lurched, and his knees felt weak. He could not help himself. He stared at her, even though it was the worst manners, and unseemly behavior for a man.

She dropped her gaze and spoke a few words to Jaelle. The servant rose and picked her way across the ground toward them. Vasha felt Stefan go tense beside him.

When Jaelle reached them, she flashed a glance at Stefan first and then regarded Vasha. This close, Vasha saw that she too, did not look frightened; resigned, perhaps. Where Rusudani carried with her a kind of uncanny calm, Jaelle looked more exhausted in spirit than anything, as if she had ceased fearing the jaran not because they couldn't hurt her, but because she was used to being hurt. All at once he wondered what Jaelle thought of them, of him, of Stefan, who every night came dutifully to help her simply because he had fallen in love with her pretty face and quiet manners.

"The princess wishes to speak with you," she said finally.

Vasha stood rooted to the ground. *She* wanted to speak with *him*. With a last glance toward Stefan, Jaelle walked back toward the princess. Vasha followed her reflexively and Stefan, not to be left out, practically trod on his heels.

Because Rusudani was sitting, it was polite to sit, cross-legged on the ground three strides from her. Jaelle knelt equidistant between the two and Stefan hovered, undecided, and then took up a position a step behind Vasha, kneeling as well. Vasha smelled the faintest aroma of incense, or perhaps it was her scent, the exhalation of a khaja perfume. He felt dizzy, she was so close beside him. The rest of the world vanished, and Rusudani regarded him steadily, with interest but without fear.

She spoke, and Jaelle translated. "Princess Rusudani wishes to know who you are, and what your name is, and why you led the expedition that rescued her from the Lord of Sharvan."

Words caught in his throat and he could not speak. He dropped his gaze to stare at the hem of her skirt. Stitched along the hemline ran a series of sigils, embroidered in pale gray thread against the plain dark blue of the fabric, a practical color quite at variance with the wealth of jewels she

wore. Her feet stirred, shapes molding the curve of the skirt
into a new contour. His elbow, shifting, caught on the hilt of
his saber, and he realized with a flush so strong that it made
his heart pound that he could mark her right now and with
that mark make her his wife.

By jaran law. Lifting his eyes to look at her, at her lucid
expression, at her right hand resting lightly on the tiny
knife suspended from a gold chain around her neck, he experienced a revelation: Marking her would be an incredibly
stupid thing for him to do.

Even by becoming the husband of a powerful khaja princess, he could not force the Orzhekov tribe to look more
kindly on him. He could not make Ilya Bakhtiian love him
as a son.

Still, he succumbed to temptation. He wanted to impress
her. "Tell Princess Rusudani," he said, proud that his voice
barely shook, "that my name is Vassily Kireyevsky, and I
am the son of Ilyakoria Bakhtiian."

The world had long ago ceased holding any surprises for
Jaelle. She had, by necessity, learned how to measure men:
Some wanted companionship on the long road, others a
hard-working, uncomplaining girl to do their washing and
bring them wine; a few cared mostly about their pleasure in
bed, but those rarely expected her to do any other work.
Once she had taken a hard slap from a merchant rather than
hire herself to him; later, along the train of gossip that
passed down through the women who followed the caravans,
she had heard that he had beaten a girl to death.

But to have this slender, unexceptional jaran man sit down
modestly beside her and quietly announce that he was the
son of the great and terrible leader of the barbarian hordes
. . . that shocked her so completely that she forgot to translate his words.

"What did he say?" asked Rusudani in her cool, hard
voice.

"I beg your pardon, mistress," stammered Jaelle, self-
consciously pushing a strand of hair back under her scarf.
The two young men smelled of horse and grass and sweat,
but otherwise seemed clean, and that, too, surprised her. "He
says he is named Vasil'ii Kir'yevski, and that he is the son
of the Bakhtiian."

Rusudani's expression, always impassive, did not change.

"Do you think he is telling the truth, my lady?"

Rusudani examined the young man, who stared in his turn at her feet. The princess had the same huge, dark, lovely eyes that adorned the images of Our Lord's sister, the blessed Pilgrim, in the frescoes that told of Her life and journey. Here in the lands where the False Church reigned, there were, of course, no frescos, no images at all to spread the story of Hristain and His Sundering. But Jaelle remembered them vividly from her childhood, when she had knelt for hours in the chapel and stared at the brightly painted people on the walls.

"What reason would he have to lie?" said Rusudani at last. "But it is true that except when he led the riders I have not seen him act as a king's son should, nor do the other soldiers treat him with any deference. He does not bear the Bakhtiian's name. I do not know."

"What do you wish me to say to him, mistress?"

"Ask him what his father means to do with me once we reach his lands."

Jaelle coughed. She knew very well what was done with captured women, but the princess wore a kind of exalted calm like a mantle around her. "My lady, is it wise to ask—?"

"Ask him."

Jaelle flinched. She knew that tone from her childhood. Her mother, with her exotic Northern paleness and her compliant nature, had been a prized slave in a nobleman's house. "Yes, my lady." She repeated the question in Taor to the young prince, if prince he was.

His shoulders stiffened, and behind him, his slave stirred restlessly. "Tell Princess Rusudani that she will be treated with the respect jaran show all women," he said, for the first time sounding as curt as a prince. "Remind her that all the lands we ride through are jaran lands."

Rusudani's reply was swift. "Ask him if his father will send me back to my father, Prince Zakaria. My father will pay a handsome ransom for me."

The question brought a strange expression to Prince Vasil'ii's face. He did not reply immediately. Jaelle studied him surreptitiously. He was one of the dark barbarians, with their odd brown-black eyes and severe features. Most of them, though, like his slave, were as pale as she was, as if they shared Northern blood in common. "That will be decided by Bakhtiian and

Mother Orzhekov and Mother Sakhalin, and the Prince of Jeds,
and their council."

"Ask him," continued Rusudani in the same level voice,
"if his father would accept ransom from the envoys of the
Peregrine of the Church, for I was pledged to the service of
Our Lord as a child."

"I do not understand who is *the Peregrine*," said Prince
Vasil'ii. "But if she is pledged to your god, does that mean
she is a priest?" He looked a little angry as he said it. Jaelle
shrank back. A season ago she had never seen a barbarian,
only heard tales of them. Now she traveled with them as a
prisoner, and their arrogance and cold indifference bewildered her. Only the fair young man who helped her every
evening had the slightest measure of the humility that God
required of the faithful, but he was only a slave.

"What are you doing here, Vasha?" demanded a new
voice, in Taor.

Jaelle started. The jaran princess was the most arrogant
of the lot.

Prince Vasil'ii leapt to his feet, looking even angrier. He
directed a long comment at Princess Katherine in their own
language, to which she delivered a stinging retort. Through
all this Rusudani sat with a heron's stillness, waiting in
quiet waters for a fish to swim too near.

"I beg your pardon," said Lady Katherine to Rusudani,
signing to Jaelle to translate, "if my cousin is disturbing
you." Her demeanor was so haughty that Jaelle could easily
have believed that *she* was the child of the Bakhtiian, although she claimed only to be his cousin's daughter. She
wore a bow quiver slung over her back and she also wore
wide trousers covered by a calf-length skirt. She was truly
a barbarian!

"He is not disturbing me," replied Rusudani coolly, but
hard on her answer Prince Vasil'ii excused himself and
stalked off. Princess Katherine, without excusing herself,
chased him down, and they were not even out of earshot before they launched into a furious argument.

"Can you understand what they say, Jaelle?" asked
Rusudani.

"No, my lady, I cannot. They speak in their own language."

"You will learn it," said Rusudani, and Jaelle could not
tell whether she meant it as a command or a threat. "You

will teach me Taor." She bowed her head over clasped hands. Beyond, only half covered in darkness, the jaran princess embarked on a scathing diatribe which was interrupted explosively at intervals by the young man. "He must be a prince," murmured Rusudani into her hands, "or else he would never speak to a woman of her rank in such a fashion."

"I am surprised he does not beat her, then."

"Do not try to understand those who are above you. In any case, I have heard that the women in their tribes are queens in their own right."

Reflexively, Jaelle touched her middle finger to the tiny knife she wore on a chain around her neck. "Like the blessed Pilgrim," she breathed, and felt the vaguest stirring of an inchoate hope.

"*Not* like the Pilgrim," said Rusudani sharply, "blessed though she is. You must cleave to the True Church and end this profession of the heretic faith, Jaelle. I will go in now." Rusudani closed the holy book and with it in her hands she retreated inside her tent.

Jaelle rose, dusted off her skirt, and rolled up the blouse she was mending. At once, she became aware of the slave's presence—Stefan, that was his name. He did not move. The argument between his master and the jaran princess still raged, but at a lower volume.

As soon as she looked at him, he spoke, although like all the jaran men he did not look at her directly. "Is there any other way I can help you?" He had a quiet, modest voice, and spoke Taor as well as she did, although with a harsh accent.

Jaelle examined him warily. She recognized the look: He desired her. While it might be to her advantage to lie with a man so closely connected with a jaran nobleman, still, she couldn't see what direct benefit such a union would bring her. In any case, if Rusudani found out that she had gone back to her old profession, she would be summarily cast out. That had been made clear at the outset.

"No," she replied, and then, impulsively, because he had asked so gently, "thank you."

He made a gesture with one shoulder, an embarrassed shrug, and turned away. Jaelle skirted the princess's tent and headed out toward the trees to relieve herself. He followed her, and she stopped and turned to look at him, suddenly nervous.

He halted as well, looking uneasy. "Don't go far," he said abruptly, as if there was anywhere she could go. He walked away to the ring of guards and fell in with them. The old soldier named Zaiyt'zev let her through, seeing where she was headed, and he said a few words to her that she did not understand but which she took for the same warning as the young slave had given her. How odd that they should think so little of foreign women that they refused to look at them, and yet warn her on a dark night not to wander too far from camp. She knew already what happened to girls wandering alone in foreign lands, where they had neither family nor lord to protect them.

As she reached the line of trees and undergrowth, she clutched the Sunderer's Knife that hung at her throat and mumbled a prayer to the blessed Pilgrim, who had wandered alone for so many years in search of Her Holy Brother's remains. *She* had suffered, too, and through Her suffering taken upon herself the suffering of others. Here where the False Church reigned, they said that She was only a handmaiden, the sister who served the anointed Lord Hristain, whose Sundering at the hands of his jealous brother defined the wickedness of the world, but Jaelle knew they were wrong, that they heard the recitation of the Lord with closed ears.

Still, although Princess Rusudani was the worst kind of unbeliever, even desiring to enter the Order of Sisters who devoted their life to prayer, Rusudani had interceded with Sister Yvanne, who had at first refused to sell a holy relic to a woman she called a heretic. For that alone, Jaelle was grateful to her new mistress.

She relieved herself behind a screen of bushes and pressed farther forward, wanting to wash the smell of horses off her hands. She paused under the silent bower of trees at the river's bank and waited, cautious, to be sure no one was near. The spill of the water over rocks melded with the low whisper of the wind, except it wasn't windy. As she leaned forward, bracing herself on the trunk of a tree, the moon slipped out from behind her veil of clouds, and Jaelle saw a strange sight.

A jaran man sat on horseback in a shallow eddy of water where the river curved away out of sight. She recognized

him instantly: He was the prince who had joined them with
a troop of his men some days back. As fair as a Northerner,
he had the pride which God finds most displeasing in a
man, but he was clearly a man of consequence.

And he was close in conversation with a soldier who
wore a dark surcoat over mail. Who or what this soldier
was Jaelle could not tell, except that he was not a jaran
man. She could not hear any part of their conversation save
as a melismatic counterpoint to the river's melody.

She did not move until the clouds swallowed the moon
again and cast a cloak of darkness over the river. Then, cautiously, she retreated back to camp. The guards marked her
return but asked nothing, not even the slave, whose notice
now disturbed her. It was always dangerous to draw attention to oneself. Jaelle had learned long ago that it was better to watch and to remain silent. She did not tell anyone
what she had seen.

CHAPTER TWELVE

Meroe Transfer Station

Anatoly Sakhalin settled his daughter on his lap, switched on her flat book, and watched his wife as she laughed and talked with colleagues she hadn't seen in months. He rested his chin on Portia's flaxen hair, tucking an arm more tightly around her, and studied the scene of actors before him. He felt more lighthearted then he had in months. The Bharentous Repertory Company had taken a sabbatical while Owen and Ginny made the final arrangements for their tour into Chapalii space, and now, finally, they had reassembled at Meroe Transfer Station for their departure.

"*Kostra*," said Portia, using the khush word for "father" as he had taught her to, "let's see the war."

Anatoly gauged the distance between them and Diana, who was deep in conversation with Gwyn Jones, and called up the program. The thin slate itself had solidity and heft, sitting on his knees with Portia's little legs stuck out on either side, framing it in a "v". But the image that appeared on the flat black surface was insubstantial although it looked as if they were peering through a window into a tiny world, complete with depth and movement, a range of sharp hills and a distant city, and two armies facing off on a flat stretch of ground. Anatoly had learned to model these programs himself: The walled city in the distance was the Habakar city of Qurat, where, nine years ago, Bakhtiian had won a decisive victory over the Habakar king.

"Which ones are the bad guys?" Portia asked, and answered herself by putting a finger on the Habakar army, with its bright pennons and flags. "The *khaja* are the bad guys. They had a king and he ran away from you."

"That's right." Anatoly could not help but smile over past glory. "Now, when two lines meet like this, what should the general ask himself?"

"Hmmm," said Portia. "Why do all those soldiers there

have gray horses?" She pointed to the center rank of the Habakar army. The image was as distinct as if they were watching the real battle from a hilltop.

"Because those are the king's guard, and they all wear the same color coats over their armor and ride the same color horses to show that—"

"Anatoly!"

Reflexively, he tapped the screen to black. "Awww," complained Portia. "*Kostra,* I wanted to count the gray horses."

"Oh, Anatoly." Diana grabbed Portia under the girl's arms and heaved her off Anatoly's lap. "If you have to do this, could you not do it in public? It's so embarrassing."

"It's nothing to be ashamed of," he snapped. "It's just a picture."

"Oh, yes, just the thing for people to see: The barbarian gloating over his last battle where uncounted human beings were slaughtered. I told you I don't want you to—"

"Then what would you rather have me do? Argue with my wife in public?"

She flushed. She took in a breath and forcibly took stock of their argument and any potential eavesdroppers. Hyacinth stood close by, but after living upstairs from them for eight years, he was bored by their bickering. "Anatoly," she said in a calmer voice. "I know you've found other people through the net who are interested in war history, but most people aren't like that. It's very old-fashioned."

"And it is still new-fashioned to bring home a barbarian husband?" he asked, just to see her flinch. "Or is that old-fashioned now as well?"

"I don't like this," said Portia, and she squirmed out of her mother's arms and darted off into the crowd toward Hal.

"We agreed at the farm that we wouldn't talk about that again!" said Diana through clenched teeth. "You're not fighting fair."

"What is *fair* in fighting? I'm fighting to win." He leaned to one side, looking around his wife, to make sure that Portia had reached Hal without incident. She had, and was even now hanging on Hal's leg, an impediment the other actor took with his usual good grace: He ignored her while continuing his conversation with the stage manager, Yomi Applegate-Hito.

"Exactly! You're stuck in primitive patterns of thinking. Everything has to be win or lose."

"But, Diana, if you are fighting a war, then someone must win and someone must lose."

"That's why we don't fight wars anymore!"

"Then what is Duke Charles doing? I would call that fighting a war, to drive away the *khepellis* who have conquered these lands."

"Shhh! Anyway, that's different—"

Anatoly snorted. "Different! In what way?"

"We want to regain our freedom—"

"I want to do what I wish, and not have you tell me that you care more about what other people think of me and what I'm doing than about *me*." At once, he was sorry he had said it. Her face closed, like a blanket being drawn across a tent's entrance.

"I'm sorry," she said curtly. "You're right."

Then, damn her, she left him and went over to greet the actors Dejhuti and Seshat, who had just arrived in the concourse. Anatoly cursed himself silently. Diana was right: They had the same argument over and over again. Irked, he keyed on the screen and watched the battle play itself out in collapsed time.

"Do you mind if I give you some advice?"

Anatoly glanced up. "Yes."

Hyacinth did not take the hint. Instead, he crouched down beside Anatoly's chair. The actor no longer wore his hair blond. It had reverted to a coarse black, shorn tight against his head, and with his dark almond eyes and his yellow-brown complexion, he looked much more foreign than he had when Anatoly had first met him. Then again, most Earth humans Anatoly saw looked more like Hyacinth than like Diana, with her golden hair and light skin. "Yevgeni isn't coming with me, you know," said Hyacinth, seemingly at random. "He's off to another crafts exhibition. I'm getting a little tired of him winning all those awards for his leatherwork. He's had an offer from Passier to do his own exclusive line of saddles for them."

Anatoly endured this confidence in silence. He didn't want to like Hyacinth. He could just imagine what his grandmother would say to the thought of a prince of the Sakhalin befriending an avowed lover of men, especially a man who lived as if in marriage to a jaran man whom his grandmother had exiled from the jaran.

"At first I thought it would be impossible for Yevgeni to

adjust," Hyacinth continued. "Yevgeni was so dependent on me for everything. But it's odd that he was able to take the very things that made him so out of place here and create his own life with them. He's built a reputation for himself that he never could have gained in the jaran. Of course, he had no standing to lose. It's not as if he was a prince of the Sakhalin."

"I can't imagine that anything that an arenabekh, an outcast, like Yevgeni might do would have anything to do with me," said Anatoly, affronted.

"Yes. That's exactly the problem, isn't it?"

Anatoly closed his lips hard on a sharp retort. At the same moment, movement eddied around the concourse entrance, and with the instincts that had made him a successful actor, Vasil Veselov entered. Behind him, mobile cameras nudged up against the concourse archway, passing through nesh images of interviewers and hangers-on in their efforts to get a better angle and that one final shot of the departing star; the ephemeral escort of nesh figures halved in number, vanishing into the ether, as soon as they reached the archway, which blocked their entrance. One of the hangers-on was real, then, Anatoly noted, because she walked into the waiting area alongside Karolla, carrying a pack, with the baby in a sling at her hip. The children followed at their mother's heels. Veselov went to greet Owen and Ginny. Karolla found the nearest seat and sank down, looking tired.

"Oh, I won't say you're worse than poor Karolla," added Hyacinth, who had also been watching this display, "with her odd notions about what is due her and that awful place she's made to live in, but you're certainly no better. In your own way."

"I beg your pardon." Anatoly stood up. "If you will excuse me."

Hyacinth rose as well. "No. Now let me say this, because I'm the only other person here who's gone through what Diana is going through, and I care about her very much. Hell, I even like you. Portia deserves better than you two fighting all the time."

The mention of Portia stopped Anatoly. He looked for her. She had found little Evdokia, and the two girls were giggling at something Ilyana Arkhanov was telling them. The two boys had lost themselves in the crowd, but Ilyana herself inevitably stood out: She had her father's beauty as well as a precociously self-possessed manner. Born into the Arkhanov line, she would have been a fine candidate for etsana of the Arkhanov tribe, had her mother stayed with her family, as she should have.

"Diana is stuck with you, Anatoly."

The comment jerked Anatoly out of his wandering thoughts. "Diana is my wife!"

"By jaran law. I don't recall that she has taken any steps under Earth laws to marry you, except for the child-license certificate, and that's simply a legal agreement. I notice she no longer wears the scar of marriage."

Stung, Anatoly defended himself. "We agreed that because of her work it had to be covered up. It isn't really gone. That had nothing to do with our marriage."

"Except that she can't leave you because she's all you have here, and she knows it. I felt the same way about Yevgeni for a long time. But he wasn't too proud to change. You are."

Drilled in a harsh school of manners, Anatoly only barely stopped himself from slugging Hyacinth right there in front of everyone. But Hyacinth was a Singer, and Singers were allowed to say whatever they wanted to, even to a prince of the jaran. Even to a prince who was not a prince in these lands. Gods, he knew in his heart that Hyacinth was right. But he felt helpless to do anything about it. He had no family, no tribe, to give him stature, and wars, as Diana constantly pointed out, were old-fashioned here.

"Nor did I ask Yevgeni, obviously, to take the kind of risk you demanded of Diana, that she have a child, which we all knew would endanger her life because of the incompatibilities."

"It was her choice as well!"

"She had that child for you."

"She loves Portia! She's a fine mother to our daughter! You know it's true."

"It's nice to hear you defending her, for once." Hyacinth smiled slightly, if sadly.

Anatoly suddenly realized why he didn't want to like Hyacinth. It wasn't truly that Hyacinth was a lover of men, although that was bad enough. It was that he felt sorry for Anatoly. That was worse than any insult. "I offered my services to the Duke years ago," he said finally, roughly, "for the—"

"Yes, for *that*." They never used the word "rebellion."

"His councillors sent a message to tell me that I must wait. So I have waited. I have tried to learn about this place, even though half of it seems to be shadows and air. What else is there for me to do?"

"We are going into Chapalii space now. Finally. We'll have unprecedented access to their—well, to their lands."

"To zayinu lands."

"Maybe this is what Charles Soerensen has been telling you to wait for."

During his seven years on Earth, Anatoly had found a dark corner of himself that he had not known existed. He hated it and feared it in equal measure, but it had grown steadily. What if Duke Charles had told him to wait not because he had a jahar for Anatoly to lead at some distant point, but because he had no use at all for an exiled jaran prince? At first, certainly, Anatoly had thought that Bakhtiian's army could sweep as easily across Earth as across Rhui, since no one here seemed versed in the ways of war and no one carried weapons and there were no fortresses except as museums. He knew better now. "I—" he began, and stopped. He could not bring himself to say it aloud. *I've mounted a horse that's too wild and too strong for me to ride.* Bad enough that they all pitied him covertly. He could not stand it if they did it openly.

"We live longer. You know that. So we take longer to make decisions and to take action, because we have the luxury of taking time. We don't even know how long the Chapalii live. They seem to be even more leisurely than we are. It doesn't mean you aren't wanted—"

"I didn't say I thought I wasn't wanted! Of course I—" Anatoly broke off and lapsed into silence.

"—it means," Hyacinth went on, "a lot of things. Your people fell in love with the vision of destiny, and it's like a great engine turning at high speed. It's huge, and it's visible, and it has immense weight and force. We don't work that way anymore. The Machine Age is over. And right now, especially, we can't. We have to work in insubstantial ways. We have to work under the surface."

"You understand about the way your world is like the breath of Father Wind, all air and ghosts."

Hyacinth chuckled. "What other way should it be? No,

I'm not laughing at you. I think I see what you mean. Listen. Talk to Gwyn Jones."

"Why Gwyn Jones?"

"Because he is . . . oh, I guess I could say he is the dyan of the new jahar that's forming. A scouting jahar."

At once, Anatoly bridled. "I was a dyan—"

"In Bakhtiian's army. Were you born a dyan?"

"No! I earned the right just as any soldier must."

"Mother of Gods, Sakhalin, you're not stupid. I've seen you use the net. You speak our language very well, and I've heard you working at the Chapalii language, which most of us are too damned intimidated to even try to grasp. So earn the right here, as well. That's what I've been trying to say all along. You want them to come to you and give it to you because of who you are. But you wouldn't have expected that from Bakhtiian, or at least you say you wouldn't have."

Anatoly flared. "One thing Bakhtiian learned from my cousin Yaroslav: that a boy must earn his saber and a soldier earn his command."

"Then I've made my point."

Fuming, Anatoly found Diana in the crowd—now she was talking with the good-looking man who built the lights for the plays—and he was filled with an immense irritation that she seemed so interested in the other man. It was bad manners for a woman to flirt openly with another man when her husband was around to see. Portia, still giggling, sidled up to her mother, and Diana hoisted her up without even looking at her and continued talking, her face so animated, so bright.

Anatoly looked away. The sight of them together pained him too much. At that moment, more than anything, he wanted to ask Hyacinth: How do I make my wife love me again? But he could not.

Ilyana wondered if she could throw herself out an air lock, up here in space, on a transfer station whose knobbly docks were like blunt fingers from which the webs that connected the vast reaches of space together were woven and sent into the heavens. It just wasn't fair. She had said g'bye to Kori at Victoria Station and then hid her tears on the long ride to Nairobi Port by pressing her face up against the glass and staring out the window at the sea until her father had grown tired of entertaining Evdokia and Anton and left them in her care while he went forward to the salon car. But Kori's Un-

cle Gus had taken her aside right before they'd left and told
her that he was also negotiating for a tour into Chapalii
space; that if he managed it, he'd bring Kori with him.
Ilyana clung to that faint hope.

Darling Portia ran over to giggle with Evdokia and then
wiggled away to go to her mother. Ilyana glanced quickly
around the room but did not see Portia's father anywhere.

"Yana! My dear girl. You've grown again. How nice to see
you." Dejhuti and Seshat, Yomi and Joseph, Oriana, Phillippe,
and Ginny all came up to greet her, and Phillippe, as usual,
tugged on her braid. She would have kicked him, but that
would have been childish. Owen was so engrossed in his conversation with a man Ilyana vaguely recognized but could not
place that he only acknowledged Vasil with a sketchy wave of
the hand without giving him any attention at all. But Vasil insinuated himself into the conversation anyway. He was like
those kids who always have to be where the center of attention
is.

By now overexcited, Evdokia was beginning to run in circles, so Ilyana led her back to their mother and sat down
with her. Nipper stood guard over Karolla, who had yet to
regain her strength even though the baby was now three
months old. Nor had she begun her courses again, and because of the child's blemish, Karolla could not name the infant until she had offered the blood of her body to
Grandmother Night, so that She might forgive the blemish
on the body and allow the child to live.

Karolla gave her daughter a tired smile and let Evdokia
crawl up onto her lap. "It's a pity about them," she said.

"About who?" asked Ilyana suspiciously. She hated it
when her mother gossiped.

"That they haven't had another child yet. *Porzhia* is a
sweet girl, and they ought to have had another one by now."
She clicked her tongue disapprovingly. "It's no wonder they
argue so much."

Ilyana caught sight of Anatoly Sakhalin on the other side
of the room. Like a good soldier, he stood alert and on
guard, surveying the crowd for danger. He *was* really old, almost as old as her mother, but still . . . the boys her own age
were just so uninteresting. Most of them didn't even know
how to ride a horse. They hadn't commanded a jahar. They
hadn't captured a king. She bit at her lower lip and looked
around to see that her mother was eyeing her speculatively.

At once, Ilyana clasped her hands in her lap and fixed her gaze on her knuckles.

"If you had completed your woman's passage," said Karolla suddenly, "you could name the baby in my stead."

Ilyana felt her ears burn. She said nothing.

"A prince of the Sakhalin would be an appropriate choice for a girl's first lover," continued her mother relentlessly. Ilyana would have clapped her hands over her ears, but it wouldn't have done any good. "You are sixteen years old, Yana, and you began your courses two years ago. It's past time for your *tsadokhis* night. When I was your age—"

"You had four ankle bracelets to show you'd had four lovers. You were married just before you turned seventeen. I know. I know. You've told me all this before."

"You will show me the respect I am due, child!"

Ilyana could not stand it anymore. She leapt up and hurried off into the crowd, knowing Karolla would not follow.

She promptly careened into a man.

"I beg your pardon," she gasped, preparing to bolt.

Her victim chuckled. "If only I had that much energy. You're Ilyana Arkhanov, aren't you?"

Stuck, Ilyana slanted a glance up at him. He was the man Owen had been talking to. He had a pleasant face and an open expression, and like all adults, he looked old. Not old like dying-old, because she knew that here on Earth most people lived for a long long time without ever looking like Elders, but so old that Ilyana couldn't quite imagine that she herself would ever be *that* old. But he looked approachable. "Yes," she agreed. "I'm sorry, I don't remember you."

"No reason you should. I won't embarrass you by telling you how young you were and how much you've grown since I saw you last." He grinned, and, tentatively, Ilyana grinned back. "I'm David ben Unbutu, by the way. Pleased to meet you."

"Pleased to meet you," Ilyana echoed. "Do you know M. Zerentous? Are you one of the new actors?"

"I know Ginny better than Owen, and no, I'm not an actor. I'm—well, it looks as if I'll be traveling with you. I've done that before, when the company went to Rhui."

"Oh," said Ilyana, enlightened. "I think I sort of maybe remember you. Didn't you—aren't you the one who painted the portraits of Tess Soerensen and Bakhitiian, in Jeds? I used to come watch you paint."

Now he really smiled, so that it creased his face with warmth. "You knocked over the easel once while Tess was doing a sitting."

Ilyana giggled. "Only because I tripped. I didn't mean to, and it ruined the painting, but then you said you had barely started and it didn't matter."

"In fact, when I started over, I realized that I'd had the wrong image in my mind, so really I should thank you for it. It's as if you knocked my preconceived notions to the ground and made me rethink them."

Ilyana smiled and tried to think of something to say.

"If you don't mind my asking," he went on, "why *did* your father come back to the repertory company? I'm surprised he walked away from the string of successes he's been having."

"Uh," said Ilyana, tensing, "I dunno."

"Well, never mind," said M. Unbutu quickly. "No doubt the artistic rewards are greater. Have you heard that we're going straight to Duke Naroshi's palace? It's said that it was designed by his sister. In Chapalii culture, she's evidently a renowned architect." He hesitated.

"No one knows much about Chapalii architecture," Ilyana said into the silence, enthusiastic now. "I did my last year's depth survey on it, but there wasn't much—" Another scrap of memory swam into sight. "*You* compiled one of the files I used as a reference, didn't you?"

His eyes widened, and she saw she had surprised him. "It's a hobby of mine, yes. I know which program you mean. It doesn't get a lot of use-tags. Most people only pick and choose and browse through the upper layers. As I recall, I only got fifty complete downloads of that file all last year."

"Well! One of them was me!"

"I'm *not* going to fall into the trap of asking you how old you are," he said with a laugh. "What interested you in Chapalii architecture? The architecture, or the Chapalii?"

"Oh. I like buildings and stuff. I dunno why. It's just sort of, the way they're built, and then to look at them and I just like them, and I really like to do the unbuilding programs in nesh. That's my depth survey for this year, an unbuilding project on ancient temple complexes." She stopped, hearing how stupid she sounded.

"Have you picked any particular complexes?"

"Well, uh, I thought maybe Karnak."

This time when he smiled, he looked more like a child planning mischief than a responsible adult. "How about the Imperial Palace?"

"The one in . . . uh . . ." Ilyana felt an urgent and discomforting need to impress him. " . . . Beijing?"

"That would be interesting. I was thinking of the Chapalii Emperor's imperial palace."

"But—how could we—I thought—wouldn't that be impossible?"

"Probably. Just wishful thinking. I don't have access to Duke Naroshi's sister anyway, because I'm male."

"I'm female," said Ilyana brightly.

There was a short silence. M. Unbutu blew all his breath out between his lips and pulled a hand back through his mane of dreadlocks. The hand came to rest on the back of his neck, playing with four thin beaded braids. "Yes, you are," he said finally. "No doubting that." Ilyana felt like she'd missed something. "But I'd be happy to help you with your survey, if that's allowed in your tutorial."

"Certainly it's allowed! You're allowed to use a mentor! Are *you* an architect?" Ilyana began bouncing from one foot to the other, realized she was doing it, and stopped, fixing her feet to the ground. Her teachers approved of her ability to focus and explore, but she had never before met an adult who really truly was fascinated by architecture the way she was.

"I'm an engineer, but I have a special interest in architectural and historical engineering. A bit of a hobby. But I'll have to talk to your parents first."

"They won't care." Her mother thought her interest in buildings to be slightly obscene, and her father treated it with the same approbative disinterest with which he treated all her activities. "Are you going to stay with us the whole time?"

"I don't know about *that,* but I'd like to find out as much as I can about architectural and engineering techniques and traditions in Chapalii culture. That's why I'm coming along. It's a great opportunity. We don't truly know *anything* about the Chapalii except what they've given us permission to know. No human has ever been invited *into* a Chapalii nobleman's palace and private city before. Never been farther than certain restricted areas of port authorities."

Suddenly it didn't seem *quite* so bad to be leaving London

behind. The communique-implant on Ilyana's right ear rang, and she heard Yomi's calm voice calling them to board.

"Remember," Yomi intoned, sounding bored as she said it, "this is a Chapalii passenger liner, and if I find out that any of you haven't scrolled through the protocols for shipboard, I'll personally vent you out an air lock myself."

"I'd better go, Ilyana."

She flushed. "Everyone calls me 'Yana.' My father doesn't like—well, anyway, they just do."

"Oh," said M. Unbutu in an odd tone. "All right, Yana. We'll set up a meeting once I've spoken with your father and mother. We could do a regular tutorial if you'd like."

"I would!"

He left. Ilyana reluctantly returned to her mother, who was frantically searching for Valentin. Half the company had already filed into the port tube by the time Ilyana tracked him down.

He had shinnied past the rope barrier at the bubble that looked out onto space, and he lay on the transparent curved surface, braced on his palms and knees, staring out.

"Valentin!" Ilyana whispered, afraid someone would find him here. "Come on. We're leaving."

He mumbled something inaudible. She finally squeezed past the barrier and eased out onto the curved bubble, careful of her footing, to grab him by the back of the shirt and tug. Out here on the surface of the bubble, the stars swam in depthless night and the transfer station itself ran like a blot of darkness against the backdrop, covering stars and half of the brilliant globe of Earth. Dizziness made her sway. She yanked Valentin back and gulped down nausea, and they ran up against the barrier. It stung where the forcefield touched her bare arms and made her scalp prickle through the veil of her hair. Then they were through and out into the concourse. Valentin walked dazedly along beside her, saying nothing. She had no problem getting him in line. By the gate entrance, David ben Unbutu greeted a surprising new arrival: Margaret O'Neill.

"Mags!" He was laughing again. "You're up early, and late as usual. Congratulations on arriving before departure."

"It's too damned early in the day to be taking ship," she growled. "How can you be so bloody cheerful?"

"Oh, to be seventeen again. I've lost my heart."

"You're making perfect sense. Here I thought it was me. Where is Yomi?"

They walked out of earshot. Nipper arrived, breathless. "Oh, thank goodness, Yana, you found your brother. We'd better go. The cabin arrangements are already made."

Ilyana let go of Valentin and allowed Nipper to herd him forward. She trailed behind. Everyone was on board, except for Yomi, who ticked off the roster with the touch of a finger as each individual crossed into the port tube, the last stragglers, and Anatoly Sakhalin. Like a good soldier, he was bringing up the rear. He caught her gaze on him, smiled at her, and then looked away quickly. Ilyana ducked her head to hide her blush and hurried after Valentin.

They stopped beside Yomi. The stage manager glanced up and tapped a finger three times on the slate. "You're clear."

Nipper went on ahead. Ilyana winced as the khaja woman almost stepped on the threshold, the inch-high seal-ring that circled the port tube entrance. But her heel passed over it without touching it, and she walked away down the tube. An alien scent wafted out from the tube, like the current of a freshwater river mingling with the saltwater sea. Ilyana took in a deep breath. It was different, weird, but not unpleasant. Coming out of his stupor, Valentin grabbed her hand, and together they passed over the threshold and entered the domain of the Chapalii.

CHAPTER THIRTEEN

In the Tent of Stone

Tess arrived at Arina Veselov's tent out of breath and anxious. Irena Orzhekov stopped her. "You can't go in."

Tess's stomach twisted into a knot of fear. "I don't hear the drums. Did she already have the baby?"

Irena turned the comment away with a flick of her wrist. "She has fallen into the gods' sleep. The child has not yet come. Varia Telyegin says she has bled too much, and she no longer has the strength to push the child out."

"She can't die!" Irena put an arm around her, comforting her. Tess wept onto her shoulder. She heard voices from inside the tent, but they were indistinct, smothered by the felt walls between them. "What about the baby?" she asked finally. "If only Cara were here! Wait. Let me speak with Varia. Perhaps ..." If she could record Varia's account of the labor, then perhaps she could transmit it to Cara via console hidden in the library and receive in turn at least some advice, whether they might save Arina and the unborn child. "Perhaps I could find some answers in one of the texts in the library."

"Juli Danov and Niko Sibirin are also attending," said Irena.

"Ah, Niko, then. He can give me a detailed account."

Quickly enough, by sending a Veselov girl into the tent, Niko was brought forth. He looked tired, and when Tess set off at once toward the library, she had to stop and wait for him. He smiled wryly at her and took her arm to support himself. His halting pace depressed Tess even further.

Finally, blinking on her implant and locking off the visual, she asked him to describe the labor. As he spoke, she recorded, asking a clarifying question now and again. Niko's mind suffered from no infirmities; his account was comprehensive. Because he walked so slowly, they were only to the edge of the plaza when he finished.

"I'll run ahead and search out some texts," Tess said, impatient to be off. "If you can—"

"I can manage." Under other circumstances, he would have looked amused. Now he simply let go of her. She blinked the implant off and ran.

At the library she took the steps two at a time and cut around to the outside entrance built specially for the ke, the Chapalii exile who now lived permanently in Sarai. There were several ways to override the privacy lock that kept these rooms off limits to everyone but the ke, Tess, and the rare visitor from Earth. Tess spoke her name out loud and heard an audible click, the override signal.

As she tugged the door open, a wave of warm air spilled out from the corridor and anteroom. She had to stop for a second inside the door to adjust. The corridor was about twelve strides long, whitewashed, paved with brick. At opposite corners of the corridor wall a design grew out, engulfing the blank white of the walls with bright colors, odd shapes, and interesting textures. It had manifested soon after the ke had arrived here and now it expanded according to some unknown principle. Tess could not tell whether the ke was in the process of creating it or whether it was an organic construct that blossomed at an excruciatingly slow pace. It smelled different here, too, as if through an unseen portal the Empire touched these lands that were nominally free of it.

Tess caught her breath and advanced to the anteroom. The ke waited for her there. The ke wore gloves and long robes. Here in the private suite the ke had thrown back the hood and face-covering to reveal the slate-gray epidermis and lank tail of hair. The ke was by now so familiar to Tess that she could not help but wonder if she would find the white-skinned Chapalii males strange-looking, although in her other life they were the only ones she had ever seen.

"Assistance is necessary," said Tess at once in the form of Chapalii that the ke termed "the deeper tongue."

"What is necessary?" responded the ke, perhaps rhetorically.

Tess shifted restlessly. To her surprise and annoyance, she was finding the idiom that the ke was teaching her particularly difficult to learn. "*Arina Veselov,* a female unnamed also fertile, suffers with a difficult—" She struggled to find the right word. The closest match she could find was: "—flowering. *Niko Sibirin,* a male unnamed also learned in the art of healing, comes to consult the texts which teach of this."

The ke made no movement with head or shoulders to show agreement or negation but only said, with no inflection, "The texts will be laid out on the scribe's table as necessary."

"Yes."

The ke lifted the hood to cover its hair and masked its alien face with a veil. Once, Tess had expected all Chapalii to show her deference, because she was a Duke's sister and heir. The ke, with no further words or gestures, simply left.

Although this was ostensibly the ke's suite, built so that the ke could isolate herself according to the precepts Tess put forward for the Chapalii religion, one of the rooms was set aside for Tess's use. As soon as the ke had gone out through the interior door that led into a side room of the central library, Tess went to this chamber, a starkly furnished room with a single spot of color: a plush couch upholstered in a gorgeous red and gold fabric patterned with affronted birds wreathed by vines. Woven in Habakar, the cloth had been a gift to Tess from Mitya's wife, Princess Melatina.

"I want a call through to Cara Hierakis in Jeds," Tess said aloud as soon she shut the door.

"What level?" the console responded in its alto voice.

"Urgent. I'm uploading a file."

The implant was embedded in the hinge of her jaw. An interface melded with the exterior of the bone, accessible through a permeable membrane grown through the skin. Tess triggered the implant, pressed a node from the console against her skin, and loaded Niko's description into the console. Moments later, Cara's head and shoulders appeared above the console. Tess could see through her to the wall beyond.

"I'm in luck," breathed Tess. "I was hoping you would be in the lab."

Cara did not look up at her. She was reading the transferred account on a screen which sat out of Tess's sight. After a bit, she shook her head, and her gaze, lifting, was painfully compassionate. "If I was there," she said, and closed her lips on the thought. "But I'm not. How in hell did she get pregnant?"

"I suppose the usual way! What can you do?"

"I can't do anything, except to advise you to find the

commentary by Sister Matthia of Maros Cloister and the treatise on the womb attributed to Shakir al'Quriq. They're both obstetrics texts and one of them discusses a primitive version of a cesarean section. I gave you copies myself for your library. There's nothing else I can tell you. I spent many evenings discussing midwifery with Varia Telyegin and Juli Danov, and I think they taught me more than I taught them. Except for technological intervention, there frankly isn't anything I can do that they won't already have thought of. You know how sorry I am to hear this."

"I'll go. Niko is in the library already."

"Let me know—"

"Yes. And off." Cara vanished, her black hair and white blouse replaced by the ivory surface of the console desk. Tess took in a shuddering breath and hurried out of the room.

Even with these side trips, she arrived at the inclined table where the ke had propped up four leatherbound volumes of varying sizes before Niko did. Tess hurried outside and found him contemplating the steps. She gave him her arm, and together they climbed to the top. Inside, she found him a stool. He sank onto it gratefully and without preamble pulled the commentary by Sister Matthia toward himself and opened it reverentially. He read slowly, negotiating a crabbed script, and his lips moved as he read although no sound emerged. Tess shifted from one foot to the other.

After a bit, he glanced up at her. "Go on. You'll be happier waiting impatiently there. Send one of the children to help me back when I'm done, or better yet, Svetlana. It will do her good to learn some of these things."

Torn, Tess hesitated, then went. The ke hovered in the background, robed and veiled so that no part of her skin was visible. What did the ke think of these human visitors and of her strange and sometimes trivial duties as librarian? Tess did not know. She took the steps three at a time, leaping down, and broke into a loping run when she reached the plaza. Her mind skipped to Niko's request to have Svetlana Tagansky attend him. Aleksi's wife was almost as old as Tess; she was a practical, competent woman with a growing reputation as a good attendant at births. Tess rubbed at a pain in her side. What if Niko knew perfectly well that he was not going to live all that much longer? What if he saw every birth now, especially the difficult ones, the unusual ones, as a means to pass on the vital knowledge to the younger healer who would take his place?

Such thoughts, more than the running, made her breath come ragged. Losing Niko would be like losing her father all over again.

When she came up, panting, to the awning of Mother Veselov's tent, she found Irena Orzhekov holding a bundle: an infant with vivid blue eyes.

"I brought her outside while they prepare Arina for the pyre."

At first, the words did not register. "I have to send for Svetlana Tagansky to escort Niko back from the library," she said, staring at the infant, whose stare was fixed on Irena. "Then they can—" It hit like a shock wave. "Arina is *dead?*"

"She stopped breathing. Varia and Juli chose to attempt this cutting open that *Dokhtor* Hierakis has taught them, to see if the child still lived, although I am not sure the gods will approve of a child coming into the world in such an unnatural way."

Tess could not find words to reply. Without asking permission, she simply pushed aside the entrance flap and went in. The sheer weight of smell overwhelmed her, blood and excreta, all the leftover products of childbirth swamped by the iron stench of blood. Tess sank down onto an empty pillow and watched, stunned, while Varia Telyegin and Juli Danov cleaned up the blood and composed the body, while Varia and Arina's adopted sister Yeliana wrapped Arina in a shroud until only her face, pale, lax, and her cloud of dark hair remained unshrouded.

Then Mira was led in with her little brother Lavrenti. Lavrenti was allowed to kiss his mother, but to Mira fell the duty of braiding her mother's hair for the final time. Dry-eyed, the eleven-year-old set about this task with horrifying calm. Lavrenti huddled beside her, shivering although it was hot and stuffy inside the tent. Tess shook herself out of her stupor and moved forward to coax the boy back next to her, but he wouldn't budge. At last, Mira finished. Arina's brother and father and uncles were all long since dead. Her husband was far away, so there was no man to pull the shroud across her face in order to shield her eyes from the living world. Numb, Tess listened to women whispering in the outer chamber. Meanwhile, the two children stared. Sud-

denly little Lavrenti took the last corner of the shroud in his
right hand, covered his mother's face, and tucked the cloth
down to seal her in. He burst into tears.

"Here," said Juli Danov, her voice so close to Tess's ear
that Tess jumped, startled. "You may light these."

Obediently, Tess lit and hung four sticks of incense in
burners at each corner of the chamber. But there was nothing
else she could do. Already, from outside, she heard women
discussing where to find a wet nurse for the baby, and how
they ought to go about naming it since its mother and aunts
and grandmother were all dead and its only sister not yet a
woman. Tess went forward and kissed both children, but
they did not acknowledge her nor did they really seem to realize that she was there. Nor did Tess truly belong here, in
the tent of death, a woman who was no blood relation to the
deceased.

Wrung out and feeling utterly useless, she touched the top
of the shroud with her right hand, as a last farewell, and left
the tent that no longer belonged to Arina Veselov.

The ke, the one who is nameless, grows and lives in the
tent of stone. Like organic creatures which have ceased to
grow, stone is cold to the sight. The tent of stone, a tempo-
rary shelter which may only last a thousand orbits around
the sun, grows in a primitive fashion, by the work of hands.
This cold growth is strange to observe, awkward, tensile. A
true building grows organically and never ceases to grow,
just as it reflects the exposition of the universe. But one
mark of the half-tamed animal called early cognition is that
in building, the act of finishing also occurs, although the
civilized know that nothing is ever finished. Living things
are warm. Unliving things are cold. Thus primitives grow
buildings which are dead even as flowering occurs.

The ke perceives that the heat of the daiga—the half-
tamed animals who name themselves *human*—has left the
chamber labeled *the reading room*. Soon all traces of daiga
presence dissipate into the air. The daiga, being primitive,
have the impulse to name and to label in the same way that
bacteria have the impulse to divide. By these markers, the
web that structures the universe is constructed, although like
bacteria the daiga web is shallow, shorn of depth by the in-
discriminate quality of their desire.

Under the central dome of the library, placed on a carbon

table, sits a building by definition dead and also never living, a tiny simulation of a building that once lived. The daiga like to look at it for reasons impossible to fathom. The daiga name the building *Morava* and the simulation a *model.* Once the great palace sheltered the Mushai, but the great palace, the actual palace, has ceased living because of the rite of extinction; it has also become a tent of stone. Yet the Mushai is imprisoned within its walls and within the still growing walls of the great towers named Sorrowing, Reckless, and Shame, caught without means of escape, because the act of remembering has imprisoned the name of Mushai in the universe's binding architecture. Only the nameless are not bound by the web whose filaments secure the patterns of heat and death. Without a name there is no true existence, and yet, without a name, existence is boundless.

Existence, measured by heat, by a net of turbulence, enters the reading room. The one who is nameless but who also has brought namelessness onto the daiga called *Tess Soerensen* hesitates, a stab of time halting movement. Except in size the daiga appear alike. Nothing distinguishes one from the next, although slightly different patterns of turbulence flow through and around the females and the males, and the small ones called *children* are different again, hotter, brighter, lucency diffused across the diminutive bodies rather than focused in certain spots. At first, the ke believed that the diminutive ones were a third kind of daiga, the ones who cannot flower, but instead the daiga Tess showed how over time the children flower as buildings flower, to become daiga. In this way, as the civilized grow buildings, the daiga grow themselves. In this way the potential to become civilized manifests.

But the daiga who is nameless but brought namelessness bears a peculiar tincture of heat and lucency that leaves an indelible mark. By this tincture, the ke can recognize this daiga apart from other daiga. Tess names the daiga *Ilya,* but with the promiscuity so evident in daiga behavior, this daiga wears other names as well.

The hesitation ends. Ilya moves forward into the chamber. A flare of heat reveals that the daiga has registered the ke's presence. The warmth subsides into the usual reticulation of turbulence patching the daiga's surface. An inclination of the head, now given by the daiga, signifies notice of the ke, perhaps. Daiga are promiscuous with gestures as well, shifting legs and arms and torsos and heads in a chaotic and restless dance. This daiga Ilya knows something of the art of stillness, perhaps learned from the nameless one Tess; perhaps not. But the ke has seen only one daiga who truly understands it: the Tai-en Charles Soerensen. The Tai-en could not have passed across the threshold of rank without the knowledge of the great dance, where movement and stillness each signify particular messages. Notice is given. The daiga crosses the chamber and passes into a separate room. The tincture of heat lingers and fades, swirling into the air's ever-present taste.

Quiet reigns.

The ke picks up the four bound collections of parchment leaves. Here, also, the daiga confuse the living and the unliving. Knowledge is a growing thing, not a thing sewn into thin dead surfaces marked with scratches. Nevertheless, the books must be returned to specific and arbitrary places. By such means do the daiga order the world. As the ke circles back to examine the empty chamber, the door opens and on the wings of the air swirling in from outside, the daiga Tess arrives.

Of all daiga, only the nameless one called Tess can speak any of the civilized tongues. Thus, although the aura of turbulence patterning Tess is in no fundamental way different from that of other daiga, the ke can recognize the presence of a civilized being.

There is no hesitation. Tess crosses the room to a carbon table and sinks onto a carbon stool, which is also dead. All the furniture worn by daiga is dead. Head dropping to arms, legs drawn up, the daiga Tess forms a seamless maze to the ke's sight, hot mostly, but with the tint of cold death chasing living warmth like an echo through the pattern of the daiga's lifewarmth.

As if sight or some daiga smell has raised a signal in farther rooms, the daiga Ilya enters. There is no hesitation. Time quickens with swift footsteps. The daiga male places a hand on the daiga female, and the ke is allowed to observe the strange and disorderly communication which goes on between the two. Some of the communication occurs through the vocal boxes. The ke cannot interpret the primitive speech without aid. Nor can the ke interpret the coils of heat and cold, brightness and shadow, that flow wildly from one to the other and back again. Heat blazes and subsides on different portions of the body.

The ke has learned to distinguish male daiga from female daiga because certain patterns of heat recur more frequently and more obviously with the males, while the female daiga manifest subtler patterns. And with these two, best known, most observed, the ke recognizes iterations in the conversation of heat and cold, as if the body of the one is familiar with the complex web of the body of the other, and back again. Although how two might interweave patterns in such a fashion, the ke is not certain.

But all creatures, even animals, deserve privacy. The ke returns to the necklace of rooms in which civilization grows, the merest seedling, on the shores of this wilderness. There, on all the walls, grow restful scenes shaded in degrees of life, hot and towering, slender and warm, cool and sluggish, tinged by motifs of incandescent blue heat and smoldering orange coals, all wrapped around and penetrated by the sinuous reach of the vine of life, ever-probing, ever-seeking, ever-enclosing.

But the ke also wonders. The daiga Tess has many shades. A new one, stained with coldness of stone, has insinuated itself boldly into the pattern today. The ke examines the walls of the entrance corridor, whose slow growth is pleasing but as yet unfinished, creeping forward to overcome the chill blankness of the daiga-built walls. Satisfied, the ke walks as far as the door which is the threshold to the daiga world.

There is a hesitation. But beyond lies only the daiga world, after all. The ke could have chosen the final act of extinction. That act was not chosen, and so a different choice was made, a choice that includes the daiga world.

Opening the door, the ke sights at once the leaping, unruly heat of fire. The ke pinpoints and locks in on the distant fire, drawing the image closer to identify the source. This custom the daiga Tess has explained; the daiga name is *funeral pyre*. The pyre is an odd daiga custom, celebrating death with heat.

The ke watches in stillness. One mystery has linked up with another, thus creating a bridge across which an answer can travel. A pyre means that a daiga has passed from life to death. The stain of cold on Tess's pattern reveals that this death has touched the complex web of Tess's being. Thus are the two related. Satisfied by this small but precious understanding of the daiga world, the ke closes the door.

CHAPTER FOURTEEN

Prince Mitya's Court

They left the train of merchants at the khaja city of Parkilnous and headed up over the mountain pass into the kingdom of Habakar, riding hard now that they were free of the wagons.

At the Habakar city of Birat, Andrei Sakhalin requisitioned fresh horses from the garrison, and the Habakar governor, an obsequious merchant whom Vassily disliked immediately, slaughtered twenty cattle that evening so that the party could feast as befitted a prince and princess of the jaran. Andrei insisted that Vassily sit beside him and the governor. Princess Rusudani remained secluded in her tent, but Vasha got some little consolation out of the evening by watching Katerina outface the governor, who was alternately embarrassed by her presence and perplexed by Andrei Sakhalin's deference to her. As for Katya and Andrei, they seemed rather like two soldiers dueling with sabers, except that Andrei, instead of carrying the attack to her, used feints to draw her out.

"You're making a fool of yourself," said Vasha finally, leaning over to whisper these profound words to her at a safe moment when Andrei Sakhalin had left the feast to go relieve himself.

"You're drunk," retorted Katya. "You're jealous."

"Jealous of *what?*" he demanded, but then Sakhalin came back. Vasha could not properly leave until the others did, so he endured the rest of the feast in silence, drinking heavily.

When at last the feast ended, Vassily managed to walk out under his own power, a brooding sense of injustice weighing on him. Ahead of him, Katya laughed at something Sakhalin said, and Vasha stumbled. Stefan, appearing out of nowhere, caught his elbow and steadied him.

"You looked miserable up there," said Stefan. "Are you going to be sick?"

Vasha waved toward Katya who, with Andrei, was making a florid and perfectly obscene farewell to the Habakar governor. "How can she stand it? She doesn't even like him. She never has."

Stefan cocked his head and considered Vasha. "Is that so? That must explain why she's taken him for a lover."

"She has not!" He said it so loudly that both Katya and Andrei glanced toward him.

Stefan got a firm grip on Vasha's arm and led him away. He didn't speak until they were outside of camp. "You shouldn't get drunk. You're making a fool of yourself."

"I am not! *She's* the one—"

Then he did get sick. Thank the gods, only two of Riasonovsky's riders, on sentry duty, were around to see.

In the morning, head throbbing, he assessed the situation with cold agony as they rode away from Birat. Like landmarks, the signs sat clearly for him to recognize, now that he bothered to look: Katya was ignoring him in favor of Andrei Sakhalin although, as was only proper for a young woman sleeping with her cousin's husband, she was discreet about it.

"I don't understand it," he said to Stefan that evening when they halted for the night. "She really never did like him before."

Stefan shrugged. "That's how women act, Vasha. They don't mean it."

"No, really. When Galina married him, Katya really told me that she didn't like him."

"She's free to change her mind."

"Are you going to help Jaelle?"

"Yes." Even Riasonovsky's riders had ceased teasing him, since he so faithfully went each night to help her and so stolidly refused to be baited by their jokes.

"I'll come with you."

So Vasha went. Rusudani had a second attendant now, the young priest, Brother Saghir. Together, Rusudani and Sister Yvanne had successfully petitioned Katerina for a Hristanic priest to be allowed to go to Sarai, and since Sister Yvanne was not robust enough for the long journey, Saghir had been sent in her place.

With the priest and Jaelle as chaperons, Vasha was allowed to sit five paces from Princess Rusudani and listen to her read from her holy book. He examined her profile surreptitiously and breathed in the scent of incense that hung over her.

So he went the next night, and the one after that, and the one after that, listening to them read in a language he could not understand. They crossed the length of Habakar, rising before dawn and keeping up a brisk pace, switching horses, straight to sunset. Every night by lantern light Princess Rusudani read from the holy book before she retired for the night. Her calm voice allowed him to forget everything else, to forget what they rode toward, to forget to whom they rode . . . and what might happen when they got there.

They passed the ruins of Karkand, a plain of tumbled, cracked stone and fields poisoned with salt. Even in so forbidding a wasteland, a village grew up in the ruins, pale brick houses roofed with thick reeds dried and bound together in sheets. Gardens patched the wilderness of stone and barren earth as flowers inhabit the wild, wide plains: Startling where they showed up, bright and flowering, their contrast gave the landscape its true character.

"Do you remember?" asked Vasha, boldly pulling his horse up alongside Katya's. Now that they traveled through Habakar lands, she usually rode with the two khaja women, like an extra guard.

"There is the watchtower where Tess's birthwaters flooded," said Katerina, pointing. Somehow, the tower had survived the destruction, although the walls on either side had crumbled.

Vasha started. He hadn't been thinking of the birth, and the baby who had died. He had been thinking of the great battle that ended several days later, and of the inferno that followed it, destroying the city.

"I beg your pardon," said Jaelle to Stefan, using him as an intermediary as she now did when she wanted to initiate any conversation. "My mistress wishes to know what is this place?"

"It was a city," said Katya.

"It was the Habakar king's city," said Vasha.

"It remains as a lesson to those who would defy Bakhtiian," finished Katya.

Princess Rusudani regarded the ruins of Karkand tranquilly. She spoke, and Jaelle translated. "God shelters the righteous."

Jaelle added, in an undertone, "And the blessed Pilgrim watches over those of humble estate."

Riasonovsky rode up to investigate the delay. The soldier seemed uninterested in the dead khaja city; it evidently had no significance to him except as an unimportant marker of the course of Bakhtiian's campaign. His tranquillity of purpose had much in common with Rusudani's serenity.

They rode on. In the afternoon, they met up with a jahar sent by Prince Mitya to escort them the rest of the way to his court. In a matter of days, they arrived at Hamrat.

"I remember Hamrat from the first time I saw it eight years ago," said Katya. "It was so beautiful. All the other cities we saw were either under siege or already burning."

Vassily regarded the city with interest but without passion. "I don't remember it at all, although I suppose we must have passed by it."

"No," agreed Katya, sounding almost like her old friendly self again. "You weren't with us then."

Once, the old city had been bounded by gleaming white walls. With its new prominence, Hamrat sprawled out from the walls along the river, new buildings erected on the path of the crossroads that led to the great gates. Vassily could see the city walls and the profusion of silver towers within, as well as the massive dome of the temple, looming above the sprawl of the outer city. No wall protected these villas and environs, as if the new residents of Hamrat felt that the presence of Prince Mitya was surety enough for their safety.

Mitya's court lay slightly south of Hamrat. Called *sarrodnikaiia,* "Her Voice is Merciful," the palace's foundation rested on the very spot where Yaroslav Sakhalin had been camping when he heard the news that Bakhtiian had won his contest with Habakar sorcerers and returned to the world of the living. Now, set out among fields gone to pasture for the prince's horses, it was a new-looking place, with cold walls and a temple rising in stark white stone within the palace complex. A temple to the Habakar god.

Behind the temple lay a broad park that stretched all the way to the river. Horses grazed in the distance. In a little gazebo, painted white, Mitya waited for them, fanning himself against the heat. He sat on a wide couch, and next to him sat his wife, the Habakar princess Melatina. She wore white robes trimmed with blue crescents, her hair hidden by white cloth, but the silk veil that covered her face below the eyes was so sheer that one could see the rich rose of her lips. A small child played on a carpet at the foot of the couch, with a nurse hovering in attendance.

Mitya rose at once, seeing them. As soon as they dismounted he signaled to his guard to take the horses away. Then he came forward and kissed Katerina on either cheek, in the formal style.

"Vasha! What are you doing here? I thought you were riding with Sakhalin's army."

Vasha shook his head. Mercifully, Katya held her tongue.

"Sakhalin." Mitya acknowledged Andrei Sakhalin gravely, as one prince acknowledges another, and the older man inclined his head in return. Mitya waved toward the park. "You may, of course, camp anywhere as long as you are here. And you are? Riasonovsky? Ah. You'll find everything you need here, horses, supplies, if you're to continue all the way to Sarai."

"Thank you, Prince Mitya. We also have a khaja princess to safeguard while we are here. We are taking her to Sarai."

Mitya looked immediately toward Katya, thereby putting the matter in her hands.

"Set up the Princess Rusudani's tent next to mine," said Katya, "and maintain a guard as before."

Thus dismissed, Riasonovsky took his men and Rusudani away. Stefan glanced at Vassily, then at his cousins, and finally followed the khaja women. Andrei Sakhalin lingered a few minutes more, but Mitya merely smiled blandly at him until, taking the hint, he left as well.

"I can't stand him," said Mitya as soon as the Sakhalin prince was out of earshot. "Prince" Mitya sloughed off him to reveal the mild and rather transparent cousin Vasha knew and loved best. The three of them stood together on a tile mosaic that fronted the gazebo. Princess Melatina still sat on the couch, watching them. "The Sakhalin princes are all proud bastards, but at least the others deserve it."

"You're getting fat," said Katya.

"I am not!" retorted Mitya indignantly, although he was certainly thicker in the face. "Where is Anna?" He turned around to regard the gazebo. "Anna! Come here and greet your cousins!" The child on the carpet lifted her head, hesitated, and then, nudged by the nurse, got to her feet and carefully negotiated the stairs. "Katya," Mitya said in a low voice, "I want you to ask my mother to send someone to care for my children."

"Children?"

He flushed, looking pleased. "Melatina is pregnant again. But these khaja nurses are terrible. They tell Anna never to shout. They cover her hair and they weigh her down in khaja clothes so she can't run. Even Melatina says that a little girl like Anna, because she is a princess, ought to go veiled in public. That's not how a girl ought to behave!"

Katya regarded the child seriously. The girl hesitated again, was urged forward by her nurse, and slowly, then picking up speed, walked across the mosaic to her father. Reaching him, she wrapped her arms around one of his legs and clung there.

"I'd better take her back to the tribes with me," said Katya. "There'll be nothing but trouble for her if she's raised by khaja women."

At once, Mitya grew agitated. "Don't take her away from me!" he pleaded, reaching down to lift her to his hip. Anna circled his neck with her arms, laid her cheek against his shoulder, and stared at Vasha and Katya with dark, Habakar eyes.

"It would be better for her to go, Mitya."

"Oh, Katya, don't be mean," said Vasha. "A daughter wants to be with her father. By what right do you take her away from her mother and send her to her father's kin?"

"At least there's no doubt about who her father *is*," retorted Katya.

Vasha flushed. Gods, that hurt.

"That was unkind," said Mitya in a cool, un-Mitya-like voice, bristling with authority. "I invite you to apologize."

"You can't make me," said Katya stubbornly, "nor should you speak to me that way. And anyway, it's true."

"I am your cousin. I am older than you. And I am right."

Vasha lifted his gaze in time to see Katya wince. Very few people could make Katerina ashamed of herself.

"I apologize," she mumbled. "It was an unkind thing to say."

Vasha, still angry and embarrassed, said nothing, but Mitya seemed satisfied. "You haven't greeted Melatina yet. Katya, you come first. Vasha, you wait here for a moment." Mitya looked vexed. His voice dropped confidingly. "You went to Tess's school with her. I remember that she used to sit out under the awning with everyone else, even if she still did always wear the veil. But ever since she came back to Habakar, she's gone back to all her barbarian ways. The palace must have separate rooms for the women, and she and Princess Laissa keep separate audience rooms for women. Even though she rules as queen by law, she will not sit in open court with me and pass judgment, not even on things that by right a woman ought to rule on."

"She won't pass judgment at all?"

"Oh, she will pass judgment, but only—" He hesitated, as if the next words were too unbelievable to utter. "—only through me. Unless it is a matter she may hear and judge in the seclusion of the women's chambers. Being king here isn't anything like being an etsana's husband. It's as if I'm the etsana." Having uttered the awful thought, he clamped his mouth shut, turned, and strode to the gazebo, briskly mounting the steps to the shaded platform within. A trellis hung with vines and sprays of purple flowers half-concealed the couch and the servant women waiting in attendance.

"Even if it isn't right that a child go live with her father's kin," muttered Katya without looking at Vassily, "I still think we ought to take Anna with us. It would be worse to have her raised as a khaja."

"What about the other children? Will you take them, too? If we can only rule the khaja by force, then our rule will not last long. That is why Bakhtiian married Mitya to Princess Melatina, and why Tess married Georgi Raevsky to Isobel Santer in Jeds."

"I'm not going to marry a khaja!"

Surprised by her vehemence, Vasha laughed. For all that he was furious with her, Vasha could not help but see Katerina as the very model of what a young woman ought to be. Aware of her power, as all the Orzhekov women were, she could ride, weave, shoot with devastating accuracy, and organize the setting up and taking down of a camp. She wore eight lover's bracelets on her ankle; the first one was the one he had given her four years ago. The only thing she had not yet shown was whether she could bear strong daughters and sons, but the evidence of her mother and aunts and cousins suggested that she would. Marriage to a khaja prince would bring no benefit to *her.*

"None of them would have you," he retorted, and was pleased to see her go red. She turned her back on him and

stalked away, mounting the steps and sitting down hard on
the couch between Mitya and Melatina, not waiting for an
invitation. Mercurial as ever, she took Melatina's hands in
hers as if they were cousins and the two women began talking to one another.

After a moment Mitya got up and returned to Vasha, looking disgusted. He *was* getting thicker around the middle.
"We'll walk in the park. Katya has dismissed us." They
walked away from the gazebo along a path of smooth white
pebbles that wound through a garden and toward the palace
wall. "I thought you were to ride with Yaroslav Sakhalin's
army."

Stones whispered under Vasha's boots.

"Just tell me." Mitya had always been a good listener.

Vasha could not resist his sympathy. "I *know* the boys
coming to a jahar start by caring for the horses and then—
but I'm older than them. I don't think it's right that I be
treated like boys three and four years younger than me just
because my—because Bakhtiian refused to send me away
earlier. And Sakhalin never liked me. He didn't want me
with him, even though Bakhtiian sent me to him because
Sakhalin is his best general. But it reminded me of—!" He
broke off, unable to go further.

"Of what?" They reached a courtyard of red brick surrounded by a flowering hedge. In the center, a fountain
splashed.

"Of when my mother died and then Mother Kireyevsky
and all the others suddenly began treating me like a servant."

"Ah." Mitya led Vasha under the shade of a grape arbor.
He sat down on a wood bench whose legs were themselves
carved with clusters of grapes and leafy vines, but Vasha
was too humiliated to sit down. He hadn't known he was going to say that; it had just popped out. Now Mitya would
scorn him. But Mitya put some grapes in his mouth and ate
them, looking thoughtful. "What did you do to make
Sakhalin send you back, then? You must know that
Bakhtiian will be angry."

Vasha paced. "Stefan and Arkady and Ivan and I went out
and stole some khaja horses."

Mitya snorted. "And?"

"And? That was enough."

"Are you sure there wasn't more?"

"It isn't that we took her, Mitya, it's that she ... came along with us."

"Who?"

"Princess Rusudani."

Now Mitya looked startled, but Vasha was saved from his recriminations by the arrival of a dark-bearded, turbaned man floridly dressed in a jade-green overtunic embroidered with stylized gold suns and, under it, blue and white striped baggy trousers. He halted ten steps away and bowed low. "Your Highness."

Mitya beckoned him forward. "What news, Jiroannes? There will be a feast tonight, out in the park."

Jiroannes glanced at Vasha and away as quickly. "I will see that the pavilions are set up, Prince Mitya. Will the queen and her ladies be allowed to attend? The queen's pavilion can be set up a decent distance away—"

"No, no," said Mitya impatiently. "That is, well, my cousin Katerina Orzhekov is here. Oh, Vassily, perhaps you don't recall my chief minister, Jiroannes Arthebathes." Vasha acknowledged the minister with a nod. The minister looked puzzled, but merely bowed, saying nothing. "In any case, you must consult her as to the arrangements."

"I will ask the queen's chamberlain to deal with the matter, sire."

"Was there other news?" Mitya asked, evidently content with this settlement. "You have that look about you."

"Nothing, sire, except that my wife Lady Tarvesi ... but it is nothing."

"Ah. Is she not expecting a child?"

"She has given birth, sire."

"The baby is healthy?"

"Yes, your highness."

Mitya grinned. "Well, then, I am happy for you, Jiroannes. The gods have blessed you."

To Vasha's surprise, the minister did not look particularly pleased. "It is only another girl, Prince Mitya. Nothing to celebrate. I beg your pardon."

Mitya rolled his eyes and cast a glance at Vasha. "I have never thought it safe to begrudge the gods the gifts they choose to give us, Jiroannes."

"No doubt you are wiser than I, your highness."

"A tribe's name lives on through its daughters, may they

prove numerous and healthy. But of course, it is different with you khaja."

"Yes, sire. I hope I have not offended you."

Mitya scratched an ear. "Not at all. I hope the child flourishes. If she is too much bother to you, I am sure you could foster her to the tribes."

The expression that passed across the minister's face was almost comical as he tried to hide his dismay. "Of course, if that is what you wish. . . ."

Mitya sighed. "But you have two fine sons by Princess Laissa, Jiroannes. Surely that contents you."

"They are fine boys, it is true. But it is also said that the Everlasting God shows love for a man by granting him the strength to sire many healthy sons. Whereas I . . . the two boys, that is all, and from my other wives and concubines, only girls."

Mitya cleared his throat, and at once, Jiroannes bowed again. "Thank you, sire."

"You may go," said Mitya.

"The khaja are very strange," said Vasha once the minister had vanished behind the hedge, hoping that Mitya had forgotten about Vasha's horrible misdeeds.

"Melatina apologized to me when Anna was born."

"Apologized to you? What for?"

"That she had failed to give me a son. I was furious. What man would not want a daughter?" Mitya paused and glanced around, looking unsure of himself for the first time. "Vasha, do you wonder, sometimes, if jaran and khaja can ever truly breed together? Or live together in a land, or rule together? Or their children live as both one thing and the other?"

"But they must. That is the vision the gods granted to Bakhtiian."

"It is not so easy from where I sit," said Mitya.

They feasted that evening under white pavilions set out on the grass. In the distance Vasha saw a gold pavilion. It was empty, a reminder of the argument that had raged all afternoon about the disposition of the women. The argument had raged in Habakar fashion, delivered by messengers and go-betweens, Princess Laissa scolding Melatina for even considering feasting in public with her husband, Melatina begging Mitya to allow her to set up a tent for the women to feast separately and Mitya, of course, acceding to her wishes. Once settled, the accommodation had fallen apart when Katya declared that it was unseemly for women and men to feast separately. And when a daughter of the Orzhekov tribe gave an order, it was obeyed.

Given no choice, Mitya simply proclaimed that it was to be a family meal and thus, an intimate one. Vasha could count the number of diners on his fingers: Prince Mitya and Princess Melatina, and Melatina's young sister who lived with her at court; Princess Laissa and the minister Jiroannes; Katya, Vasha, and Andrei Sakhalin. At the last minute, no doubt to foment trouble, Katya had brought along Princess Rusudani, who sat quietly at one end of the table, Jaelle attending her. It was a quiet dinner. Mostly, Andrei Sakhalin talked. Vasha could see nothing of Princess Laissa but her dark eyes, and they made him nervous.

Servants passed to and fro, serving and removing food, lighting fresh lanterns, and Andrei Sakhalin told (again) the story of the battle on the River Djana, this time against the counterpoint of the murmuring of the interpreters. Vasha caught a moment of delicate interplay between Laissa and Melatina, and a moment later Melatina quietly suggested to her husband that it was time for the women to retire. Mitya agreed at once. To Vasha's surprise, Katerina did not object.

It was Princess Rusudani—isolated at the far end of the pavilion—whose reaction surprised him the most.

"I beg your pardon, Prince Mitya," she said suddenly. She had said not one word before this, except to acknowledge Mitya's first greeting. "I would beg an audience with you."

Mitya blinked. Melatina, who had already risen, sank back down onto her couch. "You may speak. Of course."

Rusudani's uncanny calm amazed Vasha. "In my company rides a holy priest of the Church, to whom Princess Katherine has given permission to travel to the great city of Sarai. It is my hope that Brother Saghir be allowed to meet with the Bakhtiian, that he may speak to the Bakhtiian of the true faith and expound the word of God."

"For what king is this priest an envoy?" asked Mitya.

"For no king but He who is King of all of us."

"Does this mean, then, that he is an envoy of Bakhtiian?"

Katerina coughed. Nonplussed, Rusudani simply repeated herself. "He is God's envoy, Prince Mitya."

Mitya glanced at his wife, but she said nothing. "It is a

matter for Bakhtiian. You must present your petition to him."

Princess Rusudani accepted this pronouncement with equanimity. Princess Melatina rose again, and this time in a sudden flurry of activity all of the women left, escorted by various attendants. Minister Jiroannes begged to be excused as well, and Vasha watched as Mitya by almost imperceptible means and without saying as much, convinced Andrei Sakhalin to take his leave as well.

"When did you learn to do that?" Vassily asked when they sat alone under the pavilion. Servants carried away the remains of the meal and brought a silver-plated tureen and a pitcher of cool water for the two men to wash their hands. "*How* did you do that?"

"Do what?" asked Mitya. He was a little drunk.

"Get everyone to leave like that? Even Andrei Sakhalin."

Mitya considered Vasha, frowning. "Do you *like* Sakhalin?"

"He's kind enough to me. He's very friendly, and he doesn't scorn me."

"He tolerates you because you're useful. I tolerate him because he's a Sakhalin. And he tolerates me because I'm Galina's brother."

Impulsively, Vasha blurted out the next words before he realized he meant to. "Katya's taken him as a lover."

Mitya grunted.

"Don't you care? I think it's disgusting."

"I am not about to dictate to any woman what lover she ought, or ought not, to take. Katya has spent two years with Sakhalin's army, Vasha. She has enough demons chasing her that you don't need to add to them."

"What do you mean?"

Under the lanterns, Mitya's pale hair glinted, and he looked for an instant as young as the fifteen-year-old Mitya Vassily had first met, when he came to the Orzhekov tribe eight years ago. "If you don't know, then you had better ask her."

"She won't talk to me." Vasha rested his arms on the table and stared out at the park. Wind soughed along the walls and roof of the pavilion, and the tiny silver flags trimming the open sides fluttered and stilled. A haze hung over the sky, dimming the stars. He could smell the city, now that the wind had shifted. Mitya said nothing. Vasha did not like the way the silence pressed in on them, and since he feared to talk of his own problems, he changed the subject. "Mitya . . . do you . . . are you *glad* you're here?"

"I am doing my duty for Bakhtiian."

"Yes, but . . ." A lantern guttered out, and at once the shadows shifted, spreading and altering in shape. "Are you glad to have married a khaja woman? Do you . . . do you love her?"

"Naturally I love her," Mitya said carelessly. "She is my wife."

"But what do the Habakar think of having a jaran prince to govern them?"

There was no answer for a moment and then, a soft snort. Mitya had fallen asleep.

Vasha stood up and crossed to his cousin, touching him affectionately on his fair hair, and went to stand under the line of flags. The servants had gone, all but two silent jaran guards and, farther, like the shades of ghosts, four riders at attention. It was so quiet that Vasha could hear the distant slur of the river. Closer, he heard the slip and slide of fabric.

"My lord. Mitya!"

Mitya snorted and roused. "What is it?"

Vasha, caught in shadow, turned to see Princess Melatina sit down beside her husband. Mitya draped an arm over her shoulders and pulled her close against him, murmuring something Vasha could not hear.

Melatina rested a palm on his chest. Seated thus, with the light caught on her torso, Vasha could see the swell of her belly, still slight, under the soft lines of her silk robes. "Mitya! It is unseemly to let the false prophesiers consort with the jaran."

Mitya blinked several times in quick succession. "Hmm?"

"The unbeliever. The Almighty God enjoins us to tell only the truth, and the words her priests will bring to the jaran are lies."

"My heart," said Mitya, sounding a bit annoyed, "that is for Bakhtiian to judge. I have given you your temple here in the palace. I have saved the temple in Salkh. What more can you want?" He shook his head, clearing it. "Vasha was here. Where did he go?"

Suddenly embarrassed to be eavesdropping, Vasha slid around the corner while the two of them were looking elsewhere and escaped into the darkness.

They spent one more day reprovisioning. The next morning Katerina had an ugly fight with Mitya, but in the end, when they rode out of Hamrat, Mitya's little daughter Anna went with them.

Dread overtook Vasha. They had begun the final stage of the journey. All too soon, he would come face-to-face with his father.

CHAPTER FIFTEEN

Gateway

David ben Unbutu regarded the horde of children surrounding Ilyana with dismay. Recovering, he smiled wryly. "Who are these?"

Ilyana let go of a held breath. He was going to agree. He hadn't said so yet, but she could tell by his expression that he had accepted his fate. "These are my brothers Valentin and Anton, and this is my sister Evdokia. This is Portia. She's Diana and Anatoly's daughter." She added, "She and Evdi are both four years old," and then wondered if M. Unbutu would be insulted by having the obvious pointed out to him.

"Perhaps I need to clarify my question."

"Oh, I know," said Ilyana quickly. "It's supposed to be my tutorial, but I have to take care of them, so I thought, maybe, I could bring them along, maybe, I hoped, that they could. . . ." She trailed off. They all stood in one of the passenger lounges, a rectangular room lined with benches. The alien fragrance was muted here, but then again, she never saw Chapalii on the passenger deck, so it was no wonder it smelled neutral here.

"I can take care of myself," muttered Valentin.

Ilyana bit down on a retort. "Valentin," she said reasonably, "it isn't my rules, it's the ship rules. You're not allowed to run around on this ship. Or even just sit anywhere you want to." There were not, thank the gods, any obvious neshing ports here either. Maybe the Chapalii didn't nesh.

"You're the eldest, I see," said M. Unbutu. "That puts you in charge."

She nodded warily. Maybe he did understand.

He rubbed at his chin with his knuckles. "I was going to start by discussing tension and compression, but . . . on the other hand, maybe we could build some tiered programs so that we could all follow along the same lesson at different levels."

"If you got a nesh port, I can do some building for you," Valentin blurted out. "I can build an immersion program, even."

"Uh—" Ilyana began.

"Slow down." Chuckling, M. Unbutu sat down on a maroon bench that seemed more grown out of the wall than set there and shook his head.

"What's a mersion program?" asked Evdokia.

"I got a suitcase of multiblocks in our cabin," said Portia, piping up brightly.

"Those are little blocks you can stick together any way, into people or buildings or animals or stuff," added Anton.

"Don't worry." M. Unbutu seemed to be stifling a laugh. "I had those when I was a kid. Those would be good for model building, and for the little girls—"

"I am not a *little* girl," interrupted Portia. "I'm a *big* girl."

"—for the two younger girls to play with. They shouldn't be spending all their time sunk in an immersion program, anyway." He looked at Valentin with interest. "Can you really build an immersion program?"

"Yes." Valentin's clipped reply had the effect of making the boy seem more, rather than less, knowledgeable.

Ilyana clenched her hands so tightly that her nails bit into her palms. She didn't want to betray Valentin's addiction to M. Unbutu. What would he think of them? But she hadn't expected this. She hadn't wanted to bring the younger children along in any case, but she hadn't had any choice. They were her responsibility.

"I just don't have experience teaching kids this young," said M. Unbutu with a sigh. Fear gripped Ilyana's heart. What if he wasn't going to agree? It was a lot to ask, not just that he tutor her, but that he put up with the younger kids as well. "Do you have any suggestions?"

"I could—" Valentin began.

Ilyana cut him off. "They could play some games, play with blocks, and maybe do some basic immersion programs. It isn't like we'll be on the ship for that long."

"Yes, but what about when we get to Duke Naroshi's planet? Has there been any discussion of what kind of tutorial program you kids will be on?"

Ilyana shrugged. Probably Diana had plans for Portia, but

Ilyana knew that her parents would expect the children to do their work around the tent and otherwise take care of themselves. She didn't want to say that aloud.

M. Unbutu sighed. "Well. I may have some old programs buried in my modeler, some elementary mathetics programs, that kind of thing. Valentin, perhaps your first project could be to excavate those for me."

They had been on the ship for almost a whole day. Ilyana could see how Valentin's hands practically twitched at the thought of getting onto M. Unbutu's modeler. Sure, each room had a net screen embedded in the wall, but Valentin hated flat screen work.

"Sure I can!" Valentin said enthusiastically. "But I could do a better job getting it out through a nesh port."

"Yeah, I've got one of those."

"Valentin," muttered Ilyana.

"I'll have to have your parents' permission first, though."

Valentin shifted from one foot to the other, impatient. "Sure, M. Unbutu, but you know that we did nesh work all the time at school. It's part of the mathetics program."

"Is that true?" M. Unbutu asked Ilyana.

"Yes," she said reluctantly. She chewed at her lower lip. What was she going to do? Just blurt out that Valentin was nesh-addicted? But he had to do some nesh anyway, to avoid going into withdrawal. Maybe if she could just monitor him closely enough, she could ease him off the addiction. "We do. Valentin even got a recognition for his chamber that he added to the big Memory Palace project."

Valentin snorted. "That wasn't that good. That was just our flat, with all of Mother's crazy walls and stuff."

"That's exactly the answer, then," said M. Unbutu. "I've got a partial version of the Memory Palace. We can let the younger kids explore it. There are a number of teaching chambers on different subjects embedded in one of the wings of the palace, and there's a whole wing on architecture and engineering that I was planning to use with you, Yana. My modeler is *just* capable of holding open several chambers at one time." He set his modeler on the floor and knelt in front of it, opening it up so that it resembled a flat black plus-sign against the pale marbled floor.

"Memory Palace," he said aloud. He sat back on his heels. "This is another form of architecture that might be interesting to explore. Back when computers were first developed, people built multiuser habitats out of text and explored them."

"What if you couldn't read?" asked Ilyana.

"My mother can't read," said Anton suddenly.

"Shh!" It was true. That didn't mean Anton had to tell everyone about it. Of course, Vasil couldn't read very well either, but he had an excellent memory and a fine sense of navigation, so he had learned to negotiate in a world where visual landmarks were as common as textual ones.

M. Unbutu chose to ignore the remark. "It's true that in those days people were dependent on the word for many things. Even farther back, before the wholesale diffusion of writing, people were dependent on the oral tradition for the transmission of knowledge. That's something actors still do. They're able to memorize at rates the rest of us usually can't manage, because they're practiced in the art of aural recognition."

"I'm hungry," said Evdokia.

"Evdi! We just ate." Ilyana turned to M. Unbutu. "She isn't really. She's just bored."

"I'm bored," said Anton.

"Do you have a nesh port in there?" Valentin asked.

"Here it comes," said M. Unbutu.

The lounge filled up with a gateway.

It was a pretty good representation considering that it came from a portable modeler. It only shimmered in a few places, although the sharp corners of the lounge caused the edges of the visual representation to fade toward transparency where the walls met.

A plain white arch represented the gateway into the labyrinthine sprawl of the memory palace. Literalists, Portia and Evdi clasped hands and, giggling, crossed under the arch. As they moved, the arch itself stretched out into a barrel vault, becoming a corridor lined with blank marble walls down which the visitor progressed until she reached the courtyard.

There was a moment of reorientation as the three-dimensional picture shifted, blanked out, and reconstructed a new chamber: a spacious courtyard ringed by arches and centered around a circular fountain.

Valentin sighed. "I hate this. It's so flat. It's so primitive. It's jerky."

It was true that a three-dimensional rendering that simply filled the room around you didn't have the fluidity of nesh, where an icon of yourself inhabited the seemingly endless web of cybernetic space, but it had its uses.

"We'll split up here," said M. Unbutu. "I can maintain three separate chambers. Girls, where do you want to go?"

"Dinosaurs," said Portia at once.

"Hmm. Menu, is there a Cretaceous room suitable for four-year-olds?" One of the arches turned blue. "That way. Anton, what about you?"

Anton yawned. "I don't care. I'll go with them."

M. Unbutu shifted and let one half of the passenger lounge turn into a prehistoric landscape. Quickly enough, Anton had a Tyrannosaurus Rex and a Triceratops engaged in a duel to the death, while Evdi and Portia busily constructed odd-looking dinosaurs, mixing the head of one with the body of a second and the tail of a third, giggling over the results.

M. Unbutu turned his back on the jungle and regarded Ilyana and Valentin. "Do you mind if we just use discrete holographs? The modeler can maintain three chambers, but I can't. I keep seeing both sides and overloading. We'll just blank this side of the room and build models. That's all I need to talk about tension and compression, anyway."

"If you have a nesh port, I could excavate for those programs you talked about," said Valentin.

"It's back in my cabin. Why don't you stick with Ilyana and me today? I'll bring it next time."

Valentin swallowed. "Yeah." He wrapped the fingers of one hand in his pale hair and twisted them around and around.

"Now." Freed of the younger children for the moment, M. Unbutu relaxed. "How does a structure stand up?"

Valentin took his fingers out of his hair and began chewing on his lower lip.

"Through tension and compression," M. Unbutu continued, clearly taking pleasure in this subject. "Tension is 'pull.' Compression is 'push.' Let's look at a column and an arch, which are both examples of structures that are in compression."

The Tyrannosaurus roared triumphantly on the other side of the room. Ilyana plopped down cross-legged in front of a plain Doric column and an arch bridge that materialized next to the modeler, little holographs complete in detail, if lacking solidity. Content, she listened as M. Unbutu began to discuss the compressive strength of stone. Sitting down beside her, Valentin had put on his polite mask, but he worried at his lower lip until he drew blood.

That night, she woke up when she heard the sigh of the door. She and Valentin shared a tiny four-bunk cabin with Evdi and Anton, but the two younger children slept so soundly that an explosion wouldn't have woken them up. Ilyana cracked open her eyes in time to see the dim lights of the nightshift corridor flash and disappear as the door slid shut again.

She was out of bed instantly. By the time she pulled a skirt on, belting it closed over her nightshirt, and got out into the corridor, Valentin had already disappeared.

She cursed under her breath. Kneeling, she examined the floor, but its sheen was uniform, hiding any trace of Valentin's passage. The entrance to her parents' cabin was closed. The distant murmur of voices whispered along the corridor. The air itself seemed charged, scented differently, as if during nightshift the aliens allowed a breath of their atmosphere to infiltrate the human passenger deck. Under the dim lights, the walls of the corridor gave off a light of their own, a pattern manifesting under the surface of the wall, slowly revealing itself. Ilyana stood, then headed to the left.

Whoever had designed the ship had spent more thought on the lounges than the cabins, which were cramped and utilitarian. Just as the inner walls of an etsana's great tent could be shifted around to create a variety of different chambers, so could the public chambers the humans called lounges be rearranged to create greater or lesser, or more private, chambers. Rather like, Ilyana thought, a physical Memory Palace whose walls could be altered at will.

Owen Zerentous was rehearsing Vasil and Dejhuti in a scene from *Oedipus Rex;* the actors were screened from Ilyana's view by a white trellis. The trellis spread out from a single trunk in the floor, like the ivory channels of a delta reaching for outlet in the sea. It grew into the ceiling, and Ilyana could not help but wonder if it reappeared on the deck above, or if it was, like ganglia, some kind of nerve outgrowth of the ship. She dismissed this fanciful idea and paused inside the door to see if Valentin was anywhere in the rest of the lounge, which was cubbyholed into a series of cubicles by the arrangement of walls of various height.

Owen said, "Vasil, you're not in the interactives anymore. This is theater. Use your voice and your body, not just your damned face."

Another lattice, polished and sharp like obsidian, veiled four shapes sitting around a table. Ilyana crept closer, draping herself along a bench, trying to find an angle that would allow her to see faces through the lattice.

"Let me go home," said Vasil, and she jerked, startled. Then froze, one hand clutching the curve of the bench. Her heart raced. He was just saying lines from the play. *" 'Bear your own fate, and I'll bear mine. It is better so: trust what I say.' "*

She breathed again, and discovered that she could make out the party around the table with perfect clarity: Anatoly Sakhalin, David ben Unbutu, the actor Gwyn Jones, and a woman named Wingtuck from the tech crew whom Ilyana didn't know. Sakhalin sat carelessly, one arm flung over the back of the chair next to him, the other hand resting on his belt. Somehow, the acoustics of the room had clarified as well with her change of position, and she could hear them, interposed with the soft tones of her father's voice. She could not quite hear Dejhuti, playing Oedipus the king to Vasil's blind seer, Teiresias.

"The actors and the crew are covered. They have a reason for being here, and since all of them are legitimate and only a handful actually part of the survey, the cover deepens. How do you determine which are seeking information and which are simply doing their job?" That was the woman.

Anatoly stirred. "That is one way Bakhtiian would get intelligence in a region. Not only would he interview every merchant and traveler from that place, but he would send a group of merchants out on selected routes and put spies in with them, but men and women who could also trade."

" 'You are all ignorant. No; I will never tell you what I know. Now it is my misery; then it would be yours.' "

"What about you, then, M. Sakhalin? You're neither fish nor fowl." This, again from the woman.

"I beg your pardon?"

" 'I do not intend to torture myself, or you.' "

"A figure of speech."

"I think what Wing is asking is this," said Gwyn Jones with a glance toward the woman, who flipped her long black braid over her shoulder so that she could play with its tip.

Ilyana did not know Jones well, but she did know that he was the only actor her father actually respected enough to leave alone. "Should we pass you off as part of the Company's crew?"

After some thought, Anatoly replied, more to the group at large than to Jones specifically. "It seems to me that only a fool would believe that none of the humans wish to discover more information about the khepelli. I do not believe that the khepellis can be fools, to have become as powerful as they are, to have sailed between stars and to control so many different peoples. Think of the logistics! Clearly their women are wise and efficient, to have created such an empire."

"Their women!" M. Unbutu chuckled. He seemed different. Ilyana thought him the most unpretentious adult she had ever met, diffident without being dithering, but after all these years with her father she had learned to read lines of authority, and it was clear that he sat at the focus of this conversation. Although, of course, the flurry of energy stirred around Anatoly. "We're not sure their females have any position at all, any status, any real power, in their culture."

"Is it not women who run the camp and the wagon train? It is on the strength of its supply lines that an army can move. Everyone knows that my grandmother knows how to organize a camp better than any other woman of the tribes, and it is true as well that Mother Orzhekov built the great system of logistics and supply on which Bakhtiian feeds and maintains his armies."

" *'I have gone free. It is the truth sustains me.'* "

M. Unbutu set a brown hand on the table and stared at his nails. "I saw that myself. But that doesn't mean that it is the same everywhere. We do know that Chapalii females are secluded, and that under their law a Chapalii woman who marries loses her birth status and takes on her husband's status completely and irrevocably. The judgment xenologists have drawn from that is that Chapalii females have a lesser and markedly unimportant status, compared to the males."

Anatoly digested this information in silence. "You khaja are very strange," he said at last. "It is no wonder you have fallen to the armies of these khepelli, if everything I have read about your history is true. It seems to me that you think they are khaja like you, but they might not be." He frowned.

"If only Bakhtiian and the tribes could breed horses that could sail the seas of night. . . ."

" 'Are you tempting me?' "

Jones laughed. "Now there's a thought."

"You'll have to fill me in on the joke," said Wingtuck caustically.

"Which doesn't bring us to a consensus," added M. Unbutu mildly.

"I mean to say this," said Anatoly, now addressing himself to M. Unbutu. "The khepelli must know we will seek intelligence about their Empire and their emperor. If we do not seem to be seeking such information, then they will become even more suspicious. So there must always be one person who is clearly a spy. That will be me."

"That puts you in a vulnerable position," said M. Unbutu.

Anatoly shrugged. Ilyana admired the lack of concern with which he greeted the prospect of such danger. On the other hand, he had put himself in as great a danger years before, riding, as he was now, into enemy-held lands.

In the quiet, she heard Dejhuti.

" 'You child of endless night! You cannot hurt me or any other man who sees the sun!' "

Her father's voice was oddly calm. " 'True: it is not from me your fate will come.' "

At that moment, Sakhalin turned and looked straight at her. Instantly, she realized that her thin nightshirt exposed her arms, and that the lace trim at the neck drew attention . . . but as quickly as he saw who it was, he looked away. By then the others had all seen her.

"Yana!" M. Unbutu beckoned to her. "Come here." He said it so pleasantly. But however easygoing the words, and his expression, might appear, he expected to be obeyed.

She crossed her arms over her chest and slid around the obsidian lattice, and stood there, shifting from one foot to the other while the three khaja examined her and Anatoly Sakhalin looked at her obliquely.

"Damn," said Wingtuck. "She does look like her father. Is she past the age of consent?"

"Mother's Tits, Wing," snapped Gwyn Jones. "Shut up."

"Were you looking for someone?" asked M. Unbutu.

Ilyana was struck by revelation. Looking at M. Unbutu, who had, by the evidence of two empty cups sitting by his right hand, been here for some time, she knew where Valentin was.

" '*But I say that you, with both your eyes, are blind.*' "

Ilyana gulped. "I . . . I was just looking for Valentin. He said he wasn't feeling well, but I guess he must have gone to . . . the infirmary."

"Go on," said M. Unbutu gently. "If you need any help with him. . . ."

"No! No." Freed, she backed away, bumping into the lattice. It felt warm. A hum like distant singing throbbed through her. She stepped away, smiling stupidly, knowing they were all still looking at her, hugged herself even more tightly, and sidestepped toward the door.

"Vasil," said Owen in a voice that combined patience, disgust, and excitement, "you've picked up so many bad habits in the last four years that I don't know *what* I'm going to do with you. Maybe I should have left you on that Mother-forsaken planet. I don't know where your mind is right now, but I want it here with *me!* Go on."

As Ilyana paused by the door, she saw her father direct his next line not at Dejhuti but at Owen. " '*I would not have come at all if you had not asked me.*' "

She fled into the anonymity of the corridor. There, she took in three deep breaths. She knew where M. Unbutu's cabin was. She and the children had escorted him there just hours before, while she had peppered him with more questions about suspension bridges, elasticity, and plasticity. He had only escaped because it was dinnertime. She ran. Once she had to slow down to a walk and, breathing hard, she smiled blandly at two of the actors—new ones, whom she didn't know—who were evidently headed down to the lounge for their scene. She crossed into the sleeping ring and counted doors until she stopped in front of a door as unremarkable as the rest. Not knowing what else to do, she touched the wall panel. To her shock, it was not locked. It opened immediately.

She groaned. Remembered where she was, and darted inside. The door closed behind her.

Valentin had a look of bliss on his face and a trail of spittle running down his chin. He was curled into a fetal position on the bunk, two transparent patches covering his eyes so that she could see the movement of his eyeballs underneath. Spasmodically, his hands clutched an egg-shaped control sponge that was slightly smaller than his head.

Ilyana felt sick and furious at the same time. This was the kind of stuff kids were not allowed to use. She didn't even know how to work it. Worse, Valentin had broken in here and was stealing time, blundering into places he wasn't supposed to be. She wasn't an idiot. David ben Unbutu worked for Charles Soerensen. What if there was top secret information on here? What kind of awful trouble could Valentin get in if they were discovered?

Strewn on the bed were two additional pairs of eye patches. Not knowing what else to do, she sealed one set over her eyes. It was odd to be able to see the room through the patches, even mottled with a distant, because tiny, grid. She knelt on the bed beside Valentin and twined her fingers between his, and touched the sponge.

She fell. From clear to opaque to blinding light, her sight vanished. First she felt. Wind tore at her skin and sand blasted her hands and fingers. Then she saw, first her hand and the sleeve of her school tunic, then the yellow screen of sand whipped into a wild dance. Her nostrils choked on it. When she opened her mouth to breathe, her tongue was instantly parched by the grit. Last, the sound: howling, howling. She had been here before.

"Valentin!" She didn't really say it, but the shout emanated out from her. "Valentin!"

Like a ship pitched on stormy seas, he stumbled and fought forward not twenty paces in front of her. Except it wasn't quite him. The wind had flayed the skin from the muscle and scoured through layers of tissue until bone gleamed like a beacon against the overpowering blizzard of sand. His hair was black and twisting, and as she struggled nearer, she saw it was snakes, hissing and writhing like an echo of the storm.

He turned, although he couldn't have heard her frail voice over the roar of the wind and the clashing din of earth cast up into the air. He had no face, only a skull.

"Valentin! What are you doing here? Where are you going?"

"I'm trying to get there! I'm trying to get there! Let me go home!"

She grabbed for his arm before he could walk on. Her fingers oozed through his flesh as if through butter, closing at last on dry bone. "Come home with me!"

A blast of wind caught her in the face, blinding her. The

force of it scraped her skin raw. Blood welled and dripped onto the sleeve of her blouse, mixing with the layer of grime that contaminated the pristine white cotton. Droplets of blood spun away into the storm, and she focused on one, fixed her gaze on it no matter how much it hurt as the wind screamed against her face, and willed it to wink into existence as a portal. The blood flashed scarlet, and grew, and there was an arch, the plain white gateway of the Memory Palace. She threw her body to one side, twisting, and with that torque spun them down into it.

They tumbled down the great entrance hall spanned by a barrel vault and landed in the courtyard where the fountain's cool spray bathed them and washed away the grime and washed away Valentin's horrible guise until he became Valentin again. Looking sulky, and queasy.

"Oh, gods, don't throw up," said Ilyana.

"Much you care. Why can't you just let me alone?"

"Stupid question." She stood up, keeping a firm grip on him. There were only four arches on each side of the quadrangular courtyard, but the number was deceptive. Each one split into multiple archways, so that depending on the angle at which you passed through any individual archway, you found yourself at a different destination, at a different wing of the Memory Palace. "Where's the room you built, Valentin?"

"We have to go upstream."

She let him lead her. Gods, he knew this place well. Passageways branched off into vast warrens; chambers flew past, and then at a dock they clambered onto a barge. Towed by horses up a torpid river, the barge breasted the current and sent a lazy wake flurrying out from its stern. Wings of the palace lined the river, and suddenly they swung onto a side channel, passed under a bridge, and were back inside the palace, in a dark chamber that rang with the lulling slap of water against a stone jetty. The barge bumped placidly up against a piling.

Valentin scrambled up onto the jetty. Utterly lost, Ilyana climbed out and followed Valentin down a wainscoted corridor whose windows looked out onto the ocean. They turned a corner and walked into their flat in London, with the great etsana's tent and the walls that masked the real world and pretended to show a false one instead. At once, her stomach clenched with the old familiar loathing, the awful feeling of being trapped.

"Now," she said. "We're going back to the ship."

"I don't want to," said Valentin, straining against her. "Just let me go, Yana."

"Don't you have any idea what kind of trouble you could get us into?"

He looked about to say, "I don't care," but he didn't. She dragged him over to the panel that opened the door into the hallway.

Aloud, she said, "I don't know how this program works, but when we step through this door we're going to be back in the cabin. In M. Unbutu's cabin. And the program will be over. End run."

She opened the door and stepped through.

And jerked her hands back from the sponge and yanked Valentin's hands off, but he was already blinking, awake.

"Are you going to throw up?"

He gagged. "No. Why did you have to go so fast?"

"Oh, like I want to be found here when M. Unbutu comes back. You may not care about getting tutorials, but I do!" She pulled the patches off their eyes, and stood over Valentin while he replaced everything exactly as he had found it. "Hurry! Hurry! No, you idiot. Smooth out the bed. Any fool can see someone's been lying there. Now come on."

They got out the door into the corridor. No one was around. The dim lights made her feel safer.

"How did you get the door open?"

"It was unlocked."

"I don't believe you."

"I don't care whether you believe me. So there."

Voices sounded from the right.

"Come on!" She grabbed him by the wrist and dragged him in the opposite direction.

"Slow down, slow down," he gasped. "I feel sick."

He was shaking. His forehead and neck were wet with sweat, and he felt hot. She stopped and put her arms around him, holding him.

"Valentin, why do you have to do this?"

He did not reply, just rubbed his face against her shoulder, back and forth, like he was trying to wipe something off.

David ben Unbutu came around the corner. He was alone.

He pulled up, surprised. "Well. Hello. I see you found him." His eyes widened, taking in the scene. "Is he all right?"

"Yeah, fine. I mean, no, he's sick, but everything is fine. I'm just taking him back to the cabin now."

"Oh, well. Maybe we won't be able to meet tomorrow." Was it her imagination, or did he sound a little disappointed?

"Of course we will! No, really, everything will be fine tomorrow."

"I hope so."

"Good night," said Ilyana firmly.

"Good night." He walked on, looking back once over his shoulder.

Ilyana waited until he had curved away out of sight. "I'll get you nesh time somehow," she said in a low voice. "But you gotta do it legally. You can't sneak in—"

"Just let me go home," he muttered, so she took him back to the cabin. He fell asleep at once.

CHAPTER SIXTEEN

Birbas

Tess woke suddenly. Ilya breathed beside her. He was, and always had been, an extremely quiet sleeper. A curtained alcove screened off the tiny chamber in which the children slept. She listened, but she heard nothing. It was too early for the camp to be stirring, even on the day that the women and the army would ride out to the great hunt, the birbas.

The noise came again. A cough. Tess pushed back the blankets, stood, and deftly lit the lantern hanging from an overhead pole. She looked in on the two children. Natalia slept with her limbs all akimbo, Yuri more compactly, but both of them with such angelic faces in repose that Tess's heart ached just to look at them. Yuri shifted and coughed again.

Ilya stirred and a moment later stood beside her. He slipped past her and knelt beside Yuri, gently touching the boy's cheeks with the back of a hand. "Hot," he murmured.

Yuri coughed again and woke himself up. He whimpered and licked his lips and wiped his nose on his wrist. "My mouth hurts," he said, his voice rising with a sick child's wail.

"Shh." Ilya moved his son to rest against his chest, stroking his hair. He glanced up at Tess, and she fetched a waterskin. As Yuri was drinking, Natalia woke up. Like her father, she was a light sleeper, one who woke from sleep straight into focused consciousness.

"He won't be able to ride out on the birbas, will he?" Natalia asked, cutting to the chase.

Yuri began to wail in earnest.

"Hush, little one," said Ilya. "I'll stay here with you." He looked up at Tess, anticipating her question. "The young riders and archers will have my aunt's eye on them. That should be more than enough to convince them to perform well."

That hadn't been quite the question she was going to ask, but it served to answer it just as well. Would the young riders not want Bakhtiian himself to oversee their prowess? In fact, when she could untangle herself from her Earth-bound prejudices, Tess knew perfectly well that Mother Orzhekov's stature was equal to her nephew's.

"You cry too much," said Natalia to her brother, which merely set him wailing again.

"That is enough of that," said Ilya sternly to his daughter, and Yuri was not sick enough to miss the opportunity to stick his tongue out at her in triumph. The tongue was coated with a white film.

Tess sighed. "Talia, get dressed and run and get—" She almost said Niko. But he needed his rest. But wouldn't it be worse to begin to overlook him just because he was getting old? "Get Niko." Natalia jumped up and left. Yuri coughed again. What if, this time, it was a truly serious illness? She lived with that nagging fear all the time, that and brooding over how she was going to educate her children properly. Ilya kissed Yuri on the forehead and whispered something to the boy which made him smile. Tess watched him. Ilya was impossibly patient with his children when they were sick; it was perhaps the only thing for which he had any patience. What was she going to do when they grew into adults? She did not want her children to live only in this world.

Ilya lifted his gaze and smiled at her. He seemed unconcerned about Yuri's cough and fever, but Tess had discovered that Ilya was a better judge of illness than she was. "The truth is," he said, "hunting bores me. There are some books in the library I haven't read yet."

Tess snorted. She crouched beside her husband and took Yuri's hand in hers, but Yuri had already slipped into a doze again. "Ilya, what do you want?"

His smile vanished. When he contemplated his vision, his gaze narrowed until Tess could almost imagine it as a single beam, piercing to the heart of the universe, capable of vaporizing any object that stood in its path. "The world."

It was at moments like this that Tess was forced to acknowledge that he was, in some small way, insane. Sometimes out here on the plains, she could forget his vision—or at least, not the vision, since Ilya would not have been the person she fell in love with without that vision, but the plain bald fact of what it meant.

"I was dreaming," said Ilya abruptly, "before I woke up. I had a vision of a god with four arms, and he was dancing, and as he danced he created the world. I thought, *this is a vision given to me, that with every great change comes a new making.*"

Tess hung the lantern from a pole and favored Ilya with a wry smile. "Was it a true dream or a false one?"

"The gods only send me true dreams."

She kissed him, and Yuri, and went outside. What could she say to him? Because he was right. His own children would not be jaran, not truly. Already his vision and his armies and the deadly influence of Tess and her brother Charles wove a new pattern into Rhui's history.

Outside, dawn limned the distant hills. The Orzhekov camp rose and readied itself for the great hunt. Tess greeted Niko and packed saddlebags and took Natalia out to help her bring in her string of horses. She left the horses with one of the Orzhekov boys and returned to say good-bye to Ilya and Yuri. Irena Orzhekov met her under the awning of her tent.

"Your husband is not riding out with us."

"Why is it, Mother Orzhekov, that you call him 'your husband' instead of 'my nephew' only when you are displeased with him?"

"Humph."

"He is concerned for his son."

"Ilyakoria spoils his children," said Irena firmly. Tess knew better than to disagree. But for some reason Vasha's image leapt to her mind. Ilya had never spoiled Vasha, but perhaps he had sheltered him too well. She wondered how Vasha was faring in Yaroslav Sakhalin's army, but then Niko emerged from the tent.

"How is Yuri?" she asked anxiously.

Niko shrugged. "I saw four other children yesterday with the same complaint. I am not concerned. Nor should you be."

Irena made a movement toward the tent and then checked herself.

"Are you going to go back in and try again?" Tess asked, amused despite herself.

"I know him too well," said Irena. "We are leaving now."

"I will come at once," said Tess, but she went inside the tent first. "Your aunt is very annoyed with you," she said to Ilya as she kissed him good-bye. Ilya merely smiled. He sat

in the front chamber. Light streamed in through the entrance
flap to illuminate the pages of the book he had set on his
knees where he sat in a heap of pillows. Tess could hear
Yuri's soft snore from the back. "Anatomy?"

"*On The Nature of the Body,* an old text from Byblos written by the great physician, Antomis of Thene." The book
was open to a page illustrating a pregnant woman with a
child curled up inside her. Ilya flushed suddenly and turned
the page, as if such matters were only for women's scrutiny,
but Tess thought at once of Arina, dead for ten days now.
She pressed her lips together and clenched one hand, so she
would not cry. "Do you have to go?" he asked softly.

"Yes. I'm a woman. Of course I have to go. As does most
every other person in camp, except those too old or too
young or too pregnant. Or too self-important."

"You're exaggerating."

"Yes." She relented, grinning. "I don't mind. I like it."
She kissed him a final time for good measure and left.

They spread out in a long line and rode southeast for six
days, driving game before them. At dawn of the seventh day
the jahars on the wings broke off, advancing ahead of the
center until they vanished into the rolling hills. By the end
of the eleventh day, the wings met up with each other again
to form a vast ring of riders around the chosen hunting
ground. When at last the call came that the circle had been
completed, the advance began: The circle slowly contracted
as they drove the animals before them in toward the center.

Indeed, this was the test of the birbas which Tess most enjoyed. It was forbidden to kill the game, but more importantly, it was a point of honor for each rider not to let any
animal, no matter how small, how fleet, or how ferocious,
escape out of the ring as it contracted. Children rode behind
the front lines, which were made up on this birbas primarily
of young archers and riders who would after this be sent out
to the armies in the field. What worse fate, Tess reflected,
than to prove oneself unworthy of riding with the army?

At night, a string of lights—campfires—curved off into
the distance on both sides. Tess took her turns at watch and
slept tucked in a blanket with Natalia.

On the fourteenth day as the ring contracted further and
further, she dropped back from the second rank to ride with
Natalia, who wanted to range along the ring itself.

A herd of skittish antelope had fallen back against the

line, and Natalia watched with interest as a jahar of young riders shifted and drove the animals on. A single antelope bolted for freedom, heading for a gap that had grown in between this jahar and another, but at once a flag went up and riders split off from the other jahar to contain it. Tess was, as usual, impressed by the coordination of parts.

"Mama," said Natalia, "why do women and men hunt together in the birbas?"

"It trains the army, little one. An army in the field must be able to accurately judge the ground it crosses, and in battle a jahar must judge distance and time."

"Do the khaja armies train like this?"

"I don't think so."

"Is that why the khaja must always fall to the jaran?"

"Well, that is one reason."

"Is Papa really the emperor of the world?"

Tess glanced at her daughter, but Natalia's expression was serious. "Who told you that?"

"I went to the market with Aunt Stassi, the khaja market in Sarai, and that is what one of the khaja said."

"There is a great deal of 'world' out there, Talia. You might as well call me emperor of the world, as him." It would be more true.

"Are you emperor of the world, Mama?" Natalia asked, and Tess supposed that she might well seem so, to her daughter. Or at least, to her daughter at this age. That would pass.

But the question made her ponder, and her mind wandered. How tempting it would be to enforce her views onto every society on Rhui. How hard it would be to stop once she started. Perhaps one reason she stayed with the jaran was to keep herself to some degree removed from the ability, the opportunity, to meddle outside of this one (rather significant) spot. Yet the simple fact was that even with the force of Earth's knowledge behind her, she would need an army ten times the size of the jaran army, she would need a communications network far more sophisticated, which would all have to be laid in, and she would need time and more time yet, to achieve any wholesale unalterable change in the complex web of Rhuian culture.

So how did the Chapalii do it? They did not, as far as she knew, possess a standing army with which to control their great stellar empire. They had no obvious military presence

on Earth except for the Protocol Office, which was bureau-
cratic and not military, and the security force, which was
drawn exclusively from the human population and which
worked with the Protocol Office to prevent breaches of
Chapalii law.

Yet they had crushed Charles's first rebellion decisively.
They had destroyed, or at least outlasted, the Mushai's rebellion millennia ago, but in all the stories about him Tess had
never once heard the name of a general or a battle; neither
had she found any such stories or names or titles honored
anywhere in what (presumably) little she knew of Chapalii
literature, if it was even literature as humans knew it. There
was one whole story cycle about the clever dealings of a
probably mythical merchant house called Sashena, but nothing of the noble deeds and great sacrifices of a warrior class.

A great empire thrives on movement. But a great empire
must be established somehow. It does not just spring fully
formed from the brow of Zeus or from the angry frown of
Brahma's forehead.

"Mama! Look! Look!"

Torn out of her thoughts by Natalia's shout, Tess blinked
rapidly, accidentally turning her implant on and then off in
quick succession. Slightly dizzy, she finally found Natalia's
arm and looked where the girl was pointing.

A clot of grim-faced young riders battled with poles and
the flats of their sabers against a pack of terrified, furious
sargis, wolves, who had struck out into the line.

Natalia looked pale. One of the young men had fallen
back, his right arm hanging limp. The struggle was made
more eerie still by its silence. The riders did not shout or
curse except to give terse commands.

"Should we move back, Mama?" asked Natalia suddenly.

"No," said Tess, caught up by the contest. "Those boys
would rather die than let those wolves break back through
the line. They won't get to us." Once, she had gone on such
a hunt in the front ranks; once she had turned back a great
cat, tawny and powerful. The memory made her heart pound
fiercely. "Never run away from what frightens you, Talia."

"Yuri once said he wished all the animals could get away
free."

"What do you wish?"

"I wish I was old enough to hunt."

Yipping, calling out to each other, the pack of wolves

broke away from the riders and turned and ran toward the center. Even now, as the day waned, Tess saw the grass move as animals were forced closer and closer together. Dark stains in the distance marked herds of grazing beasts driven against each other. This was not the greatest birbas Tess had ever ridden on. That one had started not with a circle but with a huge drive over hundreds of miles that formed only at the end into a circle, a hunt that had taken weeks and had taxed the army's skill at working as a unit, and under unity of command, to its limit. That birbas had been led by Mother Sakhalin, with her nephew Yaroslav and with Ilya at her side. Still, even now as they closed the ring, the ground teemed with wildlife.

They camped that night, and almost everyone stayed awake. It was almost impossible not to. Lions roared, wolves howled, and the restless, terrified calls and bleats of animals drifted on the air. Tess could smell their fear and, overwhelming it, the palpable excitement of the young women and men who were proving themselves on this birbas.

Natalia had already fallen asleep, muttering about how sorry Lara would be that she hadn't been able to go along because of her broken arm. Tess visited desultorily with Ilya's niece Nadine Orzhekov while watching the flow of visitors into and out of the field awning set up for Mother Orzhekov.

"The fact is," Nadine was saying, "that Lara's arm has healed enough that she could have come along, but I wouldn't let her. I won't trust her on a birbas until she's sixteen. She'll do something idiotic. Feodor would let her do anything. He doesn't care that she's headstrong and won't listen to reason because she always knows she can get him to do whatever she wants. She'll turn out just like—"

"Dina," said Tess abruptly, distracted by the appearance of a travel-worn old rider whom she didn't recognize in the circle of lanternlight that illuminated Mother Orzhekov and her court. "I think it's time for me to convince Ilya that you need to ride out with your jahar and get away from camp for a few months."

Nadine flushed angrily. "Don't patronize me!" Then, her mood changing, she shifted forward eagerly. "Do you think you could? I'm going crazy. I'll murder Feodor and the whole Grekov tribe if I don't get out of here. He's after me to get pregnant again. Aren't two girls enough?" Her voice was so plaintive that Tess felt suddenly sorry for her. "He's wild with jealousy that Galina has a boy, and by that no-good Sakhalin, too. He's utterly convinced that if we don't have a boy to become dyan after Bakhtiian dies that the Grekov tribe will lose all its influence again. As if they—"

"Good Lord," said Tess, breaking into this tirade. "Speak of the devil. Is that Andrei Sakhalin?"

Nadine flung her head around. "Gods!"

"What in hell is Andrei Sakhalin doing here?"

"Come back to see his wife give birth again, I don't doubt. Why else? He's certainly never distinguished himself more or less in battle than any other common soldier, so Galina is the only real power he has. Or at least, that's what Feodor thinks."

Tess snorted. "Feodor should talk."

Nadine flared at once. "Feodor has distinguished himself in battle many times! I'll thank you not to compare him to that good-for-nothing Andrei Sakhalin."

"Why is it, Dina, that you may criticize him, but no one else is allowed to?" But that was going too far. Nadine jumped to her feet and stalked away into the night. Tess shook her head and then got to her feet and walked over to Mother Orzhekov's awning, curious about Andrei Sakhalin's arrival. But he left just as she arrived, acknowledging her with a nod but nothing more, so Tess had to be content to sit down beside Irena Orzhekov's pillow.

"What is he here for?" she asked.

"He is traveling back to Sarai in order to celebrate the arrival of his next child. Tess—" Irena hesitated suddenly, and got a peculiar look on her face.

"Yes?" asked Tess after a moment when it became apparent that Irena was not going to go on.

"Nothing. Was that Nadine who walked off so suddenly?"

Nothing escaped Mother Orzhekov's keen eye, Tess reflected ruefully. "Yes. She needs to leave camp, you know."

"I know." Irena lifted a hand, dismissing all of the folk under the awning except her eldest daughter, Kira. Stassia and Sonia had stayed in Sarai, and those of her grandchildren who rode on this birbas were old enough to ride in the front ranks or else were in charge of the fires and the horses. "My nephew has developed a bad habit of keeping close to him for too long a few people for whom he feels overly responsible, and whose welfare he has taken onto himself as a gods-given obligation when in fact he ought to be freeing them to make their own mistakes and their own decisions."

"Are you criticizing your nephew, Mother Orzhekov?" asked Tess, biting down on a smile. She enjoyed hearing Irena Orzhekov cut Ilya down to size.

"I have not yet begun on you, my daughter," replied Irena mildly.

"I have argued before that it is time to release Nadine from camp," said Kira. "Birthing is difficult for her. There are enough Orzhekov children from which to choose the next Orzhekov dyan."

"Yes," agreed Irena, "but we have agreed that a child with the vision is more likely to come from the line whose grandfather was a Singer, that is, from the line of Alyona Orzhekov and Petre Sokolov."

"But Nadine has two daughters now, who will in time have children," argued Kira. "They may prove stronger. Anyway, I'm going to strangle her one of these days. I'm surprised I haven't done it yet. She complains constantly about Feodor, but the fact is, he knows exactly how to play her, so that for all that she grumbles and whines about the influence of the Grekov tribe, she still takes their side without realizing she does so."

"Nadine's strength does not lie in diplomacy," said Tess.

"Spoken kindly," retorted Kira.

"Let her go," said Tess softly. "Let her take her jahar and lead an expedition—oh, anywhere. Let her go south to Kirill Zvertkov's army, or farther south still on a reconnaissance. We know little about the lands south and east of Jeds. There are some interesting manuscripts coming north to us from Byblos." Like the anatomy manuscript Ilya had been looking at. Tess was impressed by the Byblene scholars; they were strangely ahead of their time.

"Leaving Feodor to raise the children?" Kira asked sarcastically.

Irena coughed. "In fact, Feodor is a good father. He might have made a good etsana's husband, had he only married one. He would not indulge Lara so much if it didn't irritate Nadine. But I think you are right, Tess. Nadine has given our tent two healthy daughters. If her heart lies elsewhere, then I think we may safely let her go."

Tess chuckled, low in her throat. "I know what she would

like most. Do you recall Marco Burckhardt, the khaja man
who rode with my brother's court?"

"I do," said Irena.

"The one Sonia took as a lover," Kira said.

"The same. Nadine and Marco could travel into the southern lands, or east along the Golden Road, without a jahar.
They could bring back far more valuable intelligence that
way, and travel as far and as long as they please."

"That would be dangerous."

"Exactly. Now we must only convince Ilya to agree."

"My nephew will agree once I have spoken to him."

There was no answer to that. Tess kissed Irena and Kira
on either cheek, in the formal style, and went to curl up in
the blanket with Natalia.

On the final day Tess held Natalia back from the front
ranks as the army closed the animals into an arena circum-
scribed by their own line of advance. This part of the hunt
she did not like as well, because it reminded her too much
of a siege. When Irena Orzhekov rode forward through the
lines to let loose the first arrow, as was her right and duty,
Tess could not bring herself to let Natalia, who was after all
not yet eight years old, go along and watch.

"But, Mama—!"

"It isn't safe. You couldn't see anyway."

But they could hear the howling and screams of the animals, muted by the cheers of the riders. Tess was reminded
suddenly and bitterly of the first—and as it happened the
last—battle she had actually fought in. She remembered
eleven-year-old Katerina finishing off wounded khaja soldiers with a dagger up through the palate, not enjoying it but
simply doing it because it had to be done. Was that what she
wanted for Natalia and Yuri?

Natalia, fuming, eyed her with a blend of rebellion and
resignation. She was not quite ready to go directly against
her mother's wishes. "Papa would let me go," she said suddenly, trying a new line of attack.

"He isn't here."

"I'm going anyway!"

Tess stared her down. Natalia began to sniff and then to
cry. "Oh, Talia. . . ."

"Tess! Tess!" Like her uncle, Nadine had never shown
much interest in hunting, going along mostly because it was
expected of her.

At this moment, Tess was glad to see her. "Why did you leave?"

"Nothing interesting left to watch. I think Mother Orzhekov is going to break the circle early. Talia, whatever are you crying for? Tess, did you hear about Vasha?"

"About Vasha?"

A roar went up from the assembled army. Tess grabbed for the reins of Natalia's horse and steadied Zhashi with her knees. They were not in the direct line of escape, but as the first animals broke for freedom in the gaps opening for them in the ring, it was like a force of nature roiling forth. The ground shuddered with their running. With shrieks of laughter and fierce yells, bands of mounted archers raced after the fleeing animals. The simple energy of it sent Tess's adrenaline rocketing, and she laughed. Natalia watched with wide eyes as the arena collapsed and wild animals of all sizes, riders galloping after them, dispersed back into the plains.

After a long while, the army that still remained formed into orderly groups and began the ride back to Sarai. Tess let go of Natalia's reins and swung Zhashi around to fall in beside Nadine. "Were you saying something about Vasha? Did Andrei Sakhalin bring word from his brother's army? Vasha isn't—!" She broke off, but the twinge of worry faded as quickly, because Nadine looked positively smug, as she only did when she saw trouble brewing for someone else. Yes, it was long past time to get her out of camp.

"No, Andrei Sakhalin didn't bring back word of Vasha from Yaroslav Sakhalin's army. He brought back Vasha. In disgrace."

"What! But then Irena must have known last night . . . why didn't she tell me?"

"She didn't want you riding back to Sarai to intervene, no doubt."

"It's nothing to laugh about! In disgrace. What does that mean?"

"How should I know? Except I caught up to him last night, to Andrei Sakhalin, that is, and he reports that Yaroslav was disgusted with Vasha's behavior and threw him out."

"Oh, gods. Talia, I want you to find Mother Orzhekov and ride with her."

"But, Mama, I want to ride with you!"

"Talia, my love, I don't have time to argue. Do what I say."

"Yes, Mama."

"Dina, give me your horse."

"No. You have your own string. Can I come with you?"

"Vulture," said Tess. Nadine only laughed.

Tess was far too worried to try to stop Nadine from coming with her. She did not even bother to stop to remonstrate with Irena Orzhekov, who would feel no need to defend her decision in any case. She paused only long enough to make sure that Natalia was safely under her grandmother's wing.

Then she and Nadine rode in stages, back across the rolling plain to Sarai. Even so, the jahar they followed rode faster. She reached Sarai six days later without having met up with it.

Riding up behind her own great tent, seeing Ilya's golden banner flapping peacefully at the top, Tess hoped wildly that perhaps, just perhaps, she and Nadine had beaten the jahar to Sarai. But when she dismounted and came around front, handing off her horse to one of the guards, she saw a scene that dismayed her. The ring of guards had been pulled up tight against the tent, as if the tent itself was under siege . . . or had walled itself off against outside interference.

"Mama! Mama!" Yuri ran to her from Sonia's tent. She scooped him up and kissed him. "Papa won't let anyone in the tent. He's very angry at Vasha."

Tess looked Yuri over and reassured herself that he was healthy. "What do you mean he won't let anyone in the tent?" She set him down and marched over to her awning, placing herself squarely in front of Konstans Barshai, who stood at attention, fully armed, together with nine of his men. "Where is my husband?"

"Inside the tent."

"Why? Is it true as my son tells me that he refuses to see anyone?"

"No, Cousin," said Konstans, lapsing into the formal style, so that Tess understood that he was acting wholly in his capacity as dyan of Ilya's personal guard, "he refuses to see the young man known as Vassily Kireyevsky, who has brought disgrace onto this tent."

"Where is the young man known as Vassily Kireyevsky?"

He pointed with his spear.

The central tents of the Orzhekov tribe were laid out

around the huge tent that served as Mother Orzhekov's residence. All tent entrances faced east to let in the light of the rising run, and Tess had sited her tent so that she could see the central plaza and the library to the front and, horizontally, the awning and carpets that marked the entrance of Mother Orzhekov's residence. It was unnaturally quiet for this time of day, midmorning. To the left, Sonia sat under her awning and wove. She lifted a hand to acknowledge Tess's arrival but curiously did not move to come greet her. Nadine practically bounced, she was so excited.

"That's him!" Nadine said loudly. "That's Vasha. Why is he sitting there under the awning with Niko?"

Holding Yuri's hand, Tess walked over to Mother Orzhekov's great tent, Nadine hard on her heels. It was indeed Niko, sitting composedly on a pillow and playing. . . .

Khot! Tess stared.

Vasha sat hunched over the board. He always looked intense, but sitting there playing khot with Niko he seemed to have honed that intensity to such a fine point that it was painful to look at him. He was concentrating all his attention, all his nerves, on the game itself. When he reached out to set down a stone, his hand trembled.

Niko grunted. He glanced up, took note of Tess, and looked back down at the board. "Well, my boy, I think you've won again."

A pained noise came out of Vasha's throat, forced through closed lips. Clearly, winning at khot even against as wily and experienced a player as Niko gave him no pleasure. His dark skin had a leached-out undertone, as if he were sick or sick at heart. His black hair looked unkempt.

"Shall we play again?" asked Niko in the voice he might use to quiet a nervous horse.

"Why do you keep me sitting out here?" said Vasha through gritted teeth. "I feel like an idiot."

"It's good training."

Tess could tell by the shift of Vasha's shoulders that he was about to protest. Abruptly his shoulders sagged, and he gave in. "Very well. Another game." Then, alerted by Yuri coming to crouch down next to him, he looked up and saw Tess.

He went red. His body stiffened and his expression froze into a rictus of shame and dread that struck Tess dumb.

Nadine drew in breath to speak. Vasha leapt up and fled into the safety of Mother Orzhekov's great tent.

"Vasha?" Yuri stood and pushed past the tent flap to follow Vasha inside.

"Well!" said Nadine into the silence.

Niko gathered up the knot stones.

"What happened?" asked Tess, kneeling down to help him. She was shocked to find her hands shaking.

Niko cleared his throat. "There was an unfortunate scene. That was yesterday."

"Why are you sitting out here playing khot with Vasha?"

"To make sure that everyone sees him, to see that both Stassia and Sonia Orzhekov, as representatives of their mother, accede to his presence under the Orzhekov awning."

"As I recall, Niko, you were among those who expressed misgivings about bringing a boy into my tent on the strength of khaja inheritance laws, by acknowledging Ilya as his father."

Niko smiled down at the khot board, a musing smile. Then he slanted his gaze up at Tess. "It is true I did not approve of the khaja inheritance laws then. Nor do I now. Nor will I ever. It is also true that Vassily is young and has a great deal to learn, and has conducted himself badly. But you adopted him as your son, Tess. That counts for a great deal. And, gods," he shook his head admiringly, "the boy can play khot!"

CHAPTER SEVENTEEN

A Ring of Guards

When they came across scouts from the great birbas, Riasonovsky suddenly turned stubborn.

"No," he said to Vasha, "you may not go to Mother Orzhekov or to the Prince of Jeds. My orders were to deliver you to Bakhtiian, and Bakhtiian is in Sarai. That is where we are going."

So they rode on. With each dawn Vasha grew more nervous until he reached such a high pitch of anxiety that he thought he would burst. By the time Sarai rose out of the plains, an exotic blend of jaran camp and khaja city, he could only choke out one-word answers—when anyone bothered to address a comment to him, which wasn't often.

They rode into the city. The khaja along the avenue spared them not a second glance. But as they moved into the great jaran camp, they gained a second escort: children and elders, mostly, all those who had not ridden out on the birbas and were eager for some excitement. Vasha endured their presence without flinching. First Katerina began to wave and call out to people she knew, then Stefan. He heard his own name called, but he had to keep his eyes fixed on Riasonovsky or he would not have the courage to ride up to Tess Soerensen's tent. The closer they got, the more his vision narrowed, until at last he saw the gold banner in the distance, riding ever closer, ever closer, until he could see Mother Orzhekov's huge tent beyond, could make out the colors and patterns on the walls of Tess's great tent, could see the awning itself where a dark-haired man sat on a pillow playing khot with Stefan's grandfather Niko while a soldier read to him from a report. Vasha thought he could practically read the words on the parchment, his sight had grown so keen and so focused.

Bakhtiian looked up. He jumped to his feet.

As if in slow motion, Riasonovsky dismounted and

walked forward to speak to Bakhtiian. All the while he
talked, and it went on and on and on until Vasha thought
probably the whole day had passed and another one taken its
place, Bakhtiian stared straight at Vasha.

In one more instant his father's stare was going to obliterate him. Misri stood with perfect stillness, his only ally,
even as Vasha's hands convulsed on the reins. And all the
while Bakhtiian's expression grew colder and more furious.

Riasonovsky finished speaking and, as if in precaution,
took one step back.

There was silence. Vasha hoped it would last forever.

"Katya!" That was Aunt Sonia's voice, full of joy. "My
dear girl—" But her voice faltered, swallowed by the stillness that radiated out from Bakhtiian.

When he spoke finally, his voice was not loud but so clear
and cutting, so steeped in rage, that it resounded through the
assembly.

"I turn my face away from him. I will not see him." He
turned and walked into the tent.

At once, a ring of guards closed in around the tent. Vasha
just sat there, numb. His ears filled with a roaring, like a
river rushing past. He stared at the awning. A few shapes
moved around underneath the awning, men, guards, but it
was empty of what mattered. His father had repudiated him.
His worst dream had come true.

Fingers touched his arm. He jerked so hard that Misri
sidestepped until Stefan caught her bridle and stopped her.

"Vasha! Dismount, you idiot. You'll just look worse if
you sit up there and gape. Come to Grandmother's tent."

After a moment he realized that it was *Katerina* who was
talking to him. He swung down reflexively from the saddle
and let her lead him away, but he could not help but look
back over his shoulder toward the tent. Perhaps in another
moment his father would emerge and agree to talk to him, to
let him explain what had happened, to just see—

"Vasha!" Katerina hissed. "Don't look back. Look dignified."

"I have to talk to him," he blurted out, and wrenched
away from her and half-ran back to the tent. His father's
guards crossed their spears before him. "Just let me talk to
him!" Vasha cried. "Konstans!" he pleaded, fixing his gaze
on Konstans Barshai, who had taught him saber. "Just let me
in, just—" He faltered.

Konstans, stone-faced, made no reply, only blocked Vasha's path. This time, when Katerina took hold of Vasha's arm, she got a good strong grip and tugged him along so hard that he stumbled backward, trying to turn himself.

"I said come with me, you fool!" she said in a low voice. She dragged him all the way to Mother Orzhekov's great tent and shoved him all over the threshold and inside, where he found his Aunts Stassia and Sonia and a mob of young, curious cousins.

"Go to the back, Vassily," said Aunt Sonia curtly. "We are making a bath for you. I want you clean. Katya, you will tell us what has happened."

He waited at the back while a big metal tub was filled with steaming water. No one spoke to him, not even the littlest ones. But he was glad of it, since his throat was thick with grief. He could hear a discussion going on at the front, but it passed in a haze. Someone, he wasn't sure who, drew a curtain closed, screening off the bath, and he undressed mechanically and sank down into the water. Just sat there, staring at the tent wall. It was an old panel, fading: Wolves chased a stag.

"Vasha?" The merest whisper. The curtain stirred. Yuri slipped through. "Shhh. Don't tell anyone I'm here." Yuri put two fingers to his lips and grinned. "I *missed* you. I'm glad you came back." He set his hands on the edge of the tub and leaned forward and kissed Vasha on the cheek. "Why is Papa angry with you?" It was said so innocently by him, who could not imagine his adored older brother doing anything wrong.

Vasha began to cry. The more he dug his nails into his palms, the more he bit his lower lip, to try and stop himself, the more the tears ran from his eyes.

Troubled, Yuri watched him. "Well," said Yuri matter-of-factly, "everything will be all right when Mama gets back."

Only it wasn't. Stassia and Sonia treated him courteously, even perhaps with some sympathy, but coolly. He slept in one of the side chambers of Mother Orzhekov's tent. Only three people visited him: Stefan and Niko Sibirin, and, once, Katerina, who frowned at him for the longest time and then got up and went way without saying anything. Niko made him sit outside under the awning and play khot, and Vasha's humiliation was complete, to be put on show like that. The only way to ignore the stares he *knew* were being directed at him was to focus on the game so completely that he didn't notice anything else.

That was why he never noticed Tess's arrival until she stood not four paces from him, regarding him with pity. Even with Niko's remonstrations echoing in his ears, he jumped up and retreated inside the tent, into the tiny closed-off chamber, because he could not bear to face her. She had given him everything. At that moment, sitting in darkness on a pillow, wringing his hands, he wasn't sure which was worse: his father's anger or her compassion. He sat there for a long, long time, alone. Finally he lay down. He had been strung too tight last night to sleep. Now, in the stuffy tent, he dozed.

Someone lay down next to him, embraced him, pressed against him. He rolled over. "Mmm? Katya!" That woke him up.

"Shhh."

"What are you—?" But it was obvious what she was doing. Her body was agreeably familiar to him, and his to her, as if his hands remembered their old paths better than his mind did. Gods, he was angry at her for treating him so badly for the past months, but all that suddenly didn't seem quite so important. For a brief while, he forgot the rest of the world.

Until Katerina, collapsed on top of him afterward, promptly reminded him of them. "Oh, Vasha," she said, a little out of breath still, "I didn't know *this* would happen. I'm sorry."

He ran a hand down her back, confused, and only then realized what she was talking about. He pushed her off him and she toppled back onto the carpet. "Do you mean you just came in here by way of *apology?*"

"I—"

"I'll thank you to leave me alone!" He sat up, humiliated, and began to put his clothes back on.

"Vasha" She hesitated, heard voices nearby, and hastily began getting her clothes back on. "That isn't fair."

He grunted, turning his back on her.

"Well, you can scarcely blame me for disliking the way you rode into Sakhalin's army, expecting everyone to treat you like a prince when you'd never even proven yourself yet. It just annoyed me so knowing that you'd ride all the way back here in disgrace only to have Cousin Ilya forgive you and pretend nothing had happened."

"Forgive me! Of course he wouldn't forgive me. Any fool can see that. He's furious."

Katerina shrugged on her blouse and belted it over her skirts. "It's what he always did before. Why should it be different this time?"

"What he always did before?" Vasha was so stunned by this comment that he sat and stared at Katerina, shirt hanging loose in one hand.

She pulled on a boot, not looking at him. "He's always coddled you, Vasha. I was just wrong in thinking he would do the same thing this time."

"He's never coddled me!" But the exclamation trailed off into silence, and he only watched as Katya stood up, straightened her clothes, and listened intently.

"Tess is coming inside," she said. "I am sorry. I wouldn't have been so angry with you if I'd thought Cousin Ilya would be. I just thought it would be bad for you if someone didn't make you realize that you have to—"

There was a discreet cough from outside. Blushing, Vasha tugged on his shirt, got an arm in the neck, cursed, and finally pulled it on just as Tess pushed aside the curtain and stepped inside the tiny chamber. Katya flashed her a shamefaced smile and retreated at once. Vasha buckled on his belt and hoped furiously that Tess would not notice what he was doing. Then he fixed his gaze on his knuckles. There was yet a slight sheen of the hunt on her, and it disturbed him. And he was horribly embarrassed. And terrified of what she was going to say.

"I have heard several reports," she said finally. "But I would like to hear your report."

"I made a fool of myself," he mumbled.

"I beg your pardon. I couldn't hear that."

"I don't *like* Yaroslav Sakhalin," he burst out, flinging his head up. "He treated me like—" He broke off, clamping down on his tongue. *Like Mother Kireyevsky treated me.*

"I hear that he expected you to do what every boy who joins the army does: care for the horses, help with the herds, do duties here and around for the soldiers."

"I was older than the other boys. Why couldn't *he* have let me go to the army earlier?" He hated himself even as he said it, for the whining tone.

"A good question."

He wrenched his gaze back down to his knuckles. "Whatever Katya told you is probably true. I didn't like Sakhalin. He didn't like me. We never got along. But it was stupid of me to steal those horses and to convince the others to go along with the plan. And we didn't mean to steal Princess Rusudani, too."

"I'm curious. If you'd gone as a Kireyevsky rider, do you suppose Sakhalin would have liked you?"

The question was so odd that it silenced him. Tess waited him out. "If I'd gone as a Kireyevsky rider, Yaroslav Sakhalin would never have noticed me at all, unless I distinguished myself in battle."

"Yes. Well, do what Niko says, for now, and what your aunts and grandmother say, of course. How many times did you beat Niko at khot anyway?"

"I don't know. We just played."

Tess made a little sound, and he glanced up at her and saw that she was holding back a laugh. Anger flared, but he fought it down. How could she laugh?

"Niko says you're a fine khot player. I don't take praise given by Niko lightly." She kissed him on the forehead and left.

Vasha stared at the curtain as it swayed to stillness, leaving him alone again. He had known Tess would not be furious with him, not in the way his father had been. She would scold him, take him to task, expect him to think about what he might learn from the situation—and suddenly Katya's accusation, that his father coddled him, flashed back into his mind. He had a sudden, bothersome idea that she was right. Bakhtiian did not treat him the same way he treated Natalia and Yuri. It was as if there was a line Bakhtiian could never quite bring himself to cross, as if he didn't think it was his *right*.

The thought plunged Vasha into gloom. He shut his eyes and rested his head on his hands. In the end, of course, the dream was just that, a dream. Any fool could see that he was not truly Ilya Bakhtiian's son.

Tess swept into her tent, took one look at her husband's grim expression, and swept out without saying a word to him. Sonia waited for her outside, but Tess kept walking and did not speak until they stood out on the grass between the tents, away from anyone who might overhear.

"Well?" Sonia asked.

"If I talk to him now, we'll have a fight, and he'll only get more stubborn."

"Should I go in?" Sonia cocked her head to one side. "Ah. You are right. When a man feuds with his son, it is not a woman's matter."

"I would not want to be there when Irena goes in."

"Mother may take his part in this. What makes you think that anyone in this tribe will support Vasha except for you? Has he proven himself worthy of being an Orzhekov son?"

"He has not yet been given a chance to prove himself. He should have gone to Yaroslav Sakhalin sooner or not at all."

"Why are you trying to convince *me,* Tess?"

"Niko says he plays khot much better than his father."

"I can assure you that most people in the tribes accept Ilya as his father only through his connection with you. I'm sorry, but I won't interfere, and I will counsel our mother not to interfere either. If Ilya's councillors and generals choose to take Vassily's part, then so be it. If they do not. . . ."

"What in hell's name am I going to do with Vasha if they don't? I can't just abandon him. Or, God forbid, force him to be a servant like he was in the Kireyevsky tribe. Do I send him to Jeds? Marry him to a khaja princess so he can have some kind, any kind, of position?"

Their eyes met. With one thought, they both turned and looked toward the distant scatter of tents, pitched beyond the Sakhalin tribe, that housed the khaja hostages, and now housed with them the princess, Rusudani Mirametis, daughter of Prince Zakaria of Tarsina-Kars, granddaughter of King Barsauma of Mircassia, and cousin of Prince Basil of Filis. They had heard the whole story from Katerina, corroborated in a tense interview with a deeply-shamed Stefan.

"In Erthe, in older times," said Tess slowly, "a man who captured a woman under such circumstances had the right to marry her."

"How barbaric!"

"Oh, Sonia! Is that really so different from a man riding into a tribe and marking a woman who does not want him?"

"Of course it is!" said Sonia indignantly. "*We* are not savages."

'Oh, of course not."

"It may not be your choice to make. Are you going to try to discuss Vassily with Ilya?"

"Not now. Ilya won't mind being angry with me. That would only feed his anger."

"Then wait and see what Niko and Josef do. See what his senior captains, Konstans Barshai and the others, counsel. You cannot make the tribe keep Vassily here simply because you will it to be so. The boy will never be able to live in the Orzhekov tribe now if the tribe itself does not want him here."

"I'll wait a few days. Poor child. He was already thrown out once."

"He is not a child anymore. That should be evident."

"Umm, yes. Katya has taken up with him again, I think."

Sonia did not respond to this feint, and Tess was forced to follow her meekly back to her tent and attend to more domestic chores.

Vasha endured the Orzhekov camp for another day, but on the evening of the second he could bear their forbearance no longer. He fled to the part of the camp where the khaja hostages and envoys lived. A small group of people had gathered at the end of the line of tents closest to Sarai. He paused to look them over. He was surprised to see the priest, Brother Saghir. When the priest recognized him, he smiled at Vasha, beckoning him over.

"What are these people doing?" Vasha asked him.

"They have come to receive the recitation of the Lord's Word. Some of these people already belong to the faithful, and it has been years since a priest of our Order has come among them. Others seek to learn more of God's law."

"It is good to be reminded of the gods' laws," agreed Vasha, "since it is by their favor that the jaran have gained so much."

" 'Those whom God favors have also a greater responsibility,' " replied Brother Saghir instantly. He had an answer for everything, rather like Tess did. But Vasha had never once seen Tess worship any god. "Likewise, in another place, 'If more is given you, then also ought you to love more.' If the jaran and their Bakhtiian have been given much, then by Whose hand has this been done? By the idols, by the thousand demons named as gods by the ignorant? No,

by the hand of God Almighty, Who made heaven and earth
and all kingdoms upon it, and by the grace of His anointed
Son, who was sundered and yet lived again so that we might
be granted a vision of the power of life over death."

"My father was granted a vision by the gods," said Vasha,
and then cringed, cursing himself inwardly. His father was
not his father at all; Bakhtiian had already repudiated him.

Brother Saghir nodded gravely, whether at Vasha's statement or with a mysterious knowledge of Vasha's plight. He
had a sallow complexion and black hair, and though he was
not much older than Vassily himself, he carried himself as a
man does, not as a boy. "For every man and woman there is
the hope of salvation, if he will only hear God's word, if she
will only take unto heart the Pilgrim's journey."

"Is that true?" Vasha asked wistfully.

The appearance of Princess Rusudani distracted him from
Brother Saghir's answer. She arrived in great state: Her servant, Jaelle, walked three paces behind her, and behind them
came three soldiers walking and four riding, with Stefan at
the tail end of the procession. Brother Saghir left Vasha immediately and hurried forward to bow in front of the princess. The townspeople parted to let them through, and
Brother Saghir busied himself setting out a table as an altar,
covering it with a cloth sewn of gold fabric and setting on
the cloth a large carved box and several cups.

Rusudani knelt at the front of the gathering, in front of the
altar. Jaelle knelt farther back, with the people gathered from
Sarai. Vasha sidled over to stand next to Stefan.

"What are they doing?" Stefan asked.

"They've come to pray," said the soldier in charge,
Gennady Berezin. He was Vasha's uncle by marriage, having
been married to Anna Orzhekov, the sister who had died
years before Vasha came to the tribe. "They have all sorts of
strange khaja rituals, but they can't help it, since they know
nothing of the true gods."

"They read from their book," said Vasha, desperately
wanting to impress Berezin with his knowledge. "And they
sing. Then they pour the wine on the ground. But I don't
know why."

"Jaelle says they do not worship in the right way," said
Stefan suddenly. "She comes from a different place."

Berezin snorted and Stefan looked embarrassed. "If she

worships a different God, then why does she worship with her mistress here?"

"No, it is the same God, but. . . ."

Several of the soldiers in attendance chuckled, while on the grass near the altar the congregation sang softly and rather off-key in a language Vasha did not recognize.

"If it is the same God, then how can they worship differently?" demanded Berezin. "My boy, you had better learn that the khaja are all savages. I grant you she has a pleasing enough face, but there is a proper jaran girl waiting for you out on the plains, no doubt."

Stefan clenched his hands and refused to reply.

"Have you been talking to her?" Vasha whispered in his ear.

"A man is allowed to talk to a woman!" Stefan lapsed into an indignant silence.

The soldiers settled in for a long wait as the congregation alternated singing and listening. The three on foot hunkered down; Berezin whittled at a stick of wood. The riders dismounted and led their horses around the periphery, reappearing at intervals. Dusk bled to twilight and twilight faded into night. Stars filled the sky. Brother Saghir circled the congregation with a lit lantern bobbing up and down in front of him like a beacon, and when he returned to the altar he spoke rhythmic words to the congregation which they repeated back to him.

Vasha could not help but stare at Rusudani. She swayed in time to Brother Saghir's speaking, and he had a feeling that she alone of the gathered was speaking the words to herself along with the priest. Her dark head was bent submissively, her hands clasped and pressed against her breast. Vasha felt uncomfortable all of a sudden, and he walked around a little bit to work off his nerves.

Finally, Brother Saghir poured a full cup of red wine out on the ground and first Rusudani and after her the others in turn came forward to touch the damp earth, their way lighted by Brother Saghir with the lantern. Then Brother Saghir opened the wooden box and lifted out a loaf of bread, they sang a final song, and that seemed to signal the end of their worship.

The townspeople filtered away toward Sarai. Rusudani's escort reassembled and she walked with dignity back into their guard. Jaelle, behind her, glanced toward Stefan and away. Poor Stefan looked pathetically gratified by that scrap of attention.

Suddenly, Rusudani looked straight toward Vasha. "Brother Saghir tells me you spoke with him about the word of God," she said; that is, she spoke the words in her tongue and Jaelle translated them into Taor.

Vasha was horrified and ecstatic together. "Yes," he managed to reply. By the light of the lanterns held by her escort, Rusudani's face glowed mysteriously.

"What does she say?" asked Berezin. Vasha was so thrilled by the old soldier's interest that he could hardly reply for fear of saying something stupid.

"She says, she saw, that I spoke with her priest about their God."

"And did you speak with him?"

"I did." On this ground, Vasha felt sure of himself. "It is always wise to learn the ways of the khaja, so that we may rule them more wisely."

Berezin lifted an expressive eyebrow. "That is true, and sensibly said."

Vasha felt the fierce pain of hope, like Brother Saghir's promised salvation. If a soldier like Berezin spoke in his favor ... but Berezin was already moving off, saying something to one of his riders about some of the straggling townspeople.

Rusudani was talking again, and Jaelle translated. "Princess Rusudani says that she had heard that there were followers of the True Faith among the jaran, but that when she came among you she saw that it was not so. For this reason she feared you." Jaelle looked nervous saying these words. Vasha, risking a glance full at Rusudani's face, did not think the princess looked afraid. She looked more annoyed than anything, as if she wasn't sure she could trust her servant to translate correctly. "But Sister Yvanne brought her to a fuller knowledge of God's will, and if that means that she must follow the path of the Pilgrim, Our Holy Sister, then so will she follow that path."

Berezin signaled, and the guard formed around Rusudani, herding her away. She went without a backward glance for Vasha. Vasha wanted to follow her, to speak to her again, but he did not dare to. What if Berezin did not approve? What did it matter what Berezin thought, anyway, if Bakhtiian had already turned against him?

"What am I going to do?" he asked the air, wanting to cry, but he could not.

From the altar, Brother Saghir looked up at him, hearing his tone if not understanding the words. "I will pray with you, if you wish, Prince Vasil'ii," he said sympathetically, and Vasha winced away from the title, knowing he had no right to it.

"Come on," said Stefan. "I know an inn in Sarai where we can get drunk in peace." He took Vasha by the arm and drew him away.

But Vasha shook loose of him and went over to Brother Saghir first. "I thank you," he said, not sure whether he was thanking the khaja priest for his sympathy or for his kind-hearted ignorance, giving Vasha the title he so badly wished for, that of prince, a true prince, acknowledged as such by khaja and jaran.

Then, because it seemed the best solution to his pain, he went with Stefan and got blindingly drunk.

After three days, a delegation of older men requested permission, through Konstans Barshai, who diligently maintained the ring of guards around the tent, to see Bakhtiian. Tess could not quite bring herself to go directly in with them, but she could not stand to miss the confrontation, so she simply let herself into the inner chamber through the unsewn back flap and peeked through the curtain.

There were five men, Niko Sibirin, Sonia's husband Josef Raevsky, Kira and Stassia's husbands, and Gennady Berezin. They sat, as was their right, and Josef refused help in finding a pillow to sit on until Ilya himself, shamed by Josef's blind groping, helped him. Niko acted as spokesman.

"Why have you grown angry, Bakhtiian?" he asked.

Ilya glowered at them and did not answer.

"The Habakar king fled from your wrath and came to a bad end, and now his cities and his people belong to the tribes. Our armies are rich, and with each day they continue to advance southward. People of three different faiths bow to our governors. How can you remain angry?"

Still Ilya did not reply, but his hands shifted restlessly on his knees.

"The child knows he has done wrong," continued Niko, "but now he is afraid of your anger. If you continue in this way, you will break his spirit. Let him see you."

The other men nodded in agreement. The silence lasted a long time, but these were men who were both willing and able to wait Ilya out. After a while, Niko unfolded a khot board and got out some stones and he and Josef commenced playing a game.

Yuri poked his head through the back flap, and Tess, with a hand over her mouth, waved him away. Ilya had responded to the provocation of the game by pressing his mouth together more firmly and refusing to be drawn, but like the others he could not help but watch. Josef was the finest khot player in the Orzhekov tribe. He used an unpolished set of stones, and he played by touch, his fingers fluttering across the board, lightly marking each stone as it was laid down in order to memorize its position. When the game ended, with Josef winning as usual, Ilya stirred.

"Very well."

When Niko brought him before the tent, and Konstans Barshai pulled back his spear in order to let Vasha through, Vassily shuddered, a shock wave passing through him so hard and fast that at first he could not step forward.

He heard Bakhtiian's voice say, "Send him in," and he felt for an instant as if he had never heard that voice before. Memory hit him, staggering him: Eight years ago he had stood before this tent a tribeless, kinless child of eleven, thrown on the mercy of the Orzhekov tribe, and been called in to stand before the man who would pass judgment on him with those same sharp words.

Except that in the end Tess Soerensen, not Bakhtiian, had made a choice whose repercussions had, perhaps inevitably, led him to this moment when Bakhtiian would repudiate him once and for all.

Niko nudged him, and with the old man beside him, he forced himself to push past the entrance flap and go inside. Konstans Barshai followed them in, as if to guard Bakhtiian against the threat Vasha posed, and after him a handful of other men. Vasha did not really see them.

Bakhtiian sat on a pillow, a closed book balanced on his left knee, covered by a hand, and his other hand in a fist on the carpet beside him. Vasha scarcely had time to draw breath before Bakhtiian started in.

"I have satisfied myself that the report I have heard of your behavior is true. Do you dispute it?"

Vasha shook his head numbly.

"Is this the way a child of the Orzhekov tribe is expected to conduct himself? Do we train our boys to grow up into men who will steal women out of the sanctity of the tents—"

That was *too* much. "We didn't steal her! She ran to us—"

"Silence! I did not ask you to speak. Can an army march when the soldiers will not obey their captain? Truly, 'the boy who does not respect his uncle will never learn to fight.' Is a boy's judgment to be honored above that of a man? If the children of the jaran refuse to respect the wisdom of their elders, why should the gods grant us their favor any longer?"

The force of Bakhtiian's anger felt like heat, melting him. The worst of it was, this was just the beginning.

"When the tribes first came to earth and their tents spread from the west to the east, there were two brothers, Mstislav and Daniil. Now Daniil had but a single eye in the middle of his forehead, and with this eye he could see as far distant a place as would take a man three days to ride. One day he saw a tribe riding toward them, and he spied a young woman riding in their midst who was as fair as the dawn. At once he asked his brother to ride down and see what this tribe was, so that he might marry the young woman. Mstislav agreed, and he rode down to the tribe, but coming before her, he fell in love with her as well. But because he had given his brother his sworn word, he did not mark the woman, but instead marked her older sister, who was also unmarried. Daniil rode into the tribe as well, and he marked the younger sister. So came the brothers into the tribe."

Vasha could not have moved even if he had wanted to. Although, outside, the season was turning, he found it inexplicably stuffy in the tent, and he sweated and sweated.

"Mstislav's wife bore two daughters and four sons, and Daniil's wife bore four daughters and two sons, but all those years Mstislav nursed his jealousy against his brother, and this jealousy he passed down into his sons' hearts.

"In time Mstislav passed away, but his sons nursed their father's resentment against their uncle Daniil. They did not leave to marry women in other tribes because their grievance had blinded them to their duty."

Vasha was beginning to feel faint. Sweat trickled down the small of his back. His feet felt so hot and swollen that it hurt to stand on them.

"One day when the jahar rode out to scout, Daniil saw a

jahar of an enemy tribe riding toward them, still three days off. He alerted the jahar and they turned and rode into the broken lands to protect themselves. The four brothers refused to believe him. They had seen no signs of a large force nearby. They remained in the valley where the grass was sweet and plentiful. The other jahar arrived at dawn on the third day and killed them.

"Any man I name dyan in my armies is as an uncle to you, and any boy who will not heed the word of his uncle is as good as dead to his tribe."

The tirade went on. Vasha lost track of words and then phrases and then whole portions as he concentrated more and more on simply not toppling over. He began to hear, not the words, but the spate of words and the pauses during which Bakhtiian took breath to start in again.

During a pause, a new voice broke in, staggering Vasha with its placidity.

"All of these words are true," said Niko slowly, "but what is the point of abusing the boy at such length? If you end by putting fear in his heart, then how will he ever learn what to do in war? He is young. Like an immature eagle, his first strike may fail to capture his chosen prey."

Then Konstans spoke. "Why strike with your anger against the boy? We have enemies enough. Set us loose against them, and the gods will give us greater strength, greater riches, and many more people to rule. You need only to ask, 'Which people?' and I would tell you that the king of Mircassia and the prince of Filis alone prevent us from ruling all the lands between the plains and Jeds. Let us strike at them now and with such fury that they will scatter and run and beg to become our servants."

There was a long silence.

Bakhtiian stirred finally. For the first time his gaze shifted away from Vasha. Vasha's knees almost gave out. "It is past time for me to rejoin the army, and to call in Zvertkov's army to join with Sakhalin's in the attack against Mircassia and Filis. Between those two swords, the khaja will fall." He paused. "The boy can go to Kirill Zvertkov, providing he behaves himself. He may ride with us southward until we meet up with Zvertkov's jahar."

He lifted a hand, to signal that the audience was over.

Vasha gaped. So casually came the reprieve. At first he was too stunned to feel anything. Hard on that came shame:

Shame, that Katya had been right. Bakhtiian coddled him, in
the wrong way, making things easy for him because, perhaps
. . . well, how could he know why? A real father would have
been less lenient.

But I will prove myself worthy, he said, voicing the words
soundlessly. Aware that the other men watched him, he accepted the pronouncement with a cool nod, turned without
haste, and walked out of the tent on steady legs. But it was
too much to have to face the crowd that greeted him outside.

Tess saved him, as usual.

"Come, Vasha. I want you and Stefan to attend me at
Princess Rusudani's tent."

The thought of Rusudani calmed him at once. With her serene face and composed voice as a promise held before him,
he could press through the assembly without quailing.

In the end, Tess did nothing more on that visit than establish the language Rusudani spoke, a dialect of the Yos language, confirm the princess's pedigree, and listen politely
while Rusudani, through Jaelle, begged leave to bring the
word of her God to the attention of Bakhtiian and the elders
and women of the jaran.

Vasha needed to do nothing but sit in respectful silence.
Slowly the weight of tension sloughed off him. He was surprised by the revelation that he felt more at ease sitting here
with khaja women than with the women of his own people.

CHAPTER EIGHTEEN

Duke Naroshi's Palace

From the ship, Ilyana and the rest of the company boarded a shuttle that took them down not to the surface but to a platform, like a thin sheet of glass, that floated high above Duke Naroshi's palace. Stepping out from the interior of the shuttle, she felt exposed and dizzy. It was a long long way to the ground.

"This is amazing," David ben Unbutu was saying to Maggie O'Neill. "I've never seen anything like it."

"Any idea how it levitates?" she asked nervously. About the size of a soccer field, the "plate" on which they stood seemed no thicker than a hand, and there were no railings along the sides.

"None. Goddess, if I only had access to their technology—"

Ilyana clutched Anton's wrist with a strong grip and told Valentin in a voice made brusque by fear to pick Evdokia up. It was just the kind of awful accident that might happen, one of the children plunging off the side. To her right, Diana Brooke-Holt had already grabbed hold of both Evdi and Portia.

The air smelled funny, but it was breathable.

The palace spread out below and before them, but they were still nightside and all she saw were pinprick lights and vast contours of shadow. The platform glowed with a silver tinge that echoed distant clusters of subdued and delicate lights.

One of the actors whistled, low, marveling. "Can you tell how high up we are?"

"Pretty damned far."

The musician Phillippe swore: "Tupping hells, I *hate* heights! Let me sit down!"

"Here, hold on to my legs," said Hyacinth to Anatoly

Sakhalin. Hyacinth lay down on his stomach and inched forward until he got to the edge.

"Oh, Goddess," wailed Phillippe, sitting in the very center of the crowd, hair clutched in his hands. "Don't *do* that, Hyacinth. You're making me sick."

Hyacinth grinned. Sticking his hand out, he groped forward with it, kept going until his shoulders and head were out over . . . nothing. "Yeah, yeah, you can pull me back now," he said, laughing with nervous excitement. When Anatoly had dragged him a body's length back, he sat up, smiling madly. "There seems to be a beacon, like a lighthouse, underneath us. But there's nothing around or below the platform, no forcefield, nothing."

Anatoly walked up to the edge of the platform, right up so that the tips of his boots edged the rim, and stared down into the gulf of air. Nipper shrieked and fainted. "He's right," said Anatoly calmly. "Is there some tool that can measure the space between air and land?"

No one spoke.

"Oh," said Anatoly suddenly. "The *transit.*" He unclipped his hand-sized computer slate from his belt, keyed a command into it, and held it out. Ilyana caught in her breath. With his arm extended he seemed even less stable, as if the merest touch of breeze could push him over. Nipper revived, but catching sight of Anatoly poised as if to plummet, she began hyperventilating until, mercifully, the company medic rummaged through his bag and slapped a patch on her skin. Her head lolled back, and her breathing slowed.

Anatoly drew the slate in and puzzled out the letters on the screen. The pale light turned his hair to spun gold, and Ilyana saw his lips move, sounding out the terms. "One thousand three hundred and six meters." He clipped the slate on his belt and stepped back.

The others had already clustered at the center, except for Hyacinth, on his knees an arm's length behind Anatoly. Ilyana heard the group give a collective sigh, whether at Anatoly retreating from the brink or at the appalling height at which they now stood. Without warning, the shuttle retracted its landing ramp and banked away from the platform, stranding them there. Its leaving did not rock the flat surface at all. They watched it go until the darkness swallowed it up and the last red and blue lights were lost to distance.

"Damned lucky we can breathe the atmosphere," said one

of the women sardonically. Wind gusted and died and rose again more gently. A thin strip of cloud drifted beneath the platform. It was cool, but not cold. And it was weirdly quiet.

"Now what?" asked a lonely voice in the anxious silence. Ilyana counted thirty-eight people huddled in the middle of the platform. The silver light emanating from the platform lit them from below, gilding their forms. Most of them now looked toward David ben Unbutu and Maggie O'Neill, except for Phillippe and a handful of others who had their eyes shut.

M. Unbutu lifted his hands, palms up. "I don't know. Charles was supposed to be here to meet us, and to, ah, formally present us to Duke Naroshi. We can't enter the ducal house without the formal 'crossing of borders,' that's the literal translation. It's some kind of ceremony, although I don't think retainers, like us, are truly introduced to a duke."

There was a bit of tense laughter at this comment, which Maggie O'Neill followed up. "I'm not sure we actually exist as individuals to them," she said.

A light flared on the ground. It rose and steadily approached them. One light resolved into four, four into the curve of a ship set off against stars and the pale glamour of clouds. Noiselessly, it slowed down, stopped, and drew up along one side of the platform. A hatch opened. Two figures stepped out, followed by a third. Ilyana sidestepped and yanked Anton along beside her. She had never seen Chapalii this close before.

"Anton, look, the one on the right. That's Charles Soerensen."

"Who?" Anton seemed more interested in Nipper, who was now snoring softly, than in the fantastic events taking place.

"Shhh! You idiot. The only human who has a place in the Chapalii court. Duke Charles."

Ilyana had seen him before, of course, a sandy-haired man of medium height, except there was something oddly unsettling behind his unprepossessing appearance. Ilyana always had a feeling that, like the mythic creature called the basilisk, if he looked at you in the wrong way he would turn you to stone. He was the one person in the whole universe who she suspected her father was scared of.

The two Chapalii looked alike to her, tall, awkward, and angular, but she supposed that the one who stood next to

Duke Charles must be the Chapalii duke. His skin was so pallid that he seemed to reflect back the muted light given off by the platform.

"Maggie," said Duke Charles in a low voice. Maggie O'Neill stepped forward and handed Soerensen a rod. He ran a hand down it, as if his fingers were reading something carved into its surface.

"Tai-en," he said, speaking in Anglais. "This is the manifest of my retainers, whom I pass into your hands for safekeeping while they sojourn in your lands." He held out the rod. Duke Naroshi accepted it from him and replied in Chapalii, which Ilyana could not understand.

And that was that. Duke Charles walked over to Owen and Ginny, the leaders of the Company, and conferred with them briefly while the Chapalii duke waited, oblivious to his new companions. To her left, Ilyana saw her father inching by degrees closer to Duke Naroshi. She opened her mouth to say something, but Duke Charles broke away from Owen and Ginny and headed for the little ship, David ben Unbutu and Maggie O'Neill with him.

Without thinking, Ilyana tugged Anton along behind her as she followed them. Had she misunderstood? Was M. Unbutu leaving now? It was too awful to contemplate!

But Duke Charles paused in front of the hatch. "Good luck, David," he said in a low voice. "You'll transmit to Maggie once a day if you can manage it, otherwise through the regular communiques. What do you think?"

M. Unbutu grinned. "I think I'm going to die happy." He kissed Maggie.

Duke Charles glanced back over the platform, caught sight of Ilyana, and gave her a brief nod before his gaze swept out, locked, and retreated back in again. "Hell." Ilyana was shocked to hear his voice shaking. "I'm glad to get off of here. I *hate* heights." He crossed over into the ship. Maggie followed him inside.

The hatch closed. Retreating, M. Unbutu waved at Ilyana to move back with him. The ship sighed away from the platform, banked, and headed up into the sky, which was lightening.

M. Unbutu smiled kindly at Ilyana and Anton. "Planetrise. I guess it should be some sight."

"What's planetrise?" asked Anton, but Ilyana hushed him and said, "but why did we have to come here, M. Unbutu?"

She motioned toward the platform, where they hung in the air.

"We're crossing the border, passing from one fiefdom to the other. This place is not quite in one domain or the other."

"Oh. This platform is like a crossing place. But where is Duke Charles going now? I didn't expect to see him here."

"Look!" said Anton. Ilyana turned to see her father standing not five paces from Duke Naroshi, who seemed unaware of Vasil's presence. But Anton was pointing toward the horizon. The smooth line of a luminescent ball nosed up over jagged hills. "Is that the sun?" he asked.

"No, silly," said Ilyana. "That's a planet. Isn't it?"

"Yes," said M. Unbutu. "We're on one of its moons. One of the few things we know about this system is that this satellite has an erratic orbit around the planet, so I'd guess it's practically impossible to calculate simple things like sunrise."

"Moons don't have atmosphere," said Anton stubbornly.

"Yana!" Valentin sidled over, now carrying Evdi, who stared open-mouthed at the planet rising into the sky. "Look at that, will you!"

Bronze and ivory-colored bands girdled the planet, swirling together in thick stripes, and by its light Ilyana could see the suggestion of curves and planes on the ground below, the palace taking form as if light itself brought it into being. But the glory of the great planet was its magnificent rings. The rings stretched out as far again on either side as the planet's diameter, so that the planet and rings together appeared monstrous.

"Oh, gee," said Valentin, who was never awed by anything.

Even their father simply stood and stared, forgetting how close he stood to the Chapalii nobleman. Karolla, sitting, nursed the baby, but she glanced up at intervals to look, she who never truly looked at the khaja world, who had learned to avoid seeing it. The company whispered and exclaimed to each other in a reverent hush. The planet took so long to rise that Evdi fell asleep in Valentin's arms.

A sharper light caught and splintered over the horizon, and the sun rose. It was bright, bluish-white, and small, disappointing compared to the huge planet. But the sun and the reflected light of the planet combined to bring dawn.

Ilyana's first thought was that the horizon was curved.

Then she saw the palace.

First, the sheer size of it, stretching out in a web over the land, curving away from the horizon. A huge river cut through the palace, infested with towers; a nest of towers even grew up from the middle of its confluence with one of its tributaries. Almost directly beneath them a canyon cut deep into the earth, spanned by three gossamer bridges whose arches splintered the new light into rainbows. Domes huddled in the depths.

Phillippe started to hyperventilate. A spate of wondering talk flooded the group on the platform.

"Goddess bless us," said M. Unbutu under his breath.

Ilyana had not had time to take in everything when an opaque dome coalesced over the platform and the floor sank. Her heart and stomach collided. She thought she was going to fall, but the descent was even and slow and anyway her feet seemed to be stuck to the platform.

After a long time, they stopped. An arch of silver light appeared in the opaque dome. Duke Naroshi walked out through it. Light flared around him and vanished back into gray. He was gone. The dome moved again, slowed and stopped, and the opaque wall steamed away into nothing.

They stood in the middle of ruins. The platform sank, melting into the ground until they stood on dirt. Pale crumbled brick walls surrounded them. A squat tower, half fallen in, marked a gateway. Through it, Ilyana saw green. The sky above had a hazy density, and the planet loomed along the horizon. It seemed to have sunk a bit, so that its bottom rim lay hidden behind the jagged mountains. The sun's light cast weak shadows out from the ruined walls, and a few stars shone faintly. The air still smelled funny, and here in the middle of the dead brick city it carried grit unleavened by filters or plants.

One Chapalii remained with them. He—Ilyana reminded herself that it had to be a "he"—because the females were sequestered—stepped forward and addressed himself to David ben Unbutu in Anglais made odd by his inability to sound a hissed "s." "I am called Roki. It is my obligation to serve you and these assembled people. This caravansary has entered into decay but another has grown beyond the arch." He inclined his head, an awkward gesture that looked copied, not natural, and walked away from the group toward the arch.

"Entered into decay?" muttered Hyacinth. "How old is this palace, anyway?"

"I'm no antiquary," said M. Unbutu, "but this was either cleverly constructed to look this way, or else it's been abandoned for centuries. This kind of erosion doesn't take place overnight."

Anatoly was the first to move. He ran a hand carefully along a waist-high wall, testing it. "I have seen such places in Habakar, old cities and towns lost out in the desert, forgotten by everyone except Father Wind and Mother Sun."

Diana glanced at him but said nothing.

One of the new actors said, "Father Wind and Mother Sun?" and Gwyn Jones told him to be quiet.

Finally, Yomi picked up her trunk, activated the lifts on the company trunks and boxes, and started the whole mass moving after the Chapalii steward. "Well, what are we waiting for?" she demanded of the others. The trunks and boxes floated about an arm's length off the ground, locked together in stacks and lines, and she maneuvered them out the still-intact arch and into the green.

First one, then a second, then a third person gathered together their personal luggage and either hoisted it up onto their hips or back or activated its levitation grids, and followed Yomi. Their breaking away precipitated a flood, so everyone converged on the arch at one time. Ilyana waited patiently for the congestion to sort itself out. She let Anton run ahead with their mother while she hung back, loitering near M. Unbutu, who had evidently decided to bring up the rear. That way she managed to walk beside him as they came out through the arch and caught their first glimpse of the palace from the ground.

From this angle, everything looked different. Down along an unpaved road stood another square brick caravansary, this one intact. To the left lay fields and a green park in which clumps of animals roamed, and behind the caravansary and to the right loomed a great rose-colored wall, a mass of jade towers with bulbous stems and flowering roofs, and a glass-paned dome that shimmered in sunlight. A tiny gate marked the rose wall, like a stain. Above, in the sky, the ringed planet loomed.

"That's odd," said M. Unbutu, crossing back under the arch. Ilyana followed him. "Look. From inside, you can't see the towers or the dome, and they're tall enough that you should be able to."

Ilyana gaped. From inside the ruined caravansary, she saw only dunes and a line of craggy mountains etched against a hot blue sky. Even the planet did not show. She walked back out, half expecting to find a different scene outside, as if she were caught in one of Valentin's guising worlds, but she saw the same landmarks as before. Yomi's tiny figure, attended by the levitated freight boxes and trunks, crossed under the arch of the other caravansary and disappeared from Ilyana's view.

One actor broke away from the road and trotted out to one of the fields, kneeling down to examine a low growth of green plants. "Strawberries!"

"That's interesting." Ignoring the excitement, M. Unbutu keyed a note into his slate. "Yana, you might want to note that there's a field inside these ruins that affects what we see."

"Unless it's the outside view that's wrong."

"Or some kind of massive refraction ... at this point it's undoubtedly useless to make many conjectures. We take notes. Then, if we see different parts of the palace, we can compare notes on how often this sort of thing occurs. As well as other anomalies."

Ilyana simply nodded. She was thrilled to be included, but she wasn't going to make a fool of herself by saying so out loud. They reached the caravansary in time to hear a blood-curdling shriek from inside. M. Unbutu broke into a run, and Ilyana raced after him.

"Look!" one of the young actors was shouting, sounding hysterical. "You expect me to use that?"

M. Unbutu seemed good at navigating by sound. He found the frenzied actor quickly, in a small chamber by the back gate. She stood in front of a meter-long trough. A shallow stream of water ran down it, spilling into a drain. The Chapalii steward waited by the door. He and the actor looked toward M. Unbutu, who arrived at the same time as Yomi.

"He says this is the bathroom!" said the actor. "And there's only *one!* One bathroom for thirty-eight people!"

"This is insufficient for your needs?" asked Roki. Ilyana saw an odd shade of color mottling his pale skin. M. Unbutu began to chuckle.

"How can you laugh?" shrieked the actor. "There isn't anywhere to bathe, and there're no mirrors, nothing!"

"Roki," said M. Unbutu calmly, "if you will step outside with me, perhaps we can discuss some alterations."

"We followed the specifications given to us," said Roki. His tone had such an odd pitch that Ilyana could detect no emotion in his voice, but colors swirled and faded on his face, and she knew that the Chapalii were sometimes called chameleons by humans because they shifted color according to their mood.

But outside another controversy swirled, rather like a physical expression of the steward's consternation.

"There isn't any food!"

"Of course there's food, you idiot. There are gardens and herds."

"Oh, yes. I want to watch Thea butcher one of those sheep."

"Fuck off."

"Now, let's all calm down—"

"I thought the Chapalii were supposed to be so damned advanced."

"What? You thought the food would just come out of thin air? I don't think even they've managed that level of molecular transformation."

"Shut up, Thea. But it's true, Ginny. We came here expecting that these things would be taken care of. There isn't any one of us here who knows how to exist in such primitive conditions."

Ilyana had never figured out exactly how much Anglais her mother understood.

"First we must set up my tent," said Karolla with calm authority. Yomi emerged from the caravansary, M. Unbutu looked around from his conversation with Roki, and slowly a hush fell over the assembly, which had worked itself to quite a pitch.

"Then we will gather under the awning and I and the elders will decide which men will go to the herds, which women to the gardens, and how the women will divide up the stone chambers which must serve as your tents."

To Ilyana's utter astonishment, they all obeyed her as unquestioningly as if she really was etsana.

Anatoly dumped his saddle, bridle, and saddlebags on the floor of the chamber which now belonged to his wife. He laid his saber down on top, the crown of his possessions.

"I don't understand why you insisted on taking those with you," said Diana.

"There are horses out in the park," Anatoly retorted. "Didn't you see them?"

She ignored him. "Help me with the cots." She had chosen a room without a bed built in. As Anatoly unfolded the cots, he reflected sourly that she had probably chosen it in order to have an excuse to sleep alone: Each cot was meant for a single person.

Portia came in, poked around the room, then grabbed her box of molding blocks.

"Where are you going?" Diana asked sharply.

"Out to the tent. Yana said I could."

"Go with her," said Diana to Anatoly without looking at him.

He frowned, but he grabbed a halter, took Portia's hand, and went out. She chattered happily as they crossed the caravansary courtyard and under the arch to the outside. Anatoly said "yes" and "no" at intervals, but he wasn't really listening to her. He was furious with Diana. Yet, stepping out into the open, he felt relieved of pressure. The open sky was refreshing. The sight of a tent set out in the open, where it belonged, acted as balm to his soul. Children played under the awning. Ilyana looked up, seeing them, and waved, then abruptly looked embarrassed and turned her attention back to the little ones. It bothered Anatoly. Girls her age were supposed to act like women, not like boys. Portia pulled out of his grasp and ran over to the tent to plop down beside Evdokia.

Karolla emerged from the tent, discussing something with Yomi and Ginny and the eldest of the women actors, Seshat. The women nodded, came to some conclusion, and the khaja women left, greeting Anatoly as they passed.

Karolla caught his eye and, obediently, he walked over to her. They had achieved an understanding early on, nothing codified but rather understood through a shared belief that someone must hold to the ways of the jaran and must teach these ways to the children. Even while Anatoly could not approve of Karolla's leaving her mother's tribe, still he valued her adherence to tradition.

"Walk with me," she said quietly. They walked out into the park. Anatoly studied the horses, a small herd of seven: four mares, two foals, and a stallion. The lead mare was a handsome creature, big-boned and sturdy and from what little Anatoly had seen of her so far, not one to take any nonsense from the others.

"My servant will supervise and tutor the younger children now," began Karolla, "but it is my hope that you will take some interest in Valentin."

"I will keep an eye out for him," agreed Anatoly cautiously.

She cleared her throat. "There is one other thing. It is past time for my daughter to celebrate her tsadokhis night. Because she is a daughter of the Arkhanov line, it would be appropriate for a prince of the Sakhalin tribe to be her first lover."

Anatoly kept his gaze fixed on the horses. "Any man would be honored to be your daughter's tsadokhis choice."

"I beg your pardon for speaking of these things so baldly. But you have seen as well as I that Yana has lived too much in the khaja world and has had no older girls to emulate. It is wrong that a girl should reach her age and not arrange with her aunt for her flower night. So I must act."

They had come close enough to the horses now that by mutual unspoken consent they both halted. The stallion circled warily, but the lead mare lifted her ears and ambled toward them.

"Of course," said Anatoly softly, watching the mare, "no man would wish a girl to feel that he was forced on her."

"She admires you," said Karolla flatly, "but she acts as a boy would act admiring an older woman, shying away, waiting for her to approach him."

The mare had a black mane and a chestnut coat, and she halted six paces from them and eyed the humans curiously but without fear. Anatoly knew an invitation when he saw one. Karolla calmly handed him an apple she had evidently taken from the gardens, and with it he approached the mare. She deigned to take the offering and to let him introduce himself. He let her sniff the halter and then he pulled it on over her head. Clearly she had been ridden before. A half grown filly came up and shied away, skittish, and the other mares cropped at the grass. Anatoly heaved himself up onto her back and swung a leg over. Waited. She shifted but seemed content.

Karolla had another apple and a bridle. Now she walked over to the nearest of the other mares. Soon enough, she, too, was mounted. Anatoly grinned. Together they rode back toward the tent. The rest of the herd followed at a distance, except for the stallion, who trumpeted his displeasure at this desertion. Anatoly's mare merely quirked her ears.

"It's no wonder you prefer me to him," said Anatoly to her. "I'm much better-looking."

She flattened her ears briefly, and he chuckled.

Karolla came up beside him. "If I arrange her tsadokhis night, will you agree to act as if she had already lain flowers beside your saddle?"

The children saw them. Portia leaped up, shouting, "Papa! Papa!" and Valentin hoisted her up and shushed her. Ilyana stood up as well, her face alight with pleasure.

"Oh, Mama! Let me ride!" she called. "No, I'll go first, Evdi, and then I'll take you."

She disappeared inside the tent and came out a moment later with a saddle. Karolla dismounted. Anatoly watched as Ilyana swiftly made the acquaintance of the mare, a compact roan, and saddled her and mounted.

She shot a glance toward Anatoly. "Race you!" Urging the mare forward, she put it through its paces, getting acquainted. After a bit, she encouraged it to run. Like any jaran girl, she knew how to ride. Her braid bounced on her back and she laughed with joy.

Anatoly sighed and dismounted. He tossed the reins to Karolla. "Let me get my saddle. We'll let the children ride."

"Do you agree?" asked Karolla quietly.

Gods, it was tempting. Any man would be tempted. But what Karolla suggested went too far. He could just imagine what his grandmother would say about it. "If she places flowers beside my saddle, I would be honored by her choice. But if she does not wish it, then even by your request I cannot act. I beg your pardon."

Karolla simply nodded.

They let the children ride for a while, then turned the horses loose.

It rained in the afternoon, so they were all stuck inside the warren of rooms that made up the caravansary. There were many arguments, mostly about rehearsal space and if anyone knew when they were expected to perform. Portia splashed in puddles in the courtyard until Diana yelled at her to come in under shelter, and David ben Unbutu found some kind of interface to a map of the palace under the gazebo in the center of the courtyard.

But only three people could stand out of the rain under the tiny gazebo roof, and so many of the actors began quarreling about right of place that David told them all to go away. He did not precisely lose his temper, Anatoly noted; instead he spoke so softly that they had to stop talking in order to hear him. Anatoly sat on a bench and watched the spectacle. Most Earth khaja were quite patient—it was something he admired in them—but many of the actors were not just young but nervous, and that made them irritable and quick to take offense.

Diana took Portia to bed. The rain slackened and gave out, and Anatoly walked into the courtyard and leaned over the gazebo railing. The map looked like a mosaic made of thin lines of light, but each time David touched an intersection of lines an image rose out of the floor, mist rising and solidifying into a tiny model of a building.

"It's clever," muttered David to what was left of his audience: Anatoly, Gwyn Jones, Yomi, Hyacinth, and the woman Wingtuck. "But not very illuminating. We'll have to copy each individual item into our modeler and then assemble it as a whole."

Nevertheless, they watched with interest as, one by one, insubstantial edifices formed on the mosaic and melted again. Much later, Anatoly went back to Diana's room, half expecting to find flowers beside his saddle. There were none, of course. He was surprised at how disappointed he was.

He took off his boots and his clothes and lay down on a cot. He heard Diana shift, so attuned to her that he could practically feel the blanket slipping over her skin.

"I couldn't believe it when you walked right up to the rim of that platform," she whispered suddenly. "I thought I was going to have heart failure. Aren't you scared of anything?"

"Only of losing you," he murmured.

"What? I couldn't hear you."

"Why should I be afraid of anything here? If I died, no one would miss me."

"Oh, Goddess, now you're feeling sorry for yourself again." She shifted to turn her back toward him.

"Diana!"

"Shhh. You'll wake Portia."

He got up and she stiffened, but he went instead to the window. The clouds had blown off. Three small moons chased after them across the sky. Earth had never seemed quite as *different* as this. He felt lighter, almost buoyant, something to do with gravity and the size and density of this moon. He stood there until she fell asleep.

He woke when the first slivers of light pierced through the window. Going outside, he caught and saddled the chestnut mare and rode toward the distant rose wall, toward the dark slash that marked, perhaps, a gate. It loomed greater and ever greater, much farther away than he had first judged. When he reached the base at last, it blocked out half the sky; it practically seemed to curve inward at the top. The mare grew skittish, so he dismounted, hobbled her, and walked the rest of the way. The air hummed, a tingling on his skin.

The dark slash was not a gate but an opaque window, a huge block of ebony stone. The wall itself was translucent, and through it he saw another world colored rose by the substance of the wall. Beyond, in that other world, it rained. Tentatively, he reached out and touched the wall. Hard. Still, the material had some quality that made him feel as if with the right kind of pressure he could push his way through.

"Anatoly!"

He turned.

Two riders approached. One was khaja; he could tell by the seat. As they neared, he recognized David by his profusion of black braids. The other rider was Ilyana. Anatoly cursed under his breath. He was too old to become infatuated with a girl half his age. He knew very well that part of it was a reaction to Diana's turning away from him, and yet, he was perfectly within his rights to admire a beautiful young woman and even to hope that she might honor him by choosing him as her first lover. It wasn't unknown for a man to find more gratifying love with a lover than with his wife, but, gods, at least he expected his wife to respect him.

"How do you know the map in the courtyard is a real map of the palace?" Ilyana was asking as they came within earshot.

"We don't, of course. Find anything interesting? Did you do a scan for the composition of the wall?"

"No," said Anatoly. "I wouldn't understand the figures. See how the wall curves. It's raining on the other side."

"I think we're under a dome," said David. "It would make sense, given that they would have a different composition of air to breathe—close to what we're used to, I'd guess, since they can exist in Earth's atmosphere without any evident aids. That doesn't explain the trick with the platform yesterday, though."

"The air is singing." Ilyana put out both hands and touched the wall. She shut her eyes as if to listen better. "It's just like that trellis in the ship: It's as if something is pouring through this. I almost feel like it's talking to me."

She shrieked and jerked back her hands.

"What's wrong?" David demanded, taking hold of her arms. All three of them took quick steps backward. The wall remained. Beyond, it rained, while the air remained clear and warm on this side of the wall.

Ilyana gulped down air. She leaned her head unselfconsciously against David's chest, and it was David who, a moment later, let go of her and stepped away.

"It was so odd," she said finally, turning to look at the wall. "It was hard like stone when I touched it. Then when I began to listen I really did feel like I could just hear what it was saying if I focused right. I felt like I could hear this tone. I thought it was the beat of a drum, and the wall began to melt away under my hands, like I could all of a sudden push through to the other side." She paused and smiled apologetically. "It scared me."

David pulled on his braids—'*locks,* he called them—and frowned. He turned and walked over to the wall, placed both hands on it, and shut his eyes. After a while he opened them. "I feel a humming. That's it. Anatoly?"

"Just the humming. But when I touched it, I felt as if I should be able to push through, if only I could understand it."

Ilyana cast him a grateful glance. He forced himself to meet her eyes and smile reassuringly at her. Gods, she was scarcely more than a child.

"Well, Yana," said David, "do you want to try it again?"

She smiled nervously. "Do I . . . do I have to?"

"Of course not!"

"No. Not right now." She hesitated. "You know what else?" Her words were tentative, groping. "It was like I had started opening a door into a room, only just as I looked I realized that the room was way bigger on the inside than it could be from the outside." She faltered. "Does that make sense?"

Anatoly exchanged a glance with David. "We could ride the wall," Anatoly said. "If it is the wall of a dome, it must circle around until we reach this spot again."

"Yana?"

She bit her lower lip, shook her head. "I have to go back. Mama is expecting me."

"Tell the others where we went, then," said David as she went back to her horse. As she rode away, he turned to Anatoly, and for an instant Anatoly thought he was about to say something about the girl, but he did not.

Instead, the two men began their ride. Anatoly enjoyed being out here, exploring. He taught David some songs, and they discussed how to take readings on the slate and why the rose wall might appear to run in a straight line, from a distance, and yet prove, as they rode, to be curved.

It took them the rest of the day, riding at a steady clip and stopping several times to rest and water the horses at streams which were too convenient to be natural, to circumnavigate the dome, for that was what it proved to be. The distant, craggy mountains were simply part of the barrier, steep cliffs that from a distance gave the illusion of naturally sloped hills.

At dusk they reached the slab of ebony stone again. It was night by the time they got back to the caravansary. Two moons lit their way, and as they dismounted and unsaddled the horses, rubbing them down and turning them loose, a third and a fourth moon broached the horizon and rose into the starry sky.

"What do you think?" asked Anatoly.

"I don't know," admitted David. "It could be that Duke Naroshi is protecting us in some way, from other Chapalii, from a poisonous atmosphere, from getting lost. It could be that we are prisoners. It could be he just doesn't want us wandering around in his palace without his knowing where we are. He knows we'll try to spy on him. Why shouldn't he try to stop us?"

"Then what did Yana hear?"

David just smiled wryly and shook his head. "That one I won't even guess at."

CHAPTER NINETEEN

Leavetaking

"I'm not going with you," said Tess. She braced herself for Ilya's reaction, but he merely glanced at her. He had been preoccupied and moody ever since Vassily's return, but he refused to discuss it. At times like this Tess found his autocratic nature especially exasperating. Then she chuckled.

He stopped packing his saddlebags. His look was question enough: Why are you laughing at me?

Tess knew it would be impolitic of her to tell him that she didn't mind him acting autocratically toward others, only toward herself. "Take *The Recitation*," she offered helpfully. "I've read it."

He hefted the book in his left hand. Princess Rusudani had presented it to him as a gift. It was an ordinary looking book except for the gilt lettering on the cover. "You've read it?"

"I read it in Jeds." And as an intellectual exercise, she'd drafted an essay comparing elements of the Church of Hristain with elements of Mediterranean religions: It was almost as if three puzzles, of the ancient religions of Christ, Isis, and Mohammed, had been mixed together and reassembled in a new form. "Of course I've read the commentary by Sister Casiara on the nature of the Pilgrim."

Ilya thrust the holy book into one of the saddlebags. "Then I will be able to debate its finer points with Princess Rusudani."

"Ah. So you are taking her with you."

"When we defeat the King of Mircassia, I must have a claimant to put on the throne in his place."

"She is not necessarily a partisan for our cause, Ilya."

"Not necessarily. But she is now under my control."

Tess hesitated, then broached the subject she and Sonia had once discussed. "You could marry her to a jaran prince."

"I will do that, naturally," he said without looking at her. "But I'm in no hurry. Mircassia must fall first."

"Marry her to Vasha." There. Now she'd said it.

"I do not choose to discuss Vassily Kireyevsky."

"Stubborn bastard. You're very annoying when you're in this unreasonable mood."

He finished packing his bags. Finally, he spoke. "We should have let Nadine foster him."

"He's your son, Ilya."

"He has no father."

"You know I'm right."

"Gods, Tess! Must we have this argument again? He was spoiled by his mother and he expects the same treatment now that he is a man. A prince! He's worse than Andrei Sakhalin."

"I resent that! He is not worse than Andrei Sakhalin. Nor have I seen to his education for eight years and had him turn out *that* badly. Do you know what is wrong here? *You!* You could never make up your mind, and so you always treated him too gently. You have to treat him as you would any son of yours."

"If any son of mine behaved as he has behaved, this is how I *would* treat him! He will act as my servant until I turn him over to Zvertkov."

"After what he went through as a boy! That's cruel. He'll hate it."

"His behavior is a disgrace to this tent! He will obey me."

The passion of his statement took Tess aback. Abruptly, she felt optimistic, and she hid a smile from him. He could not appreciate humor when he was angry. If Ilya was this angry with Vasha, there was hope for the boy. Because the truth was, Vasha would never be accepted as a soldier on her say-so. He must have a man's sponsorship, and without uncles or cousins, he had only his father, problematic as that relationship was. Just as a girl became a woman through the agency of her female relatives, so a boy became a man with the support of his male relatives. That was why there was no worse fate for a child in the jaran than to be orphaned, to lose not just parents but the entire kin-group.

"Once you've completed the campaign," she said, changing the subject, "I will sail south with the children and meet you in Jeds."

He kissed her absently and hunted around the tent for something he was missing. Of course such a separation seemed natural to him. Jaran men rode away from the tribes all the time, to go to war. They had themselves been separated for months at a time on three occasions in the last eight years. *I should be used to it by now,* thought Tess, but somehow it always felt like a foretaste of death to her. She would never get used to it.

But Ilya was, in a sense, already gone. Once he had made the decision to launch the final assault on Mircassia and Filis, his mind had gone to the war. Now his body would follow. Anyway, she had received two more cylinders from Charles. This would give her the freedom to explore them. She felt guilty at once for thinking it, as if she wished to be rid of him.

From the inner chamber, she heard him voice a soft exclamation: He had found whatever he was looking for. Curious, she pushed aside the curtain and looked in to see him weaving one of her hair ribbons into his belt buckle. He glanced up at her and suddenly looked self-conscious. Gods, he hated being caught out. But Ilya was never one to stall or retreat when attack would serve just as well.

"Where are the children?" he asked.

"Katya took them out on a little birbas, out in the park."

"Well, then." He crossed to her and firmly pulled her into the inner chamber, letting the curtain fall closed behind her. "Since we leave at dawn tomorrow, and there will be a late and public celebration tonight. . . ."

"You don't have to make excuses to me, my heart. I think it's very sweet that you're taking one of my hair ribbons with you as a token." He ignored her, intent on undoing her belt. "Lest you've forgotten, you have to take my boots off first."

In answer, he picked her up and dropped down onto the pillows with her. She kissed him, and partway through the kiss she was struck as if physically with a premonition that something horrible was going to happen to him, that she would never see him again. She broke off the kiss and cupped his face in her hands, staring into his eyes for so long that he stilled to match her silence.

"What is it?" he asked softly, slipping an arm more firmly around her, gathering her closer against him.

The idea of asking him not to go was so ludicrous that she smiled wryly and kissed him again, murmuring, "I love you" several times in order to make him understand how much she did love him. And at least, moving there among the pillows, she knew without a doubt that he understood what was in her heart.

So at dawn the next day the army rode out, twenty units of a thousand soldiers each, half of them archers, and of those archers, a full third were young men a year older than Vasha who had trained with saber and bow. That first day, Tess could not bear to let Natalia and Yuri out of her sight. But there were the two cylinders from Charles to distract her, there were administrative and judicial disputes in Sarai to oversee, and, five days after the army had left, a cryptic message from Cara Hierakis: "Coming north. Expect me any time within the next sixty days."

Galina Orzhekov gave birth to a healthy infant son. After the requisite feast, Andrei Sakhalin announced that he was taking a hundred riders and riding south after the main army.

Later that night, after Natalia and Yuri were asleep, Tess was interrupted while reading one of Charles's reports. She blinked off her implant and said, "Come in."

To her surprise, Katerina pushed aside the entrance flap and entered, alone.

"Hello, Katya. I thought you'd still be with Galina."

Katerina did not reply immediately. She prowled the room, examining each object in the outer chamber with a niece's disregard for any lingering possessiveness Tess might have managed to retain after twelve years with the jaran.

"Do you think Galina really loves him, or just thinks she has to because she had no choice but to marry him?" Katerina asked suddenly.

"If she loves him, does it matter why?"

"You don't like him, do you?"

Tess quirked a smile but refused to reply.

Katya sat down abruptly in the other chair. Stood up. Sat down. Clasped her hands together on the table and fixed Tess with a stare. "I took him as a lover, on the ride back here."

"Katya!" Tess was surprised to discover that this shocked her. "You could have hurt Galina deeply by that." But even as she said those words, she realized that she was shocked more by the prospect of actually lying with Andrei Sakhalin, whom she found acutely unattractive, than of the unlikely prospect of Galina feeling betrayed by an affair that had occurred hundreds of miles away.

"All he ever does is talk about himself. Just like Vasha. Vasha is becoming just as boring as Andrei Sakhalin."

Tess winced. "That comparison is unfair to Vasha!"

"Ha! You *don't* like him."

"If you *dare* repeat that, young woman—!"

"Of course I won't!" Katya lapsed into a morose silence. She stood up again and prowled the chamber. Tess did not bother to watch her; it only made her dizzy. "Vasha was so stupid," Katya said finally. "He always felt sorry for himself. He arrived at Yaroslav Sakhalin's army thinking everyone should treat him like a prince, and he'd never even fought in a battle."

Tess heard a quaver in Katya's voice, like a hint. She seized on it. "You fought."

There was a long silence.

A *long* silence.

Tess rose to face her. There is a moment before dawn of a drawn-in breath, as there is before speaking; so Tess waited for light to breach the horizon. Katerina lifted a hand to trace the gold designs inlaid in the quiver hanging against the wall. The gesture, oddly tender, was the only sound in the chamber.

"My lover died in my arms," she said. "Cut down by khaja arrows."

"I'm so sorry."

Katya flashed her an angry look. "No one understands!"

"Oh, Katya! I'm truly sorry, you must know that. But do you suppose that you're the only person—"

"Don't mock me! Have you ever watched a loved one die of wounds right in front of you?" Her indignation was palpable.

Tess sighed, unable to be angry with her. "Your uncle Yurinya died just so, my child, defending me." Just like that, the image of Yuri lying in the grass as life and blood leaked out of him slammed into her, as clear as if her implant had flashed on with a reconstruction of the scene. Tess had to steady herself on the back of her chair.

Yuri. He lay utterly still. There was a transparent cast to his skin, to his pale lips. His eyes fluttered and his lips moved. The scent of blood and grass drowned her. He lifted

one hand and held it, wavering, searching for her ...
searching. ...

Katya stared as if she had just that moment realized that someone else could suffer as she suffered.

"I'm sorry, Katya." Tess wiped away her own tears with the back of one hand. Nineteen was too young to see death so violently and so close, no matter how good the cause. Any age was too young, to have your best loved comrade die despite the full force of your own will that they, by God, just *live*, just hang on. "I know it doesn't make it any easier to know that other women have lost lovers and husbands and brothers, but still it's true that you aren't alone. If that helps."

"I am alone." Caught in profile, Katerina looked tired, beaten down. The Orzhekov women were known as a handsome line, but it was intelligence and vitality that made them attractive more than the simple physical prettiness that had—for better or worse—graced the line of Sakhalin princes. Katya's grief was raw and terribly affecting. It drained all animation from her. Tess went to her and rested a hand on her shoulder.

"Oh, Katya—"

Katya jerked away from the touch. "I can't tell *anyone*," she gasped, gulping down dry sobs.

"Katya! Oh, gods." Tess took hold of her, as she would of a small child caught up in uncontrollable fears, and held her with an iron grip. "You must have loved him very much."

"I yelled at her, 'Don't leave me, don't leave me.' But she just looked at me and said, 'It hurts so much. I just want peace.' When she died I died with her, because I could never share my grief with anyone else, I could never share our love and give it life by remembering it to others." She broke into racking sobs, burying her face in Tess's shoulder. "Oh, gods. Promise me you won't tell my mother."

"I promise." She let Katya cry. When the sobs quieted, Tess stroked her hair. "What was her name?"

There was a pause.

"Mariya. Mariya Sakhalin. Grandmother Sakhalin's youngest sister's youngest daughter. She was sent out to her uncle Yaroslav's army when she was sixteen, a year before I got there. We were put in the same jahar—"

She began to talk. And talk. Tess sat her down and held her hands, and Katerina talked fast, and low, and fiercely, as

if she feared that this was her only chance to share her love,
to truly mourn. For as the jaran say: "If you hold your grief
to yourself, you double it." As Kirill Zvertkov had said to
Tess after her brother Yurinya's death: "You might as well
be dead, too, if all you care for is your own grief." But how
could Katerina share her grief when she would be condemned for it? Tess felt a grotesque compassion for little
Katerina—no longer so little—who had borne her sorrow
like a burden for so many months, alone, who could only
unburden herself to her khaja aunt, who alone of all her relatives would not, just possibly not, judge her harshly for
loving another woman when she ought to have been loving
men.

She also felt a little bored. Katya was no different in this
respect from any other callow youth, transported by her first
serious love affair. She could go on at length about her lover's fine qualities and the stupid little endearments they had
made up for each other and the three arguments (the only
ones they had ever had). And she did go on. Tess let her,
wondering sardonically if she had ever bored anyone with
the same recitation of Ilya's virtues and the minutiae of their
meeting and falling in love; feeling the full force of the irony of the situation, that she should sit here and be bored by
poor Katya's confession of her ecstatic and passionate love
for this matchless paragon who was now dead.

After a while Katya trailed off. The lanterns burned low,
streaking the corners of the chamber in dense shadows. "I'm
going to ride south with Andrei Sakhalin tomorrow."

"Why? Your mother is so happy to have you home again.
She's certain you're staying. You've spent two years with
the archers. That's enough."

"She'll marry me off," muttered Katya. Tess did not reply,
since it was true. Katerina was nineteen, quite old enough to
be married. "She even said to me yesterday, after Galina's
baby was safely born, that when she was my age she'd already given birth to me. I hate that."

Tess sighed.

"I don't want to get married."

"Do you want to ride with the army, like Nadine?"

"No. But I don't see what else I can do."

Tess did not know what to say, except platitudes, and she
hated platitudes.

* * *

"Something is troubling my daughter," said Sonia to Tess the next morning, after they had said their good-byes and the little jahar had ridden away. "But she spoke of it to no one that I know of, not to me, not to her aunts or to her grandmother. Not even to Galina."

Tess had hold of Yuri's hand. Natalia had ridden out a ways with the older children, escorting the jahar to the outskirts of Sarai. "She will probably tell you when she is ready," she said, and hated herself for mouthing platitudes.

"May I help you with that?" asked the barbarian girl with a smile.

Jaelle did not in truth understand the exact words, but the tone and the gesture conveyed the young woman's meaning well enough. Jaelle smiled tentatively. Over the years she had grown unused to smiling. Since Princess Rusudani had come to the jaran, Jaelle had been forced to smile frequently.

The girl helped her carry water back to the princess's tent, and laid a fire for her while Jaelle rolled out a carpet and set up the awning and the quilted chair on which the princess would sit. These jaran girls went armed everywhere, quivers strapped across their backs and knives stuck in their belts. They wore striped trousers and over them a skirt split for riding, and full blouses quilted and padded like armor. In the great jaran camp in the north, the same two girls had assisted her every day, as an honor to the princess, probably, and yet always the girls went about their duties with evident good nature, including Jaelle as well as they could and even taking her down to the pond to bathe several times. Jaelle judged them to be around the same age as she was. She had learned quickly how to identify these unmarried girls from the more respectable married women. Now that they were traveling again with the army, several young women of the same type took shifts helping her. Perhaps this served as a break from more onerous duties elsewhere.

Like most women who traveled in an army's train, Jaelle knew they must also sleep with the men, and all these girls, however barbaric they seemed otherwise with their weapons, had a free manner around men that revealed that, like Jaelle, they were prostitutes. But in fact it was the behavior of the jaran men that struck Jaelle as odd. She had thought the young slave Stefan's quiet manners to be the consequence of his lowly position, but surely all these soldiers were not slaves? Granted, she had immunity because of her new status as a servant to Princess Rusudani, but not one man importuned her. Yet she knew—had stumbled across—a few trysts taking place out in the brush away from the camp.

She set the quilted chair in place under the awning and made the sign of the Pilgrim, praying to Our Lady to make clear these strange events, to grant her faithful servant good fortune at the end of this journey. After one unfortunate experience, Jaelle had learned to stay with the caravan trade. Traveling with an army's train was not so much dangerous as ... changeable, and any woman caught on the losing side was fair game. It had only happened to her once, four years ago. But Our Lady had given her a blessing to hold against the horror of the three days that had followed the lost battle: The treatment she had received had caused her to lose the child she had been carrying. Indeed, because she knew enough to cooperate with the men who had come to her, that abortion had not been as painful as the one last year, which she had procured with the aid of an herbwoman.

"I beg your pardon," said a man's voice.

Jaelle stiffened. She knew who it was, knew it instantly. She collected herself and turned around slowly. The jaran girl, lighting the fire, examined the new arrival with crass interest. Even after she got the fire lit, she showed no inclination to leave.

Jaelle clasped her hands meekly in front of herself and cast her eyes toward the ground. "Bakhtiian." She was not sure whether this was his name or a title, or both. "Princess Rusudani has gone with an escort to the church in the village." They had taken a different route south, along the coast instead of into the heathen kingdom in the highlands inland.

Bakhtiian held the copy of *The Recitation,* translated into Taor, which Princess Rusudani had purchased from Sister Yvanne and then given him as a gift in Sarai. "But you are also of the faith," he said. "I am curious about these words I read, in the third gospel, that when Hristain was brought back to life by his sister—"

Jaelle tried to hide an involuntary shiver. It was as if God had given her a sign, through this barbarian prince who, given the gift of God's word from a daughter of the apostate church, yet spoke truly. To Princess Rusudani his words would be blasphemous, of course: When the Pilgrim had bathed her brother in the waters of the spring, God had

turned the water to life-giving milk and thus granted the
Holy Son life once again, but according to the northern
church, the false faith that the princess professed, it was
God's doing alone, when in fact the faithful who professed
the teachings of the Anointed Church, the southern church,
knew that it was God acting through His Daughter, who partook equally with her brother Hristain of God's divine nature.

Bakhtiian paused. She did not correct him, even though
she knew her mistress would be aghast at his words. She
knew better than to go against a sign sent from God.

He went on. "—that after Hristain rose up again, and
blessed the multitudes who had come to witness this wonder,
that then—" He spoke the words without having to refer to
them in the book, which remained closed. "—'a bright light
appeared from heaven, and on this light He ascended to His
Father's house.' How is this explained, that a person might
ascend to heaven on light alone?"

Jaelle risked a more comprehensive glance at him. Even
her mother's master, a mere lordling, had traveled in greater
state than the great prince of the jaran tribes. He wore the
same clothes as his commonest soldier might: scarlet shirt,
black trousers and boots, and a saber and knife. The only
adornment on him was the embroidery on the sleeves and
collar of his shirt, a simple gold chain necklace around his
neck, and a plain green ribbon woven into the bronze buckle
of his belt. His sole escort was Stefan, except for the ever-
present escort of guards who hovered a spear's throw away.
Stefan met her glance, flushed, and looked at his boots.
Jaelle swallowed, looking about in the hope that her mistress
might be returning. It was never ever wise to attract the attention of powerful men. "It is Princess Rusudani who was
educated in a convent, my lord. I cannot interpret the words
of the holy book."

"But surely you have an opinion?"

"God has great powers, my lord, which lie beyond the understanding of men. It is our duty to be faithful to His
word." And because the princess was not there to hear, she
added, "And to Our Lady's example of endurance and fidel-
ity."

He grunted. "Ask Princess Rusudani when it might be
convenient for me to visit her, to ask her of these things."

"Yes, my lord."

God and Our Lady were merciful. He took himself off.
The jaran girl at the fire swung into step with him and began
flirting so outrageously with him that Jaelle was amazed by
her audacity. But it was true he was a handsome man, and
not nearly as old as she had expected him to be. And so
strange, too, to speak to her so casually, to ask her *opinion!*

"Would you like to go to the church? I could escort you
there."

She had been so intent on Bakhtiian that she had forgotten
about Stefan. An odd impulse struck her, and she tried out
a smile on him, and promptly regretted it. He practically
stammered, he looked so taken aback.

"I . . . I . . . perhaps you . . . I thought that . . ." Words
failed him.

"*Are* you a slave?" she asked suddenly, wondering why he
had not left with Bakhtiian.

"Am I a *what?*" he yelped. Bakhtiian's escort had moved
on, after Bakhtiian, and the young woman who had helped
her now chatted with a guardsman at the tail end of the procession, having evidently given up on her flirting with the
prince. He tried the word out, as if he thought he had misunderstood her. "*Slave.* A slave? Certainly not! I am the
grandson of Nikolai Sibirin and Juli Danov, who are both
great healers, and elders of the Orzhekov tribe, as well." For
an instant he looked her full in the face, and whatever he
saw there made him clench his hands. "I beg your pardon!"
he said in a tight voice, turning to leave.

Jaelle's mouth dropped open, she was so surprised. "Wait!
I . . . I beg your pardon."

He stopped but kept his back to her.

"I only thought . . ." She cursed herself. Suddenly she
didn't know what to think. How could he not be a slave?
What other man would help a whore, unless he had hoped to
sleep with her? Except he had never once asked. . . . She
didn't want him to leave, not thinking badly of her. "I
thought you must be a slave. I beg your pardon for offending
you."

His stiff shoulders relaxed, and he turned. "Why did you
think I was a slave? I suppose you can't know—only prisoners or people who have in some way betrayed the tribe are
made servants in the jaran. And a *slave*—doesn't that mean
another person owns you? Tess said that a master can do
anything he wants with a slave, even kill him." He grimaced.

"Only the gods can hold a person's life in their hands. It isn't granted to men."

"God grants us our fate, and we must suffer it gladly, and with faith."

"It is true that the gods gave Bakhtiian a vision. That is why all the khaja kingdoms are falling before our armies."

Jaelle made the sign of the Lady in front of her chest. "Your gods are false gods. If God chooses to punish His own people, it must only be because we have sinned and deserve to suffer his wrath. You are merely the instrument of God's will." Then she wondered why she had said such a thing to a man who could probably kill her on the spot, if she offended him.

But his lips quirked. He had a rather sweet smile. She hadn't noticed it before. "That is true. The gods have given us their blessing."

How could she have ever thought him a slave? she wondered now. He had the same unseemly arrogance as the rest of them.

The clatter of horses interrupted them: Princess Rusudani had returned. Jaelle told her at once of Bakhtiian's request.

"We will go to him," said the princess.

"My lady, he asked when it would be convenient for him to visit you."

"A jailer visits those he has imprisoned. We will attend his court."

They came to Bakhtiian's court just as the lanterns were being lit around the awning that sheltered him. He sat on a pillow, and the young man who claimed to be his son, Vasil'ii, lit those lanterns and brought cups and a leather flask filled with the drink they called *komis*. He acted, in truth, more like a servant than like a prince's son. Two of the women archers came forward and checked the princess and Jaelle for knives before letting them go forward.

Rusudani knelt on the edge of the carpet. Bakhtiian gestured for Vasil'ii to bring forward a pillow for her to sit on. Jaelle knelt at a respectful distance to one side. The holy book lay open on a pillow beside him.

"I give you greetings, Bakhtiian," said the princess, and Jaelle translated, "and I render thanks to God Who has brought me from my father's house across great distances to the tents of the jaran. I pray to Hristain, under Whose dominion we all live and die, that He grant you a long life."

"I have a question." He quoted from the gospel of the witness of the light that took Hristain to Heaven. "How is this explained, that a person might travel up into the heavens on light alone?"

"God's power is great," said Rusudani, "and by God's will alone any man can ascend to heaven, should he only hold to the laws which God passed down through his holy book to us."

Bakhtiian tapped his fingers on the open pages of the book, looking thoughtful. It was strange to sit so near him. He had a stern face, bearded and dark. His gaze was piercing. "I have ascended to the heavens," he said softly, "when the gods took my spirit from my body and lifted me up to their lands. That is how the Singers of our people make their journey. Do you mean that this man you call both Hristain and the Son of God traveled himself up to the heavens, body and spirit together?"

"God lifted him, Bakhtiian. He ascended on the light. That is the account given us in the holy book."

He made some comment in his own language to his son, who stood like a slave behind him. Vasil'ii shook his head. Bakhtiian turned back to the princess. "Did the bright light on which Hristain ascended to heaven leave a mark of its burning on the ground? After he had gone?"

"The gospels do not speak of any burning. But God's hand is so powerful that he might blind us with the brightest light without leaving behind the least trace of its passing. In our pride we seek to imitate God's power, but all power granted us on earth is granted to us by God."

Bakhtiian ignored these protestations of God's power. "In this book—" He tapped the pages again. "—there is no mention of burning, it is true, except that three of the accounts of Hristain's ascent into the heavens mention the light. But might there be other stories, other accounts of the same events?"

"*The Recitation* is God's holiest book. In it God speaks to us through his chosen witnesses."

One of the lanterns flared and sputtered out. Jaelle took it as a sign. She felt her heart pound in her chest, drowning the world for an instant, and then it steadied and faded. She translated Rusudani's words, but she went on, speaking her own words. "There is an account of Our Lady's travels, my lord, as spoken by The Pilgrim herself and written down by a foreign scribe who came to the knowledge of God through her ministry. In it she speaks of the light that took Hristain into Heaven, and of the fire of God's eye that scorched the earth beneath."

His gaze fastened on her. She felt acutely uncomfortable. "What is this account? Why is it not in this book?"

Jaelle clasped her hands hard in her lap. Rusudani already was looking at her, looking puzzled, looking . . . suspicious. "It is called the *Gospel of Isia of Byblos,* my lord."

Rusudani leapt to her feet and raised a hand as if to ward off Jaelle. "How dare you mention that heretical work!" Jaelle shrank back, murmuring a prayer to the Pilgrim. She had not realized how much Rusudani could understand. "Isia's false words brought about the breach between the north and the south. She is anathema." Jaelle had never seen Rusudani look so angry. "Granting divinity to Peregrina Pilgrim, when all know she was, like the Accursed One, daughter of the shepherd Ammion."

Jaelle drew herself up. Her covenant was, first of all, to God. "How could she have been the daughter of Ammion when she was twined in the womb with the Holy Son, born with him wrapped in the same caul? How else could she have sought and found his sundered remains? How bathed him in the life-giving milk, if she did not partake of God's holiness as well?"

"Heretic! Apostate! I have endured your company thus far, hoping to bring you into the True Faith, but I will endure it no longer! You are henceforth cast out from my service. If God has mercy on you, you will learn humility."

Stunned, Jaelle clutched the cloth of her skirts in her hands and prayed.

"What does Princess Rusudani say?" asked Bakhtiian mildly. His arrogance was so complete that no disturbance troubled him.

But at his words, Rusudani's enraged expression changed. She stilled. She drew her hand back to her side and after a long pause, her lips moving in a prayer, she sank back down on to the pillow.

Jaelle felt the fierce pain of victory. God had made His judgment. For Princess Rusudani could not speak to them except through her. Here, with the jaran, she was not expendable.

CHAPTER TWENTY

The Recitation

"Kireyevsky! Fix my bridle."

After six hands of days riding south with Bakhtiian and his army of twenty thousands, Vasha no longer flinched when his father spoke to him.

"I want to sit down."

Vasha took the bridle, slung it over his shoulders, and rolled out the carpet for his father to sit on, tossing down three pillows, since Ilya would inevitably have visitors now that they had halted for the night. He examined the sky, decided that probably it was going to rain, and set up the awning as well, then his father's traveling tent. Got him komis, and something to eat. He had grown so efficient that now Bakhtiian rarely spoke to him at all.

When all these things were taken care of, he lit the lanterns and sat down on the farthest back edge of the carpet, got out a new strip of leather, and began to fix the bridle.

Two of the commanders, Nikita Kolenin and Vladimir the Orphan, had come by, and they sat, laughing and talking about men's concerns. Vasha saw that the komis was running low. He jumped up and refilled the flask, having to search some way through camp to find more. When he returned, Bakhtiian took the flask from him without a word.

But in some ways it was a blessing. At first, each time his father had spoken to him had felt like a stab into his flesh. Now his father's presence was merely like salt poured continually onto an open wound.

A rider appeared, dismounted, and hurried up to the awning.

"Bakhtiian! Andrei Sakhalin is riding in with a jahar of one hundred, from Sarai."

Ilya raised his eyebrows, but he did not look overly surprised. "Send him in to me when he arrives." He glanced back at Vasha.

Vasha ducked away from his gaze. He knew what was expected of a servant. He lived in a kind of numb haze, trying to anticipate every task so that he need never actually be ordered to do anything. But he got up and trotted out to find more komis, and more food. He knew by now which of the soldiers and archers were sympathetic to him, and which ignored him.

Returning to the awning, he was brought up short by the sight of Katerina sitting perfectly at ease between her Cousin Ilya and Andrei Sakhalin. He swore under his breath. But, gods, he didn't intend to let her defeat him. Taking in a deep breath, he walked forward and without meeting anyone's eyes got out cups and poured komis all round. Then he sat down in his usual place and went back to the bridle.

"I am surprised to see you here, Sakhalin," Ilya was saying, "but I am overjoyed to hear that the gods have granted Galina another healthy child."

"Even if it was only another boy," added Katya.

"A boy may do his part by riding in the army." Sakhalin sipped at his komis, unnettled by Katya's remark. "I rode to Sarai to witness the child's birth. Now I am returning to my garrison in Dushan. I have received word of a revolt being instigated by the king's younger son, Prince Janos, and I think I had better get there quickly and execute him. That should discourage any others."

Vasha risked a glance at his father to see how Ilya would take this remark, but Ilya said nothing. The lantern light cast him into high relief, and Vasha wished fiercely, painfully, that he, too, might be able to sit so still and without comment or action invest his surroundings with the weight of his authority, as his father could.

"What do you intend, Katya?" Bakhtiian asked instead.

"I am returning to my jahar."

"Your mother says it is time for you to get married."

"Marry me to Prince Janos of Dushan, who is about to be executed. That would please me."

"A not unthinkable idea."

Katya's features underwent a swift change. She leapt to her feet and stalked away from the gathering without a word.

"Surely you can't mean it?" asked Sakhalin, sounding almost nervous.

"I know nothing about Prince Janos of Dushan. If he is a troublemaker, then certainly you must execute him. But he may have other motives. A son without prospects who has strong feelings might be amenable to other kinds of alliances."

"Ah," replied Andrei Sakhalin in an odd tone. "Well, I will ride with you as far as Parkilnous. After that we will ride west to Dushan."

"You honor us by your company," said Ilya so blandly that Vasha could not tell whether he was being polite, sincere, or sarcastic.

Sakhalin made his good-byes and left.

"You don't mean it, do you?" asked Vasha into the silence. "That you would let a khaja prince marry Katya?"

"Why not?" Ilya did not look at him. He opened up his copy of the holy book Princess Rusudani had given him. He always started at the same place: the account of the ascension of Hristain into the heavens. "It might prove to be a worthwhile alliance."

"Aunt Sonia would never agree. Mother Orzhekov would be furious. It is one thing to say that women have no choice in marriage, but quite another to force a jaran woman to accept the attentions of a khaja man, prince or not."

"Have you fixed that bridle yet?"

Vasha winced. Ilya went back to reading. After a bit, another commander came back. Vasha was glad of the excuse to leave, but he had no sooner gotten out of earshot than he was waylaid by Katerina.

"What are you doing? Acting as Bakhtiian's servant? How can you stand it?"

Vasha stiffened. "I survived two years as the most despised member of the Kireyevsky tribe. I can survive this."

"It's disgraceful how he treats you."

"He may treat me any way he wishes! It's his right—"

"—as your father? Do you think anyone acknowledges the connection?"

"Katerina Orzhekov, I politely request that you *leave me alone*." He brushed past her and kept walking. To his vast surprise, and disappointment, she left him alone.

Indeed, as they rode on, one day passing into the next, she kept herself to herself. Eleven days later they rode into Parkilnous, and the city elders begged Bakhtiian to allow them to present him with gifts and to lay down a feast in his honor. Vasha served his father at the feast and managed to overhear one elder whispering to another about a traveling friar who had been imprisoned for preaching a false gospel about the imminent end of the world, in which God would obliterate the sun in a blinding flash of light and bring Heaven to earth.

He related this information to his father when they rode back to camp that night. In the morning, Ilya sent a message to the elders asking that he be allowed to speak with the arrested man. Andrei Sakhalin arrived to make his farewells just as the messenger returned with the elders' reply.

"They've sent him where?" Ilya asked, annoyed.

"He was sent away two days since, Bakhtiian," said the messenger, one of Konstans Barshai's guardsmen, "in a cart, bound for a place called Urosh Monastery, where the khaja priests will pass judgment on him."

"You are interested in this khaja criminal, Bakhtiian?" asked Andrei Sakhalin, sitting down suddenly.

"I am interested in certain words it is reported that he has said, yes. I would like to interview him."

Sakhalin took his quirt out of his belt and drew it through his hands. "Urosh Monastery lies about seven days' ride off the main road that the army is taking south, but it does lie in territory I control, and I am riding that way in any case."

"Why would he be taken there?"

"The dyan of their priests lives there. He is named in their tongue a *presbyter*. He came to the king's city to give his respects to me, which he did with proper humility. He was an old man, but my interpreter said that he had no sons or grandsons to follow after him, that it is their way to elect a new presbyter from among the ranks of the most worthy after he is gone."

"I must think about this."

Sakhalin rose. "I will ride with the army one more day, then, before I turn west."

Ilya gave him a curt nod but scarcely noticed his leaving. He saddled Kriye himself, forgetting that usually he had Vasha do it for him, and rode that day tight-lipped and preoccupied. That evening when they halted for the night, he sent Konstans Barshai to ask Princess Rusudani to attend him.

"You're still thinking about the khaja priest, aren't you?" asked Vasha.

"I am thinking about the bright light that appeared from heaven. Here, give me that carpet. I'll unroll it."

"Tess taught us that the khaja might think the words our gods have spoken to us equally strange to what we think of theirs."

"Certainly that is true. But eight years ago the captain of a group of jaran riders who found my wife wandering out in the hills beyond Karkand saw a bright light in the sky which vanished just before he found her. That same night Tess's brother Charles disappeared. I thought nothing of the captain's report, until I read these words."

Vasha could see that his father was in the grip of one of his obsessions, and he knew him well enough to know that he would be impatient and cross until he had found some satisfaction. Aunt Sonia had once told Vasha that Ilya had gone for years in this state, until the tribes had united utterly behind him. But more importantly, Ilya was talking to him. "Do you think the khaja god came down and lifted Charles Soerensen up into heaven?"

"No." Having unrolled the carpet, Ilya rose and began pacing, slapping his gloves against one thigh. "I think he went to Erthe."

"What was the bright light?"

"I thought the captain who gave me the report saw the city burning from a distance, and mistook it. Now . . . I don't know. He also said there was a freshly burned patch of ground in the valley in which he found Tess."

Princess Rusudani arrived, attended by a jaran girl who now helped her around camp. Jaelle, who had been given her own tent by Bakhtiian in recognition of her status as a valued interpreter, arrived a moment later. The two khaja women glanced at each other, and Vasha was surprised to see the princess look away first. Ever since the awful scene many days ago, when the princess had fallen into a rage and screamed words Vasha did not understand at her poor servant, Princess Rusudani had seemed less calm, less sure of herself, but Jaelle had oddly enough become more confident, and had even (according to one of the archers whom Vasha lay with occasionally) begun working very hard to learn khush.

Stefan appeared and threw himself down beside Vasha. He touched Vasha on the shoulder and leaned in to whisper in his ear. "Is there something wrong with Katerina? She asked me to lie with her last night."

Anger shot through Vasha. He hooked his fingers into his

belt, a better choice, he thought, than slugging his best friend. "And?"

"But all she did was cry and hold on to me. She told me that you said you never wanted to talk to her again. Is that true? It made her very unhappy."

Princess Rusudani and Ilya exchanged formal greetings, translated through Jaelle. While Rusudani spoke, Jaelle glanced up once, swiftly, to mark Stefan's presence.

Vasha shoved Stefan away. "You're too ugly for any woman to want to lie with anyway, except as a brother," said Vasha in a low voice, weirdly happy about the story Stefan had just told him.

Stefan snorted. "That isn't what Valisa Savko told me."

"I don't believe it. Why should *she* bother with you? You're not even a soldier."

Stefan smirked.

"Liar!"

Ilya glanced back at them. Vasha clamped his lips shut over his next words: Why should beautiful Valisa Savko, whose prowess with the bow was legendary and who was famous for having single-handedly killed ten khaja soldiers with ten successive arrows, want to lie with *Stefan?* Many young women had approached his father on this journey south. Only Valisa had actually gotten inside Bakhtiian's tent.

Stefan merely looked smug.

Vasha wrenched his attention back to Princess Rusudani.

"I lived for ten winters in the house of God," she was saying, and Jaelle translated.

"You were sent there as a child," Ilya said.

"I was."

"I have seen that you are wise in the ways of your church, because of your education. You can read and write?"

"These things I was taught at the convent. But God has not yet granted me the glory of being invested as a sister in the faith. My knowledge is insignificant next to God's glory."

"But you have heard of the *Gospel of Isia of Byblos.*"

She made a gesture with one hand over her chest and shot an angry glance at Jaelle. "It is a heretical text. The Accursed One seduces men with false words and false prophets."

"Yet there are some who believe it is truth?"

"They have strayed from the True Church."

" 'They have strayed from the True Church,' " Jaelle translated, "So speaks Princess Rusudani, but it is not so, my lord. The Anointed Church follows the word of God faithfully. The northerners have broken with His covenant by refusing to acknowledge—"

Rusudani began to speak harshly, drowning out Jaelle's words.

"Silence! I do not care to listen to you disparage one another. You will translate my words faithfully."

"I will, my lord," said Jaelle meekly.

"I wish to hear about the *Gospel of Isia of Byblos*."

Rusudani touched the knife that hung on a chain at her neck. "I have not read it, my lord, only heard of it so that I might not fall into error."

"You heard the story of the man who was taken away to Urosh Monastery, Jaelle. Is there such a story, of a great blinding, in Isia's gospel?"

"Not as it was read to me, my lord, but I am not educated."

"Ask Princess Rusudani."

Rusudani hesitated before she spoke. "The heretical gospel speaks only of Hristain's ascension and his sister's ministry. But in recent years a new heresy has spread northward from the lands where the apostate church holds sway, speaking of a light that flares in the western oceans and of angels whose glowing wings track across the sky, and how these are signs presaging the second coming of Our Lord, the Son of God."

"Those words Princess Rusudani speaks," added Jaelle. "But I have also heard it said among the caravan women that His sister, the Blessed Pilgrim, has already descended from Heaven and walks the earth even now, preparing us for His coming and the final days."

Ilya considered for a long time. He took a sip of komis, and Vasha refilled his cup. "I will go to Urosh Monastery and speak with this prophet."

"Let me go as well," said Rusudani instantly, "so that I may guard you from his lies."

The passion of her plea took Vasha aback.

But Ilya had withdrawn his attention, wrestling with new preoccupations. "Stefan, escort the women back to their tents. Kireyevsky, you will attend me." He rose and walked away through camp.

Vasha hurried after him. "Wouldn't it be wiser to wait? When we reach Jeds, we could ask that the holy women admit us to the great library in Jedina Cloister. Surely they will have books that would answer your question. They might even have this gospel that Jaelle speaks of."

"Men aren't allowed to set foot in the cloister, and I do not intend to force my way into a women's sanctuary. But I can enter Urosh Monastery."

The idea sprang to mind easily and pleasantly. "Princess Rusudani can gain admittance to Jedina Cloister for us, if it is true that she lived for many years in such a cloister in her own land. Or Tess could."

Ilya fixed him with such a look, suddenly, that Vasha shrank back. "I will speak with Andrei Sakhalin. Send Konstans to me as well. Then brush down my string. Look Kriye over particularly. He was off on his right foreleg today."

Stung, fuming, Vasha walked away, not too fast but not too slow, either. But he went and found Konstans Barshai, and made excuses to himself that he would care for the horses after he escorted the captain over to Andrei Sakhalin's tent.

Konstans did not like Ilya's idea either.

"I will take five hundred men," said Ilya.

"You should take one thousand, the whole guard," argued Konstans.

"Why not the whole army, then?" Ilya retorted.

"No need for that," Andrei Sakhalin said, smoothing over the tension. "I have already sent word ahead to my garrison that I am riding through this territory. I travel with only a jahar of one hundred. My men control this area. There will be no trouble."

"Five hundred men, then," said Ilya. "We will travel swiftly. It would be best if Princess Rusudani rode with us as well. She can speak to them, and to us through her interpreter, and because of her rank and her position in the church the khaja priests will be more likely to accede quickly to our request."

"She is a valuable prize," said Andrei Sakhalin. "Is it wise to remove her from the protection of the army?"

"If you do not control these lands, Sakhalin, then it is not wise for me to make this journey."

The two men looked at each other, and they seemed without moving or speaking to contest. Vasha had watched Ilya do this to lesser men—proving his right of place—but he had never seen him do it to a Sakhalin prince.

"Of course I control this region," said Sakhalin stiffly, looking angry. But he had spoken first, and defensively, and thus given right of command to Ilya.

"She will ride with us. How are the khaja to know she rides with us now? They must still believe she resides in Sarai. Kireyevsky, go tell Katerina Orzhekov that she will attend us as well, to show the khaja priests that the princess has been granted the protection of our women." He looked at Konstans, allowing his captain the final word. "Is there anything else?"

Konstans' expression could have been carved in stone, it was so still and so disapproving. But he made no further objections.

So it was decided.

At dawn, leaving the banner with the main army, Ilya split off from the main road south with an escort of five hundred of his personal jahar and headed west with Andrei Sakhalin and his one hundred riders. Vasha went with him, and Stefan managed to attach himself to Vasha at the last moment.

Autumn covered the land in browns and faded greens. It was a rough, dreary landscape, tracts of dense forest interspersed with lonely fields and an occasional village. No one bothered them. When they stopped at night, Andrei Sakhalin commandeered food and forage at the nearest village or isolated manor house, and the Dushanites gave it over without protest, seeing the staff that represented his authority to oversee this region in the name of the great jaran conqueror, the Bakhtiian.

The troop of riders made good time. Vasha half expected that they would overtake the wagon carrying the accused friar, but they did not. They reached the vale that sheltered the monastery in the late afternoon on the fifth day after leaving the army.

The size and grandeur of Urosh Monastery surprised Vasha. Surrounded by a low wall, the complex of buildings was laid out neatly, centered on a long building anchored by two towers: Vasha recognized its type from Jeds: It was the church, built of stone. The rest of the buildings were timber.

Cattle lowed, and shorn fields striped the land around the
wall.

He and Katerina had called a truce.

"These khaja priests hoard their gold in their churches,"
she said to him now. "I'm surprised no one robs them."

"Would you rob a Singer?"

"Of course not! Anyway, Cousin Ilya has already made a
decree exempting khaja priests from taxes." She urged her
horse forward down the slope that led to the field on which
Sakhalin had halted his men. Some had begun pitching tents.
"I suppose it speaks well for the khaja, then, that they honor
their priests enough to grant them both respect and wealth."

"And immunity from thieves?"

Katya grinned at him suddenly, and he felt the spark of
her laughter catch on him. She had been so quiet the last
five days, riding in silence alongside the other two women,
attending to herself and assisting Princess Rusudani, who
had clearly never learned how to take care of herself. He
smiled, and as if she knew what he was thinking, she gestured toward Rusudani and Jaelle, who rode some ways in
front of them.

"I think all khaja noblewomen must be poorly educated.
That's what Mama says. She says Tess was the same way
when she came to the jaran, not knowing how to care for a
horse or to prepare food or weave or shoot, although I do admit that the princess can use a knife."

"Khaja have slaves to do all their work for them." Her
words stung a little, though. He didn't like to hear her criticize Rusudani. "Perhaps they think it isn't fitting that noblewomen wait on themselves."

Katya snorted. "No wonder they're so weak. Do you suppose
any soldier in this army would respect Bakhtiian if he could not
care for his own horse, repair his tack, and know whether or
not his saber was balanced and sharp? Jaelle is much more like
a proper woman. She can take care of herself."

Stefan had been silent until now. "Do you think jaran
women respect her?"

"I know nothing of her parents or her tribe. She has never
spoken of them to me. But you must know, Stefan, that she
was a *whore*—" She used the Taor word. "—before she became an interpreter."

He got a little red. "I know that Tess says that among the
khaja a whore is a dishonored woman who lies with men for

gold, but Tess also says that such women are merely surviving in the only way they can and it is not the *women* who ought to be condemned."

"She has always done her share of the work," said Katya, as if that settled the matter of Jaelle's character.

Stefan looked pleased.

Here at the edge of the great field that fronted the monastery's outer wall a second road intersected with the one they had traveled on. The second road led away to the southwest, back into the forest. Ten of Sakhalin's riders vanished into the gloom of the trees. Vasha looked back to see the telltale white plume of Konstans' helm at the rear of their party. Konstans pulled up his horse and gazed after the riders who had gone into the forest. After a moment, he came along after the main group.

It was difficult to pass through the mob of horses that crowded the field as the jahar arrived and settled down. Since every man had two and perhaps three mounts, and some of the fields beyond still wore a coat of unharvested grain, there wasn't as much room to spread out as was proper. Flanked by Vasha and Stefan, Katerina pushed her way through and came out to a relatively clear space where Ilya, still mounted on Kriye, was having an uncomfortably polite disagreement with Andrei Sakhalin.

Ilya had taken off his helmet and held it tucked under one arm. "I will go in now with you. There is no reason I can't interview the accused man tonight, allowing us to leave again in the morning."

Sakhalin shook his head. "Of course that would be the swiftest way, Bakhtiian, but there are certain traditions which are best followed in Dushan. King Zgoros makes no request himself. He always sends ahead an envoy to make his will known. He does not go to others, they come to him. If you go in yourself, you will be considered no better than a servant. Let me act for you. I will bring the presbyter out to wait on you. Thus will he understand your power."

"So be it."

"It would be well," added Sakhalin, "if I took Princess Rusudani with me. No woman wishes to remain with a jahar when she could spend the night in the tents of her own people."

Katya's head snapped up. "I grant her the protection and good name of the Orzhekov tribe. That is sufficient."

Sakhalin dropped his gaze away from her at once. He hesitated, shrugged, and rode away with ten of his riders. They passed in through the stone archway that was the only opening in this stretch of wall. Mounted, Vasha could see over the wall, which came up to Misri's withers. Like any khaja town, the buildings inside appeared crowded together, but they had an orderly look to them. All the paths were straight, and the church itself was impressively tall, with a high, peaked wooden roof.

"I beg your pardon, Cousin," Katerina said in a low voice to Ilya.

Vasha looked at them in time to see a glance flash between them, she and Ilya, and his lips quirked. He seemed amused. "I would never presume to correct Mother Orzhekov's representative. But perhaps it is true that Princess Rusudani, because of her own customs, would prefer to rest for the night inside the monastery walls."

"I will bring her over," said Katya.

"I'll go get them," said Stefan quickly, and dismounted, tossing his reins to Vasha. Katya did the same, following him.

Konstans Barshai appeared, white plume bobbing. He took his helm off and surveyed the field with disgust. "These khaja never have enough pastures. I have posted sentries and sent out a few scouts. I would prefer to send more out, but it would be an insult to Sakhalin, since he's already sent many of his men to reconnoiter."

"Find room for the horses, and forage," said Ilya. "That is my first concern."

Konstans nodded and rode away, clapping his helmet back on. Ilya dismounted finally, giving Kriye over to Vladimir. "Kireyevsky, give Vladi your horses as well. Put out my carpet."

Most of the riders had nothing with them except their horses, the armor they wore and weapons they carried, and a pouch and flask for food and water. Ilya had brought an extra horse to carry a carpet, pillows, and an awning, and Vasha set these out beside the handful of tents pitched by Sakhalin's men.

As he threw down the first pillow, he heard Rusudani's voice and then Jaelle's translation.

"—and that is the dormitory and the refectory, those roofs

beside the church. They enclose the inner *claustrum*, which only the monks may enter."

"Have you been here before?" Katerina asked, with some amazement.

"I have not. Many years ago, in the time of Saint Benaris, the blessed founder of the holy Orders, the presbyters held a great council and prepared in court the plan to which all monasteries and convents have since been built. Those that could. Even I have heard of Urosh Monastery, which is famous for its adherence to this holy design."

Ilya had already seated himself. Rusudani took her place on a pillow next to him with a kind of exalted grace. Jaelle knelt beside her, and Stefan hovered behind Jaelle. Katya halted beside Vasha and gave him a look, which he could not interpret.

"Katerina Orzhekov has asked if I wish to enter the protection of the monastery, but you must know that women are not welcome within the walls, except in times of extremity. There is a guest house outside the north wall. But—" She hesitated and glanced toward Katerina. Swallowed. "In Dushan, I would prefer the protection of jaran."

"Why is that?" Ilya asked.

"Many years ago my father had reason to quarrel with King Zgoros. I would not necessarily be welcome here."

"Yet you came with us willingly, even asked to."

Her lashes shaded her eyes as she fixed her gaze on her clasped hands. "I wish only to save you from error, my lord."

"Ha!" said Katya under her breath, and Vasha glanced at her, but her expression gave nothing away.

"When did your father have this quarrel? What was it over?"

"I was very young, my lord. It was before I entered the convent."

"By whose hand were you sent to a convent at such a tender age?"

"By God's Hand. He sent me a vision when I was a child. So my father gave me to the convent."

The locus of Bakhtiian's attention, still focused mostly outward, keeping track of the settling in of his jahar on the field around them, changed abruptly when Jaelle translated these words. "You are a Singer?"

"I am dedicated to God's service."

"To a woman or a man whom the gods have given a vision we give the name, a Singer."

Rusudani looked up and met Ilya's gaze. Something passed between them. That moment of intimacy flooded Vasha with wild jealousy. "You were granted a vision," she said.

"I was."

"Only God grants true visions."

"And my vision has come true. Just as Mother Sun spreads her rays in all directions, so my power is spread everywhere, and so my armies march as with the rising sun."

"All that comes about, comes about because of God's will."

Ilya smiled. He lifted up his right hand and held it out, open. "The gods gave us different fingers to the hand, and so did they also give different ways to jaran and khaja. Is this not so?"

She hesitated, looking angry.

Ilya went on. "Why did you leave the convent?"

A pause. She looked up at him again. "I did not leave. I was taken. My father promised me to the church, but some men do not respect the sanctity of God's house."

"That is certainly true."

"The Lord of Sharvan sent his men to take me out of the convent. He wanted to marry me."

"You did not wish to marry him?"

She caught in a sharp laugh. "Why should I wish to marry any man, when I could be a bride to Hristain himself, and dedicate myself to His service? Nor would my father ever have sanctioned such a match. The Lord of Sharvan is a bandit, nothing more."

"Yet you are a valuable woman."

Both she and Jaelle looked startled by this comment. Finally, Rusudani nodded. "It is true, my lord," she said at last, "that you married the Prince of Jeds' sister, who in her turn became prince when her brother died. But I have never heard that the jaran take more than one wife."

Vasha thought he would choke. Was she actually suggesting that his father might want to marry her? Did she want him to? He eyed his father surreptitiously. He was a good-looking man; everyone said so. A woman might desire him for that alone. But he was far more than that. Rusudani had not spared the least glance for Vasha since this journey began. Gods, why should she? For a moment, Vasha hated his father for that.

Ilya coughed into his hand. "No, indeed," he said mildly. "It would be more than a man could bear. It is bad enough having to please your sisters and aunts and cousins. You had been captured by the Lord of Sharvan, then, and were being taken to his holding?"

The abrupt change of subject threw Rusudani off. She looked down at her hands again as if recovering her composure. She had beautiful eyelashes, and the soft curve of her lips made Vasha's palms damp. "That is true," she said finally.

"Then who were you escaping from? Who were the men who attacked the holding? Why would you run from your father's men?"

"They were not my father's men. Otherwise I would have run to them instead of to . . ." She looked up at Vasha. Her gaze seared him. "Is it true he is your son?"

"You don't know who attacked the holding, or if you were the object of their attack?"

"I cannot say, great lord."

Ilya blinked. "You know whose men they were."

This sort of tense silence had the interesting quality of magnifying nearby sounds, so that abruptly Vasha could hear horses and laughter and a man singing a lewd song. Afternoon had faded toward dusk, and the sun dipped down below the wall of forest, shading the road west. He felt Stefan's body next to him, and on the other side, could sense Katya's breath, in and out.

"I know, or at least I could guess," she admitted at last. "I am not a fool. I was betrothed to him as an infant, but the betrothal was annulled when God marked me for the convent."

"What is his name?"

A shout came from far away, and Vasha heard Konstans barking an order, but he could not make out the words.

Ilya waited.

Khaja were very strange, Vasha thought as he watched Rusudani struggle with herself and then, giving in, look up. They only looked you in the eye after you had beaten them. Except Tess, of course, but Tess was different.

"Prince Janos of Dushan," she said in a low voice.

Hard on her words a cry rang through the gathered riders.

"Stanai! Stanai!"

The quiet scene centered on the carpet dissolved into confusion. A sudden maelstrom surrounded Vasha. Ilya jumped to his feet.

"Get that helmet on!" he snapped at Vasha as he fastened his own over his head.

Katya moved in a blur. She shoved Vasha and Stefan off the carpet and grabbed it by the edge. "Off!" she shouted to Jaelle. "Quickly! Get under it!"

Vasha gaped, but Jaelle moved swiftly enough, crouching on the grass and dragging the carpet up over herself and Rusudani for what little protection it afforded.

A sudden dark shadow covered the sun with the whirring of thousands of wings. Stefan yelped, staggered, and fell to his knees. He clapped a hand over one ear. Blood leaked through his fingers. Ilya had vanished. Men, mounted, pushed past, but already the screams of horses shredded the late afternoon stillness.

Katya wrenched Stefan's hand down from his head. "Just flesh. It will only bleed. Get your helmet on, you idiot." She slipped her bow from its quiver and fitted it with an arrow.

Another flight of arrows darkened the air.

And there was his father, on Kriye, with Konstans beside him.

"No," Konstans was saying, "these aren't bandits. We have been betrayed. Look there."

Already the jahar had arrayed into ranks while Vasha and Stefan stood gaping. Already men had fallen under the awful rain of arrows. Another flight fell. Metal rang on Vasha's helmet, and he started, coming out of his daze. He stared down to see two arrows sticking out of the quilting of his heavy coat, and an instant later he realized that something wet was running down his skin. He yanked out one arrow, but it had no blood on its tip. Twenty paces away, a horse reared, screaming, and threw its rider. Stefan moved, bolting for the horse.

Katerina swore. "Get up, you idiot," she said, and he felt Misri's comforting bulk shoulder against him. Reflexively he mounted.

Up the slope, coming out from the encircling forest, coming down the roads, and appearing all at once at the farthest edge of the fields surrounding them, appeared a phalanx of spears and shields escorted by rank upon rank of armored riders. No banner flew to identify them, but there were many, many more than Ilya's five hundred riders. The last trail of the sun glinted on their helmets and on the bright points of their spears and swords.

"At least half of Sakhalin's riders have vanished," added Konstans in a voice so calm that he might have been talking about the layout of a khot board. "I believe we are surrounded."

CHAPTER TWENTY-ONE

Flower Night

Ilyana woke up suddenly. For some reason she had been dreaming of Kori's Uncle Gus dancing the part of Lord Shiva, exotic, uncomfortable to watch yet impossible not to watch; but even as she remembered it the dream faded and vanished in the dark rather stuffy air of the tent. Abruptly she knew what was wrong: Valentin was gone. It was so still that above the quiet breathing of Evdokia and Anton she heard footfalls on the path outside, scritching on pebbles. She got up, checked the little ones, and slipped a skirt on over her sleeping shift.

Ducking out through the entrance flap, she was disoriented for a moment by the dark square of the caravansary in front of her, by the pale globes of moons in the sky above, by the slash of distant wall and ridge, by the faintest nimbus glowing in the air above which, as she oriented herself, she realized was the energy field of the huge dome which contained them. Valentin's nocturnal escapes were so much a part of her life that she had forgotten where they were, and when she remembered it, she felt a thrill of excitement: They were the first humans to set foot on a Chapalii Duke's private planet, in his very palace, or at least, in as much of it as they were allowed to see.

Valentin disappeared inside the gateway to the caravansary. She followed him. Pebbles slid under the soles of her feet and, as she passed under the gateway, became stone paving.

At first, halting inside the courtyard, she did not see him. He was hidden in plain sight: crouched in the gazebo, fingering the latticework with desperate concentration. His hands shook. When she came up behind him, he turned, starting. The gazebo's lattice shone with just enough of an unnatural glow that Ilyana saw sweat break on his forehead, running down his neck.

"What are you doing?" she whispered.

"There's a nesh port in here somehow," he muttered, turning back to the latticework. "I heard M. Unbutu say so yesterday to Gwyn Jones. It must go with the map or something. I gotta get access, Yana. I can't stand it anymore."

She knelt beside him. "But Valentin, if there is one, then it was built by the Chapalii. That would be dangerous to—"

His hands, sliding over the lattice, abruptly stopped, and his face altered expression so quickly that she gasped out loud. Then he was gone. Not his body, but his mind. Spirited away from her so utterly that her limbs froze in terror.

Traceries of light shifted along the mosaic floor of the gazebo, and an aroma like incense brushed past her, fleeting, like a glimpse of a butterfly. She touched Valentin's shoulder. A thrumming caught up in her blood, and she could almost see what he was seeing, as if the contact through their skin was enough to link her in as well. She smelled, suddenly, the scent of heat baking on stone.

She jerked her hand away. The movement woke her out of her stupor. She had to find M. Unbutu. She knew which tiny room was his: They had held tutorials there the last five days. Like all of these rooms his was screened off not by a door but by a curtain. She hesitated, fingers brushing the coarse weave, then coughed and said, softly: "M. Unbutu?"

No answer.

"M. Unbutu?"

From the other side she heard the sound of a person grunting in his sleep and shifting. She glanced up and down the corridor and slipped inside, pressing back against the cold wall.

"M. Unbutu. I'm sorry to disturb you, but—"

"Hmm?" He woke up suddenly and sat up. She could see him like a bulky shadow, his wild hair, his naked torso, against the faint gleam of light that came in through the open window. "Yana!"

The room wasn't large. If she took a step forward, she could touch him. He peered at her through the gloom. The silence was a third presence in the room. Ilyana felt acutely uncomfortable for a reason she could not understand.

"Uh, Yana," he said finally, sounding very odd, "I don't think you should be here."

She got her breath back. "It's Valentin. He's been caught in the gazebo. I think he's neshing."

He began to stand up, froze, and said, "Yes. I'll be there in a minute."

She felt herself flush. Too mortified to speak, she stepped backward out of the room and fled down the corridor, back to the courtyard where Valentin crouched, locked into his strange union with the latticework. A striped moon hung squarely above the courtyard. Stars blazed. Valentin was unnaturally silent, only the lift and fall of his chest revealing that he still breathed. Ilyana shifted from one foot to the other, and back, and back, and waited forever.

M. Unbutu's white shirt and trousers appeared like a pale flag at one corner of the courtyard. A moment later she saw the shadow of his face and hair. He hurried over and halted an arm's length from her.

"Oh, Goddess," he exclaimed under his breath. "I see what you mean. When did this happen?"

"It just did. But when I touched him, it was like I could almost nesh *through* him, the connection is that strong."

"I don't know how that could be. But why would he risk neshing on a system we know nothing about and which might be antipathic to the human mind? Valentin is not stupid."

Under her bare toes, the gazebo tiles felt slick, almost damp. She chewed on her lips.

"Oh," said M. Unbutu suddenly. "He's addicted. The signs all point to it, once you think to put them together. So *that's* why my portable nesh was tampered with on the ship out here. I thought it was odd."

Ilyana cringed.

When he spoke again, he sounded angry. "Why isn't he getting help? Your parents must know how dangerous—"

"They don't understand."

"They don't understand? Yana, do you know that nesh addiction can kill?"

She gulped down panic. "Yes."

"Oh, Goddess, of course you do. I'll have to talk to them."

"No. Don't. They really won't understand. But . . . maybe you could help me."

"I'm not licensed or experienced in—" He glanced at her and stopped. She felt more than saw him wince.

"There isn't anyone else to help him anyway, not here."

"Yana! Your parents have to—"

"Don't you see? They already know, they just pretend that they don't. They can't. They can't help him!"

He swore, something long and convoluted, under his breath. "We'll discuss this later. Right now we'd better get him out of there." He placed a hand, fingers splayed, on Valentin's back. Ilyana's eyes had adjusted to the dark well enough that she could see details now: The way M. Unbutu's eyes began to track something that wasn't there; the way his nose twitched, sniffing. He licked his lips, and with his free hand reached and touched something that didn't exist. With an effort, he dragged his hand away from Valentin's back.

He whistled softly. "Damn me to hell. I don't know what kind of interface they're using, but that field is emanating *through* him somehow. All I got was shadows, but still . . . you know we just can't pull him away."

"I know. I've done this before. Gone in myself and guided him out."

"We'll have to try. But I'm going with you."

She swallowed. Her throat was dry. "He might not look like himself."

"Oh, tupping hell. You mean he guises, too? I thought they'd stopped letting minors do that."

"Yeah."

"Sorry. I'm not usually that naive. All right. Take position on either side and imitate how his fingers are positioned. Wherever we end up, stick with me. We will not split up."

She nodded and knelt beside Valentin, making sure she didn't touch him. M. Unbutu knelt on his other side. Valentin breathed. A breeze had come up, and it tickled the stray hair that had escaped from her braid and lay now along the back of her neck. She placed her fingers on the latticework.

A great web, thrumming with light, set over (into?) an abyss of endless nothingness. Ilyana stood on a strand of light and it pulsed with the warmth of blood against her bare feet, filling her, drawing her in.

She dissolved into sound.

"Valentin!"

She stood in a vast echoing space ringed with pillars of black stone. She was alone. A floor of obsidian stretched out to the pillars, and above and beyond was a darkness so absolute that it had texture, as if it was a dome of velvet. Then she smelled Valentin's trail. Or not him, precisely, but camel, and knew that it marked his passage through here.

She followed the foul smell, walking carefully, and just as she crossed between a set of pillars she heard a stutter in the thrum that lay so quiet along her consciousness that she had forgotten it was there until it was, so briefly, interrupted.

"Yana!"

She turned. M. Unbutu ran over to her. When he halted beside her, he took hold of her wrist. His hand was solid, warm.

"Complete perceptual immersion. We could just as well be here in the flesh." He dropped her hand and tapped at the pillar instead. "Solid. I just spent about an hour wandering around a huge reconstruction of what must be the palace here, about waist-high models, just amazing. Needless to say, I was the only living soul there, and there was no obvious way out."

"But I just got here. I mean, just a minute ago we were in the gazebo."

"Huh. I found this, though." With great care he fished into a pocket and drew out . . . nothing. She looked closer and saw that it was a short strand of blond hair. "Do you think it's Valentin's?"

"How could a nesh lose a piece of its hair?"

"Can't. How could I have noticed it? But I did, and as soon as I picked it up it gave me a kind of pulling field, as if I could suddenly sense where you were. That's how I found you."

"Quick!" The camel scent was moving off. "He's this way—"

She stepped off between the pillars only to realize that she was stepping into nothing

Winds buffet her. Sand stings her face. This place again, the barren, storm-wracked desert. Always this place. She gropes blindly and finds a solid hand and grasps it as if it were a lifeline. Its fingers work in hers, but the storm is so fierce that she cannot even see the person beside her, so hard does the grit and sand batter her eyes and grind and groan in the streaming air. The wind howls.

They emerge into an eddy.

"This is his place," she cries, cracking open one eye that swells with tears, aching and dry. M. Unbutu holds tightly on to her and stares at something ahead. The blistering sand

doesn't seem to bother him as much, but his lips are shut tight against it. "He always comes here."

"Look," he murmurs, awestruck. "He's building it."

She lifts her chin against the weight of the wind and squints upward, toward the hills. But they aren't hills. They are detritus, they are the streaming wind that pours out of the back, the arms, the legs, the head, the whole being of the slight adolescent boy trudging forward head bent slightly as against a steady grinding force and that wind is both the storm and the desert he leaves behind him.

She gulps in sand and chokes on it. "Oh, gods. Is this what's inside him?"

The boy presses forward, receding from her, and the wind moans and shoves her after him and thrusts her back, caught in the whirlpool of his creation. A blinding light frames Valentin's fragile outline, as if he is the conduit through which it passes.

"It's like the old conundrum," says M. Unbutu, canting his voice high to pierce above the torrent, "about gravity and time and the edge of the universe—that explorers could never find the edge of the universe because their very presence, their mass, would cause the universe to keep expanding in front of them because of their gravitational field."

"How do we get him back?" she wails.

"Formless matter. It's like the formless matter out of which Earth, the universe, any cosmological order is made."

She realizes he isn't listening to her. She drops his hand and plunges forward into the maelstrom. Sand pelts her. Pebbles scrape her skin. The dry barren heat is overpowering. Sheer frantic force of will brings her to Valentin in sixteen agonizing steps. She grabs his arm and tugs him to a stop. What else can she do?

He strains away. "Let me go. Let me go, Yana. Can't you see it? I'm almost there."

She sees nothing but light. Stillness shudders into being around them.

And there, maybe, something golden, like a shimmer, like a golden sea seen through a tiny, distant gateway.

She hesitates. She can feel the strength of his yearning, can taste it, like the husk of grass on her tongue.

"Yana! Valentin!"

M. Unbutu is solid. His hands have weight where they close on her arm and pull Valentin into her. He swears.

*"We're going out of here." His tongue wets his lips. "I don't
know how the hell you did this, Valentin, but—" As he says
the last word the stream of sand still pouring out of Valentin
coalesces and begins to form an archway, turns into wood,
and then Ilyana smells the leafy mold of thick vegetation,
rotting.*

*"Damn it," say M. Unbutu mildly, surprised. "Oh, well.
Good enough. Through here."*

Valentin goes meekly.

*They step through into a pocket of dense jungle. Vines
trail down from tree trunks that shoot up into a dome of
leaves. The vines twine and curl and form a lattice and they
place their fingers on the latticework*

Ilyana heard the softest scrape of a shoe on stone and she
started back, but the three of them were alone in the courtyard. Valentin slumped backward and she caught him, and
together with M. Unbutu eased him down onto the smooth
mosaic tiles. She still smelled the desiccating heat of the
sandstorm.

"M. Unbutu, how did he do that? What was he doing?"

"If we're going to try that again, you'd better just call me
David. The formal style takes too damned long."

"We're going to do that again?" She hesitated, tried out
the word "David" on her tongue, and decided just to not call
him anything unless she absolutely had to.

"You don't want to?" He laughed under his breath, and
she realized with a shock that he was exhilarated.

And that she was, too. If Valentin could do that, could
she? Could she pour light through her and create a world?
"Well. Yes. I'd like to see that model of the palace."

"I'd like to see if we can use it to get through to the real
palace, even in nesh form."

At that moment, Ilyana knew that she was part of the conspiracy. She felt suddenly very . . . adult. "Yes," she said
fiercely. "Oh gods. We'd better get Valentin back to my
mother's tent."

Anatoly watched from the shadows as Ilyana and David
supported Valentin between them and helped him off toward
Karolla Arkhanov's tent. When the courtyard was empty, he
emerged from behind a column and examined the gazebo
and the latticework wall. It hummed in the way the great
wall that anchored the dome hummed, but although he had

seen the way their hands clutched it, he was not so foolhardy as to make such an expedition alone.

In the morning, he woke to exclamations coming from outside. Portia and Diana were already gone. He dressed quickly and ran outside to find the Company gathered along the east wall of the caravansary, facing the gardens. Yesterday a bank of green shrubs had grown here. Today they had all come into bloom at once, white flowers with a scattering of crimson blossoms at their center, forming a shape that Anatoly vaguely recognized as glyph, something Chapalii, he thought, but he found it difficult to remember visual markers of language.

"What kind of flowers are those?" he asked, coming up alongside Hyacinth, who looked flushed.

"Flower night," said Hyacinth. "That's how Roki translates the glyph. It's a summons."

"A summons?"

Already Yomi was calling out orders. Several of the younger actors were shaking out skirts and gowns, hanging them out in the open air on a line set up by some of the techs.

"To perform." Hyacinth paused, slapping his fingers on his cheeks, eyes wide. "Tonight!" He laughed. "The bastard made us wait so long to even get here at all, made us wait weeks here, you'd think he'd give us more notice. Not even a tech rehearsal. We don't even know what kind of space we'll be performing in."

"He is zayinu."

Hyacinth lowered his hands, glanced at Anatoly, and grinned. Anatoly grinned back, realized what he had done, muttered an excuse, and went to find Diana.

"I don't have time for you right now," Diana said, catching sight of him before he'd even said a word to her. She was helping shake out costumes. "Yana already took Portia. Maybe Yomi has something for you to do."

But he was superfluous. The repertory company was like a well-honed jahar, adept at working together. His presence would only throw off their drill. Even David, by virtue of his relationship to Charles, fit in with them. Anatoly did not. And while it was always appropriate for a man to take care of young children, it certainly would be unseemly for him to do so in the company of an unmarried young woman to whom he was not related.

So he went out to the horses and rode the mare he now thought of as his. A summons meant, of course, that the zayinu duke Naroshi commanded the Company to come to him. How would he bring them there? Where was he? Anatoly rode at once to the great slab of ebony stone embedded in the rose wall. Was this the doorway through which they would pass? Through the rose wall he saw the blurred lines of the other world, drowned in rain.

He dismounted and went to lean against the rose wall where its color changed from rose to ebony, an abrupt break, like a seam. Through the wall he could make out ... towers, a host of spears thrusting up into the sky. He had seen a gathering of towers from the platform hovering high above the palace, when they had first come here. The foundation of those towers had been lost beneath the confluence of two rivers, and yet in the map in the courtyard of the caravansary, there was a similar nest of towers which rose from a spit of land bounded by rivers: Was it possible that some catastrophic flood had risen and covered them? But that meant, then, that the map in the courtyard might not be accurate.

Only the khaja put their faith in maps. The land changed over time, over the seasons, and over the lifetime of a man. Anatoly knew better than to trust anything he had not seen with his own eyes or heard from the wisest elders, and even then, nothing truly remained constant except the plains themselves.

And he thought bitterly of Diana.

The humming pitch of the stone changed. He ran to stop his mare from bolting. A shudder shook through the ground, running up through his boots, up through his whole body, like the charge of the air in a lightning storm out on the flat plain.

The gate opened, just opened, dissipating into the rose wall, leaving a gap the width of eight horses riding abreast through to the other side. Hot, humid air spilled out, spattering him with warm rain and the sheer weight of heat and dampness. In the world beyond it rained in dense sheets, pounding rain, like the thunder of hooves of an army charging into battle.

He got on the mare and rode for the opening. He did not get there in time.

A great vehicle appeared, a barge, filling the opening. The

mare shied and reared. As he fought to hold her, the barge moved through, floating above the grass, and the opening sealed shut behind it. Water poured off its sides, sprinkling the grass, and then it was dry, gleaming, a boat flat on both the bottom and the top, with a silver railing wreathed in white and red flowers. It was empty. It sailed off over the grass, leaving a wave of wind in its wake. Anatoly could do nothing but follow its trail back to the caravansary.

By the time he got there, the company was fitted up and mostly onboard. Most of the actors were chattering with excitement, voices loud, faces flushed. He left the mare waiting and ran to find Diana.

She sat on the prow, a calm eddy in the midst of the wild stream of movement around her, her skirts arrayed around her and her expression distant, contemplating not the far line of wall but something else, something unseeable, unknowable. Then she caught sight of him.

"Thank goodness, Anatoly, I was wondering where you were." Gods, it hurt, the leap of hope in his heart any time she gave the slightest smile to him. He walked over to her, careful not to let the hope show on his face. "Portia is staying with the other children, and I wanted you to know where she was in case she needs anything. They don't want anyone except the Company to come this time, because it's the first time. They're being extremely careful about protocol."

"I thought I might come with you."

"You can't."

She sat above him on the boat, not looking particularly sorry about it. She was so beautiful, in her khaja gown given life by her presence in it. "What play are you doing?" he asked dutifully.

She pulled a face. "*The Tempest.* You know, the one about the magician Prospero and the island he rules through his magic, and how his enemies are shipwrecked on that island and he rights old wrongs done to him. Charles Soerensen told Owen and Ginny to play it for our first performance. I suppose . . ." she canted her voice lower and leaned down toward him. He had not truly grown used to the immodest clothing khaja wore: Her gown was cut so low that he could see the swell of her breasts. ". . . it's meant to be subversive."

Caught by a sudden overwhelming impulse, he stood on tiptoe, steadied himself with one hand on the side of the barge and with the other hand stilled her chin, and kissed her on the lips.

"Anatoly! You'll ruin my makeup." But she laughed. "If only you were playing Ferdinand instead of Vasil. He's too old for the part, but he's so damned pretty. He would have done better as Ariel—that's the spirit who is servant to Prospero—but he just couldn't do it."

"Why do you wish I was playing Ferdinand?" Anatoly asked suspiciously.

She gave him her most brilliant smile, and moved slightly to make room for Vasil Veselov, who appeared at just that moment to strike a pose, standing, at the railing. "Because I'm playing Miranda, Prosper's daughter, you idiot, and she and Ferdinand fall in love with one another."

"Sakhalin," said Vasil, acknowledging him, and went back to his pose, adjusting his sleeves to drape over the railing.

"Veselov, surely you will bring back a report to me," said Anatoly, "of what you see."

Vasil glanced at him. "I'm not in the army anymore."

Anatoly grunted under his breath and then, to his surprise, Diana got to her knees and leaned down toward him, ducking under the railing. He lifted his arms and caught her and swung her down from the deck into his arms. She was giggling.

"I'm not going to sit next to him," she whispered, leading Anatoly away to the back of the barge. "He hogs every scene he's in, and especially entrances." Pulling him against her, she pressed her lips against an ear. "Don't talk about reports and scouting," she breathed, so close against him that he almost forgot to listen to her words, "not to Vasil. He isn't part of it."

"Diana," he murmured.

She broke away from him. "You will remember that, won't you?"

"I am not a fool, Diana! But Veselov was in Bakhtiian's army once. Surely he still feels loyalty to his people—"

"Vasil feels loyalty to no one but himself. Don't be naive. Himself and perhaps, just perhaps, the memory of what he once shared with Bakhtiian. Oh, stop getting that stubborn look on your face. I don't care whether you believe it or not, or if it offends your prim sense of virtue, it *is* true. I get so tired of your oppressive moral code. Give it up, Anatoly. Haven't you learned anything?"

"I will thank you not to insult my—"

"Oh, you're impossible to talk to." She turned and walked over to the barge, leaving him.

As usual, Hyacinth had listened in. He was crouched about twelve paces away worrying at his shoes—if one could call those lavender cloth wrappings on his feet shoes. His clothes were absolutely obscene. He stood up, revealing bare chest and wings made of a glittering fabric like gems spun into silk.

"May I give you a piece of advice?" Hyacinth asked.

"No!" growled Anatoly, and stalked off.

He unsaddled the mare, brushed her down, and let her go back to the herd. She was reluctant to leave him at first; she liked him—which was more than he could say for anyone else—but finally she kicked out her heels and ran off. Anatoly watched the barge go from a distance, garlanded railings and the splash of colors that was the Company in their costumes, the bleaker black figures of the techs in the center with their boxes and props.

Leaving the caravansary almost empty. He heard the children's laughter as they ran after the barge, waving and calling and halting finally to watch it shrink as it sailed away over the grass. Soon it would pass beyond into the other world, a world he might never be permitted to visit.

But, gods, he was determined to get there somehow. He wandered into the courtyard. Dust motes drifted down in shafts of light, playing over the surface of the mosaic map in the center of the gazebo. Anatoly stopped in front of the latticework. Perhaps he could go *there* with the boy. With Valentin's knowledge of that way of traveling, and with Anatoly's knowledge of intelligence and scouting, they could pierce the wall, they could discover the secrets of the palace.

He heard a footfall and turned, caught a glimpse of a skirt, then nothing. It was silent in the caravansary, empty of life. Everyone, even David, even the khepelli steward, had gone, leaving only Karolla and her khaja servant and the children. And him. The afternoon light mellowed, ripening toward evening.

At last he sighed and went back to Diana's chamber, pushing aside the curtain to go in. Stopped dead in his tracks.

Color flared in the dim room. Lying next to his saddle rested a bouquet of freshly picked flowers. Flower night. His heart racing, he bent down to pick them up. Their smell was heady and intoxicating. He stood there for a long time, until shadows filled the room. Finally he stirred, putting on his other, fresher shirt, wiping the dust off his boots, running his finger through his hair. Then, clutching the flowers in his right hand, he went in search of Ilyana Arkhanov.

CHAPTER TWENTY-TWO

The Surface World

Karolla sat the children under the awning after they had eaten dinner and set each of them a task: Valentin to polishing the worn leather of a bridle, Anton to embroidery on a square of cloth, and Evdokia and Portia to try their hand at spinning. Nipper tied off the ends of a fringe rug, and Karolla took the baby from Ilyana and settled down to nurse her.

"Go on," she said in that tone that Ilyana knew meant she wanted no arguments. "Go out. You have little enough time to be on your own."

Ilyana hesitated, but she wanted to get away from them. She walked away down the road that led to the ruined caravansary. The wind curled in her hair, and she hummed to herself, happy to be alone. Three moons chased each other across the sky, and the barest curve of ring rimmed the western horizon, the great planet hunkering down to its nightly rest. It was warm. She smelled the exuberant scent of night-blooming flowers, their perfume coating the air.

The ruins threw intriguing shadows over the ground. She wandered through them, tracing a ridge here, a ledge there, finding a single white blossom framed by a ring of stone worn down until it lay even with the earth. She bent to explore it with her fingers, the rugged stone, the loamy dirt, the supple petals of the flower, gray-white as if they had been formed from the palest of ash.

And she heard her name, soft, on the breeze. "Yana. Ilyana."

She did not recognize the voice at first. She stood up and saw him, walking toward her through the quiet ruins. In his right hand he held a bouquet of flowers.

Flowers.

"I'm returning these to you," Anatoly said, and held them out to her.

She froze.

"It is a great honor for a man to be a young woman's first chosen," he went on, his voice as soft and caressing as the breeze, "and a great responsibility." He sounded as if he had said these words before. But what girl wouldn't want a man like Anatoly Sakhalin as her first lover?

She lifted her eyes finally from the flowers, white with a center of red, and he dropped his gaze away from her at once. A moment later he looked at her.

She had an instant of blistering revelation, that washed over her like heat. He *desired* her. *He* desired her. She simply could not move.

He smiled, slightly, the merest uplifting of his lips, as if he understood something she did not. He took a step toward her, a second, and lifted a hand, brushed it along her shoulders and settled it around her, comforting, except that now his whole side touched her and he was warm and solid and she was utterly terrified. It had been safe to become infatuated with him when he was on the other side of a room. This wasn't safe.

"Look there," he murmured. "A fourth moon is rising."

When she looked up, he kissed her. It was the briefest touch, gentle, not insistent. Her heart pounded in her chest. She wanted to kiss him again. She *wanted* him.

And why not?

Even though she knew who must have put the flowers by his saddle, why not? Everyone else was gone. What better night than this night? The actors had said the summons translated as "flower night" also. She summoned up every bit of courage she had and tilted her chin up and kissed him. And he responded.

Ilyana had such a vivid flash of her father, intertwined with that awful khaja man dressed up in jaran clothing, kissing him, caressing him, that she started back, shaking.

"Yana?" Anatoly did not reach for her. He just stood there, quiet, steady. The moons illuminated his face, a handsome face for a man as old as he was. She suddenly wondered if her father had ever tried to seduce him. Flinched to even think of it, knowing that her father surely wouldn't be that stupid. Anatoly Sakhalin came out of the old traditions, schooled by the strictest taskmaster of all: Mother Sakhalin. He scarcely spoke to Hyacinth and Yevgeni, except to be scathingly polite. Like Karolla, he held to the old ways even in the new land. The old ways, like flower night.

Except that now all she could think of was her father. She could not get him out of her mind, him and that man, him, the way his body moved. She gulped down air. Her cheeks burned. She had to say something, anything.

"I'm sorry." Her breathing came in ragged bursts. "I didn't—I mean, if I did, it would be you, but—" She broke off.

He glanced down at the bouquet and up again at her. His expression changed to the stiff arrogance of a Sakhalin prince; he looked mightily annoyed. "You didn't put these flowers there." Then he swore.

Mortified, she fled.

But no matter where she fled, it didn't matter. In the end she had to go back to her mother's tent.

She stopped under the awning. The younger children were asleep, and Valentin lay on a pillow with the baby snuffling on his chest. Nipper was gone. Karolla looked up at her blandly.

"I want to talk to you alone," said Ilyana in a low voice.

Valentin shut his eyes and pretended to be asleep, making little snoring sounds.

"You put those flowers by his saddle!" Tears came, hot, to her eyes. "How could you?"

"It is past time—"

"I don't *care* if you think it's past time. It's *my* time. It's my choice."

"You don't want to lie with Anatoly Sakhalin?"

"Not tonight! I wanted to go with the actors. I wanted to go with David!"

"David ben Unbutu?" Karolla considered this, frowning. "He's not jaran, but if you won't have Anatoly Sakhalin, I suppose he'll do well enough. He is one of Soerensen's trusted captains, and I suppose if he was good enough to be Nadine Orzhekov's lover, then he is good enough for you, Yana."

Yana shrieked in wordless fury. "That isn't what I meant! How could you? How could you? I hate you!" She burst into tears and despised herself for doing so. She wanted to run anywhere, as long as it was away, only there wasn't anywhere to go.

"Unnatural child," said Karolla calmly. "It is selfish of you not to be done with what other girls celebrated long before. The baby needs a name, and I have not yet offered blood to Grandmother Night."

"All you think about is yourself! Papa would never have done something like this to me!"

Valentin snorted.

Ilyana would have slapped him, except he had the baby, who had woken up and was beginning to complain.

"That is enough, Valentin," admonished Karolla. "Ilyana you will apologize to me."

"I will not! You're the one who should apologize to me."

They stared each other down. Finally, Ilyana spun and ran away around the tent. Except there really was nowhere to go. She sat down, arms wrapped around her knees, out in the midst of the gardens, praying that no one—gods, especially not Anatoly Sakhalin—would come looking for her.

Two moons set and a fifth rose up over the horizon by the time the Company returned. She saw a glow in the distance and then heard them, laughing and singing, their celebration like a scent on the wind. She swallowed sobs and pressed her fingers into her eyes to stop more tears from coming. She had never felt more alone in her life.

"I want to go home," she said in a small voice, except she could see her mother's tent as a hulking shadow not one hundred paces from where she huddled. That was all that she had of home. Before that, they had been outsiders living with the Veselov tribe, on the sufferance of Arina Veselov, and before that, a dimmer memory, outlaws, riding with a tribe that was not truly a tribe, only a collection of people united in their goal to kill Ilyakoria Bakhtiian. Before that—but there was nothing before that. Karolla Arkhanov had turned her back on her mother and aunt's tribe before Ilyana had been born. She had turned her back on them to follow her father and her husband, and so sundered her children forever from their true home.

"I'll never forgive you for that," muttered Ilyana fiercely and buried her head against her knees, shuddering, clutching herself against herself, holding on.

Rain misted the ground and swept away, leaving its cool touch like a distant memory.

"Oh, dear," a woman said. Ilyana jerked her head up. David and Diana stood not ten paces from her.

"What are you doing out here?" David asked kindly.

She burst into tears.

He took a step toward her, hesitated, and looked at Diana. "I'd better get her father."

Ilyana was crying too hard to protest.

Diana knelt beside her, embracing her. "Dear child. Do you want to talk about it?"

Ilyana could only bawl. "I can't," she gasped out. "I'm so unhappy."

"Oh, Yana." Diana sighed deeply. "So many of us are. I'm so sorry. I wish there was something I could do."

They stayed that way until Vasil came. Diana retreated quickly, leaving them alone. Vasil pulled Ilyana to her feet unceremoniously and studied her while she gulped down sobs and wiped her nose with the back of one hand.

"I'm sorry," she stammered. "I don't want to get your costume wet."

He hugged her. "Yana! Someone can clean it. Why are you crying, little one?"

She shrugged in his arms.

"Next time I'll see that you come with us. You can stay backstage with the techs. It was marvelous, Yana. The house had perfect acoustics. I walked all through it before the audience arrived, except for the boxes that were sealed off, and I even saw the box set aside for Duke Naroshi. I took off one of my rings and left it in his chair."

"Papa!" Appalled, she pulled back and stared up at him.

"Yana," he said gravely, "you must learn the basic lesson that those who have power will use it, and those who don't must learn to control those who do. You and I have nothing—"

"We're pretty," she said bitterly, choking down sobs. "Everyone says so." Anatoly Sakhalin had thought so, staring at her in the moonlight.

"No, we're *beautiful*. Never forget that. That's what sets us apart from others and makes them desire us. Duke Naroshi is a powerful man—"

"He isn't a *man,* Papa. He's an alien."

"It doesn't matter. People are the same everywhere. They want the same things."

"Charles Soerensen didn't want you, did he?" she asked suddenly. "Or you wouldn't care about Duke Naroshi. Papa, that's disgusting."

"That Soerensen wasn't interested? I admit it puzzles me, but it isn't worth dwelling on. Naroshi must have better connections with the Empire. Perhaps I can even be introduced to the emperor himself."

"And then what?" Ilyana asked, curious despite her heavy heart. "What would you do?"

But he got that look on his face and he let go of her and stared at the stars. One of those stars probably was the star around which Rhui orbited. "I would have him give me Rhui," he whispered, "and everything on it, to do with as I wish."

He fell silent. She did not interrupt him.

After a long time, he looked down at her. "Why were you crying, Yana! You shouldn't be unhappy."

"Do you think I'm too old to be—? I didn't know and then—" She broke off, bit her lip, and could not go on.

"You're not making any sense."

But she just couldn't tell him. The words choked in her throat and she knew it wasn't right. A girl wasn't supposed to speak of these things to a man. She should have an aunt to confide in, a grandmother, a cousin. Gods, she couldn't confide in Diana about *this*.

A memory struggled up from the depths, of Arina Veselov's good-natured and thoughtful brother Anton, who had died in the battle at Karkand: She could have confided in him. He had been like an uncle to her. She could trust him. As she looked at her beautiful father, who watched her with what was truly sincere concern, insofar as he was capable of feeling concern for people other than himself, she understood that she could never trust him or confide in him.

"I'm just lonely sometimes, Papa, here."

"We're going to be here a while longer. We might even be able to tour farther into the Empire after this. Perhaps we could send to your friend Kori's parents and see if she wanted to come spend some time with you. Would you like that?"

Ilyana wondered suddenly if Kori had had her flower night yet, in the time she'd been away, even though she knew it was done differently with Kori's people. Would Kori, given the chance, choose someone like Anatoly Sakhalin as her first lover?

"I'd like that," she said.

"Perhaps Duke Naroshi would like a dance troupe to perform here," mused Vasil. He took her hand and together they walked back to the caravansary.

Anatoly waited until Ilyana had vanished into the darkness before he moved. Impulsively, he flung the bouquet into the air and flowers scattered down around him, flecking the dry earth. He walked back to Diana's chamber, stripped, and threw himself on his cot, tossing and turning, furious with Karolla Arkhanov. Furious with himself. Poor Ilyana was just a pawn tossed between them. It wasn't right. It *was* right; any man accounted himself honored to be a girl's first chosen lover. But it wasn't right that he, Anatoly, should put his frustrated love for Diana onto Yana. She was a beautiful girl, unspoiled, hardworking. In the tribes, a hundred young men would be competing for her attention by now, and her mother would have to be careful that some reckless young rider didn't just mark her out of hand. But she was little more than a child. Truly, she was still like a child in some ways. However beautiful she might be, she was not a Singer. She was not Diana.

Thinking of his wife, it almost seemed that he had made her flesh. The Company had returned. He heard their gay laughter and the bright sound of their singing, a tribe unto themselves, rejoicing in a victory. He refused to go out and join them—an outsider—in their celebration.

After a long long time, Diana pushed aside the curtain and slid into the room, giggling, disheveled, sounding drunk. The sleeves of her gown had slipped so far down that he could see the gleam of her shoulders, pale, inviting, in the moonlit chamber.

"Are you awake?" she whispered, and then went on, either knowing he was awake or not caring. "It went wonderfully. The Duke built a wonderful theater, just for us! Do you know that there were separate boxes for the males and the females I'd guess of highest rank and the female boxes were shielded so we couldn't see them, but they could see us or at least they must have been able to and the house was just filled with Chapalii, although I suppose they must have been all males in the house because they don't mix, do they?" She laughed under her breath and leaned down over him. "Anatoly, you're naked! Ummm. Here, help me off with this—"

He needed no more invitation than that. He drowned himself in her.

"You're serious tonight," she said later, still brilliant with her Singer's glory.

"I love you," he said desperately.

"Oh, Anatoly."

But her expression betrayed everything. She did not truly love him anymore, as a wife loves a husband. She pitied him. He shut his eyes, as if that could obliterate the awful knowledge. And he made love with her anyway, because it was all he had.

"Oh, Goddess," said Diana in the morning, tucked in close beside him. "I have a headache." She smiled at him, bleary-eyed in the bright shafts of sunlight that streaked the chamber. "I'd forgotten how much I like you," she added, and rolled up on top of him and kissed him, brushing his hair back from his temples.

"I am content," he replied softly.

"Are you? You have to be bored here. I'm sorry you ever left the tribes."

He winced.

"No, I don't mean it like that. I wish you would stop feeling sorry for yourself all the time. I know we . . . don't always get along now. But with the tribes you had something to do, you *knew* who you were and what part you played."

"Even if it was a part you despise? That of a soldier?"

"Oh! You idiot! I fell in love with you *because* you were a rider. I just don't like you dragging it out all the time."

"You don't like me teaching Portia the things I gained respect and glory doing with the tribes."

She placed a hand firmly over his mouth. "I am *not* going to argue with you. It just went so well yesterday, that I refuse to blacken today by having the same stupid argument again."

"All right," said Anatoly, encouraged by her mood, liking it, and never one not to press an attack when he saw he had an opening, "then perhaps you had better remind me again of the obligations a husband owes to his wife."

"Hmm."

Someone rapped loudly on the wall beside the entrance to the room. "Di-aaaaaa-na."

"Go away," she said.

"Whatever you're up to in there," added Hyacinth cheerfully, "and I'm only sorry that you're not going to invite me in to join you, we're having a Company meeting in one hour. So don't say I didn't warn you." He stamped off, deliberately being loud.

Diana giggled. "Anatoly, your expression!"

"I don't find his jokes amusing."

"Hyacinth is a good, decent person, and much the wiser for what he's been through. I really am tired of your endless prejudice against him just because what he is isn't accepted by the jaran. It's so *medieval*. But go ahead, say it anyway." She rolled off him and swung her legs over, perching on the edge of the cot. She was very distracting, sitting there naked, gold hair unbound and falling down over her shoulders. When he said nothing, she turned to look at him inquiringly.

"I don't want to argue with you today," he said.

They examined one another for a long while, while the light shifted and altered, heralding planetrise. Finally, getting impatient, he caught her by the waist and pulled her down against him. It was, for a little while, almost like it had been at the beginning of their marriage.

Thus fortified, Anatoly could watch her go to her meeting with equanimity. He went to confront Karolla Arkhanov.

Taking her aside, he said, "Never do that to me again."

"If my daughter refuses to do what is right—"

"Never do it to me, or to any man. A young woman must choose in her own way and in her own time, and it is not fitting that I, a man, should have to tell this to you, her mother. But since there is evidently no one else to do so, I must."

She looked chastened enough that briefly, he felt sorry for her, until she went on. "You don't understand how difficult it is to raise children properly, here. You have a khaja wife. Your child is already half khaja. Mine are not."

Anatoly sighed. He caught sight of Valentin, loitering under the awning, looking their way with the bored curiosity of a boy who had nothing better to do. Of Ilyana he saw no sign. "You are right," he said suddenly, seeing his chance. "I will take Valentin off your hands right now."

She looked relieved. "It would be well. He and his father . . . do not always get along."

He nodded to her and walked over to the tent. Valentin eyed him dubiously. "Come with me," Anatoly said.

"I don't want to."

"In the tribes, a boy would never dare to speak that way to his elders."

Valentin stubbornly did not reply, but he looked nervous. Anatoly knew well enough that the boy needed to push, wanted to, but was scared to.

"It is not only disrespectful," added Anatoly, "but it is impolite."

"What do I care?"

Anatoly studied him. He was a thin child, with a lean face that always seemed to be hungering after something. Not a boy to be reasoned or argued with, not a boy to be cowed into obedience. "You care because if you learn your manners then I will take you along with me to scout."

Valentin glanced toward his mother, who was carefully ignoring their conversation. "What do you mean, to scout?"

"I am scouting the Duke's palace."

"You can't get out of the dome." Anatoly let that one lie. After two blinks of the eye, Valentin got an odd expression on his face. "You don't mean in the surface world, do you? You mean through the nesh link."

"You have used these words before. What is 'the surface world'?"

"You wouldn't know, would you?"

"I'll have to come back another day."

"No, wait. I'm sorry. I just meant, most people don't know that it's all just like a top layer, *here,* that is, not *there.*" He hesitated. "You don't nesh much, do you?"

"No. I like things that have weight, that are solid. How can you trust a saber that isn't really there?"

"It doesn't work like that. There's way way more *there* than there is here. That's why we call this the surface world."

"We?"

Valentin shrugged, looking coy. "Other people."

"Other people who also go into the world where nothing is real?"

"It *is* real. It's more real—" Valentin trailed off and glanced again toward his mother and then, oddly enough, at the great tent rising behind him. "It's more real than this." He looked up at Anatoly measuringly. "I'll show you. If you want."

"If I am to scout, I must have a guide who can show me

how to find the landmarks in that other place. In a year or two more, if we were with the jaran, you would be sent to another tribe's jahar, to learn how to care for the horses and the weapons, to learn what it is to be a rider."

"I don't want to be a—" He stopped himself. He was learning. "I'd like to go with you."

"Then you will. But first you must learn to saddle a horse."

Valentin went pink. But he didn't protest.

The days went by. Valentin got thoroughly sick of the horses—Anatoly could tell—but the boy did not complain. The Company rehearsed *A Midsummer Night's Dream* and *Prometheus Bound,* and the fragile truce he and Diana had patched together held. Portia was happy. Ilyana avoided him.

Eight days after the first summons, a second came. That evening after the actors left in the barge, Anatoly met Valentin by the gazebo.

"What you gonna do with that saber?" Valentin asked, stopping in his tracks, eyes wide.

"A scout always goes armed."

The boy was so excited that he was shaking. "Say good-bye to the surface world," he said cheerfully. He twined one hand around the latticework.

"Wait. We must have a plan of action. What we will do if we are separated. How long we will reconnoiter. How we will return."

Valentin's mouth was thin and pale, lips pressed tight, and his eyes had a feverish light in them. "Just hold on like this," he said hoarsely, and he was gone.

Gone. Like a Singer, his spirit had left his body. Anatoly had seen a Singer in the midst of her trance, and all at once he wondered if it would be impious for him to try to follow on the Singer's road. He was not a Singer, he had never been called, nor had any Sakhalin child been marked by the gods for the Singer's calling for generations upon generations. It was the price they paid for remaining first among the tribes.

But he knelt down anyway, steeling himself, and placed his fingers on the latticework in the same pattern as Valentin had. Reflexively, he shut his eyes.

Nothing happened. Until he realized that he was mounted, and wearing armor. He opened his eyes, seeing first his hands on the reins and then, at his mount's shoulder, Valentin, peering up at him.

"I waited for you. Wow! Where'd you get that stuff? And the horse! Are you guising?"

He knew this mare. She was his favorite, not for beauty— she had no looks to speak of—but because she was a canny, vigorous, and stubborn campaigner. She had been mortally wounded at the battle outside Salkh. He had put her down himself, and she had burned on the great pyre of the dead, at his order. Now she flicked her ears, waiting patiently for his signal.

"How can I be wearing my armor?" Anatoly asked. "I didn't even bring it off Rhui. I brought only my saber and my saddle." Then he realized that Valentin himself was wearing, not the blocky tunic and knee-length pants that seemed to be the uniform of children on Earth, but the sort of clothes a jaran boy might wear.

"If you're not thinking about it when you go through the lock, then I guess you could come out on the other side looking like you think of yourself in your own mind. Is that how you think of yourself?"

Anatoly glanced down, seeing the lamellar stripes of his armor, polished leather and strips of metal. It felt light and entirely natural. He lifted off his helmet and noted the white plume, signifying a commander of highest rank, which adorned it.

"I had not yet earned a white plume, but had I returned to the army it would have been given to me, as well as an army of my own."

"Why'd you come to Earth, then? You didn't have to, not like me."

"You didn't want to leave Rhui?"

Valentin shrugged.

"It is proper that a man go to live with his wife's tribe." Valentin hesitated. "Can you show me a battle?"

"I don't have my slate with me."

"Neh. You don't need that here. You can make anything."

Anatoly lifted a hand to silence the boy and surveyed the landscape, except it was like no landscape he knew. It looked rather like the floor of the gazebo, white tiles spread out into a foreshortened horizon, their pale edges squared off in a seemingly infinite grid.

"There is nothing here."

"This is just the gateway. It's the second layer, it's nothing, it's all possibility. You gotta make something. Just think about something you seen once, and it'll start forming. That's what makes this nesh so neat. It must be something the Chapalii know how to do. It's like a Memory Palace, only way better."

"What is a Memory Palace?"

Like all Singers, Valentin shone with light when he spoke of the things the gods had gifted him with knowledge of. "It's a place set into the nesh where you can build easily, like the code or something is set in place so you can construct on top of it instead of having to create a basic environment first. But this place is even easier than that. You just form it in your mind and it begins to take shape right here. I mean, it's not that easy, but you can—what would you build? What would you like to see? Where would you like to go? Is there some place you'd like to go back to?"

Back to the scene of his greatest triumph, the battle of the Aro River, where Kirill Zvertkov's army had swung wide to find a crossing downriver while Anatoly had driven his troops over a heavily defended bridge against the Lion Prince's personal guard.

Diana had told him once that a memory was just a pattern of electrical impulses, a chemical code acting within a portion of the brain. *Now the battle rose up around him, he in the swirl of riders breaking past the bridge and fanning out to meet the disintegrating line of resistance. He pulled up, the boy hanging on to Sosha's bridle and staring, so as not to endanger the child. A thundering announced the arrival of the Xiriki prince's brother, with his thousand guardsmen arrayed in the blue of the Khai lineage, adorned with crescent moons on their silk surcoats.*

They hit the front rank of the jaran riders, and at once there came the ringing of sword and saber, lance and shield, and arrows rained down on the khaja lines from the archers posted behind the front ranks. There he had fought, coming once within striking range of the Xiriki princeling: He thought he could see the golden plume of his own helmet, won by right of arms and by right of his Sakhalin name, bobbing in the center of the thickest knot of fighting.

The noise itself was deafening, but Sosha stood her ground, solid, afraid of nothing. More jaran riders poured over the bridge and swept out to push the khaja flanks back, and back, and although the engagement here would go on for half the morning already he saw the Xiriki camp where

*the khaja had foolishly trapped themselves within the tight
circle of their own wagons, like animals in a corral. Already
he saw Zvertkov's army coming up from the south and the
two armies—his and Zvertkov's—combining to surround the
encampment, dust and arrows and the constant clatter of
battle hanging in the air round them.*

*And the panic, the rout, while the Lion Prince fled and his
brother alone with his picked troops tried to hold off the
pursuit, but it was already too late, because the khaja were
already defeated in their hearts and maddened by fear. The
jaran riders had slaughtered the fleeing soldiers with less
trouble than it took to kill the most placid grazel, leaving
bodies strewn for a day's ride westward like the broken trail
marking their defeat. . . .*

The swirl of the battle faded, and the actors became insubstantial ghosts and, at last, faded into the white tile grid.

"Hey, cool! Can we do it again?"

Anatoly stared at the blank landscape. He didn't want to
do it again. It was boring. It wasn't real, it was worse, it was
just something that had already happened, that didn't mean
anything now. "It's like being dead," he whispered. "This
isn't right. We must leave here. This is not the place where
the Singers go; it is the land where the demons live."

"No, no." Valentin tugged on Sosha's bridle, looking worried. "We can't go now. I'm trying to build a bridge to the
other land."

"What other land?"

"The deepest one. It's hard to get to. But I'm almost
there. I really am—just let me—"

"No."

"Just let me—"

"No, Valentin! When you ride with the jahar, you obey
the dyan instantly."

"But I know how to get to the map!" Valentin sounded
desperate, and Anatoly almost gave in, but he had no idea
how much time had passed in the real world. Suddenly he
wondered what lay beneath this grid. Another world? A
deeper world?

"We must go back. But we will come here again, to the
place where you say there is a map."

Valentin let go of the bridle and stepped back, and
Anatoly braced himself in the saddle, expecting the boy to
flee. But instead a plain stone arch coalesced on the grid and

Valentin retreated through it and was—gone. Quickly, Anatoly rode after him.

And opened his eyes.

The latticework wavered and then steadied into a white web, solid under his fingers, and he let go. Valentin was coughing and gulping, but he managed a weak smile.

"Did I do all right?" he asked.

Anatoly frowned. "What is wrong?" But even as he said it, the boy's color got better and he wiped his mouth and stood up, looking fit enough.

"Next time we can go straight to the map. It's like a big thing, like a model I guess Yana would call it." The boy paused suddenly. His lips twitched. "Is it true that my mother gave you flowers so you'd think Yana gave them to you?"

Anatoly flushed. "I would never presume to criticize a woman, but that was ill-done of her. Do you understand why?"

"Yana is in love with you," added Valentin with all the wicked glee of a younger brother revealing dark secrets.

Anatoly flushed even more, and was grateful that it was dark. "Do you understand why?"

"Yeah, yeah. It's supposed to be the girl's choice. That's not how they do it on Earth, though."

"How khaja do it is not my concern." He cocked his head to one side. "Did you hear that?"

"Yeah. I heard it before. They're all back. I wonder how that barge floats. David says it isn't mag-lev."

Anatoly jumped back from the latticework just as the first figures came through the archway that led into the courtyard. There was no celebration tonight, but a more combative feeling, as if the actors wrestled with what they had wrought this night and what they might hope to achieve in the future.

"Valentin! Hello. Anatoly." David paused beside them, peering at them curiously. In the luminescent glow from the gazebo, his expression looked quizzical. "Shouldn't you be in bed, Valentin?"

Valentin hesitated, glanced at Anatoly, then mumbled a good night and left.

David waited until the boy was gone and the actors had faded into their rooms or settled down in the far corner of the courtyard to talk. "I hope you didn't find him here."

"I used him as a guide."

"You *what*?"

"If I cannot get through the dome, and if, as you suggest, only certain portions of the palace are even habitable by us, then I must scout inside, by using the nesh."

David considered. "Fair enough. But don't take the boy. Please don't."

"Why not? It is time he had something to do, that he began to learn to be a man."

David pulled a hand through his hair. "It isn't that easy. Neshing makes him ill. He's too young to nesh except on a supervised and extremely constrained basis. He's gone far too far already, and it could actually kill him."

"Truly?"

"I don't know. I only wormed this information out of his sister a few days ago. I don't know how bad it is, and Yana claims that their parents are incapable of safeguarding him. So I guess that leaves . . . me."

Anatoly bowed his head. He thought about the hungry look on Valentin's face. "Perhaps you and I can find a way to guide him out of his need for the nesh. What we saw in there wasn't real."

David shook his head, not quite grinning. "It depends on what you're looking for. Frankly, I think it might be possible to use this nesh port to scout the palace. We'll have to arrange something. But not tonight. I'm tired."

"The play went well?"

"How to know? It went. Good night."

Diana, laughing, came in through the arch with the lighting designer, waving at him, and went out again. Out beyond the arch music started up, a guitar and hand-drums, a chant.

But Anatoly didn't really see her, although he lifted a hand in greeting and left it half raised, then curled it into a fist. The sharp satisfaction of purpose flooded him: Valentin said there was a map somewhere below the surface world. David said it might be possible, within the nesh lattice, to truly scout the palace.

He intended to do so, even if he had to do it alone.

CHAPTER TWENTY-THREE

The Altar

For the length of a drawn-out breath, Vasha saw everything as if it had stilled and frozen: The ranks of khaja infantry, drawn up with shields and spears around their position. His father and Konstans, oddly calm in the center of the maelstrom. The ranks of riders, trying desperately to form up in the too-small space. Stefan holding on to a panicked, wounded horse. Rusudani peering out from underneath the shelter of the carpet.

Katerina, magnificent, like a child of the gods caught forever in the act of aiming her bow. She fired.

The world dissolved into action. Arrows showered in, and again, and again, striking freely into the mob of remounts. The horses went mad with terror. Within moments, the jaran riders fought as much to maintain a line against the frenzied horses as against the khaja soldiers. Horses screamed. Pelted by arrows, Stefan ran out to the carpet and dragged it backward toward the wall, shouting at the two women to come with him. It was the only haven.

"Drive them!" Konstans was shouting. "Drive them against the shields."

But already men went down under the endless rain of arrows. Already arrows stuck out at every angle from Ilya's armor, from every man's armor. Horses bucked and bolted. Any man who fell was doomed to be trampled, and even when one knot of riders forced a wild group of stampeding horses into the khaja infantry, they could not press their advantage when a gap opened; by the time a second group of riders fought through to aid them, the gap had closed up again.

Katerina fired steadily, but without any real effect, until a shower of arrows pelted down around her. Her horse reared, screaming, and she was thrown.

Vasha scrambled down at once. A stumbling horse struck

him on the shoulder and he staggered, then grabbed Katya
and dragged her up, yelling at her. "Come on! Get back up!
You'll be trampled." He was furious, because he was terrified that she might be dead.

They turned, but both their horses had gone. "Back to the
wall!" Vasha yelled. He had to yell, the noise was deafening.
A horn blew. He heard an advance called, although he could
see nothing but a wall of horses, mobbing, milling, staggering and collapsing.

It was utter chaos. Only Ilya and Konstans remained in his
sight, battered but still upright. Vasha came up against the
wall and heard a woman saying something but just then, to
his horror, Kriye pitched forward and Ilya vanished, tossed
over his head. A flurry of riders, those who could press
through, converged on the stallion.

Princess Rusudani was crying out something. "She says
we must go inside the monastery walls!" shouted Jaelle.
"We will be granted sanctuary there."

"I won't leave the riders," said Katya grimly. She surveyed the wreckage of the field, looking for a new mount.
True to her training she gathered up arrows from the ground.

Vasha watched as the khaja soldiers moved down the distant rise. Already he could see their front rank in patches,
through gaps in the jaran riders where men and horses had
fallen. A bay struggled to his feet and dropped again. Farther, on the edge of the carnage, a man in the red and gold
surcoat of Ilya's guard crawled, dragging his legs, found a
saber, and hoisted it. Infantry men reached him, and there
was a flurry and then, nothing. The khaja pressed forward.

With the khaja moving in, the arrow fire lessened and the
fighting drew out in knots of wild melee, spears and swords
clashing, shouts and cries.

"We must go within the walls," repeated Jaelle, looking
frantic. "If we can reach the church, God will grant us sanctuary!"

Stefan tugged on Vasha's arm. "We'd better go!"

"I won't leave without my father!"

He saw Konstans' white plume, caught in an eddy of men
retreating step by slow step from the advance. Clots of riders
threw themselves into the fray ahead of this eddy, as if to cut
it off from the khaja, and by that, Vasha knew that Konstans
must be protecting Ilya.

Vasha ran forward as Stefan pulled Rusudani and Jaelle

up and dashed for the stone gateway that led into the monastery grounds. An arrow jammed into his armor, pricking his ribs, and another skittered off a boot and spent itself on the ground. Katya was right behind him. She found a stray horse, wild-eyed but unhurt, and she yanked its head down and mounted. It sheered away from her, and she fought it back and began firing into the soldiers nearest the final knot of jaran riders.

Vasha reached the guardsmen and at once one of the men, seeing him, shouted something about the gate and the wall, but Vasha, almost as frenzied as the wounded and dying horses now, fought through the press of animals and found—

oh, gods

—his father slumped over a saddle as if he were dead.

But he wasn't. His eyes were closed and he breathed, hands convulsing on the reins. Vasha grabbed the reins and tugged the horse toward the wall. He could feel the battle like another man's breath on his back, it was so close behind him, fought more quietly now, with fierce concentration on the part of those riders still left, those few.

Konstans shadowed him. There was a shout, a rush, and Vasha got pushed all over the place as he strove to reach the wall. Ilya shoved himself up, raising his saber, and Vasha wasn't sure what he saw first: the infantryman or the spear that took Ilya in the side.

Vasha dropped the reins and struck the soldier, first with the flat, not meaning to, but it only staggered the man and then Vasha hacked and hacked at him.

"Enough!" Konstans's voice was so eerily calm that it was frightening. "Get him out of here, Vassily."

Vasha stared over the dead khaja soldier, who lay crumpled at his feet. There were maybe fifty riders left, and far away to the right a knot of twenty slowly being overwhelmed, fighting furiously, fighting like madmen.

"Go!"

He saw the gateway. Stefan peered out at him and grabbed the reins out of his hands. Vasha looked down and realized that there was blood all over his hands. Ilya slipped. Vasha shoved him back up onto the saddle, cursing, praying under his breath.

"This way!" said Jaelle. "Princess Rusudani has gone ahead to make sure the doors of the church are open."

Vasha followed her into the maze of stone tents, bewildered and terrified. Stefan led the horse. Vasha held his father onto the saddle. He could not even tell if Ilya still breathed.

Behind them, the last of the riders poured through the gate and turned to make a final stand. Konstans pulled back with about half of those left, following Vasha. Arrows rained down into the monastery grounds.

A cowled man stared at them from a doorway and shrank back inside. Smoke curled up from a roof, but it wasn't fire. *Hearth,* thought Vasha, his mind wandering. "It's from the hearth," he said. "They cook inside their houses over open fires."

No one answered him. Perhaps they hadn't heard. Stefan was limping. The whole world, this tiny patch of ground that he set each foot on, was hazed. A cobblestone. An arrow embedded in the dirt. The hem of Jaelle's skirts trailing on the stones, muddied. A cluster of grass growing up between huts. A bird taking flight from a green sward. The struggle at the gate, distant behind them, unrelenting, a constant surge like the ocean, swelling over him in waves.

"The khaja are climbing over the walls," said Konstans conversationally. "Boris, take two men and cover—"

"Yes." Riders moved away.

"Leonid and Piotr, ride ahead and be sure that the khaja woman has found the church. It is that place there, with the great towers. Guard the door."

Two horses passed him, but Vasha could not look up from his feet, from the stone path trimmed with moss, from the way each boot set down and found purchase and moved him forward. All he could feel was the weight of his father against his shoulder. Blood trickled down his left hand.

He prayed to Grandmother Night. "I will give you anything," he whispered, "even my own life, if only you will keep my father alive."

They turned to the left.

"Edvard, wait here and alert us when the gate is breached."

Vasha knew that the gate would be breached only when all the defenders had died. It seemed odd, though, that he could feel nothing about it.

"Thanks be to God, Who has protected us this day," said Jaelle in a low voice.

Vasha looked up to see a flight of steps that led to a set

of huge arched double doors, set into the towering church. Rusudani stood poised on the steps, brilliant in the dying sunlight from the west, and beside her stood a khaja man in strange jeweled robes, with a funny hat on his head. He knelt in front of her and kissed her hand.

Edvard shouted. Vasha turned and saw the rider breaking toward them. Then Edvard jerked, jerked again, and fell from his horse. His helmet tumbled off onto the ground. His horse slowed, stopped, and stood in the road, confused.

"Up the steps," said Konstans. "Go, Vasha!"

Rusudani had gone white, but she did not cry out. She spoke quickly and fiercely to the old man, but he shuddered. She shook off his hand and beckoned to Vasha.

"Come!" she said in khush. "Come. Follow."

They stumbled up the steps.

"Leave the horses," said Konstans. "They're no use to us now. Leonid and Piotr, you must try to get through, to return to the army. May the gods be with you."

The two riders reined about hard and rode away around the church. Vasha knew they would not get through. Surely the khaja commander who had ordered this would expect such an attempt. He took each step one at a time, each one an effort. The khaja churchman watched them go by with rheumy, frightened eyes.

The great doors yawned open, and Vasha followed Stefan through them. The horse shied, but Stefan spoke softly, calming her, rubbing her. Dimness shuttered them, except for a blaze of candles at the far end. A second arch led them farther in, and then the roof leapt up into a great gulf of air, as if the heavens had invaded. Benches stood like soldiers in ranks all the way up to the altar.

There, framed and illuminated by candlelight, Rusudani knelt and prayed at the white stone altar, under the image of Hristain sundered and made whole again.

The horse, unsure of itself, came to a halt. While Stefan coaxed it, Vasha looked back. He heard a murmuring from outside like the muttering of the storm-swept sea, like the roar of fire, like the ominous rumble of a blizzard blowing in. Two men detached themselves from the ten or so riders remaining at the door and ran—one limped—to Ilya.

They lowered him down from the horse and did what Vasha had not yet managed the courage to do: They laid him on the floor and checked to see if he was still alive.

"He is still alive!" Vladimir shouted back toward the door. Vladimir's right arm hung twisted and useless. He glanced up at Vasha. "Where can we find safety for him?" No panic, just a question.

"Jaelle," Vasha said in Taor, "where can we hide him?"

"This is a church! No one will harm him in here."

From the door: "Go see to your cousin," said Konstans. "There's nothing more we can do. Drag Izyaslav in, and we'll shut the doors. If they burn us down, then we'll go to the gods having fought well."

The doors scraped shut and, with a resounding thud, closed.

From the altar, Rusudani spoke, urgently beckoning them forward.

"You must bring him to the altar," said Jaelle, catching her urgency in her tone. "God Himself has decreed that blood must never be spilled in His sanctuary. God will protect you."

"You shouldn't move him too much," protested Stefan as the two riders hoisted Ilya and hauled him up the aisle.

The door shuddered behind them. Again, cracking. The khaja were trying to break it down. The riders dragged benches in front of it, heaving them along. One rider lay on the ground. Vasha could not tell if he was dead or not. The sound of hacking echoed through the great lofty expanse of the church.

They lay Ilya down beside the altar, and Rusudani knelt beside him, praying.

"Is he alive?" asked Katerina.

"Katya!" That stirred Vasha out of his numbness. He stared at her, but she was real. She stood two paces from him, studying Bakhtiian with a weary gaze. She had blood on her face, and she cradled her left hand against her chest. Vladimir knelt on one knee, testing his grip with his left hand on his saber, and the other man—a younger man, come recently into Ilya's guards, a Vershinin son—winced, testing his weight on his leg, and then leaned on his spear. Both of the riders gazed steadily at the door. They knew what was coming.

"It isn't true," said Stefan. "They'll kill us all anyway."

"It would blaspheme God's holy word!" Jaelle knelt as well, on the other side of the altar from Rusudani, and folded her arms over her chest. "We will be safe here."

The church lay around them, silent except for the echo of the doors being cut down. Strange faces peered at them from the gloom, faces carved into the pillars that held up the ceiling, and light splintered in through windows drawn of a thousand colors, fading, muting, as the sun set. Vasha smelled sweet incense, and leather. Dust swam in the gold streams of light that filtered down from the clear shaft of the window that rose above the altarstone. Footsteps sounded, measured, and the creak of armor. Vasha marked Konstans approaching them by his white plume.

"He yet lives?" Konstans asked quietly.

"He lives," said Vladimir.

The simplicity of their loyalty staggered Vasha. They said nothing more. They needed to say nothing more. That Bakhtiian yet lived, might live still, was all that mattered.

The two khaja women, he and Stefan and Katya, and, in all, ten riders plus Izyaslav, who lay dying in the entryway. He found his voice suddenly. "Where is Andrei Sakhalin?"

"He's run like the rat he is," said Konstans calmly. He favored one leg, Vasha saw now, but if the wound pained him, he did not show it on his face. "He has betrayed us to the khaja. I only hope that I can someday tell Yaroslav Sakhalin what his baby brother has done, and have Andrei there to witness the telling of it."

The door splintered, sharp, and an ax blade bit through. A shout rose from outside.

"Kill the horse," shouted Konstans. He slanted a look down at Vladimir. "I leave him in your hands."

Vladimir nodded.

Konstans walked back down the length of the church. Vasha could barely make out two riders as they killed the mare right in front of the door, where it made yet another barrier. They overturned benches, made a great obstacle with them, and settled in with their spears. Konstans knelt beside Izyaslav and, with a deft move, slit the wounded man's throat. He rose and backed away, taking a place at the back rank.

The door splintered again, and again, wood spitting out in chunks now, cracking and fragmenting until the first man-sized hole was formed. A spear met the first khaja soldier who ducked through. Outside, they kept hacking. The next time, four men pressed through, and the fighting was quiet, intense, grunting, a terse command, a shriek of pain and the sheer bitter cold fury of the last jaran riders fighting to save their dyan.

Jaelle prayed, hands clutched at her chest. Rusudani rose to her feet as the khaja soldiers came through and fell, came through and fell—but they wounded one rider, then a second. There was a rush. They fell back, and now Vasha saw only three jaran standing. The doors had fallen to nothing, and the last scraps of them were torn down by men out of reach of the jaran spears. On the stairs outside, torches blazed and rank upon rank of soldiers stood, waiting to come in.

Katya took aim.

"No!" Rusudani restrained her. Katya's eyes blazed, and she looked ready to punch the other woman, but Rusudani kept talking.

"Listen to her," pleaded Jaelle. "What she speaks is truth. You must trust in God to grant you peace and safety."

Katya snorted and lifted her bow again, and again Rusudani restrained her.

"Let me go!" Katya snarled.

"But you see," said Jaelle, rising as well. "No one comes through the door. They wait, because they do not wish to violate the Lord's holy refuge."

From the door, a voice rang out. In Taor.

"I am sworn to kill the man known as Ilyakoria Bakhtiian. His life alone I must have. The others I care nothing for."

"Who are you?" asked Konstans. He stood in the central aisle, flanked by the last two guardsmen left standing, the cousins Nikita and Mikhail—Mitenka—Kolenin, men who had ridden with Bakhtiian since they came of age to ride, men who had been with him since the beginning of his great ride, his unification of the jaran and the khaja lands beyond. They were all of them armed only, at last, with their sabers. Between them and the door lay the wreckage of their final defense.

A man resplendent in a coat of mail stepped into the doorway, flanked in his turn by men bearing torches. The light shone and scattered off his helm. He wore a bright red cloak trimmed with silver brocade, and the clasp winked and sparkled; even at this distance, Vasha could see that it was encrusted with jewels.

Katya shook off Rusudani's hand and lifted her bow.

"Katya," said Konstans coolly, in khush, without turning

round, "I think you would do well to save your arrows for those who will need them more later." He took one step back. "Nikita. Mikhail. Move back." He pitched his voice loud again, replying in Taor. "Come forward and name yourself. If you can best me here, then surely the gods favor you."

"I am Prince Janos of Dushan." The khaja prince let his men clear a path for him, rather than trying to pick through it. Close behind him came the khaja holy man, babbling on about something.

"He says," Jaelle murmured, keeping up a constant translation, "that it is against God's law for men to profane the church with fighting."

"What does Prince Janos say?" asked Vasha, glancing at Rusudani, who was white-lipped and frozen, staring at the scene.

"God forgive his arrogance. He says that he will sort that out with God once he has done what he came here for."

"If I agree to fight you," said Konstans, "what surety will you give me that the rest of my people will pass unharmed and alive from your hands?"

"I need give you no surety." Prince Janos halted in the open aisle, hefting his shield on one arm, drawing his sword with the other. "I grant you only a warrior's death. The rest of them are in my power."

"If I kill you?"

"Then they may go free, if they can win free."

Konstans said nothing, but attacked.

Vasha had watched men duel with sabers. Konstans was among the best. But, unhorsed, he was hopelessly outmatched by a man with a shield and a straight, heavy sword. Janos absorbed hits to his shield and armor and simply pounded Konstans with the weight he brought to bear. That the fight lasted as long as it did only attested to Konstans' skill, and to his desperation.

He died well.

There was silence in the church. The hall filled with Prince Janos's soldiers. Suddenly, Vasha could hear Ilya's labored breathing, like the talisman of hope, the slender thread on which all of their lives hung.

Rusudani pushed past Katerina and stood full in the line of sight. She lifted her chin. Vasha admired her courage.

"Prince Janos," she said coldly, regally.

He stepped back from Konstans's body, but he did not lower his shield or sword. "Princess Rusudani. I hope you have not been harmed."

All translated by Jaelle in a whisper, a hush sounding underneath the shuffle of feet and the settling of dust and the darkening as twilight infiltrated the church, covering them as in a shroud.

Rusudani did not bother to reply to that pleasantry. "If you have accomplished what you came here for, then perhaps you will leave us and go on your way, having profaned God's house."

"I admire your piety, Princess, but I do not have the luxury for piety now. I have a war to fight."

"Against the jaran? You are a fool, then. You will never defeat their—"

"I have made my peace with the jaran, Princess." He looked down at Konstans's body one last time, then signaled for his men to remove the body. "My war is in Dushan. You yourself must know that you are now the most valuable piece on the board. That is why Presbyter Matyas has agreed to marry us."

"Marry us?" She blinked, taken aback.

"Yes. I am not leaving this church until the vows have been spoken and sealed. Our parents betrothed us years ago—"

"A betrothal my father renounced when God called me and I entered the convent."

"—a pledge not broken in my eyes, Princess."

"Let lie until it became expedient for you to renew it."

"No less expedient for me to renew than for the jaran to wish to add you to their considerable possessions." He pointed with his sword at Konstans' body. "Were you to marry him? To give him the key to Mircassia?"

"No. He was already married."

Prince Janos surveyed the altar. Vasha could practically see him counting the survivors and weighing what to do with them: Kill them now, or later. His gaze wrenched to a halt on Katerina.

"What is this? It is true, then, that the jaran are such barbarians that they take their women to war with them?"

Rusudani's voice grew even colder. "Barbarian or not, the women of the tribes have taken me in and given me protection, by the laws they have received from their gods, which

they follow better, Prince Janos, than you obey the laws set
down by God and the true church. This is not any common
woman, but Katerina Orzhekov, a princess of the Orzhekov
tribe."

He examined Katya a few moments longer with all the
immodesty of a savage. Katya glared at him, fingers caressing the string of her bow. Finally he looked away from her.
"And these others?"

For a searing instant, Rusudani's gaze touched Vasha and
seemed to ask something of him. He could not tell what.
"Loyal soldiers."

There was a long pause. "I will spare the woman, then,"
said Janos, "but the men must, of course, die."

"Give me their lives as a token that you will treat me as
a wife, not a servant."

He looked surprised at that, and actually lowered his
sword slightly, aware that Nikita and Mikhail stood about
six paces from him, still armed. "You will marry me, then?"

"I was not aware I had any choice, Prince Janos. You have
hundreds of soldiers with you. I have only my faith in God,
which I trust will shelter me through adversity. And I have
what power my birth has brought me, which you can be sure
I will use to make your life difficult if you do not grant me
the respect I deserve."

Janos smiled. Evidently he found this amusing. "For that
price I will spare them. Our bargain will be sealed with my
morning gift to you." She flushed, although Vasha did not
understand why those innocuous words would upset her.
Janos switched to Taor, speaking to the men. "Put down
your weapons, and I will spare your lives, by the grace of
Princess Rusudani."

There was a longer silence. Nikita and Mikhail and the
Vershinin son all looked toward Vladimir. Vladimir glanced
down at Bakhtiian, and reflexively Vasha did so as well.
Ilya's eyes were open—*open!*—but he made no movement,
no sign, and Vladimir glanced away as quickly, looking uninterested. Then, deliberately, Vladimir and Nikita nodded at
each other. Janos marked, surely enough, the man the others
obeyed. Vladimir tossed his saber down on the stone step
that fronted the altar, and Nikita and Mikhail followed suit.
Reluctantly, the Vershinin son threw down his saber as well.

"Stefan, Vasha, you, too," said Vladimir quietly.

It was hard to let go of the saber. Especially since it had

been a gift from Ilya, four years ago. But Vasha did so. He
set it down, and at once felt entirely vulnerable.

There was another pause.

"Katerina Orzhekov," added Vladimir, "I beg you, put
down your weapons."

"No," said Katerina hoarsely. "I will not give my weapons
over into khaja hands." But her hands shook as she unstrung
her bow and put it back into its case, which hung over her
back.

Janos watched her closely, and when she was done, he
sheathed his sword and handed his shield over to one of his
men, and lifted off his helmet. He was not, oddly enough, an
ill-favored man. Vasha marked that with a kind of detachment.

"Now you are the Princess Rusudani's slaves," said Janos.
"Be grateful for her mercy." He gestured, and his men
shoved Nikita and Mikhail over to one side. Vasha helped
Vladimir and Stefan shift Ilya away from the altar, over into
the shadows, where he might escape notice.

Stefan knelt. "I need cloth to bind the wound," he muttered. "I have to get his armor off."

Ilya's face was white, drawn, but his eyes were still open,
and he watched the strange ceremony that proceeded at the
altar.

The presbyter began to chant, speaking words in a sing-
songy voice. Rusudani placed her hands on the altar, but she
did not look at the man who was becoming her husband: She
kept her eyes fixed on the image of Hristain, whose eyes
gleamed eerily in the light from the candles and torches, as
if He, too, were watching, marking, all that passed at his altar.

Katerina slid over and knelt beside Ilya. She took out a
knife—there was a bit of a stir when one of the khaja soldiers noticed she had it, but she glared everyone down, and
when she began to use it to cut through Ilya's surcoat, slic-
ing it into strips, the soldiers relaxed and, maintaining their
guard, let her alone.

So while Rusudani was married to Janos in the flickering
light, serenaded by the rustle of armor and the expectant
mass of victorious soldiers looking on, Stefan eased Ilya out
of his blood-stained armor and bound the wound in his side.
Blood leaked and slowed and was covered under red silk.

Ilya breathed harshly, in and out, his gaze fixed on the swaying of the presbyter's odd hat.

"Not good," breathed Stefan finally, "but not as bad as I feared." He glanced toward the altar and caught Jaelle's eye. She still knelt, halfway between the clot of jaran and the altarstone itself, trying to look unobtrusive. Now she sidled over slowly toward them, seeking safety in their company. When she came close enough, Stefan put out a hand and touched her arm, comforting, and she smiled wanly at him and closed her other hand over his, and held on.

"So the ceremony finishes," she whispered, while the presbyter droned on in his sonorous voice, and two priests brought forward a cup out of which both Janos and Rusudani drank, Janos looking triumphant and Rusudani looking . . . exalted and defiant. "The words are much the same, although they speak them out of ignorance. 'Thus by this drink from the holy cup of Hristain's suffering are you sealed, thus by this chain are you bound together as wife and husband, never to be sundered in this life.' "

Vasha felt Ilya stir, and he looked down at once and saw Ilya looking up at him, puzzled. His expression looked odd, until Vasha realized that the pupils of his eyes were different sizes. Vasha took hold of Ilya's hand, and Ilya lifted his other hand and rubbed his eyes.

"Shh," hissed Vasha. Ilya stilled and shut his eyes.

Janos stepped back from the altar and spoke, giving a command.

Jaelle started, jerking her hand away from Stefan. All the color leached out of her face. She looked into the dark church, at the flames dancing around the assembled men, many of whom stared now at her. "I beg of you, your highness," she pleaded, "grant me the mercy God shows all His children. Do not throw me to the wolves."

Rusudani spoke.

"What is she saying?" Stefan demanded.

A discontented murmur rumbled through the assembled soldiers. Jaelle's breath gusted out of her all at once. "Princess Rusudani has interceded for me, may God bless her. I am to attend her and Princess Katerina until we reach Prince Janos's city."

Prince Janos gave a series of orders to one of his captains, who eyed Jaelle avariciously. Then, escorted by the abbot and four soldiers, he and Rusudani left the church.

Vladimir nodded to Vasha, and Vasha got an arm under his father and hoisted him to his feet. Ilya staggered and then, with a huge effort, got his feet under him while the khaja soldiers muttered and pointed at him. Vasha feared that they would want to kill him because of his wounds, but in the end the soldiers simply led them out of the church, through the dark maze of the monastery, and into a small wooden hut.

They closed them in there, in a place that smelled of hides and earth, and as Vasha helped his father lie down he heard soldiers muttering outside, laughing, calling out, as they settled into guard duty.

"Let me look at him again," said Stefan, crouching beside Ilya. It was so dark in the tiny hut that Vasha could only see Stefan as a black shape moving against the darkness.

"How is your arm?" Katya asked from the other side of the hut.

Vasha heard a caught-in gasp and then Vladimir replied, "Better that we leave it as it is until there is light to see by. It's broken, and the shoulder is out, but I'm not going to bleed to death."

"Let me at least try to pop the shoulder back. Nikita. I'll brace him and you—"

"Of course."

There was a moment of silence. Vladimir cursed sharply.

"That's done it," said Katya. "What of you others?"

They talked on, tallying their wounds, none of them as serious as Bakhtiian's, while Vasha sat beside his father, holding his hand, and listened as Stefan made a running commentary in a low voice, touching Ilya here and here, avoiding the actual wound, trying to coax Ilya to speak, but Bakhtiian said nothing. Vasha could tell he was awake, though, because of the way he breathed, and the way his breathing shifted, quickened, and slowed as Stefan probed.

A thin sliver of light showed abruptly under the door, and a moment later it was thrown open, illuminating them. Vasha blinked furiously. Stefan sat back at once on his heels. Katerina rose imperiously.

The captain stood there. He glanced at them, eyes lingering longest on Katerina, but he spoke in their tongue to Jaelle. Her hands were in fists, but she rose.

"What is it?" asked Stefan.

"I am to attend the princess," she said, but her voice quavered and she looked afraid. She went with the captain without another word. The door was set to, enclosing them in darkness once again.

Time passed. The others slept, those that could, and it was otherwise silent. Vasha could not sleep. He held onto his father's hand and now and again addressed a question to him, but Ilya never answered. Outside he heard the soldiers on guard, talking in their khaja tongue. There was no way to mark the stars or the moon. Only the soft sound of breathing and, once, a moan from one of the sleeping men, marked the night passing by. After a long while, Ilya's breathing slipped into the shallow rhythm of an unquiet sleep. In the darkness, Vasha felt alone except for the touch that linked him to his father.

Jaelle did not return.

PART TWO

The Dominion of Time

▼

CHAPTER TWENTY-FOUR

The Perilous Frontier

Niko Sibirin died unexpectedly on a day noted for many strange and unlooked for occurrences.

Tess woke alone. Natalia had gone last night to sleep at Svetlana Tagansky's tent, with Svetlana and Aleksi's daughter Sofia, and Yuri was, in Tess's opinion, an obscenely early riser. She had trained him to wake, dress, and sneak out of the tent without bothering her. He was rather like his father in that regard, except that Yuri, unlike any other child in camp, would ask to go to bed as soon as he was tired.

"On the other hand," she said to the dim ceiling of her tent, having gotten in the habit of talking to herself in the years since she'd had the implant, "that must seem no odder to everyone than my habit of sleeping in."

She got herself up reluctantly, dressed, and walked out to the pits, now built over and made much more presentable looking, with runoff and a ramp. Three khaja laborers worked now, shoveling nightsoil for the fields into a cart. They glanced up at her and as quickly away; like most khaja men living near the jaran, they had learned to be circumspect around jaran women.

On her way back to the tents, she passed Galina, who looked like she, too, had just woken up.

"Did the little one sleep poorly last night?" Tess inquired.

Galina threw her an eloquent glance. She had dark circles under her eyes.

"You look tired. Shall I take Dmitri for a little while?"

"Oh, yes," said Galina gratefully. "I just nursed him. I heard there's a new train of merchants come into the marketplace."

Tess tied the sling on and settled Dmitri in it. He was not even two months old yet, a rather querulous child and a fussy eater, so that he demanded to eat frequently but wasn't growing very fast. Galina looked tired and dragged out most

of the time. "Then it will be a pleasant change for you to go
down with a friend and look at the cloth stalls."

"I'd like that!" replied Galina, looking relieved to be free
of her son.

Tess wandered back to the tents, seeing Galina's older boy
running with the mob of young children who moved like a
perpetual motion machine about the camp. Yuri was with
them, and today, evidently, Natalia and Sofia and Lara had
been put in charge of the younger children, because they
were there as well. Tess greeted her children with a kiss,
greeted the others with hugs and kisses, and told Lara firmly
that she was not allowed to let the younger children whack
each other with wooden practice swords.

Sonia looked up from her loom and waved at her. "Good
morning!" she said cheerfully as Tess stepped in under the
awning. "What game has Lara devised this time?" Tess explained. "Ah. Earlier, she wanted to divide them into
jahars, which would have been fine except she insisted that
hers always be the strongest so that she could always win."
She shook her head. "I don't know what to do with that
child."

"Send her off to Uncle Yakhov and let her spend her days
with the horses. That would keep her happy."

"It isn't really suitable training for a girl. . . ."

"Sonia, I don't think Lara will ever have the patience to
weave or spin. You can't make a duck hunt like a hawk, nor
a hawk swim like a duck."

"True enough. I'll speak to Mother about it. Natalia and
Sofia would not be nearly as wild without Lara's influence."

"Talia is *not* wild."

"Not at all, my dear. I see you took the little one from
Galina." Tess bent down so that Sonia could peer into the
sling. Dmitri was sucking on his knuckles. His eyes were so
brilliant a blue that they startled. "Looks he'll have," commented Sonia, "but I hope he outgrows that disposition. So
like his father's."

"Sonia! You might have a child as fussy as this one,"

Sonia ran a hand over her rounded belly. "I hope I have
been faithful enough to the gods' will that they choose to
grant me as easy a child as my other four have been. In any
case, I am a much better judge of men than Galina, poor
child."

Tess laughed. "I'll let you congratulate yourself in peace, then. I'm going to the library."

On the long walk across the plaza, Dmitri fell asleep, lulled by the movement.

The ke did not meet her in the entry hallway, but Tess noted a new growth, a fretwork pattern of turquoise glass and black marble, pushing out into the white space. She passed into her own chamber and saw the message light blinking. Sitting down in front of the console, she triggered the message.

A woman's head and shoulders materialized above the console.

"Soje!" exclaimed Tess happily.

Sojourner King Bakundi smiled as if in answer, although this message had to have been recorded days or weeks earlier. "Heyo, Tess." She lifted a hand. "I'm calling you from the perilous frontier." Tess smiled and shifted in the seat so that Dmitri could rest on one hip. "I wanted you to meet the newest member of our clan, Tess. This is Imani King Oljaitu."

The recording device pulled back to take in Imani sitting in Sojourner's lap. Imani was about six months old, fat, happy, with a nap of curly black hair and a perfect mocha complexion.

"I know you heard the news about her birth, but I haven't had time to send you a decent image of her yet, so here it is. We're back on the flagship after a one month holiday with my clan, which was wonderful except there's a running feud between my sister Candace and my cousin Buru over—"

As she kept talking, the frame broadened to include her husband Rene. He sat in a chair next to her, face composed with a diplomat's polite interest. He wore a cranberry-colored cutaway jacket, unbuttoned to reveal a double-breasted striped waistcoat underneath. Rene was a dandy, not the kind of person Tess would ever have thought of Soje as handfasting with. Tess got a message from Sojourner about four times a year, always with Rene in tow, and Tess had learned that she could follow the current fashions by studying what Rene wore in the transmission. She had seen this waistcoat before, but the jacket was new.

"As it happened," Sojourner was saying, "we had transferred for a three day stint onto the Echido barge Usendi, and since I was three weeks to due date we left the med-tech behind on the flagship, and there I was standing on the bridge when my water broke! You've never felt embarrassment until you've stood in a puddle of your own amniotic fluid among a crowd of polite aliens. The worst part was having to explain what was happening! Then you should have seen changes in their facial tints." She chuckled. "They hustled me off to the female chambers and while we were sending for the med-tech a ke came in and—"

With Sojourner well launched on her anecdote, Tess focused in on Rene's hands. That was the new sartorial addition: The tightness of the jacket sleeves was relieved at the wrist by four buttons, left open to reveal a hint of white ruffled shirtsleeve. He had fine hands; Tess had learned to admire them, although she had never yet met him in the flesh. Now, he began to tap on the arm of the chair, as if whiling away the time while Sojourner gossiped.

Tess opened her own screen and, concentrating on his fingers, began to take down the message he was sending to her in Morse Code. Primitive, but useful. Sojourner cheerfully talked on and Imani chimed in with occasional comments in fluent babble.

single level of encryption. message begins. transport codes delivered in tripartite sequences. top level unknown. second level public record. third level coded to house sequence. no further levels noted.

Dmitri woke up and began to fuss. Tess flipped off the message and bounced him a little, and he calmed down, but when she switched the message to run, he began to fuss again. So, giving up, she rewound to the beginning and stood rocking back and forth to keep Dmitri soothed and just listened to Sojourner's gossip, which was, always, entertaining. She could come back later to decode the entire message.

By the end of the tape, Dmitri was fussing in earnest. Tess locked the message onto a cylinder and then left the library and took the northwest avenue that led to the marketplace. It was a dreary day, overcast and muggy. A great flank of clouds pushed in from the west. Despite that, the market was filled, and Tess pushed and squeezed through the crowd until she reached the bazaar of the cloth merchants. A crowd had gathered here to listen to a man in a plain gray robe who was, evidently, preaching.

Curious, Tess paused to listen, bouncing Dmitri on her hip to keep him quiet.

"... and when it comes to pass that the angels shall descend from the heavens, then, in the hour of the fourth book, all illness shall be razed from the land, and in the hour of the third book, all famine shall be razed from the land, and in the hour of the second book, all war shall be razed from the land, and in the hour of the first book, death itself shall be lifted by the glorious hand of God. So shall these signs be seen in the pilgrimage of His Daughter as She wanders, so do the smallest of miracles appear to mark Her wanderings: Has not the winter past been mild and the crops abundant? Has not the hand of war brought peace? Does the tiny babe not thrive that would have perished before? Those touched by Her mercy must thrive, even the heathen, who are themselves a sign of Her coming. How else would the jaran have conquered so much so swiftly if God had not granted them His Grace, for that they signal the coming of the Merciful Age once again? Is not their *bakhtiian* a man of a full hundred years of age who yet appears to be a young man of thirty?"

Tess started. She always made it a point to invite churchmen and holy men and women to audience, but this was an apocalyptic prophecy she had certainly not heard before. She studied the man's plain robes and finally saw the tiny knife hanging from a chain around his neck: that and his lack of beard or mustache marked him as an adherent of what she called the Hristanic Church. She wondered what Brother Saghir, who had already founded a congregation of the True Church in Sarai, would think of this man's prophesying.

"Tess!" Galina emerged out of the cloth merchants' bazaar.

Tess slid away from the crowd and went to greet her.

Galina displayed several bolts of cloth. "See, isn't this blue pretty? It came all the way from the Yarial Empire, across the Golden Road."

"Or so the merchant claimed," put in her more skeptical companion, a Danov granddaughter.

"No, look at this weave. Do you see how the thread is—"

The intricacies of weaving were too much for Tess, and evidently the two young women had argued over this point already.

"Dmitri is hungry," Tess broke in.

Galina sighed. "Very well. Will you carry this back to camp for me, Aunt Tess? Elena is already weighted down with the rest of the cloth."

Tess exchanged the baby for the cloth, and rather missed the warmth of the infant. She drifted back to listen to the preacher again.

"Just as you have come to this city that lies on the edge of the wilderness, so do we all live in the great city being built by God, at the edge of the time of the ending of the Accursed Age and the dawning of the Merciful Age. There will be much grief and sorrow, but there will also come the burning light of God that will cleanse us of all—"

A figure passed under the arches leading into the cloth merchants' bazaar. Tess stepped away and peered after it. Those Habakar women who had come to Sarai with their husbands or fathers dressed modestly in public, but the same could be said for all the khaja women here. A few wore veils, many covered their hair, but most had adopted the jaran custom of free passage for women. This figure, unusually tall, was covered from head to foot in heavy veils.

What on earth was the ke doing out in so public a place?

Tess darted after her. She ducked and weaved through the crowd and managed to follow the ke all the way through the cloth merchant' bazaar into the court of the spice merchants (where she sneezed at least three times) and passed into the dim arcade sheltering the Scribes Guild. The ke stood before a nondescript stall, but turned, anticipating Tess's arrival.

"Here is a manuscript you will wish to acquire," said the ke at once, as if she had known Tess was following her.

In the first Chapalii world Tess had learned, no Chapalii would have spoken before Tess, heir to a duke, did; it had taken her a long time to get used to the ke's casual assumption of equality between them. *But that's what I wanted,* she reminded herself, stepping forward to examine the stall.

The scribe looked nervous, sitting at a table illuminated by two candles protected by glass shutters and what light penetrated the inner depths: Scribes never worked out in the elements, but the outermost and innermost stalls were always reserved for the poorest or least established scribes.

"You're new here?" Tess asked in Taor.

He nodded and glanced with superstitious distrust at the ke. "This holy one is known to the scribes here. She is interested in this scroll, which has recently come into my possession." He fingered a leather sheath which, presumably, held the scroll. Tess nodded. He licked his lips and went on. "It is known as the *Byblene Gospel,* my lady."

"That's a heretical work, isn't it?"

He pulled ink-stained fingers through his black beard. "I am a good Habakar merchant, my lady, trusting in God Almighty, in whom all mercy resides. This came to me through my cousin who had it from his brother-in-law, who had it from a Xiriki merchant who had it from a captain of the jaran army who claimed to have captured it from a merchant at the siege of Targana who in his turn claimed to have been given it by a scholar from Byblos."

"What was a scholar from Byblos doing in Targana?"

"I do not know, my lady, or even if the Targana merchant received it in Targana or elsewhere. There are a few words in the Vidiyan script, here—" He helpfully held the scroll up toward one candle. "—which may be in the hand of the Targana merchant. Scrolls from Byblos are uncommon, my lady. This one has particular value because a translation of the Byblene script into Habakar has been interpolated between the lines."

"Who did the translation?"

"I cannot answer that question, my lady, but I can only assume that the Targana merchant did so. It is a careful translation, worth more than jewels."

"But then why would he have written this inscription in Vidiyan? Why not translate it into Vidiyan instead of Habakar?"

"I beg your pardon, my lady." The scribe stood up suddenly, looking over her shoulder.

Tess turned to see that she and the ke had attracted a small but interested crowd, all men, some few of whom she recognized from her previous forays into this arcade.

The scribe slid past the table. Immediately one of the men came forward and there was a whispered conversation. Tess could interpret the drift of the conversation by the exaggerated expressions of shock and fear that coursed across the poor scribe's face.

When he returned to the table, he bowed several times in a most obsequious fashion. "I beg a thousand pardons, my lady. Here, let this worthless scroll be yours as my gift." He pushed it across to her.

"I'd like to see it first." Setting down Galina's cloth, Tess

eased the scroll out of the sheath and unrolled it, peeling off
the layer of oilcloth. It was good quality parchment, and the
quality of the lettering was remarkable: elegant and clear.
Even the interpolation had no smudges. "What is this
worth?" Tess asked the ke in Chapalii.

The ke studied it. "In barter or in coin?"

"In coin."

"Two *yekh,* by the standard devised by the civil adminis-
tration here in Sarai."

"That much?"

"It is a good quality of reproduction, for these primitive
methods, and the text itself is both rare and has arrived here
from a considerable distance."

"You can be sure of that? Do you think it actually origi-
nated in Byblos?"

The ke extended a hand, gloved, of course, and the scribe
took one step back, caught himself, but did not move forward. She ran two fingers down the parchment, which Tess
still held open. "It is woven of different fibers. It is more sophisticated in manufacture, like the four other artifacts of
Byblene manufacture which have come to the library."

"Hmm. I'll have to get a Habakar interpreter who can
help me translate it into Rhuian. It will make a fine addition
to the library." Tess rolled the scroll back up carefully and
tucked it into the sheath, rummaged in her pouch, and came
up with two of the newly minted *yekh*s. She set them down
in front of the startled scribe, smiled at him, and picked up
the scroll and the cloth.

"That is not necessary, my lady. Your presence here is
payment enough."

"I trust the transaction is satisfactory?"

He bowed several more times. "May the Almighty God
smile on your children, my lady. May he bring fortune to
your—" He broke off, looking flustered. "You are most generous and gracious. May God grant you and your husband
long life."

Tess took pity on him and left, the ke keeping step beside
her. "I didn't know you came so often to the marketplace."

"On occasion it is useful. Is there not a saying in the
Habakar tongue: 'A bird caged in luxury would rather the
poverty of the wild wood'?"

Was there a wistful lilt to her voice? Tess could not tell.
"Yet you chose exile knowing that it would bring isolation."

The ke slipped into the deeper tongue, as if the answer was too important to voice in one of the lesser tongues of what she had once called "the superficies of the Empire." "Out of exile comes true seeing."

" 'It is, only through many eyes that we can see ourselves,' " replied Tess in the lesser tongue. So few things translated easily into the deeper tongue, which as far as Tess could tell used no pronouns nor even truly recognized the existence of the existential individual.

But the reply evidently contented the ke, who said nothing as they walked down the avenue that led back to the library. They paused on the steps of the library to watch the clouds roll down over the north ridge. Tess heard the rumble of thunder in the distance.

"There will be a great storm." The ke lifted her head as if to scent the air.

Tess smiled. "I can feel it in the air."

"You can feel it?" The ke did not quite *sound* surprised, but she turned to regard Tess. Tess could just make out her eyes with their odd vertical lozenge through the thin slit in her veil. "Humans are not known for this capability."

"Anyone can feel the electricity in the air at a time like this." She paused, sorting out what the ke had said. "You can feel it as well?"

"I can see it," said the ke. As if that ended the conversation, she went up the stairs to the door that led into her private chambers.

Tess just stood there, holding the cloth and the scroll. She stared at the clouds roiling down on them, trying to imagine what it would be like to see the fields of force emanating around the storm, at the pressure and the wind and the static charges shifting and building. But didn't the Chapelii see in infrared? Last Tess had heard, most xenologists agreed that the Chapalii saw in degrees of heat. What if, like some marine creatures on Earth, they perceived electrical fields as well?

A spatter of rain drove her inside the main building.

"Tess!"

"Sonia! What are you doing here?" She needed only one look at Sonia's face to see that there was trouble. "What's wrong?" Immediately her heart froze. *Something had happened to Natalia or Yuri.*

"It's Niko. He's taken quite ill suddenly. Varia Telyegin says his heart has failed him."

"Oh, gods." Her first impulse was relief that her children were fine. Her second, fear for Niko. "Here, do you have something I can wrap these things in so they won't get wet?"

"My cloak."

They hurried out across the plaza. The wind picked up, blowing hard across the open expanse, kicking up Sonia's skirts and tugging Tess's hair out of its loose braid. Rain spattered them, but the storm didn't break until she reached Juli Danov's tent. Then, just as Tess slipped inside, lightning streaked across the sky and thunder pealed, so loud that the tent seemed to shake.

Niko lay in the front chamber of the tent, attended by his wife, two of his grandchildren, by Varia Telyegin, and by Irena Orzhekov. He breathed shallowly, and appeared unconscious.

"What happened?" Tess asked in a whisper, dropping down between Irena and Juli and grasping Juli's free hand. The old woman looked frail with worry.

"He collapsed," said Varia in a strong voice, not whispering at all. "A pain in his chest while he was consulting over a patient with me, and then he was gone, like this. It was quick, and peaceful."

Thunder boomed above them as the storm rolled over Sarai.

"The gods themselves have come to take him," said Irena softly. "Listen to their voices."

They listened. Tess wept silently as the wind tore at the tent and rain pounded on the felt roof and walls, torn by the splintering crash of thunder.

As the storm rolled away southward, Niko breathed his last and passed over into the other world.

Stunned, Tess left Juli with a few words of sympathy—she hardly knew what she was saying—and went to find her children. She found, instead, three mud-spattered riders waiting outside her tent.

"Cara!" she exclaimed.

Dr. Cara Fel Hierakis swung down from her horse, handed its reins over to one of her attendants, and shook drops of rain out of her hair. "I'd like to try those baths of yours," she said, grabbing her saddlebags off her horse before it was led away and throwing them down on the carpet under the awning.

"What are you doing here?" Tess demanded.

"Come in out of the rain, my dear. It is your tent, you know. You don't have to ask *my* permission. In fact, the weather satellites showed that the thunderstorm was coming over this area so I decided to use it as a cover, as an excuse, to fly in, having neither the patience nor inclination for the overland journey this time. So we've just 'ridden in' from Jeds, so to speak."

Tess dredged up enough wit to notice that Cara wore, rather like a halo, an aura of expectancy about her. "What happened?"

"I have braved the perilous frontier, Tess. I have crossed the river, after which there is no turning back. Now . . ." She laughed a little wildly, quite unlike Cara. "I don't know. I need to steady myself for a few days."

"Niko is dead."

That brought her to earth. "Oh, no. That's sad news, but not entirely unexpected."

"He just died, Cara! Not an hour ago!"

"Ah, Goddess. If I'd only arrived two hours earlier, perhaps I could have—"

"No, no." Tess shook her head violently and grasped Cara's hands in her own. They were cold. "You're right. Better to let him go. He wouldn't have wanted anything else."

"Wiser than most of us, I fear."

"That's true enough. Gods, I'll miss him. Ilya will be furious."

The rain slowed and gave out altogether, and a shaft of sunlight broke out between clouds. Water slid down off the awning and dripped to the ground. The air smelled fresher. Tess pushed into her tent and set the scroll and Galina's cloth down onto the table.

"Was it Arina?" she asked, turning as Cara followed her in. "The baby is well enough, although not particularly strong."

"No, I didn't come because of Arina. I'd like to change. I'm truly filthy. We only rode a few kilometers, but all through the worst of that storm. It was exceptionally exciting."

"I'll walk with you to the baths. But let me find the chil-

dren first, to make sure they weren't too frightened." They
went back outside and Tess watched as Cara swung the saddlebags over her shoulders. "What did you come for, then?"

"I did it."

"You did what?"

"I've broken the code." Cara said it so casually that the
words did not sink in. "We are no longer constrained by the
treatments that the Chapalii have granted us, to make us live
with extended youth and vitality but for only the span of one
hundred and twenty years."

"What does that mean?"

"That's the question, isn't it? The Chapalii treatments
merely postponed senescence, compressing the disabilities
and diseases of old age into the last five to ten years before
death. But the Rhuian natives were tampered with. They actually are in general less susceptible to disease, especially
given the primitive nature of conditions here, and more competent at somatic maintenance—that is, general maintenance
of the body—than the other human populations. And from
that, from the tissue and blood and genome samples, I—"

"Let me sit down." Tess collapsed onto a pillow wet with
rain.

"It's just," finished Cara, crouching beside her, "that I find it
ironic to ride in here all on fire with the prospect of immortality,
or at the least a doubling of the normal life span, only to be
greeted with the news of Niko's death. All because of unraveling a code brought to me through my interaction with the
jaran."

"Code! That's it. That must be what the tripartite sequences represent. When merchant ships transmit information through the vectors as their shipping clearance, and
send it out in three discrete bunches, it's coded to different
cycles, and thus to different end points. One is clearly some
kind of public record. One is evidently to themselves, private, to their own house affiliates. But there's a third level,
which is neither public nor house."

"What *are* you talking about?"

"If we can understand what that information is, and where
it goes, and if we can disrupt it, then we can disrupt Chapalii
shipping, can't we? By a subtler and more potent method
than outright use of force, which we haven't got enough of
anyway."

Cara got a curious expression on her face. "We don't

know how long the Chapalii live, do we? But if our life spans expand to match theirs, wouldn't that give us an equal advantage?"

"Unless a short life span, if you're aware of it, makes you rasher and more aggressive in getting what you want. If you have a lot of time, it might not seem so urgent."

"Which is one reason you could choose to stay with Ilya and the jaran."

"Yes."

"What a strange, tangled web we weave, my dear."

"There they are." Tess got to her feet and waved at her children, who came out of Mother Orzhekov's tent in a herd, gabbling and shouting. Only Yuri waved back. Natalia was too busy arguing with Lara, and the whole herd of children headed out behind the tent, intent on some goal. They did not look as if they had heard the news of Niko's death yet, or as if the thunderstorm had bothered them one bit. She gazed thoughtfully on her children as they vanished from sight. "Are you saying, Cara, that you can do this *now*?"

"I have a formula. It needs further testing and refinement, and the main problem is that actual results in humans won't be quantifiable for decades."

"So my children could live for centuries, perhaps?"

"No, Tess, not just your children. *You* could live for centuries. Perhaps. Do you want to?"

"I don't think I'm quite ready to consider that question. Could we please resolve all the moral issues involved in interfering here on Rhui as well as free ourselves from the Chapalii hegemony before we tackle that one?"

Cara smiled. "Somehow I suspect they're all related, intertwined like the many strands of a web."

"And like the strands of light that make up a web, the darkness against which the strand appears must also exist in order to set it off."

"I hate to sit on these moral questions alone," said Cara softly. "That's why I came to see you."

Tess extended a hand and lifted her up. "Oh, thank you," she said wryly. "We must go say good-bye to Niko."

"What will happen to his body?"

Tess recoiled from her. "You're not—"

"No, no! I didn't mean I wanted to do an autopsy." She looked sheepish for a moment, but recovered quickly. Already, above, patches of blue sky chased the clouds south-ward. "I just wondered, that was all."

Tess lifted her chin to let the wind stream off her face. It smelled of rain and damp felt. "They'll take him out to the plain and leave him there, so that his soul may enter again into the world in another body."

"That's right. Metempsychosis. The transmigration of souls. It's a form of reincarnation belief. But that's not what happened to Arina Veselov."

"No. She was released from this world."

"I'd like to see the baby."

"Yes. There, I see others going over as well. There will be a vigil tonight. At dawn his relatives will take him out onto the grass."

Cara went over with her. Cara was one of those people who had the art of good manners down perfectly: She stayed long enough to honor her connection to the deceased, but not so long as to imply that her connection was any greater than it actually was.

Tess stayed longer, well into the night, kneeling on the carpet under the awning, first with her children on either side of her and, later, when they fell asleep and were carried off to bed, by herself. The entrance flaps were thrown wide, to admit Father Wind, but it was still night, oddly enough, and the candles burning at Niko's head and foot illuminated him with a steady light. As if to reflect his steady wisdom in life. She wept softly, but more for herself, for losing him, than for him in death.

She dozed off finally and woke and dozed off and started awake again, hearing bells. But she had been dreaming: The scene remained unchanged, only the candles had burned to stubs.

No, there were bells, messenger bells. She stood and stepped off the carpet, into the night. The sky had cleared ut-terly, and the moon hung low, spraying its silver gleam over the pale marble dome of the library. It was cool.

There. Tess saw the torches, men loping alongside a horse. She walked out to meet the messenger, and blinked once, twice, there was something so familiar about his posture on horseback. Then he swung down and turned into the direct light of a torch.

"Kirill!" Beyond that word, nothing more came out, she was so surprised to see him.

He looked travel worn, he looked weary, he looked—gods—older than Ilya, but he still looked like Kirill, only markedly grim. Seeing her, his expression softened somewhat, although he looked almost . . . cautious.

"I came to attend my wife at the birth of our child," he said hoarsely. She said nothing. She needed to say nothing. "But I heard what happened on my way here."

There was a long silence. She took one step closer to him. "The child still lives, Kirill. A girl."

He took off his helmet and shook out his hair, pale in the moonlight, still cut short. The bells strapped to his chest and back whispered as he moved. "That is not the only reason I came. South past the desert there is a pass that leads into the eastern wilderness that borders Mircassia, or so my intelligence reports. In two or three months, when the rains have stopped, it will be passable. I can lead my army over that pass and into the heart of Mircassia while Sakhalin comes down on them from the north."

"But, Kirill—" She faltered. She felt so terrible, thinking of Arina, that it took her a moment to realize that the grim look on his face was more concern for her than distress over his own sorrow. Good reasons, both of them, but neither of them truly reasons a dyan would leave his army during campaign season, not even with a capable second to hand over into command.

"Where is Bakhtiian?" he asked suddenly, and gestured to the torchbearers to leave them. An Orzhekov cousin ran up, a boy, and took the horse away.

"He rode south over forty days ago."

"We captured a man coming down the southern caravan route, bearing a letter and a message for the Prince of Filis. I traced his path back as far as Habakar. There, I lost it."

"And?"

He closed the distance between them and halted in front of her. She smelled the rain on him, and for an instant the remembered scent of the nutblossom trees in Habakar, as if he had brought an echo of them with him.

He glanced first to the right and then to the left, and when he spoke, he lowered his voice so that she had to lean toward him to hear. "The man who dictated that letter was wise enough not to expose his own identity by using his name. Someone in the tribes has set out to betray Bakhtiian."

From behind her, like an antiphony, rose the dawn song for the dead, for the departing man, so that his soul might rise into the winds and be borne back into a woman's body and so be born again into the world. To the east, light rimmed the horizon, and the sun rose.

CHAPTER TWENTY-FIVE

The Chains of the World

The captain showed her into a bedchamber. At first she thought that he meant her to lie with him there, but the bed itself was too richly arrayed for a woman of her background. She heard voices from behind the arras.

"My soldiers deserve a reward," said Prince Janos. "Those barbarians fought like madmen. We took heavy losses."

The captain deliberately looked Jaelle over, but without malice, simply with appetite. She bowed her head and tried to look meek, and watched his boots as he went out the door.

"There is a village nearby," Rusudani replied. "Surely there are women there they can take. But I need an attendant on the ride to White Tower, and I will not take an unlettered filthy peasant woman with me."

"You said yourself the whore is a heretic. Better an honest peasant woman than an apostate."

"You have shown already how much you care for God's commandments. Let me speak plainly, then."

Oddly enough, the prince sounded amused. "I wish you would."

"If she goes to your soldiers, they'll kill her one way or the other, or at least she will be lost to me. Then it will be only through you that I will be able to speak with—" Rusudani bit off a word. "—the jaran remaining to me."

"That problem is easily solved. I'll kill them all, except the princess, and you'll be rid of them."

"You have already given me your word. Do you go back on your bargain?"

"No. Why are they so valuable to you, Rusudani?"

"Because of the power they give me over you."

He actually laughed. "Your beauty alone has power over me."

"How can you say that when you just told me that it is

true that King Barsauma's last surviving son died unexpectedly four months ago?"

"There are other claimants to the throne of Mircassia."

"None with as clear a claim as mine. Now that my brothers are dead I am his only grandchild, that I have ever heard of."

Jaelle heard soft footsteps nearing the arras, and she knelt hastily beside the bed. Nervously, she caught the coverlet in her hands and twisted it around between her fingers.

"And I am a younger brother with six nephews. You understand why we are now wed."

"Yes," she said bitterly. "But I would rather have been granted the lowliest seat in God's house than a throne in this world."

One corner of the arras twitched and was pushed aside. Prince Janos looked into the room. He wore an elegant overtunic embroidered with gold thread, and in the quiet, whitewashed room she could see his features much more clearly than she had been able to in those terror-stricken moments in the church: Like most highborn men in these lands, he had a mustache, a clean-shaven chin, and hair trimmed at shoulder length, a style that suited him. Without his armor, he looked far less massive but no less daunting. He studied her for a moment, half as a man measures how much he might desire a woman and a half as a captor discerns the worth of his captive.

"Your slave is here," he said, and let the arras fall back into place.

Jaelle let out her breath. Needing something to do, she found a basin and pitcher on a side table, and poured some of the water out into the basin. Turning around, she saw that Rusudani had come into the bedchamber. Rusudani looked at her and then went and sat on the edge of the bed.

"I will help you off with your dress, my lady, and help you wash a bit if . . ." Jaelle trailed off. Rusudani stared at the arras, seeming not to hear her. Her lips were set and pale, her hands in fists on her lap.

She was terrified.

She had spent most of her life in a convent, expecting never to wed a man. Expecting never to face this night.

Jaelle felt an unexpected stab of pity for her. After all, Rusudani had as good as saved her life. She knelt in front of her, tentatively touching Rusudani's hands, which were as cold as ice. "Shall I send for someone to lay a fire in the hearth, my lady?"

Rusudani gave a slight shake of her head. "God enjoins us to seek only that warmth which the sun, His servant, grants us. To desire more warmth than that is to care more for the things of this world than for the heavenly city which God will reveal to the faithful in the next life."

"Yes, my lady. Shall I help you with your gown?"

Rusudani neither moved nor spoke.

Jaelle swallowed past a lump in her throat and, daring much, spoke again in a low voice. "It is not so bad, my lady. Many women find pleasure in the marriage bed."

"But you do not?" asked Rusudani suddenly, and Jaelle glanced up to see the princess looking directly at her.

"I am a whore, my lady. Men seek their own pleasure in me. They do not care if I find any from them."

"Never?"

Jaelle shook her head, unwilling to say more. It was not a safe subject, and she felt more than heard Prince Janos' presence on the other side of the arras. Was he listening in on them, as she had listened in on him and the princess?

"How did you come to be a prostitute?"

The question amazed Jaelle. And frightened her. "My life can be of no interest to someone like you, my lady."

"I want to know."

Beyond the arras, she heard the sound of a door, and male voices. "I am the daughter of a slave, and your slave now, my lady."

"But you were not a slave when I hired you. You were a freewoman then, were you not?"

"Yes," whispered Jaelle with fierce pride. "I was then a freewoman."

"As was I," echoed Rusudani, "but no longer. I was free to live in the holiness of God's word, but now I am bound by the chains of this world. So be it." She stood up abruptly. "Help me with my dress."

When Jaelle had helped her off with her dress and laid it neatly to one side, and washed her hands and her face and seen her, in her undershift, put into the bed, under the coverlet, Jaelle stepped back to the foot of the bed. "What do you wish of me now, my lady?"

Rusudani had a grim look in her eye. "Send my husband in to me. You may attend me in the morning."

Jaelle nodded and, hesitating only slightly, slipped past the arras to the other side. There, in a richly furnished chamber, Prince Janos sat on a chair discussing something with one of his captains. Seeing her, he broke off and stood up. Mercifully, he spoke before she could.

"I will go in," he said. "Maros, you and Osman may dispose of the woman between you, but no more than that, and see that she is restored to my wife by morning, without harm coming to her."

"Your highness," said the captain. He was a different man than the one who had brought her here. He took her by the arm and led her out. "Prince Janos is merciful," he said to her in the hallway outside, and then he took her to the rooms allotted to the two captains.

It was true, Prince Janos *was* merciful, or at least mindful of his wife's value. As Jaelle undressed in front of Maros, she spoke a prayer to God and Our Lady, for granting her their protection, even through the offices of a heretic like Princess Rusudani. Neither Maros nor Osman were particularly rough men. They didn't even argue over who was to have her first; evidently that had been arranged beforehand. When Maros left, Osman stamped in a few minutes later, and even washed his face and hands first. He gave her wine and food afterward, and to her surprise allowed her, at dawn, to take bread and water back with her to the hovel where they had confined the others. Already Janos's army stirred, preparing to march.

The door opened onto the dimness inside the hovel. Faces turned toward the door. Four of the men scrambled to their feet. Princess Katerina came forward, and at once Jaelle offered her the bread and water. Behind, at the door, Captain Osman watched the transaction.

"Thank you," said Katerina.

"The army is leaving," said Jaelle quickly. She glanced toward Bakhtiian, who lay in the shadows. She could not tell if he was awake, asleep, or dead.

Stefan rose from his side and came over to Katerina. "Are there wagons?" he asked in a low voice. "*He* is too weak to walk. And you." His fingers brushed her arm. "Are you— were you—?" He took in a deep breath and let it out. "You have not been harmed?"

"No, I have not been harmed. I will ask Princess Rusudani about a wagon."

He smiled at her gratefully, and she was surprised by how much she cherished that smile. But they all of them regarded her with intensity. She *knew* the deception that had been practiced on Prince Janos, and surely they could not be sure, could not understand why, either she or Rusudani should protect Bakhtiian. She dropped her voice even lower. "I will not betray you."

Katerina's eyes widened, but her only reply was to briefly clasp Jaelle's hands in hers. "We will not forget," she said before turning away to distribute water and bread to the others.

As Jaelle crossed back over the threshold she glanced back in time to see Vasil'ii lift up his father and help him drink.

"They may as well kill the wounded one now," said Osman as he led Jaelle back toward the guest apartments. "He won't get far."

Jaelle found Rusudani alone, sitting in the bed with her hands clasped over the coverlet. The shutters had been thrown wide, admitting light, and Rusudani held her *Recitation* in her lap and read to herself, her lips moving silently. She looked up, hearing Jaelle enter. At once her cheeks stained red.

"I am here to help you dress and ready for travel, my lady," said Jaelle swiftly, and set about helping the princess up. She caught a glimpse of blood on the sheets, not much, but enough to prove that Rusudani had indeed been a virgin. Of Prince Janos's presence in the room there was no sign.

Rusudani readied herself quickly, finally throwing a cloak over her shoulders and pinning it with a jewel-laden brooch. Jaelle recognized that brooch: She had seen it on Prince Janos yesterday, in the church. Rusudani was clearly in a mood, but it was an odd mood, combined as much, Jaelle thought, of embarrassment as of her clear impatience to reach some goal.

"I hope you were treated well, my lady," said Jaelle finally as they paused at the door.

Rusudani flushed an even deeper red. "He was not—" She broke off. "He was not unkind to me."

"My lady." Jaelle hesitated. "The one—he is badly wounded. The others have asked if you could obtain a wagon for him."

Rusudani met her gaze, and in her eyes Jaelle could read

that in this one thing, at least, they were united. "I will see what I can do."

Osman and four soldiers waited for them in the hallway.

"My slaves will attend me, of course," Rusudani said to Osman.

"You will ride with Prince Janos, your highness. We do not have horses to spare for the prisoners."

"I will see them now!"

"I beg your pardon, your highness, but my orders are to take you at once to Prince Janos."

They found Prince Janos on the steps of the church, quarreling with Presbyter Matyas.

"I will leave twenty men, then, your holiness," said the prince, sounding annoyed, "to help dig graves and to tend those of my men who are too wounded to leave immediately, but I can leave no more than that. My forces were badly hurt. Your own people will have to do the rest. Burn the heathens, if that will make your task easier—"

"But, your highness," gasped Presbyter Matyas, "would that not be impious even for savages?"

"It would be expedient, your holiness. My own soldiers will be buried and given a mass, as is appropriate. Ah, Princess Rusudani, you have come in good time. We leave now." He turned away from the presbyter, who looked aghast at the task left to him. As well he should be. Looking up through the church doors, Jaelle could see bodies, and more bodies in a heap at the base of the stairs, and a few more trailing out along the road that led to the gate. Luckily it was a cool day, and still early in the morning, so the bodies had not yet begun to stink. Janos, mounting, held under one arm a jaran helmet, decorated with a white plume. His trophy. He tossed it to Captain Osman, and with an escort of about twenty soldiers, he started down the road toward the gate.

Rusudani and Jaelle mounted horses brought for them. By their saddles, Jaelle saw that these were jaran horses, salvaged from the battlefield, and she was certain that Rusudani's horse was the one that had belonged to Prince Vasil'ii.

"Prince Janos!" Rusudani's voice rang clearly, even above the jingle of harness and the noise of the soldiers moving off. Janos halted and waited for her. "I will need a wagon for my slaves. Princess Katherine should not walk like a common woman, and one of the men is sorely wounded."

In the harsh light of morning, he looked much sterner than he had appeared last night. "We are leaving the monastery now. I cannot afford to have my soldiers exposed to any unexpected attacks. If the wounded man is too weak, then he will die. But you are right about the princess. I will send Osman with a horse for her. She may ride with us."

"Then I will go to Presbyter Matyas myself," said Rusudani, and reined her horse around. But Janos's soldiers surrounded them, and there was no way for her to break through. In the end, she had no choice but to ride forward with him. They were his prisoners, no matter how deferentially he might treat his bride.

Fuming and pale, Rusudani rode on, back along the road they had fled in on yesterday evening. Even Jaelle, inured to death along the caravan routes, was shocked by the remains of the struggle at the gate. Brothers of the church and a handful of soldiers had pulled most of Janos's soldiers out of the wreckage, but bodies were piled three deep around the gate. Jaelle had to avert her eyes from the heaps of corpses that lined the road and surrounded the gate as they rode through.

"Whatever else they might be," said Prince Janos reflectively, "they're stubborn fighters. I would like soldiers such as these as my allies instead of my enemies."

"You will have only their enmity now that you have killed Bakhtiian," retorted Rusudani. "It was ill done."

He smiled, pulling up as they came outside the gate.

Jaelle made the sign of Sundering with her right hand and clapped her left hand over her nose and mouth. The field of battle was carnage, slaughter; men and horses strewn across the sloping ground, congregated in grotesque heaps. A young man, black hair twined into three braids, lay on his back, eyes gaping open, one hand flung out, his helmet tumbled in the dirt beside him. Another had fallen beneath the body of his horse. Arrows littered the ground everywhere, like fallen stalks of wheat. Peasants from the village worked over the jaran corpses, systematically looting them, although it was clear that they had been given orders to leave the armor and weapons for Janos's men. On a hill above, men in the brown robes of lay monks dug three great pits. Beyond, the forest lay dense and silent in the still morning air.

"Now that Bakhtiian is dead, the command of the army will pass to other men, grown men. Bakhtiian has only the one son by the Jedan princess, it is said, and that one still a child. The power in the tribes will pass to the Sakhalin lineage, and I have an alliance with a Sakhalin prince. I am safe."

"So you believe," said Rusudani with sudden fierceness, "but remember that I have been among them, and I believe they will avenge his death."

Raising one eyebrow, he looked inquiringly at her. "Do you suggest a course of action?"

Jaelle stared at her saddle and tried not to take in a deep breath. The sight and stench of death oppressed her, and it frightened her as well. The battle had gone so swiftly, to leave such appalling remains. It was truly as the Holy Pilgrim said: "It is easier to deal death than to grant life, and so has God sent us, my brother to take death onto himself and I to reveal the promise of eternal life in God."

"Let us move away from this place," said Rusudani softly, "and then I will speak to you of what may well save your life: That you have a more valuable hostage than you know among my slaves."

But her tone and her face gave away nothing. Janos regarded her with an expression so wintry that Jaelle shivered. Then, thank God, they rode on, away from the battleground.

Ilya could drink. Vasha thanked the gods for that. But he would not, or could not, eat any of the hard bread. The others devoured it, if only to keep up their strength.

Soon after Jaelle left, one of the captains came to drive them from the hovel. Vasha and Stefan propped Ilya up between them. Leaning all his weight on them, he managed to hobble along. He said nothing—he had not spoken since Kriye had thrown him—but he seemed to understand that they had to move and that he had at least to give the appearance of being able to walk. Stanislav Vershinin's leg had stiffened during the night, but he could limp along, bringing up the rear of the pathetic little procession together with Nikita and Mikhail Kolenin. A grim-faced Vladimir walked alongside Katerina, in front, forming a fragile barrier between the khaja soldiers and his precious dyan.

They plodded along the road that led to the gate. Vasha heard Nikita's voice: At each body they passed, Nikita muttered a name, marking the dead. At the gate, Vasha stared at the pile of bodies and then at his father, who seemed unaware of the corpses thrown to either side, clearing the road. Nikita kept speaking. Although he could not have been able to identify each man by sight, they were thrown on top of each other with such disregard, he seemed to know each individual who had been left to defend the gate. But even his voice failed when they crossed through the gate and set out across the field outside.

Vasha concentrated on Ilya's arm across his shoulder, on the shift of Ilya's ribs, bound by a cloth bandage, under his right hand. The back of his right hand brushed Stefan's body at intervals, as they paced themselves, balancing Ilya's weight between them, and Vasha found that comforting. A few bold carrion birds fluttered down and landed, only to be chased away by the khaja who wandered among the dead. Horses lay everywhere.

"They're digging pits," said Mikhail in a low voice.

"No. Look there. There's a pyre being built as well. Surely they would not dishonor our dead by burying them. It was their betrayal, not ours. We fought fairly."

"It was our betrayal," Mikhail reminded him.

"Sakhalin's betrayal," Vershinin spat out.

"I don't understand," said Nikita softly, "what Sakhalin thinks to gain by it. Or how he expects to explain how he escaped when Bakhtiian's force was destroyed."

Vasha felt his father move slightly, as if that comment had gotten through to him, but when he turned to look at him, Ilya's expression was washed out, taut with pain, and his gaze was seemingly fixed on Katerina's boots, pacing evenly before them.

They walked on. Vasha lifted his gaze to see a party waiting for them on the rise ahead, where the road forked into the forest. Even at this distance he recognized the prince and—thank the gods—Rusudani. His heart thudded, then jolted again as he realized that she was riding Misri! A gasped exclamation passed his lips at the same time as Stefan murmured, "There is Jaelle!"

Khaja soldiers lined the road. Behind them mounted khaja men, unarmed, drove together a herd of horses.

They trudged up the road. Vasha set his sight on Rusudani and Misri and counted in his head, each step, one hundred and three, one hundred and eighty-five, and just as they came up and stopped at the fork, their passage blocked by a troop of soldiers and three wagons bearing wounded men,

Ilya fainted. His weight sagged onto Vasha and his head lolled to one side.

To Vasha's horror, Prince Janos rode forward toward them. Vladimir took a step back, placing himself between the khaja prince and Ilya. But Janos paused, took the reins of a spare horse, and halted before them. Hope flared: Perhaps he was going to show mercy, perhaps Rusudani had convinced him to offer the horse to the wounded man.

Janos leaned forward and looked directly at Katya. "Princess Katherine. I have brought you a horse. It is not fitting that you should walk."

Vasha could not see Katya's expression, but her back was stiff. "I will ride only if the other prisoners are allowed to ride as well."

Janos raised an eyebrow. "I think not, Princess." He wore his armor, and his cloak was fastened over his shoulder with a plain bronze brooch. "The jaran are famous for their skills at riding. What if one of them escapes?"

"Then I will walk with them."

"No. You will not."

Vasha was frankly amazed that the khaja still allowed Katya to wear her quiver on her back, with arrows and her unstrung bow, and a knife at her belt. Her hands opened and closed, and her shoulders shifted; Vasha could tell by these small movements of her body that she wanted to look behind her and dared not.

"I will ride if the wounded soldiers may ride as well," she said, but even by conceding so much Vasha knew she had lost the battle.

Ilya shifted and Vasha felt him fight back to consciousness, eyes fluttering. His feet moved on the ground. With an immense effort he put some weight on them. Vasha glanced across him at Stefan, but Stefan stared blindly ahead, pretending not to notice.

"I don't have time for this," said Prince Janos impatiently. "Osman, kill the wounded men if they can't keep up with the infantry. Princess Katherine, you will ride now or you will be tied to the horse. I don't care which it is."

A horse neighed piercingly. So suddenly that the movement made Vasha flinch, Katya leapt forward with her knife in her hand.

Shouts. Soldiers broke into movement. Janos jerked his horse back, and he actually laughed as Katya's knife skidded off his mail shirt. A soldier grabbed her from behind and pulled her back, hard, then screamed as she stabbed him.

"Katya!" Vladimir yelled, but he moved back to stand more squarely in front of Ilya, and none of the other riders interfered either.

There were shouts from farther away, a flurry of movement among the loose horses, and a sudden storm blew through the ranks. A horse reared and plunged into their midst and a startled Janos was almost thrown from his own horse, who was nipped and kicked aside.

Katya was struck hard on the shoulder and, a moment later, overpowered and dragged to one side. Vladimir jumped out of the path of the horse, and Kriye stopped in front of Ilya and dipped his head, blowing, then nudged at Ilya gently.

Ilya's head came up. "Kriye," he said through cracked lips. He let go of Stefan, swung an arm awkwardly over Kriye's neck, and hung half on the horse and half on Vasha. Kriye stood perfectly still.

Vladimir swore under his breath.

Everyone was, of course, looking at Ilya now. "Oh damn," Vasha whispered, tightening his grip on his father as if that could protect him.

That any woman, and a prisoner at that, would so defy a prince astonished Jaelle. When the jaran princess leapt forward with her knife, she gasped and looked away, because Princess Katerina had been kind to her, and she could not bear to watch while she was killed.

But already Rusudani moved forward, toward the others, and then a huge altercation ensued to one side with the horses.

"He's gone mad!" one of the grooms shouted, and another man screamed, and a furious stallion drove and kicked through the soldiers like a demon. Smaller than the great war-horses, still, the black horse's rage prevailed. Until it calmed unaccountably and halted in front of—

Rusudani's lips moved in a silent word: "Bakhtiian."

Jaelle's heart gripped in fear. What would happen when Janos discovered not just the deception, but that she had known of it?

Rusudani urged her horse forward and the soldiers, startled, moved aside to let her through. "It is as I said," she proclaimed, coming up beside Prince Janos, who had fought his horse to a standstill. "You did not believe me, but it is true. The dark-haired young man is Bakhtiian's son."

Janos shook his head, clearing it. He said nothing as the horses were driven off to one side and the soldiers re-formed around him. One, cursing, had his shoulder bandaged. Swearing and kicking, Princess Katerina fought while four soldiers slipped her weapons from her. Janos examined her for a long while. The intensity of his stare made Jaelle uncomfortable. Seeing him looking at her, Princess Katerina glared back at him, but she looked tired, dirty, and beaten.

Janos wrenched his gaze away from her and looked toward the horse. "This is the stallion your drover mentioned?" he asked Captain Osman.

"Yes, your highness. Fought every man who came near him, but too fine a horse to leave behind. I had thought we could at least put him to stud."

Janos snorted. But his eyes did not leave the scene: The fine black stallion and the man to whom it had given obeisance. He turned to look at Rusudani.

"Why should a princess insist that a common soldier be honored with her? She refused to ride unless the wounded men be allowed to ride as well. How can that young man be the son of Bakhtiian? He is too old."

"He is not the child of the Jedan princess but a child by an earlier wife, or a concubine. Such a son might not be granted the preference given to the children of Bakhtiian's chief wife, but he is still valuable."

Janos studied Vasil'ii, who stared bleakly at him. "Who is this other one, then? He is dressed as a common soldier, but how would a common soldier be honored with a prince's horse? Why would a king's son carry him?"

Jaelle waited. She felt as if the world held its breath, waiting for Rusudani's pronouncement. A woman like Rusudani surely would not lie, before God.

Rusudani's face was calm, almost serene. "He is a priest of their people. A holy man, whom they call a Singer. I know of this man because—" She faltered. Janos glared at her, looking skeptical. "Bring me his saddlebags," she said suddenly.

Janos gave the order, and two soldiers edged toward the stallion, but the horse seemed content now that he had found his master. Jaelle could not see Bakhtiian's face from her position, but he did not stir. She was not sure if he was conscious.

Rusudani hesitated before she opened the saddlebags. She bit down a jubilant smile as she withdrew a copy of *The Recitation.* "You see, he reads God's holy word. I saw with my own eyes that he carried a copy of *The Recitation,* and I received permission from Bakhtiian to discuss the holy *Recitation,* the word of the Lord, with him. Think—if we can bring the jaran to the truth of God's word, what greater victory could there be?"

Janos's gaze shifted first to Vasil'ii, then to Princess Katerina, and then back to Vasil'ii. Jaelle realized that he had already dismissed Bakhtiian, that he was measuring his captives with a new eye. "What is his name?"

Jaelle gulped. Rusudani did not answer. Her lips tightened.

Janos rode forward and looked down on Vasil'ii. "What is your name?" he asked him in Taor.

"Vassily Kireyevsky," he said. His voice did not even shake. Rusudani leaned forward, her fingers tightening on her reins, eyes fixed on the young man.

"Princess Rusudani tells me that you are the son, illegitimate or otherwise, of the Bakhtiian. Is this true?"

"I would be a fool to tell you if it was true," retorted Vasil'ii.

"That would depend on if I thought you could serve my cause better dead or alive. Is it you these men are protecting?"

Vasil'ii hesitated only a moment. He lifted his chin bravely. "It is."

Of the jaran soldiers, not one moved or made a sound at this pronouncement.

"Put him in chains," said Janos to Osman, "together with the princess, and let them ride in a wagon as honored prisoners."

"Do not forget," Rusudani said quickly, "that they are my slaves. You granted them to me already."

"As your husband, I am guardian of your inheritance. But it was only the men I gave you, Rusudani. The princess is mine."

A wagon was brought forward, Katerina and Vasil'ii bound and lifted in to its bed. Jaelle shuddered, watching

Katerina, whose eyes were now cast down. She looked utterly defeated.

"What do you mean to do with him?" Rusudani asked, without looking at Bakhtiian.

Jaelle did risk a glance there. Stefan had an arm around Bakhtiian, holding him up, and she saw a glance pass between Stefan and one of the jaran soldiers. Together, they helped Bakhtiian to mount. He slumped over the black's neck, looking half dead, and Stefan remained standing beside him, steadying him.

Janos glanced at them and then, dismissively, away. "You are right. The young prince is a valuable hostage, bastard or not. After all, I cannot entirely trust Andrei Sakhalin, a man who would betray his own king, can I? I must thank you, Rusudani, for giving me this prize to hold in reserve." His mouth quirked with a glint of a smile. "But I have gained no greater prize this day than you."

Rusudani's cheeks reddened, and she bowed her head submissively. But Jaelle, this close to her, saw her eyes light in triumph. Osman called to them to march. As the column moved forward, no one stopped Bakhtiian from riding.

CHAPTER TWENTY-SIX

The Forbidden Hall

It was planetnoon, and rings striped the sky above the court-yard where Ilyana sat with her back against a stone bench and her gaze fixed on her hands. The latticework shadow plaited her fingers and arms in strands of light and dark. David was lecturing, sitting cross-legged on the white tile floor of the gazebo, but she was furious with him for letting Anatoly Sakhalin sit in on her tutorials. Only she couldn't tell David that. Not without telling him why. And if he knew, then Anatoly would know David knew by that advanced form of communication adults possessed, comprehending whole spheres of existence with glances and a few choice words.

It was so humiliating. Valentin lay stretched out on the bench behind her. He shifted, and she felt his shoulder brush her back. Right now she hated him, too, for the smirk she *knew* he had on his face. Anatoly sat to her right, but by keeping her gaze on her hands she could avoid looking at him. Her face burned.

"The original acronym for nesh was neural-enhanced simulate holo," David was saying in answer to a question Anatoly had asked, "but oddly enough, it corresponded to Jewish eschatology. . . ."

"Eschatology? I don't know this word."

Every time Anatoly spoke Ilyana winced, because his voice triggered the memory of him standing in the twilight of the ruined caravansary with flowers in his hands.

"The coming of the last days, of the end of the world."

"Why should the world end?"

"Some people believe in a time of judgment, that the world will have a death just as each individual has a death."

"But unless we are released by fire into the heavens to dwell with the gods, then we return to the earth again . . . I beg your pardon. You were speaking of nesh."

She could hear David move his head because of the quiet snap of beads braided into his hair. "In ancient Jewish mystical traditions the soul was thought to have three parts. The highest part of the soul, called the neshamah, was believed to be not liable to sin and therefore immortal, that after death the neshamoah would preserve its individual existence. It's more complicated than that, but in part because of the similarity of name, and in part because in the Jewish texts the scholars discuss the 'treasury beneath the throne of glory' and the existence of abodes that are beyond or on the borders of this world, a mystical movement developed based around the word 'nesh.' It flourished for about one hundred years after nesh first came into use and spread widely through what they then called cyberspace. The belief took root that somehow your nesh, your soul, was isolated and set free in that other place. There's still debate over whether your soul, or your guise, or the part of you that travels in nesh, can live on in nesh after you die, and so on and so forth. That's how the name stuck, or at least, that's how some people trace the name."

"It does," muttered Valentin into his hands. "The soul returns to its original home."

"What?" David asked.

"Nothing."

"Did you have something to say?" Anatoly asked quietly.

To Ilyana's surprise, Valentin heaved himself up and said sullenly but clearly, "The soul returns to its original home."

"That is a common belief," said David.

"Do you believe that?" Anatoly asked.

David chuckled, and Ilyana glanced up in time to see him smile and lift a hand as if he was warding something off. "I just collect information, I don't debate it. I have no opinions. But I will say this: Whether because of what we created or what we tapped into, there are a lot more levels in nesh than any one person can explore in a lifetime. Who am I to say?"

"Then are you one of those people, as Valentin is, who claims that this world, the solid world, is only the surface?"

David smiled at Ilyana, trying to draw her in, and Ilyana smiled wanly back at him, not wanting to disappoint him. "That old canard. I think it's founded on a misunderstanding of what reality is. The world system itself is made up of layers upon layers of complexity, grown out of billions of years of existence. Where I think that the view of 'the surface world' stumbles is forgetting that anything that is artificially constructed must have a maker."

"Like the worlds? Or the stars?"

"More like Duke Naroshi's palace. I have *faith,* Anatoly. The rest is quibbling. Obviously the world of nesh was artificially constructed, but that doesn't mean that it couldn't have existed on some level before we knew of it, or could access it, or that it might not exist on levels we're not yet aware of. But let's get back to the palace. We're going to go as a group to the map room. Anatoly, you can just look around. Ilyana and Valentin and I are going to be identifying arches. We established the chain of entry and exit yesterday, so let's all set up and meet there." He gave Ilyana another searching look, but she ignored him and moved to kneel in front of the latticework.

From behind her, David spoke again. "And as they say in old fairy stories, when you go into the haunted forest, 'stay on the path.' "

As she placed her hands on the lattice, she felt Anatoly kneel beside her, damn him anyway; even though he was an arm's length away she felt surrounded, entangled, in the field of energy that emanated from him. She closed her fingers over the lattice—

The web of light spread out beneath her, spanning oblivion. She took three steps, a half turn, and descended into a gateway which David had constructed, through which the others entered. No one else had seen the web, but she always entered through it. She did not know why.

She waited in the gateway, a street bordered by arches, most of them facades. One led into a facsimile of the Memory Palace (Ilyana wasn't sure if David had somehow installed his copy of it in here or if it already existed here); a second, padlocked, into Valentin's desert, and a third into the jungle which David had unwittingly created. After a while she got nervous. What if the others had already come through and were waiting for her on the other side? She stepped through the fourth open gate ... and stopped on a circle of black marble that lay in the center of a round plaza that marked, as far as Ilyana could tell, the dome under which the company lived. A man paused at the edge of the plaza and looked back at her. It was Anatoly. He moved, and she stiffened, but he halted abruptly, raised a hand to acknowledge her presence, and walked down one of the avenues that led out of the plaza, disappearing as it curved out of view.

The map room had grown since she was here yesterday. Buildings that had been chest high on her yesterday were now up to her chin. She smelled the faint scent of cinnamon. The air was warmer, humid.

"Where is Anatoly?" asked David, and she started and turned, flushing.

Beside him, Valentin was smirking. "Why don't you have any flowers, Yana, huh?"

"Shut *up*, Valentin, or I'll make your life miserable."

"Can't make me," he taunted, dancing away.

"Can, too, you little worm."

David cleared his throat. "Valentin, what is the difference between an arch and a vault?"

"I dunno. The buildings are bigger."

"Yes, I had noticed that phenomenon. Yana?"

"A vault is a three-dimensional extension of an arch. Why do you think the buildings are bigger?"

"They're eating our life force," said Valentin in an exaggerated whisper. "And growing."

"Gods, you're a pig today."

"No piggier than you. What's wrong? Don't have the courage to give flowers yourself?"

She grabbed for his arm, but he jumped back, spun, and sprinted toward the edge of the plaza, laughing. To add to her humiliation, Anatoly reappeared along the western avenue and halted at the edge of the plaza.

"Valentin!" he called out. "Come here at once."

Valentin jerked to a halt, froze, and oddly enough walked obediently over to Sakhalin.

"Yana," said David when they stood alone on the plaza, "why do I get the impression that something is going on of which I'm not aware? And that it centers around you and Anatoly Sakhalin? Has he bothered you somehow?"

She hated her complexion. She knew her cheeks were flaming red. Like the Chapalii, she couldn't disguise her feelings. "No."

"I know you're upset about the flower night."

Oh, gods, he did know. She wanted to sink into the ground, and pulled up that train of thought abruptly, since for all she knew it might begin to happen, here.

"I'm not sure that it's fair that you kids haven't been al-

lowed to attend any of the performances yet. Goddess
knows, it must be hard, being confined in the dome, separated from your neighborhoods and your school friends—
there isn't anyone else your age here. . . ." He went on
earnestly, but she lost part of it, she was so relieved that he
had misunderstood her.

"Yeah. Yeah, that's it. I'm a little lonely. I miss my friend
Kori. And my other friends, too, but mostly her."

"I know it's difficult, Yana. Frankly, life doesn't, in general, get any easier, although that doesn't mean it necessarily
gets worse. But you've had an incredible adjustment, you
and your family, leaving Rhui and your whole life behind.
That took a lot of courage."

Yana cocked her head to one side and regarded him. "We
left Rhui because that's what my father decided to do. I
don't know what's so brave about it."

"Trust me, Yana. You've held up well. I think you've—
well, never mind."

"What?"

He hesitated, and to her surprise went on, though she felt
that he thought he should not. "I think you're the one who's
held your family together."

She shrugged, uncomfortable, not sure if what he had just
said was praise for her or an indictment of her parents.

"Sorry. It's not my place to say anything."

"Do you have any kids?" she asked, suddenly curious.

He shook his head and for an instant Ilyana felt like she
could read him, felt as if she had picked up the words that
he hadn't spoken: regret mingled with wry acceptance.

"Were you ever, uh, married?"

"I had a partner for about two decades, and we discussed
having a child but the time was never right and then we
drifted apart. It happens."

"Are you sorry?"

"Sorry for what? Losing her, or never having a child?"

"Uh, well, I guess both."

He smiled a little. "I guess both, too. There've been a few
other women but . . . well, one in particular, but it wasn't
meant to be."

In jaran society, one never received a gift without giving
something in return. This web of obligations and gifts held
the tribes together. And anyway, Ilyana was flattered and
amazed that David would confide in her.

"I'm supposed to have my flower night," she said tentatively, and as if the words propelled her forward she began to walk. David kept pace beside her, not quite looking at her, hands folded behind his back. "But I don't want to, even though I would be married by now in the tribes."

David made a noise that signified that he was listening.

"So my mother gave flowers to Anatoly Sakhalin, but that's not what she's supposed to do, I'm supposed to, but I didn't, so . . ." She couldn't come right out and say it, and now she felt stupid. "Now I . . . feel funny, but it wasn't his fault. He didn't know."

"And the flowers signify . . ." He trailed off. Ilyana shot a sidelong glance at him and realized that he was blushing. It wasn't obvious on him unless you knew what to look for, not like on her, but she was the one who was odd in being so light-skinned. "But he's already married, Yana."

"What does that have to do with it? Mama says that a girl is usually wiser to choose a married man for her flower night because he's bound to be steadier and more experienced."

"Oh, Goddess." David clapped a hand to his forehead, now *really* not looking at her. "You're not talking about . . . oh, I see. Umm, Yana, I'm not sure this is really an appropriate subject for us—"

"I know. I'm sorry. There just—isn't anyone else to tell."

There was a long silence.

"So what happened?" he asked finally.

"Nothing happened." Immediately, Ilyana wished something *had* happened, then was relieved all over again that nothing had. "Except I told Mama not to ever do that again and Valentin told me that Anatoly Sakhalin told her not to ever do that to him again, that is, I mean, give him flowers and pretend I gave them to him."

"Is this something they do in the jaran?"

She nodded.

"I can see that you might feel uncomfortable around him." He cleared his throat. "And he around you, for that matter. Listen, maybe we should get on with our lesson. There's a good set of barrel vaults down this way."

They had walked partway down one avenue, the one David had named Palmyra Avenue for its rank of painted columns lining both sides of the road. Yesterday the columns had been about Ilyana's height; now they looked twice as

tall as she was. To her right a trio of low buildings stretched
into a strangely elongated distance, bending away over the
horizon although by all measures of distance they should
have run into one of the other avenues radiating out from the
central plaza. Banks of flowering plants flanked the buildings, claret and dusty gold and a pure, delicate orange, rows
of color too diffuse for her to make out individual blooms.

Where the avenue, seamless and white as milk, picked up
the gray stippling of granite, the columns gained lintels and
evolved into a series of archways through which a new landscape beckoned: Wind skittered across a broad courtyard
whose expanse was one huge mosaic of jewels. A scrap of
white lifted from the ground and floated up, sighed down,
and settled back on the ground, only to lift again as the wind
picked up.

"What is that?" Yana darted through the archway just as
David called after her, "Don't go through there!" and she
pulled up short and stared up, and up, and up, at the monumental palace that hulked before her, a vast building with
two wings centered on a dome that filled the sky. Six slender
towers soared up toward the heavens, ringing the great dome
at equal intervals. Yana heard David's footsteps, muted on
the gloriously jeweled pavement.

"This isn't a model at all, is it?" he said in a low voice.
"It's a gateway. I think . . . I would hypothesize, that we've
entered the nesh palace, which has somehow become pro-
portional once we left the avenue."

Ilyana gaped up at the palace. It was so huge. It was also
gaudy, stuccoed and painted in bright primary colors with a
trim of gold and silver lacework along the columns, rimming
the grand doorways, surmounting the tiered arcades that
made up the front of the wings, crawling like vines in gold
relief up the towers.

"An arch rotated three hundred and sixty degrees pro-
duces a spherical dome." She stared up at the curved expanse of the palace's blue dome, reflecting the sky.

"True. I think we should go back to the avenue and catch
our breath. I feel a little safer there."

A feather touch brushed her ankle, and she bent and
picked up a square of white silk. It fluttered in the wind, caressing her hand and twining in through her fingers. Un-
thinkingly, she lifted it to her face, brushed the smooth cloth

along one cheek, and shut her eyes, taking in a breath. And felt a presence, knew that some *thing* was aware of her. She heard, like a whisper, the rustle of a robe shifting, the murmur of layers of starched fabric dragged over the ground, and the light but deliberate tap of footsteps, nearing her.

Her eyes snapped open, but she stood alone in the courtyard with David. "Someone knows we're here," she said. Her back tingled. She shuddered and turned all the way around, but there was only the courtyard, the palace, and the arcade that opened onto the avenue. She opened her hand, releasing the square of silk, and the wind caught it and lifted it up the stairs that led to the massive doors. She followed it.

"Yana!"

"No, let me just follow it. I won't go in or anything."

David came after her as she hurried up the steps—there were a lot of them—and the doors rose up before her, pale gray touched with lavender, framed by an inscription, letters in black stone in an alphabet she did not recognize which was itself contained within a mosaic trim of stars and hexagons. The door was not solid; it was a screen, riddled with holes, and Ilyana stopped in front of it and carefully set her hands on it and peered through. She saw nothing at first. Then her eyes adjusted to the dimness within and she saw a vast hall caught in twilight, shadows and light equal presences within, and in the center a person stood, frozen, ringed by a mandala of fire.

Not a person. A statue: a man, dancing, caught in the still heart of the hall, each of his four arms striking a pose, each hand framing a gesture, one leg lifted, knee bent, the foot swept forward.

She breathed as she stared and abruptly felt as if the hall within had captured the pulse of her heart, the cycle of her breathing, and breathed with her, waiting. The statue moved.

Except no, it hadn't at all, that was a trick of her eyes. But she flashed on Kori's Uncle Gus, and recognized who it was: It was Shiva, in his aspect as Lord of Dance, enthroned in a Chapalii gallery within a Chapalii palace.

A hand touched her back and she yelped and jumped back.

"Yana!"

"You startled me," she said sheepishly. "Look in there."

David peered through the door, closing first one eye, then opening it and closing the other in an attempt to get a good look. "It's too dark. I can't see anything. I think we should go back and get the others and discuss this."

Ilyana sighed and agreed, having no choice; however mildly David might phrase his orders, they were still orders.

They found Valentin in the plaza.

"Where is Sakhalin?" David asked him.

"I dunno. I came back here to look for you guys. He kept walking on down that way." He waved vaguely toward one of the ten avenues.

"Valentin," said David, "I get a little tired of your world-weary pose. Which one? We went off the avenue and this whole place seems to be changing. I want us all out of here."

Valentin looked interested suddenly. "Oh, so I guess he shouldn't have opened that door and gone in, huh?"

"What!"

Valentin snickered.

David swore in a language Ilyana didn't recognize. "That isn't funny."

"No, no, he didn't leave. But he was making me answer all kinds of questions, so—"

"So you thought you'd be better off with us?"

"He's okay. I mean, I like him." He shot a glance toward Ilyana. "And I'm not just saying that to make you mad."

"I'm relieved," said David. "Can you take us back to where you were?"

Valentin had many faults, but a lack of sense of direction had never been one of them. Nevertheless, they walked forever down the avenue Valentin indicated and did not find Anatoly Sakhalin.

"Maybe he went back," Ilyana suggested, "and we missed him."

So they went back to the plaza, back through the gateway, and came out in the gazebo in the courtyard, sunny and warm and glowing with afternoon light.

Anatoly still knelt at the latticework, eyes half shut, seeing some other sight, and his lips moved, but no sound came out.

"Damn it," said David. "Listen, you kids stay here. I'm going in to look again."

Even Valentin looked worried now. He sat patiently beside

Ilyana on one of the benches for upwards of an hour, half-heartedly playing a mathetics game on his slate while Ilyana mended a tear in one of Evdi's shifts. Once, twice, one of the actors walked through, glanced curiously at them, and went on into the remodeled lavatories, but otherwise the faint scent of flowers drifted to them on the breeze and the planet sank in the sky, creeping below the walls, and Ilyana smelled supper cooking, some kind of meat stew whose aroma made her mouth water. She'd forgotten how hungry she was.

When David came back to them, he came back alone.

"Where is he?" demanded Ilyana.

David stared at Anatoly, who was clearly right there, fingers wrapped tight around the latticework, and yet was just as obviously utterly gone.

"I don't know," he said.

Anatoly knew very well that by conventional measurements a forest of towers that were clearly hundreds of meters high could not fit between the avenue he walked on now and the avenue that he knew lay beyond it. If the plaza was the center and the ten avenues the spokes on the wheel, it was simply impossible that those towers could be so distant. He stood with one hand resting on his saber hilt (he always wore his saber in nesh); he shaded his eyes against the sun with the other hand and studied the towers. Valentin had gone back to find David and Ilyana, but Anatoly had walked on, endlessly on it seemed, and finally the mosaic walls that lined this avenue gave out to a procession of buildings with fantastically curved roofs, all of them black or white, unrelieved by color. Then the buildings stopped, and he was left standing on a paved road that struck out onto a flat plain. To his left rose the towers. He estimated they were perhaps a kilometer away. If only he had Sosha. . . .

To his surprise, she neighed and came cantering down the road toward him. *Stay on the path,* David had said. He hesitated as the mare halted before him. Then he swung up on her and headed out over the—well, it wasn't grass, it was a gray-green plant with tiny, bulbous leaves that hugged the ground. The plants made little squelching noises under Sosha's hooves and brought a tangy scent like seawater wafting up from the ground.

As he neared the towers he was sure that these were the same towers he had seen from the platform, when they had first arrived at Duke Naroshi's planet, that they were the same towers he had glimpsed through the hazy barrier that surrounded their camp. They should have been underwater. But there was no river here.

Black, vermilion, and glass, they thrust straight up out of the ground, spears piercing through from some other place. Their shafts were pure and smooth; far above, each one terminated in a different form: a striped onion dome, a bright spire, a silver needle, a seven-storied pagoda. He counted forty-seven towers, then forty-nine, then fifty-one, then fifty, and finally gave up.

One tower stood a bit away from the others, like a sentry. He pulled Sosha up at its base, dismounted, hobbled her, and walked up to the wall. But the black surface wasn't wall, it was darkened glass. Halfway around the base stood an opening, no door, just an empty space that led inside into a corridor that spiraled in until it reached the base of the stairwell that itself spiraled up, and up. Anatoly climbed. He did not get winded, nor did his legs ache. The stairs were black and slick, like obsidian, and the walls slicker still, almost like they were wet. In the center of the stairwell a luminescent shaft of pale gray stone gave off light. He lost count of the steps, just kept ascending until he thought he must have climbed far higher than the tower itself was tall.

He came around the curve and it ended in an arch that looked onto—

He stopped dead, right before the threshold. The archway opened out onto a great hall, vast in silence, lined with statues of a hundred hues and textures: a pallid griffin; an armored warrior hewn out of wood polished to a satiny gleam; a double helix wrought in diamond; a creature like melted wax with six probing appendages; a human woman in a belled skirt and a fitted vest that revealed—Anatoly looked quickly on down the line, imagining what his grandmother would say about such an immodest display; a pattern of lights pulsing over a black base; a man with four arms, one leg frozen in a graceful sweep in front of him, the other balancing his weight on the back of a misshapen dwarf. . . .

Anatoly stepped over the threshold and into the hall. Which could, of course, not possibly be here, at the pencil-thin tip of the tower. The hall was silent, except for a faint whisper, like the slither of a snake through grass, like the hiss of sand sliding down a funnel. The noise stopped, started again, and he saw a figure moving toward him from the other end of the hall.

His heart pounded. But because he was a Sakhalin, he stood his ground and waited.

As it neared he saw that it was a Chapalii, dressed in robes that left only the creature's hands and head uncovered. Anatoly had seen few Chapalii; other alien races were more commonly seen in Earth's cities. This one must be male, although its skin had the lustrous glow of a fine pearl, less like skin and more like a smooth shell. Its stiff robes rustled as it walked, flaring out in a complicated drapery.

Ten paces from him, it stopped. He regarded it. It regarded him. Although he could not by and large tell the difference between individual Chapalii, he knew this was not Duke Naroshi. Nor did he think it was a steward.

"Who are you?" it asked in perfectly intelligible khush.

"I am Anatoly Sakhalin, a prince of the Sakhalin tribe and grandson of Elizaveta Sakhalin, etsana of the Sakhalin tribe and by her wisdom and her years foremost etsana among all the tribes."

"A prince? Do you truly name yourself a prince?"

"Who are you?" he asked, a little annoyed by this inquisition.

"You are young in your power. You are of the—" Its voice had the resonant tone of a bell, and the shadows seemed to capture and hold the echoes of its words in the dark interstices of the hall while it studied and classified him. "—human race. A male." The light had an odd quality here, planing the Chapalii's head into a smooth oval without shadow or highlight. It had a narrow face cut by a lipless mouth and its head broadened in back—or perhaps that was just a trick of the light. "How did you come here?"

"I came with the Bharentous Repertory Company. My wife is one of the Singers—one of the *actors*. I accompanied them."

It lifted one hand—elongated fingers that were, like the plants he had ridden over, bulbous at their tips—in a gesture obviously dismissive, mimicking a human gesture. *"Here."*

"Here?" Anatoly glanced back at the trellis arch that framed the doorway. "I climbed up the stairs."

"It is forbidden for males to walk in the hall of monumental time."

"I beg your pardon," he said politely, realizing that *she* must be a female, and certainly by her bearing a great etsana. "I was not aware that I needed permission to explore here."

She blinked. The movement was doubled: first a thin lid like hazy glass followed by a thicker, opaque lid. An instant later he realized that it wasn't a reflex. It was a command.

The hall of monumental time melted around him and reformed into the plaza that anchored the map room.

"My brother will attend you in the Garden of the Thousand Petals of Gold," her voice said, but she did not appear.

"When?" he asked into the air, amazed and startled.

"When you reach there, he will attend you, as is fitting."

"But how will I get there? I can't get through—"

"For a prince of the blood, the doors in a duke's palace are always open."

A wall of air hit him like a blow, and he reeled and found himself kneeling, hands clutching spasmodically at the latticework. Stunned, he lifted his head to a thousand echoing gasps, the ringing of his ears, and looked straight into Ilyana Arkhanov's face.

"Where were you?" she demanded, then looked up over his shoulder. "Valentin! Go get David, you idiot!"

Anatoly put his hands down on the cool tile of the gazebo floor. Its solidity reassured him.

"I don't know. Gods, and I've got a headache. Have you ever heard of the Garden of the Thousand Petals of Gold?"

"Anatoly!"

He turned. The movement sent spears of pain through his eyes.

"Anatoly!" Diana knelt beside him and put her arms around him. "Do you know how long you were in there?"

He knew better than to attempt to shake his head. "No."

"Hours. Just hours. It's evening. What happened? Where were you? Goddess, I was so worried."

That she was worried pleased him, and caused the headache to recede slightly. "I'm not sure," he said, and then smiled at her, and her beauty worked to soothe away more of the pain. "But I'm to meet with Duke Naroshi."

"But no one meets with Duke Naroshi," said David, above him. "No one but Charles."

"Nevertheless," said Anatoly, "I am to meet with him. I am a Sakhalin, after all."

CHAPTER TWENTY-SEVEN

Under the Protection of the Gods

Vasha had not ridden in a wagon since he was a small child. With his wrists and ankles bound, he had no way of holding on, so he jolted along and now and again was slammed against the side of the wagon. Katerina sat against the backboard. The fetters on her wrists looked like massive iron bracelets.

"Katya!" he whispered.

The bleak fury in her eyes troubled him. "We must kill him," she said in a low voice, accompanied by the steady tramp of Janos's infantry alongside the wagon, "to avenge the insult to our tribe."

"Sakhalin?"

"The khaja prince. Sakhalin will be brought before the tribes and given the sentence he deserves."

She spoke so calmly that Vasha could not bring himself to say: *If his treason is ever discovered.* He glanced back, but the other captives were lost to view, fallen back among the infantry. Was his father even strong enough to stay mounted? He could see nothing, no sign of Kriye. Ahead, Princess Rusudani rode beside Prince Janos. He watched her, her blue scarf not quite concealing dark wisps of hair, her cloak fallen in folds over Misri's sleek back.

How could she have betrayed him like that? Except she hadn't betrayed him. She had done it to throw suspicion off Bakhtiian. He felt a stab of jealousy, remembering how she had looked at his father.

"Katya," he began, and stopped, realizing how foolish it was to even want to discuss such a thing, now that they were prisoners and his father, perhaps, dying. But Katya stared at nothing; she had not heard him.

So they jolted on. He dozed, woke, and found a way to brace himself in a corner so he wasn't jostled so badly. They stopped at midday, were given ale and bread and allowed to

relieve themselves. Went on. At dusk the army halted, and
Vasha watched from the wagon as four tents were thrown
up. He saw Nikita and Mikhail and Stefan, under guard,
hauling water in to one of the tents, but he did not see his
father. After a while, guards hoisted them out of the wagon.
Bound by chains, he hobbled along after Katya. It was by
now too dark to see the other prisoners. He and Katya were
put in a tent and left there, sitting on a rug.

"The prince will ransom us," said Katya suddenly.

"No. He must know he will get the blame for Bakhtiian's
death. I think we are surety for his safety."

"It might be," she replied, musing, and Vasha was heartened by the life in her voice, "but even if Tess acknowledges
you as Ilya's child, no one else truly does."

"But to the khaja I am," he said, and could not help but
feel triumphant as he said it. To the khaja he mattered.

"That's true. Aunt Tess says that to the khaja in these
parts, it is not what woman gave birth to a child but which
man fathered it that matters. But how could you truly
know?"

"Perhaps the women here do not take lovers once they are
married."

"Barbarians!" But she gave a little laugh. "Gods! How
could Ilya have been so stupid?" Then her voice dropped.
"Listen, we must think about escaping. We must get word
out—"

Lantern light illuminated the tent walls from the outside
and voices rose as someone arrived. Katya fell silent. She
lifted her chin and glared at the entrance just as one of the
captains came in, followed by Prince Janos. A soldier stood
next to them, holding a lantern.

"You speak Taor," said Janos to Vasha.

"Yes."

"Where did you learn it?"

Vasha studied him and wondered whether it was wiser to
answer or to act defiantly. Without his armor on, Janos was
still a sturdily-built man, strong, and he did not look all that
much older than Vasha. Probably it was wiser to remind the
prince of the power of the tribes. "I learned it from Terese
Soerensen, who is Prince of Jeds."

"She who was married to Bakhtiian while he lived."

Vasha glanced at Katya, who lifted her chin infinitesi-
mally. "She was."

"And she tolerated a rival to her own children to live in Bakhtiian's tents?"

"She adopted me," said Vasha proudly.

"*She* adopted you? What does this mean?"

Vasha thought quickly. Wiser to downplay the connection, or magnify it? If Janos thought he was too important, would he kill him outright, or be more likely to treat him well? *Think like a Sakhalin,* he thought abruptly, and chose to risk the latter course. "She acknowledged me in the eyes of the tribe as Bakhtiian's son."

Janos said something in his own language to his captain before turning back to Vasha. "So your mother was a concubine?"

"What is *concubine?*"

"She was not Bakhtiian's wife."

Katya was chewing on her lower lip, and Vasha felt her alliance with him, her concentration, almost the physical act of willing him on, as a great well of strength. "She was not."

"Then you *are* a bastard."

"He is also," said Katerina, speaking up suddenly, "Bakhtiian's only adult son."

Janos's gaze leapt to her. She stared back, and Vasha could see her grow by degrees more angry as Janos examined her with immodest directness, not bothering to hide his interest. "What of you, Katerina Orzhekov? Are you also a bastard?"

She flung her head back. "Of course not! I am the daughter of Sonia Orzhekov and the granddaughter of Irena Orzhekov, who is chief etsana among all the tribes."

"I have been told that the Sakhalin are chief among all the tribes."

"They are First among the Tribes, it is true, but the Orzhekovs rule the tribes now."

"Ha!" Janos turned and addressed a long comment to his captain, in which they heard the words "Sakhalin" and "Orzhekov" several times. He turned back to them. "I beg your pardon for putting you in chains, but you understand that you are too valuable to me to risk losing."

"Among our people," retorted Katya, "a woman would never be treated in this way."

"I assure you that you will be better treated once we reach the safety of my court. Now. Is there anything you need? I will see that food and drink are brought."

"I wish the rest of our companions to be brought here to us, and to travel with us," said Katya.

"No. They are slaves now. They have a separate place."

"We need to pray, in the manner of our people," said Vasha quickly, because he could see that Katya was angry and likely to say something intemperate. "For this, I would request the presence of our priest."

"If he is still alive, I will have him escorted here by Captain Maros." Janos offered Katya a little bow—Vasha could not tell if it was meant to be ironic or respectful—and left.

Katerina took in a big breath and let it out. "That was clever of you," she said into the darkness. "Of course you aren't important, but how is he to know that? That is why the khaja are weak, that they pass everything through the male line. But if he thinks you are valuable, then you can negotiate with him."

"The Kireyevsky tribe is important!"

"It's a granddaughter tribe, you know that as well as I do. But this is something Andrei Sakhalin could not have expected: Prince Janos has an alliance with him, but Sakhalin won't imagine that Janos thinks you are also a prince."

"No doubt Sakhalin thinks I am dead along with all the rest of them, if he thinks of me at all, which I doubt. But Katya." His voice dropped. "Do you suppose that Yaroslav Sakhalin is part of the plot?"

"No. Yaroslav Sakhalin never had to throw his support behind Ilya, but he did. Why should he withdraw it now? And in such a dishonorable way? He would never do such a thing, as you would know if you ever bothered to listen to him instead of just rebelling against him."

"Let's not start that again! I think I have learned my lesson. But what does Andrei Sakhalin have to gain?"

She hitched up against him and rested her head on his shoulder. He kissed her hair, for comfort, and because with his wrists bound he could not embrace her. "I have thought about nothing else all day."

"Nothing else except the revenge you intend to exact on the khaja prince."

"It's true," she mused, "that he does not seem quite so horrible now, although he's terribly immodest. But it must be Galina."

"Galina? Oh. Of course. Sakhalin has the two sons by her,

and because Nadine has no sons, Galina's boys are as likely to inherit the dyanship as any other Orzhekov child."

"Perhaps, more likely, because their father is a Sakhalin. Surely Yaroslav Sakhalin and Mother Sakhalin will not hesitate to suggest such a course, if Bakhtiian dies."

"I don't know," said Vasha. "It seems so rash, to do what he did."

"Andrei Sakhalin is not a thoughtful man."

"Huh. I suppose you would know. You're the one who took him for a lover, which is pretty disgusting if you ask me—"

She butted him with her head, knocking him over. "I may take any man I want as my lover. He's no worse than any other."

"In your blankets, you mean? I didn't know one man was the same as another, but perhaps we all feel the same in the dark. Oof. Don't kick me when I'm down." He struggled up to sit, almost laughing. "Katya, I—" Leaning forward, his mouth brushed her cheek and he realized with a start that her skin was wet with tears. "Katya! What is it?"

"Oh, Vasha." She said nothing more, just cried silently, and the tears ran down her face and slid into his mouth.

Voices sounded from outside. She pushed away from him just as the entrance flap was thrown aside and Ilya staggered in and promptly collapsed. Impassive soldiers, stepping over him, set a flask of wine, a loaf of bread, and a hank of freshly-cooked meat in front of Vasha and put a chamber pot down against the tent wall. They skirted Ilya and went out.

Vasha flipped over to his knees and hopped over to Bakhtiian. "Father! Father!" He put his hands on Ilya's neck, careful to keep the chains from scraping his skin, and found a pulse. It raced, but Ilya's eyes were shut. Katya managed to capture the flask of wine with her fingers and she struggled over as well, her skirts getting tangled in her manacled legs.

"Here. Give him this."

They put a few drops of wine on his lips and after a moment he licked them off. They gave him a few drops more, and then he actually drank some. Katya laboriously hitched back over to the other food and pushed it back along the carpet. She tore off a hunk of bread and moistened it with wine. Without opening his eyes, Ilya ate it.

"Father," said Vasha in a low voice. "Can you hear me? Did Stefan tend your wounds?"

Ilya's lips were bled pale by the effort of eating. "Cold." His voice was so faint that the rustling of the guards outside practically smothered it. He was so weak that the guards had not even bothered to bind him in any way.

"Here," said Katya briskly, "eat some more bread." She gave him more of the wine-soaked bread and he swallowed it. "Vasha, we'll have to lie on either side of him. We don't have any blankets, and I don't think it would be wise to call attention to him."

They ate the rest of the food, saving the last of the bread and wine for Ilya, for the morning, and lay down on either side of him. Bakhtiian shivered once, twice, and took in a sharp, hissed breath, then stilled. He was cool, but slowly Vasha felt him warm, felt his body against his back like comfort, although surely it was Vasha giving comfort to his father, not the other way around.

But he remembered long ago nights, when Natalia and Yurinya were still quite small, and how the babies, as he called them, would crawl in to share their parents' blankets on stormy nights and cold nights. During the day the illusion might be maintained, that Vasha was truly part of the family, but on those nights, lying alone, knowing that Talia and Yuri could snuggle in to the safety and security of their father and their mother (Tess sometimes threw them back out; Ilya never did) and knowing that, somehow, he could not, he had cried sometimes. But now he pressed his back up against his father, giving him warmth, and Vasha felt, oddly enough, safe.

Across Ilya's body, Katerina murmured to herself. The rise and fall of her voice reminded him of Rusudani praying, but Katya seemed to be talking reverentially to someone who wasn't there; he couldn't hear the words, but he caught a name once, and again: Mariya. Her voice soothed him. His father's breathing slowed and gentled. Vasha slept.

Katya woke him before dawn. Together, fumbling in the darkness, they woke Ilya and got the last of the wine and the bread down him. When the guards came for them, Vasha drew himself up.

"This man will ride in the wagon with us," he said imperiously, and refused to budge.

Captain Osman was summoned.

Vasha broke in before the captain could even ask what was going on. "It would be a grave insult to our gods to let a priest of our people fall behind in the dust. He will ride in the wagon with us until he is fit to ride himself."

One of the guards objected.

"We don't have time," said Osman in Taor, cutting him off. "Throw him in the wagon."

So Ilya rode with them, lying on the carpet with part of it thrown over him. Kriye allowed himself to be tied to the wagon on a long lead-line.

"They're in a hurry," said Vasha, watching as the tents were thrown down and piled into wagons.

"They fear pursuit." Katya stroked Ilya's hair, and he opened his eyes, focusing on her, and shut them again. "They know that jaran riders can easily catch up to infantry."

"How soon will they come looking for us?"

Katya shrugged. "In a few days they'll wonder why we haven't returned yet and they'll send a scouting force. After that, they'll send a whole ten thousand to burn Urosh Monastery to the ground."

"And find Prince Janos's trail."

"We have only to keep Ilya alive, and to survive ourselves, Vasha. The army will come for us."

"And for the others, too."

She squinted out down the line of wagons, which had begun to lurch along the road. "Yes. But we can protect Ilya best. The others must fend for themselves, for now."

"Unless by protecting Ilya we bring him to the prince's attention."

Katerina looked down on Ilya, her face pinched with worry. Then her expression smoothed, infusing with purpose. "He's not strong enough to survive any other way. Not yet." She glanced up at Vasha. "You did well, this morning, getting him into the wagon. You acted very much the prince."

Her praised heartened him. At midday he demanded wine and food, and they got it. That night, when they stopped to camp, he demanded blankets and more food, double the amount they had had last night, and wine more suitable to a prince's taste. And they got it.

They traveled on through a wooded countryside leavened by villages and fields. Each day the army rose before dawn and marched until sunset. Prince Janos was intent on reaching the safety of his court and drove his men forward at a blistering pace. Vasha could not imagine walking for so long every day at such a pace. In the evenings he often glimpsed Stefan and Nikita and Mikhail in the distance, carrying water, setting up tents, currying horses, but after the first three days he stopped seeing Stanislav Vershinin. They never came close enough to speak with him, but now and again one would lift a hand, seeing him across camp, and he would wave back, to show that Ilya was still alive.

His father *was* still alive. For ten days he did not speak, barely moved, but progressively ate a bit more each day. Katya fussed over him in the privacy of the tent. She ripped her inner skirt into strips to change the dressing on his ribs, using some of the wine to daub clean the wound. In public, she ignored him, except to surreptitiously make sure he wasn't being jarred too badly as the wagon jolted over the ruts in the ground that the khaja called a road.

"The Habakar had better roads," Katya observed one day after a particularly bad jolt pitched Ilya into the side of the wagon. His lips thinned, but he did not cry out against the pain. Vasha admired his endurance.

"Damn it," said Ilya suddenly, eyes still closed. His hands fumbled at his belt buckle. "Where is the ribbon?"

A breath caught in Vasha's throat and he glanced toward Katya. His heart pounded fiercely. Ilya opened his eyes. Even clouded by pain, his gaze still had the power to sear Vasha through.

"I have it here, Cousin," said Katya. Her voice shook. "It began to fray, with all the rubbing, so I tied it around my neck."

"I want it," gasped Ilya.

Katya glanced around. The soldiers driving the wagons had long since come to ignore her conversations with Vasha, conducted in a language foreign to them, but now, with the addition of a third, unfamiliar voice, the man not driving turned right round and looked straight at Ilya, whose eyes were still open. The khaja soldier grunted and said something to his companion, and a flurry of talk spread in the ranks of men surrounding the wagon. Katya glared helplessly as a number of soldiers broke ranks and came over to peer into the back of the wagon. Vasha saw coins changing hands, and he suddenly realized that the khaja soldiers had been betting on whether or not the jaran priest would live. Probably the odds had now changed. He almost laughed, the thought struck him as so funny; he almost wept, out of relief, seeing that some of the khaja soldiers were angry, thinking now that they would lose their bet.

When at last the interest died down and the new round of wagering took its course and quieted, Katya undid the green ribbon and gave it to Ilya. His fingers closed over it in a grip so strong that his skin went white at the knuckles. Finally, after ages, he relaxed and tried, without success, to lace the ribbon back into his belt buckle.

"Here, let me help you," said Vasha, bending over him.

Ilya looked up and registered him, as if for the first time. "You weren't killed."

Vasha blinked back tears. "I wasn't even scratched."

"How many . . . are left?" The words came out staggered, as if it was hard for Ilya to voice them.

"Not many. Listen, Father—" Vasha leaned farther over him, twining the ribbon into the buckle and speaking in a whisper. "What do you remember?"

"Kriye. Nothing. Andrei Sakhalin must have betrayed us. That's all."

"Then remember this. The khaja who took us prisoner, Prince Janos, believes that Bakhtiian is dead, and believes that *you* are a Singer, a priest. That is why you have survived so far."

Ilya coughed, but perhaps it was meant to be a laugh. "Under the protection of the gods."

"Yes. We're headed west, but—"

"Let him rest," said Katya. "That's enough to absorb for now."

They let him rest, but over the next five days he improved so rapidly that it was almost as if, before, he had been struggling more over the question of whether to live or die than over his actual injuries. He still spoke rarely, but he ate voraciously, and finally the guards bound his wrists in rope and took him before Prince Janos. Vasha demanded to be taken as well, since the prince had ignored them since that one visit the first night of their journey, and Captain Osman bowed before him and offered to personally escort him and Katya to Prince Janos.

Janos waited inside the plain white campaign tent he used as his headquarters. It rose first of all the tents each night and came down last in the morning. The prince sat on a carved chair, with Rusudani seated beside him on a chair that bore the seal of the presbyter of Urosh Monastery on its back. Vasha recognized it from the church.

They were stopped just inside the tent, waiting while an unarmed man read to the prince from some kind of list. Behind the chairs, an inner curtain had been drawn back somewhat, revealing a wide four-posted bed covered with a quilt embroidered with gold thread. Rusudani, sitting with a book open on her lap, glanced up at their entrance. Her eyes widened with surprise and curiosity. Daringly, Vasha met her gaze briefly, but she looked beyond him and saw Bakhtiian. Her face lit; as quickly, she bent her head down to hide her expression.

When the khaja servant had finished, Janos motioned him aside. "I give you greetings, Prince Vasil'ii, Princess Katherine," he said with ominous politeness. He looked expectantly at Captain Osman, asking him a question. Osman pushed Ilya forward.

"Kneel before the prince," Osman said in Taor.

Ilya looked weak, pale, and stubborn. "I kneel before no man, only before the gods."

Vasha wanted to kick him. He slid one boot over and nudged him, but Ilya either did not feel it or, more likely, ignored it.

Janos folded his arms across his chest. His expression, a mask of icy patience, did not change.

Rusudani closed the book in her lap and handed it to Jaelle, gesturing toward Bakhtiian. Hesitantly, Jaelle walked forward. "My lady wishes this returned to you." She offered the book to Ilya. He took it, glanced at it, and tucked it under one arm.

"I could have you killed for your arrogance," said Prince Janos conversationally, "but my wife owns you now, and it is her will that you be allowed to live, so that she may instruct you in the true faith."

Ilya was a master at controlling his expression. Standing so close to his father, Vasha felt more than saw the surprise register when Janos referred to Rusudani so casually as his wife.

"I am beholden to the princess," Ilya replied.

"How comes it that a man such as yourself has learned to speak Taor so well?"

"I have been called by the gods to learn many new things."

Janos lifted a hand and spoke a few words to one of his attendants. A moment later, Konstans' helmet was given into his hands, the white plume a beacon in the lantern-lit tent. "I wonder," said Janos, standing and walking over to him, "if this would fit you."

Ilya blanched, and Vasha cursed himself silently. It was a terrible way to learn of Konstans's death. Ilya lifted his bound hands abruptly and warded off the helmet. "It is not mine to wear," he said hoarsely. "That helmet belongs to the man who earned the right to wear it."

"That man is dead," said Janos, but he smiled, slightly, and went back to his chair, and gave the helmet back to an attendant, evidently satisfied by what he had seen. "Osman, remove him. He may take food and drink to the prince and princess in the evenings, and pray with them, but otherwise, he will labor and travel with the other slaves."

Rusudani watched him go and then, as if his absence galvanized her, she beckoned to Katerina.

"Princess Rusudani asks that you come forward," translated Jaelle. "She hopes you have been well treated so far in your journey."

"I would be better treated were I to be freed," responded Katerina, coming forward to kneel before Rusudani. Janos coughed, looking amused. Katya shot him a glare and turned a softer gaze on Rusudani, who leaned down and took her hands in hers. "But I thank you for your concern."

"Tell me, Prince Vasil'ii," said Janos, dismissing the women's conversation as if it were of no interest to him, "do you play *dars*?"

"I don't know what that is."

"Lord Belos, the board." The man addressed brought forward a table, a stool, and a leather case, which he opened to reveal a board painted with white and red squares and a carved wooden box which contained small carved pieces in either white or red representing castles, infantrymen, mounted soldiers, churchmen, and princes.

Vasha ventured forward. "Yes, I know this game. In Jeds they call it *castles*."

"Sit." Janos waved to the stool. "Did the Prince of Jeds teach you this, as well?"

Vasha sat. "No. I learned it from her court physician,

Dokhtor Hierakis. She also taught me a game much like this, called *chess*, but in chess the etsana—the queen—is the most powerful piece on the board."

"It must come from a barbarian land. Lord Belos, bring us wine." Janos placed one white and one red castle on the board. "Which do you choose?"

Vasha chose red. "How did you learn Taor, Prince Janos?" he asked as he set up his pieces. Lord Belos put down two cups of wine on the little table, beside the board. The wine was steaming, pungent.

"I also learned it from a woman, from my mother."

"How did she come to know Taor?"

Janos smiled a small, secret smile. "My father's first wife was a princess from Hereti-Manas. After she died in child-bed, he needed funds more than bloodlines, since Dushan had already fallen from its preeminent position among the Yos principalities. So he married my mother, who brought with her the greatest fortune in all the Yos principalities, a fortune gained by her ancestors in the caravan trade. He ennobled her father and convinced her mother to convert from her heretical faith, but nevertheless, like you, Prince Vasil'ii, my right to the title of prince has always remained suspect because of her birth."

Surprised by this confession, Vasha glanced up and met Janos's gaze. It was even, unclouded by petulance, and permanently marked by ambition. Despite himself, Vasha could not dislike him.

CHAPTER TWENTY-EIGHT

The Garden of the Thousand Petals of Gold

They held a war council. Anatoly was surprised at how many people attended it: David, of course, Gwyn Jones, Wingtuck Lien, Owen and Ginny, a pretty young woman named Annet who was one of the actors but evidently also in on the conspiracy, Joseph, and the etsana of the company, Yomi. Anatoly had insisted that Diana attend, though she didn't want to. The story had thrown her into a belligerent mood that troubled Anatoly.

They sat in a circle in Owen and Ginny's room, and Anatoly waited politely for Yomi to open the council. A tap sounded on the wall outside. Without waiting for an answer, Hyacinth pushed aside the curtain and came in.

"Goddess," he said, having the nerve to sit down right next to Anatoly, squeezing in between him and David, "why did you all give *me* the job of throwing Veselov off the scent?"

"I didn't know he was on the scent," remarked Gwyn Jones, the actor whose quiet mien Anatoly had long since recognized as a cloud concealing a bright light.

Anatoly waited for someone to challenge Hyacinth's right to be here, but no one did.

"Veselov's not stupid." Hyacinth snorted. "He knows there's something going on that he's not part of. He hates that."

"Listen," said David. "I move we all formally recognize Hyacinth for his services in leading Veselov off the scent. Now, the question: Can we afford to pass up this opportunity?"

They began to debate. Anatoly quickly identified two factions: Owen and Ginny were against anything that might upset the delicate accommodation they had reached with

Duke Naroshi; David and Wingtuck and Gwyn wanted Anatoly to meet with Duke Naroshi as soon as possible, to follow up on this promising lead.

"Only Charles has ever met with any member of the Chapalii nobility," said David. "We can't pass this up. Think of what we could learn."

"Surely Terese Soerensen has met with Chapalii nobility," objected Owen. "Earth diplomats have as well."

"Tess is on interdiction on Rhui. She is officially dead. How will that help us? Earth diplomats as far as we can tell have the approximate status of Chapalii merchants and ship captains: above servants, but definitely beneath the nobility. Anatoly, you haven't spoken yet."

Anatoly had been wondering why Hyacinth was here. Was it possible Hyacinth was part of the conspiracy? It seemed unlikely. Yet it was true that sidetracking as persistent a person as Vasil Veselov away from a meeting like this was no small feat. "The etsana I met did not ask, she said that her brother *would* attend me. If that is her command, then as a guest in her camp, I must obey her."

A silence followed this comment.

"I don't understand," said Diana suddenly, speaking for the first time. "I thought Chapalii women were in purdah or something, that they were restricted. That they had no rights under the Chapalii legal system. Isn't it true that a female who marries loses all her status, wealth, and position from her father's house and becomes the property of her husband? So how could she—that is, Duke Naroshi's sister, if that's even who it was—claim to know what her brother will or won't do?"

Hurt, Anatoly flinched back from her tone. "You don't believe my account of our meeting?"

"You said she spoke khush! Where would a Chapalii learn khush?"

David coughed. "Diana, it's possible that that is merely how Anatoly experienced her speech."

"I'm just saying," continued Diana stubbornly, "that either Anatoly didn't understand her and the intent of the encounter, or else we've been misunderstanding something major about Chapalii culture all this time."

"Diana," said Yomi gently, "the best human and league xenologists and diplomats and anthropologists have been studying the Chapalii for two hundred years. Anatoly met—if we can use that term—this purported female Chapalii in nesh for minutes, at most. Begging your pardon, Anatoly, but I'm not sure we can give your account the same credence."

Everyone looked at Anatoly, but he steeled himself to remain impassive.

Beside him, Diana caught her fair hair in one hand and pulled it back over her shoulder, looking disgruntled by this criticism.

"Maybe so, but Anatoly was trained in a harsh school. In his world, if you didn't observe correctly, the most likely outcome was death. Even with all the prejudices he brought with him, I'm not sure he might not observe with a fresher and less prejudiced eye than all our experts."

Everyone began to argue at once. Finally, disgusted, Anatoly stood up. When he saw he had their attention, he spoke. "I beg your pardon," he said politely, "but as a commander in the vanguard of Bakhtiian's army, it is my duty to go."

"Who is Bakhtiian?" Annet whispered.

Owen swore. Loudly. "What nonsense is this! I demand we bring the matter before Soerensen—"

"Now, Owen," David began.

Anatoly pulled Diana to her feet. "We'll go get Portia and go now. I see no reason to delay."

"We? I'm not going. Portia is certainly *not!*"

"Of course we will go together. It would not be polite otherwise." Tired of all the bickering—gods, these khaja spent most of their time discussing and debating instead of acting—Anatoly took her by the wrist and tugged her outside the room. David winked at him as he left and fluidly continued the argument with Owen.

Outside, Anatoly turned to his wife. "Thank you."

"For what?"

"For defending me to Yomi."

Diana colored slightly. "They don't know you. They don't know your strengths. I know how precisely you can observe. I trust you to see things as they are. Well, most things. But you're not taking Portia!"

"I'll thank you to understand that I would not take my daughter into any situation that I judged dangerous, Diana. You khaja do not know how to conduct a war. Any fool can see that the Chapalii are more powerful. If they have not harmed us yet, then why should they harm us now? They would have acted long ago if they meant to destroy humans. In a strong line of defense, you must probe for weakness. If a scout can't sneak in, then you walk in openly, with respect, but keeping your eyes open. Every army has a weakness."

"Ha!" said Diana sarcastically. "Then what is Bakhtiian's weakness?"

They stopped in the courtyard, where they found Veselov sitting on the gazebo bench beside his two sons. They were all embroidering. Vasil glanced up and smiled winningly at them, then bent back to answer one of Anton's questions. As if he didn't care where they had come from or where they were going now. Valentin looked up and saw Anatoly. He bit at his lower lip and cocked his head to one side, seeming to ask if he could have permission to leave.

"I suppose," said Anatoly slowly, "that Bakhtiian's weakness is that he doesn't know that anything—that all this— exists outside of himself and his vision."

"He can't know. Rhui is interdicted."

"I know."

"Oh, Anatoly." Her hand, resting so gently on his upper arm, felt pitying more than comforting. "You never should have come."

"I should have been kept ignorant, too?" He watched the words make her wince. "Well, perhaps I have thought that myself, but don't you see? This opportunity is what I came for. I can feel it." He clenched one hand and saw, beyond the open caravansary gates, Portia and Evdokia running past, following by a laughing Ilyana. "Something is about to happen. And we're going. . . ." He trailed off.

David emerged from the west colonnade and smiled cheerfully at him. "They'll argue for another hour at least."

"Good. We'll go now, then."

"Uh, do you have a way planned?"

"We'll ride to the ebony gate and it will open for me."

"You seem sure of that."

"Such has the etsana decreed."

Diana gave an embarrassed smile. "I'm sorry, David. He isn't always this arrogant."

"He isn't?" David asked, and grinned at Anatoly as if only they two could share the joke; Anatoly liked him for taking the sting out of Diana's words. She looked disconcerted. David might not be a soldier, but he was a steady companion, and wise in more than just the ways of khaja engineering.

"I will go get Portia," said Anatoly, knowing better than to leave that to Diana. "David, we have five saddles. Should we take two more riders?"

"The more eyes the better."

"Then who?"

As if in answer to the question, which he couldn't have heard, Veselov stood up and sauntered over. "Is it true you've received a summons to attend Duke Naroshi, Sakhalin? I'll go."

"No."

"But of course I will. It's no trouble. I'll go get my saddle now. But you will have to ask Yana herself if you can borrow her saddle." He shot Anatoly a charming smile replete with malice. How he had found out about the whole disgraceful episode Anatoly could not imagine, but it was obvious Vasil would not hesitate to use it against him if Anatoly did not agree to whatever he wanted. Vasil caught Diana's hand in one of his, brought it to his lips, and brushed a kiss on her knuckles. "I am sure Karolla will be happy to lend you my saddle. I'll go fetch it now." He dropped her hand and left.

Diana wiped her hand on her skirt.

"I'll go talk to Yana," said David hastily. "Meet you at the horses. And I'll get Gwyn. If anyone can rein in Veselov, it's Gwyn."

"Don't bother," said Anatoly coldly. "Veselov is not coming with us."

"You can't stop him," said Diana. She laughed breathlessly. "But I'd like to see it."

"Meet me by the horses," snapped Anatoly, growing more and more irritated. He stalked off, getting his saddle and gear first and then separating Portia from Evdokia where they ran around and around one of the flower beds shrieking and giggling in a game that involved horses, dragons, and Infinity Jilt, girl-pirate, on a speed yacht race from Jupiter to the Horsehead Nebula. He went out to the horse herd, and little Sosha, as he had named his new mare, came right to him. He finished saddling her as the others came up: Diana looked cross; David and Gwyn Jones each carried a saddle, and Hyacinth tagged along after them; Veselov lugged two saddles by himself. Unfortunately Valentin and Anton had decided to come with him.

Anatoly examined Hyacinth, who stood, smirking, with his arms folded over his chest, and watched Veselov cut out and saddle a horse. He realized all at once that he didn't dislike Hyacinth nearly as much as he disliked Vasil Veselov.

"Valentin," he said, "saddle a horse for David. Hyacinth, you'll take the one Veselov is saddling."

Veselov cinched up the saddle before turning. "No, he won't. I'm going."

"You are not going."

A hush fell over the little group. The other men paused to watch, and Diana made a great show of sighing, with a woman's disgust for men's arguments.

"Listen, Sakhalin, you may be first among the tribes in the jaran, but the jaran are nothing here, and so are you."

"You are not going, Veselov, because I say so, and because the invitation was for me, not for you. Therefore I am in command. In any case, I am wearing a saber, and you are not."

Veselov snorted. "You never truly left the jaran, did you? Well, *I* did, Anatoly Sakhalin, and I find this pathetic."

"You may find it anything you wish. You are not coming with me."

"But I am."

Valentin watched the exchange with violent interest.

Anatoly dropped little Sosha's reins and crossed to stand in front of Veselov. He lowered his voice. "Do not make me humiliate you in front of your sons. Don't think that I can't."

Veselov dropped his voice as well. Out of the corner of his eye, Anatoly noted David drawing the others away, busying them with the horses. "What are you going to do? Challenge me to a duel?"

"Do you even have a saber anymore?"

That made Veselov bridle. "Of course I do."

"Who would win such a duel?"

"You would. But these khaja don't care for such displays. You are the one who would look bad, for pressing such a fight on me. I know how to play by khaja rules, Sakhalin. You don't."

"I know how to win, Veselov, and I intend to. You are only one more obstacle in my path."

"My, my, the little Sakhalin has ambition."

Anger flared and then, oddly enough, died. Veselov's insults abruptly lost their power to disturb him. He wondered, suddenly, how David, or even Diana, would handle Veselov. "What do you want?"

"A private audience with Duke Naroshi."

"Why bother to come with us, then? You won't get that now."

"You're a good looking man, it's true, but you're nothing compared to me. Why shouldn't Duke Naroshi notice me, even in a crowd?"

At that moment, revelation struck Anatoly: Veselov was a madman. Not like those Singers who, having absorbed too much of the gods' wisdom, could no longer walk straight nor speak in tongues that humans could understand, but in a tedious, small way: Unable to see past his own beauty, praised too much for charm and looks, Veselov had ceased seeing any of the world that existed outside of his own self. He thought he *was* the world.

"That is true," said Anatoly, dropping his voice to a whisper, "so you can see why I can't allow you to go with me. I am on a mission for the army, Veselov. I can't afford distractions."

"That could be true," agreed Veselov thoughtfully. "But so far I haven't managed to gain the duke's notice."

"You are trying too hard. Or perhaps he isn't interested in having a new courtier."

"That must be it. A whisper can be more gripping than a shout."

"Then you'll wait?"

Veselov hesitated.

That was all Anatoly needed. He got the others mounted and they were away before Veselov could change his mind. Portia sat in front of her father, delighted to be riding.

"What did you say to him?" David and Diana and Hyacinth asked, and then laughed, because they had said it all at once.

"What was necessary."

They rode out to the rose wall, and Anatoly let Portia handle the reins, telling her secrets about horses, and about this mare in particular. When they reached the great block of ebony stone, Anatoly pulled up in front of it. Feeling foolish and confident together, he raised his right hand and announced to the air and the wind: "I wish to travel to the Garden of the Thousand Petals of Gold."

The stone opened.

The barge waited. They led the horses up the ramp. Hyacinth's mare balked, and Anatoly had to go back and coax her up. As soon as they were all on, a cloudy skin sheathed the barge. The deck under them thrummed, and they moved forward under the wall. It was more like a tunnel, the wall was so thick, and when they came out the other side, rain began to pound on the gelatinous dome raised over their heads. Through this skin, they saw murky shapes, buildings, perhaps trees, and there, in the distance, towers. The rain came down so hard that it roared in their ears. The temperature changed at once. The air here was steamy, laden with the smell of lush and rotting vegetation. It made him sweat.

"Is it always like this?" he asked when he had gotten over his surprise.

"Yes," said Diana.

"Yes," said Hyacinth.

"But we've only made three trips," said Gwyn. "That's not a very big sample."

"It's gooey." Portia touched the dome and then tasted her fingers.

Diana yanked Portia's hand out of her mouth and wiped it on her skirt.

"Here," said David. "The two times I came along we turned at a forty-five degree angle *here*."

They did not turn.

Anatoly gave little Sosha's reins to Hyacinth and walked up to the prow, leaning against the railing. In the world outside, it rained, heavy drops drumming down in sheets. At last a pale building loomed in front of the barge and as they passed under an arch, the rain stopped pounding above them. The barge stopped, sinking down to the ground, and the dome retracted. It was still raining, but here the rain was only a fine mist. They looked out over a vast courtyard surrounded by the distant bulk of a white palace crowned with onion domes and spires. In the center of this courtyard rested a square pool, so big that the Chapalii walking on its farther shore looked no taller than hand's height. The barge sat under a gateway of horn, carved with glyphs and evidently grown either from the earth or scavenged from some gigantic monster. The pool was lined with trees whose golden flowers drifted gently down into the water, dappling it with petals. Rain stirred the surface of the water, which shone a pellucid blue under the dome of glossy clouds that covered the sky. The air smelled strange: spicy, too rich, cutting at the throat. Portia sneezed.

An island sat in the middle of the lake, its banks brilliant with flowers. It was a small island, dominated by the rush of color along its shoreline and by a belvedere sitting alone in the middle of the island, the still center of this silent scene. Nothing stirred out there. Distant figures moved along the far bank, but they seemed unaware of the presence of these human visitors.

Anatoly took little Sosha down the ramp and the others followed him. He gave the reins to Hyacinth and walked out to the bank of the pond. A lip hung over the edge. Moss grew over the white stone to brush the water. A wave rose, and suddenly a shell-backed creature broke the surface and swam over toward them. Everyone except Anatoly stepped back prudently. He merely watched as the creature came to a halt before him, its shell rising up out of the water until it lay even with the lip of stone. It had six flippers, a beaklike face, and its green shell was flat and chased across with elegant patterns.

"Is there a boat?" David asked, peering around.

Anatoly hoisted Portia up into his arms and stepped out onto the back of the creature.

"Anatoly!" Diana cried.

The creature began to swim, heading for the island, and Portia laughed with utter delight. "Look, Papa! It's eating the petals! *Gulp.*"

Anatoly laughed, hugging her closer to him. Rain misted down around them, but it was too light to be bothersome. Behind, Diana called after them, then David, but he felt it beneath his dignity to turn and answer. In any case, he was not sure enough of his footing that he wanted to risk moving. The creature swam evenly, eyes just at the level of the water, and cut through the water with becoming efficiency. Looking down, Anatoly could see only blue, endless blue, as if the lake was one facet of an enormous, fluid gem filigreed with an endless shifting pattern of crystalline raindrops. He had no idea how deep the lake was.

A single path cut down through the banks of flowers on the islands. The creature deposited them there, and there

Anatoly turned to see how his forces had chosen to position
themselves: Hyacinth and Gwyn had stayed with the horses;
Diana and David had found transport of their own.

Diana was giggling as she stepped off onto the island, her
cheeks flushed, and David looked both amused and be-
mused. They followed him up the gently sloping path to the
center of the island. No one was there. The belvedere was
only an open, roofed gallery, decorated with lush trails of
hanging flowers. It contained one chair, a mat woven of
long, broad leaves stamped with the pattern of the golden
flowers, and nothing else.

Anatoly sat in the chair, decided he didn't like it, and sat
down on the mat instead in the traditional jaran style.

"Uh, shouldn't you stand?" David asked. "It wouldn't be
polite for us to be sitting when Duke Naroshi arrives."

"I will sit here," said Anatoly. Portia came and sat on his
lap. Diana walked over to brush a hand over the flowers,
which grew up to the edge of the belvedere.

David paced. Halted. "Look!"

A procession emerged from the distant palace and came
toward them at a bewildering speed, growing so quickly that
it was as if the island moved, too. The vessel seemed at first
to Anatoly like a chariot not pulled by horses. Three figures
stood in it. David, coming to stand by him, grew increas-
ingly agitated, and Diana flushed, went pale, tried to grab
Portia away from him, then retreated to stand just behind
him.

The vessel halted at the opposite end of the belvedere and
Duke Naroshi and his two attendants stepped out.

Naroshi came forward at once. Anatoly had never seen a
Chapalii nobleman at such close range before. He examined
him intently: skin so white that it seemed to possess no color
at all; long-fingered hands interlaced in an odd fashion;
height that was not, strangely enough, matched by bulk but
rather seemed suspended on a fragile frame. Naroshi halted
five steps before him and went down on one knee.

David gasped.

It took Anatoly two breaths to sort out what he was seeing: Duke Naroshi was doing obeisance before him. A faint
hint of blue chased across those pallid cheeks and vanished.
Anatoly raised his right hand. "You may rise, Duke Naroshi,
and sit in the chair."

"You are generous, Prince of the Sakhalin, but I do not

deserve your pardon. It is my shame that I did not grant you the honor due to you when you arrived here."

He was speaking in khush, too, or at least, Anatoly reminded himself, that was how he heard it. The duke's voice was soft and eerie, like wind whistling down a hall.

"I did not wish to be known," said Anatoly. Naroshi's deference made him uncomfortable. "Please sit."

Naroshi sat in the chair, tangled his fingers together into a new arrangement, and regarded Anatoly with an impassive expression. Anatoly remembered that the Chapalii, being alien, did not have expressions that a human could read, if indeed they showed facial expressions at all. *They aren't like us,* Diana had once explained to him. But they didn't seem that different now.

"Each petal that falls into the lake of mirrors," continued Naroshi, "is like to a word of apology fallen from my tongue for this oversight."

"You could not have known." He tucked Portia more tightly against him and glanced swiftly up at David, as if to say, *I could not have known.* David, looking glazed, just stared at Naroshi.

"The emperor did not choose to let his messengers cast the recital of your visit into the waters so that I, drawing out the net of intelligence, might know of it. Such is his will."

Anatoly blinked. "I have never met the emperor."

Blue chased green chased pink across Naroshi's alien countenance. "The emperor has never brought you before him?"

"No."

Naroshi rose out of the chair, and for an instant Anatoly felt that some other force lifted him, not muscle and bone. "Then it is my duty, my honor, to send you on to him."

Confused, Anatoly hesitated, and David nudged him with a foot. "On to him? On to his ... palace. Ah, on Chapal?" A sudden wild excitement seized him, and he swallowed it back, so that he wouldn't betray himself. Portia hooked her little fingers in among his and began to turn the ring on his right hand around and around and around.

"You may leave at once. I will see that all is made ready for you." Naroshi took a step back and, clearly, paused, waiting to be dismissed.

"Wait." Anatoly stood as well, settling Portia at his waist. "Certainly I will go to meet the emperor." He heard Diana's intake of breath, but chose to ignore it. "First I want to make sure that this will have no effect on the repertory company's tour here."

"The repertory company? Ah. The theater."

"They will stay here as you had already arranged with Duke Charles, and leave only at the appointed time. I would not want to interfere with their work."

Naroshi inclined his head, as to a superior. "As you wish, Prince of the Sakhalin. All will be done as you will it."

He dipped his shoulders down, retreated to the edge of the belvedere, and, flanked by his attendants, got into the chariot. It lifted without a sound and moved backward off the island and over the lake, so that Naroshi continued to face him.

"Fucking hell!" David burst out. "They *do* have some kind of universal translator, the bastards, which means that all this time we thought they couldn't understand us when we were speaking in some of our more obscure languages, they probably could! *Merde!*"

"Anatoly," said Diana in a small voice. "He bowed to you."

"He *is* only a duke." Anatoly lifted Portia up and kissed her on either cheek. She giggled and pinched his ears. "I will have to leave you, little one," he said to her.

"Oh, Papa!" She pulled a long face. "Will you be back tomorrow?"

"Longer than that, sweet one. But I will be back as soon as I can."

"Okay," she said with a four-year-old's disregard for abstract time, and she squirmed until he let her down. She ran over and crouched down to sniff at the flowers.

"Don't touch anything!" said Diana.

"They think you're a prince," said David as if he was repeating something he had already said.

Anatoly looked at him, puzzled. "I *am* a prince."

"You're really going to go?" Diana demanded.

"Of course I'm going to go. Think of what valuable intelligence I can bring back!"

"This is very strange," said David. "To say the least."

"You think I shouldn't go?"

"By no means! By no means! It's an incredible unlooked-for opportunity. I'm just, well, I'm just a little shocked." David stepped outside the belvedere and stood in the rain, as if the warm drops could clear his head. Rain rolled down his nose and he wiped it off his face only to get wet again. "It's raining harder," he observed.

"Well, then," said Anatoly, "what are we waiting for?" He scooped up Portia and headed down the path to the shoreline.

"The turtles! The turtles! I want to be a turtle, and you can be the Daddy Turtle and Mama can be the Mommy Turtle. . . ."

"You're just going to go?" Diana said to his back. "Just like that?"

Like a courtier, David answered for him. "Of course, Di. That's his job."

She said something else, but he couldn't hear the words. He only heard that she was upset. But Anatoly already felt himself half gone, mounted and setting off at a brisk pace on this fresh campaign into unfamiliar territory.

"But I'm not male." Feeling mutinous, Ilyana crossed her arms and sat down on the gazebo bench. Adults got to do all the exciting things. "She said that the hall is forbidden to males. *I* could go."

David glanced around the courtyard, but here, in the cool haven of dawn, it was empty. There had been a party last night for Anatoly's leavetaking, and evidently all the adults had some kind of hangover. All except David, who together with Diana had been the only ones to see Sakhalin off at planetrise.

"You could not go," he said now. "It's too dangerous."

"Nothing bad happened to Anatoly Sakhalin."

"Nothing happened to him! How would you like to be sent before the Chapalii emperor all by yourself?"

"I think it would be interesting. No human has ever mapped the Imperial Palace. You said so yourself. And it would be away from here!"

"Yana! Lots of places are away from here. I don't think you quite understand. How would *you* like to be summoned before the emperor? It's not just perilous, but troublesome, and perhaps inappropriate."

"*You* don't understand about the Sakhalin. Why shouldn't he be summoned? Everyone knows that they're first among the tribes. Naturally the emperor would—"

"—would have an interest in him," David interrupted.

"Yes, yes, I've heard that before, about ten times. Ilyana, I don't think he's being shown any kind of favor. . . ."

"Of course he's not being shown favor." Gods, these khaja could be obstinate. "They're just giving him his due. And he won't be nervous. He's ridden into enemy territory before."

"With a jahar."

"Well, won't he be traveling in on a human ship? He'll have someone to guide him."

"That's true. Charles will probably lend him Branwen Emrys. She's actually an old acquaintance of Gwyn's, and our most experienced captain on that run."

"So you see!" exclaimed Ilyana triumphantly. "That's exactly why I have to go explore that hall. Someone has to. Isn't it still important for us to understand about Chapalii architecture? Anatoly Sakhalin thought that the Chapalii he met was female. Shouldn't we find out more about her, too?"

"Goddess!" David threw up his hands. "You're impossible. No, we should not. We should proceed with caution."

"*You* wouldn't."

"Yana, I am eighty-one years old. I'm middle-aged. You're just sixteen. We don't send children into danger."

"I should have gone through with my flower night. Then I'd be a woman, and you couldn't use *that* argument against me." She chewed on her knuckles. "Hmm. I could still . . ." She slanted a glance up at David. Without quite looking at him, she could see that he was growing uncomfortable. Wind sighed through the open gate of the caravansary, drifting in to rustle her knee-length tunic. David stared steadfastly at the red tile roof. The sun breached the roof's peak and spilled down over her, bringing with it a new swell of wind bearing dust, and an echo in her ears, the memory of Anatoly Sakhalin saying her name, that night. David was uncomfortable because he found her attractive. He was afraid she would ask *him*. Ilyana felt a breathtaking surge of confidence. She lifted her chin and tilted her head to one side, and smiled straight at him, knowing suddenly what it meant to be able to use beauty to get one's own way.

"Damn it!" David exploded. He jumped to his feet, stalked down the gazebo steps, and halted on the sun-bleached stone of the courtyard, his back to her. From the caravansary hall, where the actors rehearsed, Ilyana heard

Yomi calling out to someone—Yassir, the lighting designer—and she caught the sound of two women laughing in the bathroom and the splash of water into the tile cistern. On the breeze she smelled the faint aroma of the smoke of her mother's cook fire.

"There's a word for this," said David without turning around. "Blackmail."

Ilyana giggled. She felt bold. She felt powerful. And she felt a little nervous. "But, David." Her voice shook. "We *have* to do this. You know we do."

He still didn't turn around. "Let's say for the sake of argument that I agree. First, you will go together with Wingtuck Lien, and I'll go as well but only to the entrance into the hall as described by Anatoly. Second." He turned slowly round, like a leaf spun gently in the wind. His expression was harsh. "You will never again manipulate me like that. It isn't right. Yana, you're a beautiful girl and I don't think you truly realize that yet, or the kind of trouble it's going to cause you. I'm not blind. I can appreciate your beauty. I can even wish I was eighteen again, to have a chance to be the boy you pick on your flower night. But. I'm old enough to be your grandfather. So we will resolve right now that you will treat me as if I was your . . . your aged uncle, and you will consider yourself as a niece to me. You will respect me and obey me as your teacher, and I will respect you as a serious and promising student. Is that clear?"

Abashed, Ilyana glared at the pale mosaic floor of the gazebo, memorizing the thin lines that demarcated the individual tiles one from the other. She gulped down air past a lump in her throat. "Yes," she said in a strangled voice.

There was a long silence.

From out of the shadowed colonnade, Portia padded into the sunlit courtyard on bare feet, her well-worn pillow clutched under one arm. "Where's Papa?" Portia asked forlornly.

That evening David agreed to a practice run, going into the map room and returning to the place he and she had been to before: the mosaic courtyard that fronted the domed, painted palace. Ilyana climbed the steps to the latticework door and, carefully, leaned against it to peer in, to see if she could see the distant statue of Lord Shiva in the dim interior. Squinting, she saw, perhaps, a faint anthropomorphic outline, perhaps . . . a faint rustling touched her ears, like a snake sliding through grass, like the whirring of insects on a summer's night. Startled, she pushed back from the lattice door, only it gave in against her hands instead, opening away from her. Unbalanced, she tumbled inside.

David shouted behind her, but she stood in the cool, shadowed interior of the entry hall, took in a deep breath, and sneezed. The air had a rancid odor.

"Air doesn't smell in nesh," she reminded herself.

Like an echo, another voice spoke.

"Who are you?"

The shadows moved. Ilyana caught a glimpse of a smooth, lucent surface that vanished as quickly. All was still.

"I am named Ilyana Arkhanov," she replied, folding her hands in front of her in the polite fashion. "I beg your pardon if I've come in somewhere I shouldn't have."

"I have been watching you," said the voice, and the shadows rustled. "You are the first female of your kind I have encountered."

"How can you tell I'm female?"

"I study what comes before me. In your language you might say that I study structure and function, and then I classify according to design, proportions, and ornamentation."

"Are you an architect?" But she must be, if she was actually Duke Naroshi's famous sister.

"I am a builder. You must come to the hall of monumental time."

Ilyana gulped, remembering David. She glanced behind and saw him framed in the doorway, frozen, unwilling to back up but also clearly unwilling to interrupt this odd and tenuous conversation. "Right now?"

"No. This is but a simulacrum, a net beneath which lies the true form. Come to the true hall. You need only ask."

"Uh, who should I ask for? Do you have a name? I mean, if I'm allowed to ask that?"

"You ask many questions."

Ilyana heard a soft sound from David, rather like he was unsuccessfully suppressing a laugh. "Well, that's because I'm young."

"Young." The voice savored the word, as if by dwelling on it a new meaning could be built from it. "Then you must surely bring an attendant."

"Who has to be female?"

"Female or ke."

"Uh, what's a ke?"

"The nameless ones, the ones without children to carry on their names. I believe you could give this word that meaning in your language."

"Oh," said Ilyana as an idea popped into her head. She glanced again at David, wondering if he had realized the loophole that had just been presented to him. Then she turned back and peered into the shadows. "But you still didn't tell me your name."

She saw again that glimpse of luminescence, shuttered quickly, and she thought that the voice, when it spoke again, had a curiously human tone: But she knew Chapalii didn't have the same emotions as humans; they were alien, they weren't like us. All the same, the Chapalii sounded amused. "You may call me Genji," she said.

CHAPTER TWENTY-NINE

The Scent of Rain

Tess sent a rider south with the news Kirill had brought, and then there was nothing to do but wait.

"It's at times like these," said Tess to Cara one morning as they walked across the plaza to the library, "that I feel like saying be damned to all the interdiction laws and just give them decent communications. We could start with the telegraph and work up to satellite links."

Cara paused on the steps and turned to look back toward Mother Orzhekov's great tent. The gold banner at its peak flapped in the autumn breeze. "What *are* you going to do with your children?"

"I'm becoming adept at not looking at questions I don't want to answer. They're young yet. They're learning what they need to know."

"They won't be young forever."

"Who knows? If your formula works, maybe they will be."

"But, Tess, at some point you'll have to make a decision, when they get old enough to—"

"And then what will I tell Ilya? I *know* the situation becomes more and more ridiculous the longer it carries on. Let me live in peace for a while!"

"So to speak," replied Cara dryly, following Tess up the steps.

Tess nodded at the guards, opened the door, and went inside. Inside, they found Sonia playing khot with the ke. Startled by this scene, Tess halted in her tracks and Cara had to gently shove past her in order to see what was going on.

"I think I must be wearing blinders," said Tess in a low voice. "Lately I keep finding out that things are going on that I assumed weren't. Or perhaps only," she added with a wry grin, "that people are thinking and acting for themselves without consulting me first."

"You sound more and more like your brother."

"Thank you!"

Tess's exclamation caused Sonia to look up, surprised, not having heard them come in. The ke did not shift position. Sonia smiled at them and beckoned them over, but Tess simply waved at her and took Cara over to the lectern where the *Gospel of Isia of Byblos* rested.

"Cara," Tess continued as she opened the manuscript carefully, "do you know anything about how Chapalii perceive the world?"

"Not any more than you do. Isn't it generally agreed that they use infrared? That they can see degrees of heat?"

"That same night you came in the ke told me that she could *see* the storm coming in. I don't mean the clouds, but the front of the storm, as if she could see the currents. I'm not explaining myself very well. But if they can see in visible light and in infrared, why not other ranges of the electromagnetic spectrum, too? How could we detect how broad a range they could see?"

"We could measure stimulus and response, but it's difficult, to say the least, for the lab rats to conduct experiments on the scientists."

"That's a pleasant thought."

Cara glanced back at the ke, who remained intent on the game. Sonia set down a white pebble on the board, and the ke responded at once by setting down a black pebble on a different part of the board. "We already know that the Mushai or one of his followers tampered with the genetic code of the humans they brought here. Recently I've been wondering why humans intrigued the Chapalii in the first place. It's not as if we have any technological advances to give them."

"Theater," said Tess, half laughing. "Didn't you hear that the Bharentous Repertory Company finally went to Duke Naroshi's palace? Luxury items."

"Luxury items," Cara scoffed. "That old anthropological excuse. The rise of civilization, trade, and war all based on the desire to acquire cowrie shells. Huh. What's this?"

Tess pulled a finger down the calligraphed page and drew Cara's attention to the parchment set beside it. "That's what I've been doing for the last fifteen days. Translating this into Rhuian. It's tempting to read it as an ancient memory of the Chapalii and perhaps of the human arrival on Rhui. 'And a bright light appeared out of the darkest skies, and on this light He ascended to His Father's House. And the glance of God's Eye scorched the earth where His feet took wing into the heavens.' "

"It's also a common mythological trope."

"But I'm hearing this now. Preachers in the square, talking about strange lights in the sky. The second coming of the Son of God and his sister. There's certainly been more activity by our people in the last fifty years—"

"You know, Tess, in more barbaric times on Earth, doctors would confine people in small rooms if they thought they were ill, and the people so confined would begin to get odd ideas, and hallucinate. Perhaps you need a change of scene."

Tess laughed. A khaja scholar—khaja were admitted once they had gained a dispensation—on the other side of the room looked up from his book and, seeing her jaran dress, looked away swiftly. "Admit that it isn't entirely implausible. What do you know about Byblos?"

"A country in the south. Or a city. Or something in between. It's hot. Rumored to be ancient. I've mostly heard stories that have more of legend about them than fact."

"Kirill met Byblene merchants."

"Kirill. Which reminds me, Tess—"

But Tess perceived that Cara was about to ask her an uncomfortable question about Kirill, so she quickly crossed the room to look at the khot game. Sonia was an excellent player whose skill had been honed in the past eight years by frequent games with her husband, Josef Raevsky, the acknowledged master in the Orzhekov tribe. But the ke held her own. Tess did not have a sophisticated enough understanding of the game to see quite what strategy the ke was using, but it seemed to focus on spreading a wide net so as to catch as many intersections as possible. Sonia was using one of her favored strategies: marking out territory in blocks and then connecting them.

Tess watched the game while Cara looked through the *Byblene Gospel*. The khaja scholar, perhaps made anxious by their presence, left, but two other men entered, dressed in the gray robes worn by Habakar officials. They passed on into a farther room. The game continued. Tess was beginning to see that the ke had an advantage.

The door opened again, bringing with it the scent of rain, and Tess looked up to see Kirill take three steps into the library and stop, looking uncomfortable. Sonia glanced up at Tess and had the gall to wink at her, smirking.

Irritated, Tess went over to Kirill. He waited for her by the door. Silver threaded his blond hair, so pale that it blended in unless you knew to look for it. He was about forty years old now, and maturity sat well on him. His clothes were slightly damp from the rain, and all at once the faint scent brought back memories to Tess, the sweet memory of the first time she had slept with him, with the drizzle of rain outside and the muzzy smell of damp blankets and clothes permeating the close interior of her traveling tent. Gods, that had been twelve years ago, before she had married Ilya. Kirill met her gaze, and she knew instantly that he was remembering the same night.

Even more annoyed, she flushed. "What is it?"

"I've decided to ride south. I should have gone instead of the messenger."

The thought of him leaving so abruptly darkened her mood further. "You said yourself you ought to spend time with your children. What can you do? The message doesn't need you to deliver it."

"I feel responsible," he said shortly, not looking at her.

"Kirill, surely if the original message, the one sent from the north, didn't reach the prince of Filis, then Ilya is in no danger yet. He won't be in danger until he reaches Filis."

"Perhaps."

She had an insane urge to smooth the lines of grief away from his eyes. One of her hands lifted, but she snapped it back and hooked her fingers safely into her belt. "There's something else you're trying to tell me, isn't there?"

He said nothing for a long moment. Then he lifted his eyes to look straight into hers. What she read there unsettled her, not least because it did not displease her. She tried to say something, but no words came out. He turned and left the library, that quickly, opening the door into the rain and heading out into it without hesitation. Just as he had done years ago. "What's a little rain?" She recalled him saying that now, but the door shut behind him and she just stood there and finally walked over to stand next to Cara and stare at the *Byblene Gospel*.

"I won't ask," said Cara. "I like this bit where the sister—the Pilgrim, they call her—sews together her dead brother's remains with thread spun from the feathers of a sparrow, the

sinew of a deer, the scales of a fish, and the ashes of the
wooden cup in which she caught his blood. Pagan holdovers
woven into the new religion, surely."

Tess suddenly felt very tired.

"Done," said Sonia from the table. "You have me surrounded. I concede the game, and admire your prowess yet
again." She rose. "I thank you, holy one. Perhaps we may
play again another time."

The ke nodded but did not rise.

"Now I ask that you excuse me. I have duties to attend
to."

"I'll go with you," said Tess, wanting to get away.

"I'll stay," said Cara, and by that Tess knew that Cara
wanted to go into the back rooms, where the console lay hidden, and conduct business of her own.

The ke rose and escorted Cara into the back. Tess left with
Sonia. Outside, the rain had turned to mist, giving the world
a hazy shimmer.

"When did you start playing khot with the priestess?"
Tess asked.

"Some months ago. At first, you know, when you brought
her here, she stayed completely to herself, sequestered in her
private rooms, but recently I've noticed her venturing out
more. She must be becoming accustomed to our ways."

"What do you think of her?"

"She smells funny." Sonia chuckled. "What do you mean,
what do I think of her? She speaks only a few words with
which I can talk to her. She is made invisible because of her
veils. I know nothing about her or the people she comes
from. I think she is a mystery, Tess. But she plays khot very
well. I wonder if she knows any such games she could teach
me."

"I'll ask her."

"You could teach me her language, you know. Or do you
wish to keep that to yourself?"

"Hah! That's unfair!"

"Is it? But I *am* interested, if you're willing. You should
take Kirill as a lover. I don't know why you haven't already."

"Sonia!"

"I must say I find him more attractive now than when he
was younger. If you don't, I'm going to."

Tess stopped by the fountain, its base now half inlaid with

stone. Water trickled down into the hole, washing the dirt at the bottom into slimy mud. The workmen had fled to the shelter of one of the makeshift open warehouses on the other side of the plaza where the quarried stone was stored. Tess saw them sitting among the stone, chattering amongst themselves and smoking long pipes.

"Sonia, hasn't it made any impression on you, the news Kirill brought? That Ilya and the others may be riding into some kind of ambush? I'm hardly likely to enjoy myself with a lover here while my husband is in danger."

"Denying your own feelings is hardly likely to keep your husband alive, if he is truly in grave danger."

"That's not the point! Anyway, Kirill just lost his own wife. It's . . . unseemly!"

"Some men mourn the loss of a wife quietly, by withdrawing for a time from the life of the tribe. Others need the comfort of another woman. Kirill is of the latter kind, as I'm sure you are aware. In any cases, Tess, he still loves you."

"I know," said Tess bitterly.

"And you still love him."

"Which would make it all the more indescribably foolish. Don't you see?"

"Well. No. I don't." Sonia offered Tess an infuriating smile. "I'm going to get out of this rain, and I promised Josef I would teach the younger children more letters today. Are you coming with me, or do you *want* to get wet?" Sonia said it provocatively.

"I want to get wet, of course." Tess walked on beside her. "Sonia." She hesitated. "If you could be immortal, would you?"

Sonia chuckled. "That's the kind of question Ilya would ask."

"How would you answer?" Tess suddenly desperately wanted to know what Sonia would say.

"Should the moon always be full? It waxes and it wanes and it vanishes from our sight, only to be born again. That is the natural order. Would you, khaja that you are?"

"I don't know," said Tess, and could think of nothing more to say.

The ke regards the carbon board and the lines etched into its surface. Unlike living lines, these are dead. They do not shift in the flux, the ever-moving shape of the greater universe where all threads tangle and untangle, forming the web of existence. But the game is clever. The ke wonders at a stray thought: *If only,* this thought whispers. *What does "if only" mean?*

The ke recognizes a strange impulse, the wish to show this game, the laying of the stones along the lines that represent the threads that bind together the universe, to the other nameless ones, the ones left behind beyond the veil of interdiction. Like ke, the stones remain nameless. Like ke, the stones rest each on an intersection of lines, caught in the web, forming a pattern above it.

The ke has existed in this place for two orbits of the sun. A plague of restlessness has infested the alien air which the ke breathes. In the environs beyond, the daiga go about that endless cycle of agitation, of movement, like the ceaseless trembling of atoms, that confers the mark of existence on daiga life, fleeting though it may be.

More often now, the ke ventures out, careful to keep skin and face covered according to the laws of interdiction passed down from the Tai-en Charles Soerensen out of whose authority the rite of extinction did not claim the ke. Though there is, truly, no creature here with right of authority over a nameless one, still, out of respect for the Tai-en's gesture, the ke holds to the laws of the outer world.

This other one, this curious one, this daiga with the living light of flowers gracing the pattern that entwines its body, has ventured in to greet the ke with the game, which is named, in the daiga way of naming all things, khot. The game, as played with board and stones, has no life except in the playing. That is what makes it interesting.

The door opens and the daiga of flowers comes in, together with a gust of damp wind and the swirling currents of the outside air, the weather front that moves across the daiga city.

"Smell the rain," says the daiga, by way of greeting, as the ke has learned the daiga do: Stating observations as if the observation marks a new presence.

Daiga words are difficult because primitive. The ke transfers the utterance to the shallow brain and processes the words. Rain is precipitation, water droplets or ice condensed from atmospheric water vapor in such quantities that it falls to the surface of the world. Smell is ... this word takes longer to process, to identify a meaning for. A way to perceive the world by the use of nerve fibers that conduct chemical indications of *smell*.

Distracted, the ke reflects on the primitive discriminatory faculties of the daiga, who must use names to define names, and often the same name to define its own self. Each name becomes a self, as each daiga regards its own body and mind and soul as a self. That is, the ke is learning, the essential nature of daiga-ness. While ke are the unnamed stones that surround and integrate the web of the universe, while the shifting threads of that net embrace and create all that is living, the daiga like all primitive creatures seem to see the web only as discrete parts.

The daiga of flowers sits down on the carbon stool opposite the ke at the table and separates the stones into two sets by some classification that does not register to the ke's sight. Half are pushed across the table to the ke. The touch of the daiga's hands lingers on these stones the ke now handles, dissipating into the air. As has become customary, the ke places the first stone.

After that, the game develops its own rhythm. Each game, while alike, is paced differently. This also interests the ke. Like the daiga, who are all the same and yet vibrate to a slightly different tone. By such means has the ke learned to begin to distinguish between the daiga, those who come here often enough, those whom the ke sees in the outside precincts several times. Daiga seem to put great store in being recognized in this way, by the understanding of their pattern. Recognition pleases them. Daiga do not understand that strength lies in the condition of being free of names.

The door opens to admit the daiga called Tess.

"At it again?" Tess asks, naming the other daiga *Sonia*. Tess greets the ke with a phrase learned from the deeper tongue and settles down next to the daiga Sonia to watch.

The ke grows distracted from the flow of the game by the flow of communication that goes on between these two daiga. Coils of energy mingle and intertwine and separate between the two females (for the ke has identified the daiga Sonia as a female; several of the flowering daiga known as children grew out of her body). The pattern, the interplay is like that the ke observed once between Tess and the daiga who brought Tess into namelessness, the one called Ilya, but it is different as well: Just as complex in structure and movement, it does not spark such extremes. It is more temperate.

The ke wonders how to interpret the ebb and flow of these fields as they interlace.

"Sonia wishes to learn Chapalii," says Tess. "I will begin by teaching her a few words of formal Chapalii, but you understand, of course, that you can tell her nothing of the world outside Rhui."

"It is understood," says the ke, bowing to the necessity of the interdiction. A strange flutter throbs along the ke's skin. Waiting for the first words of speech that will allow rudimentary communication of a higher sort with the daiga Sonia, the ke forgets to place the next stone.

"I greet you with good favor."

"This game is named *khot* in the daiga tongue."

"I am named *Sonia Orzhekov.*"

The daiga Sonia tries to ask a question, which the ke perceives is a request for the name by which the *ke* is named. A long conversation ensues between the two females, and the patterns surrounding them become heated, bright, and excited. The ke watches their flow with interest.

At last, Tess returns to the lesson, and now the two females revert to the shallowest form of speech: objects are named, labeled, and set away as separate units. True language does not work in this wise.

The ke returns attention to the game. Swiftly the stones engulf the board. Again, the daiga Sonia concedes the victory, but the pattern that marks this daiga is not noticeably altered by the outcome. The parting courtesies in the formal style are uttered and repeated, and after a brief mingling of patterns, the daiga Sonia leaves by the door.

"Is Dr. Hierakis here?" Tess asks.

"No, *Dr. Hierakis* has gone elsewhere."

The daiga wanders off, as daiga are wont to do, being unable to maintain stillness for very long.

The door opens. A daiga enters. The ke reads the pattern and sees that this is a male. The ke deduces that the rain sensed—*smelled*—before has now begun to fall: The clothes worn by the daiga are damp from this rain; coolness steams off them in pale swirls.

This one has been here before, recently, but is otherwise new. Hesitating, the daiga speaks and then skirts the ke at a respectful distance. The pattern that coils around this one is bright, like that of the daiga Sonia, but not otherwise distinguished.

Curious—it is the failing which brought the ke to notice within the Keinaba house and thus led to the expedition to the Mushai's ancient home—the ke followed this daiga, who is not like the other daiga, what Tess calls the *khaja*, but one of the *jaran*. These classifications the ke has learned out of necessity.

Riddled with alcoves and shadowed colonnades and side passages constructed deliberately for this purpose, the ke easily moves through the library after the daiga without being seen. The laws of interdiction layer one atop the others: The private rooms are beyond reach of all daiga except Tess and those who come from the outer world; a second suite of rooms, curtained off, are reserved for the use of those daiga labeled as jaran; all other chambers of the library may be used by any daiga who receives permission.

The daiga male goes to the map alcove and draws the curtain shut. Thus concealed, the daiga paces round the big map, tracing lines as if tracing a thread that runs across the rough, frozen symbols by which these daiga represent the living world. The daiga speaks in a low voice, as if vocal sounds can convince the map to reveal its secrets, to reveal whatever answer the daiga seeks from the map. Concealed in a narrow gallery screened off by a cunningly wrought lattice, the ke watches. What makes this daiga interesting? There is no obvious answer.

But the answer comes, nevertheless.

The curtain ripples and, as an aftereffect of that ripple, the daiga Tess enters the alcove. Stops. Time draws out.

The two daiga stand there for a long time, seeming to communicate without using vocal boxes, the male by the great map, the female by the door. What they see, what they sense, the ke cannot interpret, except that their patterns are in wild flux.

Tess walks closer. The patterns which bind and define them expand, touching, and shrink back, and expand and shrink, and again, although the bodies holding those fields do not touch. They talk together, in their daiga way, and with each word a foot shifts closer, an arm leans on the table and somehow inches nearer the other, the pattern of one laps over and intertwines with the second and by degrees of greater flooding and lesser ebbing they meet.

Like the waters of two rivers flowing into the same channel, their patterns meld. Can two selves join to become one self?

The ke struggles to understand the patterns that flow and ebb around the daiga. Each daiga is separate, yet each daiga is capable of connecting with another daiga to a greater or lesser degree. Each connection builds a unique reticulation, and this reticulation has its own self, its own existence, even perhaps its own name, that is living in the bond between them.

So the daiga Tess and the female Sonia: temperate and stable and deeply bound. So the daiga Tess and the male Ilya: intricately interwoven, brilliant, and, like a tempest, in constant often joyous tumult. So the daiga Tess and this male: different again, harder to interpret.

The ke retreats, aware that to stay longer would be to violate a certain sanctity.

At first, out of habit, the ke takes that path that leads by hidden corridors and shadowed curves to the interdicted rooms, but instead the path shifts, taking the ke to the reading room. The silence inside the great domed chamber moves like breath along the walls. Going to the doors by which the daiga enter and leave the reading room, the ke opens them.

Outside, it is raining, and the rain blurs the daiga world to the ke's sight. It drums down in a steady faintly chaotic pattern of sound. No person walks outside. Inside, the ke feels lonely.

CHAPTER THIRTY

Widow's Tower

When the town and the bluff the castle stood on came into sight, Jaelle knew at once that Prince Janos was a man to be reckoned with, if she had ever for a moment thought otherwise. The town was not overly large—Jaelle had seen larger on the caravan routes, cities fattened by trade—but a stone wall ringed it, gapping only where cliffs plunged down to a river.

A stone castle, whitewashed so that it stood out like a beacon against the green-brown hills of autumn, thrust castellated towers skyward: White Tower. The army followed the road down to the town gates and they passed in procession through the town and on up a slight rise to the castle itself. It had no gatehouse, but the forecourt was defended by two of the great towers and Jaelle saw no other entrance except through the walled town.

The army dispersed in a welter of comings and goings. A grand lady came out into the forecourt to greet Prince Janos.

"My son," she said, lifting him up from where he had knelt before her. Her voice was rich and deep and she looked truly pleased to see him. A fine linen scarf covered her hair, but the bird's feet at her eyes and the lines creasing her forehead betrayed her age well enough. Her hands were white and uncallused. Coolly, she surveyed Princess Rusudani and the prisoners. Her gaze even caught for an instant on Jaelle, measuring her, and Jaelle tried as best as she could to make herself unobtrusive. Smoke rose from the kitchens. The doors to the great hall were thrown open as a line of servants carried rushes inside. Jaelle noticed at once the stink of an enclosed place, cows and horses in their bier, a mews off to the left, a kennel of hounds yipping in chorus.

"My lady," said Janos obediently. "I have brought home my wife, Princess Rusudani, daughter of Prince Zakaria of Tarsina-Kars."

Rusudani inclined her head as one equal greets another. "Your majesty."

The lady lifted one eyebrow but did not otherwise admit surprise. Jaelle was beginning to see where Janos got his temperament from. "Let us be frank, Princess Rusudani. You may address me as Lady Jadranka. I am mistress of my son's castle but queen no longer. With the coming of the jaran, King Zgoros found it possible with his new alliance to put me aside in favor of a new bride. But you will find our quarters princely enough, I believe, and I have in my household several young women of good birth who will make fine attendants for you."

Rusudani went white at the mouth, but she did not reply. Perhaps she felt further betrayed.

"Who are these others?" asked Lady Jadranka, nodding to the jaran captives, Vasil'ii Kireyevsky and the princess, who stood in the midst of guards, still in chains.

Janos gave a short bark of laughter. "The Bakhtiian is dead, my lady. That is his bastard son, and the other— You will recall that my father petitioned the jaran for a royal bride."

"I recall it with pleasure. The Sakhalin prince refused his request with great contempt."

"Bring her forward," ordered Janos.

Jaelle admired Princess Katerina for the dignity with which she walked forward in such hostile surroundings.

"This woman is Katherine Orzhekov, cousin to the Bakhtiian and a princess of the jaran tribes."

The two women measured each other, Lady Jadranka with frank interest and Katerina with the proud arrogance that all her people wore, even in such circumstances as these. But Jaelle found her attention drawn to the other participants: Vasil'ii Kireyevsky did not watch the interaction at all, because he was too busy examining the walls and the court and the layout of the buildings; Janos stared at Katerina with a hungry expression on his face, and Rusudani watched her husband, her face as blank as a sweep of new-fallen snow.

"My lady," said Katerina finally in Taor, "I throw myself on your mercy and beg that I will be treated as befits the honor and respect due me as a woman."

Lady Jadranka's other eyebrow went up. "You are an educated woman. Is it true that the Bakhtiian's wife is the Prince of Jeds?"

"It is true."

The other prisoners, including Bakhtiian, stood much farther back, by the gate, but Princess Katerina did not glance toward them.

Lady Jadranka looked back at her son. "I will have the servants clean out the top room in the Widow's Tower. She will need attendants."

So it came about that Jaelle was sent with Princess Katerina as her serving woman.

"This is truly a prison," said Katerina. She paced out the round chamber, pausing at each of the four narrow windows to peer out. A fire burned in the hearth, but she shuddered as if she were cold and went to sit on the carpet. She seemed not to notice the sumptuous furnishings, the bed curtained with fine hangings, a table and brocaded chairs, a pitcher and basin for washing, even a gilded chamber pot and a carved chest filled with furs and gowns and undershifts. Tapestries depicting a hunt hung over the whitewashed walls. "Do you know where they've put Vasha?" Jaelle shook her head. "The other prisoners?"

"When I go down to draw water for you, my lady, I will try to find out."

"Thank you."

Jaelle could not move for a moment, she was so surprised to be thanked. Then she gathered up her skirts and negotiated the twisting stair that led downward. The first landing opened out onto the chamber below, swept clean and used now for storage. She crossed it, pounded on the door, and the guards let her out onto the outside stairway that led down into the inner ward. She took her time at the well, hoping to see one of the prisoners, and she was rewarded at last when Bakhtiian himself came to the well with two buckets hoisted over a pole. He halted, recognizing her, and set down his buckets while a castle servant pulled water up from the well.

Without looking at her he said, in a low voice, in Taor, "Where is Katerina?"

The servants at the well glanced at him curiously, at his voice, at his outlandish and rather tattered clothing, stained and crumpled from the long march. He walked with a slight limp, he was thinner, but otherwise he seemed strong enough.

Rather than answering, she stared pointedly at the Wid-

ow's Tower and then took water when her turn came and returned to the tower.

"I saw . . ." Jaelle hesitated. "I saw the man who was so
badly wounded, my lady. He was getting water at the well.
He asked about you. As for the others, I dared not say anything to him."

Astonishingly, Katerina laughed, if rather dryly. "Just like
a common slave. I doubt it amuses Cousin Ilya to be treated
that way. Well, you must see what you can find out about
Vasha, where he is being held, in what condition, and about
the others, too. I will ask Prince Janos or his mother, or
Rusudani, if the priest may be given leave to visit me each
day." She pushed herself up and paced once around the
chamber again. "Gods, is there nothing to do in this place?
No wonder the khaja are weak, made captive by their own
walls."

Evening came, with a tray of food but no inquiries, no
company. Katerina scorned the bed and slept on the servant's
bed, a hard pallet tucked away under the frame. Forced to
use the great bed, Jaelle slept in a luxury she had never experienced as a free woman—only now that she was, again,
a slave.

In the morning, the guards brought food. No one came to
see them. After they ate, Katerina tried to help Jaelle gather
the dishes together.

"No, my lady, you must not. It is my duty to serve you."

Katerina flung herself down full length on the bed, sinking into the coverlet, and watched Jaelle as she collected the
dishes onto a tray. "You were a whore before," Katerina said
suddenly. "Did you do this kind of thing then, as well, or
just lie with men?"

Jaelle's hands froze. Finally, she set down a cup and
turned to face the princess. "I beg your pardon, my lady."

"Whatever for? Aunt Tess taught us all about khaja customs. Did you want to be a whore? Is that something khaja
women want to be? Or were you a slave—"

"I was a free woman until Prince Janos took us! My service was paid for!" Frightened at her own outburst, Jaelle
knelt. "I beg your pardon, my lady."

"I was going to say, were you a slave who had no
choice?" replied Katerina mildly, clearly not offended. "I
just wondered, how a woman would come to be a whore,

that's all. Forgive me if it's not a thing that should be spoken of."

"I must take this downstairs." Jaelle took the tray away, much shaken that a princess would address her as familiarly as any caravan woman addressed another. Just before she reached the landing she paused, hearing voices in the empty chamber beyond.

"Was it wise to marry the princess out of hand like that?"

A man laughed. "And you the one who encouraged me to pay that faithless bandit to remove her from the convent in the first place, once we heard about the death of her cousin? I took the opportunity that came to hand."

"True enough, Janos, but I wonder what she was doing at Urosh Monastery with the Bakhtiian?"

Feet sounded on the wooden planks of the flooring. Jaelle took a step back up the stairs, shrinking against the stone wall, but the footsteps receded, back toward the other side of the chamber.

"The jaran are not fools. They can see as well as we can that she is a prize, now that all of King Barsauma's children are dead, and her own brothers killed. She is the closest thing King Barsauma has to an heir except the nephew who is supposed to be either a simpleton or an invalid."

"Well. She is your wife now, but it seems to me you somewhat regret the act."

"I do not regret what she can bring me."

"She's well mannered and educated. She's a handsome enough girl. You can't have expected that."

"She spends most of her time on her knees praying! Or reading out of *The Recitation*. Once she has given me a son, I'll be happy to leave her to God."

"You want the jaran princess, Janos. That is obvious enough."

"God's Love, Mother, but you know very well that no man is known to have wed or even lain with a woman of that people."

Lady Jadranka chuckled as any mother might laugh at her child's sweet foibles. "Presumably a man of *that people* has."

"I meant a civilized man, of course," he said impatiently.

"Which makes her a rare prize for you, then. She's pretty enough, too, I suppose, if as brazen as a whore."

"Mother!" There was a telling pause. "You didn't see her

framed in the torchlight in the church, with her bow drawn back as if she knew how to fire it." His voice caught and deepened, and Jaelle suppressed a chilled shudder. She knew what that tone of voice meant, in a man. "I've never seen anything like her before."

"No doubt that makes her more interesting. Princess Rusudani is much better bred. You don't intend to send the jaran girl to your father?"

"Of course not."

"You must not anger him, Janos."

"I will never forgive him for putting you aside."

"I am grateful for your devotion, my son, but nevertheless it would be foolish to anger him."

"She is mine, Mother. Fairly won in battle."

"She is a princess."

"I will treat her respectfully."

"See that you do. She begged me for my protection, and God judges harshly those that turn aside from the path of mercy."

"I will show her the respect and honor due a woman in her position."

"Let me see her first. It would be more fitting."

Dust caught in Jaelle's nose and, too quickly to stop herself, she sneezed. Knowing the sound betrayed her, she took a breath for courage and went on into the room, but Lady Jadranka and the prince barely glanced at her as she took the tray by them and left it with the guards.

"You may show me up," said Lady Jadranka as Jaelle passed back by her, and Jaelle escorted her up the stairs while Janos waited below.

Katerina sprang to her feet with relief when the older woman entered. "I give you greetings," she said in Taor.

"You have everything you need?" asked Lady Jadranka, seating herself gracefully in a chair.

Katerina paced back and forth on the carpet. "How long must I stay up here?" she demanded and stopped in the center of the carpet. Lady Jadranka inclined her head, saying nothing, and Katerina began to pace again. "So it is true I am to be kept a prisoner. Do you mean to cage me here forever? I am sure my grandmother would gladly ransom me and the others."

"It is not my decision, Lady Katherine. I am chatelaine of my son's castle, nothing more."

Katerina went over and took hold of one of the bed posts, gripping it tightly. "Ah, gods," she said in her own tongue, looking around the chamber as if to measure its dimensions. "The company of my own kind, my lady. The priest, to speak the prayers of my people with me in the morning, as is fitting. My cousin, Vassily Kireyevsky."

"These requests I will bring before my son."

Exasperated by something in Lady Jadranka's reply, Katerina went over to the window and leaned out, but she could not even fit her head through the opening. It was only, truly, wide enough for an arrow to be shot out. She turned back and sat down in the bench built into the recessed stone. "A loom? I could pass the time weaving."

"A loom!" Lady Jadranka brightened. "Yes, that is something I could arrange immediately."

"And books," added Katerina, pressing her advantage.

"Books? Can you read?"

"Of course I can read. I can do accounts in Taor and I can read Rhuian and somewhat in Habakar. I could learn another language, perhaps the one that is spoken here."

Because she stood nearest the door, Jaelle heard the scuff of boots on the steps before the other women did. She whirled around in time to see Prince Janos enter the room.

"Books," he said musingly. "It surprises me that a barbarian can read."

Lady Jadranka rose at once, out of deference for her son, but she also shook her head slightly, as much amused as irritated.

"It should not surprise you," snapped Katerina, glaring at him. Her fine pale hair was pulled back in four braids, bound with ribbons, and her chin jutted out stubbornly. Jaelle trembled, fearing how the prince would react.

He simply laughed, walking a half circle around her and looking her over, which annoyed her even more. "Does this chamber displease you, my lady?"

"Any prison is displeasing, as you surely must know."

"Alas, I cannot set you free, but perhaps your time here can be made less tedious."

"Let me visit my cousin, Vassily Kireyevsky. Let the priest of my people visit me, to speak prayers with me."

"I will consider these requests."

Katerina caught back a gasp. She looked furious. She was

remarkably handsome when she was angry. Jaelle blushed suddenly and looked away from her.

"I beg you, my lady," Katerina said to Lady Jadranka, "let me see my own people."

"You must speak with my son."

Katerina had enough dignity, just, to vent her anger by sinking back down onto the window bench. Like any young caged creature as yet untamed, she had flurries of spirit followed by despondency.

Janos turned to his mother and spoke in his own language, which he knew Katerina could not understand. "If you will excuse us, my lady, I would like to continue this interview in private."

"Do nothing in haste, Prince Janos, which you will have cause to repent later." Lady Jadranka crossed the chamber to take Katerina's hand in hers, briefly, before she left the tower. Jaelle stayed by the door.

Janos circled in closer to Katerina and came to a halt four paces from her. She did not look up at him but rather at her hands. "Do you really wish for books? Can you read?"

"I can read. I wish for something to relieve the tedium. Surely you can understand that."

He took one step closer to her. Jaelle watched as he lifted a hand toward her hair, thought better of it, and lowered the hand. "Very well. I will bring you a few things myself."

Her startled glance upward seemed to satisfy him. He stepped back, took his leave, and went off down the steps.

Katerina sagged back, wedging her shoulders into the arrow loop. "What am I going to do? I'll go mad trapped in here."

Jaelle stirred the logs in the fireplace, not knowing what else to do. A shower of sparks sprayed up and died, and the woodsy smell of the fire comforted Jaelle. The rest of the day passed, but they saw no one. Jaelle fetched water for washing, but she saw none of the prisoners by the well. Food was brought to the guards and given her on a tray to carry up the stairs, and down again, together with the chamber pot, which was brought back later washed clean. The sound of feasting came from the great hall that night, but no one broke the monotony by visiting them.

In the morning Katerina toured the windows six times, peering out each one for a glimpse of town or hill beyond. Two of the windows looked out onto air, where the tower hung above the drop off to the river, and it was possible to see the river's flowing water and the far bank, even, if one pressed far enough into the crack, to see the curve of the river around the great bluff on which White Tower rested. Finally, Katerina came to rest on one of the window benches, her back to the outside world.

Jaelle busied herself shaking out the clothes from the chest. Katerina seemed uninterested in their fine quality. The smell of fur pervaded the room, and though it was chill, Jaelle hoarded the firewood she had carried up the stairs for a later, colder day. She shook out the gowns, enjoying the feel of the cloth, which was of a superior weave. Katerina sat silent, but Jaelle could feel her brooding, like a storm about to break.

"Did you ever live in a castle such as this?" asked Katerina suddenly.

"No, my lady. I was born a long way south of here, in a place called Cellio. There it is hot in the summer and mild in the rainy season, but I never saw snow until I came north with the caravans."

"Cellio! Isn't that a town in Filis?"

"Why, yes, my lady, it is." Surprised, Jaelle looked up at her.

"What were you doing there? Your coloring. . . ." She broke off and glanced away, almost shyly, then looked back. "You look more like a northerner. Aunt Tess says that in the south where the sun is brighter it burns the skin and hair darker. I have seen women and men whose skin is as black as if they had rubbed themselves all over with coal. But your hair is light, like mine."

Jaelle folded the gowns and replaced them in the chest. The silence dragged on, and Katerina regarded her with such rapt interest that finally Jaelle found herself feeling sorry for her. Jaelle had herself never lived as luxuriously as this. But a plush cage was still a cage, after all. Hesitantly, she began to talk.

"My mother's father sold her to a merchant when she was a child. She was brought south, where light-haired children brought a better price, and bought by Lord Tacollo's father, who died soon after. Some man in the villa where I was born got her with child, with me, that is. That is where I grew up, in a nobleman's villa. She was the nurse for Lord Tacollo's children. I was allowed to sit in on lessons with them for a time."

"And then?"

Jaelle clasped her hands together and stared down at her knuckles. The scars on the backs of her hands told the story well enough. "Then other things happened, my lady. They wouldn't interest you."

"How can you know what would interest me? If I didn't want to know, I wouldn't ask!"

Jaelle's gaze flew up to her. Even in broad daylight the room was dim because the windows were so narrow, but not dim enough that she could not see the pale drape of Katerina's hair and the flow of her blouse and skirts down over the stone. She had taken off her boots, and her bare feet peeked out from under her skirts and the belled cuff of her striped undertrousers. A number of slender gold bracelets wreathed her left ankle, making a soft music every time she shifted her leg.

"Must I tell you, my lady? Do you command me to?"

"Of course not! I would only like to find a friend, here, and it is usual for friends to want to know something of each other. You do not belong here either, do you?"

"No, my lady."

"I wish you would leave off calling me 'my lady.' I am usually called Katya. What would happen to you if you had not been sent here with me? Would you still serve Princess Rusudani?"

"I don't think so, my la—. I don't think so. It is not fitting that a common woman like me serve a princess."

"Then what could you do?"

Jaelle shrugged. "All towns have a marketplace, and there are always men who will pay a woman to lie with them."

"Do you like it?"

"Do I *like* it? I am free, my— That is, I *was* free, to make my own transactions. I would rather travel with the caravans and choose my own service than be a slave, even in the finest mansion, as my mother was."

"I meant, what is it like to lie with a man when he pays you? Does he love you? Is the payment only to make him have pleasure, or is there any pleasure for yourself? It must be strange. My mother always said that a woman should never take a man into her blankets whom she would not care to speak with in the morning, and I suppose it was poorly done of me to take Andrei Sakhalin—" She spat suddenly on the stone floor. "His name soils my mouth. But still, it was only out of ill temper that I did it. I must say, he scarcely gave me any pleasure at all, he was so intent on telling me about how important he was. He talked the whole time!"

The words came quickly, and Jaelle found them confusing. "You are a widow?" she asked finally.

Katerina touched her own cheek. "No."

"But you speak of having lain with men."

Katerina shoved herself up from the bench and began to pace again. "I hate this room. Gods, I hate it. All these khaja things are so heavy and so imprisoning. Why shouldn't a woman take a lover if she wishes to? A girl becomes a woman by taking a lover, isn't that true with the khaja as well?"

"When a girl is married—"

"Are you married?"

"No."

"You see," said Katerina triumphantly. "Your ways are not so different from ours. How could they be? Even if Aunt Tess says they are."

Katerina's pacing made Jaelle dizzy. "An unmarried girl who took a lover would be disgraced," Jaelle said. "She would never find a husband. Her own people would cast her out on the street for bringing shame to her family."

Katerina stopped pacing. Her expression altered. It took Jaelle a moment to recognize the emotion: Pity. "Is that what happened to you?"

Jaelle laughed harshly. "I beg your pardon, my lady, for speaking so freely, but I think your ways must be very different from ours. I never had any hope of being married. I was a slave, first in my master's house and then for a time in the mines. I was whipped often enough for trying to run away. It was only by the grace of Our Lady the Pilgrim that I chanced to grow into a face pretty enough to attract the attention of an old merchant. I traveled north with him, and he taught me Taor and a few other languages, including Yos, which is the language spoken in all the princedoms in this region. He treated me decently and fed me well. When he died after an illness, I took some of his coin, only as much as I needed, and after that I was free to sell myself along the caravan routes. But free. It was a better life than the one I had before. May She be praised for Her mercy, for it was by Her will that I escaped the other life."

"That is terrible," said Katerina.

Jaelle did not know what to reply. Katerina's sympathy troubled her. Below, she heard someone arrive, and she went to the door and opened it. Prince Janos came up the steps, carrying two books.

Katerina sprang up at once, her face alight—for the books, Jaelle thought, not for the man, but Janos watched her with greedy eyes and stood over her, one hand resting possessively on the back of the chair in which she sat down to examine these treasures.

"This is a copy of *The Recitation*," Katerina said, opening its pages with reverence, drawing a hand down the parchment as if to caress it.

His fingers twitched on the back of the chair, but he did not touch her. "Princess Rusudani gave me this copy for you. She has asked if she may visit you, to discuss the word of God."

"Of course. I would welcome her visits." But Katerina said it absently, turning to the other volume. "What is this?" She read aloud, sounding out the script. *"The Description of Travels in the Lands of the Yossian Peoples?"*

"You *can* read."

She looked up over her shoulder at him. "Why should I lie about such a thing as *that?*"

He smiled down at her. "My mother spent some years in retirement, before I came of age and she came here to act as chatelaine of the lands I inherited from her. She translated this work."

"Your mother did that? Then she must truly be an educated woman, my lord."

He smiled further and ran a hand down one of her braids, twining it into his fingers. Her face stilled. She took hold of his wrist, pulled his hand away, and stood up, moving away from him. Janos looked startled.

A guard clattered up the stairs. "Lady Jadranka begs leave to address you, my lord," he said.

Janos hesitated, then made polite good-byes to Katerina and took himself off. The guard loitered for a moment, eyeing Jaelle, and he patted the small purse looped to his belt meaningfully and winked at her, then hurried after the prince.

"Now I understand why my cousin Nadine dislikes khaja men," said Katerina explosively. But she went back to the table and sat down in front of the books. "Will you teach me the language they speak here, Jaelle?"

"Of course, my la— Of course."

"I could teach you how to read."

"What use would it be for me to know how to read?" Jaelle blurted out, then thought better of it, seeing Katerina's disappointed expression. Certainly the poor girl just wanted something to do to pass the time. "Of course."

But even with this, and the books, to occupy them, there was still too much time to fill.

The next morning, Prince Janos came again, but this time he brought an unexpected visitor and an escort of four guards.

Katerina leaped to her feet, but said nothing, nor did she rush forward to greet the visitor. It was Bakhtiian. Jaelle thought he looked somewhat neater than he had at their other meeting, as if he had taken some pains to repair his clothing and at least wash his face and hands.

At once, he and Katerina began to speak to each other in khush.

Prince Janos casually slapped Bakhtiian with the back of a hand. "While I am here, you will speak in Taor."

"I cannot pray in Taor," retorted Bakhtiian, steadying himself from the blow, or perhaps for a new one. He did not flinch from the prince's stare.

"Then you will pray silently, or not return here."

"Do as he says," said Katerina suddenly, and Janos's gaze fastened on her. That gaze betrayed something to Jaelle, who had learned over the years to measure men's desire carefully, in order to protect herself. Perhaps Janos feared the two jaran would communicate information to each other that might be dangerous, but that was not the real reason he laid down such prohibitions. He was jealous. He wanted no attention paid to her that he could not share in, no attention, at least, paid to her by another man. Jaelle shivered, abruptly afraid for Katerina.

"You have seen my cousin Vassily Kireyevsky and prayed with him as is fitting?" Katerina asked.

"I have."

"You have not been treated ill, I trust, priest of my people."

To this he did not reply, but his eyes flashed. "Prince Vassily asks after you," he said instead.

"Tell my cousin that although I am confined here against my will, otherwise these khaja treat me with the honor that befits a woman."

"I will do so."

Their gazes met. Janos watched this communication avidly.

Katerina broke off the look first and glanced toward the prince. "We will pray now."

She knelt. Never, in her time among the jaran, had Jaelle seen one of them kneel formally for prayer, but now both Katerina and Bakhtiian did so, side by side, hands resting on their thighs, and stared into the distance, into the stone which imprisoned them. Janos was patient. He waited them out. After a while they rose, and Janos signaled to the guards to take Bakhtiian away.

"I thank you," said Katerina to Janos when Bakhtiian was gone. "How is my cousin, Vassily Kireyevsky?"

"Well enough." He circled in closer to her, placing a hand on the table next to where hers rested. She looked at him deliberately and drew hers away. "You need not fear for him, Lady Katherine. I have a special interest in treating him courteously. We play dars, castles, and he is teaching me khot."

"I can play castles."

Janos chuckled. "Truly you are a woman of unusual parts. It is not a woman's game."

"What a stupid thing to say! Of course it's a woman's game, and a man's game. It's just a game."

"Do you ever think that it might be unwise to insult me?" Janos asked quietly.

"Do you ever think it might be unwise to imprison me? My mother and grandmother will not take kindly to this."

"You are only a woman, Lady Katherine. However much it may grieve them, what can they do?" With that, looking irritated, he left.

"You must not anger him," said Jaelle.

"*I* must not anger him! Perhaps he should act like a proper man and not anger me. His immodesty is disgraceful!"

"My lady, I don't think—"

"These khaja are all barbarians!"

"He could have you killed! Don't you understand! You belong to him now!"

"I belong to the Orzhekov tribe, not to a man!"

Jaelle threw up her hands. "You're aren't with the jaran now. Listen to me, Lady Katherine. You are his concubine now. You must make him wish to treat you well."

"What is a concubine?"

The depth of her ignorance astonished Jaelle. At times, it was possible to think of her like any other woman; many of the women on the caravan routes spoke Taor with accents, so that was nothing new. But now she reminded herself that Princess Katerina was truly a foreigner. "A woman who is kept by a man as a mistress, as a . . . wife, without marrying her."

"How is that different from being a whore?"

"A whore is paid for her service."

Katerina winced. "Well, he may think whatever he wishes of me. I am not taking him to my bed."

"That may be, my lady, but he intends to take you into his."

"Ha! Let him try. Barbarians!"

Jaelle opened her mouth to reply and thought better of it. She sighed and turned aside instead. "I will go down to the well to fetch water, Lady Katherine."

A whole day passed with no visitors. The next morning proved busy, however. Princess Rusudani arrived with a train of elegant serving women, and Katerina listened politely while Rusudani read from *The Recitation* and one of the commentaries.

Later, Lady Jadranka came upstairs with servants carrying a loom, which was assembled while Katerina watched raptly. As soon as they had left, Katerina began to prepare the loom, singing happily to herself. Into this gentle domesticity, in the late afternoon, Prince Janos arrived with a servant behind him carrying a finely carved wooden box with enameled hinges.

Katerina chose to ignore him, so he watched her for a long while.

"I suppose," he said at last, "that now that you have your weaving, you won't wish to play castles."

Katerina halted at once and came over to the table, where the servant had set down the box. Without asking for permission, she opened it and examined the pieces, laying them

out in proper order on the white and red squares inlaid into
the board. "Which side do you prefer?" she asked, sitting
down in one of the chairs.

He smiled. "The choice is yours, Lady Katherine."

She let him move first. The servant set out cups and wine,
and Janos drank heavily, Katerina sparingly. She played with
great concentration. He looked up too frequently, watched
her too much. Indeed, Jaelle thought it amazing, the speed
with which Katerina won the game.

"Where did you learn to play?" Janos asked, leaning back
in his chair. Under the table, his boots crept up against
Katerina's legs, and she shifted her legs away.

"From my Aunt Tess, although she isn't really that good.
I played certain travelers, scholars, merchants, whomever I
could find who came to Sarai, and others, out with the
army."

"You traveled with the army?"

She lifted her gaze and smiled, not kindly, right at him. "I
fought in Yaroslav Sakhalin's army for two years, my lord.
I have killed many khaja men, those who thought they could
win against the power of the jaran armies. They could not."

He laughed, not quite believing her. "Surely a princess of
your line would be married by now."

"I have been spared that, at least."

He leaned toward her over the table, his fingers reaching
for her sleeve, which she swept out of his grasp. "Is it true
that you rode with the army?"

"Of course! Most young women serve for two or three
years as archers. After that, most of them go back to the
tribes to marry."

He stood up so abruptly that his wine cup tipped over, but
he had drained it dry and nothing spilled out. For the first
time he looked agitated. He paced to one of the window
loops and stopped with his back to her. "So you could have
shot me, there in the church of Urosh Monastery?"

"I could have. Princess Rusudani stayed my hand. That is
the only reason you aren't dead now."

He turned back. Jaelle could no longer read the expression
on his face, but it disturbed her. He walked out of the room
without saying anything more.

Katerina stared after him for a time. Then she bit her lip
and began to rearrange the pieces, back to their starting
points. "Do you want to learn to play, Jaelle?"

"You should let him win, Lady Katherine."

Katerina folded her hands thoughtfully on the table, gazing first at the board and then up at Jaelle. "I don't think he's the sort of man who wants to be *let* win." A small smile turned up her mouth. "We will see if he can manage to win by his own efforts."

"You are playing a dangerous game."

Katerina shrugged. "What else is there to do?" She toyed with the pieces, moving them against an invisible opponent. "On campaign we used to find khaja men for me to play, and others for an audience. They always wagered against me, because I was a woman. Mariya and I won a lot of coin that way, and some chickens, and trinkets, and even a slave once, a little girl whom we gave over into Mother Sakhalin's care. So don't think I don't know how to play."

"That isn't the game Prince Janos is playing! He means to make you his mistress."

"I'm not a fool. I can see that he desires me. But his mother has granted me sanctuary, so there is nothing he can do except try to win me in his crude way. Khaja men have no subtlety. Now can we talk of something else *besides* Prince Janos?"

Jaelle bowed her head obediently, but she was afraid now, more than ever, for herself and for Katerina.

Because of the prince's unexpectedly late visit, Jaelle went late to the well. It was already dark. Two of the guards at the door propositioned her. As she waited at the well, she considered what they had suggested. Wouldn't it be wise to store up some coin, a few useful items, against adversity? But there were few places where she could find privacy for that sort of thing. As she walked back past the great hall, a man called to her in a whisper from a shadowed corner of the outside wall.

"Jaelle!"

She knew that voice. She glanced around. Shadows had thrown the whole inner ward into gloom, and there were only a few people around. Lights bloomed in half of the great towers. The cold air chilled her hands where she gripped the metal handles of the buckets. Water sloshed out, dripping on her boots, as she hurried into the shadows.

"Stefan!" Warmth swept her, she was so happy to see him. She set down the buckets.

A moment later, he embraced her, surprising her with the

strength of his greeting. He kissed her, swiftly, and she pressed against him for the comfort of it. He broke away, whispering apologies.

"Ah, gods, I beg your pardon, Jaelle. Please forgive me. I've been thinking of you constantly. Are you . . . well? Unharmed?"

"I am fed enough and left alone. But what of you, Stefan? Where are you? What has been done with you and the others? Princess Katherine—Katerina—speaks every day of wanting news of you, but she is allowed none, only assurance that Prince Vasil'ii is well."

"Didn't she see Ilya once?"

"Yes, but they could not speak together. Prince Janos remained with them the entire time." He had taken two steps away from her. She closed the gap and set a hand on his arm, then laid her head against his chest. He stole an arm around her back and breathed into her hair. Unlike most men, his grasp was gentle. But she could feel in the way his body moved against her that he desired her body.

He whispered her name again and kissed her hair, wrenched himself away. "It's no use. There isn't time for this. Who knows when we'll be able to meet this way again? Vasha is being held in the tower. There. It's called the King's Tower, and in the room beneath, his many soldiers are quartered. I sleep with him there. Ilya and Vladimir and Nikita and Mikhail are chained up at night down below, although sometimes Ilya is allowed to sleep in the solar, the room below Princess Rusudani's chamber. That one, there, the tallest tower. Prince Janos has his own rooms, but I think he only uses those for speaking with his steward and others who come in about their business. Ilya says that every night Janos goes up to Rusudani's chamber. Vladimir and Nikita serve the princess as well, carrying water and firewood, other chores. They are almost always with Ilya. Mikhail serves Vasha, as do I. Now tell all this to Katya, so she can be prepared."

"Prepared for what?"

He lowered his voice even more, and she leaned closer to hear him. He smelled faintly sweet, especially against the dour odor of the stables. Jaran camps never smelled as rank as this castle. "For anything that might happen."

"What of the other man? The other soldier?"

Stefan shook his head curtly. "Stanislav Vershinin, you

mean. We lost him on the road. He couldn't walk to keep up, so some of the guards sold him to a farmer for three chickens and some grain for their horses. But he'll have an easier time escaping from there than we will from here."

"If he lived."

"He favored the leg more than it hurt him. He knew the risk he was taking. Someone had to try to escape to get the word back to the army."

Voices sounded from the great hall. A lantern swayed to a slow pace as two guards came along the inner ward.

"Jaelle." Her name was like a sigh of hope on Stefan's voice. "If we escape, will you come with us?" He kissed her again. Then, the confession torn from him by the night air and the chance meeting, he said, "I love you."

"Who's there?" someone called.

"Where is that slave?"

He broke away, sidled farther into the shadow, and disappeared from her view. In a daze, she hoisted up the buckets and set off for the Widow's Tower. Two guards hastened up.

"What happened to you?" they demanded.

"I lost my way."

They escorted her back, and she lugged the buckets up the stairway, not noticing their weight. Setting them down inside the room, she just stood there.

"What's wrong?" Katerina asked, coming over to her. She took one of Jaelle's hands in her own, chafing it. "You've gone all pale."

"I saw Stefan."

"Stefan! How is he?" Light flared in Katerina, like hope leaping across a chasm to find a new home. "What did he have to tell you?"

Disjointedly, Jaelle relayed his news.

Katerina clapped her hands together. "You must try to meet him again. I'll send you to the well tomorrow night at this time. Surely he'll come again then, hoping to meet you."

Surely he would. He had said that he loved her. "May I sit down, my lady?" she said weakly.

"What *is* wrong? You've not taken ill have you?" Katerina led her to a chair. "You mustn't take ill, Jaelle. You're all I have."

You're all I have. "He said he loved me," Jaelle whispered, then cursed herself for saying it.

"Oh, yes," said Katerina blithely. "Stefan's been pining after you for months. I would have thought you'd noticed it before. I thought you must not care for him, since you never asked him to become your lover."

"A woman does not ask— What do you mean? You knew?"

"Stefan told me. We grew up together. We're almost like cousins, really, although, well, he's very sweet, Stefan, and he'll become a great healer just like his grandfather Niko is, in time."

It was too much. Jaelle began to cry quietly. "What does he have to gain by it?"

"Who?"

"Stefan. To say that he loves me."

"He has nothing to gain by it! He just loves you, that's all. Why is that so strange?"

Because no man had ever before said, 'I love you.' And truly, no one had ever said those words. No one, ever, in her life. She did not know what to think, what to say, what to do, what to feel. So, being practical, she wiped her cheeks dry and sniffed down the last few sobs.

"I beg your pardon, my lady."

"Ah! You khaja are impossible. Here, we'll heat some of that water and you can wash your—"

They both heard the footsteps coming up the stairs at the same time. Katerina pulled Jaelle to her feet and like comrades they turned together to face the door. Janos entered. He dismissed his two guards as soon as they had set a new flask of wine down on the table beside the board and set torches burning in the wall sconces.

"We will play again," he announced, and sat down.

Katerina, amazingly, laughed and took her place. Janos made the first move. Katerina countered.

"You are a skilled player, Princess Katherine," said the prince after a bit, "and bold, for a woman."

"You are immodest, for a man, Prince Janos, and like most khaja men your brash manners have done nothing to improve your game."

"We shall see whose game is stronger."

It grew so quiet in the chamber that the pop of the fire was the loudest sound in the room, that and the faint jingle of Katerina's bracelets and anklets and the tumble of wine into the cups as Janos poured, and poured again. He concentrated more on the game now, but after a time it became obvious even to Jaelle that Katerina was winning.

The princess sat back after she took his castle and tilted her chin back arrogantly. "If you would not drink so much, you would play better, Prince Janos. But I would still win."

He jumped to his feet and scattered the pieces with a sweep of one hand. "It is not the wine that confuses me." That quickly he circled the table and grabbed Katerina by the shoulders before she realized what was happening. "You are the most glorious woman I have ever seen." Her mouth dropped open. She looked confounded. He pulled her to her feet and kissed her hard on the mouth.

She wedged her hands in between them and shoved him away, but he pulled her back into him. She jerked her head to one side so that his kiss touched her eye.

"How dare you! You swore to your mother that I would be treated with honor."

He looked genuinely surprised. "I have treated you with honor! Be thankful I didn't send you to my father."

"And what might your father have done? Surely he would not have treated me this improperly." She half twisted out of his grasp.

He let her go, and she staggered back, looking a little stunned. "I beg your pardon," he said. "I forgot that you are an unmarried woman and not accustomed to a man's advances." Now he took her hands in his. "My father has a rare and terrible temper, Lady Katherine. You will do much better with me, although it's true I can't offer you marriage now that I am married to Princess Rusudani." He looked over at Jaelle and signed to her to turn down the bed.

This speech had the effect of rendering Katerina speechless. She was, finally, beginning to look nervous.

"Our children will be raised as if they were legitimate, and since any sons I have by Rusudani will inherit her portion, there is no reason I can't settle some of the lands and vassalage I received through my mother onto the sons you bear."

The truth was, Jaelle thought, that Katerina appeared struck dumb, as if she simply could not comprehend what he was saying to her. It was an incredibly generous settlement, although, of course, words meant nothing. A pragmatic woman at this point would demand that he set down these promises in writing, so that she could hold him to them should his infatuation wane. She wanted to tell Katerina so but dared not speak.

He took Katerina's silence for assent and bent to kiss her.

She elbowed him hard in the stomach and tore away from him. "I have not given you permission to touch me!"

Gasping for breath, he straightened up. "I don't need permission! You are my concubine now."

"I am not a concubine. You will leave my tent—my chamber—now. I wish to see no more of you tonight."

"*You* wish—" He grasped her elbows and dragged her toward the bed, while she kicked at his legs, pulled free, only to have him wrestle her down onto the coverlet. She was strong, but not as strong as he was.

"Jaelle!" she called, as if expecting Jaelle to aid her.

Janos stood, one knee on the bed, pressing her down, but he looked up and found Jaelle, who stood immobile by the fire. It took only a glimpse of his face to see that he was headed into a rare fury. "Go!"

Jaelle fled the room.

Just as she reached the lower landing she heard a crash, and she flinched as if she had been hit. She ran back up the stairs but halted on the landing. Through the closed door she listened, feeling sick inside. Grunts, a hollow thud, a woman's gasp; he cursed; something banged loudly to the floor. The unmistakable crack of a slap to the face. Katerina swore at him in labored gasps. Fabric ripped. Something was dragged over the floor, followed by another thud, and then Janos swore again, sounding even angrier.

The struggle went on and on and on. Why didn't she just give in? How could she be so foolish? Janos wanted to treat her well, that was clear; Jaelle knew that his offer was unbelievably lavish, torn from him no doubt by his desire for her and, as it was with so many men, the ridiculous belief that the one thing he could not have was worth more than the treasures he held in his hands.

After a while Jaelle could not stand to listen anymore, and anyway, the two torches in the stairwell were failing. She picked her way carefully down the stairs and waited.

And waited.

It was dark in the lower chamber. Sounds from above were muffled by the plank flooring and the carpet. Torchlight flickered under the door to the outer stair. It was cold. She heard the guards talking outside. Mildew wafted out of the shadows, and she coughed. The damp air of coming winter seeped in through her kirtle. She had not thought to take her cloak. She sneezed and wiped her nose.

Upstairs, the door scraped open. Light gleamed on the stairwell, pooling and expanding as someone came downstairs. When Janos, holding one of the torches, came into the lower chamber, Jaelle gasped. The play of shadows gave him a grim look. His lower lip bled. It looked bitten through. His clothes hung all at random, and his fine tunic was not belted now; as he passed Jaelle, she realized that it was torn, a gash on the left side. His hair looked as if a storm had blown through it. His left ear trickled blood, and he favored one leg. He pounded on the door.

"Open up! Get me some wine!"

The door opened. He stamped out, his fury a palpable force that lingered even after he was gone. The door shut, and the bar grated down, thunking into place. Jaelle groped back up the stairwell, which was now black as pitch.

In the upper chamber, two torches threw inconstant light over the room, which lay in shambles. Katerina lay on the bed, dressed only in her undershift, silent, staring at the dark cloud of the bed canopy above her. At first Jaelle thought the shadows marked her face with peculiar shapes, but it was a bruise, already purpling, on her cheek. She had a black eye. Soft noises came from the bed. After a moment, Jaelle recognized them: Katerina was weeping with rage.

Jaelle brought water and a cloth and dabbed down Katerina's swollen face, washed her hands and arms, and lay a cool cloth over her blackened eye. Then, from all over the room, she gathered up Katerina's clothing, most of it torn, some just scattered as wind scatters leaves over the ground. She set the chairs and table upright and searched out the game board and pieces, counting them off. Two were lost: one had gotten flung into the fire and was scorched. She pushed a new log onto the fire and let the heat warm her face.

Behind her, the bed creaked. Jaelle started up, but Katerina had only heaved herself up onto her elbows. Moving stiffly, she rolled off the bed and stood up. She moaned and swore softly in her own language, then limped toward the fire. She made it as far as the carpet before she sank down into a despondent heap on the floor. There was no mark of virginity on the coverlet. The chamber smelled of sweat and exertion. Outside, a hound yelped and stilled. One of the torches guttered out, smoke steaming into the chamber and dissipating.

Half of Katerina's hair hung down loose, the kind of hair that gives pleasure to the hands and skin. The other half was still braided.

Jaelle took a comb from the chest. "Let me fix your hair," she said softly. Kneeling behind Katerina, Jaelle tentatively touched the end of the last braid, then, more bravely, unbraided it and began to comb out Katerina's long, thick hair. Katerina sighed and leaned back against her. She was no longer crying and slowly she relaxed. The heat of her skin through the thin undershift warmed Jaelle far more than did the heat of the fire.

There was no hurry. Slowly, Jaelle combed it out, breathing in its scent, like the distant grass of the plains. Katerina found one of the game pieces, a bold knight, stamped down in the fringe of the carpet. The firelight flickered over them, and all the while as Jaelle rebraided her hair, Katya scraped the beautifully carved piece on the plank floor, back and forth, back and forth, until its face was obliterated.

CHAPTER THIRTY-ONE

The Fierce Dance of Bliss

"I am sorry," Karolla announced as the family sat under the awning eating supper together, "that Anatoly Sakhalin has gone."

Ilyana stiffened, but for once her mother's comment didn't seemed directed at her. Instead, Karolla watched Valentin, who sat playing with his meat but not eating any. The skin under his eyes looked bruised, it was so dark. Twice in the past six days Ilyana had caught him in the middle of the night at the latticework nesh, but she didn't wake up every night.

"I'll eat his if he doesn't want it," said Anton, and grabbed for the meat.

"Pig." Valentin swatted his hand, and Anton wailed. Evdokia stuck her thumb in her mouth and began sucking determinedly. The baby slept in a sling against Nipper's chest, but even so, the khaja woman leaned over and pulled Valentin's hand away from his brother.

"Now now," she said in her most irritating remonstrative voice, "your brother is quite right, Valentin. If you won't eat your food, it mustn't go to waste."

Valentin jerked away from her and scuttled back. "Don't touch me!"

"Valentin!" said Karolla. "Your manners."

"What gives *her* the right to tell me what to do? She isn't even part of the tribe, except I guess *he* porks her once or twice a month to keep her happy."

Nipper gasped and flushed.

Vasil, who had been ignoring the interplay, as he usually did, turned right around and slapped Valentin on the face, hard. "Get out. Don't come back until you've learned some manners. Never speak to a woman in that way. You're a disgrace."

Valentin leapt to his feet. "You're the disgrace! I hate

you! I'm never coming back, ever." He spun and ran off around the tent.

Ilyana began to get to her feet.

"Yana," said her father softly, "we're not through eating yet."

"But, Papa—"

He just looked at her. She sank back down and ate. The food tasted like ashes in her mouth. Anton ate every scrap on Valentin's plate as well as his own, and Evdi sucked her thumb. Karolla discussed making felt for rugs with Nipper, and the baby woke up and demanded to nurse. Ilyana felt sick to her stomach.

She gathered up the wooden platters and took Evdokia aside to help her clean them. Karolla only expected them to be scraped clean before they were put back in the chest, but Ilyana had eaten meals over at Kori and other friend's houses too many times now not to find that embarrassing. They went to the washroom, where they found Diana, Portia, and the lighting designer, a broad-shouldered man with a gorgeous mahogany complexion and old-fashioned glasses.

"Good evening, Yana," said Diana cheerfully. She didn't seem very despondent over Anatoly's absence. Portia sat on a stool clutching her pillow, and Evdi sidled over next to her and just stood there, sucking her thumb. "They're a morose pair, aren't they?"

"Uh, can I leave Evdi with you for a little bit?"

"Of course. But don't forget I've got rehearsal at oh twenty hundred."

"I won't. I'll come get both of them before then. Thank you."

The lighting designer smiled kindly at her, and as she left with the platters she heard him say to Diana: "I feel sorry for that girl."

Ilyana flushed, horrified by his sympathy, and stopped outside the door to catch her breath.

"Her father's a criminal. He ought to be confined to the madhouse."

"Hush," said Diana. "Don't forget Evdi is over there. And I think it's unfair. Vasil is self-absorbed and tiresome, but—"

"He treats his children horribly."

"I know he neglects them . . ."

"Sells them off to the highest bidder, you mean. Surely you know about the boy."

"Yassir, this isn't the sort of thing we should talk about in front of the girls." A pause. "Valentin, do you mean? You forget I knew them back when they were with the tribes. Valentin's never gotten on very well here, but that isn't just because of his father. What about him?"

"Di! You live in the same house as them! He was practically being raped by that perverted old financier from the Hoover Institute of Interactive Studies."

"I don't believe it! He's barely thirteen years old."

"I don't have any proof. But I by damned almost caught her at it once, that was when they were doing the prototypes for the actie the Hoover wanted Veselov to do on Genghis Khan and he'd asked me to come in and do the lighting on the set pieces. Anyway, I laid plans to try to get evidence so I could file a third-party complaint, but then she got called away on something, the whole project got put on hiatus, and we came here. You really didn't notice anything wrong?"

"Hyacinth complained about a lot of the people who went over to their flat. I admit that some of them were the kind of people who made you want to wash your hands after you shook hands with them, but ... really, Yassir, I don't ... not that I don't believe you, but. . . ."

"We techies sometimes hear and see things other people might not notice. Did I ever tell you about the time that I overheard Veselov offering his daughter's virginity to—Goddess, what was his name?—that cultural minister assigned to Soerensen's entourage by the protocol office, a lecher if I ever met one, in return for getting Veselov secretly onto ... what's the name of the planet they come from?"

"Rhui," said Diana in a hollow voice. "He couldn't have said that."

"Neh. Not straight out. But there were a lot of unspoken things being said. Something about a traditional ritual for a girl coming into womanhood and how one man was picked for the honor, that kind of thing. I assume the minister never managed to complete the transaction."

There was a silence.

Bathed in shame, Ilyana fled. She was too furious, too humiliated, to go back to her mother's tent, so she ran out to the ruined caravansary instead, a haven now that Anatoly Sakhalin wasn't around anymore to make it unsafe.

Oh, gods, was it true? Had her father really betrayed her

like that? How much worse than what her mother had done
. . . at least her mother had been trying to help her, however
awkward and disgracefully it had been done. At least she
had picked someone like Anatoly Sakhalin.

Shuddering, Ilyana recalled the minister: He stank of oil,
and his hair always looked greasy, and his skin had the same
bloated, pasty white film as uncooked rolls glazed with egg.
And now—oh, gods—now she understood why he had spent
so much time looming over her for that month—what was
it? a year ago now—when the interactive institute Veselov
was working for had done that adventure actie on Tau Ceti
Tierce at the same time Soerensen was in residence.

Pebbles skittered. Sand crunched under boots. She whirled
around, but saw nothing. Movement flashed in the corner of
an eye, and she spun. She heard him panting.

"Valentin! Come out here."

Nothing. Silence. But she knew he was there. She could
feel him watching her from his hiding place along one of the
walls.

"Oh, Valentin, what good does it do you to hide out
here?"

But why should he go home?

"I wish I had gone with Sakhalin," he said from the shadows, and she ran toward the sound of his voice only to have
him dart away from her and vanish into the underground entrance to the storage rooms, cluttered with fallen brick and
huge, immovable *pithoi*.

If they had been with the jaran, it would have been the
next step in his education, that he ride out under the supervision of an officer, in the train of the army, to care for the
horses and the gear of the soldiers.

She leaned into the cavernous opening. "I promise you,
Valentin. When he comes back, I'll tell Mother and Papa—"
Faltered. That was no good. "I'll talk to Sakhalin himself,
really I will. I'll tell him you need to go, anywhere, to get
away."

His figure shifted in the blackness, but came no nearer.
"Will you really? Even after what happened with your
flower night?"

Ilyana imagined how utterly awkward and mortifying it
would be to approach Sakhalin after what had happened. But
no one else could help Valentin. "Yes. Even after that I will.
I promise you."

"Well. All right."

"All right, then. Come out. I'm not going in there after you. I'll get all dirty, and so will these dishes, and anyway, there're spiders in there."

"I'm not coming out. Just let me stay here, Yana. Don't make me go back. They won't care, anyway."

"I can't drag you out. Oh, all right, sulk out here if you want to. It'll be cold at night."

"It doesn't matter. Cold doesn't matter." His voice sounded eerily disembodied, echoing through the underground vaults. "It's only the surface world."

She would have thrown up in her hands in exasperation, but she was still holding the platters. Instead, she left him there.

But in the morning she found time to sneak him out a platter of food, which she left by the empty cistern. That night when she went back, half of it was eaten. She left fresh food and a flask of water. She went again the next morning. The flask was gone, so she left another one, but the food hadn't been touched.

"Where's your brother?" David asked when she arrived for her tutorial. "I didn't notice him around yesterday, and we had a tentative tutorial planned on early computer architecture, but he never showed up."

"I dunno." She could hardly face him. Did other adults besides the lighting designer Yassir, someone she had seen around a fair bit but didn't really know except to say hello to, know all about the awful bargains her father was trying to make? Did everyone know? "He had a —" But if she said that Valentin had had a fight with their dad, then maybe David would blurt out all the horrible secrets that he knew about her and her brother. "He isn't feeling well."

David blinked at her, and she got the feeling that she didn't lie very well. "You'll let me know if you need any help, won't you?"

"Uh. Yes."

He sighed and shook his head. "So. I think we should strike while the iron is hot."

"What does that mean?"

He grinned. "We've had three days to let our—your—encounter with *Genji* sink in. It's a big step, but it worked with Sakhalin. I think we should go."

"Yes," said Ilyana, who wanted nothing more than to get as far away as possible, even if it was only for a little while.

David borrowed Vasil's saddle, since Sakhalin had taken his saddle with him, and together they rode out to the rose wall with Gwyn and Hyacinth in attendance. Gwyn had to get back for rehearsal, so Hyacinth agreed to wait with the horses for as long as he could.

Ilyana stood in front of the wall and said, in a trembling voice, "My name is Ilyana Arkhanov, and begging your pardon, I've been invited to visit, er, Genji, in the hall of monumental time."

The wall clouded and vanished and a barge appeared. This one was smaller. Stairs extruded, and David waved at Ilyana to stay back so that he could enter first, but she followed on his heels and found a circular chamber domed by a low, cloudy ceiling and ringed with a bench. She sat. David, after a hesitation, sat. The barge rose, and rose, and rose, and Ilyana realized that they were flying.

"This is interesting," said David. "The other barge glided. It rested on some kind of cushion of air and never left the ground. Why is this different?"

"Maybe we're going farther away." She set a hand on the curve of the dome. "Oooo. It's gooshy and sort of sticky."

"Yana! Get your hands off that."

She giggled. "You sound like Diana. She's always telling the girls not to touch things, like the things will bite back."

"Things do bite back sometimes."

The ship banked and rose higher and Ilyana slipped off the bench and landed on the floor. She laughed, as much out of nervousness as surprise, and hoisted herself back up on the bench.

"My point exactly," added David, and steadied himself on the bench as the ship banked again. He shoved his heels into the floor but almost slid off, and then did when he started laughing because Ilyana had slipped off again. So they were laughing when the craft came to a halt so abrupt that Ilyana felt like she'd slammed into a wall. The entryway slid open and Ilyana scrambled for purchase, but there was nothing to hold onto, everything was smooth.

The opening gaped onto a gulf of air. About twenty paces away, if one could walk on air, the tip of a steeple ended in a jeweled peak, like emeralds winking in the sun. Farther, she saw the stubby top of a glass pagoda, and the curling black and red stripes of an onion dome, and nothing beneath. From this height she could not see the ground, and she felt herself slide slowly, inexorably, toward the opening and the inevitable death plunge to the ground. She didn't grab for David because she didn't want to drag him with her, didn't even dare look toward him for fear of losing what little purchase she did have. The craft cycled a quarter turn to the left and suddenly a towering wall of smoky glass blocked out the light.

The floor settled and the door lined up with a two-meter-high arch set into the glass tower. Gingerly, Ilyana stood up and walked over toward the opening.

"Don't go too near," whispered David.

"That arch is open, I think," answered Ilyana in an equally quiet voice, as if loudness might send the craft into a death spin. "But there's like two meters between it and us. I can't jump that far. Do you think—"

A sound teased at her ears, the whisper of soft paper being crumpled, the flutter of the leaves of a paperback.

"Come over," said a voice, hanging on the air like a breath of wind.

Ilyana swallowed. "I would, but I can't jump that far, and neither can my ke." She flashed a glance back at David, but like a cornered rat, he had fixed his gaze on the immediate threat: the craft's open hatch and the empty air beyond.

"Ah." The sound was more an exhalation than a word. The craft slid in toward the tower. Ilyana felt as if it were pushing against a thickening cushion of air, and it finally came to rest about half a meter from the wall and the open archway.

She did not wait to think. She pushed off and took the step—it took forever and ever hanging above the chasm—and threw herself forward into the round chamber of slick black stone, landing on her knees. The stone was hard and cold. She crawled on her hands and knees into the center and then, remembering, looked back. She was alone. The craft hung outside, swaying slightly as if in a breeze.

"David? David!"

At last he appeared, teeth clenched. He made an ungainly leap, pitched forward and stumbled into her, flung himself down on his rump, and just sat there, panting and laughing weakly.

"What an entrance," he said finally as he pushed up to his

feet. "The Chapalii must not get vertigo." The little ship
backed away as if repulsed, lifted up soundlessly, and vanished from sight. "I'm not sure I can get back the same way
I got on."

Together they looked around the room: A featureless, circular chamber of black stone that looked like obsidian. A
single gray disk resembling the color of the tower's outside
walls marked the center of the room. The archway through
which they had come was the only outlet.

"We'll step on that thing together," said David, and taking
Ilyana's hand he led her over. As soon as they stepped onto
the disk it sank down into the floor. Ilyana held her breath,
but the rate of descent remained steady, and her stomach
didn't leap up into her throat. It just went down and down
and down for what seemed like eternity.

"Sakhalin said he came up a staircase," whispered Ilyana.

"But that was in nesh. Your legs could climb this high in
nesh, but it might be more difficult in the real world."

She shivered, thinking of Valentin, who seemed more and
more to think that the real world was irrelevant. "Valentin
ran away. He's hiding in the old caravansary."

"Had a fight with your father?"

She nodded, unable to speak past the sob catching in her
throat.

"I'll see what I can do," he promised, resting an avuncular
hand on her shoulder.

At her feet light exploded. As if they were emerging from
a vertical tube, they sank down into empty air and settled
onto a floor of granite. Above, in the ceiling, a round shaft
bored upward into blackness. They stood in a gray-toned entry hall. Behind them lay a wall of granite. Ahead stood a
portico lined with columns.

"Come on," said Ilyana, wanting to get it over with. She
started forward, took the steps with gusto, and halted staring
into the next room.

"Well I'll be damned," said David. "It's Karnak."

It was. An avenue of ram-headed sphinxes dressed out of
red-rock sandstone led through a pale stone land that
seemed, just barely, to have a roof far far overhead, streaked
with a delicate filigree of cirrus clouds. They walked down
it. There was no dust, nor did the Nile River flow past behind them.

But as they approached the pylon, the monumental brick

wall that marked the entrance to the temple, Ilyana saw a slight shine in the gateway, a whispery gleam. There, waiting for her, was Genji.

David gulped down a sound in his throat. Ilyana just stared, even though she knew it was rude.

Genji looked a little like a Chapalii male who had been shined until he glowed; yet it wasn't a gaudy kind of light but more the soft richness of a pearl. Her head was narrow, her mouth like the opening of a clamshell, her skull behind the slender face swelling into a very inhuman but subtle bulge to the sides and behind. Her eyes were faceted like crystals. When she spoke, the sound seemed to emanate from her throat, not from her mouth.

"I welcome you, young one. The ke may wait here at the gate."

She turned. Her robes were like banners of silk swept up by the wind. They murmured with the crackling of a thousand distant campfires or the muted fall of a stream over rocks. Ilyana squeezed David's hand and bravely walked after Genji.

Massive walls loomed on either side, pierced by a doorway whose lacework trim bled a ghostly light into the passageway. Passing through the door, they came out into a vast hall. It was so big that the single statue placed in the middle of the hall could have been any size. Ilyana simply could not estimate its dimensions from where she stood now.

"The anteroom to the hall of monumental time," said Genji.

"Anatoly Sakhalin said there were a lot of statues in here," said Ilyana, looking around and feeling faintly disappointed. She had thought maybe there would be odd, exotic, alien things, something no human had ever seen before. The distant statue she recognized, even though it was small: It was Shiva. Or maybe, she thought wildly with a half hysterical gasp, it was Kori's Uncle Gus, frozen in the act of dancing the part. She squelched the thought and concentrated on Genji, who after a pause now began to reply.

"*A-na-to-ly Sa-kha-lin.*" She pronounced each syllable so distinctly that at first Ilyana didn't realize that she was repeating the name. "The prince of the Sakhalin, who has now gone to approach the emperor. You know him?"

"Yeah. I'm, uh, sort of related to him."

"You are his sister."

"No. More like a cousin."

"This word, cousin, denotes a genetic relationship?"

"Well, not really. I mean, maybe. I'd have to ask my mother if there was any marriages between the Sakhalins and the Arkhanovs, which there probably was at some time, but it's more that the Sakhalin tribe is First of the Ten Elder Tribes and the Arkhanovs, and the Veselovs, that's my father's people, are two of the younger of the Elder Tribes." Then she felt like an idiot for babbling on and not making sense. Why would Genji possibly be interested in a bunch of barbarians on a backwater planet?

"Like the ten princely houses recognized by the emperor. Of course, one of the princely houses passed through the rite of extinction just moments ago—or perhaps that was several years by the way you would reckon time. The emperor will no doubt be pleased that another princely house has risen so quickly into the vacuum created by the rite of extinction."

It took Ilyana some moments to sort this out, because she wasn't quite sure what a rite of extinction was, except for what she knew about trilobites and dinosaurs. "Don't you reckon time the same way I do? I mean, isn't there only one way to reckon time?"

Although she hadn't really noticed it, they had been walking the entire time, as if with seven league boots covering more ground than they ought to have been able to.

Genji extended an arm. Her sleeves were as much an extension of her robes as discrete sleeves, extending all the way to the floor. Cloth whispered. "Here is Lord Shiva, in his aspect as Nataraja, Lord of Dance. With this dance he can both create and destroy the universe."

Shiva stood poised before them, his body circled by a mandala-ring of fire. His skin was a lovely burnt golden-brown, except of course it wasn't really skin. He was a statue cast of bronze. The statue was about two meters high, the same height as a man and the same proportions, except he had four arms.

Ilyana walked a ring around Shiva. The graceful play of his four arms fascinated her. He balanced on his right foot on a dwarf, the demon of forgetfulness, and his left leg swept upward in an elegant line that, frozen, yet suggested the essential dynamism of the dance. "But he's just a statue," she said.

"Is that all he is? Language is simply a map by which we

make sense of the world. The world exists outside of language, just as the dance of destruction and creation, the great cycles of time, exist outside of the linear time in which the brief flashes of consciousness you call an individual life are measured."

Ilyana shivered. Genji made her feel so . . . insignificant. "Do you live a long time?"

"Time is a language by which you measure the world. Even the speech by which you communicate measures space as linear time. You depart. You progress. You arrive. The speech begins and it ends. It unfolds with the expectation that there will be completion."

"Oh. Right. Are you immortal?"

"Not even the stars are immortal."

Shiva regarded this exchange with raised brows and a half smile, simultaneously delighted and aloof. But of course, he was just a statue. He was made that way.

"Kori's Uncle Gus—Augustus Gopal, well, I guess you wouldn't know him—says that dancing is the oldest form of magic. He said that with enough power he could dance the universe into and out of existence. That's why he did the Shiva piece. Well, you wouldn't know about that either."

"Do you seek to learn this knowledge of the dance? It is not mine to teach."

"Neh. I mean, when he dances, it's beautiful, but after it's over there's nothing left. It's like a cloud. It takes shapes, but there's no solidity to it, it just dissolves. That's why I like buildings. I'm studying architecture with Dav—with my ke. I guess it always seemed to me that buildings last longer than anything else, even than the civilization that built them."

Ilyana caught a sense from Genji that she was pleased in some alien fashion: whether for the clever answer or the choice of buildings over dance, Ilyana didn't know.

"Temporal power is indeed both fleeting and insignificant." Genji began to walk again, toward the far end of the vast hall, and Ilyana followed her, followed the rustling of her robes, a little sorry to be leaving Shiva behind, with his lithe young body caught in stillness while still in motion.

"But we remember the names of people who lived before, in our history," Ilyana objected.

"Names are names. Language is a map, and if the map loses meaning, or the map is lost, what is left?"

"But people don't think about what's going to happen after they die. They live now, while they're alive. Well, I guess they could hardly live any other way. But I was named after a man who is leading a big really big army to try to conquer the world." She frowned, a trifle annoyed with the implied suggestion that human pursuits were somehow trivial. "Even in the Empire, don't the lords and dukes and princes try to, I dunno, try to become more powerful? It must mean something to them, just like it does to humans."

"To what end? A mighty civilization could flourish for ten million years, as you reckon time, in some far corner of the universe and yet never meet another intelligent species. Did not your philosophers wonder if you were alone in the universe? Is it not mere coincidence that your ten million years have overlapped with ours, and in such close proximity? It would have been far more likely that you grew and flourished and faded into nothing and thought yourselves always alone, while a billion years before another species rose in a distant galaxy, asked the same questions, and died, and a billion years later in another place, the same process occurred. So you might not be alone, but separated by gulfs of time and space that can never be bridged."

"Then you might just as well be alone, wouldn't you?"

"The void is like the fathomless waters of a pure ocean, and there universes float, coming and going, a fleet of exquisite but frail boats. Here we pass through into the hall of monumental time."

Ilyana paused and looked back toward Shiva, who remained, as ever, soaring in perpetual motion and eternal stasis ringed by the fire of cosmic energy. "But I thought Shiva represented time."

"So he does. But the Nataraja dances death and creation, the eternal recurrence of the rhythm of what you call nature. Pass through."

Ilyana walked through a low doorway that barely cleared Genji's head and found herself in an even vaster hall, if that was possible. Beyond, a cliff dominated the chamber. It was so tall that its height was lost in clouds. Cut into the stone, in relief, was a huge image of Shiva, sitting cross-legged, one hand raised, palm out. The great hall smelled dry, almost metallic, and Ilyana realized all at once that the usual spicy scent she associated with Chapalii air was absent.

"There sits Lord Shiva in his aspect as the supreme Yogi.

On the tower of ice called Mount Kailasa, he meditates upon the eternal. He is both unchanging and unchanged. There he will sit while one hundred civilizations rise and fall, while vast reaches of space are explored and abandoned and an immense net of light spreads its tendrils between thousands of star systems and then collapses back in on itself until it is only a weak flame burning at a single point, soon to flicker out from lack of fuel."

"He looks very calm," said Ilyana, staring up at the rock face. She liked the dancing Shiva better.

"His disinterest is truly divine."

"But if nothing is immortal, then how long will he sit up there?"

Genji turned away and walked back toward the doorway that led them into the hall of the dancing Shiva. She seemed amused. "Temporality has so little to do with the massive presence of eternity, Il-ya-na Ar-kha-nov. Like imaginary space, it is infinite, all-encompassing."

That made Ilyana think of Valentin. "Uh, I always wondered, I mean, I know you have nesh here. Some people—" Fleetingly, Ilyana wondered if Genji could read minds and know she was thinking about her brother. "—some humans, that is, they think that the imaginary space of nesh is more real than here, the real world. But maybe that's like these two kinds of time—what you said—linear time that moves and monumental time that really isn't time but just *is*."

"Building occurs as a biological process," answered Genji. "All of what we call life is a building, a fine edifice that rises and decays and vanishes only to rise again in a new form, balanced against the static repose that is the meditation of Shiva upon the eternal, the fathomless waters."

"I remember what this is called," said Ilyana, pausing in front of Shiva dancing and then running to catch up with Genji, who had kept walking. "Kori and I did a project together on her Uncle Gus's set of dances. *Anandatandava,* the fierce dance of bliss. Shiva's dance is him doing five things at once." She bit her lip, trying to remember it; she felt impelled to impress Genji with her knowledge. "He creates, maintains, veils, unveils, and destroys his creation, which is the world, but at the same time he grants release to the person who worships him."

"Here is the gate, and your escort. You will visit me again."

"Uh. Yes, I will."

Genji turned away. The soft rustling of her robes skittered through the hall, the faintest of echoes.

"Wait," said Ilyana, aware of David standing in the shadow of the passageway. She gathered up her courage to ask the question she had most wanted to but had not been sure she *ought* to or was allowed to ask. "I just wondered, why did you ask me to visit you?"

"Because you came to my notice."

"Well, uh, how come you have a human creation in this hall?"

"Learning begins with what is familiar, and what is simple." Genji moved away, back into the hall. The dark floor was polished to such a sheen that the colors in her robes seemed to scatter and flash along it as she departed.

David came to the very edge of the passageway but did not set foot in the hall itself. Ilyana hurried over to him.

"It's like teaching me about architecture by beginning with compression and tension instead of right away starting to build a Gothic cathedral, isn't it?" she asked him.

"There's a Gothic cathedral in here?" he demanded.

"No, just Shiva."

They emerged from the pylon and walked back down the avenue of ram-headed sphinxes. "I hope you're going to tell me what happened, Yana. You were gone for four hours."

"Four hours! It can't have been that long."

"Did she give you any idea why she asked you to come visit her?"

"I dunno. I think she's curious about human females."

"What did you see?"

"We looked at two statues of Shiva, and talked about time. We saw Shiva as Lord of Dance and the other one was him sitting on a mountain meditating."

David cracked a smile, beginning to relax finally. "I always liked the statues of Shiva and Parvati best. Well, anyway." He seemed embarrassed suddenly. "Do you know how we're getting back?" They came out onto the portico and descended the stairs to the granite entryway. The gray disk waited patiently for them.

"I guess the same way we came in."

"Oh, wonderful," groaned David, eyeing the disk with loathing.

Ilyana hesitated before she stepped onto it. "You know

what else, though? It was like Genji was giving me a lesson. And she wants me to come back."

Startled, he examined her for a long moment, making her uncomfortable. "No doubt Shiva told her he's lonely," he said and then, at once, "Sorry."

Quickly, he stepped onto the disk and she jumped on after him. The plate began to rise and soon was swallowed up in the glass tower. "That's great news," he finished, and said to himself in an undertone, "Goddess, what an idiot you are, David."

Ilyana stared at her feet, dim now, since they were surrounded by the black tunnel. The only illumination came from the ring demarking the boundaries of the gray disk. She had remembered who Parvati was: Himalaya's daughter, who was so beautiful that Shiva loved her divine body without respite for a thousand years. Blushing, she tried not to think of the dancing Shiva, but the more she tried not to, the more she did think of him, his graceful limbs and slender torso, the sensuous flow of his hands.

At last, they emerged into the tower chamber. The little ship was waiting for them, docked now so that only a hand's width line of air separated the ship from the ledge. Ilyana crossed over and sat on a bench and spoke not one word the entire journey back, even though she could tell David was burning to know what had happened. She just could not bring herself to talk.

When they arrived back at the dome, Gwyn was waiting instead of Hyacinth. His rehearsal was over for the day and Hyacinth had been called. The sun was setting. Only the planet's great rings peeped over the horizon. One moon gleamed softly in the sky.

When she got back to her mother's tent, Valentin had not come home. Nor, when she went out to the ruined caravansary, had he touched the food she'd left that morning.

CHAPTER THIRTY-TWO

The Game of Princes

Vasha looked forward to the games of castles he played with Prince Janos. They were well matched, and sometimes a game went on all evening while the women sewed quietly on one side of the room and Rusudani read aloud in her melodious voice from *The Recitation*. She had several attendants now, but they all looked alike to Vasha: khaja women with dark hair and the irritating habit of covering their mouths when they were amused, as if it was impolite to laugh out loud. This time spent in the solar belonging to Janos and his lady was also the only time Vasha saw his father, who usually stood at attention, face blank, near the princess.

During the day Vasha languished in captivity, locked in a stone tower with nothing to do and often no one to talk with, since Stefan and Mikhail had servant's duties to attend to. Vasha quickly figured out that khaja princes did not wait on themselves, so after the first two days, in order to maintain the charade, he did not attempt to help the others.

Now, on the evening of his sixth day in captivity, he sat with his boots drawn up on the stone bench that overlooked the only true window in the room and wondered why he had not been summoned to attend Prince Janos. He heard the door being unbarred, and he stood up. The door opened to admit his father, carrying a tray of food and wine. Vasha hurried over at once to take the tray from him, then stopped, because the guards were looking on. Ilya set the tray down on the table and the guards shut the door on them.

Vasha did not quite have the nerve to embrace him. Nervously, he hovered next to him. "Sit down, Father," he said, pointing to the chair. "You're still thin. You must eat more. Are they feeding you enough?"

Ilya did not reply. Instead, he went to each window in turn and looked out, studying the ground below. One recess had been completely opened into a window divided into nine panes which looked down over the inner ward and the well and outbuildings.

"That's where I sit most of the time," said Vasha, "there on that bench. I see you down below." He did not add that watching his father at the well was, besides the one glimpse he'd had of Rusadani crossing the inner ward, the part of his day he most looked forward to.

Ilya sat down on the bench abruptly and just stared out the window. Vasha brought the tray over to him. "You must eat something." He set the tray down on the bench beside Ilya's knee. Ilya glanced up at him. His gaze was searing. Vasha flinched back, and an instant later realized that the anger wasn't for *him,* it was for their captivity. "Please take something!" Vasha snapped finally, wondering if his father's wits were addled. "It's too dark to really see much anyway. Sometimes I see you picking up pebbles from the dirt."

Ilya took a piece of bread from the tray and examined it. "Vladimir and I play khot," he said, and Vasha breathed a sigh of relief.

"Perhaps you'll bring the stones up here so we can play."

Ilya's lips quirked, but it was not a smile. "I do not command my own movements," he said softly.

"Gods, you must hate that," Vasha blurted out, and at once was sorry he had said it. Ilya began to shred the slice of bread into small pieces while he stared out through the cloudy panes of glass. His fingers ripped at the bread with fine fury. "Don't waste the food!" scolded Vasha, picking up each scrap as it fell to the bench and the plank floor. "How Tess puts up with you I'll never know."

Ilya dropped the rest of the bread, jumped up, and began pacing. Watching him, the grim, arrogant set of his mouth, the crisp authority of his stride even clipped by the size of the room, Vasha wondered how anyone could possibly mistake him for anything or anyone but Bakhtiian? Prince Janos was not, perhaps, quite as astute as he seemed to think he was. Ilya continued to pace. The silence grated on Vasha's nerves.

"Have you seen Katya?"

"I saw her yesterday morning. She is being held in ... there." He crossed the room to one of the arrow loops. "You can just see the tower through here. We could only speak together in Taor, so we could say nothing useful, since the khaja prince stayed with us the entire time. Someday I am going to kill him."

"Isn't it a bit hasty to assume that he'll serve us better dead than alive?"

The glance Ilya shot him would have burned a lesser man to ash, but Vasha was beginning to have the glimmerings of an idea about his father, and it not only surprised but strengthened him: Ilya had a touch of madness in his mind, and without Tess around to steady him, he was becoming trapped in the whirlpool of his own rage and frustration. There was a pause. Vasha carried the tray over to the table, and without being asked, Ilya sat down to eat with him.

"What do you mean?" Ilya asked finally after he had demolished most of the food, which Vasha kept pushing onto him.

"He doesn't hate the jaran. He's just ambitious."

"He killed Konstans and half of my jahar."

"No. Andrei Sakhalin killed them by betraying you to Prince Janos. But what if you could make Janos an ally?"

"Impossible." Ilya pushed away and strode back to the window bench. Sitting, he was lost in shadow.

Vasha took the wick of a second lantern and lit it from the first, throwing a new pattern of shadows into the room. "But if you—" he began, and stopped, studying his father's face. Ilya looked as impervious and unbending as the stone walls of this tower prison. Perhaps it was better to 'wait to expand on that train of thought. "If you brought stones in, if you can come up here again, we could play khot."

"I hear you are a good khot player."

The praise stung. "You might have played me yourself to find out, not just heard it from other people!"

Ilya winced and turned away to cover it, but Vasha caught a glimpse of his expression, and it startled him: Ilya looked ashamed. Vasha steadied himself on the table with one hand. When he was in command, Ilya seemed invulnerable and unapproachable. Now, here, Vasha felt for the first time as if he might come to understand his father.

"Are you ashamed of me?"

"Why should I be ashamed of you?" Ilya demanded irritably.

Vasha hesitated, then boldly went on. He had nothing really to lose, anyway. If he was Janos, and an army came to rescue his prisoners, he would kill them out of hand and be done with it. "Because I'm a bastard. Because I'm not truly your son."

Sunk half in shadow, Ilya's face yet captured enough light to highlight the sweep of his hair and the dark line of his beard, a little ragged now, growing longer than he liked it, to soften the profile that so often Vasha had seen present a hard, unyielding face to those men *he* had taken prisoner. One of his hands played with the green ribbon woven into his belt buckle. "Tess says you are truly my son."

"Tess is very kind, but she is khaja. I am jaran."

"By the laws of the jaran it is true that you cannot be my son, but I was the man who was lying in the blankets of your mother when the winds breathed your spirit into her body."

Vasha shivered. Cold leaked in through the windows and rose up from the stone under his feet. There was a small hearth in the room, laid into the wall, but it had not been lit. "Would you have married her? My mother, I mean?"

"No." Ilya stood up abruptly and hurried over to the window loop that looked out onto the tower where he had said Katerina was being held. "I see torches there. Someone is coming out, but I can't see ... only the light. Damn it. I don't trust him."

"Trust who?"

"Trust a khaja prince with Katya in a locked tower."

"Father! Lady Jadranka granted women's sanctuary to Katya. I know khaja sometimes treat women badly, but—"

"Gods! You spent time in Jeds. Don't be so naive, Vassily."

"They aren't *all* enemies, as you should know!"

Behind them, the door banged open and Stefan came in loaded down with firewood, which he dropped with a splintering thud next to the hearth, blowing grit out of his face and brushing chips off his clothing. Seeing Ilya, his face lit, but he glanced back at the guards and said nothing. A man Vasha recognized as the khaja priest assigned to the women stepped into the room and beckoned to Ilya, barking a command that included Princess Rusudani's name. Perhaps Ilya had relaxed a little, even engaged in a conversation as perilous as the one he and Vasha had embarked on; now he stiffened and Vasha saw it all crack away from him to show the brittle fury underneath. As he passed Vasha, Vasha reached out and brushed his hand; the gesture startled him. Then he was gone.

"Do you see my father often? Outside?" Vasha asked Stefan as soon as the door slammed shut. "How does he seem to you? Does he seem well?"

Stefan shrugged. "He's still a little weak from his wounds, but he healed well. Otherwise . . . he's quiet. He doesn't say much. Now that you mention it, he rarely talks at all. Mostly what we say between us comes from Vladimir, if I see him."

"I think he's going mad. Gods, I hope Stanislav Vershinin escaped those khaja he was sold to. If the army doesn't get word of this soon. . . ."

"And manage to track us down here," Stefan added helpfully.

"What does he do all day? My father, I mean."

"What does a slave do? Hauls water. Hauls wood. I've gotten to work in the stables a bit, which is a blessing, although these khaja horses stink from being shut up. They don't let me ride. I saw Nikita, too. He's been sent to dig ditches outside the walls, and he was filthy. They never let him wash. What Bakhtiian does I don't precisely know beyond that. Vladimir says they often stand in attendance on Princess Rusudani. Unarmed, of course. That's why they've been allowed to clean themselves up a bit." Stefan was rather disheveled, in fact, but spoiled the effect by whistling as he piled the wood into the hearth.

"Why are you so damned cheerful?"

Stefan smiled, looking rather foolish. "I saw Jaelle. She embraced me, Vasha! I kissed her!"

"Did she have news of Katerina?" Vasha demanded, annoyed at Stefan's good fortune and by Ilya's insinuations. He tried to imagine Rusudani embracing him, but he could really only picture her leaning over her *Recitation,* reading from it, her lips moving and sometimes the tip of her tongue licking out to moisten her soft upper lip. . . . "You could have told me about Katya first!"

Stunned, Stefan turned round and gaped at him. "She didn't say anything about Katya except that they're fed enough and left alone. They're in the tower—" He paced over to the window. "Well, you can't see it from here."

"You can see it through that window. She said they'd been left alone?"

"Yes." Stefan did not go look at the tower. He seemed distracted. "I told her I loved her, Vasha."

Relieved and irritated, Vasha went and kicked a log. It

hurt his toes. "This is all very well, Stefan, but we've got to escape before my father goes mad." Stefan's face fell, and suddenly Vasha felt guilty for ruining his friend's pleasure. He had never before heard Stefan talk this way about a woman. "Do you think she loves you?"

"I don't know. How can you tell with these khaja?"

"You must find a way to meet her again. This time we'll have a message ready to send to Katya through her."

"Oh, yes," said Stefan dreamily. Abruptly he laid his hands on the paned glass and stared down into the dark ward. "Gods, how I hate being a prisoner."

"Can you get me stones for khot? It would give me something to do."

Stefan pushed away from the window and came back to help lay the fire. "Poor Vasha. At least I get outside. You must hate this tower."

"I don't see any use hating it. We're here, and we'll stay here unless we find a way to escape or the army finds us. Or . . . or if I can convince Prince Janos that it would be in his interest to release us. All of us."

"He'd be a fool to do it. Bakhtiian will gather an army and ride right back here and kill him. He has to."

"But what if we can make him an ally?"

Stefan just shook his head. "Sometimes I think you're half khaja yourself, but I suppose that must be because of Tess. Such an insult can never be forgiven."

"But it doesn't have to be that way!" Vasha insisted, and then gave up. The door opened. Vasha turned toward it eagerly, hoping it was the guardsmen to take him to the solar, but it was Mikhail, come to take the tray away.

To his great disappointment, Vasha was not summoned that evening, nor the next. Nor did Stefan manage to meet Jaelle at the well. But Stefan did gather up pebbles from outside and they used charcoal sticks to draw a grid onto the floor near the fireplace, and there they sat and played, Vasha against Stefan and then against Mikhail, and then Stefan against Mikhail while Vasha watched impatiently and whispered suggestions to Stefan until Mikhail, laughing, objected that it gave Stefan too great an advantage to have Vasha's advice.

It was here, the third evening after Ilya's visit, that Prince Janos found them. Vasha judged it better to allow Janos to approach to observe the game rather than to attempt an un-

dignified scramble to his feet. In any case, he was simply so
much better a khot player than Stefan that it didn't take him
long to finish engulfing Stefan's stones.

"I have seen the other slaves playing this as well," said
Janos, "but I still don't understand the point of the game."

Now that Janos had addressed him, Vasha stood. "The
purpose of the game is to take control of as much of the
board as possible."

"Ah."

"We must play again, you and I."

"I had hoped for a game of castles this evening."

"I would be honored."

In this way, Vasha played to the other game, the game that
Janos himself had introduced: That Vasha was, not a prisoner, but an honored guest. Together they went to the solar,
and here, where the lighting was better, Vasha noticed that
the prince's face looked rather battered. His lower lip bore a
fresh scab, still healing over and somewhat swollen, and a
greenish-yellow bruise peeped out from under his hair up
against his left ear. They sat down at the table and a steward
set out the game.

They began to play.

"Back when I still lived at my father's court, I was noted
as a man who could defeat men twice and even three times
my own age at this game," said Janos. Vasha glanced up at
him. It seemed unlike Janos to feel obliged to brag about
himself, and in any case, the women had not yet entered the
room. Besides his stewards and Mikhail, who had come
along as Vasha's attendant, there was certainly no one to impress. "You are also a shrewd player, Prince Vasil'ii."

They played for a while in concentrated silence. Then
Vasha moved a knight to threaten Janos's castle, and said,
"Andrei Sakhalin may not have as much backing as you
think, Prince Janos, whatever he's told you."

Janos grinned without looking up. "Which game are we
playing, Prince Vasil'ii?"

"The game of princes, Prince Janos. Is it not said of castles that a king's son should learn it who wishes to learn the
art of ruling?"

"The philosopher said, 'Any game played by princes must
teach strategy.' Who is this Sakhalin you speak of?"

"Only Andrei Sakhalin could have given you the information that Bakhtiian rode to Urosh Monastery. Sakhalin also

administers the territory of Dushan for the tribes, and often resides near your father's court. You are indeed a shrewd player, Prince Janos, among the best I have played, but I hope you have not been misled by the Sakhalin prince into thinking he can deliver on promises he may have made to you."

"What brings on this sudden solicitude, Prince Vasil'ii? My abbot takes your knight."

"My lion shield takes your abbot."

" 'Act not in haste what you may later repent,' as my mother has often advised me," said Janos, with an odd catch in his voice that Vassily could not interpret. He moved his gryphon shield forward.

Vasha realized immediately that he had been rash to drive his knight so far over to the other side. He chuckled. "I would hate to lose a good opponent, Prince Janos. Shrewd players are not so easy to find."

Janos glanced up at him, and again Vasha glimpsed an unfathomable emotion in his expression that he concealed quickly. "Do you know other shrewd players, Prince Vasil'ii?"

"The Prince of Jeds is a shrewd player, Prince Janos, and she supports me."

The door opened, bringing the smell of cold air trapped within the stone walls of the stairwell into the warm chamber. Lady Jadranka and Princess Rusudani entered with their entourage. Janos rose to greet them, and Vasha rose as well but did not approach them. The ladies settled down onto their couches and chairs, and various stewards and guardsmen took up stations around the room. Ilya and Vladimir came in toward the end of the procession, and Rusudani beckoned them over to take up a station near her. She seemed, Vasha thought, to be sending some kind of signal—to whom? To her husband, that she would choose her own guards? To the others, that these foreign slaves somehow distinguished her? Or to Vasha himself? He tried to catch her eye, but she had already bent over her reading.

The presence of the women was like an overpowering perfume in the room, they came in so laden with scent, and the soft murmuring of their voices made Vasha long for home. *Home.* For the Orzhekov tribe, for his cousins and aunts, if he could truly call them that; for Yuri curled up asleep in his lap and Natalia chewing on her lower lip as she considered her letters or what move to make next when he taught her khot.

"Even if it is true that you have the backing of the Prince of Jeds, her husband is dead. What power is truly left her?"

The comment surprised a laugh from Vasha. "What power is left her? The power she inherited from her brother when she became prince of Jeds. The power lent her by the support of my grandmother and aunts. *She* is the one who built Sarai. I don't think—" Vassily was not used to thinking so much so deeply and to having revelations so often. "She wears it lightly, but I don't think there is anyone in the tribes as powerful as she is. Gods, Andrei Sahkalin has no power except what his marriage to my cousin Galina brings him! But that is true of any man." He looked up to meet Janos's gaze only to find Janos gazing at him with a look of complete incomprehension on his face. After a moment, Vasha judged it polite to turn his attention away and study the board. In fact, Janos had not beaten him, but a series of six or seven moves, if not countered, would render Vasha helpless on the left flank. "The priest of cups moves two squares."

Janos propped his chin on his hands and stared at the board. Without looking up, he said, "Are you married?"

"No." Vasha tried to but could not stop himself from glancing over at Rusudani. She came to a break in the verse and, to his surprise, beckoned Ilya over to her. Ilya knelt before her.

Janos glanced toward this affecting scene. "Your priest refused to kneel before me, but I see him there, now, kneeling in front of my wife."

"She is a woman."

Rusudani handed Ilya her copy of *The Recitation,* the one that had been translated into Taor, and, evidently, bade him read it aloud. Without demur, Ilya settled cross-legged onto the floor in front of her and took the book in his lap. The women murmured and stilled. When he began to read, they hushed completely and leaned forward in unison rather like a stand of grass grazed by a stiff wind. His voice was steady and rich.

" 'So it came to pass in those spring days that Ammion the Shepherd took the flocks to the hills, where the streams ran cold from the winter snows, and left his wife and her son alone to care for the garden and the hearth.' "

"I have heard that the jaran take more than one wife," said Janos.

"Certainly not. A man may marry again if his wife dies, but taking more than one wife is a khaja custom."

"Khaja?"

"A person who is not jaran."

"Ah. But I am khaja, and we do not take more than one wife. It is enjoined in the holy book that each man must cleave to one woman so that from their union may come children blessed by the covenant of God."

Vasha smiled wryly.

"But in truth," added Janos, "it is as easy for a man like my father to shed a wife if she has no one to speak for her as it is for you or me to shed our clothes before we lay down into bed at night."

"Ha! I knew you were barbarians. Begging your pardon, Prince Janos. The gods have enjoined my people that once the mark is made on a woman's face by a man, only death can sunder their partnership."

"What mark?"

"When a man chooses a woman to marry, he puts the mark on her. He cuts her, on the cheek." Vasha drew a line down his own cheek, to demonstrate.

Janos looked faintly horrified. He coughed. "Begging your pardon, Prince Vasil'ii, but I scarcely think you can call us barbarians if you perform such acts of mutilation on your own women."

" 'Now there came in those days to that country a storm brought forth from the strife of men. Death came to that country as the scythe harvests the wheat, as the wolf strikes down the lamb. Death came to the valley where the garden and hearth of Ammion were tended by his wife and her son. There came to her in those days an angel, and under his wing she sheltered. His wing was as bright as the strike of lightning and where it hung over the garden and the hearth like a pall of incandescent smoke no army dared approach.' "

"Knight takes cups," added Janos.

Vasha moved his priest of swords three squares, without comment. He was still smarting. It had never before occurred to him that it might seem barbaric to mark a woman for marriage.

"What happens to a woman of your people if she never marries?" asked Janos suddenly.

Vasha knotted his fingers together, knowing the answer to this question all too well. "It is a shameful thing for a woman never to marry, unless she becomes a priest. She can have no children . . . or if she does have a child because she has not listened to the wisdom of the mothers, then that child is forever shamed for not having a father."

"Ah," said Janos, as if Vasha's reply answered some question for him. He studied the board in silence for a long while. "I left court when my father put aside my mother," he said at last, in a soft voice, "because I could not bear to see her shamed, and because my brothers ridiculed me for being no better than a bastard. I swore then that I would never put aside the woman I married, even for a great prize."

"I would think that there is no greater prize in khaja lands than Princess Rusudani." Vasha fingered the pieces he had taken from Janos and judged it politic to add to this comment, in case he had somehow betrayed himself. "Her grandfather is the king of Mircassia, and by blood right can she not claim that throne for herself, even in khaja lands?"

Janos glanced toward his wife, who was modestly watching Ilya's hands tracing a slow zigzag path down the text of the holy book.

" 'It came to pass when the harvest was brought in and Ammion returned from the hill-country, that he found his garden and hearth untouched by war but those of his neighbors shorn to the ground. He found his wife giving of their harvest to his neighbors, and she was great with child. 'Whence came this harvest and this child,' he asked. 'For I have been gone all those days when I might have sown the fields, nor in all the years of our marriage have you conceived, but brought me only this branch from another tree and now a new acorn swells.' And she replied, 'I have sheltered under an angel's wing, and of his bounty do I bring the harvest of God to all those who reach for it with empty hands.' "

"Only a fool," said Janos, "would wish to put aside a woman whose birth and inheritance are as providential and as crucial as hers." He seemed almost to be talking to himself. Vasha agreed, taking advantage of this opportunity to look at Rusudani, but dared not say so aloud. Janos sat back abruptly and tossed his head, shaking something off, and with a finger he worried at his wounded lip. "How does a man make this mark on the woman he marries?"

"With his saber."

"Your women do not object to this?"

"Women have no choice in marriage." Vasha did not choose to remind Janos that Rusudani had also had no choice.

"Prince of swords advances two squares," said Janos.

Vasha bit down on a smile. He moved his remaining knight so that he cut off Janos's prince from his castle. "Do not trust the prince who rides without an army behind him, Prince Janos. Just as your gracious mother could be put aside, as you said yourself, because she had no family to protect her, so can a man claim to be more powerful than he is. It will go hard on his allies when his weakness is revealed."

Janos saw at that moment the feint Vasha had planned, and the way he was trapped; it would take several moves yet, but his prince was hopelessly out of position now to protect the castle. But he only smiled. "You are a rare player, Prince Vasil'ii."

"I thank you," said Vasha lightly, "but the fact is, my cousin Katerina is much better than I am. If you brought her here in the evenings, you and I might test our skills against her."

Janos's expression startled Vasha. For an instant Vasha thought he had offended the khaja prince. Then, horrified, he wondered if Ilya's suspicions had been correct.

"That is not possible," he said curtly. "She is too valuable . . ." He broke off and seemed to reconsider his words. "She must remain in seclusion. If my father was to get word that I held a jaran princess here, he would send men to take her away, and I could not stop him without declaring war on him outright."

"I beg your pardon." But the confession made Vasha's heart pound, and not just because it confirmed his belief that Janos was, in his own way, an honorable man. Janos was so close to rebellion against his father as made no real difference. That was a weakness that could be exploited. Ilya just did not understand. Now that Janos was married to Rusudani, who had that strong claim to the Mircassian throne, it would be foolhardy not to lure Janos into an alliance with them.

" 'When the first snows came, she brought forth the child, and Ammion repented of his anger, for he saw that his wife had spoken the truth. He begged God for forgiveness. They named the child Loukios, for he wore the light of God on his brow. And the angels came in hosts, and the heavens about the garden and the hearth rang with light.' "

"However," said Janos, "you have forgotten your center and let it weaken. Prince of swords advances two squares and places your castle in siege."

Vasha swore at himself inwardly, but in the end he had to concede the game to Janos.

"We will go hunting together, Prince Vasil'ii," said Janos when the guards arrived to take him away to his tower prison.

The next day, Stefan and Mikhail were sent out to dig ditches, and Ilya brought him his food. Ilya was in one of his stubborn moods, unwilling to talk except to annoy Vasha with some sharp questions about Katya, and whether Stefan or Mikhail had caught even a single glimpse of her or her servant. He seemed disinclined to appreciate Janos's efforts to shield Katya from his father. Finally, Vasha convinced Ilya to play khot. In this way, undisturbed, they whiled away the afternoon.

But the truth was, Ilya was only a decent player, not truly any better than Mikhail or most of the other men in the army, who played khot habitually but without the concentration and patience necessary to make one a master of the game. Vasha was a trifle disappointed in his father.

CHAPTER THIRTY-THREE

Bearding the Lion

Anatoly stood with a chasm under his boots. The walls of the observation pod were so clear that he could not perceive them except for their solidity. He crouched and ran a hand along the gently sloping floor, curving up all around him to the shimmer of light that rimmed the entry lock. His other hand strayed away from his body and he pulled it back and hooked his fingers into his belt. Below, hanging in nothingness with the spray of stars as its backdrop, the shadow of the transfer station flashed and came to life as the sun rose around the planet Devi. Everywhere he saw ships locked into ports sewn into the skin of the great rings that circled the station. They winked at him, creatures of plastic and steel and other substances he had no name for; unlike horses, he could not name their breeds.

The lock coughed open and a woman stepped through, re-oriented herself, and with her sticky boots squelched down around the curve of the pod, halting two strides from him. She looked slightly ridiculous because her thick curly hair floated in all directions around her face, but she grinned companionably at him, and Anatoly reflected ruefully that he probably looked much the same. As was proper for a soldier on campaign he was letting his hair grow out in the traditional manner, but it wasn't yet long enough to braid properly.

"There's actually a way to gravitize these pods," she said, as if she had read his mind, "but people like the old-fashioned romanticism of zero-gee. Of course, microgravity technology is all borrowed technology and some people would rather keep our pristine but backward methods. No one's ever seen a chameleon in zero-gee." She stuck out a hand. "I'm Branwen Emrys, by the way. I'm captain of the yacht that'll be taking you to Paladia Major, and the emperor."

Anatoly knew his khaja customs, or at least some of them. He shook her hand, noting her straightforward manner with relief. Like a jaran woman, she expected to be treated with respect; he could see it in her eyes and in her bearing. "Thank you. I am Anatoly Sakhalin. Can you pick out your ship from the herd?"

She laughed at that, but in a pleased way. "Oh, yes. I'd know *Gray Raven* anywhere." She opened the pouch on her belt and pulled out a pair of *binoculars,* handing them to him. "Wind the strap around your wrist so it doesn't float away from you. I always forget that, myself." She crouched down, pressing a finger against the clear floor. "I'll point at her."

He stuck the instrument to his eyes but saw only black.

She coughed. "There's a button under the left thumb that triggers the lenses, and you can adjust for distance and focus with your forefingers on the left and right stem. It's already pretty well adjusted for these conditions."

Suddenly, a ship sprang into being, so close that Anatoly started and at once was looking at a different ship, a blocky looking gray hulk that bore two distinct scars on its hull. He scanned along the ring, marking several different ships until the yacht appeared again. She was neither large nor blocky, like many of the other ships docked here, but like the finest horses in Bakhtiian's army she looked sleek, beautiful, and strong.

"She comes of good stock," he said finally, lowering the binoculars and giving them back to Branwen. "But I don't understand why these ships must look each so different from the other, most of them anyway, and why some are so ugly."

"It depends on what they're used for, who makes them, how much you're willing to pay for advanced modifications, and how vain the owner is. A ship in a merchant fleet needs to be utilitarian, to have a large cargo capacity relative to crew and engine space, and possess reliability over looks and in some cases speed. Courier ships need speed above all else, and fail-safes. Yachts need speed, with comfortable interiors as a usual premium, and in my case with downside capabilities." She paused. "That is, they need to be able to land on planet if necessary. That means they need a different kind of design. Most of the ships here are only spaceworthy. It's always nice to have a look at her from the outside first. Shall we go?"

He followed her, squelching, to the entry lock and heaved himself over into the press of gravity. He was awkward, crawling up and over onto the entry deck, a little dizzy with the shift, but as he took off his boots he watched her surreptitiously. With a neat twist, she landed on her feet. He admired her grace. She took off her boots and put on a pair of shoes that looked more like slippers than anything. When he had put on his boots and hoisted his saddle and saddlebags up on his shoulder, he looked at her expectantly.

"Where's the rest of your gear?" she asked.

"This is everything."

"Oh. There are weight limits, but so few of us manage that level of efficiency. Is that a saddle?"

"Yes."

They stood alone in the entry deck, sealed off from the pod and from the station by doors. She seemed hesitant to leave.

"Listen," she said finally, "the truth is I arranged to meet you here in order to warn you. No one else was going to do it, but I, well, anyway, I didn't think it was right to let you walk into that mess without knowing what you were heading into."

"What mess? I beg your pardon, M. Emrys, but I just disembarked two of your hours ago from Duke Naroshi's ship and found your message waiting for me at the docking portal, so I came right here."

"Please call me Branwen. We go by first names on my ship out of courtesy to the pilot, who doesn't have a surname. But no one caught you on your way over here?"

"Was someone trying to?" Put on his guard by this conversation, he began to wish he had belted on his saber instead of strapping it, as was polite, to the saddle bags.

"You're a bit of a celebrity, in certain circles, those that have gotten word of what happened."

"I sent word to no one."

"Word got sent to Charles Soerensen, so that he could arrange transport for you, and he by law, by human law, had to divulge the information to certain councils, all of whom have sent representatives to get a piece of you."

"Get a piece of me?" It occurred to Anatoly that Duke Naroshi's behavior, alien though he might be, was more comprehensible than the behavior of these khaja.

She chuckled. "As big a piece as possible. You've just become very very important, Anatoly Sakhalin."

Branwen had not exaggerated. Anatoly smelled them before he saw them. Like most transfer stations, Karana Station had an exterior ring of docks, with warehousing and living quarters in the tubes that led in to the central sphere. They took the slidewalk out the "z" axis to the quarter ring where *Gray Raven* was docked. When they passed through the seals onto the lofty ring concourse, Anatoly scented a crowd even over the dry taint of recycled air and the tang of ship fluids. Where the ring curved up, he saw seven knots of people arranged in a semicircle around one of the pier entrances.

"Why did none of these people meet me when I arrived, if they're so eager to see me?" he asked.

"The 'x' ring is restricted to Chapalii traffic only. None of these people can get in there. And they didn't have any way of knowing when or where you'd arrive."

"You knew when."

"Not when. But I figured out where."

"How?"

Branwen smiled. "That's what Charles Soerensen hires me for."

"You aren't part of his tribe?"

"Of his tribe?" She thought that one over. "No. *Gray Raven* is a freelancer. We've just been working for Soerensen for a long time now."

"And you are working for Soerensen now?"

She nodded and waved him forward into the crowd.

Khaja were very rude. There was a moment when he and Captain Emrys forged through the crowd in silence. A moment later someone recognized her, made some connections, and then everyone began to talk at once, mostly *at* him. This would never have happened in the tribes, where people knew to respect a man's silence. They jostled his saddle, and some idiot even made a grab for his saber, as if to find some leverage with which to stop him. Anatoly pressed through ruthlessly and grinned when he heard a few yelps of pain. Then, mercifully, they escaped the crowd through the pier doors and Anatoly relaxed.

"I wouldn't," said Branwen, evidently reading his thoughts. "It just gets worse inside. Those were just the hangers-on. There's a whole 'nother crowd indoors, the mucky-mucks."

"I beg your pardon?"

"The ones we couldn't keep out. The ones whose presence here might make the wrong people ask the right questions, which is why they're inside not outside. They're waiting for you in the lounge."

His ears popped as the seal equalized and the inner doors exhaled open. Branwen hustled him through the entry bay and when the trapezoidal door slid up into the wall above and they stepped through into a passageway, Anatoly was assaulted by three things at once. He smelled broiling meat, so strong that his mouth watered. Blond wood-paneled walls curved away down the passageway, so starkly out of place on a ship that sailed the oceans of space that for an instant he thought he had been transported magically back to the palace in Jeds. A black-haired youth galloped up and ran into him with all the gawky splendor of a boy who has just attained his first adolescent growth spurt and not yet learned how to control it.

"*Madrelita!* Benjamin just sold the protocol officer those two cases of Martian whiskey he salvaged from the breakage."

"The ones that got contaminated with green dye?" Branwen demanded.

"Yeah. He told her it was that color because it was a special rare vintage ... uh, does whiskey come in vintage or is that wine?"

"Never mind. Goddess. Oh, well. It tastes the same and we need the space."

"I beg your pardon," said the youth, turning to apologize to Anatoly and fixing him with a bright, interested stare. A moment later the boy recalled how inhumanly shy he was and looked at his feet.

"This is my son, Moshe," said Branwen with a fond smile. They didn't look at all alike. In fact, Moshe reminded Anatoly of someone, but he couldn't figure out who.

"I am honored to meet you. I am Anatoly Sakhalin."

"I know," said Moshe, who was still examining his cloth slippers. "You're from Rhui."

"Time for that later," said Branwen. "Are you hungry? Whatever else he might be, Benjamin is a good cook and I thought you might want to face the inquisition on a full stomach. I don't know what kind of food you got on a Chapalii ship."

"I am hungry," Anatoly admitted, who had learned at his grandmother's knee never to refuse when a woman of another tribe offered you food. She led him around the bend and up two flights of ladders to the galley, Moshe trailing behind like an eager colt.

They fed him steak so tender that he was almost tempted to be greedy and ask for a second, but he restrained himself. One by one, as if the entrances and exits had been rehearsed, the crew arrived to meet him: the man cooking, who was evidently the quartermaster, the pilot, the engineer, and a big, broad-shouldered woman who dwarfed Anatoly in both weight and height. But he was used to that. Most people in the khaja lands beyond Rhui were bigger than he was.

Polite souls, they allowed him to look them over, looked him over in their turn, and took themselves off so he could eat in peace. Except for the engineer, who had to be chased away when he launched into an excited exposition about some new kind of *meaningless word* that he was experimenting with on the *untranslatable* system.

"Sorry," said Branwen after they'd all left. "Florien means well, but he hasn't figured out when it's time to quit. Engines and computers always want tinkering with. He doesn't always understand about people. Are you about ready to beard the lion in his den?"

"What lion?" Anatoly asked. Regretfully, he took in a last breath of the delicious aroma.

"Have another steak," said Branwen suddenly, and of course, because she was a woman, it was polite to do so. "Moshe, go see if Summer needs any help with the cargo." Moshe had been slumped in a chair pretending not to pay attention. Now he jumped up, made polite good-byes, and fled the room.

The lion was Charles Soerensen. As in a comedy where timing is everything, he came into the galley on the heels of Moshe's exit. The other time they had met, Soerensen had boasted a retinue of three alert aides. This time he was alone.

"I beg your pardon, Captain," said Soerensen, "for barging in, but I wanted to talk to M. Sakhalin alone before he meets the others."

"What others?" Anatoly asked between mouthfuls.

Soerensen had impressed him as a man who understood and obeyed the laws of common civility. That he did not do so now meant, probably, that he judged the situation to be dire.

"Laetitia Nge Oumane from the Xenology Institute. Philomena Crohmaalniceanu, a senior diplomatist from Concord-in-Exile as well as her counterpart from Earth Protocol Office, Etienne Tan. A security official from Protocol, Abigail Pandit, whom you should not trust. A member of the shadow cabinet, whom you should, Yoshiko Sung Shikibu." Soerensen smiled slightly. "And a barrister, Tobias Black, who specializes in thorny legal issues like this one."

"Of course I appreciate your interest, and I remain indebted to you for your help eight years ago when I left Rhui, and for the transportation which you are granting me now, but what do these other people have to do with it? Why should I speak with them?"

"They act, to a greater and lesser degree, as representatives of the League."

"I am a prince of the jaran. I have no allegiance to the League."

"You're human, M. Sakhalin, last time we checked. Surely that gives you allegiance to the other humans living under the Chapalii yoke."

Soerensen's placid manner was deceptive. Anatoly had learned to judge men and he could see how powerful a man the duke was: powerful enough to seem mild. Soerensen sat quietly in his chair, feet hooked casually behind the chair legs, and allowed Anatoly to examine him. Eight years ago the duke had affected a beard and mustache. Now he was clean-shaven.

"Of course I will give you a complete report when I return," said Anatoly, reluctantly bowing to Soerensen's authority. "But my final report will be reserved for Bakhtiian and my uncle Yaroslav."

Soerensen coughed into a hand. "M. Sakhalin, do you still believe that Bakhtiian is somehow going to conquer the Chapalii Empire? I thought you understood he won't ever leave Rhui. Nor can you return to Rhui. Nor can any report you deliver which alludes to space and the true nature of the empire and our lives here be allowed to reach him."

"By whose order?"

"By mine."

"It is to your advantage to use Bakhtiian to unite Rhui while you bide your time here."

"It is."

"What if I discover intelligence that will give your League an advantage?"

For the first time Anatoly heard a trace of emotion in Soerensen's voice: Impatience. "I need to make you understand that it is *your* League as well. Bakhtiian's army is great, but it can't defeat the Chapalii Empire with sabers and horses. We have begun to put into motion a painstaking plan that will take years to come to fruition. That's what I need your help for. That's where all our attentions must be focused."

"I know of your sabotage plan, and admire it, but my first loyalty must lie with Bakhtiian."

"M. Sakhalin, let me be frank." Anatoly could see that Soerensen was becoming a tiny bit annoyed, although the duke did not let the emotion modulate the cool tenor of his voice. "It is at moments like this that I wonder if you are ready to have an audience with the emperor, if your understanding of the situation with Rhui is still so . . . simplistic. Rhui is interdicted."

"To protect it from the Chapalii. But the longevity treatments which I received are part of a study being conducted by Dr. Hierakis in Jeds, are they not?"

Soerensen blinked. "Yes, they are."

"Or is Rhui interdicted to protect you from what lives on its surface?"

"What do you mean?"

Anatoly pushed the plate away and rested his forearms on the smooth tabletop. "You are a duke in the empire, I believe, M. Soerensen. I am a prince. I have now seen how a duke in the empire treats a prince. I agreed to let your people transport me to Chapal because of my loyalty to Tess Soerensen and to your alliance with Bakhtiian, but, in fact, I do not need your help. I discovered something interesting on the voyage from Duke Naroshi's palace here to Devi: I could go anywhere I wanted on his ship. Anywhere. There was not a single place forbidden to me except some few chambers whose heat or radiation or foreign air would have killed me. I acquired the coordinates of his palace, and of the lands—the planets and systems—that lie within his dukedom. These include Earth, of course. I acquired a full manifest of the shipping tables for his merchant houses. I have this information in my saddlebags." Captain Emrys made a gulping sound, like an exclamation swallowed before it could form into a word. Soerensen showed several subtle changes of expression, each one covered over by the next. "I admit that most of it is concealed in languages I do not know how to read, but I gained it as any scout attempts to gain intelligence for the army which he runs before, not necessarily knowing the full worth of what he obtains. When all of these, and whatever else I may discover once I am on Chapal, are given to Bakhtiian, and he can marshal the forces you and Tess Soerensen surely will provide for him, knowing his talent for generalship . . ." He paused for effect. "Or are you afraid to let him off Rhui?"

Soerensen steepled his fingers and gazed at Anatoly, his chin resting on his fingers. He had regained control of himself. His stillness was, in fact, his strength. "You're an anomalous case. I don't know what laws *do* apply to you."

"The laws of the jaran."

"Those laws don't apply here." He attacked from an unexpected direction. "The truth is, that it is Tess's wish to keep Ilya Bakhtiian ignorant of space and of life out here."

This information bewildered Anatoly. "But why should Tess Soerensen choose to keep her husband ignorant? It would be like leaving your most promising child untaught. It would be like leaving your strongest tribe out on the plains, all unwitting of the great war driving out beyond the frontier."

"It would be like keeping a delicate scroll filled with rare poetry and ancient knowledge away from an open flame, so that it won't burn away to nothing."

Anatoly sat back, dumbfounded. It took him a moment to find his voice. "Is that meant as an insult?"

"I suppose it might be, at that," agreed Soerensen, thereby making it difficult for Anatoly to direct his anger at *him*. "It is the current state of affairs. I need to keep Rhui interdicted for my own reasons, the ones you already understand: so that we can use Rhui as a base for the sabotage network and for Dr. Hierakis's research without the Chapalii being able to investigate or even thinking it worth their notice."

Anatoly was still angry about the insult to Bakhtiian. No doubt Soerensen counted on it. After a moment, he sorted through all that had been said, collected himself, and spoke.

"You expect me to accept your authority as if it was Bakhtiian's authority."

"You are young to our worlds, M. Sakhalin. You know that yourself. What I want is for you to do what you're best at: I want you to scout. You have the opportunity. You know how to make the most of it. When you return—" The unspoken alternative *if you return* hung in the air between them. "—I would ask that you meet with me first before making any further decisions or actions."

"I agree, out of my loyalty to Bakhtiian, whose ally you are." It was as much as Anatoly was willing to give up.

"Thank you. And you'll meet with the others in the lounge?"

Anatoly did not want to meet with the others. They were not a council of elders nor of dyans, as far as he understood khaja custom. They held authority under a different guise, and he did not feel beholden to them. But he was beholden to Charles Soerensen.

"I will."

Soerensen thanked him again and left. Anatoly finished his dinner in silence.

Branwen showed him into the lounge. Soerensen introduced him to the participants, and Anatoly noted at once the complex undercurrents of hostility, curiosity, and anxious expectation that flowed around the room. Pandit and Tan seemed united in opposition to Soerensen but at the same time kept making asides to Anatoly about how eager they were to work with Anatoly, seeing, perhaps, that he might become important. Pandit even asked him if he knew Vasil Veselov, which idiotic question he sidestepped. Crohmaalniceanu and Shikibu were clearly allied with Soerensen but not subservient to him. Black held himself away from alliances and in general said little, and the xenologist Oumane obviously cared nothing for any of the others and seemed intent on impressing on Anatoly how little he knew about the Chapalii and their culture and how easily his ignorance could create a disaster. But, in fact, except for Soerensen, they all patronized him one way or the other, either by being suspicious, condescending, or too friendly.

Anatoly did not like being condescended to. Nor did he appreciate being thought stupid simply because he came from a culture they thought primitive. He took refuge in silence for the rest of the long meeting. He maintained a serious expression and nodded his head when it was appropriate. Inwardly, he burned with anger.

Because he had learned manners in a harsh school, he stood when they left, but he did not escort them out of the ship; that was not his prerogative, nor did he intend to show them any such favor. Soerensen wisely took up the rear, but his only comment was to let Anatoly know that the yacht would leave immediately.

Finally, Anatoly was alone. He had too much nervous energy to sit still; he paced. Quickly enough, though, the lounge seduced him: lean chairs carved of ebony wood and smoothed into a sheen so perfect that he had to touch them; a drop-leaf table of a wood so pale that it could only have been placed here to contrast with the dark chairs; two couches that splashed a rich blue into the monotone setting. Anatoly ran a hand up and down the fabric absently, feeling the soft weave.

"Screen," he said. One wall faded from white to a flat, expectant gray. "Outside cameras. No sound."

The wall lit to show the concourse, narrowing in on the crowd that still hung around outside the pier. But the edges of the crowd frayed and shrank as the main players emerged from the pier and marched off with their respective entourages, and the last hangers-on shuffled off discontentedly as the big woman cycled the outer lock shut and sealed the cargo hatch. Anatoly sank back into the couch that faced the wall and leaned his head on the curve of a plush pillow, kicking his legs out in front.

"Flight plan of *Gray Raven,* last five ports and all subsequent stations between Devi and Chapal. No voice."

The picture split into four smaller rectangles, showing a star chart, vector calculations, a basic quartermaster's log, and a web of numbers and lines which Anatoly did not quite understand.

The door opened and Moshe ducked inside furtively. He stood there without speaking, biting a knuckle.

"Yes?" Anatoly asked, a little amused by his behavior.

Moshe removed the knuckle. "We're about to unlock. You should really get in a crash seat. There's a couple tucked away into the stern if you don't want to sit on the extras up in the bridge." He shook his black hair out of his eyes and grinned.

And Anatoly had it: He'd seen that smile before, although never, of course, directed at him. The resemblance was suddenly clear, although he couldn't imagine how it had come about. "How do you know about Rhui?"

Moshe looked pleased and embarrassed. "I was born there."

"Born there!"

"My biological mother died right when I was born, she was a native Rhuian like you, and Dr. Hierakis took me away and when I was two years old Branwen adopted me and I've been here on *Gray Raven* ever since."

In cases like this it was always rude to ask after a child's father, since it was clear that some kind of illegitimacy was at work, but Anatoly had an idea that the boy wanted him to ask. "What about your father?"

Moshe's face lit sweetly. "Oh, he's a grand adventurer. Just like you. I mean, I don't think he's been in wars or anything, but you're both scouts in a way, only he's an explorer. Maybe you even know him?" He bit at his lower lip self-consciously. "I mean, I know it's a big planet and there isn't any reason you should ever have met him but I know he traveled with the jaran for a while. Madrelita tells me all about what he's been doing whenever we get a dispatch or at least she did, but now I can read them myself, the ones that aren't classified."

A shudder rang through the ship. The intercom snapped into life and Anatoly heard a man curse in a foreign language and then a woman laughing, and then Captain Emrys, sounding amused, said: "Oh, shut up and get the second cable uncoupled. Summer, what's your status?"

Summer—that was the big woman—reeled off a string of numbers while Anatoly examined the illegitimate and evidently abandoned son of the man who had been his greatest rival for Diana's affections.

"I have met Marco Burckhardt," he said finally.

"Will you tell me about Rhui?" asked Moshe, by which Anatoly heard him to mean: Will you tell me about my father.

"All hands take your places," said the captain over the intercom in the bored voice of someone who has said those words so many times that they've lost their meaning. "That means you, Moshe. Quit bothering our guest, if that's what you're doing." But her tone was gentle. "Or at least show him where he can strap in."

Anatoly got up from the couch and went over to the door. The boy was as tall as he was already, and bound to grow more. He looked like his father, especially through the eyes, and Anatoly recalled with an amazing flash of jealousy how much he had disliked Marco Burckhardt. But like Valentin, this boy had neither father nor uncle to direct his education, although it was true that the khaja educated their children differently.

But still.

"Of course I will tell you about Rhui," Anatoly said, and let Moshe show him to the crash seats. As the door closed behind him, he saw the screen in the lounge blink off and the roll of numbers and destinations vanish into a gray sheet. They were on their way to the heart of the Empire.

CHAPTER THIRTY-FOUR

A Twist of the Knife

The sound nagged her through her dream, chasing her down a knife-edge ridge while a wind streaked the sky with silver threads and the land beneath shone with the scattered remnants of the burning tails of comets. Tess woke up with a headache, convinced that someone had put a call through to her on the console in the library. She knew she would not be able to sleep again until she checked.

She eased out from under the warm and now heavy arm thrown across her torso, but where Ilya, once fully asleep, could sleep through the worst storms and commotions and her nightly peregrinations, Kirill woke instantly.

"What is it?" he asked.

"Just going out." She pressed a finger to his lips, and he shut his eyes and was back asleep within seconds. Ilya, once woken, would have stayed awake. Gods, she missed him, and yet at the same time, she wasn't sorry to have this time, however brief it might prove to be, with Kirill.

She dressed quickly, slipped into the outer chamber, and kissed both sleeping children. Throwing her cloak over her shoulders, she went out into the night.

It was bitterly cold, courtesy of a sudden cold front that had swung down on Sarai from the north yesterday. The sky had the hard glare of glass, punctuated by the stabbing light of the stars and wandering planets. Her eye caught on a faint star moving across the heavens; a ship must be in orbit. What did the priests of Hristain think of such sights? Did they think an angel traversed the sky, on an errand for God? What did Ilya think of such sights? She couldn't believe he never noticed such things. She shook off the thought with a toss of her head, greeted the night guards, and struck out across the plaza to the library.

She banked her path left, toward the side entrance, but

stopped in front of the steps. Through the stone grill that surmounted the double doors, she saw the gleam of light. Who was in the main hall of the library at this hour? It must be the ke. She went up the steps. The small door inlaid within the great double doors opened noiselessly and she slipped inside.

It was the ke. She played khot at one of the tables—with Sonia.

Hearing Tess's footsteps, Sonia looked back over her shoulder. "Oh, hello. You couldn't sleep either?"

"What are you doing here?" Tess demanded. Her headache had subsided to a dull throb.

Sonia rubbed her skirt where it curved over her belly. "Too uncomfortable to sleep. And we'd left off right in the middle of an exciting game. What are *you* doing here? You never have trouble sleeping that I know of."

"I woke up."

The ke pondered the board and did not respond to the conversation nor to Tess's entrance except to mark her with a nod of her head. Tess glanced at the layout of the stones: They made a pleasingly chaotic pattern, scattered across the board in odd polymorphic shapes of white and black. The ke finally placed her hands one on top of the other on the table. It was the closest Tess had ever seen the Chapalii come to using the hand gestures that were a vital part of at least one strata of Chapalii society.

"The game is yours," said the ke in passable Rhuian. Her accent was uncannily sterile.

Sonia smiled with satisfaction.

Tess was stunned. In formal Chapalii, she said, "How did you learn to speak Rhuian?"

"A method exists to accelerate language acquisition," replied the ke in formal Chapalii.

"I thought daiga languages were considered too primitive to be worth learning."

"They are, but. . . ."

Tess would never have said that she *knew* the ke well, nor that in the three years the ke had lived here in Sarai and Tess had been able to see the ke frequently that she had gained any significant understanding of the ke's personality, if indeed the ke had a personality in human terms. But Tess had never seen the ke quite so hesitant before. She waited.

"This nameless one wished to speak with the daiga Sonia, so the program was activated."

"I enjoyed our contest, holy one," said Sonia smoothly in Rhuian, politely ignoring the interchange. "Perhaps we may play again."

"Tess wishes my assistance," said the ke, canting her veiled head so that she appeared to be looking at Tess.

"No, no," said Tess hastily. Gods, what would she say to Sonia, then?

But it was too late. "Where are you going?" Sonia asked with apparent innocence. "May I come with you?"

Tess swore under her breath in Anglais. She met Sonia's clear-sighted gaze, and it was like being slugged. She knew Sonia very well indeed after twelve years, knew her well enough to read many things from her expression alone. Sonia knew damn well what she was asking. She knew Tess was concealing something, and whether through chance or choice or simply the restlessness brought on by her pregnancy, she had decided to force the issue now.

Except she had left Tess the option to say "no."

The word came out of Tess's mouth before she knew she meant to say it.

"Yes." Then she blanched. But it was too late.

Sonia cocked her head to one side, regarding Tess quizzically. She stood up and shook out her skirts with the same brisk gesture her mother used, and she waited. The ke stood also. After a few moments, Tess managed to get one of her feet to move. Her thoughts raced wildly, jumbling in on top of each other, but like the throb of her headache, one emotion drowned out the others finally: Relief. Whatever the consequences, she had finished with deception. Taking hold of Sonia's hand, she led her back to the ke's suite, past the anteroom and into the private office. A lit bar on the console bled a line of red into the darkened room: a call had indeed come in.

"Lights," said Tess, and the walls lightened until they shone with a soft white glow.

Sonia shook free of her hand and walked over to touch one wall. But she said nothing. Instead, she turned to survey the chamber: the long bank of the console, the shining walls, a wooden table with two chairs, and the red and gold couch.

"This is the fabric that Mitya's wife gave you," said

Sonia, going over to run a hand down the curve of the couch. Her voice sounded very odd in this room, because Tess had never expected to hear it here. "I always wondered what became of it. It's very fine. It's a shame to hide it in here."

She did not need to say aloud: Why *do* you hide it in here? The jaran had many small formalities with which they smoothed over the constant rubbing of lives lived in close quarters, and it was not unknown for a woman or man to simply ride out for hours, seeking solitude. But to have a private chamber, closed away, must seem inexplicable. Privacy lay outdoors, cloaked by the anonymity of the sky.

Sonia grinned. "You khaja are very strange." She brushed a hand over the console, and Tess saw how she started and, more curious now, slid her fingers along the pale gray surface, tracing around the pads and bars without touching them. "What is this? The walls, the way they light without a flame, and this table, they all remind me of things I saw at the shrine of Morava."

Tess finally found her voice. "They are like. I have to get a message." She joined Sonia at the console. Gave a great sigh. "Sonia, there's a great deal I haven't told you."

"I had figured that out for myself."

"Play incoming message," said Tess in Anglais.

The air spun into a cloud above the console and coalesced into . . .

"Charles!" said Tess, startled to see her brother. These days he rarely sent direct links to her.

Sonia stared.

"Hello, Tess," said Charles's image, which seemed to rise from the console. Sonia crouched down and peered up the incline of the console, as if to see where he was hiding. "I have important news about Anatoly Sakhalin. He went with the Bharentous Repertory Company to Naroshi's palace, and ran into Naroshi's sister in nesh, which led him to an audience with Duke Naroshi. But the odd thing is, Naroshi honored Sakhalin as if he was a prince, and he—Sakhalin, that is—has been called to appear before the emperor. As you can imagine, this has thrown the council and the Protocol Office into an uproar, and I want you to be prepared in case some idiot tries to come nosing around on Rhui. It's unlikely they'll get through. I'm going to add security at all gateways onto the surface, but forewarned is forearmed. I will give you an immediate report when he returns. If he returns. Of course we don't have a clue what the emperor intends, if indeed he intends anything at all. Nor do I have any real assurance that Sakhalin will behave in a rational manner. He intends to issue his full report to his uncle and Bakhtiian, but I can prevent that. The Interdiction proceeds normally for now. A more extensive report will arrive in coded bursts over the next two days. Soerensen off."

The image froze, Charles's torso and head resting a finger's breadth above the gray sheen of the console. There was silence in the room. The ke waited, a cloaked backdrop. The thin whine of a fan buried in the machinery hummed away, oblivious to their measured breathing.

"He is not truly there," said Sonia finally. "How can he appear to you so?"

"It's a message, sent from far away."

"Sent from across the ocean? What carries it?"

"I guess you could say that Father Wind carries it."

"But that is not what *you* would say."

"No."

Sonia rapped the console's surface gently with her knuckles. "Are there other things hidden in here?"

"Yes."

The console was backed up against one wall, but Sonia got down on her hands and knees and investigated all its angles and shadows. She found the latch that opened the catch-door, and popped it. Tess did not need to cross over to her to know what she saw inside: the modeller banks themselves, sealed away from air and dust and the corrosive sweat of human hands. For a long time Sonia crouched, chin on hand, and peered inside. She did not try to touch anything. After a while, she rose, carefully closed the door, and walked over to the couch. She sat down.

"What message did he send you? He spoke of Anatoly Sakhalin."

Tess sighed and sat down next to her. The ke, silent, unmoving, remained standing by the door. "A strange message, in truth. The Chapalii emperor has sent for Anatoly Sakhalin to appear before him."

"Ah," said Sonia wisely. "He has learned that a prince of the Sakhalin resides in his country."

"Uh, well, it's not quite that . . . simple."

Sonia chuckled. "Is it ever? Does Ilya know that your brother sends you messages that are carried on Father Wind? No, of course he does not."

"I can't—"

"You needn't make excuses to me, Tess. If this is some kind of khaja magic—"

"It isn't *magic.*"

"If this is some kind of khaja tool, a way to send messages faster even than our post riders, then it is perhaps no wonder that you keep it to yourselves."

"You have kept nothing to yourselves," said Tess miserably, "not from me, at any rate."

"We don't need to."

Tess had to laugh, because even Sonia wore arrogance like another suit of clothes, as all the jaran did. "Can you forgive me, Sonia?"

"For what? I have never forgotten you are khaja. That does not mean I love you any less."

"For lying to you."

"Have you lied to me?"

"More or less. I'm not really from Jeds. I *am* from Erthe, but she doesn't truly lie across the seas. Or at least, not the ocean as you know it."

"Are you sure you want to tell me this?"

"Yes. No. Yes. I don't know. I'm just tired of hiding the truth."

Sonia looked up, examining the ke. "As the holy one is hidden, in plain sight, but concealed by her robes."

"Huh. Perhaps."

"You are with us, but part of you remains unseen."

"Not all the threads in a rug are visible."

"Ah. You mean to best me at my own game. If Erthe does not lie across the ocean, then there are only two other places it can lie, if it truly exists: in the high mountains that lie south and east of the plains or else in the heavens, where the gods live."

"It does not lie in the mountains."

Sonia crossed her arms over her chest and for a long, uncomfortable moment examined Tess skeptically. "Are you saying that you come from the gods' land?"

"Are you saying that you find that unlikely?" Tess demanded, and could not help but laugh.

Sonia smiled. "Yes. Why should the gods disturb themselves in our affairs, in any case? Why would they look like us?"

"You have your own story, of Mother Sun sending her daughter to the plains—"

"Tess. That is a story. I have read enough to know that peoples in other lands have each their own story, about how they came to be. I would be as likely to believe the Hristanic story of how God allowed his only son to be mutilated and dismembered and strewn about the land like any piece of offal, and then appeared to lift him up to heaven afterward on a beam of light."

"You don't believe in the story of Mother Sun?"

"Of course I believe it. But not in what you khaja would call the literal truth, not like a child believes, not like even Ilya himself believes—" She stopped suddenly. Her eyes widened. "Gods!" Sticking her little finger in her mouth, she worried at it while she squinted at Tess. Finally she withdrew her finger and wiped it dry on her skirts. "Do you believe in that story, Tess?"

Tess let out a great sigh and sank her weight onto her knees, hunching over. "No. And yes. Mother Sun sent her daughter down from the heavens and that daughter fell in love with a dyan of the tribes and brought him great victory. Well, it isn't that far from the truth. If you leave out Mother Sun."

"I would never leave out Mother Sun, having a great respect for the power of the gods. If this is true, or a way of telling the truth using what words we have, then it is no wonder you have concealed the truth from Ilya. He would be furious."

As answer, Tess kept her gaze fixed on her hands, wrapped in a tight knot between her knees.

"Are there truly lands in the heavens?"

Tess nodded.

"Is that where your brother went? What kind of lands could they be? How could you travel there? It is said the zayinu have great powers, but I always supposed these to be hidden tools. The only magic I have ever seen truly work is the magic performed by the Singers. Are your people very powerful? Does this empire of zayinu really exist? Well, that is a stupid question, I suppose, since this holy woman stands here with us now. I beg your pardon." This last addressed to the ke. "I can understand that you would not tell Ilya, Tess, but why not *me?*"

Tess's throat was choked too closed for her to speak, and only after a few tears ran down her cheeks could she manage to get out a handful of words. "I'm sorry."

Sonia put an arm around her. "Oh, don't cry. What's done is done. And I suppose the threat to Ilya is worse."

"I'm not threatening Ilya!"

"That's not what I meant. I meant that if you threw this knowledge at Ilya's feet, he would take it as a threat. Ilya does not like to feel that there are others who are as powerful as he is. If he cannot reach them, then he might feel ... diminished."

Tess was sniffling steadily now, feeling quite sorry for herself even while another part of her writhed in confusion. Was it right to tell Sonia? Would Sonia not tell Ilya? Now that Sonia knew, was it right not to tell Ilya? Now that the Interdiction was breached, where would it end? "I feel dizzy."

Sonia removed her arm and patted Tess's hands reassuringly. Except shouldn't it have been the other way around: Shouldn't Tess have needed to comfort poor Sonia, who ought to have been shocked to hear that her sister had descended to the tribes from the heavens? "There, there. You need not tell me everything. I am patient. But in the meantime, may I come in here now and again and see what else is hidden within this table? You spoke words to make this message from your brother appear. Look how like him that picture is, and yet it cannot be him. It has no substance. It isn't solid. If I put my hand up to touch it, I think I could reach right through him to the wall."

"There is a lot in that console," said Tess lamely. "You may come, with me or with the ke. But only you, Sonia. I'm not ready for more than that now. Well, and Aleksi, when he is here, or with Dr. Hierakis."

Sonia rose and walked over to stand in front of the console. "Or any of your people, I would guess, those that come from Erthe?"

"Yes. Oh, Sonia, what am I going to do about Ilya?"

Sonia shrugged, looking more interested in the console and its secrets than in the fate of her cousin. "Ilya is not a fool."

Panic flooded Tess. Her heart raced. "Do you mean he's asked you about me? Said things? That he doesn't trust—"

"No. I only meant that Ilya can add up in his own mind the sum of all your stories. He must come in his own time to a decision to face the mysteries that you have not yet explained to him. When he does, he will make it obvious to you that he is ready to hear them. I see no need to hurry him. Ilya is a very powerful man, as you and I both know. That does not mean he is not, in his own way, fragile."

"What if he hates me for it, when he learns the truth?"

"Tess!" Sonia turned right round and regarded Tess with no little disgust. "My dear sister, you are wise in many ways, but sometimes you are no better than a tiny child who thinks the camp centers always on her. But at least there is hope the child will grow out of it! Now, you will tell me how I may find what else is hidden in this table. Does it only make pictures? No, Charles spoke as well, so it must also make words."

Feeling meek and chastised, Tess heaved herself up from the couch. "Let me start with a map. Call up a map of this continent." Charles vanished, to be replaced by a rounded map of the continent on which the plains and Jeds lay. "Here are the plains. Here is Sarai. Here is Jeds. You have sailed to Jeds. You can see how these lines—"

"I know what a map is."

"I beg your pardon! Call up Rhui." The map receded and became the planet, wrapped in blue waters and mottled with three continents. It rotated slowly. "Here is that same continent on the planet my people call Rhui. A planet is a nonluminous body that revolves around a star. Show the Delta Pavonis solar system. Here is Rhui, and there is the sun, and here are other planets, like Rhui. And beyond even that, there are other solar systems like this one, including the one I come from."

"This is not like the model of the universe that Aristoteles or the Praetor Sivonis propose. But it is rather like the one I read of in Newton. Why should I believe you, Tess? It is very strange. How can these *planets* hang there without falling? What are they resting on? Who stokes these fires in the *stars?*"

Tess cracked a smile and wiped the last moisture off her cheeks. "Actually, there's no reason at all for you to believe me."

"I can see only three possible explanations. You are mad, and truly believe what you are saying. You are so thoroughly deceitful that you hope to deceive me, but in that case, why attempt such a wild story? It would almost be easier for me to believe that you had been dismembered and sewn back together. Or you could be telling the truth."

"You have not asked about the ke. Why she is veiled."

Sonia inclined her head respectfully toward the ke. "I beg your pardon, holy one, for ignoring you. I have not asked about the holy priestess because it is not within my rights to ask about her. If her gods demand that she cover herself, then who am I to gainsay them?"

"It is not her gods. It is I. It is the interdiction imposed on Rhui by my brother. The ke remains veiled because— well—" She lifted a hand along her face, as if lifting away a piece of cloth.

"Do you wish the veil lifted?" the ke asked in her uncanny voice. Tess nodded. The ke lifted the veil away from her scaly face.

Sonia started and looked embarrassed. "I beg your pardon, holy one," she said finally. "You look very . . . different." She glanced at Tess. "She cannot be the same sort of zayinu as the khepelli priests. Her skin is gray, and theirs . . . is more like ours, except for the colors."

"She is of the same kind. She is also Chapalii. The males and the females are shaped differently."

"That is not precisely correct," interposed the ke fluidly. "The difference does not lie in the male/female axis, as you daiga seem to think it always does."

Because they were speaking in Rhuian, Sonia could understand them. She looked from the ke to Tess, from Tess to the image of Rhui and its sun floating above the console. "If you are not from this *planet,* then why should the zayinu be? Why should they be even from your *planet?* They could be from somewhere else, and you might know as little about them as I know about you."

Struck by an odd tone in Sonia's voice, Tess tapped the mute bar and the room dimmed down. The ke pulled the veil across her face. "That's quite true, actually, but you almost sound pleased by the prospect."

"I'm only human, Tess. Of course I forgive you, but that doesn't mean I'm not also angry, a little hurt, and I'm not so noble that I don't mind seeing you caught in your own trap."

"Ouch. The arrow hits its mark."

"As it was meant to." Sonia smiled, but not enough to take the sting out of the words.

"It's the middle of the night. Do you suppose I might go back to bed?"

"No doubt it is more pleasant there than here," said Sonia provocatively, and by that Tess saw that she was forgiven.

They left. The ke stayed behind, and Sonia walked with Tess across the plaza. Both women were too sunk in their own thoughts to say much, a commonplace about the cold weather, a question about Stassia's plans for supper the next day. On such rocks the ships of thought borne out onto tumultuous seas foundered. Sonia kissed her on either cheek and left her to go into her tent, alone.

Kirill woke up when she slid into the blankets beside him.

"What's wrong?" he asked, sensing her mood. He curled an arm around her. He was warm.

"What would you say if I told you right now that I'd lied to you about where I came from? And what I came here for?" Tess felt as if she was flinging herself off a cliff blindfolded, hoping there would be a soft landing underneath to cushion her fall.

His breath tickled her ear. "I would ask you what your reason was, to tell a false story in place of the true one."

"You would." Tess smiled wryly into the darkness. "Let's go to sleep."

"As you wish," he said, amused or curious she could not tell. Kirill never let things he could not help bother him. That was one of the things she loved him for.

He fell asleep far more quickly than she did, and when she finally did sleep, she slept so soundly that she did not notice him leaving.

In the morning, she threw herself into the most mundane chores because it helped her calm her thoughts. It was too much to assimilate, too much to accept, that Sonia had stood in her private office and seen the planet Rhui revolving around its sun.

The messenger found her by the far stream, washing clothes, pounding them clean against the rocks. It was good, mindless hard work. It soothed her, and she could do it alone. She heard the bells and straightened up.

It was Gennady Berezin, son-in-law to Mother Orzhekov,

one of the old guard in Ilya's personal jahar. One of the guards. Her heart clenched in fear. Only the worst news would drive a soldier in Ilya's personal guard to leave Bakhtiian and ride the long road north. She could not make herself ask for the message. He gave it to her anyway.

She didn't even remember his words. She could see his face as he spoke, the words must have registered somewhere, but she became fixated on one bell, silver where the others were bronze, out of place but signifying a message from the highest quarters. He stood so still that the bell did not even shift, not at all, until the wind picked up or was that only her swaying on her feet?

Five hundred men had been ambushed and killed. That was a shame, certainly. But it happened in war. People were killed in war. Who was killed? she asked, but that was only a memory of asking, long ago, twelve years ago now when Ilya had come, the messenger, to tell her that Fedya had been killed in a battle, in an ambush. This was nothing like that. This was nothing like that.

A light danced in front of her, and she saw the knife with which she had stabbed Mikhailov. No, it was Leotich she had stabbed. That was a long time ago.

Why was Mother Orzhekov cutting up herbs with that knife in the flickering lantern light of the tent? What had happened? Why did everyone look so worried? How had she gotten here from the stream? Where were the clothes she had been washing? Someone was crying, but she couldn't tell who it was. Finally she lifted her head. Oh, gods. Yuri was crying, gulping down sobs in one corner, and Natalia had a grim look on her face, far too unchildlike, while she wrung out a damp cloth to give to Cara Hierakis, who put them on her mother's forehead. On *Tess*'s forehead. Tess shifted, pushing herself up on one elbow, and at once Natalia pressed up against her.

"Mama?" she asked, seeking comfort.

Tess pressed the heel of her left hand against her forehead. Spots flashed and faded in front of her eyes. She felt nauseated. Her neck hurt.

"They burned down the monastery," said Sonia, who stood by the entrance talking to someone outside. Lights shone in on her face, the only thing in the chamber that was not shadowed. "And killed every man they found. Though it was a just reward for their treachery, it will not bring Ilya or my daughter back."

The gift of memory.

Now Tess remembered what the messenger had told her. Now she wished that her mind had been scoured clean.

Ilya was dead. Killed in an ambush, and half his jahar with him, and Katya and Vasha and Niko's gentle grandson Stefan.

"No." Sitting up, she almost vomited, her head reeled so wildly. She groped for her boots. "I must ride south. I'll have to find him. They mistook it. It wasn't really his jahar. He escaped. Someone must have escaped. They just need better guidance. I mean, what proof do they have?"

"Tess." Mother Orzhekov grabbed her wrists. "Lie down."

"Let me go!" Tess screamed. Natalia began to cry, and Yuri had dissolved into great hiccoughing sobs, but Tess was so furious at Mother Orzhekov that she could not get her wrists free and she began to pound her hands against the floor over and over again. "Let me go, let me go." Except Mother Orzhekov had already let her go, but she couldn't stop hitting the floor, beating it until she was dimly aware that her hands hurt but she kept on, she had to keep on because somehow she knew it was her fault, if only she had told him before. "I did this to him! I did this to him!"

Sonia, then Cara, tried to grab hold of her arms, but Tess flailed on and on and finally they had to bring in Stassia's husband Pavel, whose blacksmith arms could curb even her wild fury.

She panted and struggled and gave up, and after a few moments of her stillness he let go of her, staying close by.

"I *will* ride south tomorrow," said Tess stubbornly. Belatedly, she remembered her children. She looked around for them, and as soon as she found them with her gaze, they threw themselves across the room and into her arms.

"You have been raving all morning, my daughter," said Mother Orzhekov in a colorless voice like that of a Chapalii nobleman. Dried tears streaked her face. "You will sleep. If I and the Dokhtor judge you well enough, then you will ride south." She tipped a cup up to Tess's lips. Tess knew better than to fight, and anyway, her arms were full with her two children. Ilya's children, who would never see their father again. Who could not die so young, because she had made Cara give him the drink of youth. Oh, gods.

"I will ride south," she insisted even as the herbs took hold. She sank down into sleep, Yuri and Natalia crushed against her, but one last thought chased after her, nagging her, tormenting her: This was her punishment for telling Sonia the truth.

CHAPTER THIRTY-FIVE

Lord Shiva Dances

Things began to fall apart when Yomi found out that Valentin was living in the ruins.

"I really can't just stand by and let him live like an animal," Yomi said to Karolla. Because she was wise, Yomi had come alone to talk to the other woman; Nipper had taken Anton and Evdokia away, and Ilyana sat next to her mother with the infant sitting on her lap. Still nameless, the child could now sit up by herself, chubby arms reaching for anything bright, and everyone called her Little Rose for the birthmark on her cheek.

"He has chosen to leave my tent," replied Karolla. "He can return when he is ready to apologize to his father."

"Karolla. I understand that by jaran law you have certain ways in which you live." Yomi took in a big breath and, letting it out, went on. "But we have other laws. I would be criminally negligent to allow this to go on. He's only thirteen."

"He's almost fourteen," interposed Ilyana.

"And if it comes to that," added Yomi as if Ilyana had not spoken, "since it's come to light that Valentin has run away, I've heard some other disturbing rumors ... but if we can resolve this to everyone's satisfaction, perhaps—"

"Are you threatening me?" Karolla demanded.

"I am speaking as one etsana would to another. I am concerned. Others are concerned. People are aware that this is going on and they are talking about it. It's simply unacceptable that Valentin lives out there in those catacombs. Let him come in and live in the caravansary. Let him stay with some of the actors. Diana and Yassir have both offered—" She broke off abruptly, looking embarrassed for no reason Ilyana could discern, then continued. "Diana has offered to shelter him for the time being."

"I will speak with my husband."

With that Yomi had to be content. She left, but she did not look happy.

"How dare you speak of this to khaja!" Karolla hissed as soon as the other woman was out of earshot.

Ilyana started as if she had been hit. "I said nothing! Don't think that just because they're khaja they don't have eyes. People go out there all the time to—" She swallowed the word she had been going to say, but it was too late.

"And the child remains unnamed because of your stubbornness. I am disappointed in you, Yana."

Stung, Ilyana sniffed back angry tears. "It isn't fair that you be angry with me! *I* didn't argue with Valentin. I didn't make him run away. He ran away because no one tries to understand him here. He ran away because—" But words failed her. She could not bring herself to incriminate her father.

"Here comes your father," said Karolla, like the knell of death. "He looks angry. See what your friendships with the khaja have brought us."

He did look angry. Ilyana pulled the baby against her as if the child could shield her; and the baby did, in a way, because Vasil had an aversion to the little one, with her unsightly blemish, so unlike his other, more perfect children.

"What is going on?" Vasil demanded of his wife as he came to a halt underneath the awning. "Why is everyone in the company interesting themselves in our personal affairs? I was taken aside by—" He looked so angry that for an instant Ilyana thought he was going to spit. "—by Hyacinth, that meddling—" Ilyana didn't recognize the khush word he used, but Karolla flinched. "Then Gwyn Jones mentioned that he'd caught a glimpse of Valentin! I don't want my family to be the common gossip of every lowly tech and giggling inconsequential actor in this company!"

"Mother Yomi just came by to speak with me."

Vasil threw up his hands in a theatrical gesture.

"It's your own fault," Ilyana blurted out. "You shouldn't have fought with him."

Vasil turned a stare on her that froze her. She felt like the most insignificant worm underneath his harsh gaze. He had never ever looked at her like this before. "Can this be my daughter?" he asked in a whisper that nevertheless resounded like a shout.

"But it's true," she stammered, determined to go on.

"He's addicted to nesh. He'll never get cured if you don't try to get help for him."

Vasil's expression did not change, nor did he look away from her.

"A child who will not live by the law of the tribes becomes an outcast," said Karolla sternly. "It has always been thus, and it will remain so. Khaja may have their own laws, but they do not apply to us."

"Of course they apply to us! We don't live with the tribes anymore. Oh, why can't you see?"

"Apologize to your mother, Yana."

Infuriated by their obstinacy, Ilyana lost her temper. "I won't! I have nothing to apologize for. Oh, gods, you just won't listen."

"Yana!"

"And you never call me by my full name! Never! Are you afraid to say it?"

Karolla slapped her, hard.

Vasil's face whitened with rage.

Ilyana realized she had gone too far. Only she didn't really understand how, or why. The baby hiccoughed with fear and began to wail. Looking at her father's face, Ilyana was suddenly terrified. Pressing Little Rose against her, she scrambled to her feet, dodged him—he grabbed for her but missed—and ran, the baby screaming the whole time, for the safety of the caravansary. He wouldn't make a scene in there. He just wouldn't.

He didn't follow her. Not yet, at any rate. She sat down, panting, on a bench in the courtyard, and endured a few curious glances from passersby by pretending not to notice them. She bounced the baby on her knee until the little one quieted and fell asleep. After a while, David came out, deep in conversation with the tech Wingtuck. Seeing Ilyana, he broke off and excused himself.

"What is it?" he asked in a low voice, coming up beside her.

"Nothing. Just sitting here."

"Don't lie to me, Yana."

"Why won't they call me Ilyana?"

"Who?"

"Anyone. My parents."

"Well . . ." Like most adults, he had a way of rubbing his face with a hand and hesitating when he hoped you would get sidetracked by the pause and let the conversation move on to safer topics.

"My father loved him. You think I don't remember him, but I do. He loved him more than he loved my mother or even me or any of us, his children, I mean. But not in a good way, like Hyacinth loves Yevgeni. So why did he name me after him? Why won't he call me by that name?"

There was a long silence. Wingtuck, standing in the corner of the courtyard watching them, shrugged, lifted one hand in a wave, and walked away, out through the gate.

"Ilyana," said David finally in his solemn adult voice.

"Don't treat me like a child! I'm sixteen! I'm not a baby."

"Did you just argue with your parents? Everyone is talking about Valentin. I stopped a couple of the actors from setting out to capture him."

"That would be really stupid," said Ilyana, alarmed. That would only drive Valentin further away.

"I know. I told them so. Don't worry, they're not going. And he's barely eating any of the food you take out to him. Ilyana. Ha!" He sat down beside her, a half smile on his face. "Did I ever tell you about the time I thought that Ilya Bakhtiian was going to kill me? Tess got dead drunk and I let her sleep it off in my tent, only in the morning when I went to get her, Bakhtiian saw her and me coming out of the tent together. Goddess, I thought he was going to kill me on the spot."

"Why would he? Women can take lovers if they wish to."

"I didn't know that then."

The baby breathed softly in the silence. Outside, by the flower garden, some of the actors and techs were playing soccer. She could hear their shouting and laughter. "What was he like? They never talk about him."

"Oh, Yana, he's not someone you can explain in a few words. How do you know about him if they don't talk about him?"

"I told you I remember him. I remember what he looked like. What he felt like, I mean, to be near. He didn't scare me, but he was like ... like standing outside to watch a storm come in." Sitting there, her feet in sunshine and her face in the shade, she realized something else. "In a way it's like he's always with us, even though he isn't here. Can that be?"

"Some people always remain with you, even when they're a long way away. Even if you never see them again."

"Do you have someone like that?"

His mouth tugged up, but he didn't quite smile. He looked sad, but not bitter. "Yes."

"Sometimes," said Ilyana so low that she could hardly hear herself, "I think my father wishes that I was his child by Bakhtiian. I mean, if they could do that kind of thing, if they could have done it there. I think that's why he treats me better than the others. But I don't think I'm his favorite any more." To her horror, she felt tears sliding down. She wiped her free hand fiercely over her cheeks.

"You did have an argument."

She nodded, unable to trust her voice.

"I don't know what to tell you about your father. I argued with mine often enough when I was about your age. But maybe we can do something to help Valentin. I don't know how long he can survive with that little food, but I do know that he must be going through nasty withdrawal symptoms from nesh. By your own account it's been—what—ten days since he ran away? Sooner or later he's got to come out, if he hasn't already. He'll come here, at night, to get onto the nesh. I don't know where else he could find a link."

"So we set a trap to catch him? Then what do we do with him?"

"I don't know. Feed him. He's always been so damned thin it hurts me to look at him. Now that everyone knows, I think—well, you know we are allowed to send a message out every five days, to Maggie, who's monitoring us for Charles. I could put in a query about nesh addiction, how to treat it."

"I don't know. I just feel like it would be a bad idea."

"Be that as it may, I don't see how doing nothing is going to help him now that it's gone this far. You have to accept that your parents won't or can't help him. If they can't, if they won't, if it's gotten this bad, then someone else has to. He's ill, Yana. I remember that the company took responsibility for you, for your family, when you left Rhui. I'm sure that is partly what motivates Yomi now, that sense of responsibility."

"But he won't want any of you."

"Damn it! It doesn't matter what *he* wants. Hell, ask Genji for a ship to get him off planet. We can ship him off after Sakhalin. He'll listen to Anatoly."

"I'm sure Valentin will be all right if we just leave him alone for a while," said Ilyana lamely. The baby turned her head and now her sweet breath blew moistly in, and out, on Ilyana's neck. She snuffled and sighed in her sleep, stirred by tranquil baby dreams.

"I'm sure he won't. Now it is agreed that we'll monitor the latticework, and try to capture him?"

She couldn't say yes. She couldn't say no.

"Very well," he said, accepting her abstention and making the decision himself. "I'll talk to those I trust, and we'll start sentry duty tonight."

They sat there for a long time. The sunlight crawled up her skirts and touched her belt before the baby stirred and, waking, began to smack her lips, searching for milk. "I'm afraid to go back to my mother's tent," Ilyana said, admitting finally to the most immediate of her fears, which all seemed to be crowding round at an accelerated pace.

"Stay with Diana tonight—uh, no." David looked shamefaced. "Umm, let me see. Well, listen, you can have the cot in my room and I'll sleep with Gwyn and Hyacinth. I'll take Little Rose back to your mother. No need for you—oh, hell." He stood up abruptly and took the baby from her. Ilyana sat on the bench and watched him carry her out through the gate. The baby began to fuss and then to cry, and then distance drowned her cry and Ilyana sat and listened to the soccer match and to a friendly burr of voices from another room and to a rustling like the thin noise of wind through sparse leaves.

"Genji," she said aloud, and wished suddenly more than anything else that she could be away from here, that she could vanish into Genji's halls.

She snuck outside through the back gates, straightened her shirt, and walked, quickly at first and later, when the caravansary was distant enough, more slowly, trudging toward the far far distant wall of the dome.

The barge came to meet her.

It took her to the jeweled forecourt of the huge palace, ringed by six towers, where she had first heard the rustle of Genji's robes. But this was the real palace, even bigger than she had imagined it, muted by a cascade of rain, endless sheets of it, drowning the jewels and the stuccoed walls as if it meant to wash them all away.

Walking from the barge up the steps, she did not get wet, although no awning sheltered her. But the rain struck on either side of a dry path, and up this dry path she walked, shielded by some trick of the air. Genji stood on the other side of the door, her robes a bell-like shadow behind the screen.

"You come alone, little sister," said Genji in her odd voice, precise in enunciation but shot through with a drone, like insects on the wing.

"Is that okay?" Ilyana barely managed to force the words out of her mouth, she was so afraid she would be sent back. She couldn't bear to go back, not yet.

"How long can you stay?"

"Forever," said Ilyana fiercely. Then felt guilty. "No, not really. I have to go back after a while. My brothers and sisters need me."

"You are eldest."

It wasn't a question, and yet it was. "Yes."

"It is well you have come to me. There is beauty and wisdom in your art, but you are still young."

"I haven't done any art," begun Ilyana, and then realized that Genji was talking about humans, not about her. "Is that why you keep the statues of Shiva here? I mean, in this palace, not right here."

"*Keep?*" Genji pronounced the word carefully, as if considering its flavor on her tongue. "This idea of *keep* to retain as a possession, no, I keep nothing. Ah, but I love this imprecision. Each word bears a multitude of meanings. To celebrate or observe. In this way I *keep* Lord Shiva, just as I keep the ritual of Passing."

"You can also keep someone company. Uh, what's the ritual of Passing?"

"All things pass from one state into another."

"Is it anything like the, uh, the rite of extinction?"

"It is not unlike that rite, which like a sun seen in water only reflects the original. The rite of extinction has a use for those who feel it necessary to create passages they can manipulate." She turned and began to walk. Ilyana walked beside her, noticing how the Chapalii glided more than strode, sort of like when she and Kori skated on their frictionless skates, covering the ground not in jerky impacts but in a smooth sliding motion. Genji seemed to be waiting for Ilyana's response, and finally, because Ilyana had none, she decided it was better to admit it than to pretend to knowledge.

"I don't understand that."

"No, perhaps you cannot," said Genji, but not in an insulting way.

"Why not? Why couldn't I, I mean?"

"You yourself will pass through rituals of passing, and in the end through the rite of extinction."

"Does that mean death?"

"Termination alone does not always bring extinction. Perhaps, like Lord Shiva, you are not doomed to be obliterated."

"I hope not! That sounds pretty awful."

Ilyana felt more than heard amusement in Genji's voice. "To be nameless can be a form of freedom."

"Yeah, maybe it can," Ilyana retorted, "but I notice that you use a name." Then regretted saying it, because it was so presumptuous.

Genji did not answer because they passed under an arch. Ilyana paused and glanced back into the great entry hall they had left behind: Hadn't the statue of Shiva dancing been in that hall the last time she'd looked?

"I am not bound by the same rites."

"Oh, right," exclaimed Ilyana, feeling that she had stumbled upon a revelation. "Because you live longer." The next words died in her mouth as she stared down the hall they now stood in. *This* was the hall Anatoly had described, lined with statues and strange sculptures, there Shiva (she picked him out at once) and across from him a translucent sphere of light pulsing chaotically, and farther down, more and yet more, receding into a distance that seemed actually to curve away along the moon's vast surface, except Ilyana knew she couldn't possibly see that far. "This is the hall of monumental time. But I thought the other one with Shiva on the cliff, on the mountain, was the hall of monumental time."

"This is the hall of memory, which is but one wing of the palace of time. Walk with me."

They walked in silence. Ilyana stared at the statues, but Genji did not seem inclined to stop and explain anything. Finally, the thought that had been nagging at Ilyana surfaced again, and she gave up trying to hold it in. "But if you live so long, wouldn't that mean that you would even live longer than the emperor? But if you live so much longer, how come you let him rule?"

Genji folded her hands together, the thin pale fingers as delicate as lace over the stiff jet fabric of her robes. "What makes you think the emperor rules over me?"

"Well, doesn't the emperor rule over everyone? I mean everyone, everything, that lives within Chapalii space."

"Time creates space."

"Are you saying that if you live outside of time, then you live outside of space, too? But that doesn't make sense. Then how come you can be here with me? You're in space. You're—" Impulsively, without realizing what she did, Ilyana reached out and touched Genji's hand. Gasped, jerking her hand back. Genji's skin was hard, ossified, and as smooth as a pearl. "You've got a shell!"

Genji laughed. Not in a human way, forcing breath out through her vocal chords and mouth and nose, but in a Genji way, amused and delighted. "You are quick in your curiosity, little sister."

"I'm sorry."

"We will turn aside here. You will come back again?"

"I have to go now?"

"Many of your hours have passed. Did you not say you have brothers and sisters to care for?"

Ilyana sighed, but it was true enough. The memory of them settled onto her like a burden. "Yes. But I *can* come back again?"

"Yes."

They passed through an arch, crossed a hall carpeted with white pebbles, and came out at the far end of the jeweled courtyard. It was still raining. The barge, like a well-trained horse, was waiting for them.

"Why do you want me to come visit you?" Ilyana asked, hesitating before she stepped out into the rain. It flooded down like heat, drenching the world.

"Because you interest me. I am a builder."

Ilyana shivered. Here, in the gray light of a downpour, that sounded rather ominous. "Are you going to design me into something new?"

"Buildings grow. They are not forced."

"But then what is your talent? I thought you were an architect. Didn't you build this palace? Design it? Make it, uh, grow this way?"

"Ah. You speak of the shaping hand. It is true that what I touch is forever after marked in some fashion by that touch."

"Does that mean I will be, too?"

Genji did not smile. Ilyana was not sure she could. But she inclined her head slightly and steepled her fingers, three fingers, two opposable thumbs on each hand.

"You already are."

"What makes you think," Ilyana asked, feeling pleased with herself, "that the emperor rules over her?" She settled herself more firmly on David's cot and folded her hands smugly on her lap.

"Don't distract me!" David snapped. "We've got enough trouble without you running off without telling anyone where you were going. You should have heard—well, anyway, it didn't help the situation!"

She sagged back to lean against the wall. "Are my parents angry?"

"I *thought* they were angry before. We could have kept this under control until you ran off, Yana. Now it's all blown open. Your mother as good as accused Yomi of kidnapping you—no, she phrased it some other way—your father was last seen headed toward the ruins—"

"He'll never catch Valentin!"

"You don't understand!" David rounded on her. She had never seen him so angry before. A sob choked her throat and she fought to stop from crying. "You will stay in this room until you have permission to leave. The upshot of this whole fiasco is that rehearsals have been canceled until Valentin is found and we hold a council to determine what must be done. That's what you get for disappearing."

"But it was to see Genji!"

"I don't care if it was to see the emperor himself!" David's anger was very different from her father's: It was clean and honest, and she felt bitterly ashamed of herself for bringing it to the surface. But she also felt put upon.

"It isn't fair," she muttered. "It's not *my* fault."

"What?"

"Nothing."

David threw up his hands in disgust. "Now you sound like

your brother! Someone will bring you food later. Don't leave
this room."

He left. Hands clenched, she sat on the cot and stared at
the curtain that sealed her off from her freedom. It *wasn't*
fair. *She* had done nothing wrong. Then, chewing on her
lower lip, she began to worry about Valentin. What if Vasil
did find him? Except he wouldn't. What about Evdokia and
Anton? She hated to think of them back at the tent. It was
very quiet outside, as if no one was in the caravansary. Daring much, she got up and peeked out the curtain, and indeed,
no one was around. She thought about going out—she could
always say she had to go relieve herself—but remembering
the anger in David's face, she sat back down. In the corner
of the room, David's nesh sponge lay on top of his modeller.
Eye patches dangled in two neat rows from the sponge. She
licked her lips. She could go visit Genji in nesh.

Voices sounded in the courtyard, and she started guiltily.
Now she was acting like Valentin. It would be better to wait
and ask David's permission.

Hyacinth came in, smiled at her, and set a plate of vegetables and bread down on the chair. "Here's somewhat to
drink." He handed her a flask of juice and sat next to her on
the cot. "Yana, is it true that on Tau Ceti Tierce Helms
Arundel, the cultural minister, tried to sleep with you?"

"He hung around after me. It's happened before. I mean,
not that anything happened, just that people hang around."

Hyacinth touched her chin with two fingers and lifted her
face so that he could look at her. He shook his head. "People
don't hang around you innocently, ma chere. Not that kind
of people. Not the kind of people your father gets mixed up
with."

"Don't say anything about him!"

He warded off her anger with a raised hand. "Let's leave
him out of it for the moment, then. I guess we all just ignored the signs because there wasn't anything dramatic going on. But wouldn't you say two children running away in
the space of ten days is a bit theatrical?"

She hunched her shoulders against him.

"Yana, Yana, don't go all Valentin on me. I went down to
the catacombs last night, you know, and almost caught the
little bastard." He said the word affectionately. "I ran away
from home when I was a kid."

"You did?" She looked up at him, curious in spite of herself.

"Yeah. I always fought with my mom and dad was never around. The only one who ever loved me for myself was my grandmom. Huh." He smiled wistfully. "I ran away to live with her when I was nine years old. Never saw my parents again except once a year at the legal hearing to consider my case, which lasted until I was sixteen. There was never any dispute, though. My mon never wanted me back, and my dad dissolved the partnership and went off to the asteroid belts in Three Rings system. But you don't have a grandmother to run to."

Ilyana said nothing.

"So maybe you'd better help us try to fix what you do have. Evdi is going to stay with Diana and Portia for a few days, and I've agreed to take Anton. . . ."

"He didn't used to be such a sneak and a whiner," Yana blurted out. "Anton, I mean. But I don't—"

"You don't what?"

"I don't like Anton much anymore, and I feel bad about that. It isn't right that I don't like him. He could be better, he could be likable, if he didn't think he had to sneak and whine to get his way. He's a dishonest little pig!" Embarrassed by her outburst, she got up and went over to the window.

"That's better. Anton isn't unsalvageable. I happened to go by his school about a month before we left London, and three of his tutors talked about what a good student he is, and how well and fairly he plays with the other children. So perhaps he's only like that at home."

"Oh, you must not have talked to M. Cauley, then. She doesn't—"

"I didn't consider M. Cauley a good character witness. Goddess Above, Yana, surely you realize that M. Cauley is infatuated with your father?"

Ilyana hadn't realized that. "Why did you go by his school, anyway?" she demanded.

"I keep an eye out on you all. Just like Diana does, in her own way. And Yevgeni, as much as he is allowed," he added sarcastically.

This was a side of Hyacinth Ilyana had not expected: That, like an uncle in the jaran, he would keep a careful eye out on his nieces and nephews, awake to any problems that might crop up. She went back and sat down beside him on the couch.

"If you just stay here for a few days, and we can grab Valentin, then perhaps, just perhaps, we can smooth it all over and calm things down. But you know that Yomi is going to have to recommend a legal hearing for your family when we return to Earth, don't you?"

"Papa won't like that. Mama won't do it, not if it's khaja law."

"I just mean some kind of counseling, Yana."

She shrugged.

"I think Vasil can be brought to see that the tradeoff is worth it, family therapy of some kind. The alternative being, of course, bad publicity."

She began to chew on her nails.

Hyacinth rested a hand on her hair. "Just stay here for now, all right?"

She nodded.

He sighed, stood, and left.

After a while, she remembered to eat. No one came to see her. It got dark, and the recessed lights brightened to give the tiny room a cheerful glow. She stroked them down until they gave off just enough illumination to mark the lines of the furniture and the pale square of the window.

Later, she heard her father's voice.

"Where is Yana?"

She jumped to her feet and was at the curtain before she realized what she was doing. Her hand brushed the fabric, and its coarse folds woke her up.

Vasil had his expansive, wheedling voice turned on. "You were very fine in the scene yesterday, Diana. My, Portia looks delightful tonight. Here, Evdi, let me lift you up. Can you see the rings there, just above the roof?"

Ilyana cringed, slapping her hands over her ears, and went and huddled on the cot. Why had she never noticed before how false he sounded? She bit hard on her lip to stop from crying. Harder. A salty, hot taste trickled onto her tongue. She had drawn blood. Just like Valentin.

"I'll go crazy if I stay in here all night alone," she muttered to herself. No one came to see her. No one betrayed her hiding place to her father, who eventually went away. No one disturbed her. Two moons rose. It was quiet outside. If she slipped out by the back corridor, the watchers—

presumably they had set sentries in the courtyard—would not see her. Or she could use the nesh.

Finally, she knelt down before the modeller and sealed the eye-patches down over her eyes, and gripped the sponge, and dove in.

Disoriented. The marble gateway of the Memory Palace stands before her, but the proportions are off. She is seeing them from another height, from another body. This is not her place. She twists sideways and comes to the glowing net of lines now familiar and steps through into the map room and walks, hurrying now, faster and faster, to the palace of time, but as she reaches the jewel courtyard a wind picks up and Genji says on the wind like a cloud of insects, "Do not come to me here. You must visit me in the true palace." With a wrench like the slam of storm winds, Ilyana finds herself

walking out on the grass toward the rose wall. A scatter of lights approached her, a miniature fleet of glowing bugs. It was the barge, come to meet her. She got on, sank down onto the bench and let it take her out through the wall, the rain drumming onto the opaque roof above, drumming, lulling, loud as pans banging together but so constant that she dozed off to awaken to find the barge open, perfectly still, and she walked gingerly down the ramp and up the stairs and into the anteroom to the hall of monumental time. Shiva waited for her, alone in the immensity of the hall. Genji was not there.

She walked across the hall, her footsteps like the flutter of a bird's wings in the hollow gulf of air.

Lord Shiva stood poised with his right foot balanced on the back of the dwarf Muyalaka, the Demon of Forgetfulness. He stared serenely into the air and a nascent smile touched his lips. Ilyana ventured closer. She could almost feel the heat of the ring of fire, the arch set with flames, that surrounded him. Except it was only a statue.

In his upper right hand he held the drum of creation whose rhythm brings the universe to life, and in the palm of his upper left hand a tongue of flame flickered. Ilyana started and stared at it, but when she looked straight at it, it was, like the statue, unmoving. By this flame would the universe be destroyed in the final conflagration, or at least, that was what she remembered from her report on the dance. She was close enough to touch him now. His lower right hand, palm out, puzzled her a moment until she remembered that

it represented a gesture granting freedom from fear. She
reached for it, suddenly wanting to touch his palm, to see if
somehow that contact could bestow protection and peace on
her, but, reaching, her wrist brushed his wrist, of his lower
left hand, which pointed down to his left foot.

The touch paralyzed her. Genji's skin had felt hard, shell-
like. His, smooth bronze, was warm. Then, brought to life,
unable to help herself, she ran her fingers down the fingers
of his hand and drawn down by their texture touched his left
foot, whicn was lifted gracefully across his body almost to
waist height. Bracelets ringed his ankle, little bells, and she
handled them with her fingers, each one separate, separated
from, tinkling softly as she touched them, as if she was
bringing them to life. She traced his toes. Release, that was
what the left foot symbolized. Every least detail symbolized
something.

Standing so close, she could not help but stroke back to
the bracelets, proceeding higher, up to his knee and around
the curve of his leg. Clothed in a tiger skin draped round his
loins, he wore otherwise only ornaments, bracelets, necklaces, and a sash tied around his waist, blown away from the
body as by a sharp wind so that it touched the arch of fire.
It rippled in the wind, colored now blue like the sky and
now blue like deep water and now the pale golden waves of
grass shorn by the wind.

It was not an ordinary wind. It caressed her face and then,
increasing in strength, it began to press against her like the
storm winds heralding a gale.

Lord Shiva raised up on his toes and stamped his heel
down on the back of the dwarf, the first beat, the drum, and
the sound beat on as his fingers tapped the drum contained
within his hand. Flame leapt in his palm, springing for the
arch of flame which swelled in the tearing wind to encompass the air and the hall. So brilliant it brought tears to her
eyes. He moved, the graceful turn of a hand on the wrist, the
sweep of a leg, and spun, once around, and as he turned his
gaze brushed past her, and she staggered back from the force
of that glance, like the searing touch of a beam of red fire.

Stamping his heels, he spun, his slender limbs flashing in
the air, his bracelets winking in the light of a thousand, a
million exploding suns as here on the dancing ground of the
universe the worlds were annihilated by fire. The bells rang
down the shattering of the halls of history and the world of

time, shorn by the wind that buffeted her while she yet stood her ground and watched, with terror, with a sudden blinding passionate yearning, the dance of Shiva.

The world came apart around her.

"Not yet," said Genji. "The Kali Yuga has not ended."

Ilyana was falling, standing on nothing. Terrified, she grabbed for the sash. Substance respun itself under her feet and the hall came back into being around her like threads woven into a great rug, the age of iron. There stood Genji, in her sable robes, not four paces from her. There stood the arch of flame. There stood Shiva, still now.

But he was no longer a statue.

Genji looked at Ilyana. "You are not yet old enough to tamper with the order of the universe," she said, scolding, gentle, possibly amused.

Shiva looked at Ilyana. His eyes—she met his eyes—his gaze struck her like the resounding clap of a giant bell, shuddering through her, and she threw a hand up to ward herself but she was split with blackness, shattering her.

And she woke, clapping a palm to her forehead as if following the rest of the movement to its appointed end. She had a monstrous headache.

She lay on David's cot. The room was dark, but the merest hint of dawn traced the window. Someone hissed her name.

"Yana! Ilyana! Wake up. We've got him."

No, she wanted to say. His glance will kill you. She was lying on David's cot. She'd had a dream, or been in nesh. She struggled to get up, to roll off the couch.

Almost cried out loud. Tangled in and around her legs and waist was Shiva's sash. Blue and deeper blue and gold. A wave of light-headedness swept her, so steep that she knew she was going to faint.

But she didn't.

"Ilyana!" The whisper came again, more insistently, and the curtain stirred.

She clawed at the sash, bundling the fabric, as fine as spider's silk, up into a ball and sticking it into the waistband of her skirt, hiding it. Staggered to her feet in time to fall forward into David, who came through the curtain and caught her and set her back on her feet again.

"Come," he said in a low voice, evidently thinking she had just woken up.

I have just woken up, she said to herself, not sure whether she was speaking aloud, but he did not tell her to be quiet. He took her by one hand and tugged her outside, where they stood within the dim arch of the corridor and peered out into the courtyard. A frail figure knelt before the latticework within the gazebo. From this distance it was hard to make out details of his appearance, just that his clothes hung strangely on him, too loose.

She found her voice. "Did he just get here?"

"No. We decided it would be easier to get him into nesh and then—"

Ilyana winced and a sound of protest escaped her.

"I know, I know. I went in after him over an hour ago, but I couldn't find him."

"I could have told you that!"

"Shhh."

"Why bother! Valentin can't hear us where he is."

"No, but it's getting late, and other people—"

Other people. She had forgotten about other people. She had forgotten about everything. If she closed her eyes the whirling flash of the dance raged against the darkness, the nimbus of his hair swirling out like a crown that stretched in ribbons into space, his beautiful limbs like strokes of lightning splintering the universe.

She opened her eyes. All remained as it was, the thin figure entwined with the latticework, David's steady breathing beside her, the slow bleeding of light into the night air, presaging dawn. Someone moved back by the gateway, and then another person scuttled down the corridor toward the toilets. Water splashed softly in the cistern.

"Why, look," said a young woman's voice. "There's Valentin!"

"Oh, hell," said David in an undertone.

A shadow detached itself from the gazebo—Hyacinth— and moved to stand protectively between Valentin and the betraying voice. Light rose. Valentin's face was filthy, his hair was matted, and one of his sleeves was torn. His head lolled back, and he wore on his face the same half smile poised within serene majesty, like a mockery of Lord Shiva, like an echo. Fear seized Ilyana's heart, fear for Valentin. Fear propelled her forward just as three more of the actors came out of the bathroom and stopped to gawk, just as a single figure strode purposefully in through the gateway from outside.

He was furious. He hated bad reviews. He hated looking bad, especially in front of an audience. She knew him. She knew exactly what he would do.

"Father! Don't!" she cried, but it was too late.

Vasil shoved Hyacinth away and grabbed Valentin by the shoulders and pulled. Valentin's fingers had a death grip on the lattice. The whole structure swayed, but Valentin did not let go. Could not, because he wasn't truly with his body, but Ilyana knew that her father did not understand nesh.

Instead, Vasil got a look of stark fury on his face and yanked with his full strength. With a wrenching snap that echoed like thunder resounding in the sky above, the lattice broke off by Valentin's knees. Sparks flew up and vanished in a spray of brilliant light into empty air.

Looking stunned, Vasil let go of his son. Eyes still shut, Valentin sagged down onto the tiled ground, fingers still clutching the sundered latticework. Then he began to twitch violently, and within an instant was in the throes of a full-fledged seizure. Ilyana and David reached him at the same time, and David held him down, getting kicked several times for his pains, while Ilyana pried his fingers off the lattice one by one. When the last one came free, scraped down to blood, Valentin ceased moving and just lay there, limp, like one dead.

"Oh, gods," cried Ilyana, looking up at her father, glorious in the rising sun. "You've killed him."

CHAPTER THIRTY-SIX

The Code of Law

For six days they were left alone in the tower chamber. Food was brought to them—a pittance, bread and water—and once a day a servant took the chamber pot away and emptied it. Another servant brought wood up, just enough, if rationed properly, to get them through the day and evening. More than once the guards suggested to Jaelle what she might do with them to get a few scraps of meat or vegetables for herself; to her surprise, she refused. She was not sure why, only that it had something to do with the way Princess Katerina shared out the portion equally and ate her bread as if it were a feast.

Katerina wove, taught Jaelle to play khot, and in her turn learned the Yos language from Jaelle. She read the book of travels twice (it took Jaelle an entire afternoon to puzzle out five pages), and brooded over *The Recitation,* listening with the obsessed interest of a person who would go mad without something to focus on to Jaelle's scathing denunciations of the apostasy of the northern church.

"Their copy of *The Recitation* does not include the 'Gospel of Elia,' or the 'Testimonies of the House of Narsene.' "

"What is the house of *nar seen?*" Katerina asked.

"A merchant house with whom the Peregrina—the Pilgrim—traveled while she was searching for her brother. In those days whole families would move together along the trade routes, and one such house sheltered the Pilgrim. Their testimonies of her miraculous gifts were bound by the law of the anointed church into *The Recitation.*"

"Then why aren't they in this copy?"

"Because the northerners are heretics." Jaelle was getting tired of repeating herself. Princess Katerina could read like a scholar, play castles like a man, and learn languages with the skill of a merchant bred to the caravan routes, but she could not understand the simplest explanation of heresy and the apostasy of the northern church when it sundered itself from the true and anointed faith of the southern church. "They may call themselves the true church, but they speak with the Accursed One's mouth."

"Who is the accursed one again? Oh, yes, the older brother. 'Fathered by an unholy man.' But they came of the same mother, so I cannot see why they should be treated differently."

Katerina sat on the window bench, as she often did, as close as possible to light and air, a stone's width from freedom. The bruises on her face had mostly faded, and once her shock had faded she had stored her anger neatly away inside herself, as the caravan women learned to do when they were cheated of their pay or forced by a soldier. But she still paced the circumference of the chamber many times each day, and the pattern emerging on her loom was a pleasant blue and green mat shot through with sharp red bolts of lightning.

"Because Hristain and the Pilgrim were the children of God, not of a man. The Accursed One's father was merely a man, or even, some say, the Evil One himself, taking a man's form."

"I am also a child of the gods. But I cannot fly up to the heavens as your Hristain did, nor can I turn water into milk or sew a sundered body into a living one."

"But God did not pour His essence into you."

"But if God poured his essence into some body, then that body would be God, would it not? Not a true person anymore."

"No, no. Hristain is both God and man."

"How can one person be two things?"

"It is the mystery of two natures in one substance."

Katerina giggled.

"It isn't right to mock God's holiest mysteries! Whole churches have been excommunicated for less."

"I beg your pardon." But Katerina didn't look sorry, and Jaelle abruptly realized that the other woman was teasing her. "What does it mean, *ex communicated?*"

They both heard the guards come to attention below. Katerina leapt up from the window bench and ran to the arrow loop that overlooked the outside stairway, but she could not see the landing from there. Jaelle knew that well enough, having tried herself many times before. After a bit, a guard opened the door into the chamber, and Lady Jadranka entered. Three servants followed her, laden with wood, bags of yarn, a fur-trimmed cloak and several gowns, and a tray of meat and cheese and bread, and a jug of wine. The lady looked somewhat embarrassed.

"I beg your pardon for neglecting you, Lady Katherine."

Katerina politely inclined her head. "I give you greetings, Lady Jadranka. I hope you will let me compliment you on your fine translation of the book of travels."

Lady Jadranka allowed herself a smile. "But if you have not read the original, Lady Katherine, then how can you know that the translation was fine? I might have written anything."

"If you had chosen to write anything, then you might as well have written a book of travels under your own hand, would you not?"

Lady Jadranka covered her mouth for a moment, hiding a second smile. "It would be unseemly for a woman to advertise herself in such a coarse fashion, unless she were a holy woman writing of God's words to other nuns."

"But surely Sister Casiara of the Jedan Cloister is well known for her legal tracts and her letters on philosophy."

"I have only heard her name, never, of course, read anything she is purported to have written. She is from the south. The false words of the southern church have given churchwomen there an unbecoming immodesty in their learning."

"No more immodest than khaja men. I am sorry to have to tell you so, Lady Jadranka, since you offered me sanctuary, but your son raped me."

Lady Jadranka went very still. She signed to the servants, who surely could not understand Taor, and they set down their burdens and swiftly left the chamber.

"You need not tell me what my son has wrought, Lady Katherine, in his haste to satisfy himself. But he is a man, and men will have their way."

"Have their way!" Katerina looked like she had been slapped. "How can you say so?"

"Seven days ago, my son came late to my chamber. He was bruised and battered, and he sat at my table from Resting to Midnight writing down a list of properties and other holdings to be passed on to any sons you might bear by him. Then, when he had finished and his lip began to bleed again, he tore it up and burned it. He left then, and said nothing more of it, but I have lived too many years not to understand what was going on. By dint of his own ambition and a bit of help from my own sources of news along the trade routes, he is now married to the greatest heiress in the northern kingdoms. Yet his thoughts tend only to you. What he is offering you is a greater portion than any daughter of mine will ever see. What must you have to grant him peace of mind?"

Katerina marched over to the bed and yanked down the coverlet. "He *forced* me to lie with him. In this very bed."

"He would not have had to force you if you had not resisted. It is foolish for a woman to fight against what she cannot change. You are his prisoner."

"I am still a woman! This would never have happened among my people."

"Certainly the shame of you, if they heard of it—"

"I have nothing to be ashamed of!"

"Perhaps a princess of your royal line is not accustomed to being a concubine. I can understand your displeasure, but he is already married, and was betrothed to Princess Rusudani many years ago when she was simply another young princess to be betrothed away from her family. No one suspected then that she would become so important."

"He is welcome to be married to Princess Rusudani. I want satisfaction for his crime." Katerina was so angry that she was shaking.

"My dear girl." Lady Jadranka walked over to Katerina and drew her to the window bench, helping her sit down. Her tone was solicitous. "My poor child. You don't understand, barbarian that you are. He committed no crime against you."

Katerina's chin began to quiver. Surprisingly, she did not let go of Lady Jadranka's hands. "Do you mean that you khaja do not account it a crime when a man forces a woman? Aunt Tess told me so, but I didn't believe her."

The older woman sighed, heartfelt. "Yes, some men are punished for rape, if the act has violated the code of law. But my son took you in war. Therefore you belong to him, to ransom or to sell as a slave or to take to his bed, as he wills."

"I belong to no one but myself and my mother's tribe," Katerina retorted, but she burst into tears. Lady Jadranka soothed her, and after a bit looked up at Jaelle and signed, and Jaelle hastily poured a cup of wine and took it over to them. Katerina gulped down the wine.

"When I was wed to the king of Dushan," said Lady Jadranka, "I was as good as sold to him, my father gaining the honor of his only child elevated to such a high position and the king gaining access to my father's riches. I never liked my husband. I never cared for his attentions in the marriage chamber, but I endured them, and in return for my forbearance was rewarded with a son."

"You had no daughters?" Katerina asked quietly.

"Yes, but they are all married and gone away from me, now. In truth, when the king set me aside in favor of a princess, I was not displeased. My inheritance was safe in my son's hands. It was only Janos who took offense to his father's action, and it is true that it lowered his position at court. But he need not think of that now. Nor should you. It will not be, perhaps, the position you expected, but many would envy you."

Katerina stubbornly did not answer.

Lady Jadranka sighed, as any woman worn down by the trials of the world would sigh at a young woman's intransigence. "In truth, Lady Katherine, my son is still angry at your treatment of him. It was he who ordered that you be fed on bread and water, and be confined, to see no one."

"Then why are you here now?" Katerina asked, not without hope.

"My son has ridden out to his hunting lodge with a number of his retainers, leaving me and Princess Rusudani alone with our attendants and servants. The princess will not go against his wishes, of course, but I thought I might come up and relieve your solitude each day, bring you better food, more yarn, such things."

"Books," said Katerina instantly.

Lady Jadranka nodded approvingly. "If that is what you wish. But I can only intercede for as long as my son is gone, and that will only be for a ten-night. I hope you will be more inclined to listen to his suit when he returns."

"I will not be his mistress, his concubine, his whore, none of those khaja things. I am a jaran woman. I am not a slave to any man."

Lady Jadranka smiled wryly. "I hope you will let me be your friend, Lady Katherine. I fear that you need one here."

Jaelle desperately wanted to ask Lady Jadranka why she

was courting Katerina so assiduously, but of course she dared not. Perhaps it was only concern for Janos, that he might not be torn in two between his wife, the brilliant heiress, and the woman he was infatuated with. Any mother would do as much, and more, especially for her only son. Especially for a son who was married to a woman with a strong claim to the throne of a great kingdom. But Jaelle did not know enough of the nobility to be able to judge whether Lady Jadranka acted only out of ruthless ambition or out of a truly solicitous nature.

The prospect of riding again thrilled Vasha so much that at first he didn't really mind leaving the rest behind. But when they stopped at twilight to feast in a tent set up by servants, he felt the lack of Stefan, and he wondered how his father fared. Prince Janos seated Vasha in the place of honor, at his right side. A cousin of some kind sat on his left, and to Vasha's right sat another of the young noblemen in Janos's train, a shock-haired, hearty fellow who spoke not a word of Taor and, in the end, laughed a great deal and drank so heavily that he had to be carried off to his bed.

Vasha drank sparingly, and so was able to walk outside beside Janos without aid after the feast was over and most of the men hauled away to sleep off their excesses. Vasha thought, approvingly, that Janos was not a man to indulge himself in excesses. Rather like Bakhtiian.

It was an odd thought, strange as it passed through his mind, and that thought together with the slap of the night air and the scudding gloom of clouds that hunkered down over the torch-lit clearing ripped away any lingering unsteadiness from his mind. It had often been said, in Vasha's hearing, that Bakhtiian's only excesses were the intoxicating vision sent him at an early age, that of the united jaran tribes who were fated to conquer the khaja lands, and the perhaps unbecomingly vehement passion he displayed toward his wife. Was Janos in love with Rusudani? Vasha glanced at the other man, his profile limned by flickering torchlight. He had seen no sign of it, watching the two of them together in the solar while he and Janos played castles. Janos showed a proprietary interest in his wife and seemed to appreciate her beauty, but never anything more. Perhaps Janos was just better than Ilya at concealing his emotions.

What was Ilya doing now? Pacing, no doubt, or reading

for the ladies' amusement, caught within walls of stone. But attending on the women was probably the part of his captivity that chafed him least. Canvas rippled in the wind that was coming up, and the thin flap of a banner teased Vasha's ears, like the echo of the jaran camp, so far away, lost to him.

"Come sit with me," said Janos. He walked away through the grass to another tent, small and round. Servants swept the entrance flap aside so that he could enter without breaking stride. Vasha blinked away the brightness. Six lanterns blazed, hanging from the cross-poles. Janos seated himself at a table and a steward brought him a cup of mulled wine while a second servant pulled a chair forward for Vasha and offered him wine as well. Vasha cupped the warm mug in his hands, breathing in the spicy scent, but he did not drink. He watched Janos.

The prince flipped impatiently through a stack of documents. He separated six out and handed them to the steward. "These go to Lord Belos." He pushed three more to the bottom of the pile, pressed his signet ring in a tray of wax brought to him by the steward and sealed four others, and, last, set the remaining two documents side by side on the table and stared at them.

"Did you like your father, Prince Vasil'ii?" Janos asked without looking up from the documents.

"*Like* him?" The question surprised Vasha into taking a drink of the wine.

"You have shown remarkable tolerance toward me, considering that I am the man who killed him. So I wonder if there is a reason for that, some old enmity between you."

Vasha shook his head, not willing to trust his voice.

"Then you are polite to me only because you are my hostage? What is the custom, among your people, when one man kills another?"

"It depends. In my grandmother's time, if it was purely a matter between two men, then a man's kinsmen would avenge him. If the matter extended to the camp, then it would be taken before the etsanas—the headwomen—of the tribe, and the council of elders. There might be a fine, or in a particularly bad case a kinsman of the murdered man might be allowed to take on a vendetta. Now there is the *Yarsos,* the Code of Law, written down in a book."

"What does it say?"

"It would depend on whether the killing occurred in time of war or time of peace. Whether it was a jaran man or a khaja man who was killed."

"Then a jaran man, in time of war."

Vasha set the cup down on the table, carefully steadying it so that it would not tip and spill on the documents. He had copied enough of them, under Tess's supervision, and knew how laborious a process it was to write one out. "Prince Janos, it does not matter what the Code of Law says. This matter lies outside the Yarsos. Bakhtiian's death will be avenged by the jaran army."

"Even if that army was controlled by a man who was willing to count himself my ally? War is a hard business, Prince Vasil'ii, and if we avenged every death brought about by war, we should have no more men left to fight."

Vasha considered the khaja prince for awhile in silence. Janos, seeing that he was lost in thought, went back to studying the two documents. How would he feel about Prince Janos if Janos truly had killed Bakhtiian? How would he feel about the man who had murdered his father? But Janos had not killed him. Janos had fallen for the ruse. So what use was it to speculate on what had not happened, except to uselessly tangle his ability to think clearly? Because Janos was offering him something, and Vasha needed to know what it was, and now, of all times, not to make any stupid mistakes.

"War will come to you nevertheless, Prince Janos. Andrei Sakhalin cannot protect you from that, nor will he ever control the jaran army, and if he gave you such assurances, then he lied to you."

Janos shrugged. "White Tower withstood two sieges in my grandfather's time, and its defenses are stronger now than they were then. Dushan itself is at peace with the jaran, in return for peace. I possess two valuable hostages. I hold an alliance with a jaran prince from the greatest of the jaran tribes, by your own admission, even if you say his position is not as strong as he claims it is." He tapped the right hand document. "My wife is the granddaughter of the Mircassian king."

"This is all true, but why tell me? I am only your prisoner."

"I have here letters brought by two envoys. These two envoys are here in this camp, waiting to address me. One is from Prince Basil of Filis, sent to my father, the king of Dushan. My men intercepted him on his way north."

"That is a dangerous game, Prince Janos."

Janos fingered one corner of the right hand document. "But I have information my father does not possess. This letter comes from King Barsauma of Mircassia. His envoy has traveled many leagues, first to Tarsina-Kars, then to the convent of the Holy Knife, in the Kolosvari Hills, and thence, by other routes, here to me. King Barsauma is old, his health failing. It is never wise for a king to die without designating his heir, or else the church and the lords will tear the kingdom asunder in order to grab more for themselves. His wife bore him six children, four boys and two girls. With the unexpected death last spring of his eldest son, all of them are now dead, just as poor Rusudani's three brothers have now all died, before their time, during the ten years she was shut away in the convent. She has two younger brothers and a younger sister, of course, but they are by her father's second wife, the one he took after her mother died. So that means, of all the claimants for the Mircassian throne, only two have any solid claim. One is an invalid, a boy not more than twelve years old, the youngest child of the king's deceased brother by a vicious woman whom all say the king cannot abide. The other is King Barsauma's last living grandchild, who is now my wife."

Janos lifted a hand, and the servant poured more wine into his cup. Vasha self-consciously took a sip of his own wine, which was cold and flat; the spice had lost its flavor with the heat. Another man brought a new lantern in and replaced one whose wick was sputtering.

"King Barsauma seeks Princess Rusudani. He wants her to travel to Mircassia to be invested as his heir and to make a proper marriage. He does not, of course, know that I have already married her. Prince Basil of Filis has thrown his support behind the invalid child. He writes of this to my father, whom he supposes may aid him."

Suddenly, Janos drained his cup in one gulp and set it down, hard, on the table. He looked troubled. As well he might.

"Why tell me this?" Vasha repeated.

"You owe allegiance to neither side. Therefore, your counsel on this matter might be unimpeded by the prospect of personal gain."

"But that isn't true. I am part of the jaran army."

"What did you learn from your father? Enough to judge the strength of a position, if you had a good look at it?"

"Perhaps."

"Then judge the strength of my position, Prince Vasil'ii."

Vasha revised his estimate of Janos's condition. The prince *was* drunk, not sloppily, not overbearingly, but touched enough by the drink to confide in a man whom he knew to be his enemy, if only because he did not truly know if he could trust his allies. What worth an enemy's counsel? What was it worth risking to attempt to convince an enemy to become an ally?

"Yet you still lack something. You want something from me, Prince Janos."

Janos smiled, somewhat ironically, and Vasha knew he had spoken the truth. "I want an alliance with the Prince of Jeds."

"She will never give you one," said Vasha instantly, knowing full well how *Tess* would feel about the man who had supposedly killed her husband. Except he hadn't. Tess was pragmatic. If Vasha could make sure that Ilya was restored to her, if he could convince her that Janos would make a strong ally, because he *would* make a valuable ally. Vasha felt that he understood Janos, casting here for a way to further his ambitions, as any prince would, given the opportunity. As Vasha was, seeking to improve his own place . . . and not just, perhaps, with his captor.

It would make sense for the jaran to ally with Janos.

At that moment, watching Janos's sharp, intelligent face in the bright glare of the lanterns and the slow stir of the tent wall behind him in the rising wind, Vasha knew that *Ilya* would never forgive Janos. That Ilya himself would remain the greatest obstacle to an alliance with Janos. And it was a good alliance. It was a brilliant alliance. No need for the jaran army to expend itself on Mircassia if it was a friendly kingdom. With the proper treaties, the army could pass through the fringe of the kingdom and drive straight into Filis while the Jedan army, led jointly by the young Baron Santer and his sister's husband Georgi Raevsky, hit the Filistian princedom from the rear. Crushed by these pincers, virtually the whole of the north from Jeds to the northern plains would be under the control of the jaran.

The thought of an empire of such immense size took

Vasha's breath away. He could see it in his mind, the map
they all learned so well from the great copy nailed to a
wooden board propped up by steadying legs, under the awning that served as the school for the children of the
Orzhekov tribe. It was the empire of his father's vision, so
vast that even a messenger riding at breakneck speed, not
that any man could endure such a pace for more than ten
days, would take sixty days to traverse it.

And accomplished, here at the end, without the threat of
the powerful Mircassian kingdom, against which the jaran
army might, conceivably, break its strength. Even an army
as mighty as the jaran could stretch itself too thin. As the
empire grew, the wisest course was the one that Ilya himself
was slowly cobbling together: client kingdoms and marriage
alliances balanced against outright conquest. He had married
into such an alliance himself, even if he might try to deny,
now and again, the reasons behind his marriage. However
madly in love his father might have been with Tess, twelve
years past, he would never have married her if she hadn't
been the sister of the Prince of Jeds.

Then, with a chill, Vasha recalled his father pacing round
the tower chamber, muttering under his breath. Perhaps he
would have. Perhaps Ilya was not quite as pragmatic as
Vasha always assumed he was.

Ilya would never make an alliance with the man who had
taken him captive and killed half his guard. Never. Not even
if it meant sparing his army a brutal campaign against a
powerful adversary. *He would not do it.*

So it was up to his son to do it in his place.

Because Vasha knew, with that same instinct that told him
when he had placed a pebble correctly on the khot grid, that
this was the right choice to make.

"The jaran would rather greet Mircassia as our friend than
as our enemy, Prince Janos," he said, and by so doing, made
the first move in a new and more complicated game.

CHAPTER THIRTY-SEVEN

The Lake of Mirrors

They sat docked at Crossover Station, taking in their last consignment of human-made goods and foods, as well as five casks of Bass Ale, enough for the long haul to Chapal and back. Beyond Crossover Station lay the mysterious reaches of Chapalii space.

"And while it's true," Branwen was explaining over a supper of what Benjamin, the quartermaster, called "stir-fry," "that all known space is Chapalii space, or at least controlled by their empire, still we mark the boundaries of League space because it's familiar space, it's our space, human space."

Just as, Anatoly thought, the plains would always be the true home of the jaran no matter how far their empire extended.

"Past Crossover," she added, "as the old joke goes, you're skating on pretty thin ice." Anatoly shook his head, not understanding the analogy. "I guess that wouldn't make any sense to you," she said with a smile, thoughtfully, without the self-satisfied air of superiority so many people in the League used when explaining things to Anatoly. "We League humans have been sunk in the same cultural milieu for such a long time now, over a century, that we forget what it's like to have people come in who don't have the same markers. In the old days, even the tribe just over the hill might be wholly alien. Maybe we've lost a little of our ability to adapt to that."

"But surely you must adapt to the alien, if there are so many zayinu—so many *aliens*—in the universe."

"Not as many as you might expect."

"Or more than you'd expect," interposed Summer Hennessy, the big pilot. "If you take into account the probability of a solar system forming around a star, and a planet

falling into an orbit that is within the zone of life, and life
itself arising, and intelligent life—"

"Define intelligence," snapped Rachelle, the other pilot,
the testy one.

"—and all of that coincidentally happening within the
same time frame as human life developed," finished Summer, ignoring Rachelle's comment. "It's more likely civilizations, alien, intelligent, or otherwise, would be separated by
gulfs of time as well as space."

"Begging your pardon," said Anatoly politely, not wanting to seem as if he was interrupting the other woman,
"Captain, but then do I understand you to mean that within
League space you have a variety of routes on which you can
travel, but once beyond this station, you must follow the old
trade routes laid out by the Chapalii?"

"Exactly. I don't know how much you know about how
we actually travel in space, and how we navigate. . . ?"
Branwen kindly trailed off to leave room for him to stop her.

He just shook his head. He had traveled with the *Gray
Raven* and its crew for seven days now, and he had quickly
felt comfortable with being ignorant. Especially after the
third day, when they had had a free-for-all fencing match in
the passageways and he had not only won handily but been
feted with great good nature afterward by the others. He had
actually gotten rather drunk. The crew of the *Gray Raven*
were good people to get drunk with, like his old comrades
back in the army; he had never felt comfortable getting
drunk with the actors.

"Stop me if I start lecturing," said Branwen with a grin.

"Yes, do please stop her," said Rachelle, but she always
said things like that, and Anatoly was learning not to take
her comments seriously.

"But I'll try to make this short. I'm not sure what's going
to happen to you, Anatoly, but I've always preferred to, ah,
scout out my ground in advance, so to speak." She half
turned in her seat to face the one wall in the galley that was
not wood-paneled. "Screen, pull out a hologram. Display
standard singularity simulation. If you take a stream of photons, the particles which make up light, they'll move through
space at the speed of light and continue in the same direction
unless some force causes them to change direction. Before
we met the Chapalii, we traveled in ships that could approach but never attain the speed of light, so obviously

travel time between the stars was glacial and feasible only in the time frame of years and generations. But the Chapalli gave us relay stations."

In the three-dimensional image that seemed to extend from the wall, a stream of particles which Anatoly supposed represented a stream of photons struck a round object and shot away at a different angle.

"These relay stations create 'windows' which are singularities in the time-space continuum. The navigator—that's me—in concert with coordinates given out by the relay station, describes a velocity and an angle at which the ship enters the singularity. That's our vector; that's why it's called a vector drive. It's like entering a gravity well, which throws us to a second singularity, which has been determined by the vector at which we entered the first one. So you could enter the first window and come out in two different places depending on your vector."

"Or you could enter a window with an innocent vector and end up never coming out," added Rachelle cheerfully.

"So you must scout out these routes . . ." Anatoly hesitated. "How can you scout them, if you must know beforehand where you are going? It isn't like trying a path up into the mountains and turning back if it ends in the heights, or riding out into a desert until half your water flasks are empty, and then returning to the last oasis to try a new route."

"The truth is, we're dependent on the Chapalii for that. Or at least outside of League space. Inside League space we believe we have recorded most of the routes through space, and there do seem to be a limited number, not an infinite one. Obviously, if you have a finite number of relay stations, and not all link each to the other, there would be a finite number of routes between them. But in Chapalii space proper, we have to accept the route that is chosen for us by whatever passes for their navigational staff. For instance, the run to Paladia Minor and Major and thus to Chapal: We call it the Mirror Road because on the second jump we pass through a system where there's a mirror array in orbit, reflecting the binary star. Of course we don't know what it's for, but it's a brilliant landmark. Only this ship and two others have ever been allowed to run all the way in to the Paladias, and that is the only route we're allowed to take. We know there must be other ways to get there, since we have records from Sojourner King Bakundi and her husband, who are on the Keinaba merchant flagship, but she's got no access to navigation. She can only look out the viewports, and there aren't many of those on Chapalii ships apparently. There are a few other humans apprenticed on Keinaba ships, but only the flagship seems to go in to the Paladias."

She paused. Benjamin was still eating, spearing broccoli with neat stabs, and Florien was on comm duty on the bridge. Moshe sat with chin propped on hands staring dreamily at the opposite wall, as if he could read a secret message in the swirling wood grain.

"I don't truly understand what this means, a *singularity*. Is this something that exists already? Or is it created?"

"In the early days of expansion, after humans met the Chapalii and before the Chapalii coopted the League into their Empire, there was a great deal of debate on that very point. As soon as the League was subsumed in the empire, though, the Protocol Office put an end to public debate."

"They said it was 'unseemly,' " said Rachelle sarcastically.

"Which means the debate goes on in private," added Branwen. "Which means there's no consensus yet. Do the relay stations create the singularities? Can technology do something that massive?"

"It can't only if we suppose that technology is limited to what we understand of it," interposed Summer.

"Or are the relay stations just set up to take advantage of singularities that already exist, that have been mapped? If that's the case, are there singularities out there that the Chapalii might not have mapped which we can use, to get around them? Because they control the shipping routes, with the proverbial iron hand. Well, it's not something that any of us but Florien sit up nights worrying about."

"Oh, I do," said Benjamin, a forkful of sautéed onions poised just beyond his lips. "If I could figure it out, I'd be rich."

Rachelle snorted.

"So have you scouted no other routes in Chapalii space?" Anatoly asked.

"We *can't*," replied Branwen. "We'd certainly like to. I don't know how much you know of the history of the League and the Chapalii, but until the elevation of Charles Soerensen to the dukedom, no humans had been allowed to pass beyond the boundaries of League space at all. He was the first human to set foot on Chapal, when he went to be invested before the emperor."

"Actually everyone thought he was being taken there to be executed, after he led the failed rebellion against the Empire," said Rachelle. "Imagine the surprise when he returned as a duke."

Anatoly tried to imagine this, but could not. In fact, a wise ruler knows that it is not enough just to conquer and kill; those conquered—the right ones, chosen carefully—must be given a stake in the Empire so that it becomes in their interest to help maintain the peace. That had been part of Bakhtiian's strategy all along.

Florien's voice leapt out of the console embedded in the center of the table. "We have clearance to cross over. Window at oh nine forty."

"Shit!" swore Rachelle. "That's in only thirty minutes and I wanted to take a shower." She jumped up and raced out of the room.

"She'll take one anyway," groused Benjamin. "We can't be leaving already. There's a consignment of flower rubies I've been bargaining for down at Viery Market. They'll be gone by the time we get back."

Branwen had already stood and was efficiently clearing her utensils and plate away, stowing them in the sonic cleaner. "Summer, get the hatch cleared. Benjamin, you're going to have to do a quick run around the ship and make sure everything is batted down. Moshe—"

"We never got this short a notice before," said the boy, coming out of his reverie.

"Help Summer with the hatches. Anatoly, uh, probably if you'll clean up here and then come up to the bridge, that would be the best place for you."

He nodded and began stacking plates. It was not, truly, a man's job, but he had long since discovered that the khaja of League space did not have as strict a sense of order as the jaran did, knowing which duties belonged to which people, which was no doubt why the Chapalii Empire had been able to absorb them so easily. Finishing, he sealed all the cabinets closed and secured the chairs to the table, and then pulled himself up two flights of ladder to the bridge. Here, at about half gravity, all his movements felt awkward, although he had seen Branwen and Rachelle take leaps and bounds and spins when the yacht was in its brief periods of freefall that left him breathless or nauseated. The other two men, like him, seemed more bound to gravity.

Six crash seats ringed the bronze access tube that ran the length of the ship, from the prow all the way down to the engines. He strapped into the seat that faced the courtesy screen, as Rachelle called it: a big screen that gave the appearance of being a window onto the outside, although of course it was merely a projection. Rachelle, hair bound back in a complicated braid, was there before him. She sealed herself into her pilot's chair, a contraption that covered her hands, and an oversized visor curled out to cover her eyes. Branwen sat in the captain's chair, her fingers flying over a numerical keypad, mouth lifted in a half smile that Anatoly recognized as intent concentration. Other than the faint clacking of her fingers on the pad and the hollow thrum rising up the access tube like a distant heartbeat, the bridge was silent. Florien turned, saw Anatoly, and flipped the comm onto the open speakers, another courtesy which Anatoly appreciated.

"Hatches secured," said Summer over the comm. As if in response the station controller said, "You are clear to detach."

"All hands secure," said Branwen without looking away from the keypad and whatever the screen embedded in her chair's arm told her.

One by one, all hands reported in: Rachelle (sounding preoccupied), Florien, Summer, Benjamin (sounding irritated about his lost deal), and Moshe. Last, with a start, Anatoly remembered that he had to report in as well.

"Secure," he said, a little embarrassed. Branwen glanced up at him and flashed him a swift, sweet smile, reassuring, before she went back to her calculations.

"Detach commenced. Accomplished."

"Heading mark two seven eight," said Branwen. From the depths of her chair Rachelle responded with a word that sounded more like a click, or else a word in a very strange language. They continued to trade numbers as the yacht backed away from Crossover Station, banked, and headed out to the point where they would rendezvous with the window—with the *singularity,* Anatoly corrected himself. It was the one element of travel across the oceans of space that he had yet to get used to: For that instant, which was not an instant, going through the window, he had a notion that he ceased to exist or that he was somehow thrown into a different time. Sometimes he would see brief visions, a memory from his childhood or from a battle, or catch a remembered scent, the stench of a spoiled water hole or the perfume of grass, or he would feel the touch of a spear biting into his thigh or the touch of his wife brushing a finger down his chest. As he considered this mystery, the *Gray Raven* passed imperceptibly into the singularity.

Genji walks toward him down a corridor filled with light. Her robes fill the passageway with a sound like the laughter of wind through dense leaves.

He was back on the bridge, straining against the straps, broken out in a sweat. She had been watching him. He would swear to it. Only, how could she? It was impossible, of course. It was only a vision induced by the singularity. Wiping his brow, he glanced around the bridge, but neither Branwen nor Florien paid him any mind, and Rachelle, of course, was enveloped by her chair.

A rush of alien words spilled out over the comm. On the screen, Anatoly saw a distant blue-white sun and the graceful red curve of a planet and, closer, winking lights floating in a geometric pattern, marking some kind of station.

"Damn," said Florien. "The translation program hit the standard loop again. Has Benjamin been playing around with it?"

"I'll go real-time," said Branwen. "Signal me when you've got it running." She began to speak in standard Chapalii. Her pronunciation was rough, but the phrases slipped off her tongue easily enough, standard phrases that any human could learn. "This is Hao Branwen Emrys, of the *Gray Raven,* daiga class ship under the protection of the Tai-en Charles Soerensen. Request coordinates for the next vector."

The station remained silent for some time. By the time the alien controller replied, Florien had the translator fixed. The voice came out in a tinny monotone.

"Your registration notice is in order. No protocol request has been filed in advance."

"We are bound for Chapal, under the protection of the Tai-en Charles Soerensen, this journey authorized by the voice of the Tai-en Naroshi Toraokii. Sending clearance code now."

After another pause, the voice returned. "What road do you request permission to enter?"

"The Mirror Road, bound for Paladia Minor."

"No," said Anatoly suddenly. "We want the swiftest road for Chapal."

Branwen and Florien swiveled around to stare at him. Rachelle, of course, could not, but he heard her mutter something under her breath, and her neck—all that was visible of her—tensed.

"Who countermands the authority of the Tai-en Naroshi Toraokii?"

"I am Anatoly Sakhalin, prince of the Sakhalin tribe. I countermand this order. I am on my way to see the emperor, and I wish to reach him quickly."

"Merde!" said Florien. "I'm getting a flood of coordinates."

Branwen hunched down over her screen. "I've never seen any of these before. These are nothing like our usual coordinates."

"We're being given priority to go through." Florien's voice shook.

"Rachelle, are you on it?"

"I'm ready."

They traded numbers back and forth and the ship moved on, leaving the geometric pattern of lights behind as it arced around the gilded line, as round as a cupped hand, that marked the planet against the heavens.

They broke past the singularity. Anatoly smelled smoke, sharp on a winter's wind, and then it was gone.

"Fucking bloody hells," said Rachelle, her voice muffled through the visor. "I've never seen this place before."

"New stream of coordinates coming in," said Florien. "They didn't even ask for identification."

"And he does dishes, too," said Rachelle.

"All hands," announced Branwen, keying into the shipboard link, "we've got clearance to go forward. We'll take this next window, but then we're breaking to check for stress on the hull."

They took the next window and at once the Chapalii station control fed them a new set of vector coordinates. No one had the slightest idea of where they were, but Branwen set the modeller onto a search program and by the time they'd checked the ship twice and all had a sleepshift and a shower and a meal, she had found three probable locations.

"Based on the maps we have," she said to the crew, who were gathered in the galley over a breakfast of aebleskiver and fresh raspberry jam, "we're either way the hell beyond Imperial space or else sitting pretty more than halfway to Chapal."

"Ship's chart says it takes about forty Earth days to reach Paladia Minor," said Anatoly. "By the standard route."

They all looked at him. "It does," said Branwen finally. "If there are no delays, which means, where we stand in the queue and how heavy the traffic is that week, and if no other more important ship gets priority."

"Only now," said Rachelle, "we're the ones cutting to the front of the line."

"Anyway," added Branwen, giving him *that* look again, the one they were all giving him, as if he had suddenly turned zayinu in front of their eyes when they thought he had been human all along, "this is clearly not the standard route. No bets now on how long it's going to take."

"Twenty days," said Benjamin. "Bet it cuts the journey in half." There were no takers.

They reached Chapal three days later. Not the Paladias, which were, according to Branwen and to the navigation charts, the access routes into Chapal. The *only* access routes, according to what humans knew, their best intelligence gathered by Soerensen's people and the *Gray Raven* itself.

They just winked into the system within long range scanning range of Chapal, climbing at a steep rate so that their velocity altered perceptibly as they passed through into the ecliptic. Alarms went off all over the yacht. The steepness of the climb pressed Anatoly deep into the cushion of his crash seat and then, shifting hard, flung him against the straps. Bile rose in his throat, but he kept it down. The others on the bridge—that meant all of them, except for Florien down in the damping bay to keep a close watch on the engine fields—took it in stride, but they were experienced spacers.

Rachelle swore colorfully under her visor. "Cutting it close, aren't they? What is this—?"

She broke off.

No one spoke.

"Holy Tits," said Summer. "That's Chapal. No other planet's got that porcelain gleam."

"Lock these files," said Branwen in a low voice, "and save them with access only to the crew, and to Soerensen." She glanced back at Anatoly. "And Sakhalin," she added, as if on an afterthought. She looked wan.

"Do you know how much this information is *worth?*" said Benjamin on a rising arc.

"Your life," snapped Branwen. "It shouldn't be possible to get here that fast."

Hard on her comment, the comm snapped to life. Chapalii poured out, a stream of words gushing into the sudden silence on the bridge.

"Translation program isn't picking this up," said Summer. "It keeps bleeping unreadable."

"Oh, damn, it must be formal court Chapalii or something," muttered Branwen. "We're not allowed to translate that into our primitive tongue. It isn't seemly."

The words kept coming, a flood, rising.

"This is Anatoly Sakhalin," said Anatoly into the air. "Speak Anglais, which is the language I understand."

The words ceased.

Then, awkwardly, a voice—not filtered through a translation program—spoke in Anglais, vowels clipped and consonants rounded in an alien fashion.

"Prince of the Sakhalin, a transport is sent for you, most honorable."

"I've got incoming," said Summer at the tracking console. "On screen."

The ship that flowered into view was no bigger than the *Gray Raven,* according to the stats that scrolled underneath the screen: estimated volume, mass, length. She was atmosphereworthy, Anatoly was fairly sure, because of her sleek line and trim curves. Otherwise she was fairly ordinary. He unstrapped and rose, somewhat unsteadily, to his feet, but luckily no one was looking. They were all staring at the ship.

"How will I get across to her?" he asked. Three heads snapped around to look at him. Moshe continued to stare at the screen, and Rachelle was still concealed in her chair.

Branwen jumped to her feet. "I'll take you down. Summer, you've got the helm."

"Gotcha." Summer shifted to take Branwen's seat.

They left the bridge.

"I think the best bet would be to have Rachelle accompany you," said the captain. "She has the broadest experience of the world. There isn't much she hasn't seen, and despite first impressions she can keep her mouth shut at all the best times. You'll need supplies. It took Charles Soerensen days, waiting in various anterooms, to get in to see the emperor."

"He will see me at once," said Anatoly, surprised that she would say such a thing. "I will go alone. I don't want to argue over this."

Branwen stopped dead in the passageway and looked him over rather like a young woman examines a prospective lover. "Huh. You are an arrogant bastard, aren't you?" But she said it kindly, not as an insult. "Okay. I won't argue, but we only have six months' worth of supplies, so we can't wait for you forever. I assume you have the full text of xenology's precis of Chapalii customs and so on and so forth, so you don't commit any faux pas—uh, any mistakes, any bad manners."

"I was brought up under Grandmother Sakhalin's own tutelage. I trust she has taught me how to behave properly. Begging your pardon, Captain." Then he thought better of simply ignoring her advice. Like any etsana, she had experience that it behooved him to heed. "But of course it is only wise to take a few supplies, and the demimodeller with the xenology files, in my saddlebags, against necessity."

She brushed a few stray curls of hair out of her eyes. Laugh lines crinkled up around her eyes when she smiled, and he smiled back, liking her very much. "All right." She seemed about to say something else, but did not.

At his cabin, she remained discreetly outside while he collected his saddlebags, his saddle, and his saber, and she protested by not one word when he emerged from the cabin carrying them. Diana would have, of course. She was always embarrassed by these vestiges of his former life. They collected supplies and went down to the aft air lock. A dull, shuddering thud shook through the hull as the transport made contact. Anatoly hoisted the saddle onto his shoulder, made a polite farewell, and cycled through the air lock.

A thin tube snaked out on the other side, translucent, so that he almost felt that he was walking on the heavens themselves as he crossed over into the other ship. Stewards waited for him. They took his saddlebags and his saddle and led him to a suite of rooms that were notable mostly for the unsightly orange and pink frieze that circled the antechamber. He took refuge from its splendor in a tiny lounge whose walls were covered with a restful pale gold matting and fitted at one end with an observation bubble. They brought him three liquids in spun crystal cups, all of which were undrinkable, and finally he chased them out and told them to leave him alone until they reached the emperor's palace.

He watched their descent through the bubble, which was, alas, sealed over once they hit the atmosphere. But he had seen the great porcelain skin that covered fully half of the planet's surface: The fabled city of the emperor, as large as the great Earth continent of Eurasia. Bored and curious, he set his modeller on his knees and asked it for information on the Imperial city. It knew little enough: Theoretically the civilization of the Chapalii had risen out of the murk of Chapal and eventually learned how to sail the interstellar seas. They had, it was supposed, made a kind of shrine out of the holy ground of their birth, and their home planet had become their emperor's residence, his palace and his parks, that he alone controlled access to.

The transport set down so gently that Anatoly did not know they had landed until the stewards came to fetch him. He allowed them to carry his saddlebags and saddle because he guessed that they might think less of him for trying to spare them that burden, even if he wanted it for himself. But he refused to let any of them touch his saber, and he tucked the demimodeller into the pouch on his belt, sparing it from prying hands and words.

The ship stood on a riverbank, landing feet splayed out on the sandy bank. A delicate skiff bobbed on the waters, tied up to a pier constructed of spears of ashen wood so slight that he could not believe they could hold his weight. But he knew better than to hesitate. A transparent tube extruded from the ship, leading down the ramp and out to the skiff, where it bubbled out in the stern, a safe, malleable chamber molded to the shape of the boat. He walked out onto the pier, and a steward in silver livery helped him to a seat on the skiff, in the stern. Belatedly, he recalled that silver livery was the mark of the emperor. He kept his expression impassive as the transport's stewards swung his saddle and saddlebags onto the boat and the tube pinched closed around him, sealing him into an oval bubble. Another silver-clad Chapalii poled them away from the pier and they were off, caught at once in a swift current, pulled downstream.

On the horizon he saw towers, and beyond them, the pale glow of the city, bright even against the bright light of the Chapaliian sun. He reached out and touched the skin of the mobile chamber. It gave beneath his touch, cool, not sticky, molding around his fingers as he pushed outward, stretching with his thrust and shrinking back in as he withdrew his hand. It felt as innocuous as skin and as strong as silk, as tough as boiled leather.

He sat in silence for a long while. No one steered the skiff, which plunged along, barely rocking in the waters, down a deep channel. The boat seemed poured out of one mold of a translucent pink material shot through with a substrate pattern of hexagrams and five-pointed stars, light shifting through them as the vessel skimmed over the ever-changing waters. Finally, because neither of the two stewards attending him spoke, he did.

"How soon will I reach the emperor?"

Both stewards stood and bowed, a remarkable feat of balance on the moving skiff. "Most honorable and most high, this vessel approaches the Yaochalii's seat of honor. To the unmoving throne at the center of the universe you are being conveyed."

"You are the Yaochalii's attendants?"

The steward on the right flushed a deep red, which meant, Anatoly recalled, that he was pleased or flattered. "I am Cha Kato-ra, Chamberlain of Swift-Current Boats, and this is my cousin, Cha Tona-ra, Chamberlain of the Linked Circles of Breath. We are only attendants to the great park at whose center lies the lake of mirrors where sits the unmoving throne. You honor us by your notice, most high."

Cha Tona bowed in his turn. "Most honorable and most high, it is the craftsmen of my house who have been granted the privilege of crafting this—" The slightest hesitation. Cha Tona flushed blue up the line of his jaw, and then recovered himself. "—this *membrane,* whose substance will allow you to enter the presence of the emperor."

Anatoly laid a palm flat against the bubble. A sudden, uncomfortable tingling invaded his hand, as if the skin of the bubble was trying to sink into *his* skin. He jerked his hand back, startled. "Please explain this process to me," he said, wondering if the bubble somehow protected the emperor from him, like a shield covering potential enemies.

"Your anatomical construction does not allow you, most honorable Yao-en, to breathe the air on our planet. This membrane permeates your molecular structure and creates a barrier which then synthesizes from those elements you draw in the proper intake of oxygen and outflow of carbon dioxide and waste products which suffice daiga in their primitive breathing mechanisms."

"If I do not accept this, ah, membrane?"

Mortified, both lords—for in fact they were by grant of title lords and not stewards—flushed violet. "Most munificent and generous Yao-en, without this *kukiwa* you cannot appear before the emperor."

"Did the Tai-en Charles Soerensen accept one of these membranes?"

The question produced silence. Cha Tona placed one pale hand carefully on the side of the skiff, as if he was communicating with it. Off to the right, a massive mountain of obsidian breached the ivory shell to the city, its jet bulk wreathed with carnelian and jade towers, as slender as wands.

"Yao-en." Cha Tona crossed both hands on his chest and inclined his body in a one-quarter bow. "The Tai-en Charles Soerensen did not appear before the emperor."

"Yes, he did."

"I beg a thousand pardons for disputing your words, most honorable, most exalted. The Emperor appeared before the Tai-en Charles Soerensen in the Hall of Dukes, as is the Yaochalii's custom, but it is not his exalted flesh which appears there, but only his form."

Anatoly digested this news in silence as they skimmed onward. Waves spilled once over the prow as they took a sharp dip through a flurry of rapids, and were then sucked away through the boat to vanish, leaving not one drop of water behind. Charles Soerensen thought he had seen the emperor, and he had, in a way, but only an image of him, like a nesh image, Anatoly supposed. But not even Charles Soerensen had met the emperor *in the flesh,* as the actors always liked to say.

"I accept the membrane," said Anatoly.

No sooner had the words left his mouth than the bubble shrank around him, shrank until it hugged him and shrank further, dissolving through his clothes until he felt it like fire along his skin and stretching in through his lips and nostrils and ears and eyes to invade his whole body.

At that instant he realized he had fallen into a trap. He took in a breath, to lunge, to draw his saber and at least take them with him, but he could not breathe nor could he move, as if the dissolution of the membrane into his skin had paralyzed him. Why had he trusted them so blithely? Why had he believed that the name of Sakhalin would protect him wherever he went? What an arrogant, stupid fool.

He sagged forward, caught himself with his hands on his knees, and pushed up to sit, panting. Water flashed under the light of twin suns; he hadn't noticed the other one before. The bubble had shadowed it. One of the suns was a great, glaring thing, angry and red; the other was small, hot, and bright, with the blue trembling of flame inside it. He sat in the open air, the breeze on his face and the bitter tang of alien water on his lips, spray from the river. The two lords sat in pale splendor, each with his hands in his lap, fingers folded together in complicated patterns that reminded Anatoly all at once of the complicated braid in Rachelle's hair, made beautiful because of its suggestion of layers and sweep.

And he knew that he was the first human ever to sit and breathe unaided—except not unaided—in the air of Chapal, with the great palace defining the horizon on his right and an endless park of pink and white flowers to his left.

The river dipped, sinking beneath them, only it wasn't sinking, it was rolling on along the level ground. The skiff was sinking on an impossible strip of water that seemed to be tunneling into the river itself, as if they were contained in another, invisible bubble. The river rose around them on all sides and they raced into it, underneath it, swallowed in a darkness that roared with the tumult of waters. He felt that slight touch, like the delicate brush of a hand, that usually signaled the passage into a window.

Farther back along the tunnel, receding endlessly into the distance, stands Genji, observing him still.

The blackness sluiced away like water pouring off a duck's back and they came out of the tunnel into an eerie grotto. Anatoly pinched himself to see if he was awake. They could not have gone through a window, not *on* a planet. He was obviously hallucinating. Perhaps it was an aftereffect of his intermingling with the membrane. Only an idiot would think that such a procedure could occur without strange side effects coming after it.

The grotto lightened. They passed out under a glowing arch strung with glittering orreries onto a sunlit lake strewn with petals of gold. The light was blinding, like a thousand mirrors turned to reflect the suns.

Anatoly shaded his eyes, which helped enough that he soon discerned that the lake was vast and probably square. The shoreline rode like a thin boundary of white on the still expanse of shimmering gold. In the center rose an island, and toward this island the skiff flew, skimming over the surface of the lake without touching the surface of the water or the curling leaves of the golden petals. *It's this lake,* he thought, craning around to look behind himself, *that Naroshi's garden was set out to imitate.*

The island rose, and rose, as they neared, a shore of gleaming white pebbles bounded by an ebony wall. Enclosed by the wall stood a marble ziggurat, squares piled upon squares, receding toward a distant peak, the even line of the ascending ziggurat severed by a wide staircase as bright as diamond. The skiff slowed and coasted to a halt where a staircase that seemed to be carved out of a single piece of ivory marched into the water, receding into the depths until, farther out, its descent was shaded by petals. Anatoly wondered, wildly and at random, if there was a second ziggurat mirroring the first, thrusting down deep into the earth.

Two Chapalii in silver livery came down the steps. Lord Kato and Lord Tona stood at once and bowed to them, but the two new lords bowed in their turn to Anatoly, by which he deduced they must be dukes in the service of the emperor. To his surprise, they took his saddlebags and saddle, and when he jumped out of the skiff and began to climb the stairs, they flanked him, one on each side, bearing his worldly goods on their shoulders.

It was a long climb.

Anatoly paced himself, taking it slowly and allowing himself a pause every one hundred steps to take in the changing view. But the higher he went the more winded he got, so he mostly got the impression of a vast blinding lake surrounded by a luminous gray mist, like fog creeping in. Yet even as high as he climbed, knowing that each successive platform was smaller, when he reached the top he halted on the edge of a broad square field. Glancing back, he saw the dukes standing about one hundred steps down, waiting. Below them, a wispy strip of cloud draped the ziggurat. He did not remember climbing through it.

"Come forward," said a voice in Chapalli. Unlike all other Chapalii voices, except perhaps that of Genji, it hinted at emotion, curiosity, perhaps, or something unfathomable, in-human.

Obediently, he walked forward. This field, perhaps one hundred meters square, was as black as the void of space except for the glowing lines that crossed back and forth in a giant grid. It reminded him of a huge khot board. In the center sat a slab of jet-black stone, like an outgrowth of vacuum, only it was not a standing stone but a throne. He kept to one of the glowing lines, feeling superstitious, and as he walked he passed near a three-dimensional model of a hydrogen atom, hovering about a meter above an intersection of lines. It shimmered as he passed, spitting sparks at him. He walked on, turned a right angle, and a second, and came to a halt.

It took him a long moment to find his voice.

"Yaochalii," he said at last in his mangled accent, but he knew enough formal Chapalii, he hoped, to get by. He bowed, slightly, inclining his body at the waist just enough to show that he respected the person who sat on the throne but not that he considered himself in any meaningful way lower than him. Lifting his head, he stared.

The emperor was old. Unlike Genji, whose skin had a pearlescent hue, the emperor's skin seemed so pale, so thin, that Anatoly almost thought he could read the shape and flow of his internal organs as through a fine parchment gleaming with the faint oils of a scribe's fingers. Elaborate carvings decorated the throne, towers and orreries and molecular structures entwined by an endless looping, spiraling vine. Carved out of the ebony substance of the throne itself, they stood in relief as distinctly as if they been painted white in contrast. The air around them was as still as glass: If it moved at all, he could not perceive it.

"Welcome to the game of princes," said the emperor, and extended a hand, closed in a fist. "Here is your token. Take it, and you have entered the game."

Anatoly had learned many things from his grandmother. One was never to move in haste. "What is the object of the game?"

"To take the throne."

"Who are the other players?"

"Is it not called, the game of princes?"

"What are the rules?"

The emperor seemed amused. "That is the disadvantage of entering the game late. The first rule is that each player must learn the rules."

"What happens to you, Yaochalii, when the throne is taken?"

Now the emperor chuckled, not a human chuckle, but a rolling swell of amusement. "I am nothing. I cannot be taken. But the princes bide their time and maneuver for position, and when it is proper the Yaochalii passes through and a new Yaochalii takes his place."

"Ah. Then with what resources do I play?"

The emperor lifted his other hand. It was so pale that Anatoly thought that he glimpsed, for an instant, a shifting line of carvings through it as it carved an arc in the air, rising to touch the emperor's own mouth, fingertips brushing across his nostril slits.

"What resources do you bring with you?"

"I am a prince of the Sakhalin tribe, a captain in the jaran army led by Ilyakora Bakhtiian, a husband to the Singer Diana Brooke-Holt, a brother and a father and a grandson. That is all."

The emperor considered. Anatoly noticed for the first time that filaments grew out of his back and into the throne, as if he was somehow in symbiosis with it.

"Because you are daiga, all daiga holdings accrue to you. I have spoken. It becomes as I decree."

He said the words softly enough, but they rang like hammers in Anatoly's ears. *All daiga holdings.*

"Because you are so young as to be more like a first breath of mist born of the morning than a true, solid form, I grant you this courtesy: That any of my servants you have met and will meet this day shall enter your service, they and their houses, to the end of time. I trust this will be sufficient."

Like a flower opening to the sun, the emperor's hand opened. In his palm sat a miniature tower, forged like a castle keep, the last refuge, the stronghold. Anatoly smiled wryly, recognizing the symbol for what it was: possession of a piece of ground, meaningless to him but so utterly important to khaja of all kinds, even zayinu.

"When you take possession of this token, you will enter the game. You will continue to travel as you will, and as you must. But you will leave behind on my board a splinter of yourself, a shard, by which I may monitor your movements and amuse myself with watching your progress in relationship to the others." He waited for Anatoly to come forward.

"How am I to know the other princes, Yaochalii?"

The emperor's gaze swept the plateau. Out there, on the lines, placed on intersections just as khot stones were placed in the grid, stood a handful of images, like that model of the hydrogen atom he had passed on the other side of the throne. Images, like badges, like banners, like nesh images, each one representing one of the princely houses: a streamlined and archaic-looking rocketship, a teardrop, a blade, four strands of colored rope knotted together, an inverted tetrahedron. The other four were out of sight behind the throne.

It was time to act.

Anatoly stepped forward and lifted the tower from the emperor's hand. It was as solid as stone and as slippery as water. It throbbed in his hand, as if it linked him to the pulsing web of light on which he stood. And it did link him.

Even as he stood, breathing hard through his mouth while he felt the glare of two suns on his back and the oppressive stillness of the air on his skin, an image formed around him, a glimmering that slowly faded into being. It grew and shaded from mist to gray to the false solidity of a nesh image, superimposed over him. Startled, he stepped back, out of it, and stared at the piece that now took its place on the board.

It was a jaran rider, his saber riding on his belt and the butt of his spear tucked into the curve of his boot. He wore his hair long, in the traditional style of a soldier, three braids, and Anatoly saw there his own profile, sharpened in nesh to a brittle perfection. The mare was the image of Sosha.

Like Anatoly, the rider remained still. But of course, he could not move unless Anatoly moved. He was, of himself, nothing, nonexistent, and yet he was also, as the emperor had said, a shard of the true Anatoly. The token, the tower, remained as solid as a stone in Anatoly's hand, his passage into the game, his first playing piece, perhaps, or a reminder that what appeared as a game on this high and isolated board, here in the center of the emperor's great palace, weighed heavily on the worlds below.

A cloud drifted by, breaking up on one corner of the ziggurat and reforming into a new shape over the golden lake.

It was time to move. The emperor waited, one hand open, the other hand closed.

"Yaochalii, may I ask one more question?"

"You may."

"Do you have any favorites, in the game of princes?"

"I have none."

That seemed fair enough, assuming he was telling the truth. But at that moment Anatoly did not truly care if the emperor was telling the truth; how could any human hope to know, in any case? *All daiga holdings.* That meant that not just Earth but Rhui was his, that he was their suzerain, their governor. And that meant Bakhtiian had, in one brief stroke, in the unfolding of a single hand, won his war.

All khaja lands now belonged to the jaran.

CHAPTER THIRTY-EIGHT

An Ominous Silence

Tess liked the exhausting pace forced on her by the messenger bells. It meant she was too tired to think. She didn't mind the pain either, the scraped and sore ribs, the aching muscles, the constant rasp of her breathing as the chill air of autumn pulled the warmth out of her lungs. She had earned that pain. Like a badge, it reminded her every instant of what she had done to get herself here: She had killed her husband because she was afraid to tell him the truth.

Kirill said, once, "Tess, there might have been survivors. Two of the monks said that they saw a handful of prisoners the next day."

"Said it because they were about to be killed and they probably thought it would save their lives!"

Kirill only shrugged. It seemed perfectly logical to him that every inhabitant of the monastery had been killed after a brief and no doubt brutal interrogation. Tess found it appalling. No doubt the poor heretic who had been taken from Parkilnous and hauled off to face trial at the monastery had been killed as indiscriminately as the rest, meeting an ironic and cruel fate as the unwitting bait that had drawn Ilya to his doom. She had absorbed the full report, but she felt so detached from it that it seemed to trail in her wake, not quite connected to her. It had been thorough, in its way, information gleaned from four dozen interrogations listed efficiently, easily memorizable, so that the messenger's verbal report had tallied exactly with the written scroll.

The gods had struck down the chief holy man when he was brought before the jaran captain who had led the expedition to Urosh Monastery in search of Bakhtiian. By this, Tess supposed that the presbyter had died of fright, probably a stroke or a heart attack. Unfortunately, that also meant they had gotten nothing from him.

For the rest, they knew only that Andrei Sakhalin had

been there, not whether his troops had gotten caught and killed with the others. Fifteen monks had claimed no knowledge of the attacker, two said it was the hand of God at work, and seven had recognized the colors of the prince of Dushan known as Janos the Disgraced due to some recent upheaval at court. His troops had done their job well: The slaughter had been complete, according to all but two of the monks, the two who claimed to have seen prisoners.

Tess tried to let herself hope, but it hurt too much.

They rode. The passage of ground jarred hope out of her; the rising sun each morning leached it away, and the setting sun dragged her down into a heavy sleep bereft of dreams. She thought of Vasha and Katya, of Niko's grandson Stefan, children who had become dear to her, killed before they could reach their full growth as adults. Because she was Charles's sister, she thought of Princess Rusudani and wondered sardonically, angry at herself for her calculating mind, how great a prize they had lost thereby.

Ten days and perhaps a thousand kilometers south of Sarai, she stared at Kirill as they swung onto their horses at the posting station, their escort of Gennady Berezin and fifty riders mounting up behind them, and she swore.

"What an idiot I've been! There's no obvious reason for a khaja prince to attack the guard, even knowing whose it was, especially knowing. . . ." She could not bring herself to say *his* name. "It's irrational. It doesn't make sense. Unless he thought he was getting something. What if that something was Princess Rusudani?"

"Of course," said Kirill mildly, as if he had long since assimilated this information and stored it away for future use. "She is the key. Why else would the jaran traitor in our midst have sent a message to the Mircassian king?"

Kirill's bland demeanor irritated Tess so thoroughly that she did not speak to him for the rest of the day, but then, she rarely spoke on the long, hard ride each day. It took too much effort. It was effort enough to ride for hours at a stretch, changing horses at each posting station, forcing dried meat and sour yoghurt down her throat, drinking komis until she was giddy from it.

Nineteen days after they left Sarai they came up before Parkilnous, and two days after that, they found an outrider; by afternoon they had fallen in with the waiting army, the host with which Ilya had ridden south weeks and weeks ago, now camped somewhat off the main road south.

She held court under an awning. Every captain in that host—and there were over a hundred of them—came forward and offered her his saber, giving it up to her because of the dishonor they had each and every one of them brought on themselves by letting their dyan fall prey to a khaja ambush.

She said, each time, so that it became a mantra: "Keep your saber. You are not done with it."

After all of them had knelt before her and, with her refusal, retreated to leave room for the next one, she rose. The captains knelt in a semicircle before her and beyond them, the host of riders, gathered as close as they could. The five hundred riders from Bakhtiian's personal guard ranged around her awning, equally silent. They sent Gennady Berezin forward and he knelt before her, unsheathed his saber, and laid it at her feet, his head bowed in shame.

She picked it up and gave it back to him. "I don't want to take your sabers from you," she said, loudly, pitching her voice to carry, knowing that this man more than all the others represented the whole army, a man who had ridden faithfully with Bakhtiian from the beginning. Without realizing she meant to say it, she did anyway.

"I want revenge."

They responded with silence, ominous because it shouted approval, and a moment later with the rustling of thousands of soldiers rising to their feet, preparing to ride. After that, it was too late to call the words back. She felt, at that moment, that her assimilation to the jaran, a cleaner, more honest, more brutal life than the one she had known on Earth, was complete.

She swayed, overcome by emotion. "We'll have to ride in the morning. I'm falling asleep on my feet."

Several of the young women, archers with the army, came forward and led her to a tent. She slept like one dead.

Kirill woke her before dawn. "Come. There's news."

Catching his excitement, she jerked on her boots and belted her saber on. "What is it?"

"The rider sent out thirty days ago has returned from the court of Dushan, where he has a report from Andrei Sakhalin, who is whole and safe. Sakhalin says that he left Bakhtiian at the monastery and rode on to the court, and that

the last he saw of them Bakhtiian and his guard were alive.
So the attack must have happened after Sakhalin left. Perhaps the khaja prince saw Sakhalin leaving and thought he
could easily defeat the group remaining."

"Perhaps."

"Sakhalin also sends word that this Prince Janos is out of
favor at court, and was once betrothed to Princess
Rusudani."

"Is that so? Interesting that the princess never mentioned
that she had ever been betrothed. I wonder how her parents
came to break off the arrangement and put her in a convent
instead."

Tess's escort consisted of Kirill and two of the young
women, bright, hardened girls who had the swagger of experienced soldiers and the solicitous nature of jaran women.

But Kirill did not lead her to the awning where she would
have expected to have an audience with the messenger who
had come from the Dushanite court. He led her to the surgery tents. A host of lanterns gleamed around the central
tent belonging to the chief healer riding with the army. An
apprentice healer held the flap aside for her to enter. Inside,
lanterns illuminated the body of a young man lying on furs
in the center of the tent. She recognized him, even through
the filth. Dirt and the rust stain of old blood matted his
clothing. His hair ran gray with dust. Grime streaked his
hands and face, as if he had attempted, intermittently, to
clean them. He had only recently been admitted to Bakhtiian's jahar, a signal honor, one sought after by every
young man who had aspirations.

"Stanislav Vershinin," she said aloud, she was so surprised. "What has happened to him?" *And,* she wondered to
herself, *why have I been called in to see to him?* He looked
ill, battered, and possibly as if he might yet die.

The healer, a hardy woman in her fifties, looked up from
the paste she was pounding in a shallow bowl. "He was with
the guard that went to Urosh Monastery, Sister," she said,
speaking to Tess in the formal style.

It took Tess a long time to assimilate this information. An
old man cut away the trouser leg from Vershinin's left leg,
revealing the festering wound, scabbed over but still infected. The apprentice brought an iron pot and set it on a tri-
pod next to the Vershinin lad. Truly, Tess thought, gazing
down at the young man's pale face, his closed eyes, he could

not have been more than two years older than Vasha. The old man began to clean the wound with the hot water, and that brought the young man awake. He yelped. A second apprentice handed him a strip of leather and he bit down on it, his eyes tearing while the old healer dabbed the pus and dirt off the wound and probed delicately at it with a tiny spatula, cleaning out the infected cut. Vershinin passed out. When the old healer was done, the woman sealed the wound with paste and then bound it with cloth.

"That may save it," she said aloud, "but it's badly infected."

Vershinin's eyes fluttered open. He searched the tent, found Tess, and focused on her, blinking madly. "Alive," he said hoarsely. He licked his lips and tried again. "Bakhtiian was alive, but very bad. Badly wounded. He was a prisoner."

At once, Tess knelt beside him. Her heart pounded wildly in her chest, so erratically that she felt dizzy. "What khaja did this?"

"His name . . . Prince Janos. He married the khaja princess." He licked his lips again, and the healer gave him some of the boiled water to drink. "But it was not him. Not the khaja prince. Sakhalin betrayed us."

"Sakhalin!" That came from Kirill, who turned at once and left the tent, running.

"What of the others? You escaped. Did anyone else? What of Bakhtiian?"

Vershinin seemed to have found his strength, what there was of it. "Konstans Barshai was killed in his place."

"In his place?"

"The khaja prince thought Barshai was Bakhtiian. He killed him. A few of us were spared by the princess's hand. Katerina Orzhekov. Vladimir the orphan. The Kolenin cousins. The two boys." He blinked, eyes rolling, trying to remember something.

"Let him rest," said the healer.

"No," he said. "I must tell the rest. Bakhtiian lived, but he was badly wounded. We were all taken prisoner and we traveled, west. West. A little south. We made a plan, the other guardsmen and I. I fell behind, and the khaja soldiers grew tired of my slowness and sold me as a slave to farmers. From there I escaped."

"Good God," exclaimed Tess. "And made your way here."

"How else to get the word out? He betrayed us, the bastard. The khaja prince did his bidding and took the others. He would have killed us all except for the intercession of the woman."

"But Bakhtiian was still alive, when you left them?"

Vershinin shook his head. "Still alive, but dying, or close enough. He could not even walk. I don't know what happened to him. He was with the boy."

"With Vasha?" What difference did it make who he was with if he was dying, but she grasped for each scrap of information as if enough scraps might together form a real and solid body of Ilya, surviving.

Vershinin took some more water but did not reply.

"Where did Prince Janos take them? Do you know where they were headed?"

"To his stronghold, I think. I don't know."

"Let him rest," said the healer. "Or he will not have the strength to fight off the infection. He has done enough."

"You have done enough," said Tess to the young man, patting him on the hand. And his look, when she said it, burned her to the heart: That awful loyalty that they all gave to Bakhtiian, of their own free will. That terrible desire to prove their worth, to be part of his glorious enterprise, to win fame and to blaze in their own right, a true rider of the jaran.

She left them. She felt numb. Crossing the camp to her awning, she felt each step like the hammer of death, beating down to sound Ilya's fate: dying, dying, dying. Not even able to walk.

At the awning, they waited, the ten chief captains and ten guardsmen.

"We find a khaja guide and we ride for the stronghold of Prince Janos," she said, hearing her voice from a distance, as if someone else was speaking. "I want Andrei Sakhalin. Kirill, you will bring me Andrei Sakhalin."

"I will bring him to you," he agreed. "I will need a thousand troops."

"Take two thousand. As for the rest, we ride west southwest. As soon as camp is broken, we ride. Leave an honor guard of five hundred men to protect Vershinin until he is able to move again."

They moved, scattering to obey her commands. She just stood there, toting up numbers in her head: two thousand with Kirill, five hundred with Vershinin . . . that still left her seventeen thousand riders and archers. That ought to be enough to crush this khaja prince and get the prisoners back.

"Tess," said Kirill softly. He had remained behind. The sun rose behind him, glinting in her eyes so that she could not really see his face. It was blurred by tears, but that was only the glare of the sun. She blinked them back ruthlessly. "I told you. Ilya is too damned tough for any khaja to kill."

"Go," said she brusquely.

He went.

But the truth was, it was worse, knowing that he had been alive. But not even able to walk.

"Ah, gods," she breathed, the words torn from her by a wrenching agony so strong that she staggered.

"Aunt, are you ill?" asked one of the young archers, her hovering escort, steadying her.

Dying, Vershinin had said. It would have been easier just to know that he was dead. It was worse not knowing. It hurt too much to hope.

CHAPTER THIRTY-NINE

As Far Above as Angels

Jaelle woke to the muffled sound of weeping. Sitting up, she was at first bewildered. As she shifted, she sank farther into the unimaginable luxury of a feather bed. A feather quilt slipped around her legs and hips. How had she come into such riches? Then she remembered. She heaved herself out of bed and slowly felt her way across the floor to the servant's bed, where Princess Katerina slept. The coals glowed a dull red in the darkness.

"My lady ... Katherine ..." She said it softly, daringly, and reached out to touch the other woman's hair.

Katerina snuffled and stilled, caught a few sobs, and then began to cry in earnest. "I want to go home," she gulped out.

Jaelle stroked her hair. But the act made her nervous, because she liked it so much, sitting here close to Katerina, feeling her breath against her arm and the warmth of her body close to her own, separated only by their linen undershifts.

"I don't want to be a slave."

For some reason, Jaelle thought of her own mother, who had seemed content enough as a favored slave in a nobleman's house. She had been safe. Or had thought she was, Jaelle thought bitterly. Except it was her daughter who had been sent away, not her. But her master could have sold her away at any time. "It is terrible to live on the sufferance of others," she said finally.

"You *do* understand," breathed Katerina, catching Jaelle's hand in a tight grip. She had strong hands. Jaelle could see her face only as a deeper shadow in the shadowed chamber, lit by the banked fire and a faint nimbus of light from the moon and the torchlit walls of the castle.

Jaelle tried to pull her hand away. "You should sleep in the lady's bed," she said, as she had said every night in the thirty days they had been here. "It isn't fitting that—"

"I hate that bed," said Katerina, but whether because it was truly too soft, as she claimed, or because it somehow represented her imprisonment to Janos, Jaelle did not know.

"May I get you something to drink?"

"No. Just stay with me here. Lie down with me here, Jaelle. I'm afraid."

"Afraid of what?" Jaelle did not want to lie down next to Katerina on the narrow bed. She, too, was afraid.

"I'm afraid of becoming a captive."

"You already are."

"Not in my heart."

"Do you care for Prince Janos?" The thought made Jaelle abruptly angry.

"No. But how long will I have the strength to hold against him, if I am held prisoner here for the rest of my days? I hate the khaja."

Jaelle heard Katerina's voice catch again, fighting off tears. She lay down beside her and put her arms around her. "I will be here," she said, and wondered at herself, that she might comfort a princess. Katerina buried her face against Jaelle's neck and said nothing more, just held on to her. After a while, she fell asleep, but Jaelle could not sleep, not with Katerina so close. She had shared a bed with other women often enough, in inns along the caravan route, waiting for a new hire. It wasn't unknown for women to take lovers among themselves, as a salve against the impersonal attentions of the endless parade of men who used them and then discarded them when their destination was reached or they wanted a new face, as a way to get pleasure without the risk of pregnancy, as comfort against the hard world and the censure of both the church and decent folk. Jaelle's heart trembled within her; like a bird cupped in iron hands, she feared what it meant to love another person, whether it be Katerina or Stefan, what did it matter? She knew only that love was itself a kind of slavery. It bound you to others with chains as heavy as those wrought in the armorer's forge. She had survived this long by staying free.

For the first time in years she thought of the child. Lady forgive her, but she had been having her courses for not over a year herself when the child had caught in her; she was herself truly still a child. She hadn't known what to do, not like now, with six winters of experience of the caravan roads behind her. Now she knew where to find the wisewomen from

whom to purchase herbs and suppositories, who knew what
to give a woman to drink and where to press so as to rid her
of a pregnancy that would prove dangerous not just to her
body but to her livelihood.

She had not known those things then. She had still been
a slave at the mines, hauling water and dirt. What kind of
life was that for a child, for a child bearing a child? She had
run away, only it was worse away, there being not even the
pittance of bread and soup they gave the slaves, there being
not even the surety of a roof over her head. Then the merchant had found her, begging on the streets not five days after the baby had been born, and had offered her employment,
thinking her young and pretty, under the dirt. Thinking her
childless.

For the first time in six years, held in arms that wanted
nothing from her but comfort, she wept.

Katerina woke. "Jaelle. Shhh. What is it? What's wrong?"
She kissed her on the cheeks, like a mother might kiss her
child, taking onto herself the tears.

"God has marked me. I have sinned grievously. Ah, God,
it never truly mattered to me before."

"What is *sinned?* What didn't matter?"

Jaelle bit down on her tongue and stifled her tears. She
could not afford to be vulnerable. Katerina did not press her.
She seemed content with Jaelle's presence. After a while,
soothed by the warmth of the jaran woman's body next to
hers, Jaelle fell back to sleep.

In the morning Katerina seemed oddly heartened. When
Lady Jadranka made her morning visit, Katerina agreed to
visit the church with her and receive the sacrament, more,
Jaelle supposed, out of boredom than a true interest in salvation. Lady Jadranka had perhaps forgotten that Jaelle ad-
hered to the anointed church, or perhaps she had simply
never been told, but Jaelle was allowed to attend as well.

While Katerina was led forward to the main altar, Jaelle
knelt before the altar of Our Lady Pilgrim in a side alcove,
a forlorn and dark corner, a trifle dusty, here in the north
where the false church reigned and the priests neglected Her
worship. Jaelle folded her hands before her chest and prayed
for forgiveness for her sins. Behind, she heard the priest
droning the sacramental liturgy and she smelled like a starv-
ing woman the fragrant and holy perfume of the wine that is

the blood of the sundered Lord and the freshly baked loaf
that is His body made whole by the gift of God's mercy and
by the grace of His Sister, the Pilgrim, ever exalted for the
constancy of her faith. Her mouth watered, though she had
eaten of bread that morning.

A person moved into the alcove beside her. To her surprise and chagrin, Princess Rusudani knelt beside her on the
stone floor, hands clasped. For a long time the princess
gazed at the pale visage of the Pilgrim, whose sloe eyes
stared earnestly and forgivingly at her supplicants. Rusudani's lips moved soundlessly in a prayer. At the main altar,
the priest and his deacons began the sonorous chant of the
Bath of Healing, which even such heretics as these northerners could not omit from their service. Though Jaelle took
comfort in the presence of the Pilgrim, still, this northern
church depressed her because it was so plain, without any
bright images, and so dim. Candles flickered around the altar, illuminating the mystery of the Pilgrim's healing hands
and Her serene expression, ever aloof from the world and
yet ever bound to it in her wandering.

Jaelle shuddered. Bakhtiian had been on the trail of a heretic, a man who claimed that the Pilgrim wandered the world
again and that angels had been sighted in the heavens, heralding the return of Hristain. Was it true? Or was this imprisonment their punishment for listening to the whispers of
the Accursed One?

"Jaelle," said Rusudani suddenly in a low voice, "I do not
know who else to ask, but I think you may have heard of
such things in the life you led before." Her hands were not
clasped but clenched before her, and her face was pale, lips
thin with some overpowering emotion. "How may a woman
bind a man to her?"

From the alcove, Jaelle could not see the main altar,
where Katerina knelt with Lady Jadranka. Had Rusudani
fled from the confrontation? But she remembered the two
women being friendly before. There had been no antagonism
between them while Rusudani traveled with the jaran. But
Rusudani had not been married then, and Katerina had not
been shut away to serve as Janos's mistress.

"I am not a wisewoman, to know of such charms," said
Jaelle slowly, measuring her words, "but in any town there
is always a herbwoman. There must be one such here."

"I dare not speak of this to Lady Jadranka."

"Of course not, my lady." Of course not, if Rusudani judged that for some reason Lady Jadranka had chosen to champion Katerina's cause with her son and Rusudani wished to keep his affections for herself. Yet, glancing at Rusudani, Jælle noted that the princess wore a new gown and a wimple sewn of fine dyed linen in a blue that suited her eyes. Surely this finery came to her out of Lady Jadranka's charity. If Jadranka wished to press Katerina's suit, why would she dress her daughter-in-law in a gown that was sure to attract her son's eye? "You must tell one of your waiting women to go down into the town and ask for—"

"I cannot trust them. You must do it, Jaelle."

At what price? What if it hurt Katerina? But refusing might win Rusudani's enmity. If Jaelle helped Rusudani now, then if there was trouble she could hold this knowledge in reserve; the church frowned on the use of charms and sorcery, and Rusudani had just come out of the convent.

"God forgive me," Rusudani murmured, as if in response to Jaelle's thought. "I was pledged to wed Hristain, not any mortal man, though I had not yet taken my vows. I wished with my whole heart to serve only God. What is this that has taken hold of me? The pleasures of the flesh have seduced my body away from the contemplation of God's holy mystery, and now I yearn for the marriage bed with as much fervor as before I yearned for the sacrament. Why is God punishing me in this way? Have I faltered in my love for God in any way? Why has he visited me with this longing? I have done nothing wrong. I have not sinned. Yet when I see him, my hands tremble and my heart catches in my throat and in my mouth I taste the sweetness of honey poured as if from the lips of Hristain Himself. God forgive me."

She turned her eyes away from the Holy Pilgrim and gazed at Jaelle. Rusudani wore, on her face, such an expression of misery conjoined with joy that Jaelle felt pity for her. How had it come to this, that she, a common whore, might feel pity for a great lady, a princess, who was as far above her as the angels were above mortals? Except in this fashion, that all men were equal before God, who judged them by what He found in their hearts, that all were equal before the Holy Pilgrim, who succored each and every one who knelt before her, regardless of his station in life.

"I would help you if I could, but the princess Katerina and

I are locked in Widow's Tower. By the order of Prince Janos."

"My husband fears that his father will take her away if he discovers that she is in captivity. But Janos is gone from here. Surely Princess Katerina must want something from the market? I will speak to Lady Jadranka about it. I will ask her to send you to the market in the town."

This did not sound like a woman who considered Katerina to be her rival. Jaelle was even more confused. Rusudani looked abruptly radiant.

Indeed, strangely enough, she was not looking at Jaelle at all. She was looking past her, out between two columns toward the doors of the church. There, Lady Jadranka ushered Katerina outside into the glare of the noonday sun. Her voice carried clearly.

"Where is your servant, Lady Katherine? Ah, here, I have sent for the priest of your own people, my lady. Of course I must hope that you will come to accept the Word of God, whose mercy alone can save, but I thought you might also like the offices of your own priest, so I have had him called in from the ditch work."

Jaelle recognized his silhouette against the bright sun. No priest she had ever seen stood like a warrior, even looking like he had just come from digging ditches, which, evidently, he had. She heard the gasp that escaped Rusudani's lips as she, too, gazed on the man who stood poised between the sun and the shadowed church. At that moment, Jaelle experienced a revelation. Rusudani was not in love with her husband. She was in love with Bakhtiian.

Vasha lay on his back and stared at the heavens. At one end of the clearing, near the hunting lodge, torches burned and men caroused. He heard their rough laughter and the counterpoint of higher women's voices, laughing in answer and calling out, all in the Yossian tongue. He understood a bit of it now, enough to ask for a few things from the serving man assigned to him. Enough to politely extricate himself from the attentions of the khaja women who had been invited into the camp to amuse the men. He was not sure whether these women were whores, like Jaelle, or just common women from neighboring villages who had been given no choice and were now, most of them, making the best of it. No doubt they would be paid handsomely. Or, he thought, hearing an echo of Tess's sarcastic descriptions of what she called "the rights of women in khaja lands," they would be paid by being left alone until the next time Janos and his men visited this lodge.

It was a dry, clear night with a bright moon, still early in the evening. He lay alone in the grass, able by now to ignore the ever-present guards who shadowed him. Suddenly a faint star caught his eye. It moved. Kept moving, a speck of light following a straight path through the heavens. Stunned, he watched it make its slow way through the veil of stars. Was this truly the track of an angel's wings?

"Prince Vasil'ii."

Vasha almost jumped, he was so startled. But it was only Prince Janos. A servant cast a cloak over the grass and Janos sat down on it.

"I fear our amusements tire you, Prince Vasil'ii. Are Yossian women so ugly that you scorn them? I have heard it said that jaran men have a taboo fixed on them, that they may not touch any women but their own. Are your women sorceresses, that they have punished you in this way? But it can't be true, can it, if Bakhtiian married the Jedan princess?"

"They are not ugly," Vasha replied, and then blushed, thinking of Rusudani, who was Yossian on her father's side. He sat up. "But it is not our custom to . . ." He did not know how to phrase it, how to avoid insulting Janos. "It is not a man's place to be forward with a woman."

"Be forward with her?"

"To press himself on her. To . . . well, that is a woman's place, to tell a man she is interested in him."

"But I thought you said women have no choice in marriage, by jaran custom."

"I'm not talking about marriage, although it's true what you say. I'm talking about taking lovers."

"Taking lovers!"

"I don't know what the khaja custom is in this matter, although Tess says that usually—" He broke off, not knowing how to phrase what Tess had said in such a way that it wouldn't offend Janos. Tess did not mince words when it came to customs she did not approve of, and she could go on at length about the way the khaja treated women and slaves and what she called "peasants." "But in the jaran, a woman is expected to take lovers as she pleases. It is not a man's place to ... uh ... approach a woman."

Janos did not reply immediately. Vasha craned his head back and searched the sky, but the moving star had vanished. Now he wondered if he had dreamed it.

"I don't understand what you're saying," said Janos finally, slowly. "A woman may take lovers?"

"Yes."

"But then how can a man know if her children are his? And how can a man be sure that the girl he takes to wife is a virgin?"

"What is a *virgin?* Oh, I remember what that is." Unable to help himself, Vasha chuckled, then clapped a hand over his mouth. "I beg your pardon. I just think khaja are very strange, sometimes."

But Janos did not seem amused. "Do you truly mean that jaran women, whether married or unmarried, may take lovers?"

"Yes."

"Barbarians!" Janos muttered under his breath. Then: "I beg *your* pardon, Prince Vasil'ii. This lack of modesty among your women must distress you, after you have seen how decorously women behave in our lands."

"Those women aren't behaving very decorously," Vasha pointed out, nodding toward the hunting lodge.

"They are peasants. They don't matter. I meant women of good breeding, like Princess Rusudani. Like your cousin, Princess Katherine."

Vasha snorted. "Oh, I admit that Katya doesn't show off her lovers like other girls do, but I can hardly imagine that she wishes to become like a khaja woman." Abruptly, he was sorry he had said anything. Janos looked thunderstruck. The khaja prince shifted uneasily on the cloak, took a hank of cloth in one hand, and twisted it into a knot. He began to speak but stopped, seeming to reconsider his words.

"I wish to understand you, Prince Vasil'ii. It is a custom for most jaran women to take lovers while they are still unmarried?"

"Yes, and after they are married as well, but then usually only if their husband is riding out with the army. Of course a woman cannot be expected to wait for months at a time for comfort while he is gone. But it is always impolite to flaunt an affair in front of one's husband. If a woman refused to behave circumspectly in such a matter, then the etsana of the tribe would take her to task. Otherwise there might be strife between the wife and the husband, and perhaps between her family and his."

"But ... but how does a woman show a man that she is interested in him?"

"She tells him. She asks him to her tent, into her blankets. Dances with him. Gives him a gift. I don't know. There are a thousand ways. Just as there are a thousand ways a well-mannered man can show a woman that he is interested in her without being immodest."

Janos sat for a long time in silence, contemplating his hands by the light of the full moon. He had broad, sturdy hands, and the back of his left hand was scarred by an old wound, the slash of a knife, perhaps. Vasha looked back up at the sky, but the stars remained fixed in the great wheel of night. No angels flew.

"It is time to return to White Tower," Janos said abruptly. He stood up and called to his servant. "Bring our horses. Tell my guards to saddle up and to bring lanterns. We are leaving now."

"Now?" Vasha asked, startled by this sudden change of subject.

"Yes. You will ride with me, of course."

"Of course. But what about—"

"Lord Belos can bring the rest tomorrow, when they have recovered. We are leaving now."

Vasha was not about to argue. His serving man brought his horse and his saddle bags. They left, but they made slow progress and once the moon had set they had to stop for the rest of the night in any case, hunkering down in blankets by the side of the path that served as a road through the forest.

Janos rode hard in the morning, more like a jaran man than a khaja prince, changing horses at noon and leading them on like a man driven forward by demons. It took two days more, but they reached White Tower on the afternoon of the second day, riding in through fresh embankments thrown up around the outer walls of the town. Still incomplete, the ditches and palisade swarmed with men hard at work under a pale autumn sky streaked with clouds.

Scarlet flashed. Vasha saw his father on the lip of a half-dug ditch. Vasha winced, to see him digging like a common slave. Although no member of the tribes shrank from honest work, this labor seemed demeaning. His wrists were loosely shackled, as were his legs: not enough to prevent him from working, but enough to constrain him against escape. Gods. Ilya surely chafed under such treatment.

Vasha reined his horse aside and made for his father. Shouts followed him, then Janos's voice, ordering the guards to stay back. By the time Vasha came up beside the ditch, Janos had come up next to him. The guards trailed behind, fanning out into a semicircle. But Ilya dug steadily, his back to them, pitching dirt into a small wheeled cart. He seemed deaf to the world.

"Father!" Vasha said in khush. "Father, speak to me."

At first he thought Ilya hadn't heard him, although how he could fail to hear him Vasha could not imagine, how he could fail to notice the guards and the presence of all those horses. Finally, stiffly, Ilya slacked off and turned slowly around. Looking up, he had to squint into the sun. His eyes registered Vasha and then he looked at Janos, and then away. Not insolently. Ilya never did things insolently; he was too powerful for that. Dismissively. He turned his back dismissively on Janos and went back to work. But Vasha could read as if like a book the muscles in his back, the choppiness of his movements: He was strung so tight with anger that he seemed about to burst from it. At that moment, Vladimir scrambled up out of the ditch, looking over the guards, marking the prince and where he sat mounted. He casually placed himself between Ilya and Janos and began to dig as well.

"Are your people all this insolent to their betters?" asked Janos. "How can you rule them, if this is so?"

Ilya stabbed at the earth with the shovel, chipping clumps of dirt that flew into the air.

Vasha gulped down a lump in his throat. "He is a priest, Prince Janos. It offends the gods to put him to this kind of work. I would advise you to let him return to serving Princess Rusudani and reading from the holy book."

"All able-bodied men have been set to work here."

"I don't see you digging, Prince Janos."

Janos was too surprised by this suggestion to respond.

"In any case," added Vasha, changing tactics, "it would please me. He is a holy man, what we call a *Singer*, and it pains me to see him working here in chains like a common slave."

"Very well. As a favor to you, Prince Vasil'ii. You may have one other to serve you, the young one. The rest must work out here."

"Thank you," replied Vasha, surprised in his turn.

Janos spoke to the guards, and an overseer was found to come unshackle Ilya. Vladimir stayed beside him, digging steadily so as not to arouse suspicion.

"Take him away and allow him to clean up," said Janos. Ilya was led away. He had not looked at Vasha once in all that time, nor at Janos, only at some point in the middle distance where nothing existed.

"Vladimir, you are well? Nikita and Mikhail? How are they treating you?" Vasha asked quickly, in khush, not knowing when he would get another chance.

"We are treated fairly enough, Vasha," said Vladimir without looking up, knowing better than to pause in his work. "They need us healthy to dig these defenses. They aren't fools. They know that the jaran will come sooner or later. But look to your father, Vasha. He is half mad."

"We must go," said Janos.

Vasha rode away with him, glancing back once to see Vladimir pitch a shovelful of dirt into the cart. From this angle he could see into the ditch, where a line of men worked planting stakes. A few women moved among them, hauling water in buckets. He thought he glimpsed red shirts down there, Nikita and Mikhail, but he could not be sure. Then it hit him. Vladimir had said: *your father.* In this extremity, without thinking, the rider had acknowledged their relationship. Vasha felt dizzy with joy.

"Are all your priests, your *singers,* as insolent as this one?" Janos asked suddenly, bringing Vasha back to earth.

"They are the chosen ones of the gods, Prince Janos. They are not insolent. But they serve the gods, not men. It would be as if . . . an angel descended from the heavens and was chained. We treat our Singers, our priests, with respect. We honor them."

Janos laughed. "Then your priests are holier than ours, Prince Vasil'ii, for ours spend most of their time fighting over what benefices they may wrest from the king and what portion of the taxes they may siphon off from those levied on the merchants. A lord may buy an abbacy for a younger son, and a bishop may sire a son by his mistress and call him a nephew and thus favor him with gifts and a bishopric of his own."

They rode in under the gates and forged through the narrow streets, the guards clearing the way before them.

"But surely that is not true of all of them. Princess Rusudani seems sincere in her faith." At once, Vasha berated himself for speaking her name. It seemed that he could not have a conversation with Janos but that he would mention her. Surely Janos would notice and become suspicious.

"She is devout, it is true, but her place is in the world, not in the convent."

Vasha sighed. "When may I see my cousin?" he asked as they came into the forecourt and dismounted, giving their horses over to the hostlers.

"When it is safe to do so. You will attend me at supper, Prince Vasil'ii."

Then he was gone, surrounded by servants and the steward of his castle, come to greet him. Beyond, Vasha saw Lady Jadranka appear with two serving women as escort. Janos turned aside to greet her. Four guardsmen escorted Vasha away to his tower. A bath was poured for him, and he luxuriated in it, getting out only when Stefan, covered with dirt, was let in.

"Here." Vasha jumped out of the huge tub, sloshing water on the floor. "You look awful. Take a bath."

Stefan did so gratefully while Vasha dried himself and a serving man brought in clean clothing—khaja clothing—and took away the other.

Vasha shut the door behind him and leaned against it. "Tell me everything."

"What is there to tell?" Stefan sighed and sank deeper into the water, up to his neck. His bent knees stuck out along the opposite side. "Ah, it's still warm. They're digging a third defensive perimeter. We are slaves, so we were sent out to aid them."

"Were you chained?"

"No, I was not. Only Ilya and Nikita, Ilya for resisting the overseer and Nikita for taking the whip in Ilya's place when the overseer struck at him."

"Oh, gods. Don't they know better, Vladimir and Nikita and Mikhail? If they show him too much preference, if they protect him too much, then the khaja will surely become

suspicious. I have tried as well as I can to make them believe he is a priest, a holy man—"

"He *is* a holy man, Vasha, or have you forgotten that he
is a Singer?"

"No, of course not. But—"

"Vasha, Bakhtiian is half mad. They have to protect him
or he'll get himself killed. I think—" He faltered, grabbed
the bar of soap floating in the by-now muddy water, and began to wash his hair.

"You think what!"

"I think he wants to get himself killed. He can't endure
captivity. If he dies, he has to die in a fight."

"Oh, gods."

"And you? What of you?"

"We went hunting. Some man killed a boar with a spear
and all the others congratulated him. Others shot deer. I was
not allowed a weapon, of course. They had birds that they
had captured and tamed and bound by ropes tied to their
feet. Janos offered to let me fly one, but I refused." He shuddered. "It was terrible to see, imprisoning hawks and eagles
in such a way."

"Like your father," said Stefan. He rinsed his hair and
stood up. Water sluiced down off him, and Vasha handed
him a towel and rooted around in the chest to find him a
clean set of clothing. Luckily he and Stefan had the same
build, so that the clothes brought for Vasha fit Stefan as
well. Stefan put on the breeches and knelt to wash his own
clothes in the tub. "Have you seen Katya? Or . . ." A betraying pause. "Jaelle?"

"No. Nor heard anything about them. I'm to go in to supper
with Prince Janos tonight. I will ask him again, or perhaps I can
ask his mother."

Stefan smiled slightly without looking up from his washing. "Perhaps you can ask Princess Rusudani."

Vasha kicked him halfheartedly, but he was too happy to
see him to truly be angry at him for the remark. And he was
too worried about his father.

"Bakhtiian saw Katya," said Stefan. "Lady Jadranka had
him called in. That was five days ago. But he's said nothing
of the interview. He hardly speaks at all."

"I will get him to talk."

"I hope you can. Will you send me down to the well,
please, in case I might see Jaelle there? If only we had

something to send to Katya, I might be allowed to deliver it."

"I'll ask tonight."

But he had no chance to ask. He was escorted to dinner at the great hall and placed at the high table, to Rusudani's left, two places away from Prince Janos. The envoy from Mircassia sat on Janos' right, with Lady Jadranka beyond him. Vasha ate steadily while Janos remained immersed in conversation with the envoy and occasionally turned to address a question to his wife. Rusudani seemed preoccupied, glancing now and again toward the door that led into the inner ward and thence to the kitchens, from which the servers came and went with food and wine. She caught Vasha's eye once and immediately blushed prettily and stared at her plate. She was picking at her food, moving it around with her knife. Vasha recalled what Janos had said about the women of his people.

"I greet you in God's name, Princess Rusudani," he said haltingly in Yos.

Startled, like the deer he had seen flushed out of thickets in the forest hunt, she looked up at him, away toward her husband, who spoke earnestly with the envoy, and back at Vasha. "I hope you will *something or other* to my husband, Prince Vasil'ii," she said in a whisper. "I did it *something or other* your father."

He smiled blankly at her, transfixed by the mention of his father and by her beautiful eyes and sweet curve of her jaw. Remembered himself and looked down at his plate and the remains of a hank of meat.

"Do you understand me?" she asked slowly.

He shook his head. "Little. Only little."

She glanced toward her husband again before leaning further toward Vasha. She wore a faint scent like rose water. His pulse raced. When she spoke again, she spoke slowly, pausing between each word. "I spoke a *something* to save your father. Can you forgive me?"

"Yes!" Vasha was ecstatic that she had been thinking about him at least as much as to feel that she ought to apologize, he supposed for convincing Prince Janos that he, not Bakhtiian, was the valuable hostage.

"I hope," she added, "that Janos *serves* you with *honor.*"

He wasn't quite sure about some of the words, but he assured her that it was so as much to see the grace of her smile

as because Janos had, in fact, treated him well. Then, recalling his conversation with Janos about women and their
lovers, he felt abashed and lowered his gaze away from her
to stare at his trencher. Among the jaran, it wouldn't truly
matter if Rusudani was married to another man. He might
still hope she would take him as a lover. Now he understood
why Tess said that marriage was a prison for women among
the khaja. Which made him think of Katerina, locked in her
tower.

"Princess Rusudani," he began.

A crash came from the anteroom. A man shouted, and
they heard more shouts, some scuffling. The steward rushed
out to the high table. He looked outraged.

"He *something* to pour wine for the high table, my lord.
He threw the *something* against the wall. I beg your pardon
for the *something*. I will send him to *something*."

Rusudani came to life. In a low but determined voice, she
ripped into the steward. Janos started to defend the steward,
but Rusudani cut him off, saying something about her servant and the respect due to her. She rose. All those seated at
the high table were by now silent, watching this altercation.
Janos glanced toward the Mircassian envoy, then made a
gesture with one hand to the steward, who escorted
Rusudani out into the anteroom.

Janos leaned toward Vasha. "Your priest is refusing to
serve wine at the table, Prince Vasil'ii. Is this also a task
which is beneath his dignity? Even though he is a captive
and a slave, on my sufferance? I could have him whipped
and put in the dungeon for such disrespect."

"Among my people, Prince Janos, Singers are ruled only
by the gods."

"You are no longer among your people, Prince Vasil'ii,
and this man is too proud. You will speak with him. He must
understand that whatever honor he receives among your people, here he is merely yet another servant. If he obeys, he
might hope to better his position."

Vasha wanted to laugh, but not because he found Janos's
words amusing. It was impossible. Perhaps the young man
known as Ilyakoria Orzhekov might once have been the kind
of lad willing to endure such trials for the hope of future
gain; the man who had earned the name Bakhtiian, he-who-
has-traveled-far, would not. Stefan himself had said it: He

would rather die than accept that another man ruled over him.

But there was no harm in using this opportunity. "It would be better for him to speak with my cousin Katerina."

Janos began to shake his head, then halted. Rusudani came out of the anteroom. Bakhtiian followed her, carrying a flask. His expression was a mask, frozen, and Vasha saw deep in his eyes a hint of the furious madness that raged within him. He was taut with it, strung so tightly that soon the pressure would break him.

"How is it that he will obey her and not me or my steward or my captains?" Janos asked.

"Because she is a woman, Prince Janos. All men must show the proper respect toward women."

And what man would not wish to make as beautiful a woman as Rusudani happy, thought Vasha, averting his gaze and staring down at his hands, embarrassed to be seated here in a place of honor while his father, a Singer chosen by the gods, ruler of the greatest empire he knew of, served wine at the table.

They retired to the solar after supper. Here Rusudani received the envoy and his letter for the first time. She read it carefully. No emotion troubled her even countenance, but her hands trembled slightly. Once she glanced at her husband. Once she glanced toward Bakhtiian, who stood near the door. Last, finishing the letter, she looked up briefly at Vasha. He was gratified by her attention.

The envoy indulged himself in some personal effusions toward Rusudani. Vasha found that he could follow the gist of the conversation: the king speaks fondly of her; he hopes she can hasten to the court; certain arrangements for her journey and for her arrival had been made, too complicated for Vasha to understand.

"How soon can you make ready to leave?" Janos asked.

Surprised, Rusudani looked to Lady Jadranka, but the older woman merely shook her head. "I have little enough in my possession, my lord," she replied softly. "How soon can an escort be made ready for me and those servants I choose to take with me?"

"I will escort you myself, of course, my lady. We will leave in three days."

"The prisoners?"

"I will leave Lady Katherine under my mother's care."

"Prince Vasil'ii will travel with us, then," she said with quiet authority.

So it was decided.

"I will make sure you come with me," Vasha said to Stefan when the guards returned him to his tower chamber.

"That's all very well, but what about Bakhtiian? What will happen to him? What if the army manages to trace us here only to find us gone?"

"We can't expect to be rescued. I have already spoken with Prince Janos about the possibility of an alliance."

Stefan stared, but any reply he might make was interrupted by the arrival of the khaja priest, the one who ministered to Lady Jadranka and her women. He wore a mask of disapproval as three guards dragged in Ilya, whose arms were bound behind his back.

"My lord," said the khaja priest in his stiff Taor. "Princess Rusudani entreats you to speak with this vassal and urge him to take heed of his life. He was whipped by Lord Belos for disobedience and then he struck at Lord Belos. It will not do, but Princess Rusudani hopes that God will see fit to bring this man to the true faith, so she asks you to intercede for him."

Forced to his knees in front of Vasha, Bakhtiian glared at the priest.

"I will speak with him," said Vasha. The khaja left. "Father! You'll get yourself killed if you keep on this way!"

"Untie me," snapped Ilya. Stefan began to unknot the rope. "You went hunting with Prince Janos. What did you learn, of him, of the land hereabouts? Is there any news of the army?"

"No news of the army. Of the rest, I can fashion a map in the ashes for you to see. Of Janos. . . ." Vasha paused while Ilya stood up, shaking out his arms, and began to pace out the room. He had a welt on one cheek, red and swollen. "We are traveling to Mircassia. We leave in three days. Princess Rusudani is to be invested as the heir to King Barsauma, and Janos is to be her consort. She is sympathetic to us, Father, and Janos's position at his father's court is not strong, so it will be in his interest to make a treaty with the jaran. That way—"

"Janos will get no treaty from the jaran."

Vasha flinched as though hit. "But Father, an alliance with

Janos and through him with Rusudani and King Barsauma will allow us to direct our forces against Filis, and as well, once we are in Mircassia and the treaty is sealed—"

"By whose hand?"

"By mine, representing the jaran." He hunched his shoulders, expecting his father to scold him for his presumption or, worse, to laugh at him. But Ilya, strangely, said nothing. "After that, that might give us, or at least you, the opportunity to return to the jaran army, with a copy of the treaty."

Ilya stopped in the center of the chamber and turned a burning gaze on Vasha. He looked more than a little crazy. "Tess will come for me."

"Tess probably thinks you are dead."

"She will still come."

"Even if she does, the alliance still is wise. Imagine if Mircassia is our ally and not our enemy."

"What of Katerina?"

"She is to stay here under the protection of Lady Jadranka when we ride south."

Ilya snorted. "And what do you think of that, my boy?"

Stung, Vasha strode over to the window loop and strained to see Katerina's tower, but he could only see the stairs that wound up the parapet. "What ought I to think of it? She will be as safe as any of us are."

"You don't understand the khaja, Vasha. She is not safe at all. She has already been *raped*." Speaking in khush, he switched to Rhuian, and it took Vasha a moment to understand the word.

"What do you mean?"

"What do you suppose I mean? Prince Janos raped her. He means to keep her as a mistress. She told me herself. I saw her once while you were out plotting treaties with the man who forced her."

"I didn't know!" Vasha cried, horrified. How could such a thing happen to a woman? How could Lady Jadranka have let it happen? How could *Janos* do such a thing . . . but there his imagination failed him. He could not conceive of Janos, whom he liked, whom he had many reasons to like, forcing a woman. It was inexplicable. It was impossible. But if it was true . . .

And yet . . .

Too overwhelmed to speak, nevertheless one thought intruded insistently into the chaos of his thoughts.

"But even if it's true," he muttered, bracing himself against the stone wall, "It still makes sense to make the alliance."

"Tess has taught you well," said Ilya bitterly, sarcastically. "That was truly spoken like a khaja." And in the next breath: "She will come for me." Abruptly he sat down on the bed and began to talk to himself. "A bright light appeared from heaven and on this light he ascended. Father Wind knit a rope and Mother Sun cast a spark on it from out of her eye and glowing it reached down to the tents of the people, and up this rope climb those whom the gods have marked for their own. Farther he climbed than the angels, whose wings shone in the air with the glory of God's light and filled the heavens with the light of a thousand campfires. By this light you may know him."

Vasha sidled over to Stefan. "What's he doing?" he whispered.

Stefan put two fingers over his mouth and drew Vasha aside, away from Bakhtiian, but Ilya seemed to have forgotten they were there. "He began this about ten days ago, after he was beaten by the overseer, when Nikita tried to take the blows for him. He just goes on like this, as Singers do sometimes, speaking words that the gods have poured into them."

"As far above as angels, he surveyed the lands, and by this sign he recognized his fate, that the sword given him would carve from many lands one land for is it not said that where the gods touch the earth then must all rivers run like the wind and the few shall become the many and the blind shall see. And out of this dispute did Mother Sun exile her only daughter to the earth and sent with her ten sisters who bore the ten tribes of the jaran. And the dyan of the first tribe fell in love with the daughter of the sun. She refused him, as any heaven-born creature must. He led his jahar into battle and fell to a grievous blow. Wounded unto death, he begged her for healing. Healing him, she loved him, and together they made a child."

Suddenly he leapt up and began to beat a fist against the wall, as if trying to batter it down, over and over again. Vasha jumped forward, to restrain him, but Stefan caught his arm and dragged him back.

"Let him alone. You must let him alone, Vasha. He'll just rage worse if you try to stop him."

So Vasha watched helplessly as his father bloodied his

hands against the unyielding stone. After a while Ilya slumped down and sat staring at nothing.

"Father," Vasha said, bringing him water, but Ilya would not drink or even acknowledge his existence. "Father, if Tess comes, you must have the strength to leave this place." Ilya stirred. "Father. Please."

And, finally, he drank.

Jaelle and Katerina watched from the tower the commotion caused by Prince Janos's arrival at White Tower. That evening, two servants brought a magnificent tray of food from the feasting that was, evidently, going on in the great hall.

"He will come to see you tomorrow or the next day," said Jaelle, feeling that she might broach this subject now with Katerina. "It would be prudent of you to greet him kindly."

"You think it would be prudent of me to allow him to lie with me, don't you?"

Jaelle hesitated.

Katerina touched her hand, her fingers tracing her knuckles. "You must tell me what you truly think, Jaelle. It does me no good if you are afraid to speak freely."

"What he has offered you is generous. You must make him write it down in a contract. That way you are protected if he ceases to love you. That is your great advantage, your only one."

"My only power is that this man desires me?" Katerina snorted. "That is a sad state of affairs." Her expression softened, and she clasped Jaelle's hand firmly in hers. "But that is all you have had, is it not?"

Surprised and abashed, Jaelle could only nod.

"Well," said Katerina, "I can endure anything, knowing you are my faithful friend." She leaned toward Jaelle, like a lover easing toward a kiss, and stared at her intently. Jaelle felt dizzy, felt a wash of unexpected heat flood her, but she did not know what to say only that she had to say something, for what if Katerina drew back, recoiling from her silence?

"I am," she said, her voice so faint it seemed to die into the air. "I am your faithful friend, Katerina."

Voices sounded on the stairs below. Katerina let go of Jaelle's hand and leapt to her feet. Moments later, the door

to the chamber was unlocked and swung open, and Prince
Janos entered.

"I have come to play castles with you." He handed his
cloak and gloves to a servant. A second man hurried forward
and piled more wood on the fire so that it blazed up. Jaelle
hastily cleared the tray away, but it was taken from her by
a servant and she was left to watch while Janos sat down at
the table and began to set out the pieces, pausing once to examine the knight whose features had been scraped away. He
placed it on the board, making no comment. Servants
brought wine and steadied the fire and fled. Finally, Katerina
walked over to the table and sat down in the chair opposite
Janos. She was not afraid to look at him directly. Jaelle admired her for that.

"I have learned one thing," said Katerina, picking up the
faceless knight and setting it back down, centering it precisely in its square. "That I cannot stop you. You may come
here. I will play castles, since I am bored."

Now he looked up at her, searching her face, his gaze uncomfortably fixed on her. "And my other suit?"

"You did not ask before."

"I am asking now."

Her eyes were as blue as the winter ice. "By our laws, Prince
Janos, a man who forces a woman is put to death. You are so
marked now. I will never invite you to my bed, not now, not
at any time, ever, from this day to the day I die."

"What if I married you? You would have no choice in
that, would you, nor about lying with me in my bed?"

"You are already married."

"But if I was not," he pressed, "and I chose to marry you,
then what?"

"Then you would be a fool for losing Princess Rusudani."

"But you would be mine."

Katerina shifted in her chair, looking, for once, at a loss
for words. "I want to see my cousin," she said in a low
voice.

"Become my mistress of your own free will, and this will
not be denied you."

Katerina laughed, sharp and surprised. "Is this how khaja
men court women?"

"It is your move," said Janos, indicating the pieces.

"You cannot defeat me, Prince Janos," she said softly, almost like a warning. But she moved a piece. "Your mother

has treated me kindly. I would like to send my servant to the marketplace to buy her a gift, in thanks."

"With what will you buy this gift?"

She slipped a fine gold necklace off her neck, handling it as if it were the merest trinket. "She may take this to trade."

He hesitated, hand poised over a foot soldier. "Very well," he said, moving the piece one square forward. "She may go tomorrow."

"You will purchase a suitable gift for Lady Jadranka," said Katerina in the morning as she helped Jaelle on with a cloak, "perfume, perhaps, or a fine bolt of silk, if they have such a thing for sale here. Then you must find a healer ... I don't know what the khaja call them. A woman or a man who can give you herbs, *trefin* or *enefis,* perhaps they know of others here, that will prevent a woman from conceiving. You must know of such things."

"I do."

"If there is coin left, then buy something for yourself."

"Good wool cloth," said Jaelle instantly. "Winter is coming on."

Katerina laughed and kissed Jaelle on the cheek. "You're very practical. My grandmother would like you." Abruptly she flushed and released her, and Jaelle, equally flustered, took a step back. "Go on. The guards are waiting."

In the chamber below, Lady Jadranka waited for her. "I had hoped to persuade my son to allow Lady Katherine to go on an outing, but I see that she has convinced him to let you go to the marketplace for her. I will go up."

Outside, Rusudani just happened to be crossing the courtyard with her ladies, heading for the chapel. She halted and approached Jaelle. "This is Lady Katherine's cloak," she said, fingering it. Taken aback, Jaelle stood stiffly, but Rusudani nudged her gently, her hand hidden in the folds of the cloak, and passed her a little bag filled with coin. "I see that Lady Jadranka has persuaded Janos to let you out to the market."

Jaelle took refuge in silence, not sure anymore whose cause she was furthering. She had an idea that Katerina would not approve of her seeking out a love potion meant to work on Bakhtiian, and at the same time, she wondered if Rusudani understood Katerina's position in relation to her own; certainly she must know nothing about the troubling questions Prince Janos had asked about marriage last night.

The outer ward was alive with activity. It looked rather like the great courtyard of a caravansary when a large caravan was making preparations to set off. By the armorer's forge, she saw Stefan helping to hold a horse while it was shoed. Setting down a hoof, he looked up and saw her, and his face lit. Without meaning to, she smiled at him, forgot herself enough that she slowed down and received, for her lapse, a groping hand from one of her escorts.

"Move along," the man said, feeling for her breast.

She jerked forward away from his hands and resolutely looked forward, away from Stefan. "I am Princess Katherine's servant, and I am to be treated with respect," she said haughtily, and to her surprise the man moved away from her.

They went out through the gates and down into the town that lay at the foot of the castle. The guards remained civil to her, as if her reminder had refined her status in their eyes: no longer a common whore, she was now a serving woman important enough to be noticed by Lady Jadranka and Princess Rusudani. A servant whose complaints might conceivably be brought to the attention of the prince.

In the marketplace they shadowed her but left her alone to browse and bargain. She was ill-used to such luxury. She haggled over perfume, enjoying herself, and haggled further, in a kind of three-way bargaining with a perfumer and a neighboring jeweler, over the price of the necklace. In the end, she got the perfume, some coin, and, the greatest prize of the transaction, the direction of an herbwoman who was known to be discreet and reliable, and who knew a bit of the trade language.

On market day Mistress Kunane conducted her business from a stall in vegetable row. Bundles of herbs hung from her cart, fragrant even in the open air.

"I come from the castle for herbs to sweeten my lady's chamber," said Jaelle. Lowering her voice, she added, "and herbs for myself, to sweeten a man's heart."

Mistress Kunane did not reply at once. A robust woman, she eyed the guards fiercely, as if she intended to take a stick to them. They backed up four steps. Then, pinching off herbs into a cloth bag, she examined Jaelle's face and cloak and clean but mended gown. "A girl as pretty as you has everything she needs to draw a man to her."

"Alas, Mother, not every man loves with his eyes."

The herbwoman grunted, but she seemed amused. "You are a foreign woman. Did you come in with those foreigners that was brought in by the prince, God save him?"

"I am. I'm desperate for love of him, Mother."

"More likely it's your mistress, whoever she may be, who is wanting a man she ought not to be looking at. There's naught I can do for that."

"But you must, Mistress. What will I tell her otherwise?"

"Tell her that a man's heart is best left untouched. Is there aught else I can get you?"

By now Jaelle was feeling desperate. "But can't you give me something? I must have something to take back to her." Behind her, the guards were growing restive, trying to listen in. "There is another thing . . . if I get with child I'll lose my position and the master will throw me out on the streets. . . ." The lie came out easily, but soon as it was said aloud it took on a horrible significance. *If I get with child.* She flushed, the heat like pinpricks along her cheeks.

"Tell me the truth," said Mistress Kunane. She took her walking stick and struck the nearest guard on the forearm. He yelped and jumped back, and the rest of the guards, startled as well but also chuckling at his discomfiture, moved away again.

"I am just a serving woman, Mother. I have been sent here to procure these things, one for a woman who will suffer needlessly if she gets with child, the other for . . . I don't know what will happen if the other gets no satisfaction, whether she will blame me or go another way to get what she wants. Please, Mistress."

"The holy church enjoins against love potions. I cannot help you, child, only give you sweet herbs to scent the body. As for the other—"

The great bell in the church tower tolled, drowning out the cheerful noise of the marketplace. Once, a second time, and a third, then a pause the length of three rings. And again. And again.

"Ten coppers for the lot," said Mistress Kunane. Jaelle scarcely had time to give a single silver coin into her hand before the guards grabbed her bodily and hustled her away. All around her, merchants closed their shops and windows were flung shut and bolted. The harmonious undertone of market day erupted into a frightful roar, as if a wave had burst onto a peaceful shore. The bell rang, and paused, and rang again, on and on.

"What is it? What's wrong?" Jaelle shouted, but the guards were intent on getting back into the castle and dragged her along, ignoring her questions. Once in the outer ward they simply left her to fight her own way through the surging crowd of servants that swamped the courtyard. By the armory, a growing knot of men formed, and Jaelle saw at once that the armorer's apprentices were passing out armor and weapons.

"Jaelle!" Stefan slipped an arm around her and steered her toward the inner ward. "They've forgotten all about me. Can you get me in to see Katya?"

"I don't know. I don't think so. What is happening?"

Then of course she knew. Stupidly, she had forgotten that it might come to this. His face was exultant, alight.

"They're coming," he said. "The army is coming."

"There he is!"

"You will not be abandoned," said Stefan just as the guards reached him. He did not fight as they dragged him away toward one of the towers, toward his prison, but his look struck her to the heart. *You will not be abandoned.*

For a moment she thought that Janos's people might have forgotten her as well, but the truth was, she was no longer entirely insignificant, left to make her own way. One of the guards on the steps saw her before she could duck away and hide by acting busy, and yet she could not regret it when the door opened into the tower chamber and Katerina came running to her.

"What is happening?" Katerina asked.

"The army is coming."

Katerina laughed, fairly crowed, and kissed her with delight. Below, White Tower prepared for war.

CHAPTER FORTY

The Golden Sea

Ilyana sat vigil at Valentin's bedside while the adults argued outside in the courtyard.

"You are not taking him anywhere without our permission," said her father. "Not off this planet, not until the company has finished its run here."

"Shut up." That was David. Ilyana flinched. She had never heard him so angry before. He walked around in a cloud of anger now, ever since the horrible moment when Vasil had jerked Valentin's body off the nesh lattice. "Now, Yomi—"

"Did you hear me?" asked Vasil.

"You're no longer a player in this discussion, Veselov," snapped David.

A scuffle ensued. Ilyana heard a grunt, several gasps from the onlookers, and a few choice swear words.

"Let him go, Gwyn," said Yomi in a tired voice. "Vasil, you either agree to sit and listen, or I'll have to ask Yassir to put you under house arrest. He did his public service in the constabulary and is still deputized."

Karolla said, in khush, "This is women's business, Vasil. You must wait patiently until it is your turn to have your say."

"What about the others? I must defend our honor, Karolla."

"We cannot expect that khaja will behave with equal courtesy. Now sit, husband."

Ilyana heard the rustling of the company taking positions once more, a few coughs, a nervous whisper. They began to debate again: Maggie O'Neill is coming down on a shuttle, bringing a more advanced stasis bed. She should take the boy back to a class one trauma center. He shouldn't be moved; we have to find his nesh first. That comment produced a whole new debate, about body and spirit and whether it was true that the spirit lived independently in nesh which accelerated into a full fledged argument about gnosticism, superstition, and the technology of nesh, most of which Ilyana could not follow.

Oblivious to this, Valentin's body respirated, hooked up to the bed. It gave him fluids. What else it did, Ilyana was not sure. She was not sure if he was breathing on his own or if the bed was doing that for him, too. But without the bed he would waste to nothing and die. His knees were already curling up toward his chest. Sometimes his hands twitched. She could see his veins through the pallor of his skin, a web of blood linking him to the world of breathing.

David came in and sat down beside her. "I can't stand to listen to that any more." He looked at Valentin and away, unable to endure the sight of the boy's flaccid, empty face.

"Let me try to find him in nesh," Ilyana pleaded.

"No. *No.* Anyway, the nesh screen is broken now. You can't reach him."

"I could use your nesh."

"That wouldn't do any good. It isn't connected to the nesh they have here in the palace."

"Yes, it is," she blurted out, then blushed, having betrayed herself.

Mercifully, David only gave her a look. "Others have tried. They found nothing."

"They don't know Valentin, they don't know this palace like I do."

"How can we let you go, after this happened?"

"I'm not addicted to nesh. I'm not going to lose myself in there. I'm the only one who can find him."

"And then?"

"Maybe I can convince him to come back."

"He has sustained systemic nervous system damage. Maybe he can't come back. Oh, Goddess." He pressed a palm on his forehead, as if massaging a headache. "I can't believe I'm saying this, as if Valentin even exists in any form inside nesh. Yana, he's gone. He doesn't somehow exist independently in nesh. He's in a coma, he has brain damage. There's no magical formula to reunite body and spirit in some kind of dualistic orgy. We have to get him off planet and to a trauma center."

"But you can't take his body away from where he lost his spirit—"

"Yana! There isn't some part of him that's lost in there. It's a myth. If he's going to recover, he can do it only under advanced neurological treatment."

"At least you could let me try."

He hesitated, and by that she knew she had won. "All right. We'll do it tonight, in here. I'll go in with you, and Hyacinth will monitor the connection."

Yomi came in. "Yana, your mother wishes to speak with you. I'll go along, if you'd like."

"No. I can go alone." Ilyana stood up. "Where are the children?"

"Evdokia seems to be fine with Portia and Diana, but Hyacinth finally had to take Anton back because he was acting up so badly. It's difficult to know what is the right choice to make. I did my public service in the constabulary, too, but on a counseling beat, so it isn't as if I haven't seen this kind of thing before."

"What's going to happen, when we get back to Earth?"

"Your neighborhood constabulary will be notified and your family will be assigned a monitor and an advocate. For now, I've taken responsibility."

"I should have said something sooner," muttered David. He reached out and tentatively brushed a strand of Valentin's pale hair back around the whorl of an ear, then withdrew his hand, looking uncomfortable. Looking guilty.

"You have my permission to beat yourself about the head and shoulders," said Yomi sardonically, but her gaze, resting on the boy, was mournful, and she shook her head. "Go on," she said gently to Ilyana. "Get it over with. That's a pretty belt. Is it a silk scarf?"

Ilyana gave a stiff smile and backed out of the room, crossing her wrists over the sash, which she had wrapped around her waist. She found her mother at the tent.

"Ah, Yana, sit down here beside me."

Ilyana shook her head and remained standing on the edge of the carpet, not coming in under the awning. Little Rose lay on her back on the carpet, staring at her fists, and Anton lay on his stomach, reading from a flat screen.

"You will sit," repeated Karolla, an edge on her voice.

"I won't."

"What have I done to deserve this disrespect from my eldest daughter?"

"What have you done! Is it true that you let that financier

get close to Valentin, to use him? That you knew about it
and let it go on?"

"It is usual for an experienced woman to initiate a boy—"

"She was *using* him. She was molesting him! A woman
like that would never have been allowed near a boy his age,
in the tribes."

"You know nothing about life in the tribes, Yana! You
think you know, but you have no idea—"

"I don't think it's anything you'd ever dare tell my grandmother, if you saw her now, that's what I think!"

"If your grandmother saw what an insolent, disrespectful
creature you have become, then it's true she would wonder
where I had failed, in teaching you manners, child. This is
what comes of allowing you khaja friends and khaja school-
ing."

"That's all that saved me!" Ilyana retorted, then faltered.
Her mother had retreated so far from her, into some other
world, like Valentin into nesh, that she realized she could not
reach her. She wanted to ask, to accuse, to find out if it was
true that Vasil had tried to bargain her away to the cultural
minister in exchange for smuggling him onto Rhui, but she
could not. She could not bear to know. There, coming out of
the caravansary, came her father.

Ilyana fled from him, ignoring her mother calling after
her. She ran to the ruined caravansary, where the sun beat
down on the worn walls and baked the scent of dust into the
air. She sat down on a tumbled lintel and leaned her head
back against a brick wall. Shutting her eyes, she imagined
the walls built back up, the courtyard alive with carts and
animals, merchants haggling over marching order and horses
drinking from the trough. She built a greater caravansary, a
whole complex of them, gateways for a thousand caravans
departing for other countries, for other planets, for worlds
inside and outside nesh. The sun's warmth kissed her face
and slowly slid down her body until only her bare feet lay
within its glow. Her toes worked at the dirt, wearing away a
hollow in ground worn level and hard by a century of traffic.
Except there couldn't have been any traffic here, could
there? What caravans would have come through this place?
Where would they have been going?

Where was Anatoly Sakhalin right now?

She covered her face with her hands, ashamed at herself
for thinking of him. What would it be like, if he had not al-

ready been married? If he had married her? She would have her own tent, and even within her mother's influence, she could take the younger children into her tent and Anatoly could have fostered her brothers. It was true that in many ways he held to the old ways as firmly as her mother did, but he seemed able to move between the worlds, to make enough compromises, to understand that there must be flexibility ... to understand that it took both compression and tension, push and pull, to make a building stand upright.

She heard the whisper of soft bells. Jerking her hands down, she stared at the opposite wall where a shadow loomed, a man's shadow, to her right, poised back around the corner. He had a lithe body, a head crowned with a braided headdress, and four arms. The shadow did not move. Neither did she. Paralyzed, she tried to wish herself into stone, but she wasn't in nesh. She remained flesh.

Finally, panting, she forced herself up. She refused to wait in fear. But as she moved the shadow moved, somewhere in the lane behind her, and she darted around the corner to see what was there, but all she caught was the shadow of movement, a whisper of bells moving away into the dark belly of the catacombs. Her heart was thudding so loudly in her chest and in her ears that it drowned out the noise of the world. What if she hadn't pulled her hands down and looked right at that moment? Why would a statue be wandering in this caravansary? How could a statue wander at all? Or had she only dreamed it?

The sun was setting. Its light glittered on the rings of the planet, pale arches like delicate bracelets in the sky. Like the ankle bracelets jaran girls wore, to signify how many lovers they had taken. In a ditch, a straggling line of weeds boasted tiny flowers, closing now as the sun left them. The wind came up. She felt alone and utterly isolated.

"I can't go back," she said to the air. "It's not my home anymore."

Like an echo, caught in a maze of rooms, she heard the distant murmur of bells. *It is never wise to attract the notice of the gods.* She bolted. She ran all the way back to the other caravansary and finally halted, out of breath, outside the curtained doorway of the room where they had installed Valentin.

"I could have done something about it," David was saying. "Goddess, I knew, and I didn't *do* anything."

"No wonder you're angry at everyone else," replied Hyacinth.

"Oh, hell, it's true. I'm just so furious at myself."

"You couldn't have known this would happen."

"That's what we always say, isn't it?"

"I can see you're in a self-defeating mood. I won't trot out the rest of the cliches, then. We're not going to be here much longer, though. I know Owen is angling for us to tour farther into Chapalii space. What's going to happen then?"

"Maybe the best thing for those kids would be to stay on Earth and be fostered to someone else, with Veselov a good long way away from them."

"Veselov won't be touring with the company again."

"Why not?

"You don't know? You can't see it? He's lost it. He doesn't know how to act anymore, only how to pose. Owen is thoroughly disgusted with him, but he's contracted to the end of *this* run."

"Well, whatever it takes, we need to keep him away from those kids."

"Do you blame him more than her, then?"

"Yes, I do. What a self-centered egotistical bastard he is. Karolla is just so self-negating as to be a cipher."

"Oh, I would say that she's as inflexible. No, I'd say she's more inflexible. Don't forget I've lived upstairs from them for seven years now. I like to be generous and spread blame around. Listen, David, have you ever visited their flat? No? Let me just say that they made their bed and now they're lying in it."

"That didn't happen to Yevgeni."

"Only because in the end we got up enough courage to admit that we couldn't do it on our own."

"But Sakhalin never got counseling that I know of, nor did Diana ever go to the constabulary and ask for an advocate."

"That's true. Anatoly Sakhalin may be an arrogant bastard, but if you prod him enough, you can at least get him to think. But there's going to be hell to pay between him and Di when he gets back. I think she's going to file for a dissolution."

"Oh, no."

"Oh, yes. David, I hope you're not blind enough to have missed that she's taken up with Yassir. The lighting designer.

So Anatoly will end up paying the price one way or the other."

"And what about Ilyana?" David asked.

Ilyana pushed through the curtain and went into the room, not wanting to hear whatever Hyacinth might say about her. "I'm ready," she said. "I'm ready to go for Valentin."

She walks the web of light and drops down into the hall of memory. David is not with her. She remembers seeing him place his hands on the nesh sponge, remembers a finger placed against hers, the comforting warmth of his body next to her, remembers Hyacinth holding one of Valentin's hands against the sponge, just in case, but now she is here, alone, falling into the cavern of time, where Shiva danced the anandatandava in the hall of consciousness within the heart of woman, within the heart of man.

"I'm looking for my brother," she says desperately, for Genji is there, her robes rustling with a thousand small voices as she moves from a lit corridor out into the grand hall. "He got lost in here."

"It is careless to lose a brother," says Genji. "They are difficult to replace."

Ilyana wants to ask her if she has lost brothers, but she is afraid to, because here in nesh even more than out in the surface world she is aware of the passage of time, of the incremental slippage that drags Valentin farther and farther away from her, falling into the deepest wilderness, unmapped, much of it as yet unmade, formless. . . .

"I know where he's gone," she says aloud as she realizes where he must be. Without thinking, or with thinking but without forethought, she builds the gate to the memory palace out of the seamless black floor and walks through to find David standing in the courtyard. "We have to go to the desert," she says. "That's where he went. He went to the desert."

So David takes them through the shortcut he built, the vine lattice which passes through the stultifying humidity of the jungle and then into the sere heat of the endless, empty plain. Here it is flat, packed sand in a parched monotone extending to the horizon. Nothing stirs. She sees no sign of life.

"I don't see him," says David needlessly. "There's nothing out here."

But there is the smell of baking heat, and the sour taste of grit, and the biting sand that gets into her ears and rubs in the collar of her blouse and blisters the soles of her feet. And there, half hidden in a tiny drift of sand, dried camel droppings. This is still Valentin's land. His soul still exists here.

"Not here," she says, remembering. "He's trying to get through to somewhere else." Through the storm.

She stretches out her hands, her fingertips. She reaches for the sand, feels its grain, its silicate structure. In true nesh, she could not alter the constructs of another person's habitat, but this is not true nesh, this is another type of nesh entirely, formless matter inhabited by a trace of Valentin's soul.

She draws the sand up into the air and calls the wind from the north, blowing down upon her, she draws it through her until she is scoured clean inside and herself becomes a gateway. She pushes forward into the storm which is also herself. She forms in her memory the image of that place that Valentin struggled toward, the golden sea—not, as she had thought, that bronze gold undulation of endless sand which is the desert, but a moving sea rippled by currents of wind.

She battles forward, but the way is made easier because someone has already forged this path, she is only rediscovering it for herself, Valentin has already come before her, she can see the signs of his passing like an echo of his being. The golden light glares brighter and brighter until she has to shut her eyes against the blinding glare which is both of her and outside of her. The wind howls, screaming against her, the sand tearing her to ribbons. Then she feels the hot breath of a summer wind and she throws herself through, heedless of David struggling behind her.

And she is out on a golden plain flying above it like a bird. She is a bird. She is a fledgling eagle, soaring above a sea of grass. Sharp-sighted, she can see three days' ride away, and there, beyond the swell and ebb of the ground and the endless motion of the wind through the grass, she sees a tribe moving.

Swifter than horses, she wings toward them, spying them out. As with any tribe, there are women and carts and children and the men of the jahar, dressed in the pale and bright surcoats of Bakhtiian's army. There is her uncle, Anton Veselov, just as she remembers him, and beside him, a far mistier memory, is her grandfather, Dmitri Mikhailov, Karolla's

*father and the man who led the final, failed rebellion against
Ilyakoria Bakhtiian in the tribes. And there, riding beside
the men with her bow strapped across her back, is Valye
Usova. A herd of horses and a bigger herd of glariss, bleat-
ing and trotting in the familiar unruly mob, trails the line of
wagons. An old woman drives the lead wagons; Ilyana takes
a moment to recognize her. It is Mother Sakhalin, ancient,
surely dead by now . . . but of course the others here are
dead, too. She swoops down and as a child in the second
cart points up into the heavens, marking her descent, she
sees the driver of the second string of wagons: Her aunt,
Arina Veselov. And riding beside her, an old but hale man,
the healer Nikolai Sibirin whom she vaguely remembers.*

*Ilyana feels a terrible fear. She feels as if the heavens are
contracting around her, but the sky remains cold and piercingly blue, as infinite as the grass. She lands, fluttering, on
the second wagon, perched on the rim of the wagon beside
Arina Veselov, who looks at her with grave eyes.*

*"Where is Valentin?" Ilyana asks, but it only comes out as
a shriek, an eagle's call, fierce and challenging.*

*"A spirit is visiting us from the heavens," says Niko
Sibirin.*

*Despairing, Ilyana flings herself skyward and flies, any-
where, away, not wanting to watch the tribe as it rides on
across the golden sea of grass. Was this what Valentin
wanted?* I want to go home, *he had said. The tribe continues
on its way, receding into the distance behind her.*

*But there, a tiny speck in the grass, comes a rider. She
wings closer, dives, heart fluttering in her chest with excitement.*

It is! It is Valentin, riding a young bay mare.

"Valentin!" she cries in her eagle's voice. "Valentin!"

*He does not heed her. She swoops down, but he is intent
on riding. He marks her only as a great bird, a spirit, watching from the heavens. His face is alight. Like a stone in her
stomach, Ilyana realizes that he is happy.*

"Valentin! It's me. It's Ilyana. Come back. Come back."

*But he keeps on riding, and though she tries, she cannot
transform herself here. She is an eagle, a spirit, come from
another land. She flies along with him until the wind picks
up, driving her backward. Battling against it, she loses
ground, he recedes from her, and she is torn away, sucked*

back through, and the plain is swallowed up in a howling storm of sand and grit battering against her and she feels a firm hand pull her back into the smothering haven of the jungle and she walks two steps, weeping, down the marble foyer that passes through the gate of the memory palace.

Weeping, Ilyana let go of the sponge. "He can't hear me! He couldn't hear me, he just kept on riding!"

"Where did you go?" David asked in a hoarse voice. "I couldn't follow you."

"Goddess," swore Hyacinth, fainter. "You've been gone for hours. Take some water."

"He's trying to go home," said Ilyana, and then she was sobbing so hard that she could no longer talk.

CHAPTER FORTY-ONE

A Taste of Betrayal

Guards took Vasha to the battlements and there he found Prince Janos surveying the army that, three days after the first alert, now surrounded the town and castle of White Tower. Staring at Janos's back, Vasha tried to imagine the khaja man forcing Katya, but he could not. Another khaja man, perhaps, but not Janos. Anyway, Katya would never let such a thing happen to her. Janos swung around, and Vasha was abruptly reminded of the bruises Janos had received before the hunting trip, as if he had fallen down . . . or gotten in a fight.

Seeing Vasha, Janos beckoned him to the wall. "How can you advise me, Prince Vasil'ii?"

Rather than speak to him, Vasha stared down at the army laying siege below: tents set up outside of catapult range, the sheer number of horses, and farther back, at the limit of his vision, the sudden onset of industry where the engineers would be directing the building of siege engines, towers, and the other paraphernalia of war. As a strike force setting out to join Yaroslav Sakhalin's army, this group had no such weapons with them, but they knew how to build them, how to draft the local peasants to do the work under the supervision of soldiers. He knew this force, of course, knew the banners and recognized the colors: there, the red and gold of his father's personal guard, the half that had stayed with the army and thus not perished in the ambush; there, various tribal colors. But most startling, flying among the banners, was the eagle rising, wings elevated and displayed, the heraldic device of the Prince of Jeds. Tess had come for revenge.

"I can give you no advice," he said finally, miserably. "Those are my own people." He wanted to ask about Katya, but he dared not.

"I don't want to fight them. My defenses are strong, but

as you can see they outnumber me. Is that banner not the banner of the Prince of Jeds? I would choose to negotiate. You know that is true. I can offer them an advantageous alliance. What can I send them as surety for my good will?"

Vasha almost said, 'the priest,' but discarded that idea. It was dangerous now to bring too much attention to Ilya. In any case, the army below would not be in a mood to negotiate. "Send an envoy. That is all you can do. They will not grant you terms."

"You seem certain of that. I would send you, of course, but I must hold you in reserve. I hope you take no offense of it."

"I take none. But there is one thing . . ." He met Janos's gaze. "Free Princess Katerina. That would show you mean well."

There it was, the knowledge in his eyes, that easy to see once you knew to look for it. Janos turned away from Vasha, hiding his expression, and Vasha was swamped with something like grief, a taste of betrayal. So it was true. Janos, decent to him, had raped Katerina. How could one man contain two such faces? And what of Katya, who was, Vasha supposed, never more to be spoken of between them? Janos looked out over the jaran army, the abandoned fields, and the clouds approaching from the east. Vasha felt the first spray of rain, a mist, dampening the stones.

"I will go down now," said Janos to his guards. "Prince Vasil'ii, you will attend me, I hope."

It was not a request. Clearly, Janos did not intend to give up any of his hostages. Nor, Vasha reflected wryly, would he have done any differently in the same situation. Except he would never, ever, force a woman to lie with him. Worst of all, following Janos down the narrow, slick steps, Vasha realized that he could not bring himself to hate the man, only the deed. And by thinking that, he might as well himself have betrayed Katya.

Tess sat under her awning and watched the khaja envoy approach her through the rain. She had sited her tent so that she could see the castle and the hastily-completed defensive works thrown up around the town. The rain gave them a blurred appearance, deceptively soft and welcoming. Because it was growing dark, and the lanterns threw light no farther than the square of her carpets, she did not realize until the envoy ducked under the awning that the man wore the badge of the Mircassian king.

"Why does a Dushan prince send a Mircassian envoy?" she asked, too impatient to waste time on the niceties.

The man bowed, gave his name and title, and looked, not surprisingly, a trifle nervous. "I had arrived at White Tower on other business," he said, recovering his smooth manners, "and volunteered to act as go-between. Prince Janos wishes to know why you have invaded his lands and surrounded his castle."

Tess scowled. "You may take this message back to Prince Janos. If he surrenders himself into my custody, I will spare the town and the castle and everyone who has taken refuge within the walls."

"Your highness—"

"I am not negotiating. Take that message back to him. I want a reply at dawn tomorrow." She gestured to one of the guards to escort him away. Given no choice, he went.

As soon as they were out of earshot, Gennady Berezin crouched down beside her. "You did not ask about hostages."

"Had I asked about them, Prince Janos would know that I knew that he had that power over me. Now he must play that piece himself, in an attempt to counter my first attack."

"If he does not agree to surrender himself? In his position, I would not."

"I know nothing of Prince Janos, whether he is shrewd or foolish. I can only try to force his hand, make him show his full strength early rather than late."

The soldier waved toward the castle. "His position is strong. I am sure we outnumber him, but he is protected by a ditch, a moat, and stone walls."

"Perhaps by more than that. Princess Rusudani is the granddaughter of King Barsauma of Mircassia. A Mircassian envoy comes forward as a representative of Prince Janos. That suggests to me that Janos knows what he possesses, if indeed he possesses the princess. But where else would she have gone? She surely was captured at Urosh Monastery. And if he has jaran hostages as well—"

But there, having said it, she had to stop. Hope pierced her as painfully as any spear might; she felt it physically, she could not speak. She had not spoken Ilya's name in days, as if by speaking it she might somehow release it from the earth and lose him, lose any hope of him.

"We will wait," she said at last. "Prince Janos knows why we want him."

After delivering his message, the Mircassian envoy retreated to the hearth, warming his hands at the great fire as if within its halo of light and heat he might find safety. Except there was no safety to be had within White Tower. Vasha sat in a chair, idly fingering the game pieces, and watched Janos pace the length of the solar and back again. Katya had fought, of course—Vasha was sure of that—but Janos must have overpowered her. And then—but beyond that Vasha could not go. Just could not. Janos looked preoccupied, grim, but not remotely like a man so monstrous that he would force a woman.

"Where is my wife?" Janos said suddenly. A servant scurried out. Sometime later Princess Rusudani swept in, attended by her women, by two guards, and by Bakhtiian. She looked cool and elegant except for two spots of color burning in her cheeks. Ilya held a copy of *The Recitation* in one hand and he stared fixedly at it, seeming not to see the room or Vasha.

"You will attend me," Janos said to her as she entered. She sat down in her chair and began to embroider, the other women arranging themselves around her. They were unnaturally quiet, as if fear kept them from speaking, and finally Rusudani nodded toward Ilya and he opened *The Recitation* and began to read aloud from it in a low voice.

Janos sat down opposite Vasha and set the pieces up for a game. "The Prince of Jeds refuses to negotiate," Janos said.

Ilya's voice faltered. Rusudani signed to him to set down the book, and she began to embroider again, head bowed over the fabric.

"The jaran will not negotiate, my lord," said Vasha.

"What would they do if I surrendered?"

"They will kill you." As Vasha said it, he looked up and saw Rusudani's gaze fixed on them. She glanced away at once, toward Ilya, who stared blindly at the open pages of the book. He was not reading but listening. "But they would also spare the town and all inside."

"Would you surrender yourself under such circumstances?"

"Do you intend to?"

"No. I simply wondered." He beckoned to the Mircassian envoy, and the man crossed the room to stand beside him. "At dawn you will go to the Prince of Jeds and inform her, graciously, that I hold Prince Vasil'ii and Princess Katherine, and that I am willing to enter into negotiations in return for her consideration of an alliance with Mircassia."

To Vasha's surprise, Rusudani stood up. "I am the heir to Mircassia," she said clearly. "Do you intend to negotiate without consulting me?"

Janos rose at once and went over to her. He took her hand and led her to the table. "You have been ten years in the convent, my lady. You have no experience in this. Lord Belos, bring Princess Rusudani some wine."

Her presence affected Vasha so strongly that he had to bow his head. From under his lashes he watched her drink, the curve of her lips on the rim of the glass, the slight movement of her throat. She was so close to him that he could easily have touched her, as Janos touched her, keeping one hand firmly on her as if to mark that she belonged to him. For even more than the hostages, Rusudani was the prize that could save Janos's life.

When she had finished drinking, she spoke, slowly enough that Vasha understood the gist of her words. "My lord husband, I would send the priest to the jaran as surety for your good faith. Give him to them to show that you mean to keep to any treaty you might agree to. Perhaps they will forgive you for ..." She broke off, found her voice again. "For the other. For what transpired at the monastery."

"No," said Janos flatly. "I would be a fool to give up even one. Lord Belos, see that the jaran priest and the others, the soldiers, are put in the dungeon. We may have a use for them later."

Color rose in Rususdani's cheeks. "They are my prisoners, not yours, to dispose of."

"Is it not said in *The Recitation* that a woman ought to be subject to the greater wisdom of a man?"

"Prince Vasil'ii, I appeal to you. Is such a thing said of women among the jaran?"

Her plea startled Vasha, and he stood as well, aware of how near she was. He did not look at her but at the pieces lined neatly up on the gameboard. "No, Princess Rusudani. A woman is subject to no man's authority, except—" He faltered, remembering his conversations with Janos. Remembering Katerina.

"Except her husband?" Janos asked softly.

"Except, at times, that of her husband," Vasha murmured.

Rusudani's hand moved into his field of vision and retreated, and he felt her shift, her movement like a wave against him.

"Lord Belos," said Janos, "see to your duty."

The steward bowed and left.

"All that you have," said Rusudani softly, "came to you through women. I trust you remember that."

"What I have, I intend to hold on to."

Vasha lifted his eyes and met Janos's gaze squarely. He had the sudden, appalling thought that Janos meant, not his mother's lands, not his wife's inheritance, but Katerina. Could it be that Janos *loved* Katerina? But how could a man both love and rape a woman? It was impossible. He must be either lover or rapist; he could not be both together.

Vasha risked a glance at Rusudani, so close to him now that if he leaned forward he could kiss her on the mouth, but she was not looking at her husband. She looked beyond him, at Lord Belos, who brought forward three guards to escort Bakhtiian away. Ilya merely rose and, book still clutched in his right hand, went with them, taut as any caged beast. Lord Belos followed him out.

"I will send for my mother to sit here with you," said Janos. "While we wait."

"No need," replied Rusudani. "I will retire to my chamber."

Janos watched her go. Vasha did not dare to. Finally, when the ladies had all left the solar, Janos sat down again, facing Vasha across the table. He looked restless but determined. "Shall we play?"

That night a footstep sounded in the stairwell, and a scratch came at the door. Jaelle swiftly slid out of Katerina's embrace and got up, pulling a cloak around her. A moment later the door opened. Princess Rusudani slipped inside, holding a small lantern, and held two fingers up to her lips. Lowering them, she untied a small pouch from her gown and held it out toward Jaelle.

"Do not ask questions," she said in a low voice, glancing toward Katerina, who still slept, worn to exhaustion by her endless pacing on the day just passed. "In the morning you will go down to the gates and tell the guard who wears a blue ribbon tied at his belt that you have my leave to go down to the market. You will find the herbwoman and from her you will get a drink, herbs, whatever she might have, that will cause men to sleep, enough for at least twenty men. There is more than enough coin. Get other herbs as well, the love potion if you can, or else that which whores take so that they will not conceive."

Jaelle glanced up at her, surprised that a convent-raised woman would know of such things, but Rusudani was in the grip of a passion and seemed oblivious to her.

"Tomorrow evening, after supper, I will come here with my attendants to visit Princess Katherine and to read from *The Recitation*. You will give me the herbs then. I will find some way to distract the others so that you may give them to me without them noticing."

"How did you get past the guards tonight, my lady?"

Rusudani's gaze did not leave Katerina, and Jaelle grew even more nervous. "Does she love him?" Rusudani asked suddenly, ignoring Jaelle's question. "Does Princess Katherine love my husband? I am not blind. I know he has taken her as his concubine. He is not an ill-favored man, and he can be gracious, when he chooses to be."

Only the banked coals, a dull, somber red, and the flickering candle flame gave light to the room. Rusudani's face glowed, shadowed and illuminated together by the flame from her lantern. The rest of the room was dim, unreal. Jaelle did not know what to say. In any case, Rusudani needed no reply, no acknowledgment. She went on.

"I hold no grudge against her. Like me, she was taken by force. I would only regret it if what I must do now will cause her pain." She turned, and her eyes were lost in shadow. "Take the pouch. Do as I say. We will meet again tomorrow night."

Then she was gone, closing and barring the door behind her, like a dream. So long did Jaelle stand there in the darkness, wondering if it had been a dream or a true visitation, that finally Katerina stirred from the bed, murmuring, and Jaelle jerked guiltily and went back to curl under the warmth of the covers. Reflexively, not truly awake, Katerina pressed against her and draped an arm over her, taking comfort in Jaelle's presence, as she always did now.

Did Katerina love Janos?

Jaelle felt Katerina's breath against her neck. No, she did not love him. Jaelle knew that to be true. In some odd way he interested Katerina, appalled her, fascinated her; in a very obvious way he had earned her enmity. Katerina sighed and murmured words, formless in sleep but pure in tone. A lover's words. And there the words lay, once spoken, tangible things marking the quiet night chamber just as torches lit the parapets of the besieged city, so that the army outside would know that the forces inside were alert to the threat: *She loves me.*

Love is dangerous. Jaelle had only to reach out and touch the little pouch of coin that lay in the folds of the cloak. Whatever scheme Rusudani had concocted, it did not grow out of any love for her husband. But Jaelle knew that in the morning, she would go down to the castle gates and beg leave of the guardsman with the blue ribbon tied to his belt to go beyond, into the marketplace. Not for Rusudani. Once she would have said it was only for herself, to find the least opportunity to improve her lot, to put coin away for unlucky days, to give favors to others so that they might owe her one. Now, she supposed she did it as much for Katerina and Stefan, in the hope that somehow, however unlikely it might seem, what Rusudani planned might help them. But by seeking to help them, she made herself vulnerable. And that frightened her.

At dawn, the Mircassian envoy again approached the tent of the Prince of Jeds.

"Where is Prince Janos?" Tess asked without preamble. She was exhausted. She had hardly slept. Early on she had dreamed that Ilya had come back to her, as if from the dead, and after that she had been afraid to go to sleep again.

"Your highness." The envoy was sharp enough. Neither did he waste time in pleasantries. "Prince Janos offers you an alliance with Mircassia."

"How can he do so? Does he have King Barsauma's ear?"

"He has the king's heir. I can vouch for this, your highness. I was sent by King Barsauma to secure Princess Rusudani, to bring her back to Mircassia and invest her as the heir."

Caught despite herself, Tess indulged her curiosity, even though she knew that the least sign of interest weakened her position. "There is another heir, a young man, Barsauma's nephew."

"He has fled to Filis with his mother, your highness, now that he has been repudiated by the king. Prince Janos has married Princess Rusudani. He can offer you an alliance with Mircassia."

"Surely Princess Rusudani could offer this herself. *She* is the heir."

"She is only a woman—" Flushing, the envoy broke off.

Tess smiled. "I understand the situation well enough, Lord Envoy. Tell me, since it seems obvious to me that Rusudani's consort will be the king in her stead, do you think Prince Janos will meet with King Barsauma's approval? It hardly serves me to make an alliance with a man who cannot fulfill its terms. You may tell me the truth, Lord Envoy. I grant you immunity, now, and whatever may happen next."

Startled, he glanced away from her, at the camp, at the jaran soldiers, a grim-looking lot, and at the castle, which gleamed white in the morning sun, proud but not impregnable. "He is not the prince King Barsauma would have chosen, your highness, but he is well enough. The king will not be disappointed."

And so, Tess thought, the jaran could have an alliance with Mircassia and be spared fighting that powerful kingdom at all. It was a shrewd offer. It was tempting.

But it was from the man who had killed Ilya in an ambush.

Tess stood up so abruptly that her chair tipped over. A soldier caught it before it could hit the carpet and set it upright again.

"We will begin our attack at dawn tomorrow," she said, one hand clenched, "if Prince Janos does not surrender himself to us by that time. Take that message back to him."

"Do not speak in haste, your highness," said the envoy, bolder now that she had granted him immunity. "Prince Janos holds two hostages. He is willing to trade them for an alliance."

Her heart skipped a beat. At first she could not force the words past her throat. "What hostages might I be interested in?"

He took an hour to reply, a second, a million years. Now

would come the name. She waited, but he did not speak, and
then at last when she thought she would freeze, would burn,
would dissolve into nothing because she could not bear to
wait one more instant to hear, his mouth moved. He spoke.

"Prince Vasil'ii and Princess Katherine, your highness."

At first, a spike of warmth, the unspoken reply: *Thank
God Vasha and Katya are alive.* Then, she plunged into the
darkest depths. Not Ilya, and any man whether shrewd or
foolish would know enough to bargain for his own life with
the life of Bakhtiian.

She wanted to turn and walk into her tent. She wanted to
shut herself away and scream. But she could not.

"Are there others?"

"A few soldiers, your highness, servants, nothing more."

"How can Prince János prove that these hostages exist,
and are alive? One of my own soldiers must go with you
into the castle and identify them."

"I cannot agree to this without Prince Janos's permission,
your highness."

He was stalling, of course. But Janos had played his strongest card, Tess was sure of it. She still had a fresh army. She
could afford to wait one more day. "Tell him what I have
said, then. Return to me at dawn tomorrow."

He bowed.

Even after he left, she did not retreat into her tent. Out
here, in the daylight, under the eyes of the whole army, she
had no choice but to stay composed, to look strong, to keep
in control. She was afraid of what would happen if she was
alone.

Jaelle left just after dawn to go down to the marketplace.
It was easier than she had expected to get past the guards,
who had either been bribed or cozened by Rusudani, and she
was surprised to find the market in full spate, as though the
people crammed within the town chose to pretend that no
army sat outside the walls, waiting to break through. She
found Mistress Kunane and her cart. This time, without the
doubtful presence of guards, Mistress Kunane was eager to
take an overgenerous payment of coin in return for the herbs
Rusudani had asked for.

"It's for the little ones," Jaelle explained, slipping the
bundle of herbs into the pouch she wore at her belt. "They
cry all night, they're so frightened."

"Give it to them in wine," said Mistress Kunane, counting through the coin carefully. "That will make it work better."

Another customer came forward, and Jaelle escaped, relieved that the herbwoman was too busy to question her closely, as she had done last time.

Only one man could now be spared to stand guard outside Widow's Tower, and he was too preoccupied with his own thoughts to do more than take the coin she offered him when he let her back in.

"What does Rusudani want sleeping herbs for?" Katerina asked.

"I don't know."

Katerina looked thoughtful and went to stare out the slit window, where she could see the distant streaks that marked the enemy campfires.

At midday Jaelle heard the clatter of boots and armor on the stairs. The door opened to admit Prince Janos and a flock of guards. Katerina rose slowly. Then she gasped and took a step forward. She spoke a word in khush.

Too late Jaelle saw the man surrounded by guards: a jaran soldier, his armor covered by a handsome red and gold surcoat. The next instant the guards had hustled him out, and the door thudded closed behind them, leaving Prince Janos alone with the two women.

"That was my uncle, Gennady Berezin," said Katerina, surprised into the confession.

Janos circled her at a careful distance, but she kept turning to face him. "He agreed to enter the castle in order to identify you and your cousin, to take news of you back to the Prince of Jeds."

"What of the other prisoners?"

Janos dismissed them with a wave of one hand. "They aren't important. They remain in the dungeon. *You* are the one who matters." He said it warily.

"Now what do you mean to do, Prince Janos?"

"Use your life to bargain for my own."

Katerina smiled bitterly. "It is worth so little to you?"

With two swift strides he closed the gap between them and grasped her hands in his. She began to pull back, then stilled, reading a new emotion in his face. "It is worth that much to me. More than you wish to understand." He struggled within himself, his voice thick with longing, for her. Jaelle stared, seeing him stripped away to nothing, naked, as if his desperate circumstance had brought him to reveal his weakness to the woman he evidently loved. Because it was always weakness in a man to reveal that he loved a woman. A man's desire for her was the only power a woman had. "If I had only been more patient. . . ."

"It is too late for regrets, Prince Janos. You have condemned yourself."

Strange, Jaelle thought, that the woman, locked away, might seem more powerful at this moment than the man who had imprisoned her.

"Is there no hope for me?" he asked hoarsely.

She jerked her hands out of his. "I have my honor to uphold."

"It is no dishonor to a woman to be taken in war. You are mine, and I have used you more kindly than any other man would have."

"Than any khaja man, perhaps. Do not slander the men of my own people."

"But you are mine." He took hold of her shoulder with one hand and with the other caressed one of her braids, twining it through his fingers. "Is what the men of your people do when they marry, when they scar a woman's face, any better than forcing her? Had I done that to you, had I taken a blade and cut your face, would you have come willingly to my bed?"

Pale, she twisted out of his grasp, and he let go of her. "I would have no choice."

"Tell me how this is different, Katherine. We use different words, we have different customs, because we are what you call *khaja,* but for me to take you as my mistress is no different than for a *jaran* man to take you as his wife. You have as little choice in either."

Katerina crossed to the window seat, but she did not sit down. Her posture was stiff, her expression bleak. "I pray to the gods that my aunt may come soon," she said, and would not look at him as she said it.

"I fell into a rage," said Janos softly. "It will not happen again. I will not touch you again without your consent. Is that enough?"

Jaelle had to sit down, she was so astonished to hear him say it.

But Katerina only said, "No."

"I will draw up a contract—"

"I do not want your lands or your wealth."

"What do you want, then?" he asked, growing exasperated.

"I want to be free."

"Free to leave here and be scarred by a man of your own people?"

Now she turned. Her color was high. "Free even of that, Prince Janos. You are right enough, that I might as well be your mistress as another man's wife, but I will not be either!"

It was a clear, cold day outside, and harsh lines of light striped the chamber and the rug. Katerina's eyes were as cold as the sunlight, and Janos blazed, like the fire, answering her. "You will never forgive me for one night's anger."

"I can never forgive such a thing. Only a man would ask a woman to do so."

He moved. Amazed, Jaelle watched as he knelt before Katerina and lifted one of her hands to his lips, kissing it tenderly before he let it go. "I remain your servant, Princess Katherine. Always, and forever."

She looked taken aback. "Then I order you to let me go, to return to the army camped outside these walls."

He smiled wryly and stood up. "Only a woman would ask a man to do so. My castle is besieged, Princess Katherine. A man in my position does not divest himself of his most prized possession except in dire need. And I confess to you, my pale rose, that your beauty and your fierce soul will be out of my reach if I am dead."

While she stood, speechless and unmoving, he leaned into her and kissed her, then stepped back quickly, as if to avoid any blow she might throw at him. But she did not move. "No man will offer you what I do, Katherine, no man will cherish you as I will, nor will I cease my suit, so long as I live." He placed a hand over his heart and bowed, slightly, as any man ought to a princess, and left the chamber.

Dust trailed down the beams of light as the afternoon sun sank low enough to slant in through the arrowslits. The fire popped in the hearth, and Jaelle jumped, startled, and added another log to the fire.

"No man has ever spoken to me in that way before," said Katerina into the silence. Her voice trembled.

"He loves you," said Jaelle, although it was hard for her to say the words. "That is not a luxury often given to princes, or so it is said. A prince must marry for lands and alliances, a merchant for what connection it can bring him and his family. A slave cannot marry at all, except at his master's whim."

"I will never marry."

Jaelle made the sign of the knife. "Be careful what vows you make to God, Katerina. He might hold you to them."

But Katerina fixed her gaze on Jaelle, so searing a gaze that Jaelle froze, afraid to move. "Don't you understand? I don't want to marry. I don't care for men in that way, not truly." Her voice caught, but she lay a hand against the stone wall as if for support and went on. "Scorn me if you wish, but it is what I am. I could love you, Jaelle, but I will not burden you with what you do not want. I know you are fond of Stefan." She paused. "Now you know my secret. You may betray me if you wish."

Jaelle shut her eyes, then opened them, because it was cowardice not to look on Katerina, who had just offered her a glimpse of her inmost soul. "I will never betray you. I swear it, my lady."

"Could you love me?"

Jaelle flushed. "I do love you." It came out as a whisper. "But not, not as a woman loves a man. I cannot. I'm sorry."

To her surprise, Katerina's expression brightened. "Ah, gods, Jaelle, you have given me a precious gift, and I thank you for it."

After that, Katerina seemed calmer. That evening she received Princess Rusudani and Lady Jadranka with equanimity. She even agreed to read aloud from *The Recitation* that had been translated into Taor, and Rusudani took advantage of the rapt attention given to Katerina's reading to visit the screened-off chamber pot. Jaelle followed her, and there, trading places, she slipped the herbs into Rusudani's waiting hands.

"I will remember this," said Rusudani, and returned to the group seated so charmingly around Katerina.

Lady Jadranka lingered after the others had gone. "Lady Katherine," she said in her calm way, "I hope you will remember, when all this is over, that my son has treated you kindly."

"I am sorry, my lady," said Katerina, and would say no more. Lady Jadranka sighed and left, and the guards closed and barred the door behind her.

"Blow out the lantern," said Katerina, "so that our eyes may become accustomed to the dark."

"Why?"

"Because whatever Rusudani means to do, she will do it tonight. And I, for one, do not mean to be caught unsuspecting."

Gennady Berezin returned in late afternoon, none the worse for wear, and having seen but not spoken to Vasha and Katya. Too restless to sit still, Tess took a contingent of soldiers and rode a circuit of the walls.

White Tower was well placed, its west wall riding a bluff above a narrow river and the town growing out from its other sides. The docks lay within the great curve of the river out of which grew the bluff, but these river docks lay deserted now, abandoned because they had been built outside the ring of walls.

"If I had built this castle," said Tess, "I would have carved a stairwell down to the river level from the castle, as a way to get supplies. Have you scouted out the land below the west wall?"

From here, just beyond catapult range and at the edge of the docks district, the castle loomed up into the heavens, a heavy slab limned by the light of the setting sun and by the sudden appearance of torches, like stars flickering to life.

One of the captains, an Arkhanov, replied. "We can't scout there during the day. Our men are well within archery range. And at night . . . it's steep, and impossible to see."

Tess squinted at the sky. Clouds covered the east, drowning most of the sky, but a crescent moon lay just out of their reach. "As soon as there is the least bit of light, send men in. Try tonight, a preliminary expedition."

"Will you make an alliance?"

"If I do not, will Prince Janos kill his hostages? I must think about it. We will hold a council tomorrow."

In the last light of day, they rode back to camp. Tess ate mechanically, because she knew she ought to, but she was by now too tired to sleep. She sat in her chair under the awning until her hands got cold. But once inside the tent she felt choked, trapped, and so she grabbed a blanket and went outside again. She sat down again, nodded away into sleep, woke up with a start. Jumped to her feet. The night guards looked at her, questioningly.

"Gods, I need to walk."

One of them fell into step beside her, and with his comforting presence, she walked through camp and out to the sentry line nearest the town. Here, in the concealing darkness of night, they stumbled across several interesting diversions, common enough in siegework: Among a contingent of Farisa Auxiliaries, they found two prostitutes from the town who had sneaked out to make a bit of coin.

"Send a man to follow them back in, as far as is safe" said Tess to the embarrassed captain. "See if we might be able to get a group of men inside the town that way."

A farmer was selling chickens, but he was not from the town; evidently he had been selling to the army for several days, coming in from the countryside. A robust herbwoman pushed a cart over the rough ground, peddling her wares, and in another jahar, farther on, the soldiers were goodnaturedly trying to chase away a boy of about eleven years.

"He wants to hire himself out as a servant," said the captain. "We think he came from town, but we're not sure. There're some straw tents down there by the river banks, with a few khaja left in them, those that didn't run inside the walls. He might have come from there. No one wants the lad, poor thing. I don't suppose he has any family left, or he'd not be wanting to leave his home."

"Will anyone take him on?" Tess asked, feeling sorry for the scrawny child who lingered just within the glow of a fire. A soldier threw him a scrap of meat, and he wolfed it down.

"Just another mouth to feed," said the captain, "and who knows if he can even ride? We don't have any use for a khaja child like that."

"There's one more post beyond you?" Tess asked.

"One more, and then the river bank."

A sentry's voice broke the quiet. "Stanai!"

There was a general rustling all round as soldiers sprang up, and the captain and the night guard hustled Tess back a few steps. A male voice said, loudly, "Gods, another woman! Those khaja men must not truly be men if they keep their women so poorly satisfied that they all have to come out to us."

"Aye. You don't see jaran women running to *them*."

But the voices stilled. Tess craned her neck and finally stepped out around the captain to see what had caused the sudden hush. Two fires down, a woman scrambled up a bank and into the circle of light lent by burning timbers. She was no prostitute, not gowned that richly, with her hair discreetly covered with a shawl. In one hand she clutched a small book. With the other—

Tess's heart lurched. "Vladimir!" She said it loudly, but it came out a whisper. He looked like hell, but he was alive, setting the woman on her feet so that, as she turned to look behind her, Tess saw her face.

Princess Rusudani.

The sight galvanized Tess into action. She strode forward. "My lady! Princess Rusudani. What are you doing here?" *What is Vladi doing here? Who else . . . who else?*

Rusudani shook out her skirts. Eyes drawn down by the action, Tess saw that the fabric was wet and muddy to the knees, as if she had slogged through stagnant water. But the khaja princess looked up without the least sign of distress at her disheveled appearance. Indeed, she looked positively triumphant.

"Your highness," she said, but as a challenge. In the last months she had learned to speak rough but serviceable Taor. "I come to make alliance with you."

"Your husband has already offered an alliance."

"I am not interested in what Prince Janos offers. He took me by force. I drugged the guards and the guards in the dungeon and these men fight the guards at the river stair. So I come to you, as God has willed. I want alliance with the jaran that is of my own making."

"There he is," said Vladi. "Stefan has him."

To Tess, seeing and hearing Vladimir was dreamlike. He didn't seem real. He couldn't be real. Along with the others, he was dead.

"They whipped him last night," said Vladi matter-of-factly to Tess, as if to explain something she ought to understand, but she did not know what he was talking about. "Gods, the stubborn fool would always talk back. You must speak to him, Tess. No one else can. He isn't himself."

Tess was so disoriented that at first she did not see the man himself, only the two figures helping him up the bank. She thought the odd murmuring that flooded around and past her was the spill of the river, though its speech had not seemed so loud to her a minute before. But it came from the jaran soldiers, and it crested back, farther still, moving away into the camp like a wave that swept all before it. He came full into the firelight, and Nikita and Stefan, his escorts, dropped their arms away from him.

"In token of my good faith," said Rusudani clearly, almost as if she was gloating, her face shining in the firelight, "I release you."

She was not talking to Tess.

Ilya was alive.

Or at least a man who looked like him was. He had the same deep brown eyes, the same face, scored now with a grim expression, that Tess dreamed of every night, when she dreamed at all, when she was troubled by dreams.

He said, in Ilya's voice, "Mikhail waits at the river gate. Send twenty men, not more than thirty. Get them up the stairs quickly and inside the walls and they can open the gates. Ready the army. We strike now."

Then, and only then, he looked at her.

"Oh, gods," she said, because it *was* him. She staggered. The strength that had kept her going forward for the last many weeks drained out of her in one instant. Her vision blurred, and she thought she was going to faint.

Limping, he crossed the gap between them, but only to put a hand on her arm, marking her. "Tess," he said. That was all.

He let go of her and limped over to Vladimir, giving him directions.

Tess stared, unable to take her eyes from him. Already, around her, around Ilya, around Rusudani, men moved. A group of them followed Vladimir off into the night, and others hurried off toward the main camp.

"He wanted to lead the raid himself," Nikita was saying to someone, "so I threatened to hamstring him if he wouldn't listen to reason. It was his crazy ideas that got us in this trouble in the first place."

Out of the buzz, Tess picked up, again, the slow song of the river, out of sight in the darkness. High up to her left, a handful of torches shimmered and blazed on the castle walls.

Rusudani placed a hand possessively on Ilya's arm, just above the elbow. "I hope you will show me to a place of safety, my lord."

Tess snapped to life. "Captain, show Princess Rusudani to my tent." Sheer, ugly jealousy coursed energy back through her, and she conceived a sudden and unconditional dislike for the khaja woman. Rusudani caught her eye, and Tess knew instantly that for the first time in years, for the first time, perhaps, since Vera Veselov, she had just gained an adversary. Rusudani did not relinquish her grip on Ilya's arm. Just then, Gennady Berezin ran up and Rusudani was forced to step away so that the two men might embrace. Even so, Ilya stepped stiffly out of the embrace, distracted, looking again and again up at the castle.

"No," said Nikita, who did not stray from his side. "You are not going in."

"I must go in," said Ilya. Two welts marked his cheek, covering the mark of marriage. Tess felt like she was looking at a stranger. He had recognized her, but that was all. Something else held him, something stronger, something that she did not share in.

"Then with the main army," said Nikita in a weary voice, as if he had argued this once too often and was finally ready to give up the fight.

"You're *not* going in with the raiding party!" exclaimed Tess. "Not while I'm here to stop you."

"I must kill him," said Ilya, but not truly to her. "I have sworn it."

In the firelight, Rusudani smiled.

Beyond, behind, Tess heard the eerie rustling of thousands of men donning their armor in the middle of the night.

CHAPTER FORTY-TWO

The Hunt

In the solar, candles guttered. Vasha drifted off to sleep, chin cupped on a hand, and his elbow slipped off the table. Starting awake, he slapped a hand down on the table to catch himself, scattering game pieces. A few fell to the floor, but they hit the carpet without a sound. He looked quickly around the chamber.

Janos stood by the hearth, conferring with Captain Maros in a low voice. Rusudani had retired to the bedchamber many hours ago, or so it seemed to Vasha, gauging time by the height of the candles. Six guards stood by the door, and two more lounged at their ease about five steps from Vasha. No doubt they were pleased enough that Janos had not chosen to send his hostage back to the tower, where it would be colder. During a siege it was necessary to conserve both manpower and wood, just as Lady Jadranka and the other ladies all slept upstairs together this night, for comfort and for safety. Janos gestured to one of his guards and the man helped him on with his coat of plates and then his great helm. Together with his captain, Janos left. Lord Belos padded over and offered more wine to Vasha, and he drank it gratefully, wondering what was going on.

But evidently Janos had just gone for a tour of the battlements, since he returned after a short time. A soldier unlaced the prince's armor and set it aside and pulled off his boots, and another man dragged out a pallet. Janos lay his sword down beside the pallet and himself, clad in hose and shirt, down on the mattress. Within moments, he seemed to be asleep. Vasha watched the chamber for a bit, but a hush had fallen. It was not precisely quiet; there was too much tension in the air for that. But it was still, like the calm before the storm.

He picked up the pieces that had fallen to the floor, knight, castle, and archer, and put them back on the game board. Then he stretched out on the rug and pillowed his head on an arm, shutting his eyes. Someone draped a blanket over him. A log shifted on the fire. A guardsman whispered. A spear haft thumped gently on the floor as a guardsman changed position, and mail chinked, overlaid by the brief scrape of plate against mail as another guardsman moved. A man coughed.

Vasha drifted off to sleep.

Jaelle started awake, but it was only a log slipping on the fire, rolling down into the deepest coals and sending a spray of sparks popping out from the hearth. Katerina had dragged the table closer to the fire. By the light of two candles she played castles against herself, moving first a white piece, then a red. Her hair was neatly braided, the braids thrown back over one shoulder. Although she wore a gown, she had put her jaran women's trousers—fuller than men's trousers above the knee and narrow at the ankle, sewn of striped fabric—on underneath. A cloak lay over the back of the chair.

"Aren't you going to sleep?" Jaelle asked for the fourth time.

Katerina stood and walked to each of the arrowslits in turn, pausing longest by those that looked over the river. She cocked her head to one side. "Did you hear that?"

Jaelle did not hear anything.

Katerina crossed to the arrowslit that looked out over the courtyard, her figure a swathe of shadow against the darker stone. She leaned forward, and suddenly she went taut.

"Look!" she whispered.

Jaelle scrambled up from the pallet, untangled her legs from her skirts and hurried over to Katerina, who moved aside to make room for her. She peered out through the slit, eyes already adjusted to the darkness. She saw a length of wall, rimmed with torches that illuminated the guards standing at attention, watching out over the walls toward the besieging army beyond. And below, a shadow crept along the wall beneath, slipping in and out of patches of night. A slim scar of metal caught briefly in torchlight and winked, and was still, swallowed up in shadow again.

"They've come," said Katerina, turning and walking calmly back to the chair, where she lifted the cloak off and swung it around her shoulders. Her voice was calm, but her body trembled.

"Who has come?"

"The jaran."

"How would they get inside?"

"Why would Princess Rusudani buy sleeping draughts if not to drug guards? There must be a second entrance, a side gate, a water gate. Other fortresses have fallen by treachery from within. I have seen it myself. Hush."

They listened but heard nothing except a hound yipping, the brush of wind across the slate roof, and the slow murmur and snap of the fire. Distant, a new, fainter sound carried in to them, a muted rumbling.

"It must be the gate!" cried Katerina, and she ran back to the arrowslit, squeezing herself forward into it as far as she could. Jaelle pressed in behind her, but could see nothing.

And there, rising out of the darkness as piercing as light, came the clarion cry of a horn, sounded in alarm. It cut off abruptly and hard against it rose the sound of fighting, distant at first, coming closer.

Katerina wedged her head into the opening and yelled, down toward the courtyard, words in her own language, that Jaelle could barely understand: "Stanai! I am here! Look to me here!"

She shoved herself out of the window seat. "Put your cloak on!" she cried. "Get ready!"

Jaelle could not move. She could scarcely breathe. Katerina moved to the fire and stuck a long, arm's width log into the flames, getting the end to catch and burn. Jaelle realized numbly that she was preparing a weapon.

Shouts rose from the base of the tower. There came a sudden burst of fighting, followed by the pound of footsteps up the stairs. Shocked into action, Jaelle grabbed her cloak from the chest just as the door burst open.

"Come," said Katerina. That was all. No other word was spoken as she entered the ranks of her people and, vanishing into them, started down the steps toward the battle now raging throughout the castle.

Jaelle hesitated. She glanced once round the chamber, luxurious in its way and familiar in its trappings, and then at the foreign soldiers who waited, impatiently, for her to move. But her decision had already been made. She had already in every important way changed her allegiance irrevocably.

She shrugged the cloak over her shoulders and followed Katerina down the stairs. The jaran soldiers closed in at her back protectively, and in this way they left Widow's Tower behind.

Vasha dreamt of bells, ringing to signal the coming of the jaran army. Except it was not the bells. It was the clatter and pound of the armorer's hall, the incessant, uneven clash of hammers on iron, the birthplace of swords.

He woke up. In the unearthly quiet of deep night, he could still hear the distant hammering from the armory, plying their trade on through the night. Boots pounded outside. A horn rose in alarm, cut off abruptly. On the pallet on the other side of the solar, Janos sat up, shaking sleep away. The door burst open, and a guardsman tumbled in.

"My lord! Your highness! Captain Maros, the gates are open! We're being attacked."

Hard on his heels came shouts from below and a sudden flurry of swords clashing. Vasha's guards leapt forward and hauled Vasha to his feet, pinning his arms behind him. At once, four guardsmen went out the door. Janos got to his feet and grabbed his sword.

"Tie his hands," he said, nodding toward Vasha. "Belos, get my mother, and my wife."

Lord Belos hurried out. From outside the door, guards shouted in Yossian. Janos fumbled for his boots, but Captain Maros backed away from the door, shoved the prince's boots and brigandine into the arms of a soldier, and jerked the prince toward the door.

"No time," he said, and something about the river, too quickly for Vasha to understand. Dragged along behind, Vasha caught a glimpse of men fighting at the base of the stairs, on the level below. His heart leapt. Jaran men, some auxiliaries stabbing with short swords, fought with grim intensity below, caught against a cul-de-sac in the stone fortress.

"This way," said Captain Maros. Swearing, Janos followed, down a different stair, deeper into the stone walls. Belos caught up with them. His gambeson was ripped and blood stained his right shoulder.

"The women are *something*," he said. Vasha heard another melee off to his left. A handful of guardsman joined them; their leader babbled to Captain Maros, and in the resulting

pause, while Maros and Janos and the new captain threw
words back and forth at each other, Vasha's guards trussed
his arms up behind him.

Silence fell over the group, Janos and Vasha and perhaps
twenty men. "My wife?" Janos asked.

"Gone," Belos said distinctly. "The other woman, your
mother, the guards . . . asleep . . . not wake them."

A shout carried in to them, huddling here where stairway
and wall split into three passageways. Bells began to ring
from the town, and two horns blew almost in unison, farther
away, from the town walls. A tide of noise hit, carried outward from some new conflagration.

"This way." Captain Maros gestured to the stair that led
downward. Three soldiers headed down, but Janos did not
move. He stared up, back the way they had come. For now,
it was silent up there. As an afterthought, he tugged on one
boot, then the other.

Moments later, two of the soldiers returned. ". . . river
stair . . . blocked . . . jaran . . ."

". . . fight our way . . . town . . ." said Captain Maros.

"Princess Katherine," said Janos quietly.

"Too far . . . across the courtyard . . . dangerous."

Swords rang in the corridors above them. Men shouted,
drowning out the distant swell of sound that came from the
town itself. Among the shouts Vasha heard khush words:
"Left, go left. This way. No, pull back."

"We must go, my prince," said Captain Maros desperately, tugging on Prince Janos's arm. "They are inside the
castle and the town."

For one more moment, timeless, Janos did not budge, still
looking up, toward the solar, toward his bedchamber.

"We have been betrayed," he said. At last he moved, and
his men formed a silent shield around him as they headed on
out, seeking a safe passage, seeking escape.

Rusudani saw Bakhtiian off as a queen sees off her champion. Torn between fury and fear, Tess mounted up beside
Ilya. He accepted her presence beside him without a word,
as he would with any of his soldiers. She felt frozen inside.
People in captivity formed strange bonds and stranger alliances, and for the first time she realized that Rusudani offered Ilya more than she could, an entire kingdom.

"Oh, God, Tess," she muttered under her breath, "you fool."

One of the captains called the advance, and they rode forward, slowly into the night. Ahead, she heard fighting, sounds familiar to her now: the clash of swords, the rising howl of the town coming awake to its peril, horns and bells and the roar of fighting and shouting and sobbing and the sheer grief of a people newly torn by war.

The ditch was now interrupted by bridges of hastily piled-up dirt, and they had to wait while they funneled through the two bridges over the moat. Tess eyed the walls uneasily, but already the fighting moved away from them, farther into town, and as their party moved under the gates and into the eerily deserted streets of the town she realized that she did not need to worry about Ilya getting caught in a melee. However much he might fulminate, his guard would see to it that he remained far from the real battle. They did not intend to lose him again, even if they had to let him assuage his wrath by pretending to let him join in the assault.

She did not speak to him. She was afraid to. He seemed so strange, so distant. His eye roved restlessly, catching on a torch bobbing along a farther portion of wall, skimming over a darkened doorway, touching her, marking her, and then away, back toward camp and then up, again, as always, to the pale sheen of the castle itself, thrust up into the heavens. He was mumbling something, but it sounded like nonsense to her: angels and burning lights and a sword from heaven. Abruptly he stopped speaking. After that he remained silent while his guard pressed cautiously forward through the empty, winding streets and they heard the fighting recede before them. A roof caught fire, another.

A group of riders burst through a narrow alley and were upon them. Tess raised her saber, instinctively pressing her horse out in front of Ilya, to protect him. But his guard fought with relentless concentration, cutting the khaja soldiers to pieces before them. A few arrows fell, spent, across her horse's withers, and once she held, across a distance, the staring eyes of a man just stabbed, before he fell from his horse. Otherwise, she and Ilya were caught in a shifting eddy, shielded, untouched.

Of the town's inhabitants, she saw no one. Every house was shut tight, every shutter sealed. For the most part, the riders ignored the houses except when a stray arrow flight came too close; then six of them would split off to go look for the culprit. In this way they wound into the heart of the town.

A new clot of riders clattered up a main avenue, plumes bobbing.

It was Gennady Berezin. "We tried to close the castle off, but the prince has escaped into the town with some of his men."

"Seal off the walls," said Ilya instantly. "Make a ring of riders. We'll surround him and drive him in toward the center. He must not escape."

Riders scattered through the dark streets. Auxiliaries came forward, dismounted and carrying lanterns. Pace by slow pace, winding through streets empty of life, leaving knots of guards where the line had to be broken, they pressed forward, meeting another line, calling out in the darkness because there was no light for signaling with flags.

Swords rang off to the right, a brutal but brief clash that receded into silence. Hooves clipped on cobblestones. A crack of light rimmed a shuttered window, vanishing as whatever people hiding in the house blew out their candle. Tess dismounted and led both her horse and Ilya's. Someone called for lanterns, and soon their way was lit again. Down an oddly straight avenue Tess saw more lights, torches, lanterns, bobbing like fireflies. A new group of jaran joined up with them, and their line deepened. She felt them like a mass around her, powerful, unyielding, implacable. Bridles rang. Leather armor squeaked. She could almost hear breath like the exhalation and inhalation of a single monstrous predator hunting down its prey.

Stars glimmered above in the rents between clouds. The air was cold and damp. Distant, like the noise of the river, she heard the sustained clash of swords. Behind, each street was left behind in silence. Once, turning round, she saw four dark figures, misshapen by bundles thrown over their backs, slip from a house and head, quickly, furtively, for the distant gates. Two riders broke off to go after them, but after a moment, Tess saw, they let them go. The important quarry lay in the center.

They closed at last around the central marketplace, a grassy commons now ringed with torches and lanterns and blackened by bodies strewn like so much refuse in toward the very center of the square, where the town's well rested. Trained by many a birbas, the jaran soldiers had let no one through. Now they had herded what remained of the khaja prince's guard into a corral made up of the jaran army itself. She heard fighting still from the castle, but it seemed contained within the castle walls.

The last melee dissolved as the jaran riders, alerted to Bakhtiian's presence, pulled back, and the khaja soldiers formed up around the well. Tess assumed that Prince Janos himself stood within that ring of guards, shielded by his men just as the jaran shielded Ilya. A few diffuse flights of arrows sprayed out from the khaja ranks, but they did no damage.

Ilya raised his right hand. Beside him, Nikita called out a command, and a sudden fierce stream of arrows poured into the khaja formation. Men fell and were dragged back, their place taken by others. At the very center, men threw up shields, protecting the prince.

"Advance," murmured Ilya, so low that Tess barely caught it.

Pouring arrow fire before them, the jaran soldiers advanced. The khaja soldiers fought as fiercely as cornered animals. No quarter given. None received. They fought, all of them, in desperate silence except for grunts and shouts of command and the occasional scream of a wounded horse. The ring of torchlight gave it all an unearthly quality, shimmering and insubstantial.

Ilya held back from the fighting, but even if he had wanted to go forward, he was hemmed in by a stubborn and immovable line of his own guard, who still had no intention of letting him near the fighting. There came from the direction of the castle a new tumult of riders, and the guard braced themselves, but it was Vladimir and what was left of his men, those who had broken in through the river stair.

"Ilya! Aunt Tess!"

Katerina rode at the front, mounted awkwardly because of her khaja garb, a gown hiked up to reveal trousers underneath.

"Thank God, my child," cried Tess, and went to hug her, but Katerina would not dismount. She stared at the knot of bitter fighting, the slowly shrinking circle as the jaran pressed farther in, as the khaja, one by one, died.

"Where is Vasha?" Katya demanded. "Is he here?" She

turned in her saddle to look at the woman behind her, a khaja woman, Tess saw. A moment later Tess recognized her, the interpreter, but she could not recall her name.

"Where is Vasha?" Tess asked.

Vladimir shook his head. "Not in the tower where he was imprisoned before. We have taken the castle and searched most of it. Dead, hiding . . ." He lifted a hand. "Or there, with the prince."

"Break off the fighting," said Ilya, although Tess hadn't realized he'd even been listening.

It was not so easily done, not with horses caught in tight quarters, not with corpses and wounded thrown as obstacles across the ground. Perhaps they took as many casualties pulling back as they had coming in, Tess thought, but by now they had done as much damage as they needed to.

As much, perhaps more, if it was true that Vasha was still a captive. It might be too late for Vasha. Certainly it was too late for most of the khaja soldiers. There were, at most, two dozen left standing.

Ilya urged his horse forward. He had been forced to wear guards' armor, a plumed helmet and a gaudy surcoat, quite unlike the plain rider's armor he preferred. Tess stuck beside him, and Katya, foolish unarmored Katya, rode up next to her, refusing to go back even when Tess yelled at her. Still, Katya was in some measure protected by Nikita and Vladi and Mikhail, who surrounded her.

"Tell them," said Ilya, "that I wish to speak with Prince Janos."

"I will go," said Katerina, and rode out in front of the ranks, unshielded, unafraid.

"Katerina! Come back!"

She ignored him. Strangely, a quiet fell over the square, as if her presence was what everyone had been waiting for, as if her presence would make all the difference. She reined in her horse halfway between the jaran line and the khaja soldiers. She had, Tess saw now, a bow and a quiver of arrows strapped to her back, gleaned from some unknown place.

"Where is my cousin Vassily Kireyevsky?" she called out. Lanterns flickered. No reply came. A breath of air swirled past, rustling the tunics of the dead.

Ilya kicked his horse forward suddenly. Cursing, Tess went after him. She wondered if she was the only person in this entire tableau who was terrified. Everyone else seemed preternaturally composed, as if they all knew their destined parts, and she alone did not know hers.

The outer ring of khaja soldiers did not move, but movement swirled in the middle. Two shields parted to reveal a man, an ordinary enough man except that, as he took off his helm, Tess realized that he wore no armor, that he was, in fact, only half clothed in hose and shirt, like a man who had been driven untimely from his bed. He was looking, not at Ilya, but at Katerina. Beside him, arms caught behind his back, stood a disheveled Vasha. He stood straight, without fear, and Tess felt a sharp stab of love for him, admiring his courage.

"I claim my right to take his life," said Ilya as he reined in beside Katya.

Katya lifted a hand. Her voice was hard. "Cousin, he is mine. *I* claim his life, as is *my* right."

What right? Tess wondered. To her astonishment, Ilya hesitated and, with an infinitesimal nod, gave in.

"What do you mean to do with him?" Ilya asked.

"If he will give up Vasha, then I will make a bargain with him." Katya unsheathed her bow as calmly as if she meant to take archery practice. "If my hand does not kill him, then none will."

When they hit a group of jaran fighters defending the forecourt gate, Vasha knew that he would probably die. He hunkered down, keeping his head protected as well as he could, tucked in toward his right shoulder. He fixed his gaze on his boots. Better not to see the blow that took him. Bodies shoved past him, and he was borne first forward and then back by the tide of the sortie. Going out, coming back in, suddenly surging out and they were through, pounding over the drawbridge and down into the shelter of the town's winding streets and narrow alleys. He ran with them because a man prodded him with the haft of his sword, and because to halt was to be trampled or killed on the spot. After all, Vasha reasoned, as long as he was alive, he was still alive. He could still escape.

"Put on this helm, my lord." A soldier handed a battered helmet to Prince Janos. The strap was broken, sheared through, but he stuck it on his head anyway. A flight of arrows pattered over them from the castle walls, but whoever was shooting was shooting into the dark, and although one man cursed, he was only grazed in the arm.

"No lights," said Captain Maros. A soldier extinguished the last torch.

In darkness, they forged forward. They were not looking for a glorious death. These grim men wanted to get their prince out of here, away. Vasha understood irony. Janos's soldiers were as devoted to him as Ilya's were devoted to their Bakhtiian. It was the ultimate test of a prince's stature, that his men would rather die than betray or abandon him, even in such hopeless circumstances. Yet someone had betrayed them.

Janos whispered to Lord Belos, and Vasha heard Lady Jadranka's name twice, and that of Rusudani only once, but said with a bitter anger.

"This way." Captain Maros led them into a pitch-black alley. Vasha stumbled over the rough stones. His guard grabbed his elbow and heaved him up.

"Shall I kill him, my lord?" asked the soldier.

"No," said Janos.

"Hsst." Captain Maros halted them. "Riders, that way. We'll go left."

They went left, down a broader street, and Captain Maros tried to find a route up to the rooftops but the first man to the roof was shot, suddenly, an arrow piercing him from several houses on, where torches illuminated a pitched roof and several dark forms.

"Cursed by the moon," said Captain Maros, for the clouds had uncovered the crescent moon, and there was just enough light to see figures, however shadowy they might appear against the night sky. Farther, toward the town wall, smoke rose, licked upward by flames.

"Riders," hissed another soldier, one of the pair bringing up the rear. "Behind us."

"We must take shelter in one of the houses," said Lord Belos.

"We'll be trapped," said Captain Maros.

"We must go forward," said Janos. "We must break free of the town. At the docks we can get a boat." So it was decided.

They slanted right and almost ran into a line of jaran auxiliaries. Leaving four men to fend them off, they ducked into a narrow lane, fetid with garbage and urine. Vasha's shoulder scraped along the wooden frames of houses, burning his skin under his shirt until blood welled up. Once they ran into a second group of Janos's men, who related how they had escaped from the town gates, words Vasha could not follow.

While they talked, Vasha inched sideways, toward a break in the alley, but a soldier nudged him with the flat of his sword. These weren't careless men.

Left with nothing else to do, Vasha cocked his head and listened. Somewhere, out there, the jaran army fought its way into the town. He wondered if they had rescued Katerina. He wondered about his father. Was Ilya still alive? Was it safer for him, chained down in the dungeons? Or would he simply be an easy target for a guard seeking a last act of revenge? Had Stefan died with him? What had happened to Rusudani?

There was, for a time, a restless surging noise all about them, the inconstant swell and ebb of battle, but it faded away, as if the battle had gone elsewhere or ceased altogether. More men joined them as they edged farther into town, but these were poorly-armored townsmen. He caught snatches of conversation in frantic Yossian, not enough to place it together. Evidently most of the townspeople had barricaded themselves inside their homes, trusting to their wood and stone tents to grant them safety from attack. What else could they do?

"Move left," said Captain Maros. "No. Back. Riders ahead."

Slowly, Vasha realized that it was unlikely, if so many jaran soldiers infested this town, that they would glimpse but not engage so many successive troops of jaran soldiers.

"If we can get through the marketplace," said Lord Belos hopefully, "then there are only four streets to the dock gates."

In one direction, always, the way was free. They were being driven. Vasha lifted his head and watched the others, watched Janos, his face dim in the night, watched Captain Maros, whose pale surcoat moved like a ghost through the dark streets, hugging the walls, seeking safe passage. They did not suspect.

Not until they came out into the marketplace to find at least fifty of Janos's men, forming into ranks around the central well, the pivot on which the market commons was fixed. By then it was too late. By then, they were surrounded. Vasha smiled and then bit the smile back, ducking his face to hide it.

When at last the torches and lanterns marched out from
the streets and alleys that poured into the market square,
when the shifting mass that was the jaran army settled into
a circle around them, Captain Maros jerked Vasha over to
him and laid his sword along Vasha's throat.

"Shall I kill him, my lord?" he asked. He sounded, finally,
angry.

"No," said Janos. "That would be the coward's way."

Arrows came. Vasha threw himself to his knees, but the
arrows thudded harmlessly on the shields that had been
thrown up to protect Prince Janos. Farther out, the soldiers
were not so lucky, but they struggled to regain their formation. After that, Vasha could not see, but he felt the khaja
soldiers tense, felt and heard the rumbling advance of the
jaran army, felt the impact, crushing him from all sides, as
the two groups engaged.

Caught in the very center, he pushed himself up again, so
that he would not get crushed. He set his feet against the
ground, letting the shifting of bodies move him one way two
steps, back three, two staggered steps to the left and a sway
back to the right. Sword struck sword. Men cried out, small
grunts and surprised cries, and now and again a horse
screamed in pain. He felt the sheathed tip of a knife brush
his fingers and vanish, tantalizing but out of reach. He was
helpless. Somehow, being helpless made him less scared. All
he had left was his dignity.

A strange hush fell. Out of the feral silence came a voice,
clear, muted by distance and the shifting ring and clank of
armor on the soldiers surrounding Vasha.

"Where is my cousin Vassily Kireyevsky?"

It was Katerina.

"Put down the shields," said Janos.

"But, my lord—"

"Put them down. I wish to see her."

As if a scythe had cut through them, the shields came
down, and looking past Janos's shoulder, Vasha could see—

Gods! Not just Katya, but Ilya, and Tess, too, exposed in
front of the circle of riders. At least Ilya and Tess wore armor and helms, although their faces were, of course, plain to
see; a coif of mail protected their ears and the back of their
necks. Katerina had nothing but cloth to protect her. She
moved in her saddle and reached behind her back, pulling

out a bow, then an arrow. She lay them across her thighs with the sure ease of a competent archer.

"Kneel," said Janos. The front rank knelt so that he could see Katerina more clearly. He had already taken off his helm. Vasha dared not move. He simply stood, trying not to think what could possibly happen now. Rope dug into his wrists.

"I hold Prince Vasil'ii here beside me, Princess Katherine," he shouted. "Better that it were you."

"Let him go free," cried Katerina, "and I promise you that I alone will have the killing of you."

A murmur broke out through the ranks, stilled.

"What of my men?" Janos shouted, but his face shone.

"They have served you faithfully. For that, if Prince Vassily goes free, they shall live."

"No, my lord," said Captain Maros at once. "It would be our shame—"

Janos lifted a hand. Maros fell silent. "Prince Vasil'ii, why is the priest with her? Who is the other—is that the Prince of Jeds?"

Vasha did not answer. Nor did he need to. Janos looked back at him and at once the obscuring piece on the board was taken, leaving the last position exposed.

"Ah," said Janos. "Now I understand. So I had him in my grasp the whole time." Vasha said nothing. "Are you truly his son, or was that a lie also?"

"I am his son," said Vasha, knowing it was true.

Janos turned back to face the jaran army, to face Katerina. "Very well. I accept, but on one condition."

She nodded, either accepting the condition unsaid or allowing him to continue, Vasha could not be sure. Yet that nod seemed to seal the bargain between them. Even across such a gap, they communicated without words, playing out a different game, one that Vasha did not understand.

"One arrow," cried Janos.

She lifted the arrow that lay across her thighs, lowered it, like a promise. "Let him go!"

"Let him go," said Janos to his men. No one moved. "Let him go!"

"Your highness!" protested Captain Maros.

"My lord," murmured Lord Belos.

"We are dead otherwise," said Janos harshly. "She may even wound me, with one arrow, but even if she could kill

me, it is more likely that pity, or even love, will stay her
hand. Our bargain is already sealed."

Maros laughed. "Do you trust this barbarian woman, my
lord?"

"I do," said Janos. "I trust her to keep her word. Let him
go."

They shoved Vasha forward, and he came out from the
front ranks and saw his father glaring at him. Pulling his
shoulders back, Vasha did not deign to run; he walked deliberately, not looking back until he had come almost to
Katya's horse. There he paused, half turned, in time to hear
her speak.

"One arrow will be enough."

"What if you miss?" Tess asked, sounding, Vasha thought,
curious more than anything. Ilya looked brittle with anger.

Katerina just smiled, but she did not take her eyes from
Prince Janos. Nor did he take his eyes from her. He watched
her, lifting his chin, as a brave man stares down his fate.

She drew. She aimed. She fired.

His head snapped back. Fletchings protruded from his
throat. His body, shorn of its animating force, collapsed to
the ground like an empty cloak.

CHAPTER FORTY-THREE

The Law of Becoming

Anatoly Sakhalin sat in the lounge of the *Gray Raven* and stared at the wall. The wall stared back at him, mute. It did not actually stare, of course. He only imagined it did, knowing that it contained images inside it, scenes in three dimensions, messages from people remote both in distance and time, an encyclopedia of human history encapsulated into a cylinder the size of his index finger. It even contained a nesh port, although on the *Gray Raven,* drifting in space, any neshing he might do was limited to the net space available shipboard.

But the wall remained mute because it contained no answers for him. Not any more. Information. Questions. Communications. That was all. That was no longer enough.

For two days he had shut himself off here in the lounge. Moshe left food four times a day. The small door in the corner led into a smaller lavatory. The crew of the *Gray Raven* allowed him his privacy. On a Chapalii ship he could have commanded privacy; here he could only request it. For some reason, the distinction comforted him.

At first, returning from his audience with the emperor, he had tried to make sense of what he now ruled. *All daiga holdings.* In addition, three dukes, known as Tai, and all that they possessed; five independent lords, known as Cha, and all that they possessed. Star systems on a map, diagrammatic models of cities and warehousing capabilities and charts of mining projections and designated routes along the net of singularities.

Individually, he could make sense of each one. Together, they overwhelmed him. After twenty hours of that he had slept for ten. He had tried other ways of organizing his holdings, of compressing them to manageable proportions, but after eight more hours he had given up and spoken the word that snapped off the wall.

He set a plate on his lap, broke a square of crumbly *corn bread* in half, and spread butter on it. It was a little dry. It had been sitting on the side table for hours. But the butter was sweet.

"Oh, gods," he said to the wall, which as usual refused to reply. As miraculous as these modellers, these computers, these imagers and recorders and encyclopedias and nesh worlds were, in the end, they were only tools. Like a sword, you had to know how to use them. Like a needle, they only served to pull the thread through the cloth: The pattern you embroidered had to come out of your own mind. Like a loom, they were of themselves empty until the human hand, the Chapalii hand, the hand guided by intelligence, strung the warp and wove the weft.

He missed his daughter. In some ways Portia was the only tangible thing he could trust, a part of himself without being his possession. And she loved him freely, fully, and without the least duplicity, as only a child can. He missed his sister Shura. She and Portia were the only creatures in the universe that he loved simply because they existed. Without them, he felt alone.

"Put a call through to Captain Emrys," he said to the wall.

"Yes?" she answered immediately, as if she had been waiting for him. Probably she had. What else was there for her to do, here in orbit around Chapal, suspended while she waited for him to act?

"I would like to meet with you and the others."

"When?"

"Now, if you can."

Which of course they could. They assembled quickly. Benjamin brought freshly baked apple fritters, fried to a golden brown, crunchy and sweet. No one ventured to sit on the couch beside Anatoly. Rather, they arranged themselves in a semicircle in front of him. Summer sat cross-legged on the floor and worked on a basket, weaving reeds together; able to sit still, she could not abide quiet hands. Rachelle draped herself dramatically over a chair, pretending tranquility, but he could see how tense she was. Florien sat on one arm of the couch, eyes shifting all over the room as if he was looking for something he had lost and would spring up in one moment to get it. Benjamin finished a fritter, licked his fingers, and began on another. Moshe stood, fidgeting, by the door. Branwen flopped down on the other couch. He watched her longest; she was relaxed, comfortable in her body, but alert.

They knew what he was. He had told them. At first they had not quite believed him, but after the flood of messages and the arrival of over a dozen Chapalii craft in parallel orbits begging for instructions or for a visitation from the great lord, they had to accept it. Now they surveyed him warily, except for Branwen who, thank the gods, merely looked patient.

"You know what I have become," he began. "But I don't know what to do now. What I knew, what I learned, with the jaran has taught me many valuable lessons, but only some of them apply here. I can't know everything. I can't oversee everything. I can't make every decision. All I know is that my first loyalty lies to my own people, to the jaran, and every action I take must be to their benefit."

"What about the rest of the human race?" asked Rachelle. "I'm not working for Charles Soerensen because I like being a lapdog to the Chapalii, you know."

"Rachelle," scolded Summer. "At least let him state his case."

Anatoly leaned forward, bracing his hands on his thighs. "What benefits the jaran will most likely also benefit all humans, certainly more than it will the Chapalii. But for me to make any great plans now would be hasty, to say the least. To act rashly in war is to invite disaster."

"Are we at war?" asked Summer.

"I meant it as a . . . as a . . . an old saying. . . ?" He glanced toward Branwen for help.

"An aphorism?"

"Yes. Thank you."

She smiled. The lift of her mouth calmed his nerves.

"But that isn't what I need to say," he went on. "No prince remains prince without a court. No dyan remains a dyan without a jahar. I don't have a jahar any more, and, gods, I need one now desperately. I have to protect myself by surrounding myself with people I trust, who will trust me, who will give me sincere and truthful advice whether or not they think I might like hearing it, and who I know will not betray me, for any price, at any cost. Where can I get such people?"

He let the question hang for a minute before answering it

himself. "I would like to start with the *Gray Raven*. With you."

"What's in it for us?" asked Rachelle.

"Could I get access to even more Chapalii nodes?" asked Florien.

Benjamin took two fritters and bit down hard on them.

"Where do you stand on the rebellion?" asked Summer. "It's not necessarily in your interest anymore to support freedom for us daiga, not if you're a prince among the Chapalii and can rule us all however you like."

Moshe gaped, gulping down an exclamation.

Branwen said nothing, just watched him.

"I did not seek this," said Anatoly. "You know that's true. But now that I have it, I must use it wisely. Surely, if you think you have cause not to trust me, you would rather put yourselves close enough to watch what I do rather than having to suffer my decisions secondhand? I would ask that you make an oath to me, as I would make one to you in your turn, for your service, your knowledge, your life if necessary—"

"What duration?" asked Rachelle.

"For the rest of your life would be best, of course, but I could only ask that of jaran. Ten years, to start? Twenty would be better. But I will only take your oaths if they are given freely, if you give yourselves to my service freely. In return, I will rely on you, I will take your advice, I will see to it that you are taken care of. But if I ever find that you have betrayed me, I will kill you."

Benjamin coughed down his last mouthful of fritter. "You can't do that! There's a law against murder. There's due process. . . ." He trailed off, wiping powdered sugar off his mouth with a cloth napkin.

"That is true." Anatoly lifted both hands, palms up. "I will study these laws further, and leave them in place, and respect them, but Summer is right. They do not apply to me."

"Shit," said Rachelle. "The little bastard's right. He can do whatever he damned well pleases." But then, deliberately, she winked at him.

Anatoly grinned, knowing that he had one on his side. "Of course, by only accepting your freely given oaths, I accept also that you may freely leave, so long as you tell me openly and we fix between us any due compensation and an agreement about what you may and may not do afterward which might jeopardize the security of my position."

"Hey, Florien, no selling tech secrets to the competition."

Florien blinked in his absentminded way. "Rachelle, someday the evil spirits will get you."

"I hope so."

"We'll have to discuss it," said Branwen suddenly, cutting into this interchange. "We vote on things here."

"I know that," said Anatoly. "I'll go back to my cabin and wait for your decision."

In his cabin, he took off his boots, lay down on the narrow bunk, hooked his hands under his head, and stared at nothing. After a while, he rolled onto his right side and fished out the castle piece, setting it on the floor.

"Show me the board." At once the flat black game board flowered into existence, contained in its grid of glowing white lines. The horseman had moved two intersections away from the emperor's throne. The piece shaped like a teardrop had moved closer to him, and another piece, shaped like a blade, had moved farther away. The others had not changed their position from the last time he had looked.

All daiga holdings. Should he simply go down to Rhui and report in to Bakhtiian, handing these lands over to him, as was his duty? Or should he claim them for the Sakhalin tribe, as was his right? Except without Bakhtiian and his vision, without Ilya's marriage to Tess Soerensen and the intervention of Charles Soerensen, Anatoly would never have left Rhui at all, never left the jaran, never known that khaja lands flourished beyond the plains, that worlds and stars existed beyond Rhui and Mother Sun.

A bell rang at his door. He closed his hand over the castle piece, concealing it, and the game board vanished. Lifting his hand, rolling up to sit, he said, "Enter." The door slid open and Branwen walked in. That was one of the many things he liked about her: She never hesitated. She knew this was her ship, and however powerful he might be now, prince of the Sakhalin, prince in the Chapalii Empire, it was still *her* ship. Like an etsana, she understood where her power lay, and that she alone could wield it.

She sat down on the end of his bunk. Like a woman, she did not ask for permission. His feet brushed her hips, but she did not move away from their touch. Her brown hair curled down over her shoulders. The soft white light emanating from the bunk's ceiling washed the red highlights to silver.

"It was unanimous," she said. "Rachelle tried to vote twice, to make sure she won." She grinned.

Anatoly liked her grin. "You're teasing me. You didn't tell me which way they voted."

"Someone has to make sure you don't fuck up. We just appointed ourselves. Ten years, barring catastrophic changes, as long as you keep to your end of the bargain. To be reconsidered at the end of that time."

She stretched her long, lean legs out in front of her and rested a hand just below his knee, as if balancing herself there.

"That is acceptable." He was almost painfully aware of the warmth and pressure of her hand on his leg. It had been so long since a woman had shown him spontaneous physical affection.

"I don't normally do this," added Branwen, "and I know you're married, but you've sustained a shock. And you look like hell."

"I do?"

But those were the last words he said for a while, because she leaned forward and kissed him on the mouth.

Valentin died three hours after Diana and Portia left Naroshi's palace. Both events came abruptly, as if an unseen communication had triggered them. Ilyana had not gone to see Diana off; she had been too busy consoling Evdokia for the loss of her best friend. And anyway, an undercurrent of hushed arguments and frowning looks had swirled through the company since planetrise. As usual, no one bothered to tell Ilyana what was going on, but she heard enough to guess, eavesdropping.

"She would cut out like that with only two performances left."

"Give her a break, Annet. Gives you a chance to shine, don't it?"

"That's true. Though playing Zenocrate to Veselov's Tamberlaine is more like punishment."

"Yeah, he *is* flat. I don't see why everyone says he used to be such a promising actor. He's just a slut."

"He'll go back to the acties, I bet."

"We can hope."

And another pair, in another place.

"It's about time she did something, instead of just sneaking around with Yassir. I feel sorry for that poor husband of hers."

A snort. "Serves him right, the arrogant *tvut*. He's so polite he'd freeze your blood to ice, and all like he's doing you a favor. D'you think it's true he saw the emperor? Nah. Why him, and not anyone else?"

"Cos' he's a—what—a prince?"

Gales of laughter, which annoyed Ilyana more than the comments about her father had. But they broke off soon enough. "They got a message in this morning something urgent. That's why La Brooke left."

Only two performances left. Sitting beside Valentin's couch, she shut her eyes and tranced out on his breathing. Monitored by the bed, his exhalation and inhalation soothed her because of its regularity. His body had curled even farther into a fetal position, and his right hand had ceased twitching, as it had been all yesterday.

She didn't want to leave. She didn't want to go back to London, not really, except to see Kori and her other friends, but that's where they would go, if he could get around M. Pandit. But wherever they ended up, she could not bear going on day after day like this with her parents, even with an advocate in tow, to monitor their psychological health.

Valentin let out a breath. There was silence. She thought at first that she had dozed off, but she hadn't. He had stopped breathing.

She jumped to her feet and bolted for the curtained door. When her hand touched the cloth, she froze. They would come soon enough. An alarm must be going off on Yomi's slate. But why hurry them? They would just force Valentin's heart to start up again; they would plug his brain stem into an artificial stimulator, and he would live, mindless, against his will, through the machine. She turned and stared down at him.

His face was slack, empty. All the mobility of expression that made him Valentin, little pest, favorite brother, had vanished when their father had severed him from his soul. His lips still had the pale rose tint of a delicate shell, but even that seemed to drain out of him as she watched, as he cooled. His life slipped away, and she let it go. When they all came running, it was too late to try to bring him back.

"I fell asleep," she lied, starting to cry. She did not have to lie about her grief. They left her alone to weep while they conferred over the body. She went out to sit in the courtyard. The sun warmed her, and she took off her boots and let its heat linger on her toes, on her ankles, on her knees.

"Yana!"

She flinched and tugged her trouser legs back down to her ankles.

"It is unbecoming to expose yourself so shamelessly," snapped her mother. "But I suppose that now that you have gone to live in . . . a man's tent, that you no longer feel constrained to behave like a good woman."

"I'm not sleeping in a man's tent! I'm just using David's cot. He sleeps somewhere else."

Karolla hefted Little Rose up onto her shoulder. The baby's presence was itself an accusation. Unnamed still, because of her sister's stubbornness. But Karolla said nothing more. She walked over to the group gathering outside the room where Valentin lay.

They were arguing over what to do with the body. Ilyana spotted David's thick crown of braids in the throng and sidled over to his side, squeezing past some of the others to reach him. She used his body as a shield from her father, who stood next to his wife, confronting Yomi.

"He must be left on the plains," Karolla was saying in her pedantic way, "so that he can be born again into the world."

Into which world? Ilyana thought. *This world? What would he become, born back onto an alien moon? An alien himself? A ghost crying for its true home?*

"He must be taken back to the plains," repeated Karolla stubbornly.

"To Rhui?" Yomi asked. "You know that is impossible."

"Then at least back to Earth. Surely even you barbarians have places where you lay out your dead so that Father Wind may cleanse their souls and return them to living."

Someone whispered: "What does she mean, cleanse them?"

"I don't think he wants to go back to Earth," said Ilyana suddenly, stepping out from behind David. Everyone else started, except David, who had known she was there. "He hated it there. I think you should burn him. He wants to be released."

"That is not our way," said Karolla. "He has not earned release."

Vasil just looked at Ilyana, as if she was a stranger to him.

"I don't care about *your* way. It's what he wants. *Your* way is what killed him."

"Who gave you the right to speak such accusations? His body must be given to the wind so that his soul may be returned to the earth."

"Let him go! Why won't you just let him go? You don't care about him, only about yourself."

David grabbed Ilyana and dragged her back before her mother could slap her.

Karolla whitened. In khush, she said: "I cast you out of my tent. You are no longer my daughter."

Ilyana gasped. She looked toward her father, but Vasil's face was cast of stone. He deliberately looked away from her.

Karolla went on, inexorably but with a weird dignity, her words spoken almost by rote, as if memorized from some similar ceremony she had witnessed, she had endured, many many years before. "I declare you tribeless, motherless, kinless. Wander where you will, you shall find no welcome by this fire."

Stunned, Ilyana could not move. David led her away, and she simply walked with him, nerveless, numb. Like rock, she felt nothing, but a sharp blow would crack her.

David sat her down on a bench in the sun. "What did she say?" he asked.

She shook her head. She could still see the knot of people, shifting nervously now that an explosion had occurred that they could not interpret. She could still see her father's golden head, turned away from her.

David pulled her to her feet and guided her out of the caravansary. "What was that all about?" he demanded when they came out onto the dusty road that led to only one destination—to the ruined caravansary. A road that led nowhere. The planet loomed in copper glory in the sky. The sun splintered its rays through one of the outer rings, scattering light in odd fragments over the flat landscape. Out in the grass, the horses grazed peacefully, calm in the golden haze of the sun.

Ilyana broke away from David and ran. At first, anywhere, away. He came after her, but she was younger, not as fast in a sprint, but she had more endurance and she had a head start.

"Genji!" she called into the drowsy air. "Help me."

The barge came for her. She clambered in, slipping once on the stairs in her frantic haste, and the hatch closed behind her to the sound of David cursing her in at least three different languages. Then she left him far behind. The craft slipped through the rose wall and rain poured over it, coursing down its ribs, splattering the dense glass. Clouds obscured the sky, as they always did. Here, in Naroshi's palace—in Genji's palace—it was always raining.

The barge halted and she tumbled out. She had never seen this place before. Rain drenched her, but it was a relief because the air stifled her with its heat and humidity. She stood in front of a small tile-roofed cottage in the middle of a clearing surrounded by jungle. She was soaked to the skin before she finally worked up enough courage to go inside.

She had to push the door open. She stood dripping on a mosaic entryway. What had she expected? A magical hut that, tiny on the outside, opened up into vast ballrooms on the inside? It was just a single room, about fifteen meters square, with no furnishings except a single shell-like chair placed in the center of the mosaic floor. The tiles in the floor had an odd quality of shifting every time Ilyana blinked, like the pattern of stars as seen by a ship in transit.

Genji sat in the chair. Her eyes were open, but she didn't seem to be inside them. Ilyana waited. Water puddled at her feet and, slowly, dried up, sucked away into the tile floor. Her clothes lightened as the moisture evaporated out of them. It was oppressively hot. Ilyana looked up to the high beams that straddled the open room, beams as dark as ebony wood. When she looked back, Genji was watching her.

Ilyana opened her mouth to speak, but no words came out.

"I have been traveling with your cousin," said Genji. She did not rise from the chair. Ilyana realized abruptly that fine filaments bound her to the chair, wispy strands as delicate as a spider's web.

"My cousin?"

"Prince Anatoly. Why have you come, my child?"

She had enough strength left to take three steps forward before she collapsed into a heap on the floor. The mosaic was cool against her skin, but as hard as her mother's heart. Ilyana had no tears left.

"I have no mother," she whispered, staring at her hands. She lifted her gaze to take in the smooth cascade of Genji's night-blue robes, her pale shining alien hands curved lightly over the arms of her chair. "I have no tribe."

"You will stay with me."

Eyes wide, Ilyana stared up into her face. Not a human face, not even precisely a face by human standards, but no longer completely strange. A chill struck her, and she shivered, but it passed, soaked up by the heat. "Forever?" she asked, and her voice quavered, lost, and vanished. For an instant, she was terrified. She passed through to resignation and then at last, because she was young, threw away all her fears, consumed by an intense curiosity.

" 'Every change is merely part of a mystical pattern,' " said Genji. "You will stay for as long as need be."

"We must go home," Anatoly told his jahar. "We must consolidate our position before we attempt any campaigns."

"Where is home?" Rachelle asked. "I mean, this ship is my home. Where is yours?"

"The plains," he answered, but his own reply puzzled him. How could he govern his principality from the plains, unless he built a khaja tower with which to communicate with the universe beyond? "But I think it would be wise," he added, temporizing, "to go first to Charles Soerensen."

Branwen caught his eye and lifted her chin, which meant she agreed with him. He smiled back at her. He appreciated her gesture of the night before. He had no doubt it would be repeated, or at least he hoped it would. So few khaja women knew how a proper woman ought to behave.

"We're being hailed." Florien tapped one ear with the heel of a hand. "I'm not hearing this right. Isn't a *Yao* a prince? We've got a prince wanting to come on board. Or at least, that's what it says."

"I will meet him. . . ?" Anatoly looked questioningly at Branwen.

"Route them through the starboard lock. That's the hold you first came in through, Anatoly. I'll send Summer down with you, for brawn, and I'll monitor from up here with Florien and Rachelle. Ben, you stay in reserve. Moshe, out of sight."

Anatoly went down to the forward hold with Summer. After a long wait, the lock cycled open and two Chapalii

stepped through. Anatoly hesitated, then noticed that they
wore the tunic and trousers that identified them as stewards.
They bowed to him. After a moment two robed Chapalii
stepped through. He waited and they bowed to him as well.
Last, a single Chapalii cleared the lock and halted to survey
the plain metal hold. Anatoly could not, of course, read this
creature's expression, and in any case he had learned that the
Chapalii did not have mobile enough facial muscles to express emotion through facial quirks and tugs. Nor did the
Chapalii show the least trace of color on his pallid skin. All
that distinguished him was his plain black robe and the teardrop pendant hanging from a chain around his neck. Anatoly
waited, not wanting to make the mistake of bowing to a
Chapalii of lower rank. He supposed that such a gesture
would be fatal.

The Chapalii did not acknowledge him. Instead, it
prowled the hold, touching every surface, picking up any
loose objects and examining them closely. Only a noble of
equal rank to his own would dare to be so rude.

"I am Anatoly Sakhalin," said Anatoly into the silence.
"Do you have a name or title by which I might politely address you?"

The prince did not bother to look at him. He was too busy
trying to pry open one of Benjamin's crates of sherry. "If
you can discover it, you may use it."

"Excuse me," said Anatoly, irritated by this crass tres-
passing. "That crate contains valuable and fragile goods
which are the property of one of my soldiers."

The prince looked at him. He had an ovoid head and a
single smear of permanent color on the left side of his hairless skull, where a human's ear would have been. Except for
that, he looked much like Naroshi: big-eyed, albino pale,
with a slit mouth and three translucent ivory ridges lining his
neck between his jaw and his shoulder. *Like gills,* Anatoly
thought, recalling images of fish and newts from Portia's animal program. Without replying, the prince headed for the
door that led into the rest of the ship.

Anatoly moved to block him. "No. I'm not inviting you
in."

The prince inclined his head. Perhaps the gesture was
meant as a compliment. Perhaps not. Behind him, his retainers stood in silence, fingers curled together in artful patterns.
"The Tai-en Naroshi lies within my house. Now his daiga

holdings have become yours. Don't believe that I will forget this."

Without waiting for Anatoly's reply, he turned and walked back into the lock. His retainers followed him out, and the lock cycled shut.

"They've detached," sang Florien's voice over the ship's com.

"Hell and blarney," said Summer. "I've never seen one of those chameleons be just plain rude like that. How can *that* be a prince?"

Anatoly felt a shudder through the hull as the prince's ship removed its grip from the *Gray Raven*. He wiped his mouth with the back of a hand. "Only a prince can afford to be that ill mannered," he said, and was abruptly reminded of some of his uncles.

"Now I remember why Earth got rid of this hereditary aristocracy business," said Summer. "What a jerk!"

Anatoly chuckled.

Summer glanced at him. "Too bad you're not my type," she added, and with that ambivalent praise left hanging in the air, they left the hold.

They took the fastest route back to Odys, which meant four days to Crossover and a much slower eighteen days to Odys.

"If they've got shortcuts built in," said Branwen, surveying the three dimensional chart of their progress, "then they only exist in old imperial space."

"Or they only exist going to and from Chapal," suggested Florien.

Anatoly said nothing, he only listened.

In orbit around Odys, he and Branwen transferred to a shuttle and were ferried downside. Anatoly flipped through the viewscreen, but Rhui was out of sight, far away around the ecliptic, on the other side of Mother Sun.

Charles Soerensen greeted him personally on the landing pad. As well he might. He looked . . . wary, as a man looks who is confronting an animal that he is not sure has been tamed. Anatoly greeted him politely and waited for him to make the first move. After all, Anatoly now held an insurmountable position on the board. And Soerensen knew it.

"We need to talk," said Soerensen blandly, waving him toward a ground car. "But first, you have a visitor."

He said no more, just made small talk, and when they reached the great shell of his palace, he led Branwen away and left Anatoly at the door of an informally furnished room, plain white couches overlooking two walls of windows that opened onto the flat vista of the tule marshes.

The woman and the child inside did not see him immediately. How tender the mother was, kneeling to let her daughter whisper in her ear, smiling fondly as she replied to the question; how sweetly the child kissed her on the cheek and led her by the hand to look out the great floor-to-ceiling windows that let in light and sky.

How beautiful they looked together. He could not help but fall in love with Diana all over again, seeing her framed against the heavens.

Portia turned. "Papa!" She ran into his arms.

He swung her around and kissed her a hundred times, until, squealing and giggling, she begged to be put down. But after he put her down, she wrapped her arms around his leg and clung to him, grinning with sweet ferocity.

Diana did not come over to him. She hesitated, and he just stood there, dumb with longing, stricken with foreboding.

A woman Anatoly vaguely recognized appeared in the doorway. "Here she is," the woman said. "Portia, dear, did you want to come get that surprise you made for your father?"

Portia did not want to leave, nor did Anatoly want to relinquish her, but he could see that this was some elaborate play staged by Soerensen, by Diana, by this woman, and at last he pried her off and sent her on her way, promising to come straight to her. Thus fortified, she went willingly.

He turned to his wife. "No greeting?" he asked lightly. He wanted to embrace her, to wrap himself in her and let her, for a time, relieve him of the terrible burden that the emperor had placed on him. She did not move. She did not smile her glorious smile. She offered him no light, no warmth. She stood stiffly, as if willing him to ignore the curve of her body under her dress.

"I had to tell you myself," she said haltingly. "Is it true? What they say of you? That what happened. . . ? Are you really . . . named a prince by the emperor?"

"Yes."

It was like talking to a well-meaning stranger.

"I'm sorry, then, to dump this on you now. But there's no

point in waiting. It'll just make it harder for Portia later." She let out a breath. Even at three body lengths from her, he felt its finality. "I've retained an advocate and she will be serving dissolution papers on our marriage in two days."

"But, Diana ..." Floundering, helpless, he could only stare at her.

"I'm sorry," she said, and he knew then that her decision was as irrevocable as the emperor's.

CHAPTER FORTY-FOUR

Confession

Jaelle sat alone under an awning in the middle of the jaran camp. Soldiers had hustled her here last night, back through the ranks of jaran soldiers who were streaming into White Tower, and dumped her. She supposed she was now a prisoner of the jaran, rather than Prince Janos. What had happened to Katerina? Did Stefan still live?

With dawn, the stream of soldiers outward from the camp ceased, and a few casualties came in, but otherwise a hush fell with the sun's rising. Jaelle shivered, pulled her cloak more tightly around herself, and shut her eyes. She could not sleep.

"Jaelle! You will attend me."

Rusudani stood under the awning of a neighboring tent. Jaelle rose hastily and hurried over to her.

"Tell these guards that they are to escort me into the castle. I have spoken to them, but they cannot understand me. I do not speak Taor as well as you do. Yet." A sharp glance from the princess served to remind Jaelle that Rusudani had not yet forgotten her former dependence on Jaelle's translations, and how Jaelle had defied her.

"Yes, my lady." But the jaran soldiers could not understand her, either. Evidently none of them spoke Taor. She attempted a few words in khush, but these also failed to produce any effect.

"I will go to the castle!" Rusudani proclaimed.

"Do you think it is safe, my lady? There may still be fighting."

Rusudani gave her a scornful look, hoisted up the trailing edge of her gown, and began to walk. Her jaran guards had phlegmatic temperaments. They simply found horses, mounted everyone up, and in this way they went into the town, which lay deathly quiet in the morning sun. The gates were held by jaran soldiers. After a brief exchange,

Rusudani's guards escorted her straight up the embankment that led to White Tower. Rusudani dismounted in the outer ward and Jaelle followed her in to the great hall. There was gathered the remnants of the castle's population. Lady Jadranka sat with austere dignity in her chair. She looked washed clean with grief, and her hair uncovered, had gone to white at its roots. Janos's seat was empty.

Rusudani swept up the hall and mounted the two steps that led to the dais. She approached Janos's chair and surveyed it. Jaelle, behind her, saw Lady Jadranka's mouth tighten.

"You have no right to sit there," said Lady Jadranka, her voice rimmed with frost.

Rusudani turned and examined her coolly. "I may do as I please. This castle is mine, now."

Jadranka stood up slowly. Yesterday, she had moved like a much younger woman. Now she looked as frail of body as a crone. But her voice lacked no power. "It is not yours. It reverts to me. You gained none of his inheritance by marrying him."

An odd expression colored Rusudani's face. "Where is your son?"

"He is dead. I had supposed you had heard already, since it was by your hand that he was betrayed."

The word hung in the air, proclaimed loudly enough that Jaelle cowered, expecting Rusudani to reply fiercely. Instead, voices swelled in the anteroom and a delegation clattered in: The jaran had returned from securing the town. At once, the Mircassian envoy rushed forward and knelt before Rusudani, watching her warily, head slightly bowed. She gestured to him to move aside.

"Jaelle, you will translate what I cannot understand. Mind that you do it faithfully, or I will have you killed."

"Yes, my lady."

Jaelle watched them come forward. They did not look like supplicants, although Rusudani pretended to receive them as such. To Jaelle's surprise, Bakhtiian was not with them. Instead, the Prince of Jeds stopped before the dais, escorted by two jaran soldiers.

"I see you have taken possession of the castle, Princess Rusudani," said the Prince of Jeds. She still wore armor, strips of leather and plate decorated with red ribbons, and had her helmet tucked under her right elbow. Without giving

Rusudani time to reply, she turned deliberately to Lady Jadranka. "You are Lady Jadranka? My niece, Princess Katerina, has asked to be remembered to you, my lady. She begs for your forgiveness, and asked me to tell you that the insult to her honor dictated the outcome."

Lady Jadranka inclined her head slightly. She swallowed, but it was a moment before she could speak. "It is too early to speak of forgiveness. I do not hold Princess Katherine responsible for the fall of White Tower."

The words blew a chill through the hall.

"Where is Bakhtiian?" asked Rusudani, cutting into the conversation.

As if her question summoned him, he appeared, limping. He looked grim and rather wild. He, too, wore armor, more elaborate than that he had worn when Janos and his men had ambushed him at the monastery. It made him look like a prince. Prince Vassily attended him, hovering by his side like an overprotective father. Lady Jadranka's eyes widened as she realized who he must be. But she said nothing.

Bakhtiian made a comment, curt, to the Prince of Jeds in the language of the jaran, and she flushed, so slightly that Jaelle would not have noticed it if she had not happened to be looking at her directly at that moment. Princess Rusudani had eyes only for Bakhtiian. She fairly drank him in.

"Who does this castle belong to now?" demanded Bakhtiian.

Lady Jadranka rose slowly. "It is mine, sir, inherited from my father, since I was his only child."

Rusudani looked furious, but she held her peace. Prince Vassily glanced at her, away, and back at her again.

Bakhtiian inclined his head respectfully toward Lady Jadranka. "I have prisoners to give into your hands, my lady. If you will give me your oath and sign your name to a treaty letting there be no feud between your house and mine."

"How can I promise that? Janos was my only son."

"By what means will you make war on me, Lady Jadranka? You cannot. Out of respect for you and your grief, I will leave this castle standing. Otherwise I would burn it to the ground."

"The prisoners knew, all of them, did they not?" she asked. "All but my son knew that you were Bakhtiian. He would have killed you otherwise."

"But he did not."

"But he held you prisoner." The barest smile creased her face, and Jaelle saw Bakhtiian whiten, as if at a blow. "With that memory, I will have to be content. I cannot forgive, Bakhtiian. But I will sign your treaty. Certain of my ladies have whispered to me that it is likely that Princess Rusudani is pregnant with my son's child. For that child's sake, I will swear an oath to hold you no further to blame, as long as I receive in my turn your oath to leave these lands alone and to give me the child, whether boy or girl, to raise in my son's place."

"I give you the child willingly," blurted out Rusudani. "I want nothing from your son, least of all his child."

Lady Jadranka's expression did not alter. "Then let it be so."

Prince Vassily touched Bakhtiian's elbow and whispered in his ear. Bakhtiian shook off the hand impatiently. He looked, to Jaelle's eye, quite transfigured from the man whom she had first seen at Sarai: There, he had reminded her of a steel sword, dangerous, sharp, but clean of line, and strong. Now, he seemed brittle and on edge. Before he had overawed her, but his power had seemed tempered by a glint of humor and a deep sense of control. Now, he scared her, because she could not predict what he might do next.

"What about me?" demanded Rusudani. "You owe me your life."

"Are you sure you want me to—" Jaelle whispered.

"You will speak exactly the words I speak, Jaelle!"

But, like a man well used to deciphering many languages, he had already understood her.

"What do you want from me, Princess Rusudani?"

The Prince of Jeds stood stiffly. A gulf seemed to separate her from Bakhtiian and Rusudani, though there were scarcely three arm's lengths between them.

"I am King Barsauma's heir. Any alliance with me is worth a great deal."

"That is true."

"I can give you an army and passage into Filis, as well as control of caravan routes that lead into the lands south of Mircassia, past the great waste."

"Of course it is in my interest to want these things. But surely you must want something in return."

The silence drew out in the hall until even the soldiers shifting, nervous or bored, in the back stilled and waited.

Jaelle felt a chill envelop her. She had a sudden foreboding that Rusudani was going to say something foolhardy and perilous.

Rusudani had the wisdom to lower her voice, so that only the six of them closest to her could hear.

"I will be queen of a country greater than all of the Yos principalities together, greater than all the western merchant cities, greater than Filis, greater than Jeds. Why should I not have, as husband, the only prince as powerful as I am?" Deliberately, she did not look at the Prince of Jeds.

Nor did Bakhtiian. His gaze remained fixed on a point just behind Rusudani's head, crowned with a gold-threaded shawl that almost covered her thick black hair. His eyes blazed, as if seeing some vision of a great alliance sealed by a royal marriage, the beginning of a powerful dynasty that would rule a vast empire.

Prince Vassily looked like he had been struck.

The Prince of Jeds looked gray, but she said nothing. Rusudani clenched her left hand triumphantly. Still, no one spoke. Like a storm rising, the tension rose until it engulfed the rest of the room.

Bakhtiian stirred. He glanced, curiously enough, at Vassily.

"I regret that I cannot give you myself, my lady," he said politely, quietly, and, continuing, spoke abruptly louder so that his voice filled the hall. "But you are right. It would be fitting if you married my son."

Rusudani shut herself away in the solar and would not be moved. Jaelle escaped her by simply staying behind in the hall, unnoticed and unasked for in the furor that arose after Bakhtiian's pronouncement.

"Tess?" Bakhtiian was casting about, searching for his wife, but she had vanished. "Tess! Where is she?" He sounded querulous and remarkably irritable. An instant later, he dismissed two of his guards and fell into an argument with his son.

Jaelle stood behind Janos's chair and tried to melt into the floor.

Bakhtiian looked up suddenly, right at her. "There is Jaelle," he said. She could not reply, she was so astonished that he remembered her name. "Vasha, take her back to camp."

Thus he ended the argument.

Vassily said one more thing to him, still angry, but Bakhtiian simply turned away and began conferring with someone else. Lady Jadranka had retired to her chamber, and the Mircassian envoy had gone upstairs with Princess Rusudani, her one loyal servant.

"I'm sorry," said Prince Vassily. "That was all very sudden."

Jaelle did not dare venture an opinion. He shrugged, led her out of the hall, and commandeered horses. Preoccupied, he did not speak. Ten jaran soldiers escorted them back to camp. There, dismounting, she found to her surprise that someone was waiting for her.

"Jaelle!" Katerina ran to her and hugged her for a long time. No one seemed to think her affection strange. "Come with me. Do come." She tugged on Jaelle's arm. "Stefan has paced a new ditch in the ground, he's been so worried, wondering where you are. Of course you can come, too, Vasha. What a stupid question." She asked her cousin something in khush, but he shook his head stubbornly and refused to answer.

Stefan was waiting. Somewhere in the tangle of tents that made up the camp they found him, working under an awning that sheltered injured soldiers. He wore clean clothes, the red and black of a jaran rider, and despite his youth he stitched up a wound with the confidence of a master healer, examined an unconscious man and shook his head with a frown, discussed a third case with an older man who seemed to defer to his judgment.

"You see," said Katerina, "Stefan will make you a fine husband. I don't expect he'll ever do much fighting. He's far too valuable for that. He will be as great a healer as his grandfather Niko Sibirin is. Or no, Aunt Tess said that Niko died, didn't she? As his grandfather *was*. Not every man is so gifted by the gods."

Jaelle suddenly wondered if her face was clean, her hair in place. She became aware that her skirts were muddy, and her hands needed washing.

Stefan looked up and saw her. Before, his expression had been fittingly sober. Now, his face creased with a smile, with more than a smile, and Jaelle felt a rush of *something*—she did not know what it was, a melting, a sudden fire washing

over her, a giddy numbness that fell away into sharp joy.
And was in an instant erased by agony.

"Marry me?" she stammered.

"He has been talking of nothing else since we were
freed," said Vassily, looking sour as he said it.

Stefan wiped his hands off in a bucket, dried them, and
hurried toward them. He practically bled happiness into the
air.

"I can't marry," Jaelle gasped. She began to cry. "I can
never marry. I have sinned, and God will never forgive me.
Please. Take me away."

Stefan halted, looking hurt and perplexed, and that only
made Jaelle cry the more. Finally, having mercy on her,
Katerina led her away and soon enough she was enveloped
in the dark tomb of a tent.

"But why?" Katerina demanded. "Why can't you marry
him? He'll just mark you anyway. How can you object?"

"He must not. You must not let him be stained with my
sin."

"But how—?"

Jaelle wiped her eyes dry. It did no good to cry. "I will
tell you. Then you will understand. You will yourself shun
me, but I beg you not to hate me. I will go back to the caravan trade. That is the price I pay for my sin."

"What is a *sin?*" Katerina demanded. "You khaja make no
sense to me." She said it fiercely, grown out of fresh pain.

Jaelle bowed her head. She could not bear to speak, but it
must be spoken. It was time to confess. "I killed my baby
child," she said, because it was easiest to start with the bare
truth. She heard Katerina gasp, but she went doggedly on,
determined to have it all out. "I was taken by men at the
mines, many times, even before my courses began. I ran
away when I realized that I had become pregnant, but life
was worse on the streets. That town was called Orontis. The
birth was hard, but the baby lived, though it was a tiny
thing, so weak it could barely suckle. Then one day
Kamarnos—he was a merchant—saw me. He saw others
first, other women, he was haggling for a woman to be his
companion all the way north to Parkilnous. In those days I
didn't know how far that was, I only knew that it was away,
that I would be fed every day and have a dry bed to lie in.
But he wanted a woman who had no child to burden her. He
saw me. He thought I was pretty, through the rags and the

dirt. He asked me. Ah, Lady, what was I to do? The child was sickly. She might not even have survived the month. That is what I told myself. I had no milk for her anyway. I wanted to live. I pinched her nose and mouth closed with my fingers, until she stopped breathing. It took only a moment. She just slipped away. God will never forgive me."

She fell silent. She was too tired to weep. She understood now that God was punishing her, by letting her glimpse safety but keeping it forever out of her reach.

"There was no one who would foster the baby?"

That surprised a harsh laugh from Jaelle. "No one wants a baby like that. At the mines, sickly babies were exposed on the hillside. No one wanted me. Why should they want a runaway slave's child? Why would they want a sick baby that would never be strong enough to work for them? Who would raise it? Feed it? You jaran are very strange." She said it bitterly. "My own mother stood by and watched while I was sold off to the mines. I had no mother, like you do, to watch over me. I had no tribe to care what happened to me, to send an army to rescue me. Only the Lady's mercy kept me alive in the mines at all. If only I had prayed to her more earnestly, I would never have gotten pregnant there."

"Katya?" That was Prince Vassily, from outside, sounding unsure.

"What is it?"

"Stefan is here with me. He wants to see Jaelle."

"Come back later," said Katerina. She put a hand on Jaelle's shoulder. "Do you love Stefan? Do you *wish* to marry him?"

"He won't wish to marry me, not after he knows what I did."

"It is not a man's right to judge. If you wish to marry him, then you must let my grandmother and his grandmother judge. How long ago did this happen?"

"I don't know. Five years ago? Seven?"

"How old were you?" Katerina sounded appalled, and Jaelle shrank away from her touch, aware that she must not allow her affection for Katerina, and Katerina's for her, to come between them and God's judgment.

"I don't know. Ten years old. Twelve. Thirteen, perhaps. That is the usual age for a girl to begin her courses, isn't it?"

"Gods. You khaja *are* savages. And there was no child after that? After that one?"

"I found out there were herbs that stop a woman from conceiving. Once I thought I got with child, so I took the seeds of the *torise* plant and was sick for weeks. If there was a child, it never came out. Perhaps God made me barren. It would be just."

"What about this Lady, this Pilgrim, you speak of? Does she intend to punish you, too?"

"You must not speak of God and Our Lady that way." Jaelle made the sign of severing, clutching her talisman knife in one hand. "It was just. Surely you must think so, too, Katerina."

"It is true that it is a terrible act to kill a baby. But Aunt Tess says that our army has killed children simply by existing, by conquering and laying lands waste, by leaving children no food to eat over the winter. So is what you did worse than that? I don't know. I killed Prince Janos, and I could have granted him mercy. Who am I to judge you?"

"*You* killed Prince Janos? But Lady Jadranka said that Princess Rusudani killed him."

"Rusudani betrayed him. It was my hand that killed him."

"I did not know you hated him so much."

"I did not hate him," said Katerina, her voice trembling for the first time. "But I had sworn that he would die for what he did to me. And because I swore before the gods, I had no choice."

"I had no choice," whispered Jaelle. "I would have died, too, if Kamarnos had not hired me. That is the truth. I chose to let the baby die so that I could live."

Katerina sighed and, tentatively, put her arms around Jaelle. "I would be like a wife to you, like a husband to you, if you would let me, but I know you do not wish it. So it's better that you marry Stefan. That way I know you will be safe."

"But—"

"Do you wish to go out and see him now?"

"No. Yes. I don't know."

"If I were Mother Orzhekov, I would see what punishment the gods see fit to visit on you. I would let you lie with the man you wish to marry, with other men, and if the gods have forgiven you, they would show their mercy by letting you get pregnant. No woman in the tribes wants her son to marry a woman who cannot give him children. But if you conceive, then why not let you marry him? In the jaran, you will not be forced to behave so barbarously. You will become a jaran woman. It will be as if your other life is gone away. You will become a different woman, a woman who never has to make such a terrible choice, to live herself or die with her child."

"How can I become a jaran woman if I do not pray to your gods? That I can never do."

"Ah, gods, you khaja! No one says you must stop praying to your gods—"

"There is only one God—"

"But you speak of three. You speak of God, his son Hristain, and his daughter the Pilgrim. That is three. I can count."

But Jaelle was too wrung out to launch into a dispute about the nature of God and the holy mystery of three being one. She rested her head on Katerina's shoulder. "Is it true, that I might live with the tribes?"

"You must go back to Sarai with Stefan."

"And you will come with us?"

"I don't know," said Katerina.

"I won't wait any longer!" exclaimed Stefan from outside. A moment later he swept the tent flap aside and barged into the tent. "Jaelle, I don't know what Katerina has been telling you, and it's true that I'll never distinguish myself in the army, but healers are as honored among my people as soldiers and ..." Enough light showed through the flap that Jaelle caught the indignant look that he threw at Katerina. "Would you go away?"

"Your manners, Stefan," she scolded, but she left the tent.

Stefan developed an alarming attack of shyness. "If you were a jaran woman, I would not ask," he said, "but ... but you will marry me, won't you, Jaelle?"

She gathered up enough courage to look at him. "If your grandmother approves of me, of what I have been, then, yes, I will." Exhausting her reserves, she clasped her hands nervously in front of her chest and waited.

He fidgeted a moment, bouncing on the toes of his boots. "Damn good manners, anyway!" he swore, and crossed the chamber and embraced her and kissed her. She was quick to respond.

Tess hid in her tent for the rest of the day. She curled up in her sleeping furs and just lay there. Her nerves were wrung out. She could not bear to face one more person. For the first time in her marriage, she was afraid that something had happened to irrevocably alter the man she had married.

At twilight, Ilya came into the outer chamber of the tent, calling for her in his usual autocratic way. She stirred, but then she heard Vasha's voice.

"Will you stop and let me talk to you?" Vasha demanded.

"What about?" Ilya's curt reply ought to have warned the young man.

"I am not happy about what you did in the hall."

"I didn't mean it. I meant to scare her off."

"*I* mean it."

"You mean what?"

"I mean to marry her."

Ilya snorted. "Then you'd better have someone taste your food."

"Father! Don't you understand what an alliance with Mircassia will mean for us?"

"Why should I merely ally with Mircassia when I could have her outright?"

"How many battles would that take you? How many soldiers would you lose? This is a much better way. If you and Katya hadn't been so stubbornly set on killing Janos—"

"Do not speak to me on that subject."

"I will speak to you! You're just angry that he held you prisoner. But he was a good man, he was intelligent, and he knew the worth of—"

"He raped Katerina, or have you forgiven him for that?"

For the first time, Vasha stumbled. "I don't know. I think he didn't mean to do . . . that he didn't know . . . that he supposed that what he did was different than how Katya saw it. What are the laws in his country? Shouldn't he be judged by them, and not by ours?"

"Most khaja laws are unjust."

"Then expand just laws over all people, but do not throw out everything that is theirs. How do you expect to hold together an empire if you show no respect for the ways of the people you have conquered? If you don't give them a stake in holding your empire together, then they will simply revolt at the first opportunity. You cannot hold all these lands together by force indefinitely. You must hold them together by other means."

Ilya gave a bark of a laugh. "Now you sound like Tess."
Tess winced, hearing him, because he sounded angry.

But Vasha's reply was calm. He sounded surer of himself
than she had ever heard him. "Thank you. You could have
given me no greater compliment. I had a great deal of time
to think while I was Janos's hostage, and—"

"And you still want to marry Rusudani?"

"I do. It is the wisest course, now that Janos is dead. I'll
ride to Mircassia with her."

"Who said I meant to let her go to Mircassia? She's worth
more to me as a hostage."

"Mircassia is worth more to us as an ally. You're just being contrary. You know it's true."

There was a long silence. She heard little noises, Ilya pacing, Ilya unrolling a scroll, or at least she assumed that Ilya
was the restless one, not Vasha. The furs in which she hid
smelled musty. In the rains several days ago they had gotten
damp and never been properly aired out.

"Then you'd better marry her before you go. Otherwise
she'll have you killed once you get there, if she finds a more
suitable consort."

"Father!"

"Do you approve of her killing her husband?"

"You would have killed him."

"That was different. He ambushed my guard and took me
prisoner. A woman does not betray her husband. Nor a husband, his wife."

"He forced her to marry him."

"Women have no choice in marriage. Gods, boy, I forced
Tess to marry me."

Now it was Vasha's turn to snort. "You did not!"

"I did! By the gods."

Tess sat up. She heard in his voice a touch of the old Ilya:
smug and triumphant.

"I don't believe it. Not of Tess. Of a jaran woman, perhaps."

"Well . . ." More rustling. Ilya was shifting around again.
She could practically hear the admission being dragged out
of him, however reluctantly. "She didn't accept it either and
told me so."

Tess heard the oddest sound: Vasha trying to suppress
laughter.

"I suppose she did," Vasha said finally. "That is why I

can't marry Rusudani out of hand. She must come to see that it is in her interest to marry me, to ally with the jaran."

"Vasha." Now Ilya's voice changed, to something far more dangerous because it trembled on the edge of control. "Don't be a fool. She doesn't want you. She wants me. It is never wise for a man to marry a woman who sees him only as an obstacle in her way to what she truly wants. She will stay with the jaran as a hostage until her grandfather dies."

When Vasha replied, his voice was so low that Tess had to strain to hear it. And was sorry she did. "What, are you like Janos? You want a wife *and* a well-born concubine? I won't waste my time talking to you any more."

The tent flap soughed down, closing behind him. There was silence in the outer chamber. Tess wrapped the furs more tightly around herself.

"Damn it," said Ilya. A moment later a faint edge of light sprang into being around the curtain that separated the sleeping chamber from the outer chamber. "Nikita! Vladimir!"

It was Gennady Berezin who stuck his head in finally. "Yes, Cousin?" he asked in the formal style.

"Do you know where Tess is?"

"No. No one has seen her since this morning in the great hall."

"Or if they have," said Ilya sarcastically, "they're not going to tell me."

"Yes, Cousin," said Berezin mildly, and by that Tess knew that he was protecting her.

"Then go out and see if you can find her, damn it. Send her here."

"*Send* her here, Ilyakoria?"

"Ask her if she will deign to see me, then! Go!" Ilya kicked something—it could only be the table—swore, and fell to muttering to himself. Angels and blinding lights and a sword made in heaven . . . Tess had heard this before. She got up on her hands and knees and swayed forward, twitching aside the back lower corner of the curtain and peeking through. By the light of a single lantern, sitting in the middle of the table, she watched him. She felt an inexplicable reluctance to go out to him, to speak to him; what if he had been changed forever? He never talked to himself like this before. Finally his mumbling trailed away. He sat in the chair, one hand on the table, holding open a scroll which he was not looking at. He was staring at the tent entrance, as if he expected a visitor momentarily.

One came. She pushed aside the entrance flap and paused, letting it slide shut behind her. She pulled her shawl down and let it drape over her shoulders, letting her thick dark hair tumble down around her shoulders. She wore no jewels, nothing to adorn her except her youth and her pretty face and her position as King Barsauma's acknowledged heir. She examined Ilya greedily. She practically licked her lips.

"What do you want?" Ilya snapped.

Tess flinched. She had never heard him be rude to a woman before.

Then, he recovered himself. "I beg your pardon," he said, standing up.

"You want Mircassia," she said, without moving.

"Yes."

"Then put aside your wife and marry me instead. Mircassia will be yours."

"Among the jaran, a man does not *put aside* his wife, my lady."

"Jeds is nothing compared to Mircassia. A few ships, that is all. I am a more suitable consort for a man of your power and ambitions."

He did not reply. They all knew it was true.

"An ambitious man would not hesitate. You served me faithfully enough while you were Prince Janos's prisoner. I spared you from worse indignities."

"I am not a lapdog, Princess Rusudani, an animal which I know khaja noblewomen like to pet and dandle and feed sweets to. Nor do I marry simply for the sake of land."

"Do you expect me to believe that? That is the only reason anyone of our station marries. The Prince of Jeds must have seemed a valuable enough alliance ten years ago, however paltry it may seem now."

"I invite you to leave, Princess."

"No," she said petulantly. "I am leaving on my own. I ride out tomorrow—"

"With what escort? How do you intend to break free of my army? You are under my control, Princess Rusudani. You will marry my son Vassily—"

"I will only marry in a ceremony in the true church!" But she sounded desperate now. She knew she had been outplayed.

"If that contents you. The boy is half khaja anyway; I doubt he will care. But be aware, Princess, that if he dies in mysterious circumstances, I will seek revenge."

She paled, and her hands tightened into fists. She bit down on one pretty lip and a tear squeezed out of one eye. Ilya remained unmoved by this display of emotion. She wiped off the tear and straightened her shoulders. "So I am to be sold off again to a man? To your empire? As if I were a common slave? Is this how you treat the women of your people? I once thought otherwise."

"This is how you expect to be treated. Janos was not a stupid man. You could have made a good marriage with him, but you chose to betray him instead."

For the first time, Tess saw Rusudani flinch.

"If you choose to act as if you are only a pawn in a game of castles, then that is how you will be treated. If you choose to act as an etsana, wielding power wisely and with the gods-granted authority given to women, then you will be respected. Nikita! Vladi, damn you!"

"Yes, Bakhtiian." Vladimir stuck his head in. His helmet gleamed in the lantern light. He glanced around the chamber and Tess had a good idea that he knew where she was, that she was spying.

"Take Princess Rusudani to a tent. Please remove her. Now. An escort of five thousand riders must be ready day after tomorrow to escort her to Mircassia, under the command of Vassily Kireyevsky."

"Under Vasha's command?"

"That's what I said, damn it!"

"Of course, Bakhtiian. And you—"

"I will continue south to Yaroslav Sakhalin's army. With them we will push on south toward Jeds. Is there any news of Kirill Zvertkov?"

"I understand he was sent to the court of the king of Dushan to bring back Andrei Sakhalin. There is no news yet."

"Then go."

"Yes, Bakhtiian."

Rusudani went unresisting.

Ilya began to pace. He looked like he meant to wear a trail in the carpet, and gods he looked exhausted. But Tess knew he would not sleep until he saw her. So she stood up, took in a breath, straightened her clothing, and—to spare his riders from his temper—went out through the back flap so that she could come in through the front entrance, as if she was just returning. Berezin nodded at her but said nothing.

Ilya was still pacing, back to her. He turned and stopped dead. "Tess! Where were you? I've been looking . . . you're avoiding me, aren't you? You're ashamed that I was stupid enough to let myself get ambushed, but I had to find out about the great blinding light sent from heaven. That was the angel . . . no, that was the other story. His wing was as bright as the strike of lightning. Except I suppose that the heretic is dead and burned by now while I was walled away in stone like any khaja slave. I had to— Kirill was with you, wasn't he? That's what they say. Are you already tired of me? Are you going to throw me over in favor of him? Ditches. I had to dig ditches. I don't know if they meant to flood them with water, that would have been the best defense unless they built a palisade. Now that Arina is dead—"

He was babbling. She walked over to him and he just grabbed hold of her as if he was afraid she would escape if he didn't hold on to her. Arms around her, face buried against her hair, he kept talking, on and on, and she let him talk. She let the words brush past her without listening to them, knowing they would make no real sense.

Because she saw now what had happened to him. Ilya could not abide, he could not sustain, the knowledge that another person controlled him, that he lay within a prison of another man's making. It had driven him a little mad. Sonia had been right: For all his strength, for all his visionary luminosity, Ilya was fragile. She had been right to protect him all along, however horrible that might seem now. She herself had imprisoned him all these years, by walling him off from the knowledge of Earth, of her brother's true position as Duke and as suzerain over Rhui and all its peoples, of the Chapalii Empire itself against which the jaran empire was like a nest of mice hidden in a drawer, a world self-contained and yet inconsequential. Ilya could not bear to be inconsequential.

"Hush, Ilya, my heart," she said finally.

"Ah, gods," he murmured in the tone of a man who has only now found the courage to confess his worst shame, "I had to obey their laws and their commands. That is what it means to become a slave. How could the gods punish me in this way? Oh, Tess, kill me rather than let it happen again."

It broke her heart to hear him. "Forgive me, Ilya," she whispered. "Forgive me."

He said nothing. She was not sure he had really heard her. He could not truly know what she was apologizing for, anyway, because she had made choices all along that imprisoned him. But she could no longer choose for him. He deserved the truth.

Twelve years ago Ilya had married her in the jaran way, giving her no choice in the matter. But he had learned that it was her choice as well, that he could not make the choice for her. Tess smiled wryly, pulling him closer against her, feeling him sigh, feeling his breath against her ear and the strength of his arms around her back. It had taken her twelve years to learn the same lesson.

He just stood there, holding her, as if he waited ... for what? For a tangible sign that she still believed in him, respected him, found him worthy, even simply found him desirable.

"I was so terrified when I thought I had lost you," she said finally, "first to death, then to Princess—"

"I hope you think I have better taste than that!" he retorted indignantly, pulling away from her.

"Such as?"

He turned his head away, refusing the bait. The flickering candlelight scored his face in light and shadow, like a painted mask. Not knowing what else to do, she kissed him. He shifted, just a little, against her, allowing himself to be coaxed. But he made her work at it. She kissed him again on the neck and moved up over the curve of his jaw to his cheek and his mouth, running one hand down his back and the other down his leg.

Abruptly, with an impatient curse, he hoisted her up bodily, carried her into the inner chamber, and dumped her on the sleeping furs. She thought, fleetingly, about what words to use when she told him the truth, what evidence to present, how to do what she knew now she would have to do. Then he dropped down beside her, and she thrust all those bothersome thoughts aside. They could wait. This couldn't.

CHAPTER FORTY-FIVE

The Crossing of Borders

People talked, their conversation like a stream flowing around him. Numb, he stared at his hands. He could not concentrate enough to understand the endless river of words.

"M. Sakhalin, are you listening?"

He jerked, startled out of his trance. "I beg your pardon," he said, not sure who had addressed him. Had the person spoken again, he could not have distinguished that voice from any of the others. He looked around the oval table, marking the people who sat here: Charles Soerensen, Captain Emrys, Soerensen's assistants Maggie O'Neill and Suzanne Elia Arevalo, a diplomat whose name he had forgotten, another man whose importance he could not recall. Usually his memory was keen. Now all he could think of was Diana's face, the way it had closed away from him, shutting him out, rejecting him, exiling him.

How could she have done this to him?

Why?

He had been a good husband to her, hadn't he? He had wanted another child. Maybe that was it. Or she had found out about Ilyana's flower night and misunderstood it. These khaja misunderstood many things. What had she said? *I've fallen in love with another man, Anatoly, a man whose life and interests are more suited to mine.* What did that have to do with anything? Of course he felt a little hurt, but a man expected his wife to take lovers, as long as she was discreet about it. He expected her to respect him. And that was the problem. Diana didn't respect him. Say what she wanted, she was embarrassed of him, of where he had come from, of what he was.

But how could she be embarrassed now? How could there be any shame in being married to a prince of the Sakhalin who had been confirmed in his rank by the Chapalii emperor himself?

"I beg your pardon, M. Sakhalin. But we have a great deal to discuss."

Anatoly looked up at Charles Soerensen. Soerensen's face gave away nothing, but Anatoly had a damned good idea that Soerensen had arranged for Diana to confront him first, to give Soerensen the advantage after. He dug down into his reserves of strength and pushed her image aside. She had already left the planet Odys. A pain stabbed through him, thinking that he might never see her again. How could it happen? How could this be? Then he reined himself in again. He had responsibilities now. Portia was still here, left with him until the hearings that would settle the schedule of parental care. She was asleep on a blanket in the corner made by the stairwell wall, her little mouth partly open, snoring softly because she had a cold. He had to concentrate. But, gods, it was hard.

"You understand," said Soerensen, "that this changes everything."

"You are no longer the most powerful human in daiga space," snapped Anatoly, and was at once sorry he had said it. It was Diana he was angry at, not Charles Soerensen.

"That is true. But I have been associated with Earth and League space for my whole life. I have risked much for them, and so they trust me, despite my position within the Empire. You're a wild card. They don't know you, and therefore have no reason to trust you. You have nothing invested in League space."

"Except my home."

"Rhui does not properly lie within League space. In fact, it isn't even in the same prefecture, since Duke Naroshi controls Earth and the other systems that make up—"

Soerensen broke off. It was the first time that Anatoly had seen him make a misstep.

"No," agreed Anatoly. "You are right. They are all under my control now."

"How do you intend to assert that control?" asked the other man. Anatoly dredged up his name and title, forcing it past the morass where all his thoughts got stuck: Diana. Diana at their wedding, so beautiful that she had taken his breath away. Diana on stage, a Singer who seemed at those times to be in direct communication with the gods.

Tobias Black. Barrister. There, he had it.

"Please, M. Black, go on," he said politely, pleased at his

little victory over his wife. Except she would no longer be his wife, she was leaving him, except how could that be when marriage lasted among the jaran for as long as the man lived or the mark of marriage scarred a woman's face, which was for her entire life? Except Diana was not jaran, and she had long since undergone *cosmetic surgery* to erase the mark from her face, because an actor must conceal such disfigurements. She had called it a *flaw*.

Portia sucked in a big, snoring breath and rolled half over, still asleep. Anatoly steadied himself with one hand on the table and leaned toward the barrister, fixing his gaze on him.

"M. Sakhalin, there is a difference between authority and power. Before the Chapalii Empire swallowed up League space, humans had after millennia of experimentation with such forms of government as theocracy, tyranny, monarchy, and communalism settled on what we now call diocracy, self-rule and community-rule in opposition and in balance. M. Soerensen remains a leader within the human community because of the *authority* he has derived from many years of service to the League and many years of proving again and again that he has the best interests of the League and humanity uppermost in his mind. The only *power* he has is that conferred on him by the Chapalii. You have no authority. You have only power. Without authority to persuade the Parliament and the citizens of League space to follow you, you must resort to force or coercion. That force can only come from the Chapalii and from those human quislings who have chosen to throw their loyalty away for the sake of short-term gain. You have a great deal of power, there's no doubt about that. You can impose tyranny on humanity if you will. You can impose any kind of rule that you wish. In my capacity as an advocate, however, I would advise you not to take that course. You will alienate most of the human populations of your holdings, and those who flock to your side despite everything will probably prove to be untrustworthy allies. M. O'Neill, you mentioned comm traffic earlier?"

Maggie O'Neill tapped her finger on the table top and squinted at the numbers called up on the luminous surface. "In the last four days we have received eight thousand and ninety-four queries to the attention of one Anatoly Sakhalin. Ah, no, make that eight thousand and ninety-six."

Eight thousand messages. How could he possibly answer each of those petitions? Anatoly stared past M. O'Neill. This oval table sat in the center of a round chamber roofed by an onion dome molded of clear glass, a material melded with plastic to give it strength to withstand the occasional typhoon that blew in over the plateau. From where he sat, he saw the tule flats extending to a misty horizon, sea and sky blending together in a distant gray haze. Soerensen's palace extended behind him, but he would have to turn in his chair to see it.

"I have authority within my own tribe," he said, "because I earned it. I will gain a base of power there first."

"At what cost?" asked Soerensen quietly.

"At what cost?"

"If you go back, what will you tell them? Will you disrupt their way of life wholesale in order to bring them off planet? How will you get them off Rhui in any case? How many ships would you need? Where will you house them? How will they adapt? If you only take some at first, then who will you take? How will you choose?"

Irritated by this lecture, Anatoly broke in. "Among the jaran, all adults have a say in decisions that affect the whole tribe, although of course the etsana and the council of elders make the final decision."

"Then what if no one wants to go? What if everyone wants to go? How will they communicate with the rest of us once they are off Rhui? Who or what will you use as interpreters?"

"There are slates—"

"You must get one for every person, then. Who will buy and distribute them? What will all these people do, who are accustomed to another life entirely? What about the khaja? What about the other continents, and the people who live there?"

"I wouldn't do it all at once! You think I'm a fool. I don't intend to act rashly. But how can I leave my people behind when I am here now?"

But perhaps it was true. Why should all of them necessarily want to travel to Earth? Valentin Arkhanov had not wanted it. Karolla Arkhanov had never adjusted; she lived by living a lie and by warping her family to match the image on her walls. Even he himself had not truly adjusted, not yet, maybe not ever. They all had such odd khaja ways out here, inexplicable to a civilized man, however primitive he might seem to them. They had it written down that all twenty-year-olds had to perform two years of community service in order

to qualify for citizenship in the League. How barbaric to
need a *law* for that, when among the tribes every child knew
that she or he had responsibilities to the tribe, that every
adult was needed for the tribe to survive.

But the tribes were small. There were so many humans in
League space that the number was meaningless to him. And,
of course, no one knew how many Chapalii there were ...
although perhaps a prince could find out. Perhaps a prince
could get a *census* of human and alien species.

He leaned over toward Branwen and whispered the idea in
her ear, and she noted it down on her slate. Realizing that
everyone else was watching him, he turned back to
Soerensen.

"Are you suggesting," he said, "that I learn more about
the League, about these worlds and the Empire itself, before
I try to bring Rhui into it?"

Soerensen smiled, touched with irony, and Anatoly saw
that while Charles Soerensen did not like relinquishing the
power he had gained, that he was willing to, or at least, willing to share it. "That had been my intention all along," said
Soerensen. "Rhui has valuable natural resources. The
Chapalii cannot interfere on her because she is interdicted.
Therefore, she makes a good base for planning a revolt
against the empire."

"Why do you want to revolt against the empire? I always
meant to ask that. The Chapalii do not rule you harshly.
They leave you your own parliament for local matters, your
lives are stable, and you go about your business much as you
did before. What is wrong with that?"

Soerensen stood up, speaking down toward the table.
"Call up a two-dimensional map of Rhui, continent A. Blush
all territories known to be in the control of the jaran."

Anatoly knew the map well, the great gulf that marked the
northern sea, the spine of mountains that girdled the central
mass of the continent, two delicate peninsulas to the southeast, and the large island in the southern sea that was home
to the mysterious Byblos civilization, known only through
the ancient scrolls and occasional merchant. He had met one,
once, many years ago when he was hunting down the king
of Habakar. He had bought an old scroll off him, but later
lost it.

The red blush marking the territories of the jaran consumed about one fifth of the continent, nestled in the central territories and advancing toward the periphery.

"Do you suppose," asked Soerensen conversationally, "that the khaja princes overrun by the jaran will give up their power willingly and happily? Do you suppose that their sons and daughters, however justly ruled they might be, will not listen to an old nurse's story of how once they ruled themselves, and think that they could again? When you first came off Rhui, M. Sakhalin, you fell in with our plans swiftly enough. You did not want to be subject to the Chapalii Empire, nor have your people be subject to it. What has changed?"

The barrister Tobias Black was wrong about one thing: Charles Soerensen knew he had power, and he had come to like having it. Yet, at the same time, he might genuinely want only to further the interest of the human race rather than his own. Self and community, opposed and yet balanced.

"I have changed," said Anatoly. "I have what Bakhtiian wanted all along. I have achieved his vision, that which he began, that the jaran rule over all the khaja lands. Why should I not lift my people up to meet their destiny?"

"At the expense of all the others?"

"Why should I care about them?" Anatoly asked bitterly. "They are only khaja. They have only caused me pain."

"I told you it was a mistake," muttered Maggie O'Neill. "You should have had the conference first and let him meet his wife afterward."

His wife. Not to be his wife any longer.

"At the expense of Bakhtiian?" asked Soerensen.

"Bakhtiian?" The question startled him, but as soon as he faced it squarely he knew that Soerensen spoke the truth. Even if the emperor would recognize Bakhtiian as a prince—and if any man had the power of a great prince, that man was Bakhtiian—there were only ten princes in the Empire, and all ten now had names again, since he had come into the inheritance of the missing prince. "It is true," he said slowly, "that despite my great respect for Bakhtiian, I do not intend to give him what I now have, nor will I relinquish my position in his favor. Why should I? Giving it would be insulting to him in any case. And while it is true that, like a Singer, the gods granted him a vision, they did not promise that he would be the one to achieve it. Anyway," he added thoughtfully, looking Soerensen straight in the eye, "if Bakhtiian came to space, to these worlds beyond, *he* would want to become emperor. He would die before he admitted it could not be done."

"You think he could not do it?"

"With what army? With what tools? This place is very different from the plains, as you yourself also know. Horses cannot ride the oceans between the worlds. Sabers cannot defeat . . ." But there he halted. "It is true that in everything I have read, all the images I have scrolled through, that you know very little about the Chapalii army."

"We're not sure they *have* an army, as we know of one. Only that when they use force, they use it sparingly and ruthlessly, and that their weapons are more powerful than those we brought to bear on them."

Anatoly looked at Branwen. "Note that down. That is something else we will have to investigate." He stood up and walked to the wall, splaying his hands on the cool glass, slightly moist inside from the humidity of their breathing.

"Papa?" Portia appeared from behind the stairwell wall, sleepy-eyed, and padded over to him. He gathered her up into his arms and turned to survey the people seated at the table. Soerensen still stood. "You are right," he said finally, reluctantly. "I can't go to Rhui yet. I have to consolidate my position here first. I have to understand what I have, what I don't have, and what I can do with it. So I leave you, Charles Soerensen, with your lands and your authority intact, and I trust you will continue to advise me without concern for whether I care to hear what you have to say. As for the rest of you, I mean that as well." Portia tucked her head into the crook of his neck and stuck two fingers in her mouth to suck on, eyes open, watchful. She was warm and solid. He wrapped her a little closer into his embrace. Be damned to jaran tradition, he thought suddenly, where the child always stayed with its mother. He would keep her beside him and raise her—let her see her mother, of course, that was only fair—but he would not give her up.

Branwen and the barrister closed their slates. They all rose, made small talk, and one by one left the room, bodies and then heads receding down the curved staircase. Soerensen lingered, staying beside the table.

"There is one other question I'd like to ask," he said.

"What is that?" Anatoly shifted Portia on his hip.

She turned her head to look out over the tule flats. "Look, Papa. Look. There's a boat."

"Why did the emperor make you a prince?"

"And you only a duke?" Anatoly smiled, to take the sting out of the words. "I don't know. Wasn't it after you became a duke that the tenth princely house was ... what do they call it? It was erased?"

"Made extinct."

"Yes. But in any case, you weren't brought before the emperor."

"But I was. I was brought into a great hall, lined with columns and floored with white tile. There were many Chapalii there, nobles, I supposed at the time, and I believed I supposed rightly. At one end of the hall rested a gilded throne, and when the emperor appeared on this throne, they knelt, and so I followed suit. After that, I was named a duke."

"Ah." Anatoly walked around the curve of the room toward the stairwell, and Soerensen turned slowly to keep facing him. "That is why you are only a duke. Women and princes need bow before no man, nor Singers before anyone but the gods."

"When is Mama coming back?" asked Portia while they were eating dinner, and he didn't know what to say to her. Nothing in his life had trained him for this. *She is never coming back.* That was what he wanted to say, spitefully, but he could not say it to Portia, who would not understand.

He tucked her into the bed next to which he had set up a cot for himself and told her a story about the jaran, how a hawk had warned a little girl and boy, a brother and sister, of an avalanche, and so saved their tribe.

"Can birds talk? Birds can't talk."

"Singers can understand the speech of birds because they are touched by the gods. That little girl and boy became Singers, and birds became sacred to the jaran."

"Mama taught me how to sing," she said brightly.

He had to turn away, so she wouldn't see the tears that came to his eyes. "Yes. Would you like to hear another story?" Knowing she would. "A long time ago, when I was a boy, my sister Shura was just the same age as you are now. One morning she wanted to go riding with me and the older boys, but we didn't want her along with us. So she—" So she had somehow gotten up onto a pony and ridden out after them, and when it had been discovered that she was missing, there had been such a wild clamor and he and his friends had gotten into such trouble for not watching over her and the whole tribe had searched frantically for the whole day only to find her at sunset sitting by a stream contentedly eating from a berry patch while her pony grazed faithfully beside her. . . .

But Portia was asleep.

He sat beside her for a long while, a hand resting lightly on her hair, watching the rise and fall of her breathing, studying the curve of her face, her lashes, the simple beauty of a child peacefully sleeping.

A child needs a mother. A man needs a wife or a sister or a mother or aunt, to whose tent he returns. Now he had nothing, only borrowed rooms, no tent, no home. Repose deserted him. He stood up, stroked up a faint illumination from the door panel, in case she woke up, and left the room. At the outer edge of the palace, a promenade overlooked the tule flats. Clouds covered the stars. The barest mist spattered the deck, and he held onto a railing and stared out into the last remains of daylight, the gray flats receding on and on until they were lost in sea and horizon and the gathering darkness.

It had been a mistake to marry a khaja woman. His grandmother had told him that all along. But she had wanted him to marry Baron Santer's daughter, in Jeds, so perhaps it was only Diana she had disliked. It was true that it was dangerous to marry a Singer. They had their own ways, their own calling, and the gods might lure them away at any moment.

I've fallen in love with another man whose life and interests . . . That was not a calling from the gods. That was just selfishness.

The wind turned and hit him in the face, bringing with it the smell of salt and of things left rotting, untended among the reeds.

But Diana had already left him once. She had told him plainly enough that she had her world, and he his. He had written to her, finally, unable to endure without her company—or perhaps it would be fairer to say that although he did truly miss her he wanted to prove to his grandmother, to the tribes, that it had not been a mistake for him to marry her. He had written, asking her to make a final judgment, that if she wanted him to, he would willingly leave the tribes, the army, to come to her.

But he had left the tribes, he had left Rhui, before he had received her answer. Now, finally, staring into the lowering night, he wondered what that answer would have been.

A door soughed open, blending with the murmur of gentle waves on the pilings below. He turned to see Branwen come out onto the promenade.

"Want company?" she asked.

He regarded her for a few moments, silent. She was an attractive woman, competent, smart, and a good companion. But she was not Diana. He respected her, but he could not love her. Nor did she expect him to. "No, thank you," he replied politely.

She smiled slightly, lifted a hand in acknowledgment, and retreated back through the door.

Ah, gods, how he wanted a family. He liked the crew of the *Gray Raven,* but they were his jahar, not his family; they might in time become friends, comrades, but that was not the same. If only Shura was here. . . .

Why not? He had not yet heard, in the twice-yearly letter she sent him through convoluted channels, that she had married. She had stayed with the army all this time, as a scribe and interpreter. Why shouldn't she leave Rhui and come to him? One person would make no difference.

But Charles Soerensen was right, too. Shura would be alone out here, with a brother but no sisters or female cousins or aunts. Was that fair to her?

Then, like a flare in the heavens, a sudden, piercing image of Ilyana Arkhanov burned before him and vanished. A jaran girl. Sixteen, or perhaps she was seventeen by now. That was a proper age for a girl to get married. She loved Portia already, and she could bring Evdokia with her, to be Portia's companion. Diana had abandoned him. It would serve her right if he turned around and took a new wife. A beautiful wife. Young, one who would want children.

"Damn it," he muttered, knowing it was unfair, and just plain mean, to marry Ilyana only to spite Diana. But he could travel to Naroshi's planet, to see her. Who would stop him?

He could send a message to Rhui, asking Shura to come to him. He could do anything he damned well pleased.

Fortified by this thought, he went back inside, stopped beside a wall panel, and called up a route to the communications center. It lay in the south wing, perpendicular to the massive greenhouse wing, buried under an astonishingly ugly rococo hall that Soerensen used for receptions of his least favored guests.

Maggie O'Neill and three techs sat in stylish chairs, scattered around the room like islands in a sea of muted gray consoles and several tables which displayed above their flat black surfaces rotating three-dimensional images of Rhui, of Odys, and of the Delta Pavonis solar system. Two long screens on opposite walls displayed two-dee images of landscapes, one from Earth that Anatoly recognized, a mountainscape of the Alps, and another from the sand pillar swamp of Tao Ceti Tierce. On a third wall a stellar chart glittered, seeming to sink three 'dimensionally into the emptiness beyond, even though Anatoly knew it was a trick of the projection itself.

Maggie jumped up and hurried over to him. "Heyo. What can I do for you? Are you here to start through that backlog of messages? If you turned each one into scroll and stacked them up around you, you'd have to wade hip-deep to get out of here. But you'll get used to it." She grinned.

He nodded politely. "No. That can wait. I want to put a call through to Jeds and Sarai. I want Tess Soerensen to locate my sister Shura."

She raised her eyebrows but did not respond. Instead, she negotiated the maze of consoles and came to a halt before one that looked exactly like all the others except for a saffron-colored jacket thrown carelessly over the chair wheeled up in front of it. Maggie hitched it out of the way. "Suzanne may have the complexion to wear this color. I sure as hell don't. I get jaundiced just standing near enough to squint at it. Here, put it over there."

Dutifully, he did as he was told, draping the jacket carefully over a nearby chair. Maggie sat down and began keying numbers into the console, interspersed with terse vocal commands.

"No one's home at Jeds," she said. "Odd. I'll leave a callback for when Cara catches up to us. Or wait, I think she was headed for Sarai last I heard. We can almost always at least get the ke at Sarai. Let me see . . ."

Anatoly leaned on the edge of the console. The thin line scored itself into the gray surface, forming a large square.

Mist coalesced up from that square, pulsing to an unheard heartbeat.

"Ah! I've got an acknowledge. On screen."

The mist dissipated to reveal a woman's head and shoulders, peering keenly and with a somewhat perplexed expression at them. She narrowed her eyes, registered Maggie, and twined a finger through one of her braids and shifted her vision to the left. Seeing Anatoly, her eyes widened.

"Anatoly Sakhalin! What are you doing there?"

For an instant he could not reply, he was so surprised to see a jaran woman using interdicted equipment. Finally he found his voice.

"I give you greetings, Sonia Orzhekov," he said.

Daiga transmissions are like a form of blindness to the ke's eyes, which are not like daiga eyes, seeing only in the spectrum of visible light. The daiga whose appearance startles *Sonia,* the name which classifies the daiga of flowers, is simply a primitive collection of impulses, not the complex ever-flowing pattern that informs the person of a biologically-present daiga. The ke cannot even tell if the daiga is male or female, the identifying marker by which the daiga put greatest store.

The two daiga speak in a daiga language. The ke does not know this language, it is not the language named *Rhuian* by the daiga Tess, but all daiga languages have primitive characteristics in common, in the way their structure has grown up as time and generations of daiga have passed. The ke shifts to the intermediate brain, seeking correspondences, similarities, alliances. Meaning emerges.

"But of course you're a prince of the Sakhalin," Sonia says, labeling this daiga. "Why shouldn't you go before the khepelli emperor? Except that Dr. Hierakis told me that Charles Soerensen does not want the khepelli to know where his people are hiding. That is why they have this . . . what is it they call it? . . . this *interdiction.*"

Prince of the Sakhalin replies. "I am now a prince in the Chapalii Empire. That means that the jaran have a place within the Empire, one without recourse to the khaja who have come down to Rhui and made their own rules for us. That means that we are now the guardians of all khaja space."

"I am new to this. I don't really understand what you are saying."

The ke sees that, without patterns to read, without the ability to read patterns, names might prove useful to daiga. Otherwise, needing to order the universe so that they can grow out of their half animal state, they could only see the universe as an undifferentiated mass of light and dark and color, edged with borders. To cross those borders, the daiga name *things*. By naming the universe, they bring it into existence.

"Who is that with you?" asks the prince of the Sakhalin.

Sonia says: "This is *the ke*." Thus does the daiga of flowers make namelessness into a name, bringing the ke into existence.

Able to see and sense in limited spectra, the daiga struggle to expand their sight and thus their interaction with the universe. Naming becomes both their prison and their key.

"How do I use this tool to speak to Tess?" asks Sonia after the daiga transmission ends.

"On this world," explains the ke, "daiga can only speak through tools, through *consoles*. Such are the rules of the interdiction. A call may be placed to *Jeds*. The daiga Tess journeys toward Jeds. The message will wait there until it is answered."

"How can a message wait when it is made of nothing permanent?" Sonia asks. Sonia is full of questions. "Even the speech with Anatoly Sakhalin vanished as soon as it was over."

"The message remains, recorded into memory." The ke touches several bars on the console. "By this means, the message plays back."

The patternless daiga rises about the console again, and the entire conversation plays out while Sonia watches.

"But how does it *do* that?" she demands, and the ke realizes with surprise—*surprise!*—that part of the daiga pattern of voice and physical body includes the force daiga name as *emotion*. To learn to recognize the patterns of emotion is to learn to read daiga patterns correctly. Then, as swift as a gust of wind, Sonia speaks again, casting off the last question. "But I must send a message to Tess. Or to Cara Hierakis. She left twenty days ago. Could her machines have gotten her to Jeds so quickly? Well, of course they could. There was that, what did you call it? She sent a brief *signal* to say she got there, but nothing spoken or written. It's just hard to . . . imagine. Even the swiftest, untiring messenger changing horses at every station would take forty days to ride from Sarai to Jeds. Yet words spoken into this tool can reach Jeds as quickly as I can speak them! I must call Cara Hierakis. Can you show me how to speak to Jeds?"

The ke considers, but neither the daiga Tess nor the daiga who had hidden the ke in the laboratory in Jeds for five orbits of the planet—for five *years*—have forbidden the daiga Sonia from learning whatever Sonia asks to learn. Nothing is interdicted from this daiga, now that the concealing curtain has been drawn aside. It is a daiga *metaphor,* a way of naming that classifies one object because it acts similarly to another. Or is that a *simile?* No wonder the daiga remain primitive. Language has taken the place of physical evolution. Naming and seeing have become *synonymous.*

"This gold bar seems to trigger the appearance of an image," says Sonia, trying to manipulate the console without instruction in order to discover the correct sequence.

The ke shows Sonia how to put a call through to Jeds.

The daiga named by the others *Cara Hierakis* answers. The two daiga converse. The ke follows the conversation intermittently, distracted by other questions.

"No, I've heard nothing from Tess, but she only had an emergency transmitter. Anatoly Sakhalin says he did *what?* That he was named a prince . . . in the Empire? That he saw a female Chapalii? But males can't cross into female territory, or at least . . . that just doesn't make sense. I've heard nothing from Charles. Oh, wait. I've got an incoming coded message, a download, from Odys. Let me call you back."

The visual image of Cara Hierakis vanishes. Sonia waits at the console, calling back old messages, watching the replay, even those in a language that evidently is incomprehensible.

"Is there an interpreter tool?" Sonia asks. "So I might understand what this woman is saying? She says Tess's name, so she must know Tess."

An image of a daiga speaks over the console, a daiga like all the rest, indistinguishable without a pattern to read. Daiga can discern subtleties in daiga morphology that allow each daiga to discriminate any one daiga from the others. Ke have no need for such fine discriminative control, brought on in the daiga, perhaps, by territorial instincts or the need to have and keep a *name,* which then grants existence.

"Is there no means within the daiga brain to translate words?" the ke asks.

"If I know another language, then I can understand it, or at least if I don't know it very well, I can think of what the meaning is in a language I do know well. But if I don't know the language at all, then I don't have any way to figure out what it means except through an interpreter."

"A daiga program exists," replies the ke, "which translates one daiga language into another. *Tess* has written such a program. Others exist."

Sonia makes a movement with the mouth that the ke translates as a smile, a daiga way of showing pleasure.

"You are my interpreter," Sonia says.

The ke pauses, startled by this new name, this new designation. What is an interpreter? An interpreter is someone who crosses borders for others, making one language intelligible to a second, making the outer world intelligible to a daiga who has lived confined to this inner one.

If it is true that this Prince of the Sakhalin has become a prince in the Empire, then the daiga naming their selves as *jaran* will need to understand how the Empire works. They must learn to name and to see the Empire. How can they learn to see it? Only through names.

The ke shows Sonia how to work the translation program, but then the ke retreats to a corner of the room and broods. The ke is not used to brooding. Ke do not brood, but this ke has crossed the border into daiga lands and can no longer go back to being a true ke.

This ke has been thinking about daiga.

Lacking deep brains, possessing only partially-formed intermediate brains, the daiga have constructed an interlocking web of names, like the great web that binds together the universe. Like a true building, this web is still in the process of growth. It is living, not dead.

Perhaps the daiga *are* civilized, but not as Chapalii recognize civilization. Civilization can manifest through more than one phylogeny.

"I am glad you are here to explain this all to me," Sonia adds. The pattern that distinguishes her to the ke's sight is bright, hectic with excitement.

The ke creeps closer to the daiga Sonia, as to warmth and light. Sonia shows neither fear nor shrinking, as many daiga do when confronted with a robed, veiled figure. The ke no longer needs veils, in front of Sonia.

"I hope you will stay with me for a while," says Sonia. The daiga reaches out and touches the ke lightly on the arm. Two patterns swirl together briefly. It is a daiga way of connecting. The ke knows this now.

This ke has become an interpreter. This ke is no longer truly nameless.

CHAPTER FORTY-SIX

By Right

According to the khaja priest at White Tower, a formal betrothal was as binding as a marriage.

"It makes sense not to marry until we reach Mircassia," said Vasha to his father. It was dawn. The army was ready to leave. They waited in front of the crushed grass where the great tent had stood. Behind them, guards rolled up the awning. "But I need a binding agreement so that I can't be thrown over once we reach there."

"Marry her and be done with it," snapped Bakhtiian, "if you mean to do it at all."

Vasha felt a flash of irritation, but he quelled it. He knew he was right; he could not help that his father felt impelled to disagree, to dislike new ways of doing things, khaja ways of doing things. He could practically hear his father add: *That is how the jaran would do it.* In any case, Vasha did not think Ilya had recovered yet from his captivity. "Let me at least tell you my reasons. First, it will give me a chance to become acquainted with her, and her with me, without being thrown at once into the intimacy of marriage. Second, if we are married in Mircassia before her grandfather and the court, the marriage will appear to have the king's sanction. Third, if we marry before the child is born, then by jaran law that child is mine. It makes no difference to me, of course. But Princess Rusudani will hate the child, if we keep it. So there will be no other objection to sending the child to Lady Jadranka to raise. She will raise it well. It will have an inheritance."

"All good points," said Tess reasonably.

Fuming, Ilya glared at her. He looked back at Vasha, and Vasha was heartened to see that the worst edge of his anger had been blunted by Vasha's words. "If you can gain Mircassia, then I don't care what means you use."

"Will you attend, then?" Vasha asked hopefully. "The betrothal ceremony? You won't be in Mircassia for the wedding."

Tess closed a hand firmly over Ilya's wrist. "Of course we will attend."

Faced with a direct order from his wife, Bakhtiian did not dare disobey, or even protest.

So, a short while later, Vasha knelt on a white cloth trimmed with gold braid before the altar in the castle chapel. His father and Tess stood behind him, as witnesses, and farther back, Katerina sat beside Stefan on a bench. Vasha did not need to turn his head to know how Katya would look, watching this: tense, impatient with her own curiosity, forcing herself to keep silent and still within the stone walls that must remind her of her captivity. But she had come to witness because he had asked her to.

Rusudani knelt beside him, her hair covered by a lace shawl and her eyes cast down toward the floor. She held her hands in front of her as if she was praying, but her lips did not move. No expression showed on her face that he could interpret.

The priest set out the written contract on a side table and had first Vasha and then Rusudani repeat the words that bound them to the contract. Vasha did not understand much of what he said, but it was short, and he repeated the phrase "bound by God's law," twice. Watching Rusudani, who did not look at him as she spoke the words in her turn, her voice so soft that it died into the loft of the chapel, Vasha was satisfied. Rusudani believed faithfully and sincerely in her God. If she swore to be bound by God's law, then she would keep her word.

Last, they exchanged rings, simple gold rings which the priest had nervously donated before the ceremony.

The priest called forward the interpreter—Jaelle, as Vasha had also requested. The khaja here gave him everything he wanted, of course.

"The wise father wishes you to come forward and mark the contract," Jaelle said. It had been written the night before. "It is usual for a young woman to have her father or brother sign the contract for her, transferring her into her husband's protection. But because she is a widow Princess Rusudani may act on her own behalf."

Vasha signed his name, to the surprise of the priest. That

Rusudani could write as well did not surprise the khaja man; he knew she was convent educated.

So it was done.

Without speaking further to Vasha, Princess Rusudani left, escorted by the two ladies she had retained to accompany her on the journey. Tess looked over the contracts, tracing her fingers down the Yossian script and glancing at the Taor translation. She sighed, at last, and hugged Vasha, who felt numb more than anything, wishing that Rusudani had at least spoken more than the required words.

"I wish the best to you, my child," Tess said, releasing him. "But now we really must all be leaving."

And that was it.

Except for Stefan.

"I'm sorry," Stefan said. "I'll come to you as soon as I take Jaelle back to Sarai, but I can't let her travel there alone."

Vasha glanced toward Jaelle, who stood by the table with her hands folded together. Her cheeks bore a delicate blush on them as she looked up at Stefan and then, quickly, away again. She loved Stefan.

"I envy you, Stefan," Vasha blurted out, then clapped his friend on the shoulder to cover his own embarrassment, to cover the words. "So you must come to Mircassia just as soon as you can, or I won't ever forgive you."

Stefan laughed and hugged him and he and Jaelle went away. They were riding north with a small escort, back to Sarai.

So Vasha was left alone in the chapel, except for the priest, who soon wandered out, still looking nervous.

Except for Katerina, who waited for him by the doors, great wooden doors carved with curlicues and two kneeling figures, holy men or women, Vasha could not be sure which because they wore voluminous robes and identical blank expressions.

"Like Rusudani's expression," Vasha said.

"You can't expect her to thank you for this," Katya said.

Troubled, he wandered back into the chapel and sat down on a bench. Katya sat down beside him. Restless, as always, she tweaked the sleeve of her blouse around and around, straightened it, and then began to tug at his clothes instead, smoothing out creases, lining the embroidery on his sleeves up so that it ran in a clean curve from his shoulder down to his wrist.

"Was it stupid, Katya? Shouldn't I have done it?"

"She doesn't love you."

"She may come to."

Katya shrugged. She hooked one boot up onto her knee and began fiddling with the laces. "I don't know. Perhaps she can't love."

"She loves—"

"Huh. Being infatuated isn't love, Vasha. You know that. You don't truly love her either. You don't know her well enough for that. How can you?"

He frowned at her, but her words didn't make him angry because they were true. "Well, do you think she will come to like me? To be a good wife to me?"

Katerina was silent for a long while. Vasha just sat there, feeling comfortable with her, as he always did, even when he was fighting with her. "Perhaps she has learned something. Perhaps not. Perhaps she will discover that it is in her interest, that it will further her ambition, to be married to you. Perhaps she will always think of you as a captor. How can anyone know, Vasha? We can't look into the future. But if you treat her fairly and with respect, perhaps she will not hate you and do to you what she did to Prince Janos." Her voice shook a little on his name.

Vasha swallowed past a sudden thickening in his throat. He took hold of her hand. "Did you hate Janos?"

"I don't know. I did at first. But what difference does it truly make to a woman if she is made a mistress by khaja custom or a wife by jaran? She has as little choice in either."

"But—"

"But what? What choice did Princess Rusudani have to marry you? You or someone else, someone her grandfather chose for her."

Vasha did not know what to reply. They sat there without speaking. The priest came in and began to light candles near the altar for the midday service. Seeing them, he started and hurried out again. Light streamed in through the high windows that surrounded the central nave of the chapel. Dust danced in the beams.

"You'll be a good husband for her, though, if she chooses to accept you," Katya said finally.

"Thank you," he said sarcastically, and she made a face at him. "Where are you going? You haven't told me. Back to Sarai?"

"No. I don't know. I'll go to Jeds. If I go back to Sarai, my mother will marry me off to some well-deserving Raevsky son."

"You don't want to get married." He didn't have to make it a question.

"Why should I want to? I don't want to go back to Sarai. I don't want to fight in the army anymore. I don't know, I don't know, I don't know." Exhausting this slim reservoir of repose, Katerina jumped to her feet and stalked up and down the aisle.

"Will you come with me?" he asked.

"Why?"

Vasha shrugged. "I don't know. Because I love you, Katya. Come with me now, help me. You can go to Jeds afterward."

She stopped dead. Suddenly and strangely, she looked sly. Like the Katya of old, who as a child loved lording secrets over the rest, loved having read a book her cousins hadn't grown curious about yet and teasing them by suggesting that it contained hideous or wondrous stories; in fact, once Vasha laboriously read through them, such books usually proved to contain nothing more than yet another dry philosopher propounding about natural history or arguing a legalistic question to death.

"I had a long talk with Aunt Tess yesterday," she said finally, her expression passing over into hesitancy, so at odds with her usual mood. "She said perhaps . . . she said she would talk to my mother . . ."

"So you do have to go back to Sarai."

"No. She said I should go to Jeds with her and that somehow she would sort it out there. I don't know, but she hinted, I think . . ." Her eyes lit, and Vasha was stricken suddenly by an awful sadness. He had lost her. He knew it with that instinct he shared with her. "I think she thinks I can sail over the seas to Erthe."

"But no one comes back from there, Katya! I couldn't bear to lose you forever."

"I'm not yours, Vasha! If I have to do this, understand it and be happy for me!"

"Oh, Katya."

She came back and sat down on the bench beside him, and he embraced her. They sat that way, silent, still, until

Vladimir arrived, in full armor, and reminded them that the
army was riding. Now.

For thirty-nine days they rode south, making good time
even though it rained two days out of every three. They
caught up with outriders of Yaroslav Sakhalin's army on day
forty and rode into Sakhalin's encampment on day forty-
two. Laid out in a neat spiral, the camp engulfed most of the
fields that surrounded a walled city. A pall of smoke lay
over the city, but Vasha noticed at once that the gates lay
open and a thin stream of people moved, in and out, cautiously going about their business.

Vasha helped Rusudani down from her horse—it was the
one liberty she allowed him. Her waist was thickening noticeably in the middle. He hovered nervously beside the
chair set up for her until her tent was erected and she could
be installed within. She lay down at once.

"Is there anything I can get you?" he asked.

She shook her head, closing her eyes. "My waiting
women will take care of my needs."

She was pale, but not dangerously so. Mostly she looked
tired. He left her lying there, one hand resting on her copy
of *The Recitation,* and went to Tess's tent.

Ilya sat on a pillow receiving Yaroslav Sakhalin's report.
Tess had her journal open on her knee and was, for some
reason, taking notes. Mother Sakhalin sat beside Tess, her
intent gaze on her uncle; like her mother, Konstantina
Sakhalin had mastered the art of sitting perfectly still, ab-
sorbing all that came before her.

". . . I sent a detachment behind the khaja lines to this
city, which is named Arhia in their tongue. The city elders
tried to buy off the detachment, but when they got news of
the battle fought on the Tarhan River, they wisely capitulated." Yaroslav Sakhalin paused, and his gaze stopped on
Vasha, who came in under the awning.

Vasha nodded coolly at him and sat down beside his father. Sakhalin glanced at Ilya, gauging his reaction, but Ilya
did not react at all, waiting instead for Sakhalin to proceed.
Without comment, Sakhalin went on.

"That battle took place five days ago. When the messenger you sent on ahead of you arrived, I decided we would
wait here. We have enough casualties to warrant it."

"I will tour the hospital," said Ilya.

Sakhalin nodded curtly. "The Estaharin prince fell in the battle. He had assembled a decent force, including the last renegades and rebels from the Yossian principalities. Two princes, three prince's sons, five dukes and eighteen lords died on the Estaharin side. He also had a detachment of Filis auxiliaries with him, but I haven't been able to discover whether they were mercenaries he hired or if they represent an alliance he had worked out with the prince of Filis. As well, the prince of Tarsina-Kars had sent a detachment of men to the muster, but he withdrew his troops when I sent him word that we held his daughter. I now understand, from new intelligence, that she is one of two claimants to the throne of Mircassia, and the one favored by the king."

"That is true," said Ilya. "My son Vassily is betrothed to her. He will marry her once they reach Mircassia."

Vasha admired how Yaroslav Sakhalin could contrive not to look surprised by this news. But Sakhalin was an old, canny soldier. He had not survived this long by letting startling news overset him.

"The main road through the pass in the eastern hills that leads into the heart of Mircassia branches off three days ride south of here, my scouts report."

"Very well," said Ilya.

"There is one other thing," added Sakhalin, glancing at his niece. "Two days ago Kirill Zvertkov arrived in my camp, escorting my brother Andrei Sakhalin."

Ilya was on his feet in an instant. He already had one hand on his saber hilt.

"No," said Sakhalin quietly, standing only slightly more slowly. "If everything that Zvertkov says is true, then it is my right, and my duty, as his relative to kill him."

"Damn it," swore Ilya under his breath, but he did not argue.

"He must be allowed to speak," said Mother Sakhalin calmly. She rose and shook out her skirts, waiting politely for Tess to finish scrawling in the journal, close the book, and toss it onto the pillow Ilya had vacated before standing herself.

"I'm not sure I want to see this," said Tess under her breath to Vasha. She let the other three go ahead. "It's going to be ugly."

"He must be punished—" Vasha protested.

"I don't mean that, not so much. I mean having to listen to the excuses he makes."

And Andrei Sakhalin did make excuses. Zvertkov and his thousand soldiers had encamped in a tight circle around a single, small tent, isolated within the ring of guards. When Zvertkov saw them, he jumped to his feet and hurried over to give Bakhtiian a hearty embrace. He did not touch Tess, but Vasha caught the glance that passed between them, fraught with unspoken words. Tess's eyes glittered with sudden tears. She wiped them away. Ilya could not tear his gaze away from the tent. His hands were clenched so tightly that his knuckles were white, and his lips were pale, set hard.

Yaroslav Sakhalin walked forward alone to the tent and twitched the entrance flap aside. He bent down, said something. After a long wait, a man emerged from the tent. Seeing Ilya, Andrei Sakhalin blinked dazedly at him, as if the sun, or Ilya's presence, had blinded him momentarily.

"What do you have to say to me, Andrei Sakhalin?" Ilya demanded, not moving. Unable to move, Vasha realized, standing so close to his father that he could have touched him; if Ilya moved, it would be to kill the man who had betrayed him.

"Why am I being held here?" demanded Andrei. "I am relieved to see that you survived that khaja ambush, Bakhtiian."

"You bastard. You set that ambush up. You betrayed me, and for what?"

"I set nothing up! Some of my own men were killed. I had gone in to see the priest—the *presbyter*—and we were attacked and I was cut off from you. I had no choice but to—"

"To run north to the court of the king of Dushan? Why not back to the army, to get help—"

"I had so few men left by then that I had to return to Dushan to collect the rest of my jahar. How was I to know if the country was rising against us? I couldn't risk the rest of my riders."

"He's mocking you," said Vasha, unable to stomach these grotesque excuses any longer. He strode forward to confront Andrei. What Rusudani had done was bad enough, betraying her own husband, but at least she had had cause to hate Janos for forcing her to marry him, for his own gain. How could Andrei Sakhalin stand there and let such barefaced lies spew from his mouth? "Have you no shame? I was taken prisoner by Prince Janos of Dushan, and he told me, and these are his very words, 'I hold an alliance with a jaran prince from the greatest of the jaran tribes.' "

"Which rules out you, does it not, Kireyevsky?"

"Andrei!" Yaroslav's voice cracked across them. "You are insolent, impenitent, and disrespectful! Answer the charge."

Andrei spit at Vasha's feet. "As if we ought to trust *his* word, a fatherless bastard, giving himself airs, thinking he's as good as the rest of us. Gods, Yaroslav, you threw him out of your army because he's worthless."

"Be careful how you speak of my son," said Ilya softly.

But it was too late, Andrei was going on. "What has happened to you, Yaroslav? The Sakhalins should have been the ones leading the army, not *him*. What is he? A lover of men, you know it's true, every one knew it, it was such a scandal. A man who would stoop to marrying a khaja woman for the territory she brought him. How can you stomach it, Konstantina? We are First among the tribes, how can you let the Orzhekov women lord it over you? You, who are now Mother Sakhalin by right? Ah, gods, the best soldier among us has already been thrown to the dogs, run out into khaja lands, never to be seen again. *He* could have done something, *he* could have been dyan over all tribes, that is why they drove him off, and gave me, like a sop, to the woman who will become Mother Orzhekov. So the rest of you Sakhalins would be content while they cut away our power from beneath us. How could you stand by and let it happen? Not just let it happen, but become part of it? You make me sick."

"Bakhtiian had the vision—" cut in Yaroslav.

"Hah! His mother's ambition, no doubt, foisted on an untried and untrustworthy son. Why shouldn't she put it into her son's head to make up a story, pretending it came from the gods? Everyone knew what a bitch she was, forced to marry that worthless Singer from a tribe no one had ever heard of and lusting all her life after a different man entirely—"

Ilya broke forward, drawing his saber.

But Yaroslav ran his brother through before Ilya could reach him. It was so sudden that Andrei's collapse was the only sound, except for Ilya's ragged breathing as he fought to control his rage.

"I beg your pardon," said Yaroslav calmly. "I killed him

so that you would not defile your saber with his tainted blood." He dropped his bloody saber on top of his dead brother. The corpse twitched once more, then was still.

"Let him be buried beneath the earth," said Konstantina Sakhalin, "so that his soul may never return to the jaran. Let his name never more be spoken within the tribes. Let it be known that there was no son of the Sakhalin tribe of this generation named Andrei. Let the memory of him cease to exist. So have I, Mother Sakhalin, spoken."

"So is it done," echoed her dyan. He signed, and guards carried the body away.

"Poor Galina," said Katya. "She was fond of him, I suppose because she saw him so rarely and because he was clever enough to be kind to her when he was with her, knowing he'd need her support to . . . whatever he meant to do once Bakhtiian was dead. To see that his sons by her became dyan over all the tribes."

She lay on her stomach beside Vasha, and he lay on his side, one arm flung casually across her back, his fingers playing with her unbound hair.

"It was stupid," said Vasha.

She turned her head to look at him. Hair spilled down over her shoulders, and he could see straight down the front of her shift to the curve of her breasts within. "Are you angry about what he said about you?"

"No. Why should I be? He's dead, and I'm alive. I'm the one is going to marry the queen of Mircassia. My children are the ones who will rule, not his."

"Don't tempt the gods," she said, chuckling.

"Katya . . ." He let a hand wander down her back, caressing her. "Oh, damn." He pulled his hand back and got to his knees, ducking his head to avoid the lantern that hung from the pole above. "I always look in on Rusudani before she goes to sleep."

"She won't care if you don't look in tonight. Or any night."

He sighed. "I *know* that, but surely if she gets used to the attentions I pay her, she'll come to expect them, even to miss them."

"You've turned into a calculating little bastard, haven't you, Vasha?"

He paused by the tent flap and grinned down at her. "You

were born into your position, Katya. I have to fight for mine." She only smiled back, forgiving him for his desertion. Then she adjusted the lantern and opened a book that Tess had just given her. Vasha could tell she was gone from him before he even left the tent.

Rusudani acknowledged him warily and allowed him to sit on a pillow at the foot of her couch.

"May I read aloud to you from *The Recitation?*" he asked. There were three copies of *The Recitation* in the tent: one in Yossian, one in Taor, and one in a language Vasha did not recognize. The interpreter told him that it was Mircassian. "Perhaps the princess would agree to teach me to read these words," he said, opening the Mircassian book.

Rusudani hesitated, then answered. "I speak them," she said. "You speak them after me."

They read five pages in this fashion, until even Vasha was both exhausted by the effort and bored by it, even with her so close to him. He bade her a polite goodnight, and she accepted it dispassionately.

A light still shone in Tess's tent, and the tent flap was thrown aside, revealing two figures seated within. Vasha greeted the guards, but he paused under the awning, eavesdropping.

Ilya sat erect in his chair, almost stiff, tapping his fingers on the table impatiently. "Damn it," he was saying, "I can't remember what the name of the nephew is who is the other claimant to the—"

"Here, Ilya." Tess pushed an open book across the table toward him. "I wrote everything down for you, all the reports."

Ilya grabbed the book and flung it across the room. It landed out of Vasha's sight with a soft thud. Then he jumped to his feet, knocking his chair over. "It's a khaja weakness, not to be able to remember things. Singers don't need scratches on paper to—"

"Ilya," said Tess patiently, although she looked grim, "you have received a shock. It might take some time for you to recover fully. This is just one way to tide yourself over until you have . . ."

He turned his back on her and stalked toward the entrance. Stopped, seeing Vasha outside. "What are you doing?"

"Spying." Vasha walked past him, into the tent. "Since

I'm leaving tomorrow, I thought I would come by and ask if you have any last advice for me." He grinned at Tess and abruptly felt wobbly enough on his feet that he had to steady himself on the back of her chair. "I'm a little nervous."

"Keep a cool head," said Tess, "don't give anything away, and watch your back. But you'll have a jahar of ten thousand. I don't think King Barsauma will try anything outright, anything direct. He'll see that the wisest course is to let you marry Rusudani, since we have possession of her and enough power to lay his kingdom to waste if we're angered. He'll hope that you die young, or that jaran power will wane quickly enough that, in time, Rusudani can throw you over for a more suitable consort. He'll hope that the jaran became embroiled in internal war, or wars with other kingdoms, and slowly leave Mircassia behind, forget about her, withdraw our troops from her because we need them elsewhere. He will bide his time, Vasha. It is up to you to insinuate yourself into Mircassian society so thoroughly, into the rule of the land, appointing the right people to the council or as governors in far-flung provinces . . . that in time you are indivisible from Rusudani's power. It is how an etsana's husband works. Although the authority is hers, within the circle of the tents, she needs him, and so does the tribe."

"You don't think jaran power will wane," Vasha said. "Even though I have read of the rise of powerful dynasties that later collapse, as in Habakar."

Tess glanced toward Ilya. "No. I don't think it will. Not for a long time."

Something in the way she said it puzzled Vasha. She sounded like a Singer speaking a prophecy. Except Tess wasn't a Singer. Was she?

"Prince Lazi!" said Ilya triumphantly. "That's his name. And his mother is Lady Apamaia. She is the half sister of Prince Basil of Filis. That is why he supports her and her son. More her, I suppose, since the nephew is evidently a half-wit."

"Don't you have anything to tell me?" Vasha asked.

His father just frowned at him. "Have your food tasted."

"Oh, gods!"

Tess shook her head at him, warning.

"Well then," said Vasha, swallowing his disappointment, his unease at his father's bizarre behavior, "I'll take my leave of you."

Tess hugged him. Ilya seemed to come to himself for a moment. He stared at Vasha for an uncomfortable while, measuring him, then patted him awkwardly on the arm. "You'll do, Vassily," he said.

Vasha practically floated back to Katya's tent.

The lantern was out. Inside, Katerina was asleep, her book clutched in one hand. Vasha stripped and lay down next to her, snuggling against her, listening to her breathing, and chuckled to himself. It was so rare to spend time with Katya when she was this quiet.

Vassily Kireyevsky led his jahar—*his* jahar!—southeast into the Hira Mountains. It took him thirty-three hard and mostly wet days of riding to traverse the mountains and the wild lands that surrounded them, and another twenty-four days to cross the populated lands, loose confederations of towns and manors and lord's holdings that were in their turn ruled by King Barsauma from his palace at Kavad.

No one bothered them. Indeed, word soon ran before them, and, as they advanced farther into Mircassia, farmers and townspeople flocked to the side of the road to catch a glimpse of the princess who was to be their next queen. Lords sent offerings of food and wine, and grain for the horses, clearly bent on currying favor.

Vasha refused none of the food, but refused to let anyone hold audience with Rusudani. She rode in a kind of a trance, caught between one marriage, whose fruit still lay within her, and the next, and the promise of becoming queen. And perhaps, Vasha had to admit to himself, she was still furious, or grief-stricken, at Bakhtiian's rejection of her. He accepted, on her behalf, several sons of noble families whose lands they rode through to serve as her pages, but he used them mostly to taste his food.

Each afternoon, after they had stopped, he would go to her tent and eat supper with her there, and they would read more of *The Recitation*. Soon he could pronounce Mircassian well, although he could by no means understand it. Slowly, after the first shock had worn off, she began to read alternating passages in Taor. Thus they passed the journey, reserved but not in open conflict. That was a beginning, Vasha supposed. Her cheeks grew plumper and her belly began to round under the folds of her gown. She appeared even more

beautiful to him, perhaps only because, so close, she remained out of his grasp.

King Barsauma sent a party of ministers and courtiers to
greet them. The city of Kavad looked odd to Vasha: It had
no walls. Only the palace, a great citadel that blanketed the
outcropping of rock that rose above Kavad, looked as if it
was fortified.

Vasha conferred with his captain, and they decided it
would be wisest to leave the jahar encamped outside the city
and for Vasha to go in with Rusudani with a contingent of
fifty men.

Escorted by khaja men old enough to be his grandfathers,
this smaller group proceeded up a broad avenue lined with
hordes of curious onlookers, passed through a double set of
gates, and were at last trapped within a vast courtyard
ringed by magnificent buildings. Mircassia was a rich kingdom, indeed.

King Barsauma waited for them in a sun-drenched courtyard. He sat in a chair padded with fine embroidered pillows.
At his back a fountain splashed and played over crouching
stone lions. He was so old that his skin was as delicate as aging parchment, all the veins showing through. A cap covered
his head, which seemed to be hairless, and the finest wisps of
white hair straggled down from his chin, barely making a
beard. Even sitting, he had a stooped back, bent by age and illness, but his eyes were like steel.

"Is this the child?" he demanded, tapping his cane on the
flagstones. As soon as he spoke, Vasha realized that half of
his face was immobile. His words were slightly slurred, but
understandable. "Come here, come here. Who are these barbarians? Which is the usurper who claims to be your husband?"

Vasha gulped. How such a frail old man could scare him,
he wasn't sure. But he did. Deliberately, Vasha took
Rusudani's elbow with a hand and escorted her up to her
grandfather. Let it not be said that Vassily Kireyevsky
shrank from confrontation.

Rusudani knelt before the old man, bowing her head.
Vasha did neither. His interpreter hung at his back, so that he
could whisper into his ear without seeming to intrude.

"Huh," the king grunted, looking her over. "Pretty
enough, but is she clever?"

At that, Rusudani lifted her head to look directly at him. "I trust I am clever enough, your highness."

"Not clever enough to avoid getting with one man's child and being betrothed within a day of his death to a second."

"It is the fate of women, your highness, to be married whether they wish it or not. I had no authority, no army, nothing save my faith in God, to protect me. But I am here, am I not? Unencumbered, except by husbands and their get."

King Barsauma began wheezing, which startled Vasha until he realized that the old man was laughing.

"Husbands are no great impediment once a woman becomes powerful enough. You are convent educated?"

"Yes, your highness."

"You can read, write, and figure?"

"Yes, your highness, and recite the *Eulysian Hymns,* and I have read the *Commentaries of Maricius,* the Hermeneutics of Silas, and the tract, "Against the Elians," by Hayyan of Sid Saffah."

"Pah. Church learning will not help you rule a kingdom. You will start by reading the chronicles and then, let me see, Lord Tellarkus can show you the roll of taxes and Lady Tellarkina can show you the women's quarters. I recommend you use her as your chatelaine; she's old and has but the one living daughter left. She'll know you can show that child favor, so she'll be as faithful to you as she can be." He gave his wheezing laugh again. "You can get a barbarian for her daughter, too. She's buried two husbands already." Like a sword's cut, his gaze hit Vasha.

Vasha stood his ground.

"Is this the lad? He's a mere pup. I thought he would be an experienced man."

Vasha inclined his head with what he hoped was regal disdain. "I am Vassily Kireyevsky, your highness. I am the son of Ilyakoria Bakhtiian, who commands the jaran army."

"Go away," said the king suddenly. "You may attend me another day."

He meant both of them, and his attendants briskly led them off. No doubt it was time for the old man to rest. Vasha glanced back as he left the courtyard, but Barsauma sat stiffly in the chair, not looking after them.

Vasha and his men were assigned to a suite of rooms that adjoined the women's quarters but did not have immediate access to them. In order to see his wife, Vasha had to wait at the gate into a second courtyard and be escorted across by beardless men armed with spears and swords curved almost into a half moon.

Rusudani received him under an arcade of columns that opened onto a garden. A phalanx of women, dressed in gowns that draped rather revealingly along their figures, protected her. Flowers bloomed, and the drone of insects mingled with the soft rush of an unseen fountain. In the Yos principalities, autumn was rushing toward winter. Here it was still summer. It was like this, he recalled, in Jeds as well; always mild.

A servant brought a chair. He sat down beside her. The women eyed him from behind fans; they whispered to each other, and pointed.

"You are well?" Vasha asked.

"I am well." Rusudani got the strangest look on her face. She glanced toward her attendants and, abruptly, ordered them to leave. When they had gone, she turned back to Vasha. Even though they were now essentially alone, with only his interpreter and the one jaran soldier allowed him, with her beardless guards and the Mircassian ladies out in the garden where they could see but not overhear, Rusudani still looked carefully around before speaking.

"He does not respect the Holy Church. They say he has not attended service in the chapel since his favorite son died. They say he cursed God for taking all his children from him, and that God punished him for his impiety by striking him down. That is why he can only move half of his face. But he has not repented from his blasphemy. What are we to do, Prince Vassily?"

Vasha could not reply for a long while. Rusudani was confiding in him! "Does it not say in *The Recitation,* that 'he who dines at Wisdom's table and drinks of her wine, will be brought to understanding through the excellence of her food'? You must strive by your own example to bring King Barsauma back to your church."

"You speak wisely, Prince Vassily, but you yourself have not chosen to sit at God's table, though you were betrothed by His laws and intend to be married by them."

She waited. Vasha was for one intense instant tempted by the perfect blue of her eyes and the delicate blush on her cheeks to throw caution to the winds and tell her that he would take part in the ritual cleansing that initiated a man or woman in to the Hristanic Church.

He bowed his head instead, briefly. "I respect your God and your Church, Princess Rusudani, but I must remain faithful to my own gods."

She did not reply at once. The sun crept in toward them from the garden, and the fountain splashed quietly.

"You have been gracious toward me," she said finally, so faintly that it was almost lost within the fountain's ripple and a breath of wind that sighed through the garden. Then she stood up and walked out into the garden. The interview was over.

By posting lookouts at all the windows in his suite of rooms, Vasha could keep an eye on most of Rusudani's forays outside of the women's quarters. In this way he managed to attend her on most of them, seeing where the chronicle was kept and where the steward had his offices, meeting the council of ministers and sitting beside her when, on their fifth day at the palace, she held an audience for the courtiers and was, perforce, compelled to acknowledge him to them all. Each night after supper he read with her, and after that he would go to the room where the great chronicle was kept, light candles, and pore through it, sounding out the words laboriously, turning again and again to his interpreter, who could speak but not read Mircassian, and together they puzzled out the heavy script and the history of Mircassia as written by its scribes.

He did not see King Barsauma nor, as far as he knew, did Rusudani. Old men dressed in elaborate court robes watched them, that was all.

On the sixth night he sat alone in the Hall of the Chronicle with the Interpreter and his favorite guard, a young Riasonovsky rider named Matfey who was, to Vasha's amusement, a nephew of the Riasonovsky captain who had escorted Vasha to Sarai after his humiliating dismissal from Sakhalin's army.

"What's that?" asked Matfey suddenly.

Vasha stood up, hearing an odd rustling and thump from one dark corner of the room. A lantern's glow traced out shadows, throwing them into long relief, and King Barsauma came around a screen. Leaning heavily on his cane, he shuffled forward until he got to within five steps of Vasha. He

stopped there. For all that he stooped now, and dragged his
left leg, Vasha could see that he had once been a tall, robust
man, broad across the chest, shrunken now more by his infirmity than by age. A servant placed a chair carefully behind him and helped him to sit. Metal gleamed in the
shadows: Barsauma's guards.

"I could have you killed," said Barsauma. "And no doubt
would save myself some trouble by doing so."

Vasha faced him without flinching. "I have my own
guards posted outside, at the doors, of course."

"Huh. Why do you come in here each night and stare at
the chronicles? I would stop you looking at the tax rolls if
I could without throwing all hell into the palace. I know
you're only looking to see what you can plunder, having this
peshtiqi interpreter count it up for you. How did you get into
the palace in the first place? How did you capture my granddaughter? What do you want, Prince Vassily? I can pay you
off, a hundred *filistri* of gold, if you will release my granddaughter from the betrothal."

"She's worth much more than one hundred *filistri* of gold
your highness."

"Two hundred, then. Bandit. I hear that one of your little
pages got sick yesterday. I hope it wasn't the food."

"I will be certain in future to eat only from my betrothed's
plate. It is an old custom among the jaran for a husband and
wife to eat from the same platter."

"Three hundred *filistri*."

"My children by Rusudani on the throne of Mircassia, and
that is the only offer I will accept."

Barsauma thumped his cane several times, hard, on the
floor. The noise resounded in the chamber, unmuted by tapestries. "Five hundred. I want no damned barbarian seated
on my throne."

"I will not sit in your throne, your highness, as long as
you are alive." Barsauma snorted, and Vasha, seeing that he
had perhaps amused the old man, went on. "Your great-
grandchildren may sit on a greater throne even than your
own."

"Barbarians can't hold together an empire."

"What if they can? Already Bakhtiian has conquered a
greater empire than any I have read of."

"So you can read. That is what Lord Tellarkus claimed,
but I didn't believe him." He motioned curtly to his servants

and they scooted his chair up to the lectern that held the thick chronicle. "Read to me. Something . . . here, this passage."

Vasha sounded it out, and Barsauma grew impatient with the interpreter's slowness and began correcting Vasha's pronunciation and then, evidently, the interpreter's translation.

"Pah. A useless man. You may keep him, but I'll get you a better."

With that, he got up and shuffled out of the hall, his servants carrying the chair behind him.

In the morning, Vasha went to the women's quarters and asked to see Rusudani. He had to wait a long while, but finally he was allowed in, to the same arcade bordering the garden, the only place she ever received him.

"You are well?" he asked.

"I am well."

"I saw your grandfather last night. He tried to buy me off."

She looked startled. "Buy you off?"

"He thinks that because I'm a *barbarian* that I can only be a bandit, and that I'd be as happy to have the gold as you."

"You did not accept the gold."

"Of course not."

She thought for a while, sipping at a cup of tea, then signed to an attendant to bring Vasha tea as well, poured from a new pot. He did not touch it. If she noticed, she said nothing. "What *do* you want, Prince Vassily?" she asked finally.

The question took him unawares. What did he want? "I . . . I want to be like my father."

"You look a little like him," she said, as if to say, *but are otherwise utterly unlike.* "What about Mircassia?"

"I wanted you before I wanted Mircassia. I swear by my own gods that that is the truth. But it is nevertheless beside the point, Princess Rusudani. You must marry me, or another man."

"You do not treat women so in the jaran."

"All woman marry in the jaran as well."

"How can you claim that the women of your people are not ruled by men?"

"What does marriage have to do with that? A woman can marry and still wield the power that is rightfully hers."

She set down her cup on the table that separated them and
touched, like a reflex, the tiny knife that hung on a gold
chain around her neck. "I am to meet with my grandfather
this afternoon. Lady Tellarkina says that my grandfather has
a Mircassian lordling in mind to marry me, a grandson of an
old retainer of his, after we have gotten rid of you. But I
know nothing about this man. He will be loyal to his grandfather and to my grandfather, to the council of ministers who
have agreed to his elevation. He will become their tool. He
will not care about me."

"What are you suggesting, Princess Rusudani?"

She met his gaze, clearly and cleanly, for the first time.
"That we marry at once."

"The baby—"

"It is Janos's child, no matter what your barbaric customs
say. As soon as it can travel, I will send it north to Lady
Jadranka. I will not suffer Janos's child to live by me. She
wants it. She may have it. But you and I will marry now,
Prince Vassily. I will not become their pawn. Better that I
ally with the jaran, who will give me a power base outside
of this court, where *I* am the outsider, the interloper, than be
isolated within the net of their intrigues."

"Once you no longer need me, will you betray me as you
did Janos?"

"He forced me to marry him. I had no choice. Now I *do*
have a choice, between you and this Lord Intavio. You have
no power here except through me, and if I had you killed
and the jaran invaded and conquered Mircassia, if they
could, they would force me to marry another jaran prince,
one I didn't know."

"I suppose," said Vasha bitterly, "that I needn't have
asked that question, because you betrayed me once already,
to Janos, when we were first captured."

Now she looked away from him. A flush stained her
cheeks. "I did that to protect Bakhtiian."

Embarrassed, jealous, he almost took a drink of the tea
just to do something with his hands. But he caught himself
in time. She saw his hesitation.

"Here, child," she called to an attendant, "bring a new
pot, and pour into both our cups from it." She emptied her
cup onto the stone paving. She smoothed a hand down over
the curve of her stomach. "Once I was content to devote my

life to God, to prayer, but God did not mean me to follow such a destiny. I am ambitious, too, Prince Vassily."

Deliberately she leaned forward, having to stand up to get her abdomen over the table, and kissed him chastely on each cheek. "We will go to meet my grandfather together."

King Barsauma heard Rusudani out in silence. Vasha could not tell if he was disgusted, infuriated, or pleased. When she was finished, he coughed. A servant hurried forward and wiped a drop of spittle from the drooping side of his mouth.

"Are you in love with him, granddaughter?" he demanded.

"No."

He grunted. "That is good. No fit marriage was ever founded on infatuation." He turned his head to glare at Vasha. His stare reminded Vasha of a vulture's, waiting until the dying animal stopped thrashing. "There are two provinces in eastern Filis that by right ought to belong to Mircassia."

"I'm sorry to hear that, your highness."

"Hmph. When your father conquers it, and has killed that heretic Basil and that puerile half sister of his, I want those provinces returned. That is the only offer I will accept."

"Then we have a bargain, your highness. But I will keep the pages."

"Ah, God," muttered Barsauma, "what has it come to, that I lose my fine sons and have to endure seeing a convent-bred child and a barbarian take my place?" He thumped his cane on the floor many times, his face getting red. Vasha wondered if he was about to collapse with a fit of apoplexy.

Rusudani reached up from where she knelt before him and took his withered hand in hers. "It is God's will, Grandfather. You will not be disappointed in us."

He settled down slowly, and his servant gave him a sip of spirits and wiped the sweat off his face and straightened his collar. Still breathing heavily, the old man measured first his granddaughter and second, Vasha. "Pah," he said scornfully. "A mere girl and a bandit." But he did not thump his cane. "Well. Qiros, come here, come here. Bring more glasses, pour all round. From the same bottle."

By that gesture, Vasha saw that he now had an alliance with the Mircassian king.

Ten days later, Rusudani was invested as the heir to the throne of Mircassia, the ceremony taking place in the great cathedral of Kavad.

Here, in the south, bordering on the heretic realm of Prince Basil, the huge windows in the church were laced with colored glass, and the afternoon sun streamed in through the windows and illuminated the interior with dazzling light.

The presbyter read the service with great flourish, and King Barsauma managed with every steely bit of will that he possessed to crown her all by himself, with one weakened and one withered arm.

Then the queen of Mircassia, her pregnancy showing through the heavy robes of state, turned to look toward her future husband. Vasha, knees trembling beneath equally heavy robes, mounted the steps and halted beside her.

So it was that Vasha came to be married in a khaja church by a khaja ceremony, to a khaja queen. He became a prince, as his mother had long ago promised him, but in the khaja manner, by right of paternity, by right of marriage to a woman, the ways that khaja measured rank. Not by jaran custom.

But he could hear the whisper of his father's words: *You'll do, Vassily.*

He was content.

CHAPTER FORTY-SEVEN

Himalaya's Beautiful Daughter

The caravansary echoed with the ghost voices of the company, long since gone back to Earth. Ilyana stretched out belly down on the bench in the courtyard, letting the sun warm her back through her silk shirt. She reveled in her solitude.

"You have been idle for fifteen minutes," said her slate. *"Do you wish to close the Karnak program?"*

She yawned. "Yeah, sure." She crossed her arms over the slate and lay her head down on them. The back of her neck between the part in her braids got sun for the first time in an hour. She tucked her chin down, to expose more of her neck to the glorious warmth.

A boot scuffed the pavement at the entrance gates.

She jerked up, swinging her legs off the bench. But it was only David. He dumped a saddle and bridle just inside the gate and walked over to her, pulling grass out of his hair.

"You were out riding. What happened?"

He rubbed one shoulder. "Damned horse threw me. It got startled. The dome came down."

"I didn't hear—"

"It wasn't the noise. It was the flash when the field was shut off. You didn't notice it?"

"I had my eyes closed." She bounced up to her feet. "But that means the dry season's here, just like Genji promised when she made us put those weird membranes on. Now we can go live somewhere else."

"You don't like it here?"

She shrugged, unwilling to admit to him that the ruined caravansary still made her nervous. She never went there alone.

"You're sure, Yana, that you don't want to go . . ."

"Home?"

"Back to Earth."

"No. I like it here, really."

"Even after two months alone? It's pretty quiet."

"Don't you like it?"

"I don't mind it, Yana, but it's generally accepted that adults can adapt to many circumstances for a finite period of time. Meditative retreats are considered beneficial to mental and physical health, after all. But you're still young—"

"As you keep reminding me," she snapped, irritated by his avuncular meddling. "I like it here just fine, thank you! It's nice to be alone for a while. And anyway, Genji says she's working on Duke Naroshi to invite Augustus Gopal here, to dance, so then my friend Kori could come visit."

"Ah. That would be nice for you."

Ilyana rolled her eyes, grabbed her slate, and stalked outside. She had been a little nervous, two months ago when the company had *finally* packed everything up and left, about staying alone here with just David. She wasn't quite sure about what, what there was to be nervous about, or if it was something about David or something about her, but that had changed. She liked David—well, in some ways she really loved him, because he showed her more attention and affection than her parents ever had. But really, he was positively becoming as tiresome as a parent, constant questions and worrying about her and wanting to know every least thing Genji said to her during their visits and if she was going out when she was coming back. It went on and on and on, so that even though there were only two of them here— just two humans, that is—sometimes she felt crowded.

Tucking her slate in her belt, she hoisted up her saddle and saddlebags and went out to the horses. She rode Sosha past the burnt circle of ground that was all that was left of Valentin's pyre and kept going, all the way to the rose wall and through the gate that opened for her. Armed now with a kind of a second skin, an invisible membrane that did something with the air, filtered it somehow, she forged forward, unafraid. Naroshi's palace was huge, and she and David were just beginning to mark out a basic map of it. But some routes she knew quite well.

Naroshi's palace lived in a jungle. The wet season lasted for five months, and the dry for six, more or less, according to human measures of time calculated by Genji. But these "monsoons" dropped as much as sixty *feet* of rain in a season, which was why Naroshi had had his steward Roki erect the dome, knowing that the humans were adapted to what Genji called a "savannah" climate.

The vegetation steamed under the sun, still drying out. The smells came so thick that they almost choked her. Animals writhed through the undergrowth, but she didn't look closely, just stayed on the path. There were more birds than she had ever seen and trees a hundred meters high, slim towers piercing toward the great rings of the planet above. The sun stood at its apex, so that she and Sosha cast a lumpy shadow that moved along on the packed earth path beneath the horse's hooves.

After about an hour, taking two right forks and one left, Ilyana came to Genji's cottage. Genji sat on a bench grown out of the limb of a tree, one hand held to the bark as if she was listening to something. Seeing Ilyana, she stood.

"Your cousin, the prince of Sakhalin, approaches this palace," said Genji calmly.

At once the equanimity Ilyana had gained on her ride was overthrown.

To hide her flush, her suddenly shaking hands, Ilyana turned aside and hobbled Sosha near a pool of water surrounded by grasses. This mundane chore settled her. Was she really so self-centered that she would think that Anatoly Sakhalin was coming to Naroshi's planet to visit *her?* Probably, if everything she had heard was true, he had to negotiate with Naroshi about the disposition of the territories, Earth and the League, that had once belonged to Naroshi and had now come into the possession of Sakhalin. She gave Sosha a final pat and walked over to Genji.

"We will go to the palace of memory," said Genji, having evidently dismissed the specter of Anatoly Sakhalin. Ilyana vowed to do the same. "One of the attendants will take the horse back." Genji's skin gleamed in the sun, faintly iridescent, the pearllike surface shot through with color in its depths. "Today we will begin to discuss the art of building."

They went in a barge, open now to the air. Ilyana hung on the railing and watched the palace skim past beneath them. The air streamed around her face, whipping her braids back into the wind. The whole palace seemed to steam, releasing months of rain toward the sun. It was beautiful.

"Will we start with tension and compression?" Ilyana asked when the barge floated down in front of the palace of memory and she could talk.

Genji alighted on the steps and waited for her. "My child, any building must start with the foundation."

Abashed because she hadn't thought of what was so patently obvious, Ilyana followed her inside without another word.

"The hall of building and the hall of time wrap around each other as in a maze," said Genji, "being necessarily intricately intertwined."

They came to a branching in the hall, and Ilyana stared to her right, where a hall receded into dim shadows. She saw the statue, lost in gloom, that stood in the center of that hall: She knew it, as a tingling on her skin. It was Shiva. He was waiting for her.

Shaking off her disquiet—or was it anticipation?—she followed Genji straight through the intersection. A pylon fronted this hall, painted with inscriptions and human figures. A statue of ibis-headed Thoth, holding a staff and an ankh, seemed to watch them as they went by. Passing through the pylon, Ilyana realized that they were in an undersized model of Karnak.

"We will begin in *Egypt*," said Genji, leading Ilyana forward to an altar presided over by a female figure carved into the stone. So this was not a precise model of Karnak, Ilyana thought, but a fantasia built on the theme of the old temple at Karnak. "Here is an altar dedicated to the goddess Seshat, the Lady of builders, of writing, and of the House of Books."

Ilyana peered at the statue. The shaded chamber muted the painted stone, a clay red dress, a headdress, the tools of her trade: a measuring stick, a square, and a triangle. At her feet lay coiled rope tied in knots at intervals. Ilyana got that nervous feeling again, as if at any moment the statue might come alive. She no longer trusted the creatures in Genji's hall. If Genji "grew" them, might they not be alive in a way that wasn't quite like a biological being?

Genji pulled a batch of scrolls, bound together by a string, out from a niche in the stone. "The legendary Imhotep was said to be the author of *The Book of Foundation for Temples,* and it is here we should start. With rock, with soils, with stability. With soil bearing capacity, soil properties, permeability and shear strength. Footing types."

But Ilyana was still staring around the chamber. The pillars were carved to look like flowers, or like bunches of reeds, painted in flat reds and greens and blues. "How come you have all this Earth stuff here? I mean, I always wanted to ask, but it didn't seem polite."

" 'I had access to all the writings of the prophets; there was nothing which I did not know of that which had happened since the beginning.' "

"What does that mean?" Ilyana reached out and, tentatively, touched the statue of Seshat. The goddess stared at her, sloe-eyed, her eyes outlined in heavy black; she wore a necklace and multicolored bands on her arms. She did not move. She felt as solid and quiescent as stone. "How do you know so much about Earth?"

"I became acquainted with daiga—with humans—when Third Brother was alive."

"Who is Third Brother?"

"His name is no longer spoken within the Empire. It is true that he transgressed the boundaries. I am sorry for his passing. I planted towers in his memory before I brought Fourth Brother out of the nidus."

"But that still doesn't tell me who he is. I mean, was."

"My brother discovered the planet which you call Earth."

"But it was the famous Chapalii traitor called the Tai-en Mushai who supposedly discovered Earth. That's why there're humans on Rhui. He transported some there during the Stone Age. Or at least, that's what I was taught."

"Yes." Genji slipped the string off the scrolls. A bit of dust came with it, and Genji used her sleeve to brush off one of the scrolls. The dust was so thick that it was caked on the papyrus, but none stuck to the sleeve of Genji's robe, and as soon as it drifted to the floor, a tiny, humming creature glided out from the walls and ate it up, disappearing back into a tiny niche at the base of the wall.

"Oh, you have dust-eaters, too," said Ilyana. "I figured you did, but I never saw any before." Then, as if it had taken that long to sink in, she registered Genji's reply. She swallowed. "Do you mean it?" Gods, what David would say when she told him! "But Naroshi is your brother, too."

"He is Sixth Brother. I confess that after Third Brother brought daiga to me, I became fond of them and learned what I could, studied, was not displeased when the emperor reabsorbed daiga territories because then I could study in earnest. It has become a bit of a project of mine. We each of us have projects. I am something of a renegade among fe-

males, interesting myself to a small extent in the activities of
the males, of the empire. I pulled . . . strings, you might say,
so that Sixth Brother would receive the daiga holdings in his
time. Now they are taken from him."

"Uh, does that make you angry?"

"Angry? What does this mean?" She had moved under a
well of light sinking down through an opening in the roof
above. This close to her, Ilyana looked into her eyes and was
puzzled to see that they looked flat. Genji did not have eyeballs. " 'A feeling of extreme displeasure, hostility, indignation, or exasperation toward someone or something.' No,
that does not make me angry. Should it?"

"I guess only if you're human, or if you wanted to be emperor."

Genji was amused. She turned to look down the axis of
Karnak; had to turn her whole head to change her angle of
vision, Ilyana realized now, because she could not roll her
eyes in her head. "I am a builder. I have told you this before.
I am training you, Ilyana Arkhanov, in the art of building."
She lifted a hand to encompass with an economical gesture
the whole of the hall. "In the time of the Egyptians, after the
master builder had completed the design she would transfer
the design of the building onto the site. This was done with
the plan net." She blinked, and beneath Ilyana's feet a grid
appeared, knotted at intervals like the rope coiled at Seshat's
feet. "The ground was staked and a cord stretched between
the stakes to delineate the outline of the building, to mark
the formative axis."

"It looks like a grid. It looks like the grid in nesh, the one
I always come through."

"The empire itself is a plan net, staked out and growing.
So are the daiga. Third Brother discovered them, although to
be fair I will say that the daiga discovered themselves. Now
they emerge onto the web of the empire, by his rash action,
by my wish to see what may come of this new building."

Genji turned and began to walk on down the axis of
Karnak, toward the next hall . . . whatever it might contain.
Ilyana hastened to follow her, the rustling of Genji's robes
like a beckoning whisper: *come see, come see.*

"I have set a new edifice in motion," said Genji without
turning back to look at Ilyana. Her voice sank into the stone,
muted by the frozen reliefs, circling round pillars, and yet
the very closed nature of the chamber amplified the precise,

clipped utterance of each syllable. "I have prepared the foundation with care, making sure it is solidly grounded. Now I will watch and see what grows."

Anatoly was truly annoyed to find the caravansary empty except for David, who had evidently been dozing on his cot.

"I didn't expect you," said David with his usual placidity. "You didn't send word you were coming."

"I came to see—" He rethought his tactics quickly. "To see Duke Naroshi. You're not all alone here, are you?" Better not to mention her name out loud, or David might grow suspicious. Nevertheless, Anatoly fingered the hilt of his saber, caught himself doing it, and withdrew his hand and hooked a thumb in his belt.

"Right now I am. Yana ran off again, as she's always doing. She's turning into a damned jaydee ... but she's all right," he added quickly. "She's just feeling her way now that her circumstances have changed so much."

"In what way?"

"You didn't hear?" David finally deigned to get up and walk out of his dark room, into the sunny courtyard. "Her mother threw her out, not just threw her but disowned her, I guess."

Two emotions hit Anatoly simultaneously: disgust and exhilaration. "That's terrible," he said, even as he thought, she would now want a new family to replace the old one. Surely the gods had meant this all along. Why, ever since he had conceived of this idea three months ago, he had barely thought about Diana more than three or four times a day, or when he was with Portia, or was being forced to read the latest draft of the accord that would protect the rights of each parent and bind them to their responsibilities in relation to the upbringing of the child.

"Sit down," said David. "You look hot. I discovered a cache of great old wine in the catacombs. I'll pour you a glass."

"No, thank you," said Anatoly curtly, but he did not move away immediately. He liked David, for one, and for another, the other man might inadvertently grant him more information about Ilyana that could prove useful: Such as where to find her.

David tucked his feet up under himself on a bench and looked guilelessly up at Anatoly. "So what's it like? I hear the emperor made you a prince? Met any Chapalii princes yet? I hear you made record time to Chapal and back, and that you got all kinds of transport information and that you agreed to let Charles stay in control of Rhui, for now, and that you've been cooling your heels on the *Gray Raven* for the last couple of months and gathering information and scouting out a site for a central—well, a palace, I'd guess you'd say."

"I was thinking of Mongolia, or Dzungaria. You're well informed."

"I have to be. As do you. What will you do after you've met with Duke Naroshi?"

Anatoly flushed abruptly. Irritated with himself, he spun and walked over to the gazebo. The latticework was shattered at the base; that he *had* heard about. "Do you have any suggestions?" he asked, to cover his discomfiture.

"More questions than suggestions. I wish you'd let me know you were coming; I'd have prepared a specific list." He sounded aggrieved.

"I can stay for nine or ten days," replied Anatoly ingenuously, planning already where he would go into seclusion for the traditional nine days; in the catacombs, perhaps. He did not want to stay anywhere near the room he had shared with Diana. It might remind him of her. Of course he had no tent. "My grandmother died," he said abruptly, sitting down on the bench beside David. "I got the news when I was at Odys." How soon would his sister Shura receive his message? Would she come to him? "Perhaps I will have some of that wine."

"I'm sorry," said David.

Duke Naroshi arrived while David was fetching the wine.

Anatoly heard a craft approaching, but he did not stir from the bench. He was learning things about these Chapalii: Let the lower ranks come to you, unless you want something urgently, in which case you could go wherever you damned well pleased, as long as your path did not take you into direct contact with another prince.

David came in with the bottle just as Naroshi entered the courtyard and knelt before Anatoly. Anatoly felt more than saw David stop, waiting about ten paces behind and to his right. He could almost smell the faint scent of wine in the dry air. Two glasses chimed softly together.

"Duke Naroshi," said Anatoly, acknowledging him.

"Your grace. I am honored by your presence."

Anatoly examined the Chapalii duke in the harsh light of the afternoon sun. His eyes were quite large, the most prominent feature in his face. A hood covered most of his head and his robes draped him from neck to toe, but Anatoly caught a brief glimpse of dark slits along his neck, like those he had seen on the Teardrop Prince. Only the skin on his face revealed anything of him, and he remained pale, controlling himself. His mouth remained fixed, except when words emerged.

When Anatoly did not reply at once, Naroshi went on. "I assure you that I am proceeding with all due haste in removing my retainers from Earth and the other daiga territories, from Sira, Ophiuchi-Sei, Eridanaia, Hydra, *In-tali-kono-ah,* and Small Rings. From Concord. From all stations and interstitial colonies."

Anatoly glanced back at David, wanting to ask: And what the hell am I going to replace them all with? Instead, he set his hands on his thighs and leaned forward toward Naroshi. "I want to see your sister Genji."

A hint of red stained Naroshi's skin, but faded before Anatoly could be sure he had seen it. Was Naroshi amused about something? "I beg your pardon, your grace," the duke said in his colorless voice. "Not even a prince of the realm may enter those halls, nor summon a female. Please accept a thousand thousand apologies from my mouth, that I may not obey your wish in this."

"I will go see her, then."

Naroshi bowed his head a little lower, as if to signify that this, too, was forbidden.

"Damn it! I have to see her." Forcing himself to calm down, he regarded Naroshi coolly. He must not get angry at Naroshi. That would be not so much bad manners as poor governance.

"Perhaps I may convey a message to her, your grace."

"All right, then. Perhaps you know the answer. I believe your sister has been watching me while I travel, watching me while the ship I travel on is within the singularities, the windows. Can this be?"

"Ships are not the only vehicles for traveling on the great web, your grace, although most creatures are limited to this mode."

One of the glasses shattered on the paving stones. "Oh, shit," muttered David.

Stunned, Anatoly finally winched himself around to see David staring gape-mouthed at the Chapalii duke. Shards of glass lay strewn around his boots, slivers winking in the sunlight. "Well," said Anatoly, looking back to Naroshi, "so Genji can somehow travel along or through the singularities without leaving this moon?"

"It is a female mystery, your grace. Only those who know the secrets of the deeper tongue can travel the web."

"Are allowed to, or are capable of?" David murmured.

"And of those who know the deeper tongue, only the builders can fathom the net."

"If your sister Genji has taken Ilyana Arkhanov on as some kind of apprentice, then does that mean she will teach Ilyana to, uh, fathom the net?"

"I beg your pardon, your grace. Although you are elevated above all but the other Yao by the Yaochalii himself, yet you and the others of your kind are still daiga. Animals are bound to the physical world. Is it not true that you can see only in the realm of what you call visible light, except with the aid of your brittle tools? As for the rest, you must ask this of your cousin yourself. She is not of my house, therefore I may not speak to her." Naroshi lifted his head. "Unless you seek to give her into my house by marrying her to me."

David hissed a sudden breath in through his teeth.

Anatoly shuddered, looking at this alien creature. But surely Naroshi had no . . . sexual designs on Ilyana. To him, surely, she would simply represent a powerful alliance with another princely house, a triumph for his house, for his prince. Who was, of course, the Teardrop Prince. Who had already stated his enmity toward Anatoly and *his* tribe.

"No," said Anatoly. "No. I think not. But I would like to see her, if you know where she is, if she is with your sister."

Naroshi waited for a moment. His gaze strayed to the broken latticework and back to Anatoly. "I am sure that my sister is already aware of your presence here. Is there more, your grace? Another way I might serve you?"

"No. You are free to go."

When he had gone, and his craft sailed off into the late afternoon sky, David sat down and laughed weakly. "Oh, Goddess, I don't know what gave me a worse turn, finding out that Genji can maybe travel through the singularities on her own, or the thought of Ilyana being married to that chameleon. Oh, Lady. Even if it was a nice Earth boy, it would *not* be what the poor child needs right now. Getting married, I mean. But I just could not reconcile that cold fish Naroshi with an ardent bridegroom having lascivious thoughts about his young bride. Like Himalaya's daughter, who was so beautiful that Shiva was tempted to love her divine body for a thousand years.

Then Anatoly made his first mistake. Surprised by David's babbling, he looked him right in the eye.

David was no fool. Nor was human nature any mystery to him. He jumped back to his feet, wine bottle and remaining glass hanging limply from his left hand. "Don't you dare! She doesn't need that. She's too young."

Anatoly bristled. "Staking out your ground?"

"She's sixteen years old! She's a child."

"My grandmother was married at—"

"And her mother Karolla had had a child by the time she was sixteen or seventeen, yeah yeah, I've heard it all before. But this isn't the jaran, in case you need reminding."

"I can do what I want."

"What the hell am I talking about?" said David suddenly, setting the bottle and glass down on the bench. "This isn't truly about Ilyana, is it, however attractive she certainly is? This is about Diana. For which I am very sorry, Anatoly."

"I don't want your pity!"

Anatoly whirled and ran out of the gate. He went out to the horses, but Little Sosha was gone, and he had left his saddle on the yacht in any case, in his haste to come downside. Swearing under his breath, he began to walk across the grass toward the ruined caravansary, the only place he could brood in peace. Shadows lengthened around him. By the road, the night-flowers began to open, their scent mingling with the smell of grass and an odd flavor in the air, one that hadn't been here before. Looking up, he realized that the air above no longer wore the faint shimmer that betrayed the presence of the dome. So many things he had failed to notice, in his haste to come downside. Insects buzzed. A horse neighed, calling out, and he turned to see Little Sosha, at a distance, galloping toward the herd. Behind her came a barge. He waited.

As he knew it would, it halted before him and Ilyana walked hesitantly down the ramp. She stopped in front of him, cocking her head to one side. Then she blushed and with an effort did not look away from him. He had forgotten how beautiful she was.

He drew his saber.

She paled and took a step back, one foot coming solidly down on the ramp. The barge did not move, floating in the air, ready to receive her.

"Don't," she said. That was all.

"Oh, gods," said Anatoly, and shut his eyes. While they were shut, he sheathed his saber. When he opened them, she still stood there. She was still beautiful. She was so young, and yet not young, having been marked by death and exile. "You have to marry," he said finally.

"Oh, gods!" She rolled her eyes and grimaced, no longer shy of him. He could see himself transforming in her eyes into another meddling adult. "I don't have to marry. I don't have to take a lover unless I want to. And I'm sorry about the flower night, but you know that my mother lied about it. Not that I wouldn't have picked you under other circumstances—" But that was too much. She faltered, collected herself, and glanced toward the distant caravansary, as if willing David to come to her rescue.

Anatoly realized that he was jealous of David. But that was a morass he did not want to step into, yet.

"I'm sorry about Diana," she said finally. "I feel really bad for you. I know you . . . loved her."

He looked away, unable to endure her sympathy.

"But . . . I was thinking, about Evdi. Maybe Evdi could be with Portia. Maybe there could be some kind of arrangement, with . . . Evdi's parents, that she could be fostered out. I think it would be better for her, and I bet Portia would like it."

"It's a good idea," he said without looking at her. "I'll see."

"And Anton," she pressed. "Maybe Hyacinth and Yevgeni could foster him for a while."

"Yes," he said automatically, thinking it was a good idea before recalling that he ought not to approve. But he did approve. "Do you like it here, Yana?"

She cleared her throat. "Yeah. Genji told me something really strange today, but interesting. It's true you're a prince, isn't it? I mean that the emperor said you were one."

"It is true that he has acknowledged that I am a prince of the Sakhalin. What did Genji tell you?"

"Well." He heard her feet rustle in the grass as, gaining confidence, she stepped off the ramp again. "She said that the empire is like a grid, all staked out and growing to fill the lines, the . . . space, I mean the grid that's already staked out. I'm not quite sure what she meant, except she talked about the net, it's like the grid in nesh. Does it make any sense to you?"

Anatoly clenched his hands. A slow smile spread onto his face. "Yes, it does. A bit of sense. It'll make more sense to others. What if she's talking about the transport system, the singularities? That would imply that the Chapalii constructed, or created, the singularities themselves, that they've already sown them, staked out the net, and now the empire is just growing to fill it. Except how far does it extend?"

"I dunno. Genji says the Mushai was her brother, one of her brothers, I mean. He was an earlier brother than Naroshi."

"But according to what we understand of Chapalii history, the Tai-en Mushai's line was made extinct."

"That's what she said. She made it sound like there were other brothers between the Mushai and Naroshi. Like she only has one at a time, like she controls when they appear, or something."

"You must ask her further about this."

"I know."

Struck by the confidence in her voice, he almost laughed. Here she spilled this vital intelligence, information that even he couldn't get, that generations of civilized khaja had not discovered, and there she stood, not truly a woman yet by jaran custom but old enough to be a woman, once she chose to cross over. He studied her, although it was not quite good manners to do so. She folded her arms over her chest and regarded him in her turn, steadily. Any man would be honored to be chosen on her flower night.

But Anatoly had a damned good idea, at this moment, that he wouldn't be the one.

"Are you truly happy here?" he asked instead. "I can take you somewhere else, see that other arrangements are made. . . ."

She threw up her hands in disgust. "None of you want to

believe me. I *am* happy here. I'm where I belong. When it's time for me to leave, I'll go, to wherever I need to go next, but this is where I need to be right now."

"Then I will leave you, Cousin," he said, inclining his head toward her as a man does toward a woman, to show his respect, "although I hope you will give me a full accounting of all that you have learned, all that you do learn, from Genji. You are our only window into her world."

"I know, and I understand."

So he left her and walked back, alone, to the caravansary.

"What will you do now?" asked David, kindly not alluding to whatever may have happened between Anatoly and Ilyana, out on the grass.

Anatoly allowed himself a few moments just to bask in the sunlight. It almost warmed him, but he felt perpetually cold these days, except when he had Portia by him. He shut his eyes and tried not to think about Diana, but failed. So he opened them and caught David watching him, with compassion on his face.

"I don't know," he admitted finally, because he had to admit it to someone. David was loyal to Charles Soerensen; Anatoly knew that. Yet David was more than that: David was simply David, a human being who was capable of caring and of understanding and of just plain listening. "I thought I knew. I thought I comprehended the worlds. It's like seeing the lay of the ground through a mist, and then having the mist lift and none of the landmarks are what you thought you knew. Suddenly you're lost, when you thought you knew the path."

"I don't envy you your position, Anatoly. Some may. That's the way of the world, that's the way of human nature. But unless you succumb to the easy road, to the abuse of power, you're not going to have an easy time of it."

"It's not that, so much. I *am* a—"

"—prince of the Sakhalin, yes, born and bred to power." But he said it with a laugh.

Anatoly tried to grin but could not. "It's that I just . . . can't . . . understand why Diana—" Here his voice broke, and he could not go on.

David put a hand on his arm, companionable. "Have some wine. Hell, forget the wine. I've got some Martian whiskey. Let's get drunk."

So they did.

* * *

Once the shock of the dry season wore off, Ilyana discovered she was tired of it. She missed the novelty of the rain. She and David went looking for a new place to live, but in the end they decided to stay in the caravansary. It had room for visitors, and it was the most humanlike structure that they found, except for Genji's monumental halls.

Ilyana studied, and rode, and visited Genji. David did whatever adults did when they were on retreat, and he faithfully transcribed her reports, asked her probing questions about what she had seen and talked about, explained a few things she had missed or misinterpreted, and sent coded messages up into the heavens to Charles Soerensen's—no, to Prince Anatoly's agents.

Ilyana did not visit the ruined caravansary, but she still dreamed about Shiva, dreamed of him dancing, dreamed of the feel of his skin beneath her fingers, dreamed the grace and power of his body. And woke up, sitting bolt upright, his sash twined around her body and her heart beating hard, sure that someone had been in her room, was in her room, but no one ever was.

But when she didn't dream about him, she woke up disappointed.

"You must learn to draw and measure," said Genji.

So David came upon her one day while she sat cross-legged on the road a hundred meters away from the caravansary. Flowers bloomed on either side of her. Their scent filled the air. Beyond them, the horses grazed. Sosha nipped at another mare, and there was a flurry as they settled back into place. Insects buzzed. Birds had flown in from the jungle and combed the grassy verge for bugs.

David crouched down beside her. She had a board across her knees for the paper to rest on, and a pencil gripped in her right hand. She frowned at the sketch.

David cleared his throat. "What is it?"

She grimaced. "It's supposed to be an elevation. You know, an image of the standing facade except I thought I'd start with something I could draw from life. Genji says I need to learn how to draw, and the Roman architect Vitruvius says that an architect must be 'skillfull with the pencil' and a bunch of other things, too, like astronomy and law and medicine and music and obviously mathematics, so I thought . . ."

"Uh. Do you mind? I have some skill at drawing, and, uh—"

"It's terrible, isn't it?"

"Yes, it is. If you're going to learn to draft, you'll have to start with the basics. But you're right to start with pencil and paper. We'll go the modeller once you've got a handle on this technique."

So they worked. After a bit, Ilyana paused and looked at him.

"I want to use your nesh, to see if Valentin . . ."

"Ilyana, Valentin isn't in nesh anymore. Please understand that. He's dead. His *neshamah,* his soul, hasn't somehow gone to a higher plane where it has found immortality."

"I thought you believed in a god."

"I believe in the divinity of the spirit, Yana, but not in the immortality of the individual soul."

"I have to do it, David. I ride past the ashes of his pyre every day. I have to find out for myself."

"I'll come with you, then."

"I'd like to go alone. You know that I'm aware of the dangers. I'm not at risk. Of course you'll monitor me."

Because there was no reasonable objection, he let her hook up to his nesh unit that evening.

She walks the web of light that Genji walks at will. But she turns away from the strand that leads into the hall of memory. She knows where her lost brother has fled.

The great desert is still today. The sun bakes the sand into a hard surface, as hard as stone and yet under her bare feet it cools, because all that is Valentin, all that made it Valentin's, seeps away without his soul to animate it. Except that can't be. He has made it, but it remains as he made it. She is the one draining it of life, of his life.

The sand grows hot under her feet so that she has to dance, hopping from one foot to the next. She waits for the storm. It comes, wailing down from the northeast, and she forges through it as through a funnel, pulling her in toward the crack of unwavering light that is the other land.

She feels the hot breath of a summer wind and throws herself through, and she is out on a golden plain, flying above it. She is an eagle. She soars above the plain, seeking, searching, and at last with her eagle's sight she sees the tribe three days' ride away.

Her shadow covers the ground below, like the wind moving over the grasses, and she flies over the line of march, jahar riders in front and archers behind, surrounding the carts that carry the children and the old people. There is her uncle, Anton, and there are men dressed in the surcoats of Bakhtiian's guard. Her aunt Arina drives a cart, and Ilyana swoops down toward her, toward the thin boy who sits beside Arina on the cart.

It is Valentin.

She lands on the wagon, perching on the rim, and she shrieks, crying to him.

"A spirit," says Nikolai Sibirin, who rides beside the wagon.

But Valentin is a Singer. He sees with a Singer's eyes. "It is Ilyana," he says to the others, and then to her, he speaks: "This is where I belong."

She cries, an eagle's call, and he smiles at her, a Valentin smile, full of impish humor and intelligence and a trace of the old sullenness, he is not free of that yet, but most of all, he looks content. He is where he belongs. As is she.

"I love you," he adds, "but I think we are going where even you can't follow."

"I'll find you," she says in her eagle's voice, "I love you, Valentin." But the cart hits a bump and jounces her off and she throws herself into the air and currents draw her upward, up and farther up. Valentin raises a hand in farewell. She circles the tribe once, but she knows that he is right. She can't follow them, not truly. They have their own destination.

The wind pulls her backward, and she gives up fighting it as the tribe recedes into the golden ocean of the plain, lost at last to her sight. The plain is swallowed up into a single grain of sand in the desert, and she walks backward, onto the web of light, and goes home.

David said nothing. He just smiled at her fondly, sadly.

Ilyana tucked away the nesh sponge, putting everything back in its place. She wiped one tear from her right eye and got to her feet and walked outside. The planet and the sun set together, their conjoined light a rich glow on the flower beds.

She took in a deep breath, letting the sharp sweetness of the flowers sink into her lungs. It was time to raise her own tent, to follow the path that opened out from her feet. It was time to begin her new life.

* * *

She rose before the dawn and came to him with flowers in offering, where he stood at the center of the universe, which is said by some to be the human heart. In the myths, Shiva dances at critical moments: in madness, on the battlefield, before his marriage. But in life, every moment can be said to be critical; all is revealed and concealed, created, maintained, and destroyed in the great dance of time.

Ilyana laid the flowers at his feet.

Shiva said nothing, standing with one foot on the back of the demon of forgetfulness, with the other foot poised in the air, his arms as graceful as any dancer's, muscled, strong, and sensuous. Nor did he look at her, or acknowledge the gift or the gesture. *Fear not.* He was just a statue, after all.

But she felt a breath of wind, disturbing the cloistered silence of the hall, and though she did not move, that breath stirred the sash that she held in her hands.

CHAPTER FORTY-EIGHT

The Revelation of Elia

They rode into Jeds on the wings of a bitterly cold and unseasonably late winter storm. The jaran soldiers rode with their felt coats unbelted so they wouldn't get too warm and those brave Jedan natives who ventured outside to watch the army enter the city huddled in blankets and looked miserable.

A few flakes of snow drifted down. Tess stuck out her tongue and with some effort got some moisture on it, licking her lips.

"In the four years I was a student here," said Ilya, "it snowed once, like this. I thought winter was finally beginning, but then of course I realized that there is no true winter in Jeds, just a lessening of the heat."

Tess waited, but he had finished. In the five months since the army had rescued him from White Tower, he had slowly gotten control back of his speech, although at times he still faltered or ran on as if he had forgotten what he was saying. His men seemed undisturbed by his lapses: Singers often behaved this way; it was the result of speaking directly to the gods. But she always admired—perhaps in part had fallen in love with—the precision of his mind, the incredible scope of his memory, and if one conceived of his mind as a web, a network of interconnected threads, then that captivity had worked like a knife slashing with random cruelness through some of the threads and not others, leaving gaps and unraveling ends.

"Jeds has grown," he said. "That second course of wall didn't even exist, and this was the hostelry district. Now it's too far within the city."

It was a residential district now, thrown up against the inner wall. Ilya did not even flinch when they passed under the massive inner gate and clattered down the main thoroughfare through Jeds, the army streaming out in their wake.

Tess had left ten thousand men encamped a day's ride away
from the city, but she had brought an honor guard of five
thousand riders and a thousand archers with her, to remind
the Jedan nobility who ruled here. Here, in the central city,
the populace had braved the cold to see their prince and her
barbarians. They shouted and pointed and cheered, and a
few bold girls—probably prostitutes—threw flowers at the
jaran men. Women and children leaned out of third-story
windows. Tess smelled a hint of smoke on the air and saw
a low pall toward the southeast; most likely a fire had caught
in one of the districts, as it often did in the cold weather. It
was always so: That one person celebrated a triumph hard
against the loss suffered by another somewhere nearby.

"Twenty-five years ago I lived as an exile, a poor student,
in this city," murmured Ilya. His gaze roved restlessly over
the crowd, over the roof lines and the farther spire of West
Cathedral and the flatter, more massive dome of East
Church, the twin towers of Market Hall and the distant blunt
spires that marked the old palace. Here, along the main thoroughfare, the old tenements had been torn down and new
buildings, the mercantile Exchange, the clothiers guildhall,
the law courts and the playhouse and the public library and
pauper's school, erected in their place. Tess surveyed these
additions—most of them completed or almost finished—
with satisfaction. She liked Sarai better, but Jeds had a certain civic splendor of its own.

She glanced toward Ilya, who was looking toward a clot
of people standing on the steps of the library. "And now
your armies control the lands that stretch from the plains all
the way south to Jeds, as you meant them to all along."

But he wasn't listening to her. He pulled Kriye out of formation abruptly and headed for the library. Jedans scattered
before his advance, but he brushed them aside without notice, so intent was he on his goal: A group of young men and
a handful of women who, by their black caps and loose,
open gowns, were university students. He reined in in front
of them. A few scuttled away, but most stared up at him
with the twinned expressions of curious children and trapped
animals. He leaned down and said something. After some
hesitation, one young man replied, and then there was a
flurry of conversation.

Tess brought the parade to a halt and was at once sorry.
Several dignitaries pressed themselves on the guards and she

had to acknowledge them. After all, her rule had benefited the townspeople as much as the nobility, and she needed their enthusiastic support to counterbalance the grudging loyalty given her by the Santer heirs and the rest of the barons and lords. So it was well past midday by the time they got out through the city and into the park that fronted the new palace.

"What did you talk to the students about?" Tess asked, having got Ilya to herself in the procession once again. Vladimir and Nikita rode in front, and Mikhail and Gennady Berezin behind.

Ilya glanced at her, glanced back toward Jeds, last glanced north, where his empire lay. His eyes burned with that inner light she knew so well. "I have questions. They and the scholars at the university may have answers. Or they may not." That was all he would say.

Old Baron Santer was now deceased. His children met Tess in the courtyard of the palace and, together with the jaran prince who had married the daughter, escorted Tess into the audience hall.

They exchanged formal greetings. Young Baron Santer looked over the jaran escort with a calculating gaze. He leaned to whisper something into the ear of Georgi Raevsky, his brother-in-law; Tess liked the intimacy they seemed to have developed. But the real power in this trio was clearly the woman. Isobel, Baroness Santer, had inherited her father's cold ambition.

"We have heard no recent news of Prince Basil's army, your highness, except that the snow still confines them in the Sagesian Pass," Baroness Santer said now. More coolly still, she inclined her head toward Bakhtiian. "Your Majesty. We did not hear how you managed to cross the hills and get past the Filistian army."

"Bakhtiian will do. We circled around Prince Basil's army, my lady, and crossed by the southern pass."

"But even in a mild winter that pass is closed by snow and ice!" Astounded, she stared at him. Several men nearby cocked their heads to listen.

"My army has yet to meet an obstacle it cannot surmount." He nodded politely at her, walked up the dais, paced around the single throne, and waved to Vladimir. "Here," he said. To Tess's horror and amusement, Vladimir

threw a big gold-embroidered pillow onto the floor beside
the throne and Ilya promptly sat down on it. Tess almost
laughed out loud at the consternation that broke out through
the hall. The bastard was throwing his weight around, seeing
what would come of it.

The Jedans did not know what to do: Continue to attend
their prince, who stood in the middle of the hall, or pay
obeisance to the man who was not just her husband but the
general of the army that lay outside their gates.

"How is it fitting to address him?" whispered Baroness
Santer, abandoning her pose of calm to show a less composed interior.

"Bakhtiian is itself a title."

Tess looked around as she said it and discovered something odd, watching the five hundred or so dignitaries and
noblemen and women gathered in the hall as they turned to
stare at the man sitting on the floor next to the throne. He
still wore his armor, boiled leather and polished strips of
plate tied with ribbons, his helmet sitting on the floor to his
left and his saber resting across his knees. Philosophy, celebrating her triumph, smiled benignly down on him from the
huge mural painted along the inner wall of the hall.

Ilya scared them.

No, it was not Ilya who scared them. They didn't know
Ilya. It was Bakhtiian who made them nervous.

Tess caught Baroness Santer by the elbow and drew her
forward to the dais. "Come, Isobel, we will be friends again,
as we were before your father died."

"When you took me to the north."

"Your husband has not been a disappointment to you, I
hope."

Baroness Santer caught herself before she looked back
over her shoulder toward her husband and her brother. "He
is a good husband," she said, clipping off the words as if she
was afraid that she would reveal something incriminating,
that she liked her jaran husband too little, or too much.

Tess mounted the steps and sat down in the prince's
throne without looking at Ilya. "Stand beside me, and as
each person comes forward, please make sure that I remember the proper name."

So she greeted her subjects, and Isobel, Baroness Santer,
gave her names and, often, a tiny squib of information with
which Tess could surprise or please each supplicant. Georgi

Raevsky wandered up to Bakhtiian and crouched down beside him, and the two men launched into an intense discussion in khush, oblivious to the formalities going on before them. The rest of the guard stood here and there, examining the mural (Philosophy's dress was, perhaps, a bit indecent by jaran standards), whispering to each other, going outside when it pleased them, stamping their feet and shaking out their armor. Katya was loudly explaining the different figures in the mural to Nikita and whomever else would listen; she was showing off, unaware that she had an audience of Jedans as well, intrigued by her armor and her weapons and her authoritative, bossy manner. In all, the jaran showed no propensity to be overawed by Jeds or its inhabitants. This was the army that had burned down Karkand, after all, and conquered at least ten cities equal to or greater than Jeds. This was really just another city. Filis had not yet capitulated. And there would be other lands.

Tess sent the presbyter of all Jeds on his way and glanced down at Ilya. He looked up at her, one hand on his saber hilt. He did not smile. He did not need to. He had Jeds. He had his empire. He had what he wanted.

But he had that same restless expression in his eyes, that odd, mad, passionate expression on his face: He wanted something else, something new. No doubt, the gods still spoke to him. No doubt, they were filling him with fresh visions.

The abbess of Jedina Cloister knelt before her, and Tess had a sudden inspiration. She, too, could use the gods. She could use them as a bridge to what she had to tell Ilya. Tomorrow, she would call Sarai and have the ke or Sonia transmit to her a facsimile of the scroll that contained the "Revelation of Elia."

Sonia was angry.

"It is time for my daughter to be married." She leaned forward so far that part of her passed out of the picture. She jerked and pulled back into focus. She was still angry.

"Katya doesn't want to get married."

"Why not?"

"Well, uh," Tess temporized, "she's like Ilya in that way."

"Ilya wanted to get married. Or so I had always supposed." Sonia rarely got mad and when she did, she fought dirty. Tess could see her gearing up for battle.

"Now, Sonia. I'm just saying that Katya is young yet and discontent . . ."

"Damn you," said Sonia suddenly. It was so strange, Tess reflected, to be talking to her this way, seeing her head and torso growing up from the console as if the rest of her sat contained within. A line of static popped through the image and cleared. "I know what you're saying. I went to Jeds when I was a girl because I was curious, because I wanted adventure, I wanted to see what lay outside the tribe. Now she wants to do the same. Let me talk to her. Tess, the others who sailed across the ocean to Erthe were told they could never come back. How can I exile my daughter like that? How can you expect me to agree to let her go, knowing I could never see her again?"

"Sonia, if what you say about Anatoly Sakhalin is true, then how can we know how much the interdiction will change? Anything could happen. There you sit talking to me across a gulf of thousands of kilometers—"

"Which reminds me," said Sonia, the anger slipping easily from her face. "How can this image travel as fast as I can speak across a distance that would take a messenger forty days riding day and night without a break except to change horses? What is this image riding? How can it travel on the air?"

"Didn't the ke explain that to you?"

"Well, yes, but—" She launched into such a garbled explanation of the ke's explanation that Tess could only look toward Cara Hierakis for help. Cara shrugged.

"Sonia," Tess broke in. "There is a tutorial encyclopedia under mathetics. Start there."

"Is it true that Newton's *Principia* has been superseded?" Sonia demanded. "I have been trying to discover how a person can travel in the heavens, but how can a ship sail on a road? How can a road hang in the air? What keeps it from falling? What is a *quantum?* A *singularity?* How can passing through a window take you to a different place?"

"Hold on, hold on." Tess laughed.

"Furthermore," added Sonia, "if you khaja could only devise a smaller tool than these stationary consoles, you could communicate this swiftly while you were anywhere! You wouldn't be tied to a building. You could somehow wear them on your backs like a quiver. Think of how an army could use it. Merchants. A mother could converse with her child—"

"Sonia. Sonia! We have thought of such things. We just don't have them on Rhui."

"The interdiction again."

Tess nodded.

"You are very arrogant to make these decisions for us," said Sonia, finally, rebukingly.

"It's true."

"Hmm. Well. This all belongs to the jaran, now, so perhaps we will change all that."

"What do you mean, belongs to the—? Wait a minute, Sonia. Perhaps I didn't understand that correctly. Are you saying that Anatoly Sakhalin was made prince over all the systems governed by humans? Earth, the League, *and* Charles's territory? Rhui?"

"Of course. All khaja lands now belong to the jaran."

"Oh, my God." Tess make a frantic signal to Cara, but Cara had heard it all before. Cara looked unimpressed. "Sonia, I will call you again. I have to ... think about all this."

"It isn't what you expected, is it?" said Sonia astutely. "But it *is* what Ilya expected, after all."

"I got the transcripts you sent. And the children—"

"As we agreed. I will bring them myself, when the weather changes and the ships sail again. Although Dr. Hierakis traveled a different way, did she not? Could we not travel in such a way, in a flying ship? I've never seen one. It would be faster, wouldn't it? Is it dangerous?"

"Sonia, I will call you in two days. I have to think about this."

Cheerful now, Sonia signed off and closed her end of the connection with practiced ease. How quickly she learned.

Tess sagged back into the chair, which gave beneath her and molded itself to the curve of her back, shifting as she shifted. "Oh, Lord, Cara, what have we gotten ourselves into? What did Charles say?"

Cara stood up and leaned onto the console, squinting at the symbols scrolling across the screen. "Tess, in a decade there's a good chance we will face a doubling or tripling of the human lifespan. Perhaps more. How can I take this as seriously? It's politics. Temporal power rises and falls in every generation. Empires explode into prominence and then collapse. Charles

Soerensen becomes the most powerful human in Chapalii space, and then he is supplanted by someone else, who will no doubt experience his own period of fluorescence before fatigue or fashion or a reversal of fortune plunges him into eclipse. But longevity will be a sea of change for humanity. We can't know how it will shape our view of life, how it will alter our philosophies. So let Anatoly Sakhalin have his moment in the sun. Let Charles put his intelligence to other work than playing duke."

"But—"

"Don't you trust Anatoly?"

"I don't *know* Anatoly, not truly."

"Don't you trust Charles? Are you afraid he lives for ruling? For power? That this will break him? Ruin him? Corrupt him somehow by turning him into a villain out to regain all he has lost? I confess he might be a bit disappointed, but he is wise enough to let it go, to find a new—Ah. It isn't Charles or Anatoly at all, is it?"

"Damn it. It will take me months to get through this transcript."

"It's Ilya. That's it. He's got it all. He's finished. He's complete. He's won. And it leaves him nothing. What will you tell him, Tess?"

Tess shook her head, unable to talk past the lump in her throat. She palmed the console and fed all the information into the chip in her belt buckle.

"What did Sonia send you?" Cara asked.

"A complete transcript of Anatoly Sakhalin's report on his visit to the emperor, points between, and what happened after that, including an addendum compiled by David ben Unbutu and Ilyana Arkhanov."

"Ilyana Arkhanov? But she's scarcely more than a child."

"Evidently she has gotten herself apprenticed to—"

"Of course. I had heard that she had met the female. She's broken past the veil. And? There's something else on the screen. It's not a transcript."

"It's a facsimile of the *Revelation of Elia.*"

"The heretical Hristain Gospel?"

"Not heretical here, remember. It's only in the northern church that it's heretical."

"What do you want that for, Tess?"

"I don't know what else, how else to tell Ilya the truth."

Cara turned away from the flat screen and looked Tess straight in the eye. Her expression made Tess horribly uncomfortable, but she forced herself to face Cara, to hear what Cara had to say, not knowing whether she truly wanted to hear it.

"Have you asked him yet, my child, if he wants to know?"

Tess found Katya waiting outside Cara's laboratory, practically hopping from one foot to the other in her impatience to talk to Tess.

"When will you talk to my mother?" she demanded. "I talked to a merchant down in the Exchange and he said that a ship is leaving for Erthe in ten days. I'll just write a letter to my mother. You know that it could take a year, it could take a hundred days even if we sent it by official messenger and it got to Sarai and back without mishap."

"And you can't wait a hundred days?" Tess asked. Most of the corridors in the Jedan palace were not truly corridors but loggias looking out onto courtyards and gardens. So it was here; however curtailed access might be to Cara's lab, even Cara liked to be able to step outside into the air. Tess had spent much of the afternoon in the lab, having spent the morning with Baroness Santer, the chamberlain of the palace, and a steady stream of visitors with legal questions. The sun had sunk below the rooftop, throwing the garden beyond into shade. A few streaks of snow patched the ground, in the lee of columns and striping the ground along the north loggia. But the weather was already turning. It was warmer now, at the end of the day, than it had been this morning.

"No, I can't wait! Well. I went with Ilya down to the university this morning—"

"You did! What did he want there?"

"I don't know. He went one way and I went another. But it was interesting. I thought—well, if I had to wait, I could attend classes, couldn't I? There were some boys playing castles in one of the sitting rooms, by a fire. I watched them for a while, but they weren't very good. They weren't even as good as Prince Janos." She flushed and broke off.

"Katya. You should tell your mother why you truly don't want to marry, if what you told me is still the truth, for you."

"No."

"It isn't?"

"It is still the truth. I don't want to marry. I don't—" She glanced furtively up and down the colonnaded walkway, but except for two jaran guards at either end of the loggia, no one was about. No one was allowed into this quarter of the palace, except those Tess or Cara had explicitly cleared. "—care for men in that way, not truly. But I won't tell her, Aunt Tess. She won't understand."

"I don't think you ought to underestimate your mother. You certainly got your intelligence from her."

"It isn't that. She would try to understand, but it would hurt her. She just isn't . . . it isn't part of her world. Is it true that, in Erthe, what told you me—?"

"That not every marriage is between a man and a woman? Yes. It's not common, but there are other ways to be granted a legal partnership."

"Aunt Tess, you must let me go! There's no place for me in the jaran. Maybe there will be a place for me there."

"If there isn't?"

"There has to be."

Tess kissed her and left her, wondering if little Katya would brave the forbidden hall and just charge in on Cara even though she wasn't supposed to. That would, in a way, seal her fate. She did not look back as she left the courtyard.

She looked forward.

She had to leave the palace entirely, go out into the park that lay on the landward side of the palace. The ring of guards waved her through, and she walked along a gravel path, the stones crunching in a soothing manner under her boots. She walked alone out here as twilight lowered down over the city and the palace. In its own way, in the three days since they had arrived in Jeds, this area had become even more interdicted than Cara's laboratory. Not a soul stirred. Behind her, the line of guards was marked by an occasional torch and, here and there, a good blazing campfire.

The tent stood on a flat sward of grass, surrounded by a bower of trees and two desiccated beds of flowers. Ilya refused to sleep inside walls of stone. It had never bothered him before.

Tess halted on the edge of the sward and examined the tent. The gold banner fluttered weakly and sagged. Far away, barely audible, Tess heard the shush and sough of the waters on the rocks that buttressed the palace on its seaward front. The awning faced her, the entrance flap thrown open so that she could see into the tent. A single figure sat at the table, a lantern burning by his left hand and another hanging from the pole above. He seemed to be reading, but he was just distant enough that she could not make out the details.

The wind picked up again, a warming front that fragmented the cold haze that had hung over the city for the last three days. Branches shorn of leaves reached into the darkening sky, black lines etched into a night-blue heaven. They shivered in the wind, shuddering against each other. Like veins, they marked patterns onto the sky, pierced by the first stars.

Like a web. Tess blinked, and her implant triggered. She glanced around, once, as she always did, to make sure she was alone.

"Run Sakhalin transcript. Seek mention of transport codes delivered in tripartite sequences." As she waited she was caught by another thought, a detail Sonia had mentioned in passing. "Open a second screen and transfer Sakhalin's description of the emperor." It came up simultaneously with an excruciatingly detailed documentation of transport codes, and Tess had to adjust her focus, dropping her gaze down to the ground, which provided a more uniformly dark backdrop, although the divided screen she read from provided its own transcript.

He sat in a throne. He was almost joined to it, as if part of a web, filaments linking his body to the stone that made up the throne itself.

"Cut in Sojourner transcript, also referenced to tripartite sequences." The sudden swirl of figures fighting the ground and the gentle sway of branches made her dizzy. She put up a hand to cover the trees and the tent, so they wouldn't distract her, and concentrated on the disembodied screen suspended in front of her.

Three sequences recorded by the relay stations as ships traveled through. One went to the public record: That was clear enough. One went to the house record, and that made sense; a ship might reserve information for its own affiliates that it would not want to transmit as public knowledge. But the third sequence, the highest level of encryption, went to an unknown destination.

She shifted her focus back to the screen detailing Sakhalin's visit to the emperor. The emperor, who sat connected to his throne by filamentlike threads. Anatoly Sakhalin had seen this female who called herself Genji in his window visions, as if she was tracking his progress as he traveled across the empire. Ilyana Arkhanov, their under-aged spy in Genji's Chapalii household, had seen Genji connected, also with filamentlike threads, to a chair, which could be a kind of console.

What if the emperor could travel the web? What if the emperor was tapped into the entire Empire, not like a brain, but like the switching board through which most information passed? Everywhere and nowhere. Everyone and no one. He would no longer be a true individual. Like the ke, he would be nameless, because he would be everywhere. It was like a metaphor: his body represented the Empire, just as, according to the Arkhanov transcript appended onto Sakhalin's transcript, the net itself might be the body of the Empire.

Nets could be cut. Like Ilya's mind, the threads severed at random intersections by the stress of his captivity.

If they could cripple the web, they could cripple the Empire. If they could cripple the Empire, they might be strong enough to simply take their freedom or at least to bargain for it while the Empire was weakened.

And Anatoly Sakhalin was now perfectly placed to set out the pieces and begin to move them. It would have taken Charles years to get the information Anatoly had so blithely included in this transcript; if Charles, the Tai-en, could even have gotten it at all. Anatoly was restricted, as far as Tess could tell, only by his willingness to throw himself into the fray and his ability to outface the Chapalii at their own game, once he had figured out how to play it. For the former, she could not guess whether he would choose to support independence or promote his own interests; as for the latter, he had already done it. It was enough to make you laugh, the sheer audacity of presenting himself as a true prince—whatever the hell that meant—to the Chapalii emperor and to expect to be honored as such. To succeed.

Could Ilya have done it? Oh, gods, was she doubting him, now? Was he less than what she had once thought he was?

She blinked off the implant and walked forward. Ilya sat with two books open and a scroll opened and pinned down by an elbow and a hand. She stopped outside the entrance flap. He did not notice her. He was talking to himself.

" 'And a bright light appeared out of the darkest skies, and on this light He ascended to the heavens where His Father dwelt. To mark his passing, the glance of God's Eye scorched the dirt where His feet took wing into the heavens.' "

He was reading out loud from one of the books; from the *Gospel of Elia,* the *Revelation.* She watched his gaze shift from the book to the scroll. He opened the scroll a bit farther by tugging his elbow down, unrolling the parchment, and sliding the scroll to the right so that the lantern light illuminated it better. His face was aglow in the light, his hair a patch of darkness shading into the shadows that filled the rest of the chamber, surrounding him with night.

" 'So will the light ... the lantern ... the *torch* of God fall to earth ...' " He worried at his lower lip with his teeth as he squinted at the scroll, translating it. Tess could not see what language it was written in. "*Descend* to earth. From the stars. From the *wandering* stars." He switched his attention to the second book. "No ... No ... Damn it." He leafed through the pages, searching for a reference.

" 'Because the fixed stars are quiescent one in respect of another, we may consider the sun, earth, and planets, as one system of bodies carried hither and thither by various motions among themselves; and the common center of gravity ... will be quiescent' ... This is impossible." With his right hand still immobilizing the scroll, he drew two other books toward him and flipped them open on top of the one he had just been looking in. "The realm of the fixed stars. The realm of the wandering stars."

Tess got a chill. He was reading astronomical texts. After a moment he shifted back to the scroll.

"The mysteries of the wandering stars are these: That they come in two types. The first are the chariots by which the angels sail upon, sail? Ride? Drive? Travel upon the roads that lead through the heavens, borne on the wings of the south wind. The second are the gates to the dwelling places of the angels. Dwelling places ... palaces ... no, more like a park or garden. Then why wouldn't the fixed stars be the gardens and the wandering stars the chariots?" He *was* talking to himself. He pulled the topmost book toward him, one of the new books. " 'In this fashion the sun and the sphere of the fixed stars remain unmoved, while the earth and the wandering stars revolve about the unmoving sun in a series of circles, each nested inside the other.' " He flipped pages further, losing his grip on the scroll, which rolled up against his fingers. " 'Suppose a man lived in the heavens and he was carried along

by their motion, and looking down he saw the earth and its
mountains and valleys and rivers and cities, as far above as
angels, might it not appear then to him that the earth moved?
Just as it appears to us that the heavens move. Unable to stand
in the heavens, we can only stand on the earth and make our
judgment.' "

Running a hand through his hair, he shoved that book
aside and pulled the last one closer to him. " 'You know
from astrological computation that the whole circumference
of the earth is no more than a pinpoint when contrasted to
the space of the heavens . . . The man who recklessly strives
for glory and counts it his highest goal should consider the
far-reaching shores of heaven and the narrow confines of
earth.' "

Abruptly, his expression changed. He flung the book
against the wall, but it only fell to the floor with a soft thud,
having nothing hard to impact. He had lost his hold on the
scroll. Turning to stop it from rolling up completely, he saw
Tess.

At once, he looked guilty. Or he would have looked
guilty, if the jaran had a concept of sin. She stepped into the
tent. He closed the three books and was about to get up
when she forestalled him by skirting the table and picking
up the book he had thrown.

"The Consolation of Philosophy? Ilya . . ."

"Give it to me," he snapped, and because he was in a
mood, she handed it over without protest.

But she could not help trying to read the gold letters labeling the spines of the others. *"On The Nature of the Heavens.
The Principia?"*

He opened his saddle bags and stuffed the books inside
them. Then he rolled the scroll up carefully.

"What is that?"

"It is an old text from Byblos, that I took from the university today. It is called *The Mysteries of Elia,* but no one
knows if it is the same Elia who has written the gospel in
The Recitation, or another Elia. There is some debate. You
know how scholars are." He did not offer to let her look at
it, which was strange of itself.

"What are you looking for?" she asked, although she already knew the answer.

He tied the scroll with a bit of string, slid it into a case,
and shoved it into the saddlebag before he straightened up

and looked at her. The light had the odd trick of making him look even younger—and he already looked younger than his years. "I will let you know, when I find it."

He said it so dismissively that Tess winced. He did not seem to notice. He rose and untied the flap, pulling it closed. The sky, the trees, the stars, all vanished, and they stood, the two of them, alone in the enclosed chamber, which seemed very small, now, and dim, lit only by the two lanterns.

He kept his gaze fixed on the flap, as though he could see through it to the outside world. "In White Tower they kept me chained at night when I slept. Always. I can still feel the shackles."

"Ilya," she began, knowing that the time had come. There was no putting it off any longer. He had already begun. It was up to her to lead him the rest of the way. "For a long time now I have been trying to think of a way to tell you—"

He whirled. The expression on his face struck her to silence. But he spoke, his voice so low she had to strain to hear it.

"I want nothing given to me, Tess. Do you understand?" He began to pace, agitated. "I am not a slave to be led about in chains, to be cosseted with sweetmeats and pats on the head so that I can pretend that nothing shackles me. If the gods have spoken through me, then let them speak. Let me obey the vision they have sent me and not question it."

"What is this, then?" she demanded, gesturing toward the saddlebag bursting with books. Books he did not intend to let her see.

"What the gods wish me to know they will allow me to discover on my own."

"Ah, gods," Tess said under her breath, watching him cross to the entrance and twitch the flap aside to look out, up, at the trees or the heavens or the dark outline of the palace she could not be sure. But she knew at that moment that if she handed him a book open to the page where the answers were written, he would close it and hand it back without reading it.

What Sonia had embraced, Ilya turned his back on.

But then her gaze caught on the saddlebags, on the tip of the scroll, which he had evidently kidnapped from the university. It was not truly knowledge that Ilya had turned his back on. Ilya allowed his gods to act through him, but no one else. Not even her. He would rather knowingly remain ignorant than learn that he was just another pawn in a greater game. That was the lesson he had learned from Prince Janos, that he could not bear to be anyone less than the king.

Unlike Charles, he could not reshape his life to a new path. That was his great weakness.

Finally he turned to look at her and smiled, almost shyly, testing the waters. "I will send a messenger north to Sarai," he said. "Sonia can arrange for someone to escort Natalia and Yurinya by ship here, when the winds shift."

Tess started, being perfectly able to feel guilty. "Yes. We hadn't talked yet about how long we might stay in Jeds."

"Filis must be conquered, once and for all, and Vasha settled safely in Mircassia. We must stay at least until those campaigns are over." His gaze strayed toward the saddlebags, but he did not add that he evidently had pressing business at the university.

"A year would be good," agreed Tess. "That would give me time to bring the nobles back to heel, call a new council, institute a few laws, strengthen the parliament."

So he drifted toward her, and she toward him, and in the end they met, commencing a new pattern. He knew that she had at least been willing to tell him the truths that she had chained him away from all these years. She understood, a bit, how close he had come to going over the edge. But Ilyakoria Bakhtiian was perfectly capable of reshaping the untenable path so that it circumvented or concealed the obstacles which might otherwise destroy him.

That was his great strength.

EPILOGUE

1

All of the Tribes

"But he's short," said the woman to her companion, not realizing that Anatoly could overhear her. The great foyer that connected the Bouleuterion, the assembly hall, with the public concourse boasted a number of interesting acoustic properties as well as the cyclopean sculptural frieze depicting the history of humanity for which it was most famous. The floor of the foyer was a mosaic map, not to scale, of the many solar systems that made up League space, and Anatoly had discovered that when he stood on the blue-white circle that represented the star Sirius he could hear the conversations of people standing within the Three Rings system, a spear throw away. It was, he supposed, an elaborate spying system.

"And that woman with him. Why, she looks positively savage! Aren't those *weapons* she's carrying?"

Anatoly glanced at Katerina Orzhekov, but Katya was too busy gaping at a relief of a woman sitting at a writing desk to listen. Her grasp of the common tongue spoken here was still shaky in any case; she had not yet completed the language matrix. Katya wore a mishmosh of jaran and Earth dress, a long skirted tunic with striped trousers beneath, boots, and her quiver and bow strapped on her back. There was a khaja law about carrying weapons in public places, but Anatoly had grown tired of obeying it, and now he didn't have to anymore.

"It's very strange," agreed her companion.

"M. Sakhalin!"

"Damn," said Anatoly, and to Katya, "Come."

She spun at once and fell in beside him as he headed for the concourse, but even so, the longer legs of their pursuer proved their downfall.

"M. Sakhalin! What a pleasure to see you here. I was so honored to meet you at the reception last month. I hope you

don't mind that I took the liberty of forwarding some of the
specs on our new line of luxury yachts to your . . . uh, your
office. We have so many models to choose from and we can
custom fit to any specification, even include, heh heh, an
archery range." The man bowed floridly toward Katerina
and, straightening, caught her disdainful expression. He
smiled nervously and shifted tactics. "Of course, M. Sakhalin, you understand that Cheng Shipyards guarantees the
highest quality, and we are known league-wide for the speed
and strength of our models."

"Thank you, M. Chandani. I assure you that we are studying the matter even now. If you will excuse me."

"Most honored, M. Sakhalin. Most honored." Bowing, the
merchant let them go, thank the gods.

"He smells of sweetcakes," said Katya in a low voice.
"All sticky and oversugared. Does this happen often?"

"It happens all the time."

"How do you remember all their names?"

"I have an implant." He tapped his temples just above his
left ear. "It records each person I meet and cross references
it with a name, and then those I don't remember on my own
can be recalled from the implant. It's very useful. They're
flattered when you remember their names, even if they must
know I have tools to help me."

They crossed through into the concourse and were at once
picked up by two of the *Raven's* crew—Summer and Benjamin—and by the ubiquitous throng of agents, hangers-on,
monitors, and official escorts that attended him whenever he
went out into public territory. A tiny globe maneuvered, trying to get a good angle on him for the vids, and Katerina
gave it a sharp whack with her bow. A few sympathizers in
the crowd cheered. Finally, they got through the concourse
and into the docking section and into the blessed quiet of the
Gray Raven.

"Am I really that short?" Anatoly asked Summer as they
cycled through the locks.

Summer grinned down at him. "Only in height, my dear.
But 169 centimeters is below average for a man. Remember,
we're used to our princes being Chapalii, and they're all
about two hundred centimeters."

"What's a centimeter?" asked Katya. "Oh, it's a unit of
measure."

"Five feet six and a half inches," offered Benjamin, who

could convert any unit, monetary or otherwise, into any other instantaneously. "Three point eight cubits, depending on the arm."

The lock opened and they dispersed into the gleaming passageways of the ship.

"Come with me," said Anatoly to Katerina. She followed him to the lounge. "Sit." He sat on the couch, she on the floor in the jaran style, watching him intently.

"You have been with me for two khaja months now. How do you like it here?"

"I love it here," she said fiercely.

"I have a task for you. Yesterday I finally got word that my message found my sister Shura, and she is now at Jeds, waiting for word from me. I want you to go back to Rhui."

Her expression fell instantly.

"Not to stay. Go back to the tribes. Bring me one hundred men and women, to be the nucleus of my new jahar. Recruit them wisely, carefully. Find the ones who are discontent, who question—not troublemakers, but the ones who are restless."

"I know how to find them," said Katya quietly.

"Don't let the others know what you are doing. Shura will help you. She, too, will know. She is one of them, as you are. If any riders live who were in my jahar before I left, and they wish to join me, bring them."

"If they have families?"

"It's true it would be best to bring younger people, those who are willing to leave the tribe and make a new tribe here. But I will not turn away the riders who served with me then. They must make the choice themselves. You, Katerina, will be etsana."

She made a face.

"No, it must be you. You came here first. You are a daughter of the Eldest Tribes."

"Your sister Shura—"

"It is not fitting that a brother and sister act together as dyan and etsana of a tribe. But you and I are cousins, of a sort, and we will do very well together, I think. I need the jaran, Katya. Surely you can see that."

She nodded, her clear-eyed gaze steady on him. "Yes. This khaja world is very strange."

But she had adjusted remarkably well. She had not come off the ship in shock, as he had. She had not retreated into a false world, as Karolla Arkhanov had, dragging her children down with her. With that same kind of preparation, with her guidance, the hundred riders and archers she brought off Rhui would adjust as well as she did. In their turn, when it was time, when it was appropriate, they could form the escort that would bring more jaran off Rhui, those that wanted to come.

Because not all would want to come. Nor should they.

"What about my cousin, Bakhtiian?" she asked suddenly.

He bowed his head, as any man does before the authority of a great etsana. "You must obey your aunt Tess Soerensen in this. I cannot interfere with her judgment."

"It's true, you know," said Katya in a whisper. "Before I left, I went to him, but he would not speak to me. I don't understand it."

Anatoly felt a pain in his heart. He made an image in his mind of the man he had admired so passionately when he was a boy, the proud dyan, leader of all the tribes, who had lifted the jaran to face their destiny. Who yet, in the end, could not face the greater truth he had inadvertently uncovered. He was, gods forgive Anatoly for even thinking it, like Karolla in that.

"He is a Singer," said Anatoly at last, unwilling to pass judgment. "He is subject to the will of the gods in a way we are not."

He went to his cabin and lay down on his bunk, palming the top screen on and flipping through the channels idly. There was a report on his upcoming appearance before Parliament, in less than two hours. An Infinity Jilt serial. An immersion mass in the Church of Three Faiths temple in Gabon, ready to trigger once the viewer hooked into the nesh. Freefall acrobatics. A historical epic called *Coming of Age in the Milky Way,* about the great cosmological discoveries at the end of the Machine Age. The usual gossip channel. A fencing match.

He flipped abruptly back to the gossip channel.

The bastards!

A crowd of mini-globes and nesh and flesh correspondents had mobbed Chancery Lane. A golden-haired woman walked down the New Court steps escorted by a husky woman with an authoritative bearing and by her father and Aunt Millie. The voice-over was blithering on about final dissolution papers and his name and something about the appearance before Parliament, but Anatoly could see only Diana. He strained to hear her through the globes that hovered around her. Only a Singer could look so composed, only Diana could manage to look so poised, so lovely. . . .

"M. Brooke-Holt! M. Brooke-Holt! We understand that your husband dumped you now that he's become so important."

"No comment," said the advocate, the husky woman, bringing up the rear while Aunt Millie and Diana's father forced a path through the crowd toward a private carriage.

"Isn't there a child involved?"

Anatoly could not see Diana's face. The advocate looked bored. "No comment," she repeated.

"Is it true that he's cut himself loose and is going to establish a harem of exotic primitives for himself, in the Chapalii style?"

Diana stopped dead and turned to fix a glare of monumental disdain on the hapless questioner. "Oh! You people are so stupid!" She turned her back on the camera, used her elbows to good effect, and ducked into the carriage. It sealed shut behind her, leaving the advocate in charge as the crowd moved back to avoid the backwash as the car rose and flew away.

Anatoly voiced the sound down and just stared at the screen, at the gray stone of the courthouse, at the bleak London sky above. He felt, at this moment, shame more than pain. He was shamed that his wife had abandoned him. Such a thing never happened in the tribes. What if they were to hear of it? Gods, he hadn't even told Katerina Orzhekov the truth, and she didn't understand the language or the tools well enough yet to discover it on her own.

Gods, what would his grandmother say? She would have accepted the emperor's benediction calmly, without surprise; it was, after all, simply what was due to the Sakhalin tribe. But she would be furious that Diana had left him—for a second time.

You should have married the daughter of Baron Santer, she would say. You look like a fool, Anatoly. It never behooves a Sakhalin to look like a fool, and especially not a man. A man must show himself courageous, trustworthy, loyal to his dyan, and responsible to his mother, his sisters, and his wife and children. But if he allows himself to be made a fool of, then no one will respect him.

Though she was dead, he could reproduce her voice, her tone, her words with perfect accuracy, because he knew her so well. He was thankful that she was dead, so that she might never have to know.

The cabin door slid open without warning and Portia rushed in, followed by Evdokia Arkhanov. The two girls screamed with laughter and threw themselves onto his stomach, knocking the breath out of him. Moshe stopped in the entrance and covered his mouth, stifling his own laughter. "Sorry," he said. "I hope we didn't disturb you."

Anatoly reached up and palmed off the overhead screen. "No." He hoisted the girls off him and sat up. "I wasn't doing anything productive. Now, Portia, you must get dressed in your fine clothes. You, too, Evdi."

The Bouleuterion was domed above and below by stars, or so it appeared to Anatoly. The spider's web of Concord, the great space station still under construction, threw odd patterns on the heavens, like etchings cut through clouded glass. Walking on the transparent floor, with only stars beneath his feet, made him nervous, so as he entered the hall and made his way through the sunken aisle to the center he kept his gaze on the amphitheater surrounding him.

Every seat in the hall was filled. At the high railings above, people stood at least three deep, judging from the heads sticking above the crowd. It was a circular hall, and the platform in the center faced no one and everyone. Four sunken aisles pierced the banks of seats into four quarters. As Anatoly came out into the middle, he let Portia down and shoved her toward Katerina, who waited in the lowest rank of benches. Portia stuck her little finger in her mouth and walked over to Katya, glancing back at her father for reassurance. When the girl sat down, wedged between Katya and Evdi, who were themselves flanked by Branwen and the rest of her crew, Anatoly strode out to the center.

He stood there alone, surrounded by over ten thousand seated assembly members doubled by a ghostly contingent of nesh and amplified by a high ring of vid globes and a hundred soft bulbs that transferred every last detail into the nesh reconstruction.

The audience kept a respectful silence, waiting for him to speak, but he could almost taste their wariness. They did not trust him. Neither did they hate him. They waited, reserving judgment.

He knelt without looking down at the void of stars beneath his feet and set the tower, his token from the emperor, on the smooth floor.

"The board," he said. "Enlarged ten times normal size."

At first he could not tell that the black field had manifested, since it blended with the heavens below, but then the grid of lines burned into view and the midnight black slab of stone that marked the emperor's throne. One by one the pieces flickered into view and solidified. The horseman had moved farther yet away from the throne, shadowed by the teardrop. The other eight pieces lay scattered across the board, marking no pattern he could discern. A murmur ran through the crowd, quieting only when he rose.

"This is the game played by the emperor and the princess," he said to his audience, which no doubt ran into the billions."

He turned slowly, a full circle, surveying the ranks upon ranks of his khaja subjects, like the ranks of an army. There, he thought he recognized the pale outline of Charles Soerensen, attending in nesh, but he couldn't be sure. There was no one who looked in the least like Diana, although perhaps she truly was here, guising in a different form. Perhaps she still cared enough about him to watch over him, now and again. But he pushed these thoughts of her aside; they were too distracting. He could not afford to be distracted.

Instead, he walked through the game, avoiding the other princes, keeping to the lines as much as he could, and made his way to his own piece.

"This is where we stand." He halted above the horseman, which half melded with him. "Where we go from here is up to us."

Here he paused, to let his words sink in, here in this hall and in every hall, every chamber, every street or corner where any woman or man had stopped to hear him, to measure him, to pass judgment. For that was, perhaps, the most important lesson he had learned from Bakhtiian: Let the whole of your people be your army, all of the tribes, and let that army follow you not just willingly but passionately, with their hearts.

He looked up and nodded, satisfied. He had their complete attention.

2

The Shores of Heaven

Vassily Kireyevsky surveyed the battlefield from the hilltop. He turned to Yaroslav Sakhalin. The late summer sun shone down, bathing him in sweat under his armor.

"His banner has fallen. The Prince of Filis must be dead."

"We will see," said Yaroslav, never one to hasten to any conclusions.

But so it proved. Prince Basil's body was dragged up the slope and displayed. A Filistian lord who had turned coat last winter, after Bakhtiian himself had ridden into Jeds and taken up the campaign personally, identified the body.

"What of the Mircassian boy?" Vasha asked, but no one knew, and when he rode down into the Filistian camp, he discovered that Basil's half sister had murdered the child and killed herself rather than fall into the hands of the jaran. It saddened him, more for the child's sake than hers.

He examined the corpse: The boy had black hair and the olive skin of southerners, and although Vasha had heard his age estimated at sixteen, the child looked younger. If he was truly an invalid, a simpleton, no sign of his infirmity showed in his corpse, except that he was small.

"What will you do now, Vassily?" Yaroslav Sakhalin asked when Vasha emerged from the tent.

"I will take the news to my father myself, before I return to Mircassia. King Barsauma is failing, but even if he dies while I'm gone, they don't dare try to unseat me, not now that we have defeated Prince Basil."

"What of your wife?"

Vasha had learned that when Yaroslav Sakhalin spoke, he usually sounded censorious, even if he did not mean to be. But the habit served him well, since it made it easy to distinguish between those of his men who doubted themselves and those who did not.

"Princess Rusudani and I have an understanding, Sakhalin. In any case, she is pregnant now—" He broke off and looked away, concealing a flush of pride. Rusudani was pregnant with *his* child.

The old general laughed softly. "All young men are full of themselves when their wives become pregnant for the first time. I am told I was insufferable."

Vasha was paralyzed for a moment by the spectacle of Yaroslav Sakhalin joking with him. Then he collected himself.

"Surely it is no more than we deserve," Vasha replied, watching Sakhalin carefully. When Sakhalin smiled, Vasha smiled in return, relieved that Sakhalin seemed amused by this weak sally. But it seemed safer to return to the matter at hand. "It is the council that concerns me. They are not content with either Princess Rusudani or myself, and in particular, with me. I have heard it said that I hold too great an influence over her, that there are too many barbarians at court. There is a young lord who was put forward as a prospective consort for the princess, but I have seen that he was posted to the war. Unfortunately, he didn't manage to get himself killed."

"I'll be sending scouting parties south, to probe," said Sakhalin. "I could use some auxiliaries."

"Yes. That would do very well. I will attach his company to your army before I leave."

So it was settled. Lord Intavio agreed to the posting because he had no choice, surrounded by the far greater jaran army in the hinterlands that straddled the border between Mircassia and Filis.

In the morning, leaving Sakhalin to mop up the remains of Prince Basil's army, which had by now scattered into the hills, Vasha took a contingent of one thousand men, half jaran riders and half Mircassian cavalry, and rode southwest, toward Jeds. Toward his father.

They came after twenty-six days of hard riding to Jeds. Vasha left his guard in the camp that had sprung up to the east of the city and rode the rest of the way with a smaller escort of one hundred picked men and twenty archers. They circled the city and went directly to the palace.

Tess came herself to greet him, where he dismounted in the great courtyard that fronted the palace. She grinned and hugged him, there in front of everyone, and a moment later

Natalia and Yuri ran shrieking from the eastern loggia and threw themselves on him, jumping on him and tugging at his armor and dancing around.

"Gods, you've grown. Stand back. Let me look at you."

Natalia stuck her hands on her hips. "Papa gave me a horse," she said. "It's a very fine horse, too, I'll have you know. And Lara didn't get one because she took Kriye out bareback and got thrown, too."

"Lara is here, too?"

"Yes, and Sofia. We all sailed south together, and none of us got sick, only Yuri did."

Yuri had already strayed off to examine the strange khaja armor worn by the Mircassian soldiers, so he could not defend himself against this slur.

"How many of the children came south from Jeds?" Vasha asked Tess.

She only smiled. "Enough. They're very loud."

"Did Stefan bring them down?"

"No, Sonia did. Didn't you hear? Stefan just got married."

"So Jaelle did get pregnant!" Vasha laughed. "That's the last I heard, that Stefan hoped it was true, but they weren't sure yet. He'll come to Mircassia then, when the child is safely born."

"And you must come in and get that armor off. I'll get you something to drink."

"Where is . . . my father?"

She hesitated, then lifted a hand in the direction of the sea. "Out riding."

"Perhaps I should go out directly."

"If you wish. What news have you brought, Vasha? You look well."

He gave a brief account of the battle and its outcome, the disposition of armies, the current mood of the Mircassian populace, which favored Rusudani and her consort, and the council, which remained suspicious.

He took in a deep breath. "Rusudani is pregnant." Unable to help himself, he grinned.

Tess raised an eyebrow. "You didn't wait long. She can't have had the other child that long ago."

"Aren't you happy for me?" he demanded.

"Now, Vasha," she said, maddeningly calm, "let's wait until the child is born to celebrate. What happened to the other baby?"

"When it was eight weeks old, Rusudani sent it north to Lady Jadranka with a wet nurse and an honor guard. It was a little boy. I left before we heard whether the child arrived safely. It was a pretty child." He said it wistfully. He had been sorry to part with the infant, but Rusudani had refused to have anything to do with it. As far as he knew, she had never come to see the baby after it had been born.

Tess put a hand on his hair, ruffling it as if he were a child, and smiled affectionately at him. "I'm glad you came, Vasha. Go see your father."

Like a good son, he obeyed, stripping out of his armor and just wearing his padded surcoat over his clothes. One of the palace grooms brought him a fresh horse, and he rode out with two escorts.

Most of the palace fronted a cliff, but to the north the ridge dropped down and melded with the shoreline, forming a broad strand at the mouth of the River Edesse. Vladimir and a handful of guards sat, some on their horses, some dismounted, at the farthest limit of solid land, keeping watch, but Vasha could see a distant figure that must be his father much farther out on the beach.

Vasha handed his reins over to his guard and headed out onto the strand. Once out of the slight windbreak provided by the last low promontory, he had to duck his head repeatedly to keep the stinging sand from his eyes.

Here, on the shoreline, the wind blew continually, just as it did on the plains. The waves came in in layers, levels building one on top of the next, sliding in over the damp course of sand and soughing away again. The wind coursed over the water, changing its color, darkening it. The constant breaking of one wave atop the next layered an endless steady crashing noise over the world, that shrank into this one stretch of sand and the gray-blue sea, stretching out to the islands that dotted the horizon, pale grey with clouds.

Ilya turned, shading his face against the wind, and, recognizing him, nodded. Then he turned back to stare out to sea. He stood at the very limit of the land, at that point where land and sea blend and become one.

"What are you doing out here?" Vasha asked, having to pitch his voice loud to be heard above the wind.

"Where did you come from?" Ilya demanded.

Vasha launched into his description of the battle, the disposition of forces, the end of Filistian resistance.

Ilya heard him out in silence. "You are well?"

"Rusudani is pregnant," said Vasha, but cautiously, not knowing what to expect.

For the first time, Ilya smiled. The wind tore through his hair, rippling his shirt sleeves all the way down his arms. "That's my boy."

Vasha could not help but laugh. "Why is it that women take the news one way and men another?"

"Women are more interested in the birthing of a child, men in the getting of it."

Emboldened by this levity, Vasha repeated his initial question. "But what *are* you doing out here?"

"I'm just wondering," said Ilya so softly that Vasha could barely hear him above the wind, "what lies beyond the sea."

"What lies beyond the sea? Don't you have enough to think about on the lands that lie between here and the plains? Half of the Yossian principalities could break away at any time, if they think we've weakened at all, and the Dushan king is still furious about losing the man who was the jaran governor there. Another of his sons is threatening open revolt against his father. And Mitya is still having trouble on his eastern border with Vidiya. Now that Filis is defeated, King Barsauma will begin negotiating over those two border provinces, and Yaroslav Sakhalin is sending scouts to the south. According to the reports we got from Kirill Zvertkov after he joined up with his army again, there has still been no recent word from the second expedition sent out along the Golden Road."

Ilya grunted. "I would take a ship to Erthe," he said absently. "Katya went, and returned, and went north to Sarai."

"When was this? Does she mean to stay? Perhaps she will come to Mircassia now."

"No. She means to return to Erthe. She'll sail from the north, she says. She may already be gone. I don't know. We haven't had word yet. That was months ago."

Vasha struggled with his disappointment and finally got it under control in time to hear his father going on.

"There is something strange about Erthe, Vasha," he said, describing his words with his hands. "I don't think it's a land like these lands. I think it is bounded on one side by the ocean and on the other by the heavens themselves, so that if a man stood on the shore he would look out into the vault of the sky, only it would lie at his feet instead of above his head."

Vasha laughed. "How could that be?" Sobering, he saw that his father was serious. Ilya was not truly looking at the ocean or listening to the roar of the waves. He was oblivious to the bite of the wind and the fine blowing sand on his skin. He had gone on a Singer's journey, traveling to lands that could only exist in his own mind or beyond human ken, in the worlds that belong to the gods.

"Father!" Exasperated, Vasha raised his voice. "Haven't you spent enough time staring out at the water? There are lands to administer *here,* right here. I have a much more detailed report to give you, and three other messengers with me, who have reports to give as well. But you only care about what lies beyond, not what you have in your hands already."

He turned, looking toward the guards who waited on the ridge. They stood there, small figures like statues unmoved in the wind. Another rider came, picking her way down the ridge. It was Tess. He recognized her at once, even at this distance.

Ilya did not reply. He did not appear to be listening. A wave ran in and crept up to his boots, then slid back, absorbed into the next wave.

Vasha shrugged finally. It was not his right to disturb the meditation of a Singer. He turned full around and began to walk back across the sand, to meet Tess. Out here the strand was flat and dry, untouched by water, and the wind hit with redoubled force, sculpting the sand into endless tiny ranges of irregular hills, running out along the strand until they were lost to distance.

"Does he come out here often?" he asked as Tess came up to him and they stopped together and looked toward the shoreline and the silhouette of Ilya.

"Yes. I've never quite figured out what he does, though, except just to look. Perhaps the constant wind out here reminds him of the plains."

"He's searching for the shores of heaven," said Vasha flippantly, still irritated by his father's infuriatingly pointless musing.

But Tess smiled sadly. "Has he found them yet?"

"Can anyone find them? I have work to do, reports to

hear, Talia and Yuri to play with. I need to write a letter to my wife. I'm going in. Are you coming with me?"

She shook her head, and he threw up his hands in disgust and went back by himself. He stopped once, when he was almost at the ridge to look back.

The sun had come out from behind the clouds and it spilled its light along the waters, turning them to a rich gold. It was beautiful, in its way, rimming the edges of the clouds with white-gold where a patch of deep blue sky showed through. As the sun sank, the golden stream of light reached and reached until it flowed forward in the waves that spilled themselves into nothing at Ilya's feet.

As if, thought Vasha, the shores of heaven had overflowed, lapping over into his world like a promise, sworn by the sun and the moon and the wind. If only Ilya would look at what lay right before him instead of always staring at the sky, he could see it for himself.

The wind picked up, blowing sand hard into Vasha's face, and he shaded his eyes and watched as Tess reached Ilya at last and reached out to touch her husband's arm. After a long pause, Ilya turned. Coming to himself, he said something to her and together they started back across the sands.

Vasha waited for them.

The Sakhalins

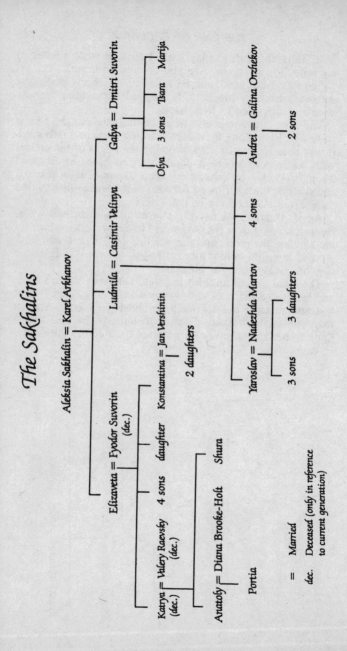

Aleksia Sakhalin = Karel Arkhanov

Elizaveta = Fyodor Suvorin (dec.)

Ludmila = Casimir Velirya

Gabya = Dmitri Suvorin

Katya = Valery Raevsky (dec.)

4 sons

daughter

Konstantina = Jan Vershinin

2 daughters

Olya   3 sons   Tsara   Marija

Anatoly = Diana Brooke-Holt

Portia   Shura

Yaroslav = Nadezhda Martov

3 sons   3 daughters

Andrei = Galina Orzhekov

2 sons

=   Married

dec.   Deceased (only in reference to current generation)

The Veselovs

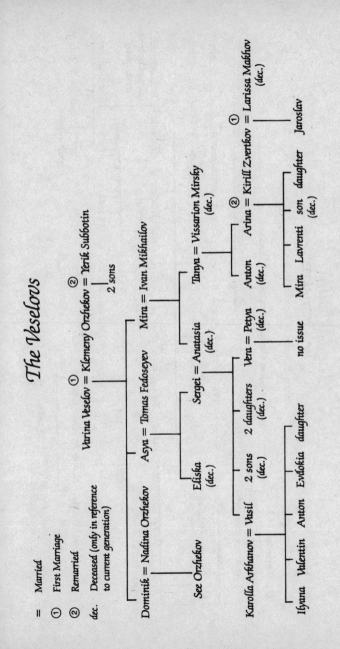

Legend:

=   Married

① First Marriage

② Remarried

dec. Deceased (only in reference to current generation)

Varina Veselov ① = Klement Orzhekov ② = Yerik Subbotin
                                          2 sons

Dominik = Nadina Orzhekov
    Asya = Tomas Fedoseyev
    Mira = Ivan Mikhailov

See Orzhekov

Eliska (dec.)
   Sergei = Anatasia (dec.)
   Tanya = Vissarion Mirsky (dec.)

Karolia Arkhanov = Vasil
  2 sons (dec.)
  2 daughters
  Vera = Petya (dec.)
  no issue
  Anton (dec.)
  Arina ② = Kirill Zvertkov ① = Larissa Makhov (dec.)

Ilyana Valentin Anton Evdokia daughter

Mira Lavrenti son daughter Jaroslav

The Orzhekovs

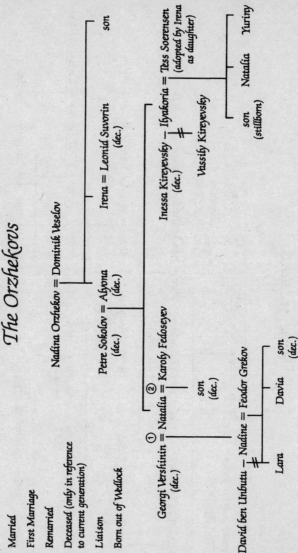

- = Married
- ① First Marriage
- ② Remarried
- dec. Deceased (only in reference to current generation)
- — Liaison
- ≠ Born out of Wedlock

Nadina Orzhekov = Dominik Veselov

son

Petre Sokolov = Afyona (dec.)

Irena = Leonid Suvorin (dec.)

Inessa Kireyevsky — Ilyakoria = Tess Sorensen (dec.) (adopted by Irena as daughter)

Vassily Kireyevsky

Natalia   Yuriny

son (stillborn)

Georgi Vershinin ① = Natalia = Karoly Fedoseyev (dec.) ②

son (dec.)

David ben Umbutu — Nadine = Feodor Grekov ≠

Lara   Davia   son (dec.)

The Orzhekovs

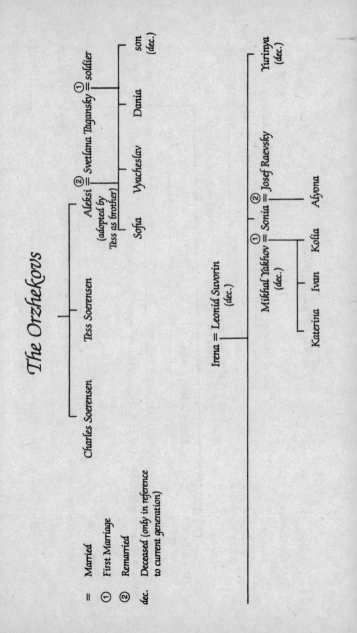

Married =

First Marriage ①

Remarried ②

dec. Deceased (only in reference to current generation)

The Orzhekovs

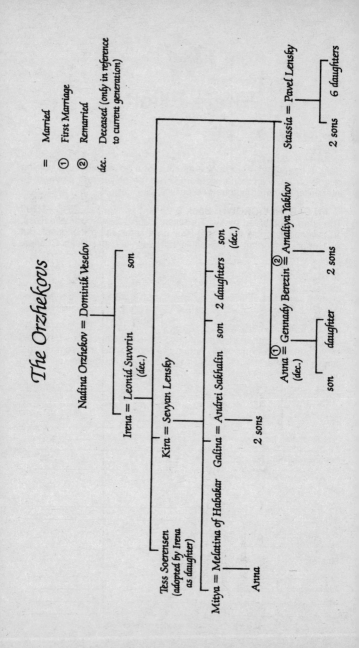

= Married
① First Marriage
② Remarried
dec. Deceased (only in reference to current generation)

Nadina Orzhekov = Dominik Veselov

Tess Soerensen (adopted by Irena as daughter)

Irena = Leonid Suvorin (dec.)

Kira = Sevyan Lensky

Mitya = Melatina of Habakar

Arna

Galina = Andrei Sakhalin

2 sons

son

2 daughters

son (dec.)

Arna = Gennady Berezin ① (dec.)

② = Amaliya Yakhov

son

daughter

2 sons

Stassia = Pavel Lensky

2 sons

6 daughters

son

Kate Elliott

The Novels of the Jaran:

☐ **JARAN: Book 1**   UE2513—$5.99
Here is the poignant and powerful story of a young woman's coming
of age on an alien world, where she is both player and pawn in an
interstellar game of intrigue and politics.

☐ **AN EARTHLY CROWN: Book 2**   UE2546—$5.99
The jaran people, led by Ilya Bakhtiian and his Earth-born wife Tess,
are sweeping across the planet Rhui on a campaign of conquest. But
even more important is the battle between Ilya and Duke Charles,
Tess' brother, who is ruler of this sector of space.

☐ **HIS CONQUERING SWORD: Book 3**   UE2551—$5.99
Even as Jaran warlord Ilya continues the conquest of his world, he
faces a far more dangerous power struggle with his wife's brother,
leader of an underground human rebellion against the alien empire.

☐ **THE LAW OF BECOMING: Book 4**   UE2580—$5.99
On Rhui, Ilya's son inadvertently becomes the catalyst for what could
prove a major shift of power. And in the heart of the empire, the most
surprising move of all was about to occur as the Emperor added an
unexpected new player to the Game of Princes . . .

Prices slightly higher in Canada   **DAW:132**

KATE ELLIOT

CROWN OF STARS

"An entirely captivating affair"—*Publishers Weekly*

☐ **KING'S DRAGON**   UE2771—$6.99
In a world where bloody conflicts rage and sorcery holds sway both human and other-than-human forces vie for supremacy. In this land, Alain, a young man seeking the destiny promised him by the Lady of Battles, and Liath, a young woman gifted with a power that can alter history, are about to be swept up in a world-shaking conflict.

☐ **PRINCE OF DOGS**   UE2770—$23.95
Return to the war-torn kingdoms of Wendar and Varre, and the intertwined destinies of: Alain, raised in humble surroundings but now a Count's Heir; Liath, who struggles with the secrets of her past while evading those who seek the treasure she conceals; Sanglant, believed dead, but only held captive in the cathedral of Gent, and Fifth Son, who now builds an army to do his father's—or his own—bidding in a world at war!

Prices slightly higher in Canada.   **DAW 211X**

THE GOLDEN KEY
by
Melanie Rawn
Jennifer Roberson
Kate Elliott

In the duchy of Tira Virte fine art is prized above all things. But not even the Grand Duke knows just how powerful the art of the Grijalva family is. For thanks to a genetic fluke certain males of their bloodline are born with a frightening talent—the ability to manipulate time, space, and reality within their paintings, using them to cast magical spells which alter events, people, places, and things in the real world. Their secret magic formula, known as the Golden Key, permits those Gifted sons to vastly improve the fortunes of their family. Still, the Grijalvas are fairly circumspect in their dealings until two young talents come into their powers: Sario, a boy who will learn to use his Gift to make himself virtually immortal; and Saavedra, a female cousin who, unbeknownst to her family, may be the first woman ever to have the Gift. Sario's personal ambitions and thwarted love for his cousin will lead to a generations-spanning plot to seize total control of the duchy and those who rule it.

- Featuring cover art by Michael Whelan

OTHERLAND
TAD WILLIAMS

Otherland. A perilous and seductive realm of the imagination where any fantasy—whether cherished dream or dreaded nightmare—can be made shockingly real. Incredible amounts of money have been lavished on it. The best minds of two generations have labored to build it. And, somehow, bit by bit, it is claiming Earth's most valuable resource—its children. It is up to a small band of adventures to take up the challenge of Otherland in order to reveal the truth to the people of Earth. But they are split by mistrust, thrown into different worlds, and stalked at every turn by the sociopathic killer Dread and the mysterious Nemesis. . . .